Fiction by Gordon Weaver

Count a Lonely Cadence
The Entombed Man of Thule (stories)
Such Waltzing Was Not Easy (stories)
Give Him a Stone
Circling Byzantium
Getting Serious (stories)
Morality Play (stories)
A World Quite Round (stories)
The Eight Corners of the World

THE
EIGHT
CORNERS
OF THE
WORLD

THE
EIGHT
CORNERS
OF THE
WORLD

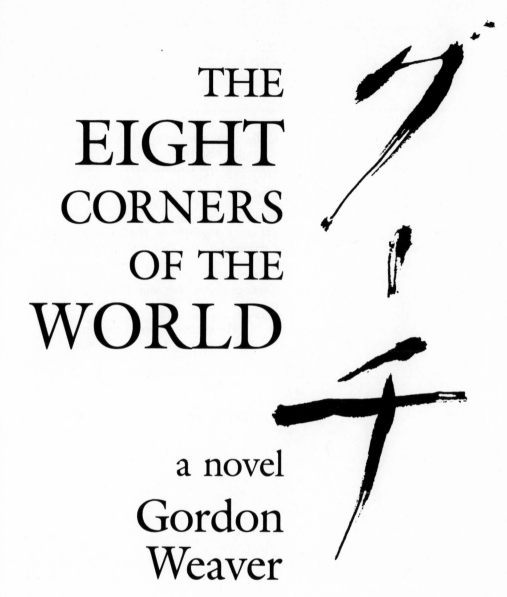

a novel

Gordon
Weaver

Chelsea Green Publishing Co.
Chelsea, Vermont
1988

First printing, July 1988

Portions of this novel, in different form,
appeared originally in *The Chariton Review,
Crosscurrents,* and *Quarterly West*

Library of Congress
Cataloging-in-Publication Data

Weaver, Gordon
    The eight corners of the world:
    a novel / by Gordon Weaver
       p. cm.
    ISBN 0-930031-16-4: $19.95
    I. Title
PS3573.E17E38 1988
813'.54–dc 19   88-17696
                         CIP

The Eight Corners of the World was designed by Georganna Towne.
It was typeset in Galliard by Dartmouth Printing Company.
It was printed on Warren's Sebago, an acid-free paper, by Fairfield Graphics.
Calligraphy by Iya Itagaki

for Judy, Kristina, Anna, and Jessica —

and for Dennis, Jim, Mike, Paul, and Tom:
the Roaring Boys of Vermont College,

and in memory of Faye Teeter, U.S.M.C.,
killed in action, Betio Atoll, 1943, and in memory
of Kazamaro "Buddy" Uno, Imperial Japanese
Army, killed in action, World War II

Not a thread in all his raiment—not a line in all the marked and singular lineaments of his face which was not, even in the most absolute identity, *mine own*!

Edgar Allen Poe, "William Wilson"

1.

Yoshinori Yamaguchi

Chukun Aikoku:
loyalty to
the Emperor
and love
of country

Says he: "*Sensei*, I am astounded!"

Says I: "Reet. But can you hack it? Is the price not right? Do you dig the concept?"

Jack, everybody gots to leave something behind when dead and gone, reet? Natural instinct of human animal shtick. Foto Joe Yamaguch ain't no exception. Best believe it, Jack!

So what do *wataschi* gots to bestow upon unborn generations of posterities of *Nihon* (a.k.a. *Dai Nippon*, reet?), much less global-wide to eight corners of the world? Plenty, Jack!

Foto Joe Yamaguch — me, how we say in *Nihonju, wataschi* — gots stuff easy to itemize in last will and testament, being of venerable (pushing seventy, Jack!) age, sound mind in failing-fast body (obesity, emphysema, renal failure, rampant cancers!). Consider:

Gots me plenty money, how we say, *genkin* cash. Located in safe-deposit vaults here in *Nihon*, stateside, Switzerland (secret account numbers to be revealed only upon ceremonials reading of said will and testament).

No joke, Jack! Bread, dough, kale, cabbage, long green (not to fail to mention also yellow, orange, red, currency species of *Nihon*, France, United Kingdom, and Saudi Arabia in addition to legal tenders of U. S. of A.).

Not to fail to mention sizable quantities of bullion and Krugerrands as conservative hedge against global inflations pressures arising from amidst incessant historical ebb-flow of international politico-economic flaps — I is talking big bucks, Jack!

Than which is not to fail to mention assets tangible than which is no sweat to convert to currency specie of choice if so desired, reet? Consider: domicile properties located in Tokyo Town (in which *wataschi* presently resides whilst awaiting arrival of Grim Reaper, Black Angel, etcetera blah,

Jack!), Hokkaido Island, Hong Kong (lease not to expire except save simultaneous with 1999 reversion of Crown Colony to People's Republic—Commie Chinks!—at which point in time situation is moot given *wataschi's* impending demise, reet?), City of Angels (L.A., Jack!), New York City Big Apple (condo in same edifice as ex-Prexy Nixon's!), aforesaid Switzerland (chalet), United Kingdom (Surrey estate), Gay Paree (luxury Champs Elysée pad)—all values of which appear perpetual in normative inflationary escalation, natch!

Also assorted motor vehicles (most leased, except save for mint Rolls Silver Dawn limo), yacht moored betwixt Ranier's and Mrs. Oona Chaplin's at Monaco marina, not to fail to mention 747 with full custom interior modeled on prototypes of Hughie Heffner and Saudi Sheik Yamani—latter of whom is casual acquaintance of *wataschi* Foto Joe Yamaguch (sorry to name-drop!).

All above which is not to mention personal wardrobe, catalogue of which same is kept by personal valet Herbert Pixton, how we say, *Igirisu-jin*, Englishman gentleman's gentleman on lifetime retainer contract exclusive to Foto Joe Yamaguch, reet?

Which is yet to mention sole distribution rights owned exclusive by Foto Joe Yamaguch (no stockholders, Jack!) via interlocking structures of Foto Joe Yamaguch Productions, Inc., Ltd., not to fail to mention G.M.B.H., assets of which is forty-six (count 'em, Jack!) feature-length *jujitsu* melodrama adventure flics—how we say, *eiga*, Jack!—starring international heart-throb thespian Mr. Ando Hirobumi, than which who is, how we say in cinema trade, hundred-per-cent boffo bankable, sure-fire certain hit, reet, Jack?

Ultimate *genkin* cash values in event of liquidation is beyond speculation, dig?

Point of above discourse (pith and gist!) is: Foto Joe Yamaguch gots him plenty he can bequest if desired, Jack!

But (sad to say!), *wataschi* gots no living relatives upon whom to bestow largesse. No son to put ritual torch to funeral pyre, no widow-wife helpmeet to grieve tearing hairs, nary chick nor child, Jack—no descendants to clap hands at household shrine and offer up Shinto shtick incense and felicities for eternity.

And do not please to jive Foto Joe as to philanthropical good works—ephemera, Jack! Endow university chairs in cinematic studies? Create scholarships for *Nihonjin* and other nationalities to pursue ambitions as producers, directors, writers, thespians? It is to laugh—as in har (hardy!) and also hee hee, reet? Than which is to say: altruism is rendered emptiness in light of overall ironics I mean to unfold hereafter! Thus: how we say, never *hochee* happen, Jack!

Than which is not to fail to mention same ethos prevails with regards to supporting endowments for public welfares—please not to con *wataschi* with respect to widows, orphans, and other assorted indigents, reet? I mean, like, I done made my nut via self-starting hustle. They is free to perform likewise!

Feel free: call me one lacking compassions for fellow man; do I care? Fact: I care not, Jack! No joke.

Still and all, gots to leave something behind, as how human impulse is to make mark during fleeting *do* of life's life and times lifestyle existence, footprints on sands shtick, as stated heretofore, reet?

So: what's it gonna be, Jack?

Dig this:

Tattoo! Would I yank your limb? Put you on? Shoot you through proverbial grease? Never *hochee*! Listen up, Jack!

Ancient and honorable *Nipponshikki* tradition amongst sailor swabbies of *Nihon*—also global-wide!—is to epitomize essence of significant life experiences as manifest in decorative tattoos, reet? As in: inscribe *Mama-san* (Mother, Jack!) in heart's shape, or perhaps name of first true love (possible irony of which is if as how romance flounders, swabbie marries another, reet?). Also to memorialize martial military services rendered to whichever nation—Yank style is bulldog crushing tank in oversize jaws, paratrooper wings displayed on bicep against backdrop of fleecy cloud, crossed rifles of Queen of Battle (infantry, Jack!), etcetera blah.

And not unknown is it that personages of eccentricity capture inner attitudes of self-irony, as in bumblebee (Big Stinger, dig?) on tip of male member—also barber pole on schlong!—fox chasing after rabbit which flees up anus—I kid you not!

Seafaring sailor swabbies of *Nihon*, Jack, exhibit elaborate distinction (most common amongst whalers and net fishermen who voyage deep waters far from Home Islands). Dig:

Early in life, upon commencement of shipboard career, sailorboy chooses, in close consultation with selected tattoo artist (myriads operate in dock and wharf environs of big port cities—Tokyo, Yokohama, Sasebo), pattern to be executed during intervals of port liberty, paying for same on never never installments plan, reet?

Aforesaid seafarer picks pattern: examples include panorama of carps swimming upstream—symbol of courage and determination (also logo, highly stylized, of Foto Joe Yamaguch Productions!), geometric chrysanthemum motifs, tigers and dragons rampant, enraged noble *samurai* defending coy helpless virgins, *Kabuki* and *No* pageants, Sun Goddess *Amer-atasu* emitting rays of celestial light, legendary depictions, as with forty-seven *ronin*, etcetera blah.

But *wataschi's* intention is otherhow, Jack!

To wit: Foto Joe Yamaguch—*wataschi*!—purposes to create personal

custom-built tattoo, reet? To which purpose I summon for personal conference in confidential confines of Tokyo Town penthouse apartments
(corporate headquarters of Foto Joe Yamaguch Productions!) one Mr.
Terada Seijo, tattooist of renown, than which whose place of business is
Yokohama wharfside district environ. Transportation laid on in form of
chauffeur-driven Rolls Silver Dawn personal limo (ref. tax-deductible
business expense — play all angles simultaneous, natch!). Beforesaid personage tattooist Terada Seijo, put cards on tea table, how you say, tushie
on tisch, strictly up-front and aboveboard shtick, reet? As follows:

Says he: "*Sensei*, I am astounded!"

Says I: "Reet. But can you hack it? Is the price not right? Do you dig the
concept?"

Terada Seijo (minimalist-stature little man, wizened, not unlike like
unto string of dried kelps, reet?): "Your life, *sensei*? You wish me to execute
a body illustration depicting the signal events of your experience?"

Foto Joe Yamaguch (me, Jack!): "Reet! You got it, *Seijo-san*! Like,
chronicle of life and times lifestyle *do* path I done followed, reet? What
wataschi has did, where, with who and how. I'm talking big picture — how
we say in *eiga* flic biz, wide-angle long shot, dig?"

Mr. Terada Seijo: little string of dried kelps corpus, bald head, sports
tattoos everywhere save except hands, face, and feets (walking billboard of
wares, reet?), so old the colors done faded, edges fuzzed, not possible to
discern whereat dragons leave off, tigers and *samurai* commence.

He says: "Are you aware, *sensei*, that a body illustration of this magnitude will require an extensive period of time for its execution? The human
body, *sensei*, will tolerate only so much violation by my needles at a single
session. It is usual, with the seafaring clientele I have the honor to serve, to
utilize twenty or even thirty years to complete the contracted design. Thus
it is, at my advanced age, I assume no new obligations."

I say: "Reet. Toxin inks introduced beneath epidermis takes time to
absorb in order to avoid lethal concentrations. Howsomever, sailorboy
swabbies also stretch duration in deference to financial exigencies, reet?
No problem for Foto Joe, strictly *genkin* cash on barrelhead, natch! Which
is not to fail to mention bonus clauses for diligence of effort and excellence
of execution, as per stated in contract proffered. Nor need you take considerations of pain attendant — I can handle pain, Jack!"

Terada Seijo, string of dried kelps, hit where he lives when confabulation turns to remunerations, reet? Artists, Jack, no matter the medium —
could I tell you some stories from *eiga* trade flic talents? High thought, not
to fail to mention noble ideals, most important except and unless subject of
yen to be garnered come to fore. Terada Seijo commences to tremble a
little, not unlike like unto mild fever's shiver, reet?

He: "Nevertheless, *sensei*, it will possibly require as much as a year or
two — "

Me: "Then let's get cracking, *Seijo-san*! Like, longest journey commences with single step, reet?"

"And I must conceive a preliminary pattern, sketch detail studies, submit for your approval—"

"Ix-nay! Not on your nelly, Jack! Like, I'll tell you as we go, follow flow of *do* as it go, reet? Existential shtick, dig? See, *Seijo-san*, I rely on memories. I mean, like, I know where to start—by time you gots that did in living colors and symmetry of line, trust *wataschi* to have next scene fixed in mind's eye. Free-association shtick, reet? I mean, you want commission, does you not? I mean, rest assured I know you the best in all *Nihon*, than which is why I am so free to offer top *yen*, reet?"

Mr. Terada Seijo, renowned tattoo artist of Yokohama, rubs bald noggin with both hands, traditionalist *Nipponshikki* gesture of self-effacement embarrassment upon hearing praise, reet?

Terada: "No frontal illustration? No arms or legs, *sensei*? Of course, nothing may be done on the hands or visage, since this is forbidden by law as constituting mutilation."

"Tell me about it, *Seijo-san*!"

Mr. Terada Seijo, famed tattooist of Yokohama dockside wharf environ, long thin fingers—so skillful with needles—shaking, Jack! On brink of closing deal of his career. More *yen* than his tiny baby blues done heretofore in life envisioned, which is not to fail to mention prospect of reputation doubtless to be won if and when he pulls it off, reet?

He says: "Dare I presume to ask, *sensei*, if it is your intention to dispose of the illustration in the customary manner?"

"I could say, like, ain't none of your beeswax business, *Seijo-san*, but I won't. To answer thus in a word: *hai*! Reet! Yes. You know it! Last will and testament, sound mind in rapidly fast-failing corpus, corpulence of which, by the way, provides maximum space for your work, contains codicil bequesting *wataschi's* hide to Wantanabe Nautical Museum of Tattoo Arts, than which I know you are cognizant of, as how I done seen some of your stuff on display therein."

He: "Do I hear correctly, *sensei*? You will allow your flayed skin to be preserved and mounted for the general public to view at the Wantanabe museum?"

"For all posterities—barring fires, natch! Are we agreed? Is we got us deal, Terada Seijo?"

"*Sensei*," says he, "I am honored! And I need only execute your ongoing instructions?"

"As per contract on tea table before us. Sign on dotted line with *hanko* signature seal. Unless you want time to consider more fully?"

Mr. Terada Seijo is honored—natch! Limns John Henry in delicate calligraphs—oh, Jack, the man got the artist's hand! Reminds *wataschi* of his old dear departed daddy's touch with ink brush on rice papers!

I think: should be, how you say, portion of confection! I feel serene confidence man can hack it, Jack! Only problem: will fast-fading corpus of Foto Joe Yamaguch, wracked by varied afflictions diagnosed and otherwise, hold out course?

Not to fail to mention Big Query: can *wataschi* slip in all ironies, of which so many abound?

Says I: "Ready when you are, *Seijo-san*! We going to start way back, circa 1928, Ueno Park, little domestic scene I gots in mind, family posed as if for still pic, maybe cherry blossoms, *torri* Spirit Gate, carp pond as background set. Can you dig it, Jack?"

What's in a name?
You tell me, Jack!
Collage: Yoshinori Yamaguchi. Me. Foto Joe.
How we say in *Nihonju, wataschi*. Me.
What's in a name, reet, Jack?

Fact is, like, how we say in celluloid world, cinema-land, film biz, it depends, man. On how you shoot it, reet? Like, what's in the frame and what's ain't. Camera angle. Depth of focus. Soundtrack (music, etcetera blah). Additional dialogue. Special effects. Like, man, what your average person, any Joe Schmoe, John Q. Public, man-in-the-street might say: depends on your point of view, reet, Jack?

I kid you not.
Dig:
Kinestasis: Yoshinori Yamaguchi.
Cut to: still photo, little pic, snapshot from the family album (than which got burned up in a big fire—I work strictly from memory, Jack— about which more later, replete with all kind of big ironies, reet?).

Where was I?

Reet. Still pic, snapshot, black and white, flat tone; zoom in to where we can see the pebble-grain paper, yellowed, curling mat, foxed corners, spider cracks in the finish. Freeze it! Gander, Jack!

What *does* we gots here?

Why, Jack, it is Yoshinori Yamaguchi! It is Mr. and Mrs. Yamaguchi's little boy, Yosh. *Yosho-san*. And his daddy and his mama and his little baby sis Iko. Yoshinori Yamaguchi. And *Papa-san*. And *Mama-san*. And Baby Sis *Iko-san*. Makes four, reet?

Context: how we say, *milieu, mise-en-scene*.

Okay, say, circa 1928. I am ten years old, man. Tokyo Town, natch. Ueno Park. Springtime, Jack. How we say, *hanami*: time to view cherry trees in blossom, lotus in bloom, listen to breeze blow through the green bamboo grass, dig? *Hanami*. Traditional shtick. The whole family—Daddy, Mama, Baby Sis Iko, Yosh (me!)—come out to see the new spring flowers, celebrate the day, Ueno Park, circa '28. Can you dig it?

Sun comes up out of Tokyo Bay, rooster crows, songbirds start in all to chirping in pine trees outside our paper house. Family wakes up, reet? Get up, roll up the beds—how we say, *futon*. Wash, dress. *Mama-san* cooks up breakfast on the charcoal brazier: soybean curd cakes, seaweed (kelps!), *nigirimeshi* rice balls, hot green tea—yum! Sun up strong now, lights up peak of Fuji in distance, warms our paper house. What's we going to do today, Jack?

"This day," says my *Papa-san*, "we shall all go together to view the cherry and the lotus in Ueno Park." *Mama-san* says as how this is a wonderful thing to do this day, for it is, indeed, *hanami*. Baby Sis Iko claps her hands for joy. And little Yosh—me, Jack!—asks can we get one of them itinerant street photographer guys to snap our pic.

Says my daddy, "And why, my son, do you wish to have your photograph taken this day?"

Says I (*Yosho-san*), "Daddy, I want to get me a pic in my school uniform with the new chevron on my sleeve. Please, Daddy," says *Yosho-san* (me!), "I mean, like, we get us a pic of the whole family, me in my uniform, put it in the album, reet?"

My *Papa-san* smiles, says as how he guesses it can be arranged; *Mama-san* smiles, says as how it will be a wonderful thing to have, a memory of *hanami*, this day, in the family album. *Iko-san*, Baby Sis, she claps her hands, says as how she want to take her dolly along to be in the pic too.

The way it was, Jack!

But first we gots this thing we do. Shinto shtick, Jack. There, in our paper house, before we can go to Ueno Park.

We all go together into this little room in our paper house, kneel on the *tatami*, straw mats, bow our heads, pay respects. Like, say hello in Shinto to the small figure of Buddha set up in a niche, how we say, *tokonoma*, in the wall, dig? *Butsudan*, family altar. Small Buddha, rice-paper scrolls, long list, names of the family dead. Paying respects, talking to the family *kami*, how we say, household spirits, reet? My daddy claps his hands to get attention of *kami*, bows his head, asks them to please bless us all and all our undertakings. Start the day off right on correct foot, Jack.

Then off we goes! Than which is not to fail to mention necessity to detour on the way to pass the Imperial Palace, stand in with *hanami* crowds across the road from the deep dry moat, high stone walls. Demonstrate loyalty and reverence for the *Mikado*, Jack!

Kowtow! Bow down low, press your visage on the cinders! We is passing the *Mikado's* house. Hirohito, man, only three years on the Chrysanthemum Throne, living descendant in direct line from *Ameratasu*, Sun Goddess. His mama, old Dowager Empress Sadako, daughter-in-law of old Meiji hisself, founder of *Dai Nippon*, still alive and kicking circa '28, Jack!

Okay. Then head for Ueno Park. Walk through Tokyo Town, rebuilding everywhere from big earthquake of circa '23 (vague memories *wataschi* little Yosh gots: much fire, noise, folks screaming in streets!) — big irony to come!

Ueno Park, cherry blossoms — how we say, *sakura* — lotus in bloom, bask in new spring sunshine, listen to breeze off Tokyo Bay blow through green bamboo grass, watch the gold carps swim in shallow ponds, *torri* Spirit Gates. Can you dig it?

Find that street photographer guy. Walking by with that big box camera, tripod on his shoulder (big irony in this to come, about which more later, reet?). Slip him a few *yen*, pose on the white gravel path, cherry tree in the background, shadow of *torri* Spirit Gate on the arched wooden bridge over shallow carp pond. Pose. Solemn, no grins in pics, how we say, not *Nipponshikki*, unseemly lack of decorum to render *sumairu* smiles in pics, dig?

Pic gets delivered right to the door of our paper house, cardboard mat, all ready for mounting in the family album — big irony! About which more to come later.

Now, gander this pic, Jack; defocus edges of frame here a sec, okay? Slow track in to extreme close-up. Freeze it! Yoshinori Yamaguchi.

Oh, he is a cute little nipper! I mean, like, looking good, man! Check them threads, Jack!

In uniform. Matriculating student in good standing (and how!) of *Aikyojuko*: how we say, Native Land Loving School. I mean: sharp. Standing tall like six o'clock, Jack! Black boots (on white gravel path, Ueno Park), toes spit-shined to look like dipped in glass, pick up highlights from bright spring sun (*hanami*, view *sakura* cherry blossoms, lotus blooms, traditional *Nipponshikki* shtick!). Trousers pressed to knife-blade creases! Stripe up the right leg means: Highest Marks for Performance in All Endeavors Undertaken — *wataschi* is not just another pretty face, reet? This little Yosh ain't no dummy, how we say, no *baka*. He cracks the books, burns midnight oils, gets studies all by heart-rote for daily recitations, dig?

Tunic buttoned up, stiff high collar holds chinny-chin-chin up high. Standing tall! New chevron on right sleeve means: Exceptional Achievement Attained Upon Most Recent Periodic Examination — *Yosho-san*, Jack, A-1 first-class overachiever! Pillbox cap with leather visor.

Do you dig it? This is me! Student Yamaguchi Yoshinori. Circa 1928. Tokyo Town. Ueno Park. *Hanami*. And Daddy and Mama and Baby Sis Iko makes four. Oh, gander!

Hard to see little Yosh's visage, but take my word for it, Jack, he is one cute little nipper! Jackie Coogan with the epicanthic fold. Mickey (a.k.a. Rooney) McGuire with straight black hair — bowl-cut, slicked down, scented, all the rage for little nippers in *Dai Nippon* circa '28. Slim and trim Spanky McFarland. Foghorn Winslow with squeaky soprano voice. Eddie Hodges minus freckles. Yellow Gary Coleman. Get the idea, Jack? Dig it, reet?

Anything else?

Oops! Almost forgot the family. Big irony. Slow track back to full shot of pic, focus, freeze.

Papa-san, Mama-san, Iko-san.

Papa-san. Mr. Yamaguchi. My daddy, Jack.

My daddy is a very distinguished gent. Speaks, reads, writes several languages – I come by my gift for the lingo honest, reet? My daddy, man! Very progressive in the ways of the outside world. No *kimono* for him, Jack! Wears western suits, vest with railroad watch on a chain, carries furled umbrella – how we say, *karakasa* – in all weathers, briefcase, sports a keen fedora, pince-nez on ribbon hooked to his jacket lapel.

Holds a very responsible position: sub-editorial desk at English-language *Japan Times*, published for the diplomatic community of Tokyo Town, dig?

Earns a good living for his family at *Japan Times* – how we say it, *saikatsu*, keeps pot boiling (tell me about it, Jack!). Makes his nut checking out the English (we say: *Eigo*) in them long editorials just starting to print in circa '28, all that *gumbatsu-zaibatsu* shtick. How we say, militarists, plutocrat cats calling for the old *joi-i*, expel the barbarians, *Yamato Damashii* Spirit of Japan, *Nipponshikki* guff stuff; how we say, Japanese system for the Japanese, maintain and enhance cultural purity of the Hundred Millions from violation by *gaijin* foreigners, reet?

Like, dig, Jack: circa 1928, *Dai Nippon* is already talking Manchuria, let's take on the Chinks, bring the eight corners of the world under one roof (*Dai Nippon's*, natch!), how we say: *hakko ichiu*. How we say in *Dai Nippon*, talking like maybe we studying a little war – how we say, *senso*, Jack.

But what's does little Yosh know, man, ten years old, Ueno Park, *hanami*, 1928?

My daddy, Mr. Yamaguchi, *Papa-san*. Head of the family. We all live together in our paper house in Tokyo Town. And when we are in that paper house, Jack, my daddy doffs his western-style threads, slips into a loose *kimono* embroidered with the family coat-of-arms, how we say, *monsho* (carp swimming upstream – means, like, courage, determination). Kneels on the *tatami* mat, takes out his rice papers, ink pot, brushes, practices his calligraphs – how we say, *sho*, reet? Than which is how I like to remember my *Papa-san*, Jack.

See, my daddy was really a poet. No jive – I come by my gift for the lingo honest! Sign of highly cultured individual, *Dai Nippon*, circa '28. My daddy composed *haiku* there in our paper house. Here's one I remember (all mss. burned up in a big fire, along with photo album — irony of which, more about later):

> What is the glory
> Of *Dai Nippon*? Flashing swords
> Or the fruit tree's bud?

Here's another:

> All I know are words,
> Shadows of the world I see.
> Ah, words! Mystery!

One more:

> My only son grows
> To manhood before my eyes;
> Such loss-gain, joy-pain!

Okay, so they lose in translation. Reet. But that is my daddy, Jack! Cut to: *Mama-san. Iko-san.* My mother, how we say, *okasan*, reet? My baby sis. Two of a kind, there on the gravel path, Ueno Park, *hanami*, cherry tree, Spirit Gate, carp pond in background. 1928.

Very traditionalist *Nipponshikki*, dig? Wear *kimono, obi* (how we say, sash), *geta*, wooden clogs. Mama's hair is high on her head, tied in a lacquered bun, powders her face with rice flour for pale complexion than which is all the rage for ladies of *Dai Nippon* in '28. Plucks her eyebrows razor thin.

Okasan. Mama! Keeps our paper house spic and span, Jack, always singing little songs she learned as a girl, about like how great it is to be the woman of our paper house, wife to a fine husband, mother to a son — *wataschi*, Jack, *Yosho-san*! — who's, like, growing into a fine man like his daddy, brings honor to our paper house (Highest Marks for Performance in All Endeavors Undertaken, Exceptional Achievement Attained Upon Most Recent Periodic Examination!). Mother to a beautiful little girl she teaches to someday be a wife and mother and keep a paper house spic and span. My mama! Sings about how she looks forward to the day she will have many grandchildren. Big irony. About which more later, reet? Mrs. Yamaguchi.

Iko-san. My baby sis, reet? Plays at dollies, clonks around our paper house in her little wooden *geta*, reet? Sings the songs she learns from Mama, all about how she will grow up soon and be a woman with fine husband and children and a paper house to keep spic and span.

My baby sister, Iko: asks me all the time to say something for her in English (*Eigo*, the lingo, Jack!). Says as how it sounds so funny, like I'm talking through my nose, a donkey's bray. Cute little nipper, my sis, *Iko-san*.

Kneels next to Mama on the *tatami*, learning how to tie off the branches of a baby tree, stunt growth — *bonsai*, reet? Kneeling beside Mama on the *tatami*, learns how to fold rice paper into birds and flowers and dragons — *origami*. Says to me, "*Yosho-san*, I shall ask my mother to teach me to make a donkey, and then you will teach me the *Eigo* words to make a funny noise for my donkey."

Says I to her . . . Jack, I do not remember what I said! Iko. My baby sister.

Anything else?

Oops! Almost forgot the lingo, man, and the flics! Big irony! Dig this:

Funny thing — funny-strange, reet? — words. The lingo, English, we say *Eigo*, reet? How we say: movies, film, the flicks, is *eiga*. *Eigo*. *Eiga*. I kid you not. Words, Jack! Big irony.

Eigo. The lingo. Oh, you best believe this little Yosh, Mr. and Mrs. Yamaguchi's *Yosho-san*, he is hot crazy cracked for the learning that lingo, the English!

Aikyojuko, Native Land Loving School, A-1 first-class overachiever — stripe up my leg, chevron on my sleeve, gots all them daily recitations by heart-rote. I could show you all my revered teachers' reports, except as how they all got burned up in a big fire, reet? Trust me: little Yosh ain't no *baka* dunce dummy, Jack! Always top marks, head of class form, great promise for future career, most likely to bring honor to family name etcetera blah.

How it were:

Kneel down beside Daddy on the *tatami* (Mama in the kitchen cooking up *nigirimeshi* rice and fish cakes — yummy! — for dinner, Sis Iko playing at dollies, singing songs). *Yosho-san* and Daddy do the read-aloud shtick, today's issue of *Japan Times* hot off the presses downtown (complimentary copy, natch!). Read all them editorials, Jack, *gumbatsu-zaibatsu* guff stuff, *joi-i*, expel the barbarians, *Nipponshikki* Japanese culture in danger of *gaijin* foreign infection, etcetera blah. Drilling them tough words with my daddy — Yosh twisting his little tongue to say the l's and r's than which is tough to extreme in *Nihonju* — how we say, Japanese lingo.

Dig:

Says *Papa-san*: "Once more, my son. Slowly this time, with care for the precise pronunciation."

Listen up to little Yosh! "Long-legged Lilly languidly and lovingly and lasciviously licks eleven licorice lollypops."

Says *Papa-san*: "That was well done. And the other, again, please."

"Rough, ribald riders rode rapidly rearward, reluctantly resigned."

"Excellent, my son!"

"Oh," says *Mama-san*, come in from the kitchen of our paper house to watch and listen whilst she pats a fish cake into shape between her palms. "Oh, soon I shall be embarrassed to speak in the presence of my son, so ignorant am I of all he learns!"

Baby Sis Iko talks to her dolly, says: "*Yosho-san* makes the noise of a donkey."

Says I: "Aw, it ain't nothing but some words. It ain't nothing but that *Eigo*." Big irony, Jack.

Eiga. Film, the flics. What it is, Mr. and Mrs. Yamaguchi's boy Yosh, *Yosho-san*, he is crazy cracked also for them flics, Jack! When not in the classroom at Native Land Loving School, keeping the shine on my stripe, glister on my chevron, when not kneeling beside Daddy on the *tatami* to drill them tough sounds, wrestle the grammar, factor syntax of them *Yamato Damashii* editorials in *Japan Times*, this Yosh is off to the flics!

Best believe. On his way across Tokyo Town, fast as his little legs will take him, *chogee* we say, off and running to Asakusa District, north of Kanda where Daddy buys all his English-language books. Asakusa, Jack, where they gots all the movie theaters, cinema houses, flics, stuck in between all the old *No* and *Kabuki* places. In a hurry to get to the *eiga*, clutching some *yen* in his hot little fist, dig?

I tell my daddy and my revered teachers at Native Land Loving School as how all them flics, how we say *hakurai*, imports from stateside, lets me practice the lingo—subtitles in English, *Eigo*, circa '28; rest of audience gots to listen to the *benshi* explain to them what's happening up on the screen. Big irony, about which more later, reet?

But it don't make *wataschi* no never mind, Jack! Homemade, *hakurai* imports from stateside, *Yosho-san* is pure crazy cracked for all the flics!

Oh, we already making great flics in *Dai Nippon*, circa 1928, all kinds. *Gendai Geki*, how we say, stories of modern life in the big city, reet? *Yakuza*, man, gangster stuff. *Jidai Geki*, historical period pieces, reet? *Chambara*, Jack, swordfight flics!

Yosho-san's personal all-time fave rave: *Man-Slashing, Horse-Piercing Sword*, come out circa 1930—now that is the real vintage *chambara*, Jack!

Great directors already coming up in *Dai Nippon* (Ozu, Mizoguchi, Kason Osanai, Daisuke Ito); studios—Nihattsu, Shochiku, Toho—cranking out flics!

And Towa Company shipping in *hakurai* imports from stateside to Yokohama Harbor—Jack, I seen them all!

Civilization, The Coward, Reaching for the Moon, The Mark of Zorro, Robin Hood, The Black Pirate, The Squaw Man, Male and Female, Blind Husbands, McTeague, Greed, The Merry Widow, Tol'able David, Way Down East, The Covered Wagon, The Four Horsemen of the Apocalypse, Salvation Hunters, Underworld, The Docks of New York, The Iron Horse, Rosita, Nanook of the North—you name it, Jack, it played Asakusa District!

And the stars, man, I seen them all! Florence Lawrence (the Biograph Girl!), Little Mary Pickford, King Baggott, Artie Johnson, Chaplin (natch!), Theda Bara, Dick Barthelmes, Charlie LeRay, Valentino (natch!), Ramon Novarro, Owen Moore, Adolph Menjou, Geraldine Farrar, Mary Garden, Alla Nazimova, Annette Kellerman, the Gish sisters, Gloria Swanson, Tom Meighan, Bill Hart, John Bunny and Fatty Arbuckle and Harold Lloyd, Keaton, man — Yosh done seen them all there in Asakusa District!

I tell my daddy and my revered teachers at Native Land Loving School as how I practice the lingo at the flics, reading them *Eigo* subtitles on the eiga, reet? *Eigo. Eiga.*

Big ironies.

And, the *benshi*, reet?

Benshi, Jack, way it were, circa '28. We don't gots no soundtracks on our homemade flics in *Dai Nippon* until maybe circa 1930. Silent flics, gots to have *benshi*, guy with great stage voice, how you say, storyteller, explains, stands up there by the screen and tells the audience what's happening, so they understand the flic, reet? Except for *Yosho-san*, natch, who can read the subtitles in *Eigo*?

Benshi: gone.

Soundtracks come to flics, puts *benshi* out of business, reet? Like John Gilbert, stateside, hello soundtrack, goodbye *benshi*! 1932, Jack, Asakusa District, all the *benshi* parade, protest soundtracks out in front of them old *No* and *Kabuki* places, *Bunraku* puppet theaters, where they playing sound flics, reet? *Kempei*, police, Jack, come in swinging batons, break some noggins, restore order, back to normal.

Benshi disappear. Like the free lunch, nickel cigar. Like Jack Gilbert stateside. Like the *oyama*, how we say, female impersonators all the *Dai Nippon* studios gots to use back then, guys dress up to play ladies in the flicks as how it ain't considered *Nipponshikki* proper for ladies to appear on big screen then.

All gone: Jack Gilbert, free lunch, nickel cigar. *Oyama. Benshi.*

Ironics, Jack!

Wataschi says the words: *Papa-san. Mama-san. Iko-san.* Ueno Park. Tokyo Town. *Hanami.* 1928.

Yoshinori Yamaguchi.

Gone.

Street photographer guy sets up his tripod, ducks under the black cloth, snaps our pic, big box camera, white gravel path, *sakura* cherry tree, *torri* Spirit Gate, carp pond. Delivers the pic, black and white, cardboard mat, right to the door of our paper house where we all live together, ready for mounting in the family album.

I work from memory, Jack!

Gone.

Because as how the pic and the family album all got burned up in a big fire. Along with that paper house. And a few square blocks of Tokyo Town. And *Papa-san.* And *Mama-san.* And Baby Sis *Iko-san.*

Yoshinori Yamaguchi. Me.

Motto: *Temei Wo Shirii*. How we say: like, total life philosophy, reet?

Meaning? Like, you gots to have a way to see it all at once, reet? But, ain't no lens on no camera makes a frame big enough, Jack!

How it are, Jack: *wataschi* Foto Joe Yamaguch strips off, assumes prone posture position (belly-down) — soft pillow for my noggin, Muzak playing Tokyo Town hit parade hits for distraction, close my baby blues, reet? Atmospherics is cool on my nudeness, chilling shiver overcomes me as Terada Seijo wipes area to be illustrated with cotton ball dipped in alcohol, than which sterilizes dermis, dig? Then I feel touch of Terada Seijo's soft crayon as he draws in rough outlines, not unlike like unto soft finger probing softer adipose.

"Do not," I remind him, "be forgetting stripe up trouser leg, chevron on sleeve, reet?"

"I endeavor, *sensei*," says he, wielding crayon, "to execute your every conception."

"Go for it, Jack!"

Wataschi feels probe of Terada Seijo's soft crayon in cushion of sausage-roll adipose at base of neck. Then the click and snap of his electric needle as he fits new point in bit, buzz begins as he flips on switch. I feel minimalist pain only as he inks in outline, buzz shifting pitch as needle rips in and out of skin — pitch shifting again as he dips point in ink pot, shifts again as he traces further outline.

"Are you comfortable, *sensei*?"

"Sock it to me, Jack!"

"You do not mind the hurt?"

"Go, man, go!"

Pains escalate a notch as Terada Seijo begins back-and-forth with needle to fill colorations in spaces — momentary respites when he dabs off excess pooling inks with swab, ink dropping like unto cool waters from needle's vibrating tip. Pains double as Terada Seijo goes over same area twice, thrice, to blend pigments, create effect of shadow and highlight. "I cannot avoid inflicting some irritation, *sensei*."

"Was I bitching? Get on with it, *Seijo-san*!"

At conclusion of session, *wataschi* radiates heat, glow of warmth swims through taut swelling surface affected. My skin feels as if how it might could burst like ripe plum in hot sun if I move too quick!

"There will," says Terada Seijo, "be several days, perhaps longer, of low-grade fever. This is your body, *sensei*, resisting the toxicity of my pigments. It will require at least twice that long before we can continue the illustrating."

"Trust me," I tell him, "to give you a yell the minute I is ready to resume, reet?"

16

"I await your summons, *sensei*," says he, bows out with minimalist kowtow crabwise backwards locomotion, clutching case of ink pots, crayons, cotton swabs, alcohol wash, electric needle.

Suffering forecast low-grade fevers, *wataschi* waits it out. Affected area (base of neck, sausage-roll adipose, reet?) remains swollen, incandescent, for six days. Thereafter, dermis surface hardens, not unlike like unto thick crust, not to fail to mention commencement of itching. I refrain from scratching only via virtue of iron-fast will powers! Aforesaid base of neck region hardens to feel of heavy wooden disk implanted beneath skin. Thereafter comes onset of flaking and scaling, shedding of skin in multi-hue harlequin scraps. Fevers dissipate. Swelling subsides, hardness dissolves, final layer of dermis peels easy in sheer strips, reet?

Tattoo remains in precision clarity, bright and subtle colorations, exquisite detail — I am talking first-class job of work, Jack!

I get Terada Seijo on horn, how you say, long distance, reet?

"*Seijo-san*, like, what you gots on agenda for the morrow, man?"

"I have only to know the hour you desire my presence, *sensei* Mr. Yamaguch."

"Reet! *Wataschi's* personal Silver Dawn Rolls limo will be at wharf dockside environ at, like, first light of sun's rays touching Fuji's peak, reet?"

"I anticipate our meeting, *sensei*."

"Anks-thay," I say, and, "And, Terada, be thinking meanwhiles in interim of venerable *Nihonjin* sport of *besuboru* — how we say in *Eigo*, baseball, reet?"

"*Besuboru?*"

"Baseball. Know anything from the *besuboru*, Terada Seijo? Not to perspire, I'll fill you in when you get here. We going to do a little scene from *besuboru* baseball, *Seijo-san*, to include caricatures of legendary famed *Amerikajin* Yank all-star stars of American League, to include Bambino, Jim Foxx, et alia, reet? Ever heard from Morris Berg — also knowed as Moe — third-string bullpen good-field no-hit catcher of Senators from Washington, *Seijo-san*?"

"*Sensei*, you mystify me!"

"Forget it. See you bright and timely on the morrow, reet?" I hang up, stand, shirtless, with back to small wall mirror, examine first-class handiwork of famed tattooist Terada Seijo, endeavor to conceive of means by which to inject striking ironics — of which are myriads! — into *besuboru* baseball depictions to come.

Than which is no easy shtick, Jack! As how: *wataschi* gots to keep big picture, totality of scope, always in mind whilst coping with individuated episodics, reet? I mean, I gots to relate particulars to wholeness of grand

17

design, strive toward entirety greater than sum of parts, Jack!

Cut to: circa 1935.

Mise-en-scene, 1935, can you dig it, Jack? *Dai Nippon* now rolling on big chauvinist binge, reet? Hundred Millions is celebrating still from seizure of Manchuria (how we say, *Manchukuo*), spoils of successful *gumbatsu* militarist aggression secured securely under thumb of *Dai Nippon* via figurehead puppet ruler Emperor Henry Pu Yi, last of old-timey Chink Manchu Dynasty, reet? Said personage raised in Forbidden City (a.k.a. Peking, a.k.a. Peiping!) by old Dowager Empress — wet-nursed till he were nine years old aged, Jack, no lie! 1931 Mukden Incident, than which was engineered by *honcho* General Tojo Hideki (nickname: The Razor!) and fellow militarist *gumbatsu* longsword rattlers agitating toward buildup for takeover venture from Manchurian fastness, aforesaid assembling later famed Kwantung Army Corps with eye peeled toward ultimate conquest of China, than which is first step in grandiose design of global-wide *hakko ichui* conquest — bring eight corners of world under roof of *Dai Nippon*, dig?

Ethos governing fast-moving politico and attendant social developments in *do* life course of Hundred Millions is derived from inspirational treatise tract pamphlet authored by obscure personage, than which whose name is Ikki Kita, than which title of is: *An Outline Plan for the Reorganization of Japan*, said tome published circa 1919.

Than which is not to fail to mention ironic side benefits of aforesaid *gumbatsu-zaibatsu* agitation, than which is marked diminishment of economics depression (global-wide event, natch, as witness Wall Street Black Monday, Bank Holiday, five-cent apples, Buddy Can You Spare a Dime?, Okie-land Dust Bowl, not to fail to mention big irony of later famed Dugout Doug MacArthur — a.k.a. $50,000 General, a.k.a. *Makassar-san!* — rousting Bonus Marcher Great War vets from Washington, D.C. shanties, etcetera blah). Evidence of economics recoveries in *Dai Nippon* circa '35 is marked slump in prices paid by Tokyo Town brothel bordellos for village girls (prostitutes, oldest profession, how we say, *moga*, reet, Jack?); previous all-timey high prices for which aforesaid was directly related to skidding silkworm cultivation and other assorted agricultural markets — new bargain cost for which reflects military munitions manufactures boom to supply aforesaid Kwantung Army in *Manchukuo* (a.k.a. Manchuria!), not to fail to mention numerous new keels laid in shipyards for expansion of Imperial Navy, etcetera blah, reet?

Primary foremost socio-politico-cultural effect of all of aforesaid is: sharpening of intensity, higher-decibel volume of anti-*gaijin* foreigner sentiments expressed publicly. How we say, *joi-i*, expel barbarians from sacred soil shores of *Dai Nippon*, foster and maintain purity of *Nippon-shikki*, Japanese culture for Japanese, dig?

18

Howsomever: Jack, what's do little *Yosho-san* know of trends of trendy fashionable momentous historical forces in motion? Like, I, *wataschi*, Yoshinori Yamaguchi, is but sixteen years old aged—sweet ten plus six (never been kissed!), reet, Jack?

Dig: in manner of busy bee (improving each passing hour!), I burn midnight oils to maintain highest excellence of academic performance as matriculating student in good standing at *Aikyojuko* Native Land Loving School, occupying top slot in First Form—stripe up trouser leg, chevron on sleeve, Form Leader by common acclaim in all subjects undertaken, reet?

Except to confess, achievement is marred by *wataschi's* failure to excel in new extracurricular *budo* studies curriculum required of all national students by force of Imperial Rescript—than which is to say: order promulgated direct from *Mikado*, reet? Regretfully, I is doing only okay, average (piss poor, Jack!) in such as squad drill, manual of arms with dummy rifle, ceremonial wielding of longsword (*katana!*), daily recitations of glorious military triumphs of *Dai Nippon* dating back to Meiji Restoration, time-honored *Nipponshikki* code of *Bushido* handed down by *samurai* traditions, loyalty to *Mikado* and love of country shtick etcetera blah, reet?

Notable failure to attain such excellence, I does contend, is due to how young Yosh's efforts is (natch!) expended fully in unceasing study of *Eigo* English lingo, Jack! Than which is to say, circa 1935, *wataschi* is well beyond concern for basic grammars and syntax, now into heavy reading of popular stateside periodical publications: *Time, Saturday Evening Post, Silver Screen, Modern Romance, Colliers, Liberty, Stars of Stage, Screen and Radio*—not to exclude, how we say, *shimbun* newspapers. *New York Times, Chicago Tribune, San Francisco Examiner* of famed Yellow Kid W. R. Hearst (noted admirer of Mussolini, paramour of starlet Marion Davies, latter frequently hinted in columns of *eiga* cinema gossip authored by L. O. Parsons, H. Hopper, et alia!). Which is to say, Jack: my purpose, circa '35, is to master idiom slangs and other eccentricities common to all lingos!

Dig it:

Typical eventide regimen routine, Jack, circa 1935: doff my school uniform in exchange for *yakuta*, how we say, summerweight man's *kimono*, as how it is unseasonably hot this autumn (circa '35, *tsukimi*, time of moon-viewing, reet?), eat dinner served up by *Mama-san* in our paper house. All together: Daddy, Mama, Sis Iko (now growed to schoolgirl aged nine years of age, about to give up playing with dollies, but enjoys still to rag big bro Yosh over humorous donkey-noise of *Eigo* pronunciations). So: chow time, supper, paper house of Yamaguchi family, circa early October of 1935 (*tsukimi* time for viewing fat harvest moons!), unseasonably warmish weathers; Yamaguchi family kneels on *tatami* mats at low table, ingests nutritional repast of steamy *nigirimeshi* rice, thick

bean-jam buns, fresh green kelps for roughage, beverage is *o-cha* hot tea—
yummy!

Sample dialogue (from memory, Jack!):

Iko-san: "*Yosho-san*, will you play at the game of *go* with me when we have finished our meal?"

Yosh (me!): "Love to, Sis, but I gots me the whole Sunday *Times* to get through tonight, chock full of reviews and publicity stills from latest *Amerikajin eiga* flics, reet? Sorry, kid, no can do."

Mama-san: "My son, I fear you will injure your health if you do not permit yourself some respite from your studies."

Yosh (me): "I'm fine, Mama. I gots to stay with it if I want to do good on terminal exams and graduate in top slot of form next summer."

Says *Iko-san*: "*Yosho-san* does not even join in the recreations of his fellow students of Native Land Loving School. He prefers to read the *gaijin Amerikajin* magazines *Papa-san* buys for him in Kanda District. His fellow students say he cannot even march correctly with his rifle, nor does he know how properly to wear his longsword."

Mama-san: "Do not presume to tease your brother." Mama says, "He studies to be a great scholar, not a soldier. I only worry that he will make himself ill."

Papa-san (looking good in his pince-nez, *yakuta* embroidered with Ya-maguchi family crest—carp swimming against current!—much at ease, looking forward to long eventide making poems with his ink and brushes, *sho* shtick): "Do we complain that our son exhibits discipline and dedication in his pursuit of learning? Does his young sister criticize him because he prefers the intricate beauty of language to the stupidly mechanical playing at soldiers and war that is surely better suited for the amusement of ignorant village boys?"

Yosh: "Reet! You tell 'em, Daddy!"

Mama-san: "You know I would not presume to criticize my only son. I am only a mother and a foolish, uneducated woman."

Iko-san: "I only teased, *Papa-san*. I am a foolish girl."

Jack: sample dialogue, as in, words to effect, reet? I gots to work from memory.

One night—I disremember which exactly!—circa autumn of '35, *tsu-kimi*, my mama says to me at dinner: "My son, will you tell me what you shall do in the year to come when you have completed the work of the first form at Native Land Loving School?"

My daddy speaks right up, Jack! "He shall of course be admitted to one of our city's seven universities for advanced studies. What else would a young man of his talent and achievement do? He has a bright future, and will bring honor to this house and to our name and to his ancestors and the *kami* to whom we pray each day for his continued success. Our son's career

20

is assured. The government will have a great need of linguists to serve in the bureaucracy as *Dai Nippon* seeks to develop relations with the nations of the world. My son," says my daddy to me, "your mother asks a question to which the answer has already declared itself in scholastic attainments!"

And I say to them—my daddy, my mama, my sis Iko—words to the effect (big *ma* moment in *do* life and times to come, Jack, vibrations of ironies impending all through atmosphere aura of our paper house!): "Mayhap. I mean, like, unless, like, I could mayhap wangle me one of them scholarships for study abroad? I mean, like, if I could glom me one of them Imperial Ministry of Education grants to go overseas, I might could mayhap go to college stateside, reet?"

Says *Mama-san*: "Across the ocean to study *Eigo* among the *gaijin* barbarian *Amerikajin*! Do not say this! It is even said that there both male and female students attend the same school! Do not say this, my son!"

Says *Iko-san* (big *sumairu* smile, laughs): "I think my brother wishes to go to Hollywood in America to seek the *hanko* autograph signatures of the actors and actresses who appear in the *gaijin eiga*!"

Says my *papa-san*: "My son, this is a bold ambition, but unlikely to come to pass. In addition to credentials of excellent scholarship, one must have influential references and recommendations. Political connections are required to obtain permission for foreign study, especially in these troubled times."

And I says to them, Jack—my family, in our paper house there in Tokyo Town one autumn *tsukimi* eventide, circa 1935 (words to effect, from memory, reet?): "Folks, I gots the grades! Good grades is no sweat! And, Daddy, you gots to know some high-power *honcho zaibatsu* with clout on account of your job at *Japan Times*, reet? I mean, like, folks, I really think it's what I'd like to do. They gots some first-rate institutions of higher learning stateside, Daddy! Harvard, Yale, Princeton, UCLA, Wisconsin!"

"I do not think I can bear to imagine my only son leaving our home to go so far away!" says my *Mama-san*.

Papa-san says, "I think not, my son. The politicians of my acquaintance are not currently in favor with our government. These are times when wise men are prudent, seldom seen and saying little or nothing. No, my son, I do not think fate intends this for the *do* future path of your life."

Says my baby sis (big *sumairu* grin): "Perhaps if you write letters signed with your blood to show sincerity, and address them to the actors and actresses of Hollywood in America, *Yosho-san*, they might intercede on your behalf?"

To which all I did riposte: "Mayhap I could get lucky. I mean, like, could *hochee* happen, if, like, it was a miracle sort of?"

"Indeed," says my daddy, "such an event would constitute a miracle."

"May such miracles never come to pass!" says Mama.

"Clap your hands, *Yosho-san*," says my baby sis, Iko, who, aged nine years of age, do enjoy to rag her big bro, "summon our family *kami*, and we will all join you in prayer to ask them to provide you a miracle!"

Big irony, Jack! Unfolding of which I delay only shortly; how we say in *Nihonju, skosh*, reet?

Dig it: circa '35 (autumn, *tsukimi*!), *wataschi*, Jack, this Yosh, sweet sixteen years aged, cracking books by flickering oil-lamp light of midnights, steady perusing them *Eigo* periodicals and *shimbun* newspapers, not to fail to mention *hakurai* import *eiga* flicks.

Jack, I seen them all! *Little Caesar, Scarface, Public Enemy, Public Hero Number 1, The Big House, San Quentin, The Criminal Code* — great *yakuza*, Jack, how you say, gangster flics, reet? Which is not to fail to mention advent of highfidelity soundtracks enabling outstanding musicals, reet? *The Jazz Singer, The Lights of New York, The Blue Angel, Morocco, 42nd Street, Golddiggers of 1933, Big Broadcast of 1932*, also mentioning comedies and human-interest yarns: *Duck Soup, It Happened One Night, Design for Living, Trouble in Paradise, Horsefeathers, She Done Him Wrong, I'm No Angel, Six of a Kind, The Blonde Venus, Shanghai Express.* To name a few, reet?

Which is not to forget emerging luminaries of silver screen, Jack: Fred Astaire and Ginger Rogers, Nelson Eddy and Jeannette MacDonald, Allen Jones, Rise Stevens, Shirley Temple and Bobby Breen, Deanna Durbin, Sonja Henie, Cagney (natch!), Eddie G. Robinson, Paul Muni, Bette Davis, Richard Powell, Ruby Keeler, Joan Blondell, Don Ameche and Alice Faye, Gable (natch!), Claudette Colbert, the Brothers Marx, Mae West, Tom E. Kennedy and Paula Casey, W. Claude Fields, Dietrich. To denominate but a sample, reet? As in, gone but not wholly forgot, reet?

Remembering also genius directors, as in Hitchcock, Howie Hawks, Jack Ford, Von Sternberg — dawn of Golden Era of stateside *eiga* flics! Which is to say, Jack, Yoshinori Yamaguchi (me!) was there! Asakusa District, every spare *yen* laid out for ducats, dig?

Than which is why, pervasive influence of aforesaid, *wataschi* Student Yamaguchi Yoshinori is thinking steady of possibility of pursuit of higher education stateside. Than which only possible possibility is touch from Fate's fickle digit, prod from toe of Lady Luck's pedal extremity, how you say: all's I needs is miracle, reet?

Big irony of which I now relate, Jack:

Autumn 1935: *Dai Nippon shimbun*, how you say, newspapers, all at once filled with reports and editorials concerning imminent arrival of barnstorm tour of Yank American League all-stars. Big goodwill visit of *Amerikajin* hardballers scheduled to come to shores of *Dai Nippon* to stage exhibitions of diamond prowess, provide instruction in subtle arts of Yank national pastime, smoothen and affix current troubled relations between

U. S. of A. and *Dai Nippon*, reet?

How you say, *deus ex machina*, than which proves to be means whereby I, *wataschi*, Student Yamaguchi Yoshinori, come to make fated acquaintance of Mr. Morris (a.k.a. Moe) Berg, third-string bullpen warm-up catcher of Senators of Washington (D.C.). Than which proves to be means by which is set into flux resultant series of events crucial to life and times *do* future lifestyle of me, Yoshinori Yamaguchi a.k.a. Foto Joe Yamaguch! Which is to say said series of *do* path twisty turns are replete with interlocked and interfaced ironies large and small, substance of which is both design and texture of my narration to come, circa 1935 to present contemporary instant.

Catalytic event (finger or toe of *deus ex machina* miracle shtick in offing, reet?): enter one Mr. Suzuki Sataro, ace sport reporter and columnist for Tokyo Town *Yomiuri Shimbun*, rabid fanatical fan of Yank *besuboru* baseball, organizer of league competitions for teams representing seven Tokyo universities.

Aforesaid Mr. Suzuki persuades employer (despite *joi-i* opposition of governing establishment to infestation of barbarian *gaijin* foreign influences) to invite team of junior-circuit American League all-stars to visit *Dai Nippon*, late autumn (*tsukimi*) of 1935, to perform aforesaid exhibition games versus seven Tokyo university squads, offer fine-point pointers coaching clinics, generate international goodwills, etcetera blah.

Dig: Morris Berg—also knowed as Moe—is included in company of genuine diamond immortals (Ruth, Gehrig, Foxx, et alia) on basis of reputed casual study of *Nihonju*, than which study Moe professes desire to accelerate in on-site context, reet? Ironics of which is: superannuated third-stringer bullpen warm-up catcher (never stroked .300!) accompanies barnstormer greats to shores of *Dai Nippon*, late autumn of '35, whereat and hereafter as I relate, fate's *do* flow paths cross for Moe and me—*wataschi*, Student Yamaguchi Yoshinori, prize performer of First Form, Native Land Loving School, fanatic fan of things *Amerikajin* via lifelong to date craze for *eiga* flics in *Eigo* lingo. Dig it, Jack! As follows:

Cut to: office environ of Mr. Nobuyoshi Muto, *honcho* head prefect of *Aikyojuko*, Native Land Loving School, Jack! I is talking called on carpet formalist *kaigi* conference of serious significance note, reet?

Assembled include (natch) Mr. Nobuyoshi Muto, said personage seated stately ensconced *honcho* exec-style behind large rosewood desk. Head Prefect Nobuyoshi is attired in new-style *monpei* garb, how we say, quasi-military pantaloons-tunic-puttees combo than which is new fashion (replacing western-style double-breasteds with vests) sumptuary norm, than which is gesture in deference to *budo* trends which is all recent rage for officialdom civil-servant factotum bureaucrat personages of *Dai Nippon*, circa 1935.

On wall behind desk, replacing no-longer-fashionable reprint portraits of A. Lincoln and G. Washington (heretofore revered as paradigm types of responsible executive leadership) is series of oversize calligraphs (bright red ink on rice-paper panels): *Chukun Aikoku, Hakko Ichui, Kodo, Yamato Damashii*, and most recent patriotic slogan, *Eija Nai Kai*, meaning of which is: ain't it good, the way things is in *Dai Nippon*, circa '35? Not to fail to mention silk national flag, *Hino Maru*. Also not to fail to mention (natch!), standard photo pic of *Mikado* Hirohito mounted regal — plumed hat, big epaulets, knee-high boots and spurs — astride favorite white horse charger named Snow White.

November 2, 1935, Jack: *tsukimi*, time of traditionalist viewing of fat harvest moons, reet?

Also present at formalist-type *kaigi* conference confabulation: personage heretofore unbeknownst to *wataschi* Student Yamaguchi Yoshinori, aforesaid oddly wearing out-of-fashion western suit (double-breasted, vest, high white collar, old school tie, furled umbrella, gray fedora hat in hand) — aforesaid personage introduced to me as Mr. Sato Isao, self-described as humblest functionary factotum of Imperial Ministry of Education, reet?

Mr. Sato Isao: smallish man, benevolent of mien, sparkly baby blues behind specs — totality effect of which appearance and demeanor masks aforesaid's impending role already underway as *deus ex machina* of significance almost equivalent to that of Moe Berg in woof and warp of life and times *do* future path of *wataschi* — who (me!) stands tall on metaphoric carpet (*kaigi* formalist conference confabulation), kowtow bows correctly — forty-five degrees! — upon introduction, waits all inwardly a-tremble in charged *kaigi* conference ambience aura of Head Prefect Nobuyoshi's office.

Here follows momentous dialogue (from memory, Jack!):

Says Mr. Nobuyoshi Muto (to Mr. Sato Isao — touch of deference in dipping head, trace of condescending *sumairu* smile, as how uncertainties of respective status of duo calls for such subtle ambiguity of interaction): "I am pleased to present Student Yamaguchi Yoshinori as a candidate for your consideration, *sensei* Mr. Sato. In my capacity as head prefect of Native Land Loving School, I am able to suggest his suitability with confidence. I am able to state that in all the illustrious history of this institution of learning, we have never heretofore boasted a matriculant of such achievement and promise. In the study of *Eigo*, it is accurate to state that he rivals even his mentors, especially with regard to idiom and other peculiarities of that barbarian *gaijin* tongue. In conventional studies, mathematics, history, geography, and the natural sciences, he is among the

24

most excellent of our many diligent students."

Says Mr. Sato Isao (to Head Prefect Nobuyoshi—minimalist five-degree kowtow bow of deference mitigated by flickering of *sumairu* sneer on thin lips): "I am impressed, *sensei* head prefect, and convey, on behalf of the Imperial Ministry of Education, sincere congratulations to you and your staff in recognition of the excellent teaching and moral guidance required to produce such a student! Student Yamaguchi Yoshinori," says he, "would seem, from your recommendation, to be the very model of perfection."

"I would be remiss if I were not to add," says Nobuyoshi Muto, "at least one qualification. Student Yamaguchi Yoshinori," he says, "has yet to apply himself with the full potential of his ability to the recently prescribed course of *budo* studies. In this regard, we must censure his apparent lack of enthusiasm, and we must continue to strive to improve his physical skills in drill devoted to both the rifle and the *katana* longsword. However, his memorization of daily recitations is as superior in this area of learning as it is in all others."

"It is obvious, *sensei* head prefect," says Mr. Sato Isao—supposed functionary factotum of Imperial Ministry of Education, reet?—"that no detail escapes the scrutiny of the mentors of Native Land Loving School! Nevertheless, I feel most confident that this young man's qualifications make him most suitable for the task we propose to entrust to him."

"It was, *sensei* Mr. Sato, my fervent hope you would find him so," says Nobuyoshi.

Dig, Jack! I mean, like, *wataschi* is at total loss as to what's what, reet? I mean, correct behavior decorums—as taught to me by my *papa-san* and *mama-san*—dictate as how I should be rubbing head with both hands as gesture of self-effacement embarrassment upon hearing direct praise, reet? Which is not to fail to mention as how decorums necessitated by called on metaphoric carpet *kaigi* formalisms situation plus standard school discipline shtick in presence of head prefect, than which is added to seen-not-heard norm for presence of adult male visitor dictates I stand tall like six o'clock, eyes-front shtick.

Than which all above is complexified by fact that this Yosh, though but sweet sixteen years old aged, ain't no dummy *baka*, reet? Which is to say: *wataschi* is full knowing something big for him is clearly in offing, Jack! Dialogue (from memory!) ensues:

"*Hai!*" says honcho Head Prefect Mr. Nobuyoshi Muto—how we say: just so, all facts, gists and piths, direct on the nob, smack dab in center of bull's eye, everything copacetic, reet? "I am in full agreement with you, *sensei* Mr. Sato, that Student Yamaguchi Yoshinori is the ideal candidate to serve in a semiofficial capacity as a representative, not only of Native Land

Loving School, but also on behalf of the Imperial Ministry of Education, the government of *Dai Nippon*, and our beloved *Mikado*!"

Jack: aforesaid utterance mentioning direct descendant of Sun Goddess *Ameratasu* mandates following shtick:

Honcho Head Prefect Nobuyoshi Muto stands up behind his big exec-style rosewood desk, turns to face photo pic of Hirohito mounted regal-style astride favorite white horse Snow White, joins me and (natch!) Sato Isao personage in formal full fifty-degree kowtow bow from waist (arms at side, Jack!) in direction of *Mikado's* photo likeness.

Reseated, *honcho* head prefect says, "Is it your final decision then, *sensei* Mr. Sato, that Student Yamaguchi Yoshinori is selected for assignment to this important mission?"

"*Hai!*" says Mr. Sato Isao.

To me (*wataschi*, Yosh, aged but sweet sixteen years!), Head Prefect Nobuyoshi says, "Student Yamaguchi Yoshinori — " I snap to! — "you have been selected to serve *Dai Nippon* in a capacity that promises great honor and glory. Are you prepared, Student Yamaguchi Yoshinori, to exert yourself to the utmost degree of your ability on behalf of Native Land Loving School, the Hundred Millions of your nation, and the *Mikado*?"

Than which utterance — natch! — compels him to get on his feet again, join me and Sato in fifty-degree kowtow bow to pic of Hirohito and Snow White on wall behind his rosewood desk, reet?

Says I (Yoshinori Yamaguchi, Jack — aged sweet sixteen years old, circa November 2, 1935!): "*Hai!*" As how, *wataschi* no *baka* fool, I does know this is shot at bluebird brass ring. "I mean, like," I say, "*sensei honcho* head prefect, you doing me great honor and all, and I, like, accept whatever, humble self and all, ready and willing, reet?"

"Commendable," says Mr. Sato Isao, than which who nods and renders *sumairu* smile at Nobuyoshi, than which who renders nod-smile in riposte — aforesaid status stature ambiguities is, like, relaxed some in satisfaction shared in satisfactory accord reached by all concerned — how we say, *enryo*, everything working out harmoniously between folks, reet, Jack?

Subsequent to which, Mr. Sato Isao lays out for me what's *hochee* happening, what's going down, reet?

"Are you, Student Yamaguchi Yoshinori, familiar with the activities of one Mr. Suzuki Sataro, a journalist?"

"Reet," says I, "Suzuki, he's the guy writes all the *besuboru* stuff for *Yomiuri Shimbun*, done gots the seven Tokyo Town universities organized for competitive play, all the time writing about as how athletic youths of *Dai Nippon* gots to get on par in sport skills with *Amerikajin* big leaguers and all, reet?"

"Precisely," says Head Prefect Nobuyoshi Muto.

"More particularly," says Sato Isao, "are you, Student Yamaguchi Yo-

shinori, aware of the impending arrival in *Dai Nippon* of the select delegation of *Amerikajin* athletes who will present a series of instructional clinics
and exhibition contests in concert with teams representating our seven
universities?"

"Reet. I been reading in all the *shimbun* of late. I mean, I ain't no
besuboru baseball fan fanatic, but I always check out all the news when I'm
reading reviews of the new *eiga* flics, and my daddy, Mr. Yamaguchi, even
did an editorial in *Eigo* for *Japan Times* about as how the international
diplomatic community shouldn't, like, mistake the sentiments of *Nihonjin*
Hundred Millions, like, not presume we was enthusiastic for decadent
gaijin cultures just because we host these *Amerikajin* hardballer barnstormers on our sacred soil. I read all about it, *honcho sensei*, big *matsuri*
gala carnival festival doings scheduled for arrival of Yank ballplayers at
Yokohama dockside and all, reet?"

Nobuyoshi and Sato exchange *sumairu* smile-nods, as how to indicate
how good I done, how good they chose from ranks of Native Land Loving
School student corps—how we say, circa '35, *Eija Nai Kai*: ain't it just
wonderful, how it is, good feelings of *enryo* satisfaction reciprocities mutually enjoyed in *yoin* resonance of *ma* moment in *do* flow of life, Jack.

"Are you familiar," says Mr. Sato Isao, "with the specific personages
who constitute the select delegation of *Amerikajin* athletes who will enjoy
the hospitality of *Dai Nippon*?"

Says I: "Like, Sultan of Swat Bambino Babe Ruth—I read in *shimbun* as
how Yankees of Big Apple Gotham New York done just give him his
walking papers and he's dickering for contract to play and also coach for
Red Stockings of Boston Beantowners. Also Iron Man Louis Gehrig,
affectionately called Lou, formerly long-timey peer teammate of Sultan
Bambino Babe, and also Jim Foxx I read some of. Also I read as how
Grand Old Man of Baseball Cornelius MacGillicuddy—knowed also as
Connie Mack—is coaching them on this *Dai Nippon* barnstorm jaunt, reet?
Like, *honcho sensei*, I try to keep up with what's happening, stay current in
the know as part and parcel of *Eigo* studies."

"Most admirable, Student Yamaguchi Yoshinori," says Sato—*sumairu*
smile-nod to Nobuyoshi, than which signals: continued satisfaction as to
choice of candidate presented for mission promising honor, glory, etcetera
blah—"And can you tell me if you recognize the name of the *Amerikajin*
athlete Morris Berg, most commonly denominated as Moe?"

"Moe?"

"Morris Berg."

"Morris Berg?"

"Moe Berg."

"Sorry, *sensei*, never heard of him. Nope. I mean, like, don't register,
reet? Morris Berg, also knowed as Moe, pure Greeks to *wataschi*. Zilch.
Zip. Not diddly squat. Who he, *honcho sensei*?"

"Morris Berg, frequently referred to as Moe, is the cause of our *kaigi* gathering here today," says Head Prefect Nobuyoshi.

"The *Amerikajin* Moe Berg is the object of the mission you have been chosen to undertake, Student Yamaguchi Yoshinori," says Sato—Imperial Ministry of Education factotum functionary. Har. Also hee, Jack! "I assure you, Student Yamaguchi Yoshinori," says he, "Moe Berg is a personage you shall come to know well!"

Big Irony in the making, Jack! Can you dig it? *Deus ex machina*. Fickle digital appendage of Fate. Caress of Madam Luck. Miracle shtick! Fundamental ironic thrust of which is: what's do *wataschi* know, reet? Student Yamaguchi Yoshinori, aged sweet sixteen years old, poised on brink of bluebird shot, brass-ring grab, wheel stopping on my numeral. Oh, big ironies to come, Jack! As how I commence to continue to relate, as follows:

"Mr. Morris Berg, ubiquitously referred to as Moe," says Mr. Sato, "is employed by the American League Senators of Washington—"

"Reet," I interject, "perennial cellar dwellers ever since retirement of star moundsman Walter Johnson, also knowed as Big Train, franchise reduced to also-ran status, as how I know from casual perusals of Suzuki Sataro's sports chat column in *Yomiuri Shimbun*, reet?"

"Washington," Sato says—raising hand like traffic cop to override interruption rudeness—"is the *Amerikajin* city wherein is located the barbarians' seat of national governance."

"Reet," says I, "D.C." As how, Jack, I is eager to display keen and alert current in-the-know info, to include both geographies and geopolitics, reet?

"Please remain silent whilst Mr. Sato expounds, Student Yamaguchi," says Head Prefect Nobuyoshi, and, "Speech is ivory, silence jade."

"Reet. Like, thousand pardons and all, *honcho sensei*."

"Mr. Moe Berg," says Sato, "is a peculiar individual." He holds a beat to see if I am staying mum as ordered, proceeds: "He is the least notorious of the select *Amerikajin* delegation scheduled to arrive in *Dai Nippon* on the ninth of November. He is quite inferior in athletic prowess to others such as Mr. Ruth, Mr. Gehrig, or the Mr. Foxx you cite. Further, unlike his athletic colleagues, he is a man of some considerable educational attainment, having graduated with honor from Princeton University—"

"Reet," I say, unable to exert respectful restraint upon exuberant tongue, "Ivy League. Go, Tigers!" I resume stony silence in response to hard look conveyed by Nobuyoshi but relax in reassurance of indulgent *sumairu* smirk bestowed by Sato.

"Equally distinctive," he says, "is Mr. Berg's very proficient facility with foreign languages, to which proficiency he has been reputed of late to have added a seemingly informal study of *Nihonju*. He has submitted a request in concert with the journalist Suzuki Sataro, forwarded to my office from the *Amerikajin* embassy, that he be provided with a companion for the duration of his visit to *Dai Nippon*."

"This Moe Berg personage," says Nobuyoshi, "alleges that the company of a native speaker of *Nihonju*, equally fluent in barbarian *Eigo*, will both facilitate the presentation of the aforesaid projected instructional clinics and exhibition contests with the athletes representing our seven Tokyo universities, even as it aids Mr. Berg in his study of our language."

"And you done choosed me for the job, *honcho sensei*?" says I—*wataschi*, Student Yamaguchi Yoshinori, sweet sixteen aged, seeing all of a sudden aforesaid bluebird in gunsight, brass ring just around next turn, door of career goals opportunity begging for knock, Jack!

"Morris Berg," says Sato Isao, "expressly requests that his assigned interpreter be someone of tender years, a student."

"I can dig it!" I say.

"Mr. Berg professes a desire to learn the state of mind of the emerging generation of *Dai Nippon*," Nobuyoshi says—whereupon he performs mock spitting on floor, traditionalist *Nihonjin* gesture of repugnance revulsion—Sato renders me tired shrug on sly, as how to say: look what's we gots to put up with, reet?

"Do you feel capable of performing this role, Student Yamaguchi Yoshinori?" inquires Mr. Sato Isao.

"*Hai!*" says I, and also, "Sock it to me, *honcho sensei*! I is your boy, best believe! I mean, like, chance to hobnob with famous legendary great Yank *besuboru* stars Ruth, Gehrig, Foxx, et alia! Earn distinctions, honor and glory shtick for family, school, and nation! Hone up on red-hot contemporary *Eigo* idiom slangs! Can do, *honcho sensei*! I mean, like, should be piece of confection for me. Milk run. Easy money. Made in shade whilst quaffing lemonade! Oh, *honcho sensei*," says I—me, Jack!—"I does dig it the most!"

Irony emerges, Jack! Than which is to say, insect in salve raises ugly noggin to cast pall on happy *enryo* satisfactory reciprocities, reet? Always a catch, reet, Jack? Dig:

"There are, Student Yamaguchi Yoshinori," Sato says, "complications."

"There are," says *honcho* head prefect, "considerations of some delicacy to be observed by one who would undertake this mission on behalf of Native Land Loving School, *Dai Nippon*, and our beloved *Mikado*." After than which utterance (natch!), Nobuyoshi gots to unseat self once more, all assembled join in fifty-degree kowtow bow to Hirohito and Snow White pic on wall, reet?

"The entire affair is irregular, and is so viewed by all in authority," says

Sato. "*Dai Nippon* strives for national cultural self-renewal in these times. The patriotic and loyal Hundred Millions enthusiastically embrace the sentiment of *joi-i* articulated by our progressive leadership, and we dedicate our energies to the achievement of total *Nipponshikki*. The impending visit of these barbarian *gaijin Amerikajin* athletes is a phenomenon contrary to these ends," says he, casts gander at calligraph slogans on wall behind head prefect's big exec-style rosewood desk.

"The actions of Mr. Suzuki Sataro in bringing these *gaijin* and their decadent sport to *Dai Nippon* will earn him only most unfavorable notice," Nobuyoshi says, "and I am confident we may trust to appropriate authorities — " renders deferential *sumairu* nod-smile in Sato's direction — "to treat him and his seditious scribblings in the *Yomiuri Shimbun* in a fitting manner when they deem the time for just retribution is at hand!"

"That is not for me," says Sato, baby blues downcast in appropriate gesture of self-effacement humility shtick, "a mere bureaucratic servant of the Imperial Ministry of Education, to say."

"The sole question that remains," says Nobuyoshi, "is whether or not you, Student Yamaguchi Yoshinori, will be able to withstand the corrupting influence of a sustained proximity to this Moe Berg personage." *Wataschi* looks at Sato; he looks back at me: as how to say, dig it, Jack, you gots to tell them what's they want to hear, reet?

I say: "Reet!" and, "Natch!" and, "*Hai!*"

I say: "Like, *honcho sensei*, trust *wataschi* to play it strictly coolish, reet? I mean, like, I will translate for this Morris — also knowed as Moe — Berg and his Yank barnstorm *besuboru* peers, do tour-guide shtick, reet? Show them all the sights, peak of Fuji in the distance, fat harvest moon of *tsukimi* hanging like paper lantern over Tokyo Bay, weekend hordes of peasant-types schlepping to Imperial Palace walls to pay homages, kiddies flying dragon kites in Ueno Park, point out dexterity of maidens engaged in silkworm cultivation, arrange ducats for *No* and *Kabuki* performances, *sumo* matches, lead field trip to nautical museums to view *irezumi* tattooed skins on display, teach them how to clap hands to summon *kami* for prayer at Yasukuni Shrine, sip *sake*, show methods of wielding *hashi* chopsticks with grace and ease, lay on formalist *Nipponshikki o-cha* tea ceremony, even host *zaibatsu*-style *geisha* party if budget permits — in short, *honcho sensei*, all standard rubberneck tourist gig!"

Mr. Sato Isao nods, *sumairu* grins, as how to say: you done real good, Jack!

Some few minimalist *ma* moments of *yoin* resonances follow, Jack. Head Prefect Nobuyoshi looks at Imperial Ministry of Education factotum functionary (to laugh, Jack!) Mr. Sato Isao; they look at me; I do not look back.

I stand tall, Jack! Straight like six o'clock, freeze baby-blue eyeballs on wall behind Nobuyoshi's exec-size rosewood desk, calligraph panels of trendy slogans, pic of Hirohito regal astride Snow White—to resist surges of mounting *hara* belly tensions, *wataschi* inwardly conjugates irregular *Eigo* verbs, rehearses definitions of past and future-perfect tenses (as memorized from reading of classic *Some Conventions of Standard English*, authored by Professor Thomas Warren, purchased for me on special order direct from stateside through English-language bookstore in Kanda District), assemble list of *besuboru* vernaculars picked up in spare-time perusals of Suzuki Sataro's sport-chat columns in *Yomiuri Shimbun*: suicide squeeze, drag bunt, Texas Leaguer, boner play, hot corner—also stove!— step in pail, etcetera blah, reet?

"Then," says Nobuyoshi Muto, *honcho* head prefect of Native Land Loving School—alma mater mine, Jack!—"you will gird yourself to be ever impervious to any blandishments, any influences of Mr. Morris Berg—more often called Moe—and his barbarian cohorts throughout the duration of your association with them, Student Yamaguchi Yoshinori?"

"*Hai!*"

"You will further, Student Yamaguchi Yoshinori," says Sato Isao, "report to me at once and in full detail any unusual or suspicious occurrence that may come to your attention whilst traveling with and among the *Amerikajin* athletes?"

"*Hai!*"

"It is not," Sato says, "that we have tangible cause to assume there is anything untoward in the inclusion of this Morris—familiar name Moe— Berg in the select *Amerikajin* delegation, it is only that his relative lack of athletic prowess, his educational distinction as a linguist, and his residence in the city of Washington, seat of the *Amerikajin* government, combine to give us sufficient cause to be alert to the possibility, however remote, that Mr. Berg comes to *Dai Nippon* for a purpose other than a trivial sporting amusement. Do you understand our concern, Student Yamaguchi Yoshinori?"

"*Hai!*"

"Then," says Nobuyoshi, "we commend you, Student Yamaguchi Yoshinori, and send you forth with our blessings on this mission of great trust, confident that you will conduct yourself always so as to reflect honor upon yourself, your name and family, Native Land Loving School, the Imperial Ministry of Education, the Hundred Millions of *Dai Nippon*, and our divine *Mikado!*"

Short silence during which (natch!) he rises, joins me and Sato in final fifty-degree kowtow bow to pic of Hirohito and his favorite white horse. After than which requisite shtick, head prefect says—all big *sumairu* smiles now, Jack, *enryo* achieved, harmonious resolution enjoyed by all assembled, reet?—"*Eija Nai Kai!*" Ain't it all just super fab, way it is here in *Dai*

Nippon, circa November 2, 1935, reet?

"*Hai!*" we say, choral-style. Hey, Jack, what's do *wataschi* know from big ironies to come, aged but sweet sixteen years old, reet?

Cut to: instance of family pride shtick, reet? Eventide of November 2, circa '35, post-prandial hour, breeze blows in off Tokyo Bay, sings in *furin* windchimes that hang on *engawa* porch of our paper house—extended *ma* moment charged by shared sense of *yoin* resonances, reet, Jack? What I mean is, *do* flow of life and times looking bright! Dig it:

Papa-san says: "My son, you have turned your father's dreams of honor for your life to a reality greater than any I dared to pray to our ancestral *kami* to grant! My heart is like a cup filled with joy, my spirit soars like a gull on the ocean wind, and my *hara* belly feels a tranquility beyond the deepest sleep! It remains to us only to beseech our *kami* for their assistance so that this venture proves as fruitful for you as it promises."

Mama-san says: "Oh my son, I am speechless! Oh, I must cover my face with my hands in embarrassment that such great fortune comes to my only son!"

Sis *Iko-san* says: "Shall you truly go about in the company of the *gaijin Amerikajin, Yosho-san*? You must remember always to carry a handkerchief to cover your nose, for they tell us at my school that the *Amerikajin* smell bad if you are close to them."

Says I (appropriate self-effacing decorum prescribed, reet, Jack?): "Aw, folks, it ain't nothing except as how I can speak the *Eigo*, reet? I mean, like, it ain't such a much except save for knowing a lot of words, reet, folks?"

Says my *papa-san*, "It is my paternal duty, my son, even in the midst of rejoicing, to caution you to conduct yourself with dignity at all times. Behave so that no slightest shame attaches to you. Bring honor to yourself and the name of our family, to our *kami*, and endeavor to earn glory for *Dai Nippon!*"

My *mama-san* can say only, "Oh, I must calm myself! I must not allow my pride to overwhelm me! Oh, I dare not permit my expectations to be so great as to tempt the *kami* of our neighbors to jealousy!"

My baby sis says, "Say again the word for the *Amerikajin* sport, *Yosho-san*. Please! It sounds so funny!"

"*Besuboru*," I tell her. "Word borrowed as direct cognate from *Eigo*, Sis, dig?" To my daddy, as we prepare to kneel on the *tatami* to give thanks due to *kami* at the *butsudan*, recite names on rice-paper scrolls listing family deceased, I whisper, "*Papa-san*, could you, like, maybe make some inquiries down at *Japan Times*, talk to folks in the know, see what you can find out about this Sato guy? I mean, if he's truly *honcho* factotum in Imperial Ministry of Education, I might could, like, work the connection for one of them big grants in aid of overseas study. I mean, it ain't what's you know, rather who, reet, Daddy?"

"My son," says *Papa-san* just before he claps his hands to get us started on thanksgiving Shinto gratitude shtick, "you shall have introduction to the greatest possible source of influence! Do you not realize, my son, you shall be presented at the Imperial Palace when the *Amerikajin* are officially welcomed?"

"No stuff? No jive, Daddy?"

Bluebird on wing. Brass ring in reach. Portal of maximum opportunities standing wide ajar, reet? Can you dig it, Jack?

Cut to: circa November 9, 1935.

Dockside environ of Yokohama harbor, Jack! Big official-style *matsuri* festive celebration doings! Toyama National Military Band on scene, standing tall, offering alternate renditions of *Kimagayo Nihonjin* national anthem and "Star Spangled Banner," reet? Hordes of elementary-school kiddies, released from classroom curricular obligations to swell progress, waving paper flags of *Dai Nippon* (how we say: *Hino Maru*) and U. S. of A., said flags on sticks furnished courtesy of Yokohama branch of *kempei* police to provide facade of welcome hospitality, not to fail to mention patina of appropriate enthusiasms, reet? Than which is not to fail to mention orderly crowd of curious citizens of Yokohama wharfside district environ—*kempei* ready (natch!) with *take* bamboo stave batons to bop noggins if situation develops unseemly disorder—assembled anxious for even passing glimpse of barbarian *Amerikajin* athletes, than which who approach dockside in passenger launch, having disembarked from ship, *Empress of Japan* (departed Vancouver, British Columbia, Dominion of Canada, late October, with Hawaii stopover), moored out at harbor berth. Interest of onlooker rubberneckers evident, as witnessed by comment *wataschi* eavesdrops, as follows:

Says heavily *irezumi* tattooed dockhand: "I have heard the *gaijin* athletes are enormous, that none is less than eight feet tall."

Says his buddy (some fewer *irezumi* tattoos visible): "It is true. Also, they are very ugly. Their noses protrude from their faces like the prows of whaling vessels."

Says old grandfatherly-aged *papa-san*: "I know nothing of this sport they play. What manner of *gaijin* foolishness is this *besuboru?*"

Casual confabulation of attendant throngs from among Hundred Millions, reet?

Official party of welcome stands tall arrayed on pier as launch approaches. Aforesaid congress includes *Nihonjin honchos* as follows: Yokohama Mayor Onishi, Kanogawa Prefectural Government Director Furukawa, attendant functionary factotum bureaucrats, lesser underlings, etcetera blah, all which who are attired in new-style *monpei* quasi-military garbs, reet?

Occupying highest stature of protocol significance status is U. S. of A. Ambassador Joe Clark Grew, than which who is attired in splendiferous formal cutaway and bowler hat, gloves and cane in hand, attended by corps of aides (cultural officer to interpret, military attache, trio of embassy clerks) aforesaid Joe Clark Grew distinguished not only via sumptuary distinction, but also from natural tallness—bowler-hatted noggin soars lofty atop surrounding *Nihonjin* noggins, reet?

Among which latter personages is not to fail to mention Mr. Suzuki Sataro, ace by-line newshawk and sport-chat columnist for *Yomiuri Shimbun*, said Suzuki dressed in western-style suit, to include knickers and two-tone shoes, shifting *hara* belly nervous fashion foot to foot, casting shy glances at *kempei* on hand, reporter's note pad and *hakurai* imported fountain pen at ready to make on-scene notes toward feature article, aided by gaggle of *shimbun* photogs with cameras primed.

And me. *Wataschi*. Student Yamaguchi Yoshinori, Jack! I is looking good in crispy clean uniform of Native Land Loving School, complete (natch!) with achievements stripe and chevron, to include badge of first form. Big day—*matsuri* celebratory ceremonial welcome doings gala!—here at last, circa November 9, 1935, Jack!

Within and beneath hubbub of nattering throng, chatter of flag-waving kiddies, blare of anthems afforded by Toyama National Military Band, here follows representational snatch of confabulation betwixt *wataschi* and aforesaid Mr. Suzuki whilst we did gander launch cutting through oily waters of Yokohama harbor.

He: "I am delighted to make your acquaintance, Student Yamaguchi Yoshinori, and I congratulate you on your selection to accompany Mr. Moe Berg and his teammate colleagues for the duration of their visit to *Dai Nippon*. You will find Mr. Berg to be a remarkably cultured gentleman. As you may know, he has even begun to study our language. I have the honor of his friendship dating from the occasion of my most recent sojourn to the United States, a visit during which I had the pleasure of visiting every *Amerikajin* city boasting a major league franchise for the sport of *besuboru*. Tell me, Student Yamaguchi Yoshinori, do you love the *Amerikajin* national sport as much as I do?"

Me: "Like, I can take it or leave it, reet? But I does dig them associated slangs! Very specialized vocabulary, reet? As in round-tripper, seventh-inning stretch, spitter and also shine ball, also knuckler, eggs of goose—signifying zilch, reet?—old automatic, not to fail to mention kill the ump! See, *sensei* Mr. Suzuki, with *wataschi* it's the lingo, *Eigo*. I do but dig *Eigo* the most!"

He: "You are a precocious young man, Student Yamaguchi Yoshinori. *Dai Nippon* has need of those whose minds are not closed, who can reach out toward international understanding in these troubled times. I am convinced the future *do* path of our beloved nation lies in peaceful and mutually beneficial relations with the *Amerikajin*. What better way to come to know and respect the *gaijin* than to participate in their sport?"

Me: "So I been reading in your column in *Yomiuri Shimbun*. My daddy agrees with you, but says, like, gots to bite tongue so as not to utter blooper these days, reet? As in: even walls of paper houses gots ears, seems like, reet, *sensei*?"

He (with glance at *kempei* cordon, *take* bamboo stave batons at ready, holding horde in place on wharf): "Your father is a wise and prudent man, Student Yamaguchi Yoshinori. It is a pity *Dai Nippon* is not governed by men who share his sentiments."

"Reet," I say, "but, like, *wataschi* don't dig politico flaps nor wrangles none, reet? My aim is to use this gig to garner me a Ministry of Education grant, not to fail to mention government permission, to go to college stateside after I graduate Native Land Loving School. I figure I gots me some clout now — pull, juice, insider connection shtick! — like with *sensei* Mr. Sato Isao, *honcho* factotum of ministry bureaucracy, dig?"

He (after pause for another gander glance at *kempei*): "I have heard of Mr. Sato. He is an interesting individual. I am not certain of his exact position in the Imperial Ministry of Education. No doubt he has considerable influence. You would do well to ask your father to ask his friends what they may know of Mr. Sato." Suzuki looks again at *kempei*, out at approaching passenger launch. "You must not fail to tell Mr. Moe Berg of your ambition. He is an honors graduate of the renowned Princeton University, where first he rose to athletic fame in Ivy League competitions. Perhaps he can provide you with a recommendation to the appropriate *Amerikajin* academic authorities."

"Reet! Princeton Tiger. Boola-boola, reet? Also Yale Old Eli — go, Bulldogs — not to fail to mention Harvard Crimson, Big Red of Cornell, also Columbia of Morningside Heights."

"Ah, me!" says Mr. Suzuki Sataro, ace newshawk sport-chat columnist of *Yomiuri Shimbun*, "That I might have your linguistic fluency, Student Yamaguchi Yoshinori! Unfortunately, I am too consumed by my *hara* belly passion for the *besuboru*, with which I was stricken almost immediately upon the occasion of my first visit to the United States. I was but a boy, younger than you, accompanying my father, who was a member of the delegation sent by Emperor Taisho with a gift of *sakura* cherry trees to beautify the city of Washington, District of Columbia. It came upon me, this *hara* belly passion, when I visited the Comiskey Park, in the company of our *Amerikajin* guides, during a stop in the city of Chicago. This was in 1920, just after the infamous affair of the treason perpetrated by the dastardly Black Hose. Despite the attendant shame later generated by the investigations of K. M. Landis, I had found a mission to guide me in the *do* path of my life's course, to bring to *Dai Nippon* a love of this most intricate and dramatic sport! Ah, me!" says he, Suzuki Sataro.

Me (craning neck in high stiff collar to gander passengers in launch now making fast by ropes alongside pier): "Reet. Like, everybody gots to do his thing, reet?"

Cut to: much faded *shimbun* newspaper clip (poor resolution due to crude printing technologies in *Dai Nippon* circa '35!), clip cut from front page of *Yomiuri Shimbun* (over feature article by-lined Sataro Suzuki—natch!) for November 10, 1935.

Which is not to fail to mention said clip comes from memory, Jack, as how it gots burned up in big fire to come, reet?

Snapped at Yokohama dockside, personages depicted are posed to memorialize momentous *ma* moment of *yoin* satisfactions of *enryo* instant of hands-across-sea goodwill cultural sport contact of U. S. of A. and *Dai Nippon*, occasion designed to usher in new era of peace, understanding, mutually beneficial cooperations, etcetera blah blah. Is it not to laugh, Jack?

Personages depicted therein is arrayed in semicircle, at center of which is feature attraction Yank delegation—big-timey American League *besuboru* all-stars, Jack! As follows:

Mr. Cornelius McGillicuddy (a.k.a. Connie Mack), all-star contingent manager, Grand Old Man of *besuboru* legends derived from long association as player-manager-proprietor of Athletics of City of Love Philadelphia. Connie Mack: very dignified in Gay Nineties style suit, string tie, stiff starched white collar, gray hair slicked down with Vitalis, parted in middle, straw boater in hands—portrait exudes aura of venerable composure, laconic unflappability in cheering crowds ambience, inanimate mien in context of solemn ceremonials, small eyes hard squinted against glare of bright sun reflecting off harbor water.

Flanking Grand Old Man Connie, left and right, are diamond stars of highest magnitude: George Herman (a.k.a. Babe, a.k.a. Bambino, a.k.a. Sultan of Swat) Ruth; Louis (a.k.a. Lou, a.k.a. Iron Man) Gehrig. Babe's visage rivals fat moon of *tsukimi* for rotundity, cheeks a glisten with perspirations, belly distending over belt like rice bag, Bambino Babe leans hard on Mr. Mack due to slight dizziness resulting from seasickness and perhaps also mild inebriation caused by eye-opener dozen bottles of Asahi beer quaffed for breakfast repast aboard *Empress of Japan*. Iron Man Lou is very photogenic, lean, tanned, shy *sumairu* smile for camera, carries Louisville Slugger bat not unlike like unto Arisaka rifle at shoulder arms, regulation Spalding horsehide gripped like fortune-diviner's globe in other hand.

To Babe's right, Vernon (a.k.a. Lefty) Gomez, Lou's teammate of Gotham Big Apple Yankees, immortal moundsman; to Lou's left, Charles (a.k.a. Charlie) Gehringer, astute batsman and sure-hand Golden Glover infielder affiliated with Tigers of Motor City Detroit; to Lefty's right is awesome hitting duo representing Amerinds of Cleveland, Earl (a.k.a. Earl of Averill) Averill and Clinton (a.k.a. Clint) Brown; Charlie's distaff personages constitute largest same-team contingent, all from Mr. Mack's Athletics: James (a.k.a. Jimmy) Foxx, Frank (a.k.a. Gabby) Hayes, Harold (a.k.a. Hal) Warstler, Joseph (a.k.a. Joe) Cascarella, Edmund (a.k.a. Ed) Miller, and Eric (a.k.a. Boob) McNair; far right, abutting Clint Brown, stands delegation from Senators from Washington (District of Columbia): fireballing pitcher Earl (no known alias) Whitehill and (natch!) Morris (a.k.a. Moe!) Berg—third-string warmup bullpen backstop.

Extreme margins of *shimbun* pic reveal motley remainder of swelled progress: Mayor Onishi, Prefect Government Director Furakawa, U. S. of A. Ambassador Joe Clark Grew, aides, attachés, functionaries and assorted factotums—not to fail to mention (natch!) Mr. Suzuki Sataro, and—last, seemingly least, down front-center due to squat stature, shoulders squared, chin up, visored cap shading eyes, hands on trouser seams (standing tall, Jack!): *wataschi*, Jack, Student Yamaguchi Yoshinori (me!))!

Which is not to fail to note details not at once apparent to casual scrutinies: on right shoulder epaulet of *wataschi's* tunic is visible the light touch of Moe Berg's hand, placed thereon just prior to *shimbun* photog's shutter click; in Moe's other hand resides large leather carrying case, within which resides 16-millimeter Stewart Warner *eiga* flic movie camera—ironies inextricably involved with which, more about later!

Stasis of newspaper photo clip (burned up in fire, all heretofore from memory, reet, Jack?) fails to dramatize cacophony of *matsuri* gala festive ceremonials context. As witness:

Constant strains of *Kimagayo* anthem alternated with "Star Spangled Banner" rendered by Toyama National Military Band, presentation of elaborate *ikebana* arranged floral bouquets to all Yanks by Miss Onishi Toshiko (daughter—natch!—of *sensei honcho* Onishi Ichiro, Mayor of Yokohama) and Miss Furukawa Tazeko (daughter—natch!—of aforesaid *honcho* Director of Kanogawa Prefectural Government Furukawa), following upon which said *sensei* personage delivers scripted speech spiel of welcome to Yanks, as follows (words to effect, from memory, Jack!):

"On behalf of our beloved *Mikado*—" sudden isolation of Yanks tall in huddle formation, as how surrounding throng is kowtow bowing full fifty degrees in direction of Tokyo Town, Imperial Palace, reet?—"and the Hundred Millions of *Dai Nippon*, I welcome our distinguished visitors. May all your days in our land prove pleasant and rewarding, and when you depart, may you take with you memories that will be a balm to your spirits in all adversities, and may your visit serve to strenthen the bonds of friendship and understanding that will join your country and *Dai Nippon* throughout future generations."

Dig: *honcho* Furukawa's scripted spiel speech is delivered in, like, how we say, High Court *Nihonju* lingo, reet? Than which dialect is standard

vocabularies and grammars traditional for usage in solemn ceremonials —
politics and diplomacies, talking to *kami* in Shinto shtick, swearing sacred
oaths, *o-miai* marriage and *kaigi* big-timey business negotiations, etcetera
blah.

Natch, Ambassador Joe Clark Grew's interpreter renders snafu-style
awkward and inaccurate translation thereof, Yank ballplayers looking on
with best possible expressions of interest, squints and scowls to simulate
sumairu smiles, reet? Example: translator factotum functionary personage
says, "The governor hopes you will prosper from your visit in future."

Says George Herman (a.k.a. Babe etcetera) Ruth: "How the hell prosper on what I'm getting paid for this bullshit, huh, Lou?"

Than which is when I eavesdrop Moe Berg mutter: "Shut the hell up,
Babe, you want to cause an incident?" and, "Grew better get himself a
decent interpreter if he wants to know what the hell's coming off over
here!" Than which is when *wataschi* must resist impulse to twist noggin
about and say, like: Hey, Moe, Honorable Mr. Berg, you saying as how
you can understand that ornate High Court dialect lingo?

Than which query I did not pose, as how big *banzai* cheer comes up
from crowd — orchestrated by waving *take* bamboo stave batons of *kempei*
police cordon — kiddies shaking paper flags on sticks, Toyoma National
Military Band playing fanfares (snatch of *Kaigun* march ruffles, reet?), all
of which brouhaha hubbub precludes *wataschi's* speculation in press of
events, reet?

Mr. Connie Mack, nudged by Moe, extracts scribbled notes from vest
pocket, unfolds same, places wire-rim specs on long schnozz, makes formal riposte in croaking voice, notes fluttering in harbor breeze, to wit:
"Ladies and gentlemen, this trip to Japan has been highly anticipated with
great enthusiasm by me and my ballplayers here. We really believe our
coming will help make us all better citizens of the world, and we look
forward to playing a lot of good ball here in the Land of the Rising Sun. I
know I speak for all my guys when I say thanks a lot for a real swell
welcome." Folds notes, removes specs, squints into sunshine, reet?

In fleeting instant betwixt translation uttered in shaky High Court
Nihonju by Ambassador Grew's interpreter and second chorus of *banzai*
cheers from assembled horde, I eavesdrop Moe Berg's aside to Mr. Mack:
"Connie, if there's one thing you're not, it's eloquent. Shit, I taught you
better than that! On the other hand, Grew's boy there's a damn joke. How
does it feel to be called a venerable patriarch of great sagacity, Connie?"

"Put a cork in it, Moe," says Mr. Mack before he steps forward to
introduce team members. Me, *wataschi*, I gots eyes only for Moe Berg —
like, the man do appear to understand High Court dialect archaisms, reet?
Moe, I is thinking, you ain't never going to palaver fluent in *Nihonju* if you
gets it all out of old books, reet? Than which is not to say it do not require
fine-tuned ear to pick up High Court like that, dig?

Wataschi's amazed dumbfoundment continues apace as intros proceed, Mr. Mack speaking without notes, Joe Clark Grew's man rendering spiels into quasi-accurate and graceless High Court, Moe Berg whispering commentaries. As exemplified in example of George Herman (a.k.a. Babe, a.k.a. Bambino, a.k.a. Sultan of Swat) Ruth. Dig:

Mr. Mack: "First off I want to introduce you probably to the greatest home-run hitter ever in the sport of baseball. This is a guy I'm glad's playing for me for a change instead of against me where he's clobbered my pitchers all the years he was with the Yankees, and incidentally he was first originally a great pitcher when he first broke into the league with the Red Sox, and also a great guy to know as a friend, and a example for youths everywhere the game's played, we call him Babe and the Bambino and the Sultan of Swat, ladies and gentlemen, the great Babe Ruth!"

Ambassador Joe Clark Grew's interpreter: "Venerable and Sagacious Mr. Mack is pleased to present to you the most renowned personage in history. His glorious triumphs have brought great honor to his name and nation. Since the origin of time, he has assumed appellations, among which are Bambino and Warrior of Large Arms. Generations revere his name in their devotions. Babe Ruth!"

Assembled throng (orchestrated by *kempei* batons, augmented by blare of Toyoma National Military Band): "*Banzai! Banzai*, Warrior of Large Arms! *Banzai*, Babe Ruth!"

Moe Berg (to George Herman Ruth, eavesdropped only by Student Yamaguchi Yoshinori, reet?): "He says you're a god they can all pray to, Babe, so try not to cuss or stagger now, okay?"

George Herman Ruth (to Moe Berg): "Screw you, Moe!" To gathered, he stands forth from ranks of peers to say, "Hey, thanks a lot, folks! I hope to hit a bunch of homers when we ever get out there on the field, and I promise to do my damn best, okay? I'm no good at speeches. I just like to give the ball a ride every time I get in the box — so, just, thanks a lot for everything, huh?"

Grew's interpreter: "The Honorable Babe Ruth pledges to struggle versus all opposition with both the strength of the arm which wields the sword and the moral imperative bestowed upon him by his venerable ancestors. He disdains words as amusements fit only for children and women."

Dockside mob: "*Banzai*, Ruth! *Banzai*, Bambino Babe Sultan! *Banzai*, Mighty Arm Which Wields The Longsword!" Kiddies jiggle paper flags on sticks; Toyoma National Military Band hits martial flourishes.

George Herman Ruth (aside to Moe Berg): "Stick that in your ass and smoke it, Moe! Did I wow 'em or did I wow 'em!"

At which juncture I am further dumbfound astounded — I mean, Jack, awe-struck, nonplussed, speechless double-take shtick, reet? — to eavesdrop, whilst Connie Mack spiels intro of Louis (a.k.a. Lou, a.k.a. Iron

Man) Gehrig, Moe nattering to self in impeccable High Court *Nihonju* dialect as follows:

"The renowned Babe Ruth humbly begs your indulgent pardon for having exhibited himself unworthily before your eyes in a condition befitting an inebriated peasant, and for revealing to his eternal shame a lack of culture appropriate only to the most baseborn among us!"

Hey, Moe, I did think, howsomever is you learned to spiel that formalist High Court guff stuff so good?

Which is not to fail to mention much hugging, slapping of backsides, mock minimalist punches to upper arms as we join official party—path through crowd cleared by aggressive *kempei*—to enter motorcars for progress to Imperial Palace, scheduled audience of welcome with *Mikado*. I sit cheek by jowl hard betwixt Moe and George Herman Ruth in back seat of latest model *hakurai* import Dodge touring car.

Remembered olfactory impression: even in open air, so wedged ensconced, I sniff sharpish odor, like unto raw beef at room temperature—Baby Sis *Iko-san* was right, *Amerikajin* do smell funny!

"The elephant," says Moe, "there next to you doing his level best to smother you to death is the famous Babe Ruth, kid. Can you say hello to Yosh, Babe, or at least grunt hello to my official guide and interpreter?"

"You're a real knee-slapper, Moe," Babe says, and, to me, "How you doing, pee-wee? Sorry if I mashed you getting in, it's a tight fit for me when you're built large."

"Pleased to meet you, Bambino Sultan," says I—*wataschi*, Jack!—and, "Delighted to extend best wishes for your hopeful new employment soon, as how Yankees of Gotham Big Apple is done give you walking papers, reet?"

Moe laughs—big hardy har har! Gives me hug. "That's a hot one! Did you catch that, Babe?"

"Everyone," says the Sultan of Swat, "is a goddamn comedian. Hey, Moe, can you tell them to get this show on the road? I'm gonna have to stop on the way and drain my lizard if this is a long haul to see the high mucky-muck."

"*Skosh* short hop," I tell them, "just down the pike to Tokyo Town, Imperial Palace, *Mikado*—" *wataschi* looks about to be certain no *Nihonjin* listening, than which would require requisite kowtow, reet?—"on hand to greet us, big ceremonials honor and courtesy national hospitality shtick, reet?"

"Hear that, Babe?" Moe says. "You're going to meet with royalty, and you just an old over-the-hill ballplayer!"

"One little Nip looks just like another," says Bambino Babe Sultan.

"Don't mind him, Yosh, he's hung over. Hey," says Moe, "could I ask you to do me a little favor to start us off with, Yosh?"

"Absotively posilutely, Moe! Name it, it's yours, reet?"

"Now, that's what I like to hear!" he says, reaches down betwixt pedal extremities, lifts up large leather case, sets it on my lap. "Would you, sort of from now on, kind of take care of that for me? Like carry it for me so I don't lose it or get it smashed in all the confusion? Guard it with your life; it was loaned to me by someone, okay?"

"With pleasure, Moe! What is it, anyhow?"

Moe laughs — hardy har! — drapes long arm around me, pats leather case gently (heavy on my lap, Jack!), says, "We're going to get along just swell, Yosh, I can always tell! That's a movie camera I got in there, Stewart Warner 16-millimeter. I thought I'd shoot me some film to remember this by in my old age. That's a good machine in there, gets sharp focus even at real long range. I'll show you how to use it if you want. You interested in cameras, Yosh?"

"Honest, Moe?" I say, clutch Stewart Warner, heavy in its leather case, close to my chest. "Honest? You'll let me shoot some film, show me how to make the *eiga*?"

"Cross my heart, hope to die," Moe says, crosses aforesaid organ with sincerity. "*Eiga*," he says, "that's movie, motion picture in Japanese, right?"

"Reet! Hey, Moe," I say, "you pronounce the *Nihonju* real good! Did you ever notice, Moe, the words, I mean, *eiga*, movies, flics, reet? And *Eigo*? English? Interesting, reet, Moe? *Eiga. Eigo.* Words, Moe, funny-strange, reet?"

"I guess," says Moe, and, "Is that a fact? No, I never really thought about it, I guess."

Says Babe: "You two start in talking that gabble-gabble Jap shit, I'm getting to hell out and riding in the car with Mack, I mean it, Moe!"

Moe laughs — big har! — says as how not to mind Bambino Babe, nobody else does, reet? And further as how he will teach me to use the Stewart Warner not unlike like unto Hollywood pro, in exchange for which tutorship as how *wataschi* can learn him some *Nihonju* vocabularies, reet? Jack: I is too happy — hog heaven, swine in excrement, lark-like, reet? — to think to wonder: how it is, Jack, somebody than which who can spiel High Court dialect don't even know from *eiga* and *Eigo*?

At which immediate *ma* moment of *enryo* reciprocal satisfactions said motorcade starts off. I sit back, ensconced, tight-scrunched betwixt *Amerikajin besuboru* sport celebs who stink from raw warm beef, gripping Stewart Warner camera close — can you dig it? Aged but sweet sixteen years, *wataschi* Student Yamaguchi Yoshinori is on way to Imperial Palace for formalist audience meet with *Mikado* — direct descendant of *Ameratasu* Sun Goddess (heir to Chrysanthemum Throne of old Jimmu, first emperor of *Nihon*, reet?) — and Morris (a.k.a. Moe) Berg going to teach me how make *eiga*, Jack!

Fast forward collage sequence, as follows:

Motorcar procession proceeding from Yokohama dockside wharf environ to Tokyo Town city limits, progress thereof slow as molasses during winter solstice due to streets jammed with rubberneckers, throngs augmented by thousands of working stiffs knocking off first shift at industrial fabrication plants along route to Imperial Palace — said route designed to impress visitors with modernist industrial *zaibatsu* vigor of resurgent *Dai Nippon*, reet? Paper streamers rain down upon us — seated in open import Dodge touring car — from windows of office buildings, how you say, tape from stock ticker *matsuri* festive extravaganza welcome spectacular. Corporate bands stationed along road offer din of anthems and marches.

Upon reaching Ginza District, rabid-fan types prove unable to maintain *Nipponshikki* decorums, enfevered by unceasing cheers: "*Banzai*, Bambino Babe! *Banzai*, Man of Iron Gehrig! *Banzai*, Noble Earl of Averill! *Banzai*, Connie Mack Eminence!" Aforesaid fans breach *kempei* security lines, leap on running boards to demand *hanko* signature autographs be inscribed on schoolbooks, scraps of parade banners, etcetera blah.

Than which is occasion of *wataschi's* sensibilities suffering further jar, resultant of witnessing Moe Berg write his name in *Nihonju kanji* ideograms, reet?

"Hey, Moe!" I shout above crowd and music clamors, "you not only spiel them High Court formulaics, you can do calligraphs too!"

Said Moe: "Not really, Yosh. Just a little trick I taught myself to make a good impression. It's all in doing your homework in advance, right?"

"You and me, Moe!" I did cry, hug his 16-millimeter Stewart Warner the closer.

Increasing press of exuberant masses of Hundred Millions almost halts our caravan in Nijubashi Plaza, entrance to Imperial Palace grounds, reet? "Ever met Hirohito before, Yosh?" Moe asks.

"Not hardly, Moe! Like, you don't even dast look at his visage when he comes outdoors in public for ceremonials shtick, reet? *Nipponshikki* decorums dictates lowered gaze, dig? *Mikado* is the deity, Moe, direct descendant of Sun Goddess *Ameratasu*, personification of glorious Showa Restoration, *Yamato Damashii*, Spirit of *Nihon*, etcetera blah. Closest *wataschi* ever gots prior to present instance was kowtowing my visage in the cinders across the road from dry moat, but rumor says he's scheduled to come to Native Land Loving School next spring *hanami* time to present pocket watches as gifts to all honors grads."

"Well," says Moe, "you won't have to wait for that, will you, kid? Here we just met, and already you're going to an audience with the Emperor. Hold on to your hat, *Yosho-san*, you ain't seen nothing yet!"

Kempei free up passage of motorcade through Nijubashi Plaza — swinging batons knock noggins, reet? Open Dodge touring car crosses stone bridge over moat. We drive into shadows cast by high rock walls, through wide gate at which stands ranks of heavy-armed Imperial Guards Regiment—Arisaka rifles with polished bayonets affixed glinting in sunlight, flash of *katana* longsword wielded by *honcho* officer-in-command. We enter grounds of Imperial Palace, Jack!

Jack: it is minimalist *ma* moment of *yoin* resonances awareness, reet? Like, different world from outside Tokyo Town. First impression thereof is sudden suspension of noise—yet still faintly audible from without high rock walls is chorus cheers (*Banzai*, Sultan Babe! *Banzai*, Lou of Iron Fabrication! *Banzai*, Venerable Sage Connie! *Banzai*, *Amerikajin* Guests of *Dai Nippon*!). Feel of silence is reinforced by growl of motorcar engines in low gears, crackle of tires on crushed seashells paving roadway we traverse, winding through decorative landscape of clipped lawns, ornamental hedges, fruit orchards—route manned by aforesaid Imperial Guards Regiment, than which personages bow low (rifles at sling arms in deference) whilst we pass, sword-wielding officer hops on running board of each vehicle to instruct respective chauffeurs as to proper speed (slow creep), maintenance of distance betwixt motorcars—dig it: collage dream sequence of sylvan glades, carp ponds, *torri* Spirit Gates, gazebos, etcetera blah.

Says Moe: "You know, Yosh, this sort of reminds me a little of Central Park, all this right in the middle of a huge city and all."

"Moe," says I, "this is *Mikado's* house, man!"

Says George Herman Ruth, leaning forward over seat to address Louis Gehrig, than which who sits beside chauffeur, "What do you think, Lou, are we gonna have a goddamn picnic outdoors or something? You think they'll give us a drink, or are these little Japs a bunch of Methodists, do you think?"

"Search me, Babe," says Lou, and, "How's your hangover?"

Says I: "Moe, Bambino Sultan don't dig it, reet? Tell him Hirohito's the deity, heir of Jimmu, father of *Nihon*, reet? I mean, failure to display appropriate decorum respects might could cause *kempei* to toss offending personage in *eiso*, how you say, jailhouse slammer hoosgow!"

"*Daijubo*," says Moe to me—how we say: no sweats, not to perspire, rest easy, reet?

"Reet, Moe! You and me. I can but trust, reet?" Moe gives me fraternalist hug; I hug Stewart Warner camera case, heavy in my lap.

Mikado's house, Jack! Big, spread out ranch style, pagoda roofs, much shrubbery, trees, total quiet—brouhaha hubbub without now-distant walls reduced to hum, not unlike like unto honeybees teasing plum blossoms, reet? Procession circles to park before palace entrance wide as *Kabuki* stage. Hosts of Imperial Household staff factotums, attired in *kimono* (no new-style militarist *monpei* garb here to diminish luster of *Mikado's* servants, Jack!), all bow forty-degree kowtows in concert as we dismount vehicles.

"Leave it in the car, kid," Moe says as I attempt to carry encased Stewart Warner camera along.

"You said guard it with my life, Moe."

"I doubt anybody's going to boost anything out of these cars right here in front of the palace. Leave it. It wouldn't look good to lug it up in front of the Son of Heaven, would it?"

After than which ensues exchange of ceremonials pleasantries with servant staff *honcho* factotum, Imperial Household Chamberlain Hasegawa Mitsuchi, than which who, after introducing hisself and leading subordinate factotums—not to fail to mention ritual coordinated kowtows, perorates as follows:

"I, Hasegawa Mitsuchi, First Chamberlain of the Imperial Household, welcome you to the abode of my celestial master, and I humbly request you, our honored guests, to permit me to escort you to the audience chamber wherein his divine presence awaits your expected arrival."

Whereupon Ambassador Joe Clark Grew's interpreter—personage name of Walter Wetherell, New England prep-school type, reet?—steps up to riposte in (natch!) faulty High Court dialect *Nihonju* lingo: "We accept the infliction of your unspeakable hospitality and surrender to your entreaty. I am the liege of the honorable Ambassador of the United States of America, and demand to speak for the members of his court and our guests, who, disrespectfully, are ignorant of language."

Moe whispers in my ear, "What do we need this crud to confuse things when we got a whiz like you on our side, huh, kid?"

"Moe," I mutter, scarce permitting lips to quiver, "fact is said Wetherell factotum personage is strictly *baka* dummy dope with High Court lingo, but seems to *wataschi* you could do the spieling just fine, reet?"

"Not really, kid. I just get the general drift enough to know this weenierind sounds like he belongs in Bellevue. I'll have to clue Grew in when I get a chance that his boy's out of his league."

But it is time to follow in wake of *honcho* Chamberlain Hasegawa within—go with *do* flow, reet? I join with Moe, Connie Mack, Suzuki Sataro, Ruth, Gehrig, Ambassador Grew, et alia, up stone steps, into cool dim-lit corridor (roof so low Bambino Sultan of Swat Babe must slouch to avoid scraping bean on ceiling), smack sound of heels (Imperial Chamberlain affects wooden *geta* clogs, natch!) on tiles echoes off close walls, into which are set periodic *tokonoma*-style niches holding burning (perfumed!) candles, corridor throughout fragrant with odoriferous incense smouldering in unseen censers—not to fail to mention also periodic Imperial Guards personages stationed at intervals, all in *kimono samurai* attire here within household, long and also short swords sheathed in *take* bamboo scabbards tucked in *obi* sashes (along with traditionalist folding fans), all aforesaid striking rigid forty-degree kowtow deferential postures whilst we proceed by.

Says Iron Man Lou Gehrig: "We should have had us a ramp like this up to the dugout at Yankee Stadium, huh, Babe?"

Says Babe: "Sing out if anybody sees the little boy's room, okay, guys?" Long corridor, Jack!

End of which is arched doorway hung with beaded curtain, held aside by Chamberlain Hasegawa to give entrance to spacious chamber—big as my daddy Mr. Yamaguchi's whole paper house! Imperial Audience Chamber is lit by rays of late *tsukimi* November sun penetrating skylight, beams thereof falling upon rock garden, miniature waterfall tinkling into shallow pool in which swim humongous gold carps, canaries chirping in cages suspended from limbs of semi-*bonsai* dwarf trees. Can you dig it? I eavesdrop George Herman Ruth: "Reminds me of a Chinese whorehouse in San Francisco I heard about once!"

"Is that the one where you got your pox, or was it the place in Baltimore lets you run a tab, Babe?" Moe says through closed teeth.

Group comes to shuffling halt, arrayed in semicircle—as in *Yomiuri Shimbun* front-page photo snapped at Yokohama dockside, reet?—by *honcho* factotum Imperial Chamberlain Hasegawa; we face similar rank of assorted Imperial Household staff *honchos* posed to receive us across minimalist space of polished floor tiles. I press forward for better view, situate self at side of Moe Berg, looming hulk of Iron Man Louis Gehrig, fidgeting mass of Bambino Babe just behind me.

Ma stasis moment of uncertainty, Jack: everybody kowtow bowing from waist, reet? I look up on sly to gander opposite row, see only *kimono*-clad factotums, dash of Imperial Army and Navy *honchos* in full dress (chests bemedaled solid, tassled longswords, high stiff tunic collars, epaulets, visored caps, gleaming knee-high boots!)—which one, *wataschi* Student Yamaguchi Yoshinori is asking hisself (natural curiosity of youths shtick) is *Mikado*?

Dig:

Celestial Presence of direct descendant of Sun Goddess *Ameratasu*, hundred and twenty-fourth successive heir of old father of *Nihon* Jimmu—*Mikado*, Jack!—manifests self: when we rise from kowtow, phalanx of dignitary *honchos* opposite bends from waist in prescribed *enryo* reciprocity, *Mikado*, Jack, Emperor Hirohito, is onliest one across audience chamber remains standing. Upright before four-panel gold-filigree screen, facing north (prescribed royal orientation), directly beneath stylized chrysanthemum shield mounted above imperial symbol of crane on far wall—*Mikado* onliest one don't gots to bow.

Big shocker, Jack! Requires double-take, reet?

As how: I seen *Mikado* heretofore only in *eiga* newsreel flics, selected short subjects run along with previews of coming attractions between

45

double-feature *hakurai* stateside imports playing in former *No, Kabuki*, and *Bunraku* theaters.

Than which is to say, *Mikado* Emperor Hirohito regal astride favorite mount (Snow White) in full military uniform, reviewing officer cadets at Eta Jima Academy, navy midshipmen on parade at Sasebo submarine base, dedications of new vessels, sword-rattle shows of tanks and artillery, awarding decorations for valor to new heroes home from Manchukuo front, *Mikado* mounted stately regal on Snow White high above folks in kowtow posture whilst factotums read most recent imperial rescript into megaphones, etcetera blah.

Which is to say: *Mikado*, Emperor of *Dai Nippon*, Hirohito in militarist full dress — plumed hat held firm on noggin by chinstrap, shoulders enhanced by thick braid of epaulets, chest swelled by rows of decorations, how you say, fruit salads, legs long in high-gloss riding boots, fancy spurs, tassled *katana* longsword — can you dig image as established in aforesaid by *eiga* flic news clips, Jack?

Than which image is all at once of a sudden confronted hard up against realities within sensibilities of *wataschi*, Student Yamaguchi Yoshinori (aged sweet six and ten years old!) there in skylighted incense-fragrant Imperial Audience Chamber, Tokyo Town, *Dai Nippon*, circa November 9, 1935, Jack!

Sad fact and truths told, Jack, *Mikado* is sole personage in chamber diminutive as me, reet? I mean, I can look direct into his celestial visage — small watery eyes behind oversize round horn rim specs, hair greased and parted western-style, twitching mouth half-hid by scraggly moustache (than which looks fake, as if stuck on with spirit gum, reet?), pale sick complexion speckled by brown moles, chin receding to brink of nonexistence. Truth told: excessively diminutive corporeal Divine Presence of Son of Heaven etcetera blah is attired in swallowtail coat, starched dickey, black cravat, pinstripe pants, tiny feets in black patent-leather pumps, itty-bitty hands folded in front of trouser fly.

Wataschi Student Yamaguchi Yoshinori thinks: this is *Mikado* of *Dai Nippon*?

Ma moment's stasis of shock-state prevails during following period of hushed silence (waterfall tinkle, canary chirps); I breath deep to recover disoriented sensibilities, rocked still by after-shock of *Mikado's* voice as he spiels scripted High Court ceremonial welcome — than which voice is high-pitch mouse's squeak, not unlike like unto my baby sis *Iko-san* when she whines through her schnozz to imitate donkey-bray sound of *Eigo* lingo, reet? As hereinafter:

Mikado: "We welcome Ambassador Grew and our distinguished *Ameri-*

kajin guests, and extend to them the hospitality of *Dai Nippon*. We are confident our mutual endeavors cannot but yield the fruit of continued positive relations between your nation and our empire."

I mean, Jack, thin bloodless wet lips move under fake-looking scraggly moustache, but them small runny eyes is blank behind oversize horn rims, diminutive corpus don't seem even to breathe inside frock coat, child-size hands clasped over trouser fly—I is wondering, is it really him, Hirohito, Son of Heaven *Mikado*, lineal descendant of *Ameratasu*, heir of Jimmu? Him?

Dig it: Palace moat, high rock walls, ornamental gardens and ponds, Imperial Guard regiment, pagoda roofs, incense fragrance, populous household staff and retainer *honchos*, Imperial Army and Navy brass hats, sky-lit waterfall and songbirds — and *Mikado*, Jack, undersize wimp-visage, squeaky squeal voice in frock coat and pinstripes, spats, fakey stage moustache and specs! Like, it is to laugh — har and hee, reet?

Joe Clark Grew's interpreter (prep-schoolish Walter Wetherell, reet?) steps forward, renders fair-to-middling full fifty-degree kowtow from waist, delivers riposte in (natch!) incompetent High Court, eyes downcast (natch!) to avoid straight look at Son of Heaven etcetera blah. To wit:

"On behalf of all worthy personages gathered in the presence of God's sunshine, in the mouth of Franklin Roosevelt, and in the mouths of Ambassador Grew and the American League warriors of repute here, I extend my congratulations to your heavenly majesty. I now demand to speak the names of the legends who reside in our midst."

"Sweet jumping Jesus! Did you hear that?" Moe whispers to me.

"Reet," I mumble, and, "Loses in translation, reet, Moe?"

As for example:

Grew's interpreter Wetherell: "I honor your divine scrutiny with the visage of Connie Mack, whose fabled exploits of execution and design create a legend rivaled only by his famed brother John McGraw, whose twin symbols inspire the worship of youth's ambition in our great landscape."

As Connie Mack steps up I eavesdrop: "Hey, Moe, did I hear him say McGraw's name in there?"

Moe: "He's trying to tell his nibs you and McGraw are famous rivals, but I think it came out McGraw whipped your ass to a frazzle every time you played the Giants. Now get up there and do like we rehearsed on the ship, Connie!"

"I never," says Connie Mack, loud enough for even Joe Clark Grew to hear — ambassador winces, reet? — "been so goddamn bored in my entire damn life!"

Said ejaculation is happily lost in final bow from *Mikado's* factotums, ensuing spiel of inept *Amerikajin* interpreter Mr. Walter Wetherell, as follows:

"I now demand you look upon Mr. George Ruth, whose valorous deeds have raised him to equality with deities."

"Babe," whispers Moe, "get your finger out of your nose, it's your turn here in a sec."

"Mr. Ruth's immortality is signified in the many names he assumes," continues blundering Wetherell factotum.

"Moe," says Babe, "what's he saying about me?"

Continues Wetherell in impenetrable High Court dialect lingo, "The utterance of his many appellations — Babe, The Bambino, The Sultan of Swat — strikes horror in the bellies of his bitter enemies, and he is one who may serve as a ghostly model for the weak and suffering. *Dai Nippon* trembles before his peerless fist!"

"Babe," Moe says when Bambino Sultan fails to step out from behind me, "shag your buns out there and do like I showed you."

"Moe," asks George Herman Ruth as I step sidewards to permit passage of humongous bulk, "how long's this bullshit go on? I got to wee so bad my molars are floating, Moe!"

So it goes, reet? Mr. Mack, Bambino Sultan, Louis Gehrig, Charles Gehringer, Earl Averill, James Foxx, et alia, than which is not to fail scripted closing spiel of thanks for audience granted, same delivered in all-but incomprehensible High Court by Joe Clark Grew, reet?

Which is not to fail to mention awkward moment during presentation of Harold Warstler. *Ma* moment's silence accompanying his kowtow is punctuated by long, low growling, not unlike like unto grinding of Dodge car's transmission gears in too rapid downshift, than which feral outburst emanates from *hara* belly cavity of George Herman Ruth — said rumbles is followed immediately thereafter by high keening whine recognizable to all in earshot as gaseous explusion — how you say, ripping fart, sounding like unto slow tearing of fine silken fabric. Than which audio gives way to fast diffusing of tangy fecal odor into heretofore incense-fragrant atmosphere.

As Harold (a.k.a. Hal) Warstler rejoins visiting delegation ranks, I eavesdrop Joseph (a.k.a. Joe) Cascarella say, "Slice me off half a pound of that Limburger next time, Babe!"

"You smelt it," ripostes Babe. "That means you dealt it!"

Says Moe Berg: "Nice going, Babe. What are you going to do for a finish, take a dump in the corridor on our way out?"

Happily, ceremonials proceed to conclusion, aforesaid anal scent dissipates via natural principles of osmosis, aided by dominant incense influences, reet?

Than which is not to forget two further instances of interest! As how:

Introduction of Mr. Suzuki Sataro, ace newshawk reporter and sport-chat columnist of *Yomiuri Shimbun*, provokes singular reaction. His good offices in arranging and promoting entire shindig is distinctly not (natch!)

appreciated by chauvinist *gumbatsu* militarist types in *Mikado's* retinue, than which who is ever alert to maintain *joi-i* anti-*gaijin* trend rampant amongst Hundred Millions of *Dai Nippon*, reet? Upon occasion of his intro by unceasingly inaccurate translator Wetherell, Hirohito spiels no rejoinder—rather, Imperial Household Chamberlain Hasegawa Mitsuchi remarks: "The *Mikado* does not read *Yomiuri Shimbun*. Mr. Suzuki may be assured that his writings are familiar to those of the Imperial Household who are charged with the responsibility of informing The Son of Heaven of interesting developments among our loyal subjects." Than which blatant snub shtick is followed by choral threatening hiss of breaths intake by *honcho* household staff ranks, said hisses accompanied by deliberate threat gestures—hands placed on ornate hilts of *katana* longswords, hard looks from visages speaking volumes at unfortunate kowtowing Suzuki.

Meaning of all which is, how you say in *Eigo*, Jack: your ass is grass, *Suzuki-san*!

Second noteworthy relevant instance is presentation to *Mikado* of *wataschi*—me, Jack, Student Yamaguchi Yoshinori! Last but not least, reet? As follows:

I note Grew's incompetent interpreter Wetherell must consult notes concealed in palm of hand prior to announcing me thusly: "I terminate our relations in the person of one Yamaguchi Yoshinori, blessed among *Nihonjin* by a tongue supple in alien words. This personage, your majesty, is said to read books. Your assembled guests hold him to their bosoms and will speak out of his mouth whilst they display themselves throughout your empire."

Eyes fixed on floor tiles in extremity of full kowtow, I eavesdrop Moe saying, "With friends like that, who needs enemies, huh, kid?" I come up slow out of bow, keep baby blues affixed fast on tiles whilst *Mikado* spiels.

"We commend Student Yamaguchi Yoshinori of Native Land Loving School, and note the symbols of scholarly accomplishment adorning his uniform. *Dai Nippon* is proud of this excellent example of our youth. He stands poised to bring honor and glory to his name and family, and to the Hundred Millions."

At which juncture, Jack, *wataschi* does depart from prescribed decorums! Which is to say: I speak out, reet? To wit:

"Like, *Mikado*, my sole goal is hopefully to glom Imperial Ministry of Education grant support in aid of higher-educational education endeavors stateside, than which is to say, *Mikado*, further study of *Eigo* in native-speaker contexts, reet? Like, *wataschi* praying daily to his *kami* for favorable response approval of petition I'll submit as soon as I garner sheepskin diploma from Native Land Loving School, reet?"

49

Extended *ma* moment of silence (*yoin* resonances heavy in scented bird-chirping air, howsomever lacking in *enryo* reciprocal satisfactions, Jack!), reet? Broken by hissing—quick, sharp breaths intakes by all *Nihonjin* present, save excepting (natch!) *Mikado*, as how Celestial Presence ain't never perturbed, reet? Followed by resumption of bird-chirp silence.

Than which impregnated pause ends only with handclap rendered by Imperial Chamberlain Hasegawa, than which is followed by *wataschi* bowing way backwards into ranks of *Amerikajin*, visage asweat with consternation approaching shame for violation of decorum protocols—I attempt to lose self within huddle of Moe Berg, Gehrig, Bambino Babe, my noggin aswim with meld of exultation and despair as we follow wake of Imperial Chamberlain escort out and down corridor to motorcars—candle illumination, Imperial Guards on duty, etcetera blah. *Hara* belly excitements is eased by Moe's aside: "That was pretty gutty, kid! I bet that's the first time anybody off the street ever spoke up to the little guy, huh?" In subsiding flux of pubescent consternation, I scarce register casual ongoing confabulations:

Connie Mack: "What I need now is a nap. I'm too damn old for all this crap, boys."

Earl Averill: "What you need is some slant-eye nookie, Connie, you'll feel like a new man."

Joseph Cascarella: "Shit and fall back in it! Piece of ass and a bicycle ride'd kill you, old man."

Earl Whitehill: "You know it's set sideways over here, don't you, Joe? Wider you spread it, tighter it gets."

Bambino Babe: "I think maybe my gut's infected or something. It's all that Jap beer I licked up on the ship, I keep having gas."

Ed Miller: "Which one was the king? All I could make out was the soldiers and all the old cobs got up like butlers."

Bambino Babe: "I'm dying to wring out my kidney! I think it's that running water I was hearing."

Louis Gehrig: "Dollars to doughnuts there's more bowing before we make it to the hotel. Moe, were you kidding when you said you have to bow to the ump before you step into the batter's box?"

Etcetera. Blah, blah, blah, reet?

Than which confabulations register only faintly—from memory, Jack!—as how I persist in mild shocks at audacity of my effrontry in speaking to *Mikado* to tout self, reet? Exchange I recall clear:

"Well, Yosh," says Moe, "you seen your monarch face to face in the flesh. Does it really blind you to look at him, or is that just the story they tell? You could have floored me with a wet noodle when I heard you pipe up about wanting to come to the states, kid!"

"Moe," says I, "I think I sticked my feets in nightsoil, reet? I mean, how you say, blotted copybook, sold ranching enterprise, not to fail to mention outdoor *benjo* toilet facility, flubbed proverbial dub, big boner play!"

"Just because you told his nibs you wanted to study the language in America?"

"You understood all that, Moe? Moe, I don't think you need no interpreter, man, you dig the lingo like native *Nihonjin*. Hey, Moe, scarce few among Hundred Millions spiel that archaic High Court dialect stuff!"

Moe Berg laughs—hardy har *sumairu* hee hee, vigorous fraternalist hug—says, "Not at all, Yosh. Like I said, I only get your basic drift. I got lots to learn. That's why I'm so glad to have you on my side! And don't worry about speaking your piece back there. If you get any static for it, let me know, I'll ask Grew's people to square it for you. When it comes to that, kid, maybe I could put in a word or two for you with the right people at the embassy could help you get the dough you need to go to school stateside, huh?"

"Honest, Moe?" Hardy har. Fraternal ursine hug.

Re-ensconced betwixt Moe and Bambino Babe (scent of warm, raw beef intensified!) in back seat of Dodge, Stewart Warner in leather case re-clutched close to chest, I ride through throbbing throngs of Hundred Millions (choral *banzai* cheers!), route cleared by efficient *kempei*, journey of but two city blocks to Imperial Hotel (designed by F. L. Wright, stood tall throughout devastating earthquake disaster of circa '23).

Says Babe: "Squirt, can we get a real drink at this fancy-schmancy hotel they got laid on for us?"

"*Daijubo* not to perspire," I assure him, "as how *Dai Nippon* boasts excellent malted beverages, as in Asahi, Kirin, Nippon, etcetera blah, than which you doubtless imbibed on *Empress of Japan* whilst en route, reet? Also available for purchase is Suntory whiskey, top-seller favorite with *zaibatsu* well-heeled high-roller types, not to fail to mention imitation scotch and bourbon blends. Not to mention *sake* rice wine vintage, than which can sneak up upon you and deliver telling blows if you ain't careful. Do you like *o-cha* tea, Sultan?" I ask.

"Screw damn tea," says Bambino.

"You're terrific, Yosh!" Moe says, hugs me tight. "We'll have a swell time, kid! You teach me the language and show me all the sights, I'll see to it you see all the games from the dugout! You like *besuboru*, Yosh?"

"I can take it or leave it," I say, and, "It's the *Eigo* I dig, Moe! I look to hone idiom slangs via eavesdropping and confabulation exchanges, reet?"

"What kind of a kid don't like baseball?" queries Bambino Sultan of Swat.

"Forget him, kid," Moe says, and, "Stick with me, I got a feeling you're going places!"

Further confabulations proves difficult to initiate or sustain in brouhaha hubbub of arrival at Imperial Hotel, than which includes vehicle-dismount ceremonials (goodbye to Ambassador Joe Clark Grew, fraudulent interpreter Walter Wetherell, Mr. Suzuki Sataro—who must dash to make column deadline for special *Yomiuri Shimbun* extra edition), cries of collective welcome resounding skyward for visiting *gaijin*.

"*Banzai*, Ruth Bambino Babe Sultan! *Banzai*, Iron Gehrig! *Banzai*, Venerable Sage Mack! *Banzai, Amerikajin Besuboru* Visitors to *Dai Nippon!*" Etcetera blah.

Wataschi's intended intention is to depart homeward to paper house, regale *Papa-san, Mama-san*, Sis *Iko-san* with whole story enlived with anecdotals, reet? But Moe Berg insists I come up to his suite for a while. "Bring the camera. We'll break it out, and I'll show you how it works. I want you to shoot some footage of the doings when we play out at Meiji Shrine tomorrow. Would you like that, Yosh?"

"Do I not!" and, "Is Pope papist, Moe?" I say. And follow after, eager to learn mechanics and operative tips for 16millimeter Stewart Warner *eiga* flic camera. "Hey, Moe," I say, "this is great day for *wataschi* Student Yamaguchi Yoshinori, man!"

Hardy har. Slap on back. Fraternal embrace. "Trust me, Yosh," says he, "we'll have us a ball! And don't worry over that little gaffe at the palace, okay? I'll get the ambassador to square it, and I meant that about pulling a few strings for you to get stateside to go to college, kid."

"Really, Moe?"

"Trust me, Yosh! And be careful and don't drop that camera or lose it someplace along the way, okay?"

"You gots it, Moe!" I say, and, "I can but trust, reet?" and, "You'll really ask Joe Clark Grew to grease Imperial Ministry of Education for me, Moe?"

Says Moe: "Not to worry! How do you say it? *Daijubo?*"

And I follow after to Moe Berg's Imperial Hotel suite, wherein he proceeds to instruct me in maintenance and operation of his 16-millimeter Stewart Warner camera—to include long range focus capacities.

"Hey, Moe," I did say, "was you as, like, shock surprised as *wataschi* to note unprepossessing wimpy dorklike look of *Mikado* in contrast to public relations image presented heretofore to Hundred Millions?"

"Kid," Moe said, "it's an old story. Almost nothing's the way it seems to be, get me? You'll get over it. Come on, let's break out that camera!"

Than which we did proceed to do, reet? Pandora's box shtick, Jack! Which is to say, big ironies associated therewith and thereafter, to include even present contemporaneous *ma* moment within which *wataschi* speaks, reet? Which is to say: what's do I know, Student Yamaguchi Yoshinori, aged but sweet sixteen years of age, Jack?

Cut to: Meiji Shrine, Tokyo Town, circa November 10, 1935. Enormous open field expanse environ prepared for inaugural diamond exhibition contest pitting visiting barnstorm Yank American League all-star hard-baller greats versus all-star *Nihonjin* contingent drawn from ranks of squads representing seven Tokyo universities—65,000 seats constructed to accommodate sellout crowd of ecstatic rabid-type *Nihonjin* fans of *besuboru*, to include even sprinkling of Tokyo international community *honchos*. Initial such event calls (natch!) for appropriate ceremonials, as follows hereafter:

Yank American League all-stars line up in front of dugout on first-base side (*Nihonjin* squad arrayed opposite on third-base line) of diamond, introduced individually over loudspeaker system, as exemplified in following example:

"We are pleased to present Mr. Connie Mack, Venerable and Sagacious Eminence of *Amerikajin* professional *besuboru* establishment, who serves as the revered mentor of our guest athletes. We welcome Mr. Connie Mack to *Dai Nippon* and extend to him the unreserved hospitality of the Hundred Millions, even as we wish him and his colleagues good fortune in this memorable athletic confrontation versus the finest young players from our seven universities."

After than which Connie Mack, attired in customary gray suit with vest, watch chain with elk's tooth adangle, starched white collar and string tie, hair slicked and parted in exact midline, straw boater in hand, bows stiff to cheering assemblage—"*Banzai*, Venerable Historic Sage Eminence Connie Mack!"—after than which Connie Mack (a.k.a. Cornelius McGillicuddy) rejoins ranks of Yank lineup, proffering final stiff kowtow of appreciative greetings to screaming throngs, reet?

After than which follows respective individual Yanks in turn—step forward, bow, *banzai* cheer: Sultan of Swat Ruth, Iron Man Gehrig, Lefty Gomez, Jim Foxx, scholar-athlete Moe Berg, et alia etcetera blah.

First-ball ritual is performed by *honcho sensei* Marquis Okima Nobutsume, newly elected prexy of recently formed Nippon Baseball Association—aside about which who is as how Marquis Okima is (natch!) also, as with Suzuki Sataro, non grata persona in *zaibatsu* chauvinist circles now exercising telling influences on government, as how this entire shtick is contra *joi-i* principle in ascendancy in *Dai Nippon* circa '35.

Marquis Okima tosses pill underhand with minimalist grace to aforesaid Mr. Mack (barehanded catch!), who in turn tosses horsehide sphere to starting pitcher Earl Whitehill, than which who takes mound to face first batter, one Masu Ueda, star outfielder and slugger-type of Asahi University Buffalo squad. Ueda bows (natch) to ump, to catcher Moe Berg (who delights audience with return kowtow!), thence to Whitehill on mound prior to assuming aggressive hitter's stance in box.

How you say, Jack: play ball, reet?

Where (you might could query, Jack!) is *wataschi*? Jack: Student Yamaguchi Yoshinori is ensconced in Yank dugout, seated on bench beside water cooler and bucket of orange slices, serving in multiform capacities as interpreter, batboy (handing requested Louisville Slugger lumber—also pine tar and resin bag—to each *Amerikajin* as he departs dugout for on-deck circle chalked in grass, reet?). Which is not to fail to mention *wataschi's* first documentary *eiga* flic assignment, lensing souvenir footage of historic game from vantage of dugout steps perch—can you dig it, Jack? Student Yamaguchi Yoshinori hoisting Moe Berg's 16-millimeter Stewart Warner. Framing significant and representative illustrative instances through viewfinder—I is making *eiga* flic, Jack!

"Don't," says Moe to me prior to warmup drills, "go and shoot all my film up at once there, okay, Yosh? We got a long tour of *Dai Nippon*, and good, fast, high-resolution film's hard to come by over here, I been told, so we don't want to run short, okay?"

"You got it, Moe!" says I, put my baby blue to viewfinder, center Bambino Babe in frame as he swings cluster of bats to loosen up.

To inculcate proper competitive spirit, I cup hands at my mouth, root for Yanks as umpire calls for inception of play: "Strike him out, Earl!" I shout into din of roaring *Nihonjin*. "He can't not hit your curve on his name-day, Earl baby! Whiff this loser!"

Which is not to fail to note it is notable as how Masu Ueda confounds my exhortation by slashing hot single through pitcher's box (Earl Whitehill scrambles to evade speeding pill) to center field—than which bingle causes marked decibel increase in crowd-noise volume, as how Hundred Millions is inclined to take first-pitch single as spiritual omen signifying victory to come, reet?

Sad fact to say: contest proves to be strictly no contest, Jack! Earl Whitehill settles down on mound, fans next two batters (Kitigawa Isuzu, second sacker of Waseda U. Frogs; Ieyasu Ito, who mans hot corner for Keio U. Dragons), allows lazy pop fly to left by cleanup hitter Aoki Sesshu, burly backstopper representing Hitsubashi U. Carp—than which fly ball is easily garnered in glove of casual-loping Ed Miller, leaving aforesaid Ueda to, how you say, die on first, reet?

"*Masu-san* done laid some wood to the apple there, huh, Moe?" I say whilst assisting him in removal of chest protector and shinguards in dugout.

"It's harder with your eyes open, Yosh. *Daijubo*, kid. These boys are sandlotters. Trust me, this'll be a cakewalk."

Yank half of first inning produces two runs, as how McNair walks, moves to third upon occasion of Charles Gehringer double off left-field wall. Bambino Sultan Ruth, up third, swings hard for fence, but suffers ignoble ground-out to short, than which permits McNair to cross platter with first marker via failure of *Nihonjin* shortstop Yoritomo Taira, golden glover errorless ace of Ibaragi U. Cranes, to hold runner with threatening look, reet?

"Tough break, Bambino," I say to mitigate his embarrassment as George Herman Ruth stomps into dugout, huffing hard despite not even legging out grounder.

"Little Jap pecker!" says Babe Sultan in reference to Takshashi Sengoku, reputed fast-baller mound ace emanating from Kanagawa U. Spiders. "Next time I'll tear his head off his scrawny shoulders at the neck if he gives me another fat one high and hard!"

Than which *wataschi* is compelled to report fails to occur despite *Nihonjin* crowd's evident desire to see fabled Babe loft one out of park. George Herman Ruth goes zero for five to earn dubious distinction of sole hitless Yank personage in context of dramatic decisive *Amerkajin* triumph.

As witness, bottom of second inning: Moe Berg reaches first upon being struck in buttock bottom by pitched ball, wild one uncorked by aforesaid moundsman Takshashi. Said phenom provokes collectivist gasp of embarrassment from 65,000 fans dismayed on behalf of *Sengoku-san* for inflicting blatant indignity upon honored guest of *Dai Nippon*, reet?

Further curious instance: as Moe trots to first, rubbing offended bun, I eavesdrop Kanagawa U. moundsman Takshashi Sengoku cry out to sky, "Oh, shame upon my head and name!"

To which Moe, assuming short lead off bag, shouts to him in idiomatic *Nihonju*, "It is no disgrace to dust a man off in this game, *sensei* pitcher!" Moe and Takshashi exchange bows to delight (natch!) of 65,000 onlookers. I is thinking (ensconced on dugout steps perch, ready to lens Moe in action if he elects attempted theft of second — than which will never *hochee* happen as how he is distinctly unfleet of foots, Jack!): this Moe Berg is one fast study of the lingo, reet?

Than which puzzlement is forgotten in catching action in viewfinder, than which is: single stroked by Whitehill, allowing Moe to reach third on weak wimpish throw from outfield, followed by McNair single scoring Moe.

Bottom line (pith and gist, Jack!) is Earl Whitehill scatters six hits (mostly Texas League bloops), Yanks (unassisted by hitless Babe) coast to 17–1 pasting of local talents.

Omnibus ride back to Imperial Hotel occasions casual confabulations:

Connie Mack: "If this is their best it'll be a slaughter against the teams these jokers came from. Maybe we better go a little easy on them, boys. We don't want to wear out our welcome."

Ed Miller: "Yeah, Babe, go easy next time, we don't want to hurt their feelings, okay?"

James Foxx: "Yeah, Babe. That one loud foul you got nearly made it into the bleachers."

"Crack wise, assholes!" rejoinds Bambino Sultan of Swat.

"You okay, Moe?" I ask, observing as how he declines to take seat in omnibus, kneads buttock with heel of hand.

"Other than a strawberry on my rump, I'll be fine, Yosh. All I need is one of your hot baths and one of those famous rubdowns Japanese women give. A hot bath and some rest. How do you say it, *yasumi*?"

"Reet," I say, and, "I am steady amazed, Moe, as how you can spiel the *Nihonju* so good!"

Hardy har har. Hug. "I got a good ear, Yosh. Hey, can you do me one favor when we get to the hotel before you head off home?"

"Name it, Moe. I am but to serve!"

"Listen, get me a batch of the latest editions of the *shimbun*, okay?"

"You can read *kanji*, Moe?"

"A little. I want to practice up in my room tonight while these jerks are out looking for the red-light district."

"Reet!" says I. "Burn midnight oils, emulate the industrious honeybee, only way to get it, huh, Moe?"

"Yeah. And be sure to just buy the papers for me and bring them right up to my room, okay?" He slips me *yen*. "I got this little thing, I have to read a paper first before anyone else does, otherwise I can't stand to read it, okay?"

"I do not dig, Moe."

"Because words are alive, kid. Don't you know that? Somebody else reads the paper first, it's like they're dead, see? Will you do that for me?"

"Never thought of it that way, Moe. Will do!" I say, receive hardy-*sumairu*-har and fraternalist hug.

"I got a little treat in store for us planned for tomorrow, kid."

"What's up, Moe?"

"Count on it. Tomorrow we're scheduled to scrimmage with the Tokyo Imperial Whales, right? Well, what we'll do, you and me, we'll let these bums play *besuboru* out there in the heat and dust. You and me, Yosh, we'll take a little walking tour of the city on our own, okay? *Sanpo*, isn't that what you call it? Would you like that?"

"Reet," I tell him, "*sanpo* stroll perambulation. But ain't we supposed to show for the game, ceremonials and all that official shtick?"

"They'll never miss us in all the fuss, kid. We'll check out the town, eat in a good restaurant. Maybe take some souvenir pictures with the Stewart Warner, huh?"

"I am but to serve, Moe," says I as omnibus pulls up at the Imperial Hotel. Hardy hardy har and big fraternalist squeeze goodbye shtick.

"You're great, Yosh! Now get me those *shimbun*, I'll meet you up at my suite, and tomorrow we'll play tourist while these dumbbells do all the sweating, right?"

"You and me, Moe!"

"Trust me, Yosh," says Moe Berg, and, "Hey, why don't you take the camera on home with you and show it off to your folks if you want, huh?"

"Reet!" says I, off and running *chogee* pace to news vendor, Moe Berg's *yen* in one hand, schlepping Stewart Warner 16-millimeter in the other, going to buy all the hot-off-presses *shimbun* for my friend Moe Berg!

Do you dig it, Jack? It were as how me and Moe was becoming, how we say, *oyabun-kobun*, mentor and pupil, senior-junior duo relationship, reet? *Oyabun* leads, *kobun* follows, dig? Oh, big ironies to come therefrom, Jack!

I say to my *papa-san*, "It only looks complicated, Daddy. Really, like alls you gots to do is look in the viewfinder, frame up what it is you want to lens, push down on the lever and hold it there, reet?" *Papa-san* looks through viewfinder at *Mama-san*, Sis Iko, and *wataschi*.

"Remarkable," says my daddy, "but I am too old to learn to care for such machinery. I prefer to write poetry and perfect my execution of the *sho* calligraphy, which is enough to fill a man's life if he is diligent."

"Very latest technologies, state of the art," I assure them, carefully replace Moe Berg's camera in its case, buckle it shut.

"Only the *gaijin* would devise such a thing," says *Mama-san*, refuses to touch it.

"Moe says it gets sharp focus even at long range. This ain't no Kodak Brownie, folks!"

"The tanned hide of the case stinks," says *Iko-san*. "Is that how the *Amerikajin* smell, *Yosho-san*?"

"No," I repeat for her, "they kind of smell like meat on a warm *hanami* day, and like from the tobacco they chew and spit when they play *besuboru*, and some from perspirations, too. It ain't so bad once you get used to it. They all put fancy grease on their hair smells like lilacs, and George Herman Bambino Babe Sultan of Swat Ruth smells like sweats all the time on account he's so fat, excepting save he says he's working off night before's booze, reet? Moe don't smell so bad because I think he takes hot baths a lot just like we does."

Says my *papa-san*: "This Morris Berg appears to be an interesting personage, my son. It is clear to me that you respect and admire him. I did not think you would prove to be so enamored of their *besuboru, Yosho-san*."

"It ain't that, Daddy," I explain. "I care about as much for sport as I does for *budo* drill with the longsword. And Moe truly ain't such a much to watch on the diamond. The only one looks worse out there is Bambino Babe Sultan, than which is mostly due to George Herman being built like water barrel with little *mimikaki* toothpick legs and tiny feets, reet? Plus he asserts as how he's only in slump. He didn't hit for squat today, but I can see if he ever catches one solid on fat end of bat, he'll give horsehide ride, reet?"

"What then does my son find to look upon with such favor in this barbarian Morris Berg?" asks my mama.

"Perhaps *Yosho-san* enjoys the odor of perspiration or sees beauty in the enormous noses of the *Amerikajin*?" says Sis Iko.

"It's the lingo, folks!" I tell them, and, "Moe, he's a true scholar, Phi Beta Kappa, digs Latin, Greek, Sanskrit — you name it, French, Spanish, Italian! And he sure digs a lot of the *Nihonju* for somebody says he needs me to interpret for him! Did I tell you that shtick he does with the *shimbun*?"

"You have said he reads *kanji*," *Papa-san* says.

"Reet," I say, "thinks words is alive, dead if somebody reads them before him. Says as how he only knows a few characters, Daddy, but, I mean, it looked to me like the man was reading right through, right to left, bottom to top, reet? I asked, but he says as how he just gets gists and piths general drift, reet?"

"Perhaps he displays the virtue of modesty," says my daddy.

"Could be," I say, and, "And, like, as how he tells me to go ahead and take this here *eiga* flic camera home to show you. Do you know how much *yen* something like this goes for, Daddy?"

"My brother has been received by the *Mikado*, yet he rejoices more over a *gaijin* camera," *Iko-san* says, laughs.

"This has been a memorable day in your life, my son," Daddy says. "You have spoken with the Son of Heaven and made the acquaintance of a man who places great trust in you. Conduct yourself so as to prove worthy of both distinctions, *Yosho-san*."

"Reet," I tell them, and, "*Mikado*, sad to say, folks, ain't such a much to look at up close. But me and Moe, we tight, folks! He is like *oyabun* to *wataschi*, reet? He's going to put in word for me via *Amerikajin* Embassy, pull wires with Imperial Ministry of Education, help me garner one of them grants to study *Eigo* stateside!"

"I do not wish to hear of this! I do not wish my only son to go so far away to study among barbarians!" *Mama-san* says, covers her face with her hands, traditionalist gesture shtick indicating woes too great to bear.

"My brother will come to smell like uncooked meat!" cries *Iko-san* — mock-woe blague shtick.

"Moe pushing from his end, contact I gots me with that guy Sato, I'm a cinch, Daddy!" I say.

"Perhaps," says my *papa-san*. Wise man, my daddy, Jack! Says: "I have made informal inquiries, but have failed to learn anything of Mr. Sato Isao from those who know the Ministry of Education. I caution you, *Yosho-san*, to behave with reserve. You know that our government favors *joi-i*. Those who ignore or resist this principle must take care not to come to the attention of the *kempei*."

"I am only a woman," *Mama-san* says, "but I fear that shame will come of this!"

I tell my family: "Aw, come off it, folks! It ain't all abouts nothing excepting save a whole mess of words, reet? What's the big brouhaha hubbub about learning to lens *eiga* flics? What's bad can happen?"

"Did not your new *oyabun* great friend and mentor Morris Berg say to you, my son," says *Papa-san*, "that words are living things?"

"Top of the morning, Yosh," says Moe when I call for him at Imperial Hotel. "Good man," says he, "I see you didn't forget to bring my Stewart Warner with you. It wouldn't do to see all the sights without a camera, would it."

"Morning, Moe," I say, and, "Where's all your *besuboru* colleagues?"

"Gone off on the bus for the game at Meiji."

"So where you want to start?" I ask. "Used to was we could of hired us a *ricksha*, excepting as how now the government put a ban on them, saying as how it's an affront to dignity of all Hundred Millions to be schlepping *gaijin* around not unlike like unto horsie pulling nightsoil excrements cart, not to fail to mention also *ricksha* being Chink in origin is unpatriotic non-*Nipponshikki*, given as we are engaged in unofficial *senso* war with same in Manchukuo, reet?"

"We can hoof it," Moe says. "I'd kind of like to just mingle with the hoi polloi and see the real Japan, okay?"

So: we just *sanpo* stroll for a while, Moe and me, nice November day (circa '35), past the Imperial Palace (Moe holds camera on me whilst I demonstrate full face-in-cinders kowtow prostration posture to high rock walls across moat), into Nijubashi Plaza, crowded as ever with vendors of pickled squid, *shimbun*, kites, yard goods, ciggie smokes, live ducks, fresh tuna, *hakurai* imported pencils, decorative *sho* calligraphs, you-name-it etcetera blah.

"Note," I say to Moe, "old *mama-san* there wearing fancy old-timey *kimono*? You want I should get some footage of her schlepping along in her *geta*? Be a nice touch, Moe, contrast to drab *monpei* tunics and pantaloons Hundred Millions of *Dai Nippon* wearing these days."

"Save it," Moe says. "Maybe some other time if we end up with film left over. Like I said, this stuff's probably not easy to come by over here, huh? A good photographer always chooses his subjects with care, Yosh."

"Reet. I mean but to learn, Moe!"

We stroll *sanpo* style into Ginza, windowshop stalls, noodle and fish restaurants. "How do you tell," asks Moe, "who's a cop if you need one in all these uniforms?"

"Easy," I explain. "Cop on beat wears armband, reet? Like unto him," I

59

say, point out officer of law directing thick bicycle traffic at busy intersection crossroads. "Guys with *katana* longswords, white shirts, and Sam Browne belts is regular military, Imperial Army, reet? Dark blue is Imperial Navy personnel off ships moored in Tokyo Bay, liberty shtick, also sporting swords. Everybody else in tunic and pantaloons *monpei* attire is plain Joe Schmoe civilians. Three-piecer western-style suits, double-breasteds with attaché cases, is most like to be bureaucrats or high-level clericals, like my daddy, Mr. Yamaguchi. Excepting if they wear straw boaters instead of fedora, mostly likely they is *kempei*, how you say, Secret Service, G-man, Thought Police shamus types. As in him," I say, nod back over my shoulder at obvious flatfeeted *kempei* functionary factotum walking half-block rearwards.

"I'll have to tell Connie about that hat of his," Moe says, and, "I saw that guy. Is he following us, Yosh?"

"Most probably." I explain: "See, Moe, big chauvinist anti-*gaijin joi-i* paranoid shtick, especially in light of Mukden thing, agitation for *senso* war against Chinks in Manchukuo, very big trendy trend in *Dai Nippon* nowadays. *Kempei* like to keep tabs on all *gaijin* personages out and about, see they don't corrupt Hundred Millions with barbarian ways and all, reet? Man," I tell Moe, "they even post up outside *eiga* motion-picture theaters, old *No* and *Kabuki* and *Bunraku* places over in Asakusa, jot names of folks going in to see import flics."

"So what are they likely to think about you hanging around with me?"

"*Daijubo* no sweats," I tell him. "Ain't no big thing, reet? As how I'm just kid, so it ain't that serious probably, dig?"

"I guess that figures," Moe says, and, "Hey, Yosh, for the fun of it, let's walk fast and get in the crowd and see if we can lose the gumshoe in all the bustle, okay?"

"Easy money," I tell him. "Anyplace special you want to go, Moe? I know all the back streets, waysides, shortcuts. I can turn *kempei* tail inside out of hisself if he essays to stick to us."

"Let's go take a look at Tokyo Bay," Moe says. "I bet we could get a nice view of Fujiyama down close to the water, film what we call a cover shot, get a vista of the whole city, Fuji in the background, what do you say, Yosh?"

"You got it, Moe!" We pick up pace (*kempei* shamus tail gots to trot to keep us in sight, *wataschi* going *chogee* pace to stay alongside Moe's long stride), cut off busy Ginza, where I take lead, effort impeded by bulky weight of Stewart Warner camera I lug, Moe Berg now close behind to follow in my wake.

We hit side streets, alleys, narrow dirt paths between close-set paper houses, reet? Folks sliding open *shoji* paper-covered sliding frame doors to air interiors via sea breezes, sweeping off stoops with short-handle rice-straw brooms, setting charcoal to burning in *hibachi* braziers in anticipa-

60

tion of noon repasts, etcetera blah. Than which is to say: swift moving spectacle of Student Yamaguchi Yoshinori (schlepping heavy *eiga* camera in leather case!) accompanied by *gaijin* westerner provokes comments in passing. As follows:

"Where do you go in such haste with the ugly *gaijin*, young man?" yells oldish *mama-san* setting rice to boil over glowing coals.

"We doing sightseeing tourist shtick, *Mama-san*, on our way to view city environ from Tokyo Bay!"

"And how is my poor house of interest to the barbarian?" she calls after us.

"This *Amerikajin* wants to, like, see the real *Dai Nippon* lifestyles with bark off, reet?" I shout back. "Up ahead, Moe," I say, "we'll hang a right. That *kempei* going to think we become flat out translucent!"

"Right behind you, Yosh! Lead the way!"

"*Sensei* Student," calls out cheeky little boy-*san* practicing *kendo* with long *take* bamboo stick out in front of his paper house, "why are you not in school, and why do you go in the company of the huge *gaijin* with such an enormous nose?"

"Show *Nipponshikki* respects!" I yell as we fly by, "I am the oustanding scholar of Native Land Loving School, and this august personage is Morris Berg, also knowed as Moe, himself a scholar of languages, professional *besuboru* athlete, an honored guest of *Dai Nippon*!"

"Yosh," Moe slows *chogee* swift pace to say, "I'd just as leave you didn't announce me to everyone we run into, okay? And I could care less what anybody says about my beak, for that matter."

"How's come, Moe? I mean, like, you're a celeb, reet?"

"It's embarrassing," says Moe Berg. "Guys like the Babe eat up publicity, but I guess I'm the shy type."

"You understood *wataschi's* confabulation exchange with that smartypants kiddie, did you, Moe?"

"No," he says, and, "but I recognized my name when you said it."

"Also insult epithet concerning your schnozz, reet, Moe?"

"Yeah, about my nose, I understood that too. But I'd rather just kind of blend in if I can if you don't mind, okay?"

"Whatever you say, Moe, you the *oyabun boss*, I'm but the *kobun* flunky, reet?" I say, and, "Moe, you gots you one fantastic ear for the *Nihonju*!"

"It's a talent," says he, "like yours. That plus studying up, right? Say," he says, "are we getting close to the bay? I can smell the salt air on the wind with this honker of mine!"

Tokyo Bay, Jack! *Kempei* shamus tail is (natch!) decidedly outdistanced, doubtless wandering confused in narrow streets, questioning householders as to direction taken by *Nihonjin* student and ugly big-nosed *gaijin*, reet? "Did I lose him or did I but lose him, Moe!" I say, catching breaths after final lope to strand.

"Kid," Moe says, "you're as smart as you look!"

Tokyo Bay: tranquil scene. Traffic on strand, lorries and horsecarts schlepping *hakurai* import cargoes up from Yokohama dockside to warehouses and rail terminal. Stevedores exhibiting heavy *irezumi* tattooed torsos load and also unload, smell of salt water tinged with dead fishes floating belly-up in oil scum, said pollutant doubtless resulting from offshore fuel tender vessels moving in bay to service fleet ships at anchor, reet? "Not much of a view of Fuji's peak from here, Moe," I tell him. "We need to seek higher elevation unless you want viewfinder frame cluttered with rooftops and telephone wires."

"Let's give it a shot," says Moe, and, "Here, I'll walk along in front of these warehouses, along past those oil-storage tanks. You get on the other side of the strand and track me until I give you the high sign to cut it, okay?"

"Whatever you say, Moe, but you won't see much of Fuji if I keep you in frame." Through viewfinder, I focus Moe as he *sanpo* strolls nonchalant past warehouses, oil-storage tanks. Navvies at work on loading platforms pause in labor to gawk, point at perambulating *gaijin*, wave at camera (me, across strand, back to fishy-oil smell of lapping bay water) — tip of Fuji is remote as backdrop to framed scene.

"Frankly dull stuff, Moe," I say, "Can't not compare with full shot of Bambino Babe swinging four bats in on-deck circle or swish pan of standing-room-only crowd at Meiji."

"I want to get the real Japan, not just tourist stuff. Hey, Yosh," he says, "what are all those big boats tied up out there?"

"*Kido Butai*," I tell him, "How you say in *Eigo*, something like, Primary Fleet Strike Force of Imperial Navy, reet?"

"Is that a fact?" Moe says.

"Than which is commanded by Grand Admiral Yamamoto Isoroku," I tell him, "than which who is *honcho* of Imperial Navy. Back in port from tour of Chink coastline undertaken to inspire fear-and-trembling shtick amongst same in case they contemplate recoup of losses suffered in big Mukden Incident of circa 'thirty-one."

"I read something about that," says Moe, "in those *shimbun* you bought for me. Which one's the *Yamato*?" I point out recognizable warships: supercarrier *Yamato* (Grand Admiral's flagship, natch), also *Akagi, Kaga, Hoshu, Miyako, Hokato*, sister ships *Horyu* and *Soryu*, attendant cruisers and destroyers.

"You interested in things nautical, Moe?"

"Only casually. Hey, Yosh, stand over there and face me. I'll get a few feet of you in front of the bay."

"Doing what? I mean, like, you want me to walk along seawall, how as if I were out for postprandial *sanpo* stroll to sniff sea airs or some such?"

"Good idea," says Moe, and, "Don't look at the camera. I'll stand over here and track you."

"I feel, like, a little silly, Moe."

"Keep walking. Don't look at the camera! You look good, Yosh. Tell me again about the boats out there."

"*Kido Butai*," I say, "under command of supreme Imperial Navy *honcho* Grand Admiral Yamamoto. Naval power of *Dai Nippon*, proud result of armaments buildup inspired by *gumbatsu* plutocrat *honchos* saying as how Hundred Millions gots to flex muscles, assert national dignity on stage of global-wide politics guff, redress grievances against Washington Conference of circa 'twenty-two when we done agreed to limit size of navy as against Yank and *Igirisujin* Limey British contingents."

"You're pretty well informed for a young man, Yosh," says Moe.

"Just words, burning midnight oils, peruse *shimbun*," I say.

"How do you feel about all that politics, Yosh?" he asks. I hear cries of gulls skimming bay's surface for flotsams, chatter of *irezumi* tattooed navvies on platforms joking over ugly big-nose *gaijin* filming student on strand, mechanical hum of Stewart Warner 16-millimeter grinding out footage.

I say: "*Wataschi* does not dig the politics guff, Moe. Me, I is interested only in the words, the lingo, not to fail to mention *eiga* flics, about which I is crazy cracked fanatic fan thereof."

"That makes two of us," Moe says.

Shooting finished, we pause to remove film magazine, reload Stewart Warner. "Now," says Moe, "what say we move on?"

"Where to, Moe?"

"I was thinking. We got us a shot of the bay, we got Fujiyama from down at sea level here, what we need now is some nice high ground where we can get us an overview of the city, bird's-eye view sort of, don't you think, kid?"

"Ichigaya Heights," I say.

"Isn't that where the Imperial Army headquarters is?"

"Reet," I say, and, "How's come you to know something like that, Moe?"

"Like I told you, Yosh," says he, "homework. I did a little reading on board *The Empress of Japan* on the way over."

"Burning midnight oils," I say. Big hardy har complete with fraternalistic ursine hug, reet?

Moe Berg says: "Come on, show me the way. We'll trek up to Ichigaya Heights. I'll show you how the long range lens works on this baby!"

"I do mean to learn, Moe!" I say, grasp camera, exposed magazine packed in case, start off for Ichigaya environ, explaining to Moe how geography of Tokyo is facile to conceive, city bordered by bay on southeast, Kanto Plain to north, Edo River on northwest, Tama on the south.

"From the air," I explain to him, "it would be strictly *daijubo* no perspirations to orient to any spot via reference to rivers, broad expanse of Kanto Plain, dig?"

"I can imagine," Moe says, "it would be pretty clear if you saw it from up above and you knew what you were looking for."

"Than which ain't likely," I did say, "as how *honcho* authorities improbable to grant permissions for fly-over to any *gaijin*, given current paranoids *joi-i* ethos."

"No," Moe says, "I don't guess that'd be possible. Too bad," he says, "you can get terrific pictures from the air with a camera like this, Yosh."

Me and Moe Berg, Jack, circa November 1935, reet? We toddle in tandem across Tokyo Town for Ichigaya Heights, reet? *Wataschi* schlepps Stewart Warner camera, Moe steady checking over shoulder for reappearance of *kempei* shamus tail. "It looks," says he, "like we ditched him for good."

"Moe," I explain, "it don't make no matter, reet? Ditch one *kempei* factotum personage, another one going to pick us up sooner or later. Even if not, *Nihonjin* folks is going for sure to report sightings of unlikely duo, than which is us, student in school uniform, *gaijin* personage. How's come you to be so worried about police presence, Moe?"

"I'm not. It's just I don't like the idea of someone dogging my tracks."

"Eccentricity shtick?" I ask. "Like unto your need to read *shimbun* first, inability to peruse same if somebody else done glommed it prior?"

"Something like that, Yosh. Hey," Moe says, "you getting hungry yet? My belly thinks my throat's cut. Find us a good restaurant, and I'll spring for lunch."

"Reet!" I say, and, "Been so long since my mama cooked me fastbreaker on *hibachi*, I could eat, how you say in *Eigo*, opposite end from out of southbound equine, reet?" To laugh, reet, Jack?

We proceed via shank's mare, traverse Jubai, Ueno, Shimbashi, Shiragawa, hit Tsukiji District, renowned for good gustatory emporia, reet? "You'll dig this place, Moe, name of Little Restaurant of Prawn and Noodle, sometime habitat of famous *geisha* such as Kiharu, not to fail to mention *zaibatsu* fat-cat clientele, perhaps on pricey side."

"My treat, Yosh!" says Moe, flashes roll of *yen* adequate to strangulate aforesaid horsie. "Money's no object, I'm on per diem."

We dine alfresco under shade of paper *karakasa* umbrella, seated western-style at table (no need to remove brogans, reet?). Big spread consists of house specialty, steamed prawns reclining on bed of *udon* noodles, pickles, *tofu* bean curds, side dish (a la carte, costing arm and leg appendages!) of *surume* dried squid, sweet *nigirimeshi* rice balls and dry chestnuts for dessert, green *macha* tea. I delight in Moe Berg's loud belch of apprecia-

64

tion of cuisine. "*Umai!*" says Moe—delicious, reet?

"Moe," I ask, "how did you learn to read menu bill of fare like that?"

"I was guessing and got lucky, kid," he says. "I really don't understand the half of what I read in *kanji*."

"You sure could of fooled waiter personage," says I, and, "And most *gaijin* folks insults *Nihonjin* via proffering *chippu* tip for good service, not to fail to mention *wataschi* is amazed at your skill in wielding *hashi* chopsticks!"

"You can read up on local customs in any tour guidebook, Yosh."

"Homeworks?" I say.

"There you go, Yosh."

We press on with *sanpo* perambulation, *hara* tummies full, through Omiri, Ikebukuro, Yoshiwara. "Here," I tell him, "is where your *besuboru* colleagues needs to come if they seek red-light *moga* slut delights of *futon*, Moe. We in Yoshiwara now. Notice ladies watching from second-story windows?"

"I noticed," Moe says, and, "*Moga*. Comfort women. Yoshiwara, it means Happy Fields, is that right, Yosh?"

"Moe, you a flat out facile genius for the lingo!"

"I work at it," says he, and, "Those jerks wouldn't know how to enjoy themselves here, kid. They like to see boobs and butts, when the secret is the nape of the neck with *Nihonjin* women, right?" Har and hee of sleaze smutty cast shared, reet?

"Notice uphill trend of topography now, Moe? We entering Kaguasaka District. Over yonder lies Imperial War College, close by, natch, aforesaid Happy Fields."

"Let's get a few feet on film here, shall we?" he says. "For transitions, so I can make a narrative when I edit my shots back in the states, okay?"

"We don't dast," I tell him. "Folks catch a *gaijin* lensing the War College, you going to see all manner of *kempei* emerge from proverbial woodworks, Moe!"

"Even if he's with a kid in his school uniform?"

"Best believe it!"

"How about," says Moe, "in that case you go on up ahead and shoot it? I'll hang back and catch up with you when you're done."

"Reet," I say, "but it ain't nothing to look at no more than all them warehouses and oil tanks down by the bay. You sure you don't want me to take you somewhere scenic, Yasukuni Shrine, for examples, where all the souls of dead from all the *senso* wars meet? Or Grand Ise Shrine, Moe, you can lens Hundred Millions on knees praying to *Ameratasu* for helpful hints on how to formulate big life career decisions, etcetera blah. Than which is not to fail to mention as how I might could arrange it for us to lens the tea ceremony in your honor, *cha no yu*, very colorful traditionalist ritual tea house, tea master performing rites dating back to Chink origins, most impressive spectacle, Moe."

"Yosh," says Moe, "that ain't the real Japan I'm interested in, okay? Be a pal, run on up ahead with the camera and get me a few feet of the War College, okay? I'll kill some time, buy the afternoon *shimbun*, catch up with you in a minute, okay?"

"You the *oyabun*, *wataschi* mere *kobun*, whatever you say, Moe!"

"This'll give me a chance to practice my *Nihonju* on my own hook, huh? You think I can handle buying a newspaper all by my lonesome, Yosh?"

"Did you get it?" Moe asks when we meet, stack of afternoon *shimbun* under his arm.

"Such as it is," I say. "*Honcho* Imperial Army and Navy officer types bopping in and out of War College, much gilt braid, many longswords with fancy tassles, incessant salutes and kowtow deferences and other such militarist guff stuff. I hope you ain't going to be disappointed when you screen the rushes, Moe!"

"Not on your life, kid!"

"You want me to help you schlepp some of them *shimbun*, Moe?"

"You handle the camera, Yosh. I'll carry the tabloids. Remember? Anyone touches the words before I do, they're dead?"

"Reet," I say, and, "Eccentricity shtick."

"Lead on," Moe says, "I'm anxious to see what Tokyo looks like from all the way up on top there."

"Reet," I say, lead on across Shibaya and Shinjuku districts, steady uphill trend of topography, to Ichigaya Heights.

Ichigaya Heights, Jack: me and Moe stand to gander vista of Tokyo Town laid out below. Imperial Army Headquarters, complex bunker-type structures, off to left of grassy knoll whereon we strike stance to enjoy view in cool shade of big pine tree.

"Can you dig the geographics now, Moe?"

"I see it," says he, extends digit to point and trace layout of Tokyo — tiny dots is ships of *Kido Butai* fleet at anchor, fuel tenders moving to and also fro not unlike like unto waterbugs on surface of tranquil carp pond, Edo and Tama rivers frame confines of municipality reaching back from bay to flat expanse of Kanto Plain. "What's the big green patch right smack dab in the middle?" Moe asks.

"Imperial Palace grounds, Moe," I say, and, "Off to right you can see road we took in from Yokohama with motorcade. Them other green swatches is big public parks, Miyama, Ueno, where my folks Mr. and Mrs. Yamaguchi used to take me and my baby sis for *sanpo* walks when we was but little nippers."

"What's all the haze over the city from?"

"Amalgam of pollutions, Moe," I explain, "charcoals smoking in *hibachi*, all the *mama-sans* getting fire started to cook up dinner pretty soon now, not to fail to mention *sento* public bath houses stoking wood fires to get hot water ready for folks, hundred and thirty degrees Fahrenheit standard."

"All those short chimneys are bath houses?"

"Mostly. Some is small fabrications factories, casting, smelters, etcetera blah, reet?"

"That's what I figured," says Moe, and, "I noticed coming up here how your factories are usually small places, no big centralized industrial area."

"*Dai Nippon*," I tell him, "small environ, cheek-by-jowl crowded, Moe. Over seventy millions, which is to 'fess up as how *zaibatsu* patriot chauvinists types yack steady about Hundred Millions, than which is only guff stuff, but we gots to think smallish here, reet? Land too scarce for household gardens, so we make *bonsai* trees, trim roots and dose topsoil with morphine to stunt growths."

"Pretty slick," says Moe, "but you'd think fire would be a hell of a hazzard with all the paper and wood houses."

"You know it, Moe! How we say, Flowers of Edo, monicker name for frequent incendiaries resultant from combo of flammable constructions, *hibachi* coals in every house, frequent wind off Tokyo Bay. Big earthquake of 'twenty-three,'" I tell him, "major damage was conflagrations following upon tremors. I was only little nipper aged but five years of age at the time, Moe, but I recalls noise, heat, folks screaming, jumping into Edo and Tama to escape inferno."

"I can imagine," Moe says, and, "Break out the camera and get a slow pan, Yosh."

"You don't want to do it yourself? I'd like, hate to be responsible for faulty footage, Moe."

"You'll do just fine," says he, and, "I don't think it'd be such a hot idea for me to be flashing the camera around here." Moe nods in direction of Imperial Army Headquarters, gaggle of *honcho* officer types dismounting staff car pause to gander our way before ascending steps, confabulating with armed sentries on duty at entranceway guard boxes.

"Whatever you say, Moe." I place Stewart Warner viewfinder to my baby blue, frame vista of metropolis, crank lever, shoot very slow pan, east to west, north to south.

"Here," Moe says, "get a few feet of me mugging for my friends back home." He assumes buffoon pose, hands on hips, jaw outthrust.

"Moe, Imperial Headquarters is right behind you in the frame. We could get us in deep tribulations, betwixt rock and hard place shtick, reet?"

"Shoot," Moe says, and, "Try that long range lens, the focus on that gizmo will get every pore in my honker. Do it quick, they won't notice." I shoot Moe, mass of Imperial Army Headquarters, sentries on duty, officers gathered near staff vehicle—trembling a tad from *hara* belly nerves, Jack! Moe grins big *sumairu* for the camera.

"I think it's going to be a little fuzzy, Moe," I tell him as we repack camera in carrying case. "Probably have to leave most of it on cutting-room floor. Sorry, Moe."

"You did swell!" says Moe, and we take off, down downward trending topography toward downtown, Imperial Hotel. "This has been a great day, Yosh!" I check back over my shoulder, sigh relief to see nobody coming after us.

"Glad you enjoyed it, Moe, but it ain't like you seen much to talk about."

"I saw everything I wanted to," he says, "and I couldn't have done it without you, kid. You're some kid, Yosh! And I'm not forgetting my promise to put in a word for you on that overseas study permission thing either! Trust me, Yosh, I'll speak to my contact at the embassy, this time next year you'll be tapped for the best club at Princeton!"

"Really, Moe?"

"Have I ever lied to you yet?"

Than which is to complete account of our day, me and Moe Berg, seeing sights of the real *Dai Nippon*, circa early November 1935—except save for awkward incident experienced in lobby of Imperial Hotel, whilst bidding mutual goodbyes until the morrow, reet?

Dig: we is just entered lobby environ. Very western-style, reet, Jack? No need to remove brogans, tables and chairs, *gaijin* personages wall to wall imbibing preprandial libations (dry martini is fav-rave circa '35!), *Ameri-kajin* musics played by three-piece tuxedo-clad combo, bar crowded with journalists, tourists, *zaibatsu* business wheeler-dealers, international diplomatic community *honcho* factotums, et alia etcetera blah. We is just heard from bellboy as how Moe's colleagues done already returned from Meiji Shrine ballfield triumphant, having whipped up on Tokyo U. Whale squad by lopsided 22–3 score in but seven-inning outing—handcuff pitching of Vernon (a.k.a. Lefty) Gomez, hitting of Gehrig, Foxx, Gehringer, Earl Averill (Bambino Babe Sultan, alas, remaining in slump, zero for five at plate!).

"Thanks again, kid," Moe is saying, "See you bright and early on the bus, huh?"

"Shizuoka on the morrow," I say, and, "Here's hoping you get better competitions from Waseda Frogs, reet?"

At which exact juncture comes gentle inquisitive voice from direct behind me, as follows: "Myriad pardons, *sensei* Student, for this disgraceful intrusion upon your confabulation with this distinguished *gaijin*, but my prescribed duties require that I ascertain information as to his activities."

68

We turn, me and Moe (combo is playing Benny Goodman swing tune, very hep, beneath which can be registered cacophony of various lingos being spoken by international types seated at tables, clustered *hara* bellies against bar, not to fail to mention rattle of cocktail shakers, reet?), confront man in posture of fifteen-degree kowtow bow of greetings — it is (natch!) *kempei* operative, as immediately evidenced in baggy suit, two-tone black-and-white shoes, straw boater clutched deferential in both hands.

"You do the talking, Yosh," says Moe as I hit twenty-five-degree bow, say to *kempei* personage:

"You ain't butting in on nothing, *sensei* Policeman! Allow *wataschi* to introduce self, reet? I is Student Yamaguchi Yoshinori, first form matriculant, Native Land Loving School."

"My name is of no significance, Student Yamaguchi," says *kempei*, "but the identity of your companion would be of great interest to me."

Upon hearing which (*Nihonju*, reet, Jack?), Moe Berg says (in *Eigo*, Jack!), "Tell him who I am, Yosh. Make me look good. We got nothing to hide, right?"

I say: "You looking at illustrious *Amerikajin* athlete and also scholar Mr. Morris Berg, commonly denominated as Moe. He is prominent member of visiting delegation Yank American League *besuboru* barnstormers, which is to say invited guest of *Dai Nippon*, than which who, but day prior to yesterday was received in official audience by none other than *Mikado*!" Whilst *wataschi* and *kempei* face Imperial Palace directional to (natch!) render kowtow, Moe adds in *Eigo*:

"Lay it on thick, Yosh!"

"Just so!" says *kempei* with breath intake hiss, and, "I am informed of the activities of these *Amerikajin* visitors to *Dai Nippon*. Are they not engaged in their decadent sport with students of our seven universities?"

"Reet," I tell him, "imparting fine pointers of *besuboru*, not to fail to mention staging entertainments exhibitions for delight of Hundred Millions, reet?"

"Higher and deeper, kid," says Moe in *Eigo*.

"What does the *gaijin* say to you?" *kempei* queries.

"Tell the little fart I'm asking what the hell does he want."

"*Sensei* Mr. Berg queries as to purpose of this confab."

"Inform the barbarian that I am charged by my superiors with verifying the details of his peregrinations this day, since it was noticed that he did not join his peers in sport at Meiji Shrine."

"He says where we done been all day, Moe," I say, look from *sumairu* smiling *kempei* to smirking Moe.

"I heard what he said. Tell him I had a strawberry burn on my ass and couldn't catch, so we walked around to see the local color while I worked out the kinks."

"Mr. Berg is hurting from minor wound suffered via strenuous exercise of sport. Long *sanpo* walk provides relief from discomfort, reet?"

At which juncture *kempei* operative personage removes pad and pencil, licks point of latter, jots note. "Just so!" he says, and, "That is precisely the report I am concerned to corroborate. Please ask the *gaijin* where exactly he went during the course of this day, *sensei* Student Yamaguchi."

"Tell him we took a damn long walk. Is that so hard for him to understand?" says Moe in (natch) *Eigo*.

I say to *kempei*: "*Sensei* Mr. Berg says as how no particular destinations in mind, no purposes except save health-restorative aforementioned exercise, reet? We done scoffed midday meal at Little Restaurant of the Prawn and Noodle, now returned for western-style dinner here, whereat he is duly registered guest." *Kempei* consults notes.

"That is in accord with reports transmitted to me. Please, Student Yamaguchi, ask the foul-smelling *gaijin* if he did look upon the ships of the *Kido Butai* at anchor in Tokyo Bay. Ask further, did he enter the vicinities of the War College and Imperial Army Headquarters?"

"I think we was spotted on wharfside and up on higher elevations, Moe," I say to him.

"Tell this turd all we saw were some boats out on the water. We don't know from nothing, right, Yosh?"

"Mr. Berg allows as how we did visit strand to inhale bracing sea airs. We did schlepp up Ichigaya Heights, but, like, he ain't gots no understanding of signficances of said locales, reet, *sensei* Policeman?"

"Perhaps," *kempei* says, makes note after licking pencil point for indelibility. Folks in lobby beginning to notice, reet? "The *gaijin* appears agitated," says *kempei*.

"The foreigner would just as leave kick your little yellow keester up between your shoulder blades," says Moe.

Says *wataschi*: "*Sensei* Mr. Berg don't, like, dig what's all the flap for, reet?"

"Like all barbarian *gaijin*, he has little understanding of the subtle complexity of administrative affairs. Do you, Student Yamaguchi, find Caucasians to be as repulsive looking as I do? The enormity of their noses is disgusting! And do they not all exude a foul stench?" He *sumairu* smiles at Moe, at internationals at tables, on bar stools.

"*Sensei* Policeman, is it, like, cool to be zinging insults at guest of *Dai Nippon*? I mean, like, such ain't *Nipponshikki* hospitalities decorum, reet?"

"You tell him, kid!"

"It is not for a tender youth to admonish his elder, Student Yamaguchi," says *kempei*—I (natch!) hit five-degree bow as indication as how I stands corrected, reet? "And wherein lies the insult when the ignorant barbarian cannot understand our words?"

"That's right," Moe says, "can't understand a blessed thing you're saying, you sawed-off little shit-ass!"

"Orry-say, myriad pardons begged etcetera blah," I say.

"Just so," *kempei* says.

"Tell him I'd like to get on with my life if he don't object too damn much, Yosh."

"*Sensei* Mr. Berg says as how he'd like to repair to his suite to perform ablutions prior to scoffing, etcetera blah, reet?"

"I require but a moment more of the *gaijin's* time. Tell me, Student Yamaguchi, what is that you carry? Is it some burden thrust upon you by this *Amerikajin*?"

Than which before I can riposte, says Moe: "Tell him it's your camera, Yosh. If he thinks it's mine we'll never get him out of our hair. What the hell's business of his is it, right?"

I say . . . Jack, I gots reasons for what I did say!

Dig: I said what I said to *kempei* because my new *oyabun* friend Morris (a.k.a. Moe) Berg treats me not unlike unto *kobun* protégé, reet? And I say it because as how I does not wish to see my *oyabun* friend Moe experience hassle with *kempei* gumshoe operative shamus, reet? And I say it, Jack, because as how for fear if I utter otherhow my new friend and mentor Moe Berg might could become unwilling or unable to employ his good offices clout influence pull grease to assist *wataschi* in garnering overseas stateside study permission and grant-in-aid, reet? Jack, I did say what I said because I is but Student Yamaguchi Yoshinori, aged only six and ten sweet years of age, circa '35 — tender innocence of youth status knows no possibilities of ironies big and small to come, reet?

I say: "*Sensei* Policeman, this is my *eiga* motion-picture camera, reet? I do schlepp it out and about so's as to make me a flic as memento memorial of this occasion, wherein I is got the opportunity to earn honor and glory for my name, family, not to fail to mention *Dai Nippon*, reet? Which is also to mention honor-and-glory shtick reflecting upon Celestial Personage of *Mikado* —"

At which juncture me and *kempei* pivot (natch!) in direction (two blocks away!) of Imperial Palace, kowtow thereto.

" — I is but trying to do good on mission assigned to serve as interpreter and guide to visiting Yank American League all-star *besurboru* barnstorm squad, motivated to said endeavor by responsibility bestowed on me by illustrious mentors of Native Land Loving School, not to fail to mention also by *sensei honcho* Mr. Sato Isao, than which who is important functionary factotum of Imperial Ministry of Education, reet?"

"Sato Isao?" says *kempei*, writes longish note on pad, reet? "Allow me to take my leave of you, Student Yamaguchi. Please convey my farewell to this *gaijin*. I have enjoyed and profited by our informative confabulation. Let me only, in departing, caution you to conduct yourself with discretion in your association with these *Amerikajin*, for their presence on our sacred soil is a cause of dismay to many in authority. Is my meaning lucid to you, Student Yamaguchi?"

"*Hai!*" I say, and, "Reet!" and exchange goodbye bows. "Moe," I commence to say, "I think we going to have us troubles—"

Than which articulation is interrupted by sudden arrival of George Herman (a.k.a. Babe, a.k.a. Bambino, a.k.a. Sultan of Swat) Ruth, said personage emerging from elevator, reet? Bambino Babe Sultan calls to us as he makes swift progress toward bar. "Hey, Moe! Where the hell where you today, Moe? You talk one of them little *mama-san* chambermaids into crawling into the hay with you?"

"Hello, Babe. I hear you put on another real stellar performance out there today."

"I think it's this Jap food, Moe. I got the runs real bad! How the hell expect me to play ball when I feel any second I'm either gonna heave my lunch or crap my drawers? Hello, squirt," says Sultan Babe to *wataschi*.

"Moe," I try to say, "we better not pull no fancy footworks if them *kempei* eyeballing—"

"Tell me about it in the morning, Yosh," he says, and, "Bright and early on the bus to Shizuoka."

"Reet. See you, Moe."

"And don't forget to bring the camera," he says, "Who knows, maybe Ruth'll even get a hit against those Frogs, you can peddle the footage to The March of Time, huh?"

"Count on me, Moe!" I call after him as he disappears in pursuit of errant Bambino Babe admidst barstool crowd.

What's else to do, Jack, excepting go home, dinner in paper house with Yamaguchi family, reet? Long *sanpo* walk, Jack, than which interim allows *wataschi* ample time in which to conjure up good story to tell Daddy, Mama, Sis Iko. Not to fail to mention ample duration in which to consider emerging implications of events up to and including lobby incident experience, reet? Not to fail to mention calculations of attendant hazards I discern manifesting, reet? Surprise, Jack: I don't see no *kempei* gumshoe shamus tail dogging my tracks as I perambulate through falling dusk's light of Tokyo Town!

Dig: omnibus ride to Shizuoka City, bright and early. Yank American League all-star barnstormers scheduled to oppose Waseda University Frogs, take *besuboru* exhibition show on road, see how *Amerikajin* sport plays hick sticks provinces, reet?

I—*wataschi*, me, Student Yamaguchi Yoshinori!—glom seat alongside Moe Berg, than which who sits by window for morn's light by which to peruse batch of early-edition *shimbun* purchased in kiosk outside Imperial

Hotel. Sky over Tokyo hazed with charcoal smoke due to *mama-sans* all over town cooking up fast-breaking scarfs over *hibachi* fires, city streets filling with pedestrian and bike traffics, Hundred Millions out to perform daily nut hustle.

I say: "Moe, can we, like, chat? As how I is some concerned concerning possible hassles impending resultant from schlepping camera round and about *Dai Nippon*." I pat Stewart Warner, secure in leather case, on my lap.

"In a sec, kid. Let me finish reading the papers, okay? If I put them down someplace, one of these yahoos is going to pick them up to look through for the funny pages, and you know what that means, right, Yosh?"

"Words all die."

"You know it!" Moe resumes perusal of editorial section of *Asahi*, skimming *kanji* ideographs with apparent ease. What's else to do? *Watas-chi* twiddles thumbs, waits on Moe Berg to finish reading *shimbun*, observes fellow passengers disposed about confines of omnibus as we traverse city limits, hit road to Shizuoka, reet?

I eavesdrop Mr. Suzuki Sataro's confabulation with omnibus chauffeur, volume of discourse unrestrained as how they disregard me as sole additional speaker of *Nihonju*, reet?

Says chauffeur: "I undertake to transport these *Amerikajin* to Shizuoka only because I am promised a *bonasu* bonus remuneration. Without this inducement, I would not subject myself to proximity with them. Their appearance is grotesque, and the stink of their bodies will surely linger for days in my vehicle."

Says Mr. Suzuki: "It is inhospitable of you to speak thusly of them. They are the honored guests of *Dai Nippon*. *Nipponshikki* dictates that we exhibit unfailing courtesy at all times."

"My omnibus smells like a slaughterhouse. I hold my breath, but when I must breathe I smell the stench of warm blood. When I take my eyes from the road, I see them in the driving mirror, and this vision causes my *hara* belly to tingle with nausea! I assert these *gaijin* assault my senses as strongly as the dirty *Eta* people who gather our nightsoil in carts!"

"I will not hear you speak this way!" Suzuki tells him. "Silence yourself or I shall report you to your superiors!"

"Tell him," Moe says from corner of his mouth to me, "to keep his eyes on the road where they belong. How is anybody supposed to read in this yammer? You might tell him for me some people think *Nihonjin* smell like fish sauce and the human waste they fertilize their vegetables with, if it comes to that."

"You caught all that guff, reet, Moe?" I say. Moe Berg looks up from *shimbun* to *sumairu* smile at me.

"I must be getting the hang of it, huh, kid? I won't tell if you don't, Yosh."

"Mum," I did say to him, "is word, *obayun* buddy pal Moe."

Do you dig it, Jack? Which is to say: significant *ma* moment of *yoin* resonances awareness on part of *wataschi*, reet? Which is to say: Jack, I think I did at long last get it, how you say, catched on, circa November 1935, omnibus interior environ, road to Shizuoka City! Dig it!

"And I," chauffeur personage is saying to Mr. Suzuki, "should feel compelled in turn to report to appropriate authorities the fact that you appear to feel perfect ease in the presence of *gaijin* barbarians! The brother of my sister-in-law is a respected member of the *kempei!*" he adds.

"Is it seemly to dispute within the hearing of a tender youth?" Mr. Suzuki says. Chauffeur personage checks me out in mirror, reet? Natch, *wataschi* looks straight ahead, conceal all awareness, as if how fascinated by vista of road to Shizuoka.

"My assigned task is to drive this omnibus to Shizuoka, and from thence to return it to Tokyo. I need dispute no further with you," says chauffeur.

"Nor I with you," says Suzuki Sataro.

What's to do, reet? Twiddle thumbs, wait on Moe to finish *shimbun* perusal, observe and eavesdrop, consider implications of situation *wataschi* begins to twig — as in, how you say, eureka! (incandescent bulb lights up in balloon over my noggin!), reet, Jack?

Up front, Venerable Sage Connie Mack (a.k.a. Cornelius McGilli-cuddy) plays cutthroat (five cents *Amerikajin* coinage per point, reet?) cribbage with Iron Man Louis Gehrig — Clint Brown, James Foxx, and Eric McNair huddle close to kibbitz.

"Fifteen two, fifteen four, a pair is six. Skunked you, Connie! Pay up, old-timer!"

"Dumb slop luck," says Grand Old Man of Sport, digs in wallet, extracts *yen* note.

"Greenbacks only," says Iron Lou, "none of that Monopoly stuff."

"I'll take your money, Connie. Deal me in," says Clint Brown.

"Anybody for a fast few hands of five-card?" asks McNair.

"Who's the old drag queen anyway?" Sage Mack says, holds up ten *yen* note to examine portrait of Emperor Taisho garbed in royal *kimono*.

"Ignore them, Yosh," Moe says to me without looking up from reading, "Consider the source."

"Sticks and stones, Moe," I say.

Across aisle, Earl Whitehill, slated to start on mound today versus Waseda Frogs, slaps tangy lotion onto pitching arm, kneads bicep. "Forget it, Earl," says Vernon (a.k.a. Lefty) Gomez, "that rag-arm is way past reviving."

"You can throw yourself out just as easy against sandlotters," Earl says.

"Baloney," Gomez says. "I went half-speed all day yesterday and they still can't hit anything that moves or jumps."

"Suit yourself," Whitehill says, "but I ain't burning up my wing just to put on a show for a bunch of Japs."

Joe Cascarella joins them, says, "You want to go over signals while we got time? Once we get there it's all bowing and scraping. We won't get the chance, Earl."

What's to do, reet? Waiting on Moe Berg to finish perusal, discomforted in eye-contact exchanges with chauvinist omnibus chauffeur personage, not desirous of initiating confabulation with Suzuki Sataro — than which who has expressed wish that I assist him with translations in conducting interviews with Yank *besuboru* greats for column he authors in *Yomiuri Shimbun* — I hop, uninvited, into aforesaid confabulation, reet?

"No need," I tell them, "to fabricate elaborated cryptic code signals, as how Waseda U. boys will not deign to attempt thefts of same from you, reet?"

"What'd he say?" Earl Whitehill says.

"Reet," I say, and, "*Nihonjin* ballplayers will not try to steal signals."

"Says who?" says Lefty Gomez.

"What's that?" asks Joe Cascarella.

"Listen to him," Moe says without looking up from his *shimbun*, "he's trying to wise you up."

"Who the hell asked you for your two bits, Moe?" Earl Whitehill queries.

"I mean, like," I tell them, "stealing is dishonorable, un-*Nipponshikki*, reet? Natch, Waseda U. coaches, not to fail to mention baserunners, will not contradict ethical decorum norms via attempt to pick off pitching signals. Honest Amerind!" I say.

"No shit?" Lefty says.

"So how in the hell do they expect ever to win any ballgames?" Earl says. "It's bad enough they don't even know to tag up and advance on a fly ball."

"They play inspirited by spirit of sport, than which is in turn inspirited by inspiration of competitive desire to excel," I tell them. "How we say, *kirijini*, means, like, give it old collegiate effort, do damndest, press on to glorious triumph even despite formidable odds against success. Ain't that right, Moe?"

"Something like that," says he, "but it's closer to the *Eigo* expression to go down swinging with your sword still in your hand, kid."

"Reet," I say — do you dig it, Jack? Thus it were, aboard omnibus enroute on road to Shizuoka City, *wataschi* did come to understand — eureka! — as how Morris (a.k.a. Moe) Berg was fluent speaker (also reader!) of *Nihonju* lingo, than which is not to fail to mention *eiga* flics we did lens with long range lens of Stewart Warner camera (in my lap, Jack!) was not souvenir footages to show folks back home! Oh, Jack, big *hara* belly dilemma, mentioning also big irony of what I did decide to do in light of awareness thereof!

"You know, Moe," Earl says, "you can be a real pain in the ass when you talk like a damn professor, did I ever tell you that?"

"Knowlege is power," ripostes Moe, "which is why you'll be up the creek without a paddle the day your arm goes on you."

"If your batting average was as big as your mouth, which it ain't and never was, you'd make the all-star team every season, Moe," Lefty says.

"Tell your boys," Joe Cascarella says to me, "it's against the law to steal bases too, then we won't have to worry about Moe here throwing the ball out into center field when he's doing the catching."

"Just for that crack," says Moe, putting down *shimbun* he did peruse, "you can catch the whole game today, Joe. Me and my buddy Yosh here will go out and see the sights in Shizuoka."

"In a pig's ass, Berg!" Joe says, and, "I played the whole damn game yesterday, it's your fucking turn to earn your keep on this gig for a change instead of sitting around on your butt reading that chicken-scratch crap while the rest of us do all the work, man!"

"Like, guys," I try to say, "*wataschi* didn't intend to instigate no rhubarb beef brouhaha—"

"Will you loudmouth assholes shut the damn hell fuck up so a man can get in a snooze!" interjects George Herman (a.k.a. Babe, a.k.a. Bambino, a.k.a. Sultan of Swat) Ruth, than which who resides in back of omnibus, whereat he has reposed aslumber since departure from Imperial Hotel, reet?

"Please, sirs," says Suzuki Sataro, joining group from up front, reporter's notebook and *harukai* import fountain pen in hands, "may I to please extract quotables for employment in feature article in preparation for publication for erudition edifications of Hundred Millions loyal readership *Yomiuri Shimbun besuboru* fans?"

"Balls!" says Iron Man Louis Gehrig, "Now you guys went and done it! He's gonna want to interview me again!"

"I said I was trying to get me some fucking shut-eye!" screams Bambino Babe from rear of omnibus, and, "Connie, is there anything to eat or drink on this goddamn jitney for a man they won't let him even get a little sleep before he has to go out and play a ballgame in the hot sun?"

"Okay," Earl Whitehill says, "if they don't steal signals, one finger for the fastball, two for a curve, and to hell with the rest of it, Joe."

"Honored sirs," Suzuki Sataro is saying in inept *Eigo* further garbled by excited tense atmosphere aura of omnibus interior environ, "direct quotables induce immediacy of drama's illusions, but please to be articulating more slower for exactitudeness of transcriptions, please?"

Wataschi catches eyes of chauffeur personage in mirror—he sneers *sumairu*, says to me, "*Sensei* Student, the *gaijin* dispute among themselves like unto housewives who strive to purchase the self-same fish in an open market! I am ecstatic that I am *Nihonjin*, and was not born an ugly and evil-smelling *Amerikajin*!"

I tell him: "They bickering about professional stuff, reet?" and, "You gets used to the smell."

Omnibus ride to Shizuoka City. Circa November 1935, reet, Jack?

Wataschi Student Yamaguchi Yoshinori, aged but sweet sixteen years old, disconcerted to max extreme at eruption of ill wills *hara* belly tensions amongst Yank all-star barnstorm hardballers, embarrassed on behalf of rude asides engendered by chauvinist chauffeur personage—which is not to fail to mention as how I is foremost preoccupied with personal ambitions to develop interpreter-guide shtick new *oyabun-kobun* camaraderie relationship with Moe Berg in direction of Imperial Ministry of Education cachet enabling pursuit of higher-educational studies stateside at prestige Ivy League institution, than which impulse is complicated by admonition of Mr. Sato Isao to report any and all untoward behaviors of aforesaid Moe Berg, than which is complicated to maximalist by *ma* moment's awareness that Moe is done faked ignorance of *Nihonju* lingo, not to fail to mention as how he done lensed *eiga* flic footages of off-limits *Kido Butai* fleet and Ichigaya Heights Imperial Army environ day before—all which is to say, Jack: *wataschi* Student Yamaguchi Yoshinori is jabbed by dilemma's horn, getting big clear vision to wit: Moe Berg is done come to *Dai Nippon* for purpose other than *besuboru* sport exhibitions, reet?

What's to do? Rat on Moe to aforesaid Mr. Sato? Keep mum confidences to self, go with *do* flow in hopes of attaining to aforestated goal desires? Let Moe in on secret to effect I is wise to his game?

Jack (sad to say!): I did sit tight on omnibus seat alongside Moe, clutch 16-millimeter Stewart Warner *eiga* camera (magazine thereof which is loaded with fresh film stocks to lens actualities footage of upcoming diamond contest versus Waseda Frogs), hope for best, reet? In midst of snafu, I did think, Jack, ride out currents of situationals, pray in silence to *kami* for favorable resolutions to all concerned, reet?

"You're mighty silent all of a sudden. Cat got your tongue, Yosh?" Moe asks.

"Orry-say, Moe. I fear creating further controversies via inserting pedal extremity in mouth, not wishing to fan flames of *hara* tensions amongst you and peer athletes." To which Moe ripostes with hardy-har laugh, reet?

"Forget it, kid! The trick is not to take these bums too serious. Come on, talk to me. Tell me what we can expect to see in Shizuoka."

"You ain't already checked it out on a map, Moe?"

"I looked, but I couldn't make anything out." Har. Hee. It is to laugh, reet, Jack?

"Not much, Moe. Shizuoka City is, how you say, one-horsie wide spot in road jerkwater provincial hick sticks, reet? Biggest thing in town is nearby Eta Jima encampment environ, humongous big Imperial Army training site for draftees, how we say, *issen gorin*, cheapest coin cannon-fodder types, than which who is assembled from all over *Dai Nippon* as result of manpower mobilizations decreed to meet needs of Kwantung Army since buildup of Chink hostilities via Mukden Incident."

"Eta Jima," Moe says, ganders out window at passing scenics — peasant-farmer types knee deep in terraced paddies engaged in final stages of rice harvest, planting wheats and barleys for winter growing season. "Eta Jima," says Moe, "Is that a fact? Well, now, that might be something worth giving a look, huh, Yosh? What do you think?" Hee. Har, reet, Jack?

"Rubberneckers not encouraged in vicinity, Moe," I tell him. "As how considered military-sensitive locale. Like, place doubtless crawling with *kempei* types taking names of personages exhibiting undue interest, dig?" Moe laughs. Har. Hee.

Says he: "Heck, Yosh, they couldn't object to an old ballplayer and his *Nihonjin kobun* buddy just out for a *sanpo* stroll to see the sights, now could they?"

"Possible," I say, "but prudence dictates we leave Stewart Warner *eiga* camera behind if we do. *Kempei* operatives very wary of snapping pics of military, Moe, big national-security shtick."

Says he: "How would I get any souvenir footage to remember it all by when I'm back home if we didn't take the camera with us, Yosh? *Daijubo*! Don't fret, kid! We'll be discreet. Trust me."

"How we going to go out to Eta Jima when you supposed to be backstopping versus Frogs in Shizuoka City, Moe?"

"Nothing to it. I'll tell Connie my behind's still sore."

"I heard that, Berg!" shouts Joe Cascarella, and, "Connie, am I the only catcher on this team, or is Berg supposed to help haul the freight too?"

"You wouldn't want me to play hurting, would you, Joe?" And, to Sage Mack, "Connie, I think I must of pulled a muscle walking around Tokyo with the kid here yesterday. I think I better sit this one out, okay?"

"You letting him get away with this, Connie?" asks Joe.

"Will you," says Gray Eminence Mack, "shut the hell up and give me some peace for a change!"

"Swell!" says Joe Cascarella. "Sure thing! Big deal Moe Berg gets special treatment all the way, right? Everybody else's got to play against the slant-eyes like we're paid to do. Jew-boy's got connections with everybody from Commissioner Landis to you to the damn American ambassador, don't you, you mockie bastard!"

"For the last time," yells Bambino Babe Sultan from rear of omnibus, "either I get some rest or I ain't playing neither! I got a sour stomach, my head's pounding, there ain't a goddamn thing to eat or drink on this cattle truck, and I'm in the worst slump of my life in case nobody noticed!"

"Cork it!" screeches Sage Mack, and, "Go back to sleep, Babe. Cascarella, you'll do what the hell you're told! If I say you catch today, you catch today! Moe," says Mack, "it don't help me none your provoking him."

"Please, honorable sirs," says Suzuki Sataro, scribbling *kanji* in reporter's notebook, "to speak in leisure. I am unable to capture verbatims for quotables at rapid pace confabulations!"

"Connie," says Iron Louis, "will you please for a change for Christ's sakes get this twerp to interview Lefty or Earl or Babe or someone else? He's giving me a headache!"

At which juncture omnibus chauffeur cackles over shoulder to me, "*Sensei* Student, witness the quarrelsome *gaijin*! Do they not remind you of barnyard geese who honk at the approach of every stranger?"

"I'll give him geese honking," Moe mumbles, ganders out window to take in passing scene of Shizuoka City outlying environs.

Wataschi sits tight alongside. Mute, thinking.

"Cat got your tongue again, kid?"

"Cogitating, Moe. Like, say, when I graduate Native Land Loving School next *hanami* springtime, say I gets lucky and glom stateside travel permission, not to fail to mention grant monies in support thereof, you think you might could use influence clouts to get me into Ivy League, even alma mater Princeton Tigers?"

"Bank on it," Moe says, and, "Didn't I tell you I'd pull some strings? Count on it, kid, you get stateside, we'll have a reunion, I'll show you all the sights there just like you're doing for me here, right? You and me, kid!"

"Some people," I eavesdrop Joe Cascarella say to Connie Mack, "sure must have a lot of important friends in high positions to get all the breaks they seem to get even if they'd rather hang out with little yellow persons instead of their own teammates is all I can say!"

"Please to repeat, please, sir," says Suzuki, "I essay verbatims!"

"Drop it, Joe," says Connie. Moe thumbs nose in general direction of colleague peers gathered on opposite side of aisle.

Wataschi? What's else to do excepting save sit tight, keep mum, hang on to camera on lap, sit back and enjoy ride—how we say, go with *do* flow of life's path, reet, Jack? I mean: I knowed what I knowed, Shizuoka City environ, circa November 1935, and did elect to proceed, reet?

Jump cuts: cinematic *eiga* flic technique to truncate narration, telescope actions, hence accelerate pace, reet? Dig:

Shizouka City, Yank American League all-star barnstormers lambast (natch!) Waseda U. Frog squad by lopsided 23–2 margin before cheering *Nihonjin* thousands, only disappointment of which exhibition is failure of Bambino Babe Sultan of Swat to homer—omnibus ride back to Tokyo Town, I eavesdrop aforesaid George Herman remark: "It's just a plain old slump. Either I'm in a pure slump or else it's this damn Jap pitching is so dead and slow, every one comes over like a change of pace. What do you think, Connie?"

Which is not to fail to mention no actuality footage of contest versus Frogs exists, as how me and Moe depart game site instanter upon arrival, Moe pleading pulled musculature, hence unable to participate on active basis, reet? Har. Hee.

And to report *sanpo* walking tour of one-horsie wide spot jerkwater hick sticks burg Shizuoka culminates — natch — in environ of Eta Jima, Imperial Army basic-training facility. Can you not dig it, Jack?

Atop hilltop, we gander panorama of barracks squares, columns of *issen gorin* dogface yardbird types marching, engaged in bayonet drill, pop of Arisaka rifles distantly heard from rifle range, chatter of Nambu rapid-fires as trainees crawl through confidence obstacle course, chants of cadence counted for calisthenics, bugle calls over loudspeakers, not to fail to mention ranks assembled for *tenko* roll musters, and also choral singing of famed *kirijini* fighting-spirit song, how we say, *Umi Yakuba*, as follows:

> If I go on the sea,
> My corpse will dissolve in the water;
> If I go in the mountains,
> My body will be covered by moss:
> I will have died for the *Mikado*,
> I will have gone with no regret!

Etcetera blah blah.

"For the fun of it," Moe says, "let's get a slow pan of this. My Christ, it's bigger than Dix or Riley, nobody'll believe me if I live to tell it!"

"Moe," I query, "what's interest about *issen gorin* to folks stateside? Besides which, we too distant to lens. And don't dast go nearer."

"Why, you seen any of our friends with the funny hats and shoes around?" says he, and, "No sweat, Yosh, you'd be surprised what the long range focus on this baby will bring in. Come on, I'll stand over here and mug for you, you can track over to me, it'll make an interesting shot to show back home."

What's to do, Jack? I crank Stewart Warner, pan vista of Eta Jima with long range lens, finish with close-up of *sumairu* smiling countenance of Moe Berg, who winks as magazine runs out. All the way back to game site to catch omnibus, I keep watch for appearance of straw boaters and two-tone brogans. Worry whilst Moe stops to purchase afternoon *shimbun* at kiosk — "Alive! These words are alive, Yosh!" — arrive dumbfounded at pure dumb luck of which is no *kempei* show on scene, reet?

"Greetings, *sensei* Student," says chauffeur personage as we board omnibus amidst final cheers of assembled Hundred Millions fans: *Banzai*, Venerable Sage Mack! *Banzai*, Man of Iron Gehrig! *Banzai*, Great Sultan of Swat Who Lamentably Failed To Perform to Expectations! Etcetera blah. "I did not observe you in attendance at the recently concluded exhibition of barbaric *besuboru*. Where have you and the *gaijin* been with the camera you carry with you always, as if you were a lowly hired porter, *sensei* Student?"

"Tell him," says Moe as we find seats amidst Yanks sprawled in sweated disarray, "to mind his own beeswax and drive the damn bus!" and, "What makes him think it's a camera? For all he knows it could be my protective cup and a change of shorts in there."

"I been escorting scholar-athlete Moe Berg on tour of Shizuoka City. He's like, real keen culture vulture for real life and times lifestyles of *Dai Nippon*, reet? Not to fail to mention wound suffered in first game prevents active participation versus Waseda Frogs."

"You can sling it with the best of them, kid!" Moe says.

Says chauffeur personage: "He does not appear incapacitated to my eyes. See how his comrades lie about in such uncouth fashion! The *Amerikajin* do not even express joy in their triumph. Tell them for me, *sensei* Student, that it is of no consequence to the Hundred Millions to suffer defeat at their hands in so decadent a sport!"

"Tell him to blow it out his ass," says Moe.

"It's, like," I tell chauffeur, "*Amerikajin* mode of decorums, reet? They hopeful of preserving *enryo* good relations with *Nihonjin* via nongloating, reet?"

"About time, Moe," says Sage Mack, "I thought we'd have to leave without you."

"Well, well, well," says Joe Cascarella, still attired in shinguards and chest protector, "if it ain't Mr. V.I.P. Moe the Berg come to ride with us ordinary stiffs back to his hotel! Wouldn't you just as leave call for a personal limo instead of having to hang around with us jerks just did nine innings with a gang of bushers my high-school team could of whomped, Mr. Bergstein?"

"Hey, Moe," says Bambino Babe, "you're a catcher, what do you think? You seen how they throw like girls, you think it's I'm just overswinging is causing me to slump?"

Omnibus ride back to Tokyo Town, reet? Moe peruses Shizuoka *shimbun*, Bambino Babe snoozes in peaceful assurance that bar of Imperial Hotel will provide take-out service to *sento* hot baths, Suzuki Sataro conducts labored interview with victorious *Amerikajin* — "I feel sure," Sage Mack says, speaking loud and slow, "that Japan will soon be able to field teams that can compete on a level of at least Class B or C ball as we know it in America."

"You better keep talking, Connie," says Iron Lou Gehrig, "cause I for sure ain't answering no more of his questions!"

"What's new in the *shimbun*, Moe?" I query.

"More of the same," says he, and, "Fighting in China's going real good for you guys at the moment, looks like."

"Moe?"

"I'm reading, kid, got to get it while the words are fresh and alive, right?"

"Moe, chauffeur personage is watching you in mirror, Moe!"

"So?"

"So he's like, funny strange chauffeur personage, Moe. I mean, uncommon vocabulary for working-stiff type, refined articulation, undue interest in you, Moe."

"Hats and shoes?" says Moe.

"Could be. How's he know it's a camera I schlepp in case, reet?"

Moe Berg lowers *shimbun* to return stare of chauffeur in mirror. Grins *sumairu*. Hardy har. "Hang in there, Yosh," he says, and, "What do we shiv a git? We ain't done anything except see the sights and take a few souvenir home movies, am I right?"

"Reet." What's else to say or do, Jack?

Jump cut: says my *papa-san*: "And what of your experience with the *Amerikajin* in Shizuoka, my son? It is not like you to be silent. Does it not go well?"

"Aw, it ain't nothing, Daddy. It's okay. Except save as how it's funny strange sometimes, reet?"

"Tell me of it," says *Papa-san*.

"Oh," says my *mama-san*, "did I not fear there might be trouble in this, that my only son would go about each day in the close company of the *gaijin*!"

"Hard to put in words, Daddy. Maybe nothing at all. Like, I'm bushed from long bus rides and walking all over Shizuoka environ with Moe Berg, reet?"

Sis Iko says, "It is that your legs are too short to keep step with the gigantic *Amerikajin*, *Yosho-san*, which so exhausts you?"

"Can you not tell your father what it is that strikes you as strange, my son?"

Says I: "Like, Moe, he don't want to play in the games, not since Meiji Shrine, reet? And the lingo! Daddy, the man spiels High Court, digs the *Nihonju* not unlike like unto native speaker, reet? And he can read them *shimbun* bottom to top, right to lefts, reet? Not to fail to mention *eiga* flic footage we shooting with Stewart Warner. What's Moe Berg need *wataschi* for, Daddy?"

"My son," says *Papa-san*, "were you not charged by Mr. Sato Isao to report anything untoward of the *Amerikajin*?"

"Did I not fear just this?" Mama says. "Did I not at once, upon seeing the *gaijin* camera in my house, know that it was not *Nipponshikki* to have such a device in the place where we eat and sleep and pray to our *kami*?"

"You see, *Yosho-san*," chimes in Baby Sis Iko, "what your love of the donkey's-bray *Eigo* has brought upon you?"

"It probably ain't nothing, folks," I say, and, "If I go fink guff stuff I don't dig to Sato, Daddy, I might could embarrass myself and *oyabun* buddy pal Moe, not to fail to mention blow my *enryo* with him, than which would put kibosh on chances of getting Ministry of Education permission and grant support to go stateside, reet? What's good of connection to Sato if it turns out nothing funny strange in all this? I don't dast embarrass Moe, Sato, Native Land Loving School, Imperial Household, you name it, Daddy!"

"My son, you give me cause for great concern," Daddy says, and, "In these times one's behavior must be circumspect. Have I not said that I can learn nothing of Mr. Sato Isao's function in the Ministry of Education?"

Jack: I did not tell my *papa-san* what's all I is done figured out, reet? As how family confabulation terminates due to my *mama-san* is started in to weep. And Baby Sis Iko ain't making no more jokers now, instead starting in to weep because *Mama-san* is weeping, and Daddy is gots to step in and say as head of household how it is foolish *baka* women only who shed tears before their flesh is burned, and so are reluctant to cook dinner over *hibachi* fire, reet?

"*Daijubo!*" I did tell my folks, Jack—what's to sweat? As how *wataschi* keeps trap shut, speak, hear, see no evils, how can I be one gets blame if anything proves amiss, reet? I is just, I did remind them, but sweet sixteen years old aged, matriculating student of Native Land Loving School, outstanding scholar of first form. I mean, like, can't no flies land on me, reet?

To which utterance in riposte my *papa-san* did quote me traditionalist *Nihonjin* bromide slogan: how you say, even monkeys might can fall out of trees, Jack!

Cut to: omnibus ride down Tokaido Highway, toward Kyoto, ancient old-timey capital city of *Nihon*. En route to Nagoya Town to oppose Ibaragi U. Cranes squad, reet?

Yank American League all-star barnstormers repose in silence, as how nobody willing to risk interview ordeal with Suzuki Sataro so early of a morn. "Honored sirs," says he, "you do not empathize my predicaments. I must formulate copy in anticipation to telephone in deadline evening press runs in Tokyo, is this not so? How, I am beseeching, honored sirs, shall by-line appear authoritative lacking verbatims to enliven historic chronicles of *besuboru* struggle soon to unfold? Hundred Millions readership desires humanity-interests angle scoops, is this not so? Routine statisticals augmenting play-by-play not sufficing, honored sirs! Mr. Mack, can you not reproach your minions toward cooperations?"

"I'm a manager, buddy, not a publicity hack."

Final word on subject is snoring snort from Bambino Babe George Herman Ruth, who sleeps in back of bus, hangover-stricken via overindulgence in *sake* served warm from bar in *sento* hot baths at Imperial Hotel. Gehrig, Earl Averill, Lefty Gomez, and Jim Foxx play at cards, observe oncoming traffic on great Tokaido Highway, peak of Mount Mihara behind us, peak of Fuji lost in morning hazes up front. I wait upon Moe Berg to conclude perusal of *shimbun*, fold and discard deceased words before I speak.

"Moe, you gonna play today, or is we touring Nagoya Town like unto how we did Shizuoka?"

"You damn straight he is!" says Joe Cascarella.

"You heard the man, Yosh," Moe says, and, "Why'd you ask me that?"

"Like, Moe, I guess I thought maybe you was more interested to lens sights than play *besuboru* versus seven universities, reet?"

"Why," he asks, "is there anything special in Nagoya I'd likely want to visit?"

"Nothing special. Not unlike like unto Shizuoka, only more of same, reet?"

"No old temples or shrines even?"

"Ix-nay. Kyoto's the place for that stuff, ancient capital city, everything preserved as was out of respects and veneration shtick for glorious heritage of *Nihon* ethos. Not even good restaurants nor night lifes in Nagoya. Nothing there unless you count Imperial Army's tank and artillery ranges, than which is just big empty space environ wherein they shoot off cannons into mountainside."

"Is that a fact?" says Moe.

"Why?" I query, look away from driver's mirror, wherein chauffeur personage attempts to catch my baby blues. "You interested in seeing big guns go boom at mountain, tanks running to and also fro over rocky plain?"

"Oh no," Moe says, "it's my turn to catch the game today. Right, Connie?"

"You bet your sweet ass it is!" says Joe Cascarella — Sage Mack does not respond, being concerned to concentrate in vain effort to comprehend semicoherent requests of Suzuki Sataro that he employ clout of his managerial *honcho* authorities to compel Man of Iron Louis Gehrig to cooperate in on-the-record pregame interview.

"*Sensei* Student," says chauffeur over shoulder as he downshifts to slow for Tokaido Highway turnoff, spur road to Nagoya, "shall you serve as the porter and guide for the *Amerikajin* in Nagoya today, just as you did yesterday in Shizuoka?"

"He's a persistent little cuss, ain't he, Yosh," Moe says.

I say, "You talking to official interpreter for Yank visitors to *Dai Nippon*, reet? I ain't subject to guide nobody out and about Nagoya Town, as how my *oyabun* buddy pal scholar-athlete Moe Berg is slated to start behind plate versus Cranes of Ibaragi University today, and *wataschi* going to occupy seat of distinctiveness in dugout, like unto what's I did at Meiji Shrine opener."

"Just so," says chauffeur personage, shoots me big *sumairu* grin in mirror. "And shall you hand to them the large wooden clubs they employ in their barbarian sport?"

"Reet!"

"And shall you, as they run about and throw and hit at the small white ball, make photographs of them with the large camera you cradle in your lap as a mother might hold her dearest child?"

"Reet!" I say to him, and, "I learning to make the *eiga* flics, Jack! Than which requires skill techniques I learn from *oyabun* buddy pal renowned scholar-athlete Moe Berg!"

"Ignore him, Yosh," Moe says, "he's a goddamn bus driver, right? What the hell does he know?"

"Reet," I say. Oh, Jack, big irony!

Long story truncated some via cinematic jump cut, reet?

Moe Berg starts as catcher versus Ibaragi Cranes contingent. Delights assembled Hundred Millions *besuboru* fans via exquisite observance of rituals — bows to plate ump, bows to each and every batter entering and departing box, renders low kowtow to ump when he's called out on strikes first time up, also when granted intentional walk by Ibaragi moundsman, who, with runners on first and third, prefers odds of facing Yank pitcher Earl Whitehill — than which strategy is to no avails, as how Whitehill belts first pitch into centerfield bleacher on but one bounce for ground-rule double, reet?

Moe proves great crowd pleaser, than which horde responds with personalized cheers: "*Banzai*, Catcher Berg Who Observes *Nipponshikki* Decorum! *Banzai*, Catcher Berg Who Combines Excellence of Athletic Prowess with Intellectual Distinction! *Banzai*, Morris Berg Who Embodies Dual Disciplines of Mind and Body!" Moe renders assemblage bow from steps of dugout after crossing plate when Whitehill's double is followed by leadoff hitter Gehringer's triple down leftfield line. Crowd cacophony almost drowns out distant thunder rumble sound, than which is sporadic cannon fire from tank and artillery ranges, reet?

"Nice going, Moe," I say, capture scene in Stewart Warner viewfinder's frame.

"Wait till you hear them if I catch one on the meat end of my bat, squirt!" says Bambino Babe Sultan as he slips iron doughnut on Louisville Slugger to begin warmup swings.

"For Christ's sake," says Sage Mack, "somebody make an out! We'll be here until they have to call it off on account of dark if it keeps up like this!" After which Bambino Sultan obliges by whiffing on slow curve, reet?

Which is to say, blow-out rout proceeds unabated until fourth inning, when Moe, after bloop single to right, attempts to stretch same to two-bagger, essaying exploitation of weak arm of Ibaragi U. outfielder, resorting to successful hook slide to evade tag. Immediately after which Moe rolls in basepath, clutching ankle—crowd is struck silent at prospect of serious injury, than which, natch, constitutes serious violation of *Nippon-shikki* hospitality ethos, reet? I focus long range lens on Moe hobbling, assisted from field of play by Sage Mack and Joe Cascarella.

"Sorry, Joe," Moe says, "looks like you'll have to pinch run for me."

"Bull fucking shit!" Joe says.

"Get out there, Joe!" Mack says, and to Moe, "You think you broke something?"

"Just a strain," Moe says, and, "Let me lean on you while I give them a kowtow, Connie."

"You for damn sure better be limping when I see you walk from now on, Bergstein!" says Cascarella on his way out to second to run for Moe.

"You okay, Moe?" I ask.

"I'll be allright, kid. Come on, help me out of here. I need to walk it off. If I sit around in the dugout it'll stiffen up on me."

"We ain't staying for remainder of game?"

"What for? You got any doubts about who's going to win? Besides, I'd hate to see you waste any more of our film on this farce. Come on, Yosh, give me a hand. And don't leave the camera behind!"

Awkward departure for *wataschi*, one arm supporting gimpy Moe, one schlepping Stewart Warner, reet? Crowd expresses admiration: "*Banzai*, Morris Berg, Gracious Even in Moment of Disabling Injury! *Banzai*, Catcher Berg Who Smiles Through Pain! *Banzai*, Scholar-Athlete Who Will Surely Recover Swiftly!" Not to fail to mention continuous background thunder rumble of Imperial Army tank and artillery ranges.

Dig ironics, Jack:

Expecting to assist Moe in cautious walk-off of sprain in vicinity of waiting omnibus, I is surprised—har!—when Moe picks up pace of *sanpo* once beyond game-site environ, says, "Shake a leg, Yosh! Let's use the time we got left for a little jaunt. I'd like to see where all the thunder and lightning's coming from."

"Your ankle ain't hurting too bad to be walking far, Moe?"

"Best thing for it," says he, and, "Keep your eyes peeled in case we pick up any funny hats and shoes along the way, okay?"

"Reet," I say to Moe, trot to keep pace with rapid striding Moe (unhampered by phony-baloney ankle injury, natch!) leading way through empty streets of Nagoya Town—shops shuttered shut in deference to game, reet?

Moe moving not unlike like unto as if he has map of Nagoya in noggin indicating most direct direction to course of tank and artillery cannon booms, Jack! Bee-line to city outskirts, climb hill, whereupon we stand under tall pines on summit to gander revealed vista of Imperial Army ranges: thunder of cannons, puffs of smoke following upon wake of muzzle flashes, eruptions of earth as missiles land on remote mountainside. Big booms, growl of tank engines as they race bounding to and also fro over rocky terrains, *issen gorin* infantry dogfaces clinging to handholds on turrets to practice armored-assault manuevers.

"Here," Moe says, "I'll stand up here, back off under the trees there while you get a sweep of this, then focus on me. I'll vamp a little of the old soft shoe for you."

"What we doing, Moe?"

"What? Come on, we got to hurry if we don't want to miss the bus, that game won't last forever even the way those kids play it."

"Souvenir *eiga* flics to show folks back home stateside, reet, Moe?" I say, place viewfinder to my baby blue, frame vista of tank and artillery ranges.

"What else?" he says, loud to be heard over boom of cannon, roar of tank engines. "Hurry," he says, "they might not appreciate us hanging around so close."

"Souvenir flics," I say, press lever, begin slow pan to encompass scope of tanks, artillery batteries, muzzle flash and smoke puff, missiles tearing up mountainside in distance. "Souvenir *eiga* footages to show home folks stateside, huh, Moe? Ain't it but funny strange as how than which all such shots include *Dai Nippon gumbatsu* militarist buildup, to include *Kido Butai* fleet, Ichigaya Heights headquarters, War College, Eta Jima, not to fail to mention here and now?"

"What'd you say?" Moe asks, winging tap routine on grass as I lens him. "I can't hear you with all the noise, Yosh!"

"Nothing, Moe," I say. As how, Jack, *wataschi* thinking: sworn duty to report aforesaid activities to Native Land Loving School Head Prefect Nobuyoshi Muto, convey particulars to Mr. Sato Isao, Imperial Ministry of Education *honcho* factotum, reet? Get word via channels to *kempei*! I is thinking: loyalty to *Mikado* and love of country, Jack!

"We better *chogee* back unless you feel like hoofing it all the way back down the Tokaido Highway to Tokyo, kid." What's to do!

I repack Stewart Warner 16-millimeter in leather case, follow after Moe.

"Moe," I query, "is you done talked to *Amerikajin* embassy about me yet? I mean, like, good word on behalf of *wataschi* in reference to permissions and grant-supports funds for stateside higher educational studies come circa 'thirty-six?"

"Oh," says Moe, "I meant to tell you. I was talking to Grew's interpreter just last night. He stopped by the hotel. Remember him, Wetherell?"

"I remember him, Moe."

"I talked to him about you, told him what a whiz you were, what a big help you've been to me, laid it on with a trowel. Trust me. He promised to speak to Grew. You're in like Flynn, Yosh!"

"Really, Moe?"

"Money in the bank, kid. Would I pull your leg? No doubt in my mind whatsoever, the word's going in at the highest level of the Ministry of Education any day now, if it hasn't already."

"For absolute positive certain sure?"

"I'll be surprised if you don't get an official letter before the tour's over. Come on, kid, shag buns, I think we can make it to the bus before the last man's out. Trust me!"

Than which I did, reet, Jack?

Which is not to fail to mention presence of omnibus chauffeur personage awaiting us when we reach game site, aforesaid resposed in squat-hunker posture beside vehicle as we quicktime on scene, crowd still cheering whilst Ibaragi Cranes mount futile last-ditch bottom-of-ninth rally, reet? "*Banzai* !" we hear, "*Banzai*, Valiant Cranes of Ibaragi University Who Strive To Overcome Insurmountable *Amerikajin* Lead!"

"Greetings and salutations, *sensei* Mr. Omnibus Chauffeur," I say to forestall queries, "me and *oyabun* buddy Moe Berg is been on briskish *sanpo* stroll to exercise injury and thusly forestall complications thereto, reet?" Riposte to which is biggish surprise, Jack, as how chauffeur personage stands up straight like six o'clock, faces Moe, speaks direct to him, harsh *budo* mannerism, reet?

Says he: "Tell me, *gaijin*, where have you been in the company of this innocent and tender youth? Have you perhaps visited the environs of our Imperial Army's tank and artillery ranges? What forbidden photographs have you taken this day, *Amerikajin gaijin*?"

"Is he talking to me?" Moe asks, and, "Tell him to take that finger out of my face unless he'd like to lose it!"

"Scholar-athlete Moe Berg says, like—" I begin, interrupted by chauffeur.

"Do not look to this ignorant schoolboy to provide your answers for you, *gaijin*!"

"—like he's indulged in but moderate exercises—" I try to interject.

"*Wakarimasen*," says Moe to chauffeur, than which is, how you say, I don't understand nothing from what you say, as in, Jack, I don't speak no *Nihonju* nohow.

"Moe Berg trying to express as how—" I start.

"And yet you are able to read our *shimbun* with such apparent ease? No, *gaijin* barbarian, I do not think you are unable to comprehend my words!"

"*Wakarimasen*," Moe repeats, grins *sumairu* leer at chauffeur, and, to me, "Get in the bus, Yosh, we don't have to talk to this crud."

"What impudence does the lying *Amerikajin* utter now, *sensei* Student?" chauffeur asks.

"Mr. Moe Berg," I say, "says he but digs only most rudimentary locutions from *Nihonju*, don't twig nothing when you talk fast, *sensei* Mr. Chauffer."

"*Wakarimasen*," adds Moe once more.

"The *gaijin* prevaricates!" shouts chauffeur, and, "Does he think I am *baka*, or even that I am but a humble driver of vehicles? Tell him I am an agent of the *kempei*, young student, and that I have reason to inquire of his activities in *Dai Nippon*!"

Than which flap — *hara* belly tensions inspiring, Jack! — concludes instanter due to arrival of Yank American League all-stars, game concluded (Yanks trounce Cranes by 30–1 — how you say, strictly laugher, *Nihonjin* fans accompany aforesaid to render polite enthusiastic send-off cheers:

"*Banzai*, Victorious *Amerikajin* Athletes! *Banzai*, Mentor Mack! *Banzai*, Pitcher Whitehill Whose Swift and Devious Delivery Baffles *Nihonjin* Batters! *Banzai*, Formidable Gehrig and Foxx and Averill!"

"Tell that driver to crank this jalopy up and get us to hell out of here, kid," says Sage Mack. "Christ, I thought it'd never end!"

I take seat alongside Moe, avoid chauffeur's baby blues in mirror as omnibus moves forward, begins return journey to Tokyo Town, Imperial Hotel, reet? "*Sensei* Student," Suzuki Sataro is saying to me, "you have missed a truly thrilling episode! Our valiant Cranes rallied to score their sole run in the final inning, and just previously the great Bambino Babe Ruth was denied a home run in his last attempt at bat by virtue of a miraculous catch in the far reaches of centerfield executed by Crane outfielder Toru Ono, whose name I shall give much prominence in tomorrow's early edition of *Yomiuri Shimbun*! Please, *sensei* Student Yamaguchi, assist me as I interview the legendary Sultan of Swat to ascertain his emotions upon this memorable occurrence!"

"Moe," I say. "Moe?"

"*Daijubo*, kid. Who cares what he thinks, right?"

"I guess."

"You only guess? Hey, Yosh, you wouldn't cause me any problem here, would you? You wouldn't mess up our *enryo*, would you, kid? We're pals, *oyabun-kobun*, right? I'm the guy's going to set you up to come to the states to go to college, remember? Ivy League?"

"I guess," and, "Reet," I say. Big hardy har, not to fail to mention ursine fraternalistic hug, reet, Jack?

"Moe," says George Herman Ruth, "where the hell'd you disappear to again? You should of seen it to believe it, Moe, I finally connect on one and this little Jap bastard in center catches it going away over his shoulder!"

"Slump syndrome in remission?" Suzuki Sataro queries in *Eigo*.

"Drouth at plate terminating at long lasts? Does Babe prognosticate resumption of vaunted offensive prowess over duration of remaining scheduled contests?"

"How's your sore leg, Bergstein?" Joe Cascarella says, and, "I didn't notice you limping a whole lot there when you climbed on the bus."

"*Sensei* Student," calls out chauffeur (what ain't such, reet?) over shoulder as we slow for turn onto Tokaido Highway, "were I in your delicate position, I should feel compelled to acquaint appropriate authorities with the activities of your *gaijin* companion this day!"

Jack: at which juncture in *do* flow of *wataschi's* life and times lifestyle I did first articulate expression of decision I is already done decided, reet? To wit:

"Jack," I did say to chauffeur what ain't, "do not be ragging me as to duties, reet? You talking to outstanding A-number-1 scholar of first form of Native Land Loving School, dig? Not to fail to mention I is, as deputed by both Imperial Ministry of Education and Imperial Household too, to conduct mission on behalf of school and nation's Hundred Millions, all which render me cognizant of manner and mode of behavior calculated to earn honor and glory shtick thereto, reet? So, like, chauffeur personage, buzz, how we say in *Eigo*, off, reet, Jack?"

"That's telling him, Yosh!" Moe says.

"Little runt peckerhead," Bambino Babe is saying, "he wouldn't of caught it on his best day if he'd of had his eyes open!"

"Permissions granted to quote quotable verbatims, *Babe-san*?" Suzuki asks.

"I suppose," says Joe Cascarella, "it's no use me bitching to you, Connie, Mr. Bergstein'll just run and tell his embassy friends on me, huh?"

"Moe," I say, "you really did put in word for me, reet?"

"*Sensei* Student," chauffeur says over his shoulder, "it is not well to insult your countryman out of a misconceived desire to curry favor with barbarians!"

"Would I lie to you, Yosh?" Moe says, and, "Trust me!"

"Would everybody," says Sage Mack, "please for the Jesus Christ sakes just put a cork in it for a while so a old man can sit back and enjoy the damn ride for a change!"

Than which we did do, Jack, all the way back up Tokaido Highway to Tokyo Town Imperial Hotel environ, reet?

"And what of this day, my son?" my *papa-san* asks me. Are you still troubled by the activities of Morris Berg?"

"No, Daddy. Everything coolish."

Mama-san says, "I shall not sleep well until this time has passed and the

Amerikajin are gone from the soil of *Dai Nippon!*"

"Soon, Mama," I tell her.

"*Yosho-san*," my sis Iko says, "tell us of Nagoya. What did you see there, my brother?"

"Nothing," I say to her, and, "Yanks done whipped up something fierce on Cranes. I saw *besuboru* is all, Sis."

"Perhaps," my daddy says, "your concerns were wholly unfounded?"

"I guess," I tell my family.

Jack: I did told them nothing. Zip. Zilch. Squat. Zed, reet? Because as how *wataschi* Student Yamaguchi Yoshinori, aged but six and ten sweet years old, is done come down on side of promise of glorious future *do* path's possibilities, reet? Because as how I did wager on Moe's clout contact with Ambassador Joe Clark Grew, not to fail to mention pipeline to Imperial Ministry of Education via Mr. Sato Isao, all which converges to create visions of overseas travel permissions and grant-support *yen*, shot at brass ring and bluebird career options, Ivy League higher educational *Eigo* studies, not to fail to mention viewing Yank *eiga* flics on first run on scene, etcetera blah blah.

What's do I know, Jack? Aged but sixteen sweet years old, *do* flow of future shines bright as personalized oyster intended for consumption of Student Yamaguchi Yoshinori, linguist and apprentice maker of *eiga* flics.

Thus it were: *wataschi* did keep silence mum trap shut, Jack! Oh, big ironicals thereby to come!

Cut to: wrap-up summary summation via jump cuts of Yank American League barnstorm *besuboru* exhibition tour of *Dai Nippon*, circa November 1935, reet? To include:

Final omnibus jaunt (new chauffeur personage, Jack!) to Omiya Town for penultimate exhibition contest matching Yanks versus Keio U. Dragons — than which game is (natch!) routine rout, Yanks 34, Dragons 4 (Gomez wild on mound, strike-zone evading Lefty's curve, hence two runs walk in) — not to fail to mention Bambino Babe Sultan reaches base twice when Dragon rightfielder muffs high flies, but Sultan continues to fail to deliver hoped-for round-tripper.

Also not failing to mention as how Moe starts at backstop, but, after fanning twice, Joe Cascarella is inserted into lineup as pinch hitter by Sage Mack, after which (top of fifth inning), I (natch!) accompany Moe on short *sanpo* stroll to downtown Omiya third-floor restaurant environ. From which elevated vantage — whilst we gorge on expensive repast of *take, fugu, matsutake, hatsugatsuo, nigirimeshi, udon*, and *o-cha* (how you say: bamboo shoots, blowfish, mushrooms, raw bonito, rice balls, noodles, green tea, reet?), Moe handling *hashi* chopsticks not unlike like unto native-born, reet? — it is possible to view and lens (via long range lens focus of Stewart Warner) panorama parade of Imperial Navy aircrafts land and also take off: Zekes, Bettys, Nakajima and Aichi dive bombers, etcetera blah.

"Pardon, please, *sensei* Student," waiter personage queries, "may I know what this *gaijin* does with his enormous camera in my humble restaurant?"

"Reet," I say, and, "This famous scholar-athlete personage, name of Morris Berg, also knowed as Moe, making an *eiga* flic as *o-miyage* souvenir to memorialize visit to *Dai Nippon*, reet? Back home stateside, his family and also friends going to gander your fancy-schmancy restaurant eatery environ, dig, Jack?"

"I understand," says waiter, "but why does he also make his *eiga* from the window of my restaurant? Does he intend also to share with his friends an *eiga* of Imperial Navy aircraft as they fly to and from the Omiya Airdrome?"

"Moe?" I say.

"Hats and shoes?" says he.

"My *Amerikajin oyabun* buddy pal shoots, how we say, footage to serve as cover shot, establish environ locale for feature of eatery interior, reet? It's, like, technical consideration of creative nature."

"Couldn't have said it better myself, Yosh," Moe says.

Cut to: final *besuboru* exhibition contest, site of which is aforementioned field of Meiji Shrine, Tokyo Town, repeat rematch pitting Yanks versus seven universities' all-stars, contest replete with concluding ceremonials.

Than which includes Toyoma National Military Band assembled behind home plate to render "Star Spangled Banner" and *Kimagoyo* anthems, game ball tossed in underhand by Ambassador Joe Clark Grew, statements of farewells and appreciations uttered by same (inept translations provided by aforesaid Walter Wetherell — me and Moe snickering, reet?), response to which is delivered by whole shebang shaker-and-mover organizer Mr. Suzuki Sataro, speaking pigeon *Eigo*, to wit:

"It is with humiliated pride to American friends who has with such graceful gestures stymied the earnest athletic endeavors of our flowering youths, thusly commanding the bridge of internationalist empathies so greatly generated by collective talents upon battlefield of sportsmanships . . . ." Etcetera blah blah blah, reet?

To include frequent kowtows: Yank all-stars bow to seven universities' all-stars, seven universities' squad bow to Yanks, Sage Mack bows to Suzuki Sataro, Suzuki to Mack, individual Yank players bow to assembled Hundred Millions upon being introduced, crowd renders *banzai* cheers to each, batters bow to ump, ump to batters, etcetera blah blah blah!

"How in the hell," says Sage Mack in dugout, "do they expect to learn the game if we spend all our time bowing back and forth?"

Ensuing contest is (natch!) strictly no contest. Yanks clobber *Nihonjin* pitching, 37–6 (Moe Berg guilty of three passed balls allowing runners to score). Sole notable incident is end of Bambino Babe's slump, which is to say Sultan swats towering homer in last at-bat.

"It had to be sooner or later!" Babe shouts as he doffs cap in response to assembled's personalized *banzai* cheer of appreciative delight. "I could feel it, Connie, it was in my timing all the time! All of a sudden, the minute he goes into his windup, I knew he was coming high and hard, and I knew the second I swung she was going for a ride! Jesus, it felt good!"

"Moe," I say as I assist him in donning shinguards and chest protector to start game, "you got a film magazine? I don't gots no film to lens ceremonials with, reet?"

"Forget it, kid," says Moe. "We're out of film, Yosh. I guess we'll just have to remember this one on our own, huh?"

"So why therefore is I schlepping Stewart Warner ever since we left Imperial Hotel this morning if you don't gots film for it?"

"It's a surprise," Moe says, winks. "I'll tell you about it right after the game, I promise. Trust me, Yosh!"

Cut to: how we say, Jack, *yoin*, moment of profound significance in sensibilities, reet? Wherein resonance in feelings, consciousness overtones, epiphanies reside, dig?

Memorial pic, Jack, snapped by *Yomiuri Shimbun* photog laid on by Suzuki Sataro to illustrate front-page by-line story rehashing Yank *besuboru* barnstorm tour of *Dai Nippon*, circa November 1935, reet? Dig:

Front and center, feets together, sole seated figure, hands holding Spalding horsehide in lap, crossed Sluggers of Louisville manufacture lying on grass not unlike like unto *samurai* longswords, is Venerable and Sagacious Mentor Connie Mack (a.k.a. Cornelius McGillicuddy), attired in customary suit with vest, high collar, string tie, hair parted down the middle, straw boater flat against chest.

Behind Sage Mack, clad in flannels game garb, stands rank of American League all-stars: Ruth, Gehrig, Gomez, Gehringer, Averill, Brown, Foxx, McNair, Hayes, Warstler, Cascarella, Miller, Whitehill. Direct center behind Sage Mack stands Mr. Suzuki Sataro, spiffy in sport jacket and knickers, golfing tam on noggin. Yanks grimmace into autumn sun shining bright on Meiji Shrine playing field — Suzuki, exhibiting proper *Nipponshikki* decorums, refrains from *sumairu* smile.

Not to fail to mention Mr. Morris (a.k.a. Moe) Berg, linguistic scholar (Princeton, class of 1923, Phi Beta Kappa, Magna Cum Laude, etcetera blah) and athlete (third-string bullpen warmup catcher for Senators of Washington, D. C.) — also clandestine *Amerikajin* espionage operative, sent on mission to *Dai Nippon* to lens assorted *gumbatsu* militarist activities, reet?

Directly before aforesaid stands *wataschi*, Jack: Student Yamaguchi Yo-shinori, attired in uniform of Native Land Loving School (stripe on leg, chevron on sleeve). Moe's hands rest on my epaulets.

Moe displays huge face-splitter *sumairu* grin of feline consuming excrement—hardy har har, also hee, reet?

Wataschi not smiling, Jack!

Because as how I did think (*yoin* resonance in *ma* moment of awareness!): *wataschi*—little Yosh, *Yosho-san!*—you is done betrayed self and name, family folks and *kami*, Hundred Millions of *Dai Nippon*, not to fail to mention *Mikado* hisself! Experiential experience, Jack, of profundities such as to linger in memory.

Than which (memory, Jack!) is required, as how photog's pic, copy of which is delivered by courier direct to my paper house next day, does not (natch!) survive big fire of April 1942, than which burned up also family photo album, paper house, and sizable section of residential Tokyo Town—not to fail mention my *papa-san*, *mama-san*, baby sis *Iko-san*! Than which said conflagration was ignited by missiles dropped from *Amerikajin* B-25 aircrafts, flying off Yank carrier *Hornet*, Jimmy Doolittle's flyboys, same guided to targets via *eiga* footages garnered by clandestine espionage operative Morris Berg (circa 1935!), also knowed as Moe, reet, Jack?

Which is to end narration of life and times lifestyle of Student Yamaguchi Yoshinori, except saving to describe fond farewells shtick exchanged with Moe Berg at Meiji Shrine field, aftermath of final *besuboru* exhibition, reet? As follows:

"I'd like nothing better," says Moe, "than to take you back to the Imperial Hotel with me, treat you to a big feed and a bash, invite your family out and all, kid, but I won't have a minute to myself between now and tomorrow when we ship out from Yokohama."

"Extensive departures ceremonials with personages of diplomatic officialdoms, huh, Moe?"

"Something like that. I've got some people at the embassy I've got to see, and there's packing up to do, and all. But I want you to know it's been real, kid! I mean it. You're a great kid, Yosh, you'll go far in this world with a little luck on your side."

"Same by me, Moe," I tell him, and, "Swell times had by all, reet?"

"And I want you not to fret yourself about anything. Know what I mean?"

"*Eiga* flic footages we did lens, Moe?"

Says Moe, "It's too complicated to explain, but believe me when I tell you it's for the general good. Maybe even the whole world. You understand what I'm saying, Yosh?"

"I guess," I say, and, "You didn't never not need no interpreter, did you, Moe? You spiel *Nihonju*, read *kanji* not unlike like unto Hundred Millions, reet? What you was needing was, like, cover, for when *kempei* and assorted informer types scrutinize, reet?"

"Something like that," says Moe. *Sumairu* grin, hardy har, hee, reet?

"Them *eiga* we lensed might could have been biggish hassle, reet, Moe?"

"*Daijubo* about the film we shot, kid. It's long gone in a diplomatic pouch to a safe place a long ways away from here."

"*Amerikajin* Embassy. *Wataschi* can dig it, Moe. But you wasn't joshing when you promised to put in word for me for overseas-study shtick?"

"Trust me."

"Then might could be we'll rendezvous anon stateside, reet?" Moe gives me big ursine fraternalist hug, *oyabun-kobun*. *Enryo*. *Ma*. *Yoin*. I did say: "Trust me to continue to strive in *kirijini* spirit of great Yank *besuboru* all-stars, Moe! I vows to burn midnight oils, exert collegiate-style effort to excel in all things, achieve glorious future time, career shtick to attain glory and honor for self, name, family, *kami*, and nation, reet?"

"You can do it if anybody can, kid!"

"Moe," comes voice of Sage Mack, "do you always have to straggle? I don't know about you, but the rest of us are due back to meet with some chamber-of-commerce biggies or whatever they call them here, okay?"

"Duty calls, Yosh."

"Reet," I say, and, "I gots a present for you, Moe," take tiny box my *mama-san* wrapped up pretty from pocket, hand to him. "How we say, *o-miyage*, souvenir, like unto *eiga* flics we did make, little something to remember trip to *Dai Nippon* by."

"You are the greatest!" says Moe, unwraps, opens box. "Hey, this is really nice, Yosh!" and, "*Hanko*!" says Moe.

"Reet!" I have gifted Moe Berg with *hanko*, how you say, signature seal, ideograph of his name in *kanji*. Very pricey, rendered in ivory. "My daddy, Mr. Yamaguchi, is done designed calligraph, how we say, *sho*, reet?"

"*Sho*," says Moe, and, "I'll treasure this, kid. I promise to sign my contract with the Senators with it if they offer me one, huh? Your old man must be quite the artist, kid."

I tell him: "My *papa-san* is a poet, Moe, always practicing his *sho* shtick, making them *haiku*. I query him, what's should I gift Moe Berg for *o-miyage* of *Dai Nippon*? My daddy says, like, he'll design *sho* of your name, and we'll get it carved in ivory, because as how, *Papa-san* says, a man's name is the man hisself, and *hanko* is seal of his word and honor, reet?"

"For sure," says Moe, and, "I got a little something for you too. You're carrying it right there in your hand right now." I look down at Stewart Warner 16-millimeter *eiga* flic camera (complete with leather carrying case, reet?).

"Really, Moe?"

"Would I pull your leg? It's yours. What do I need a movie camera for? And you've got a flair for *eiga*, kid, somebody in the embassy actually said that to me after they saw some of the footage you shot. Wear it in good health, *Yosho-san!*"

Thus hence it were, Jack, *wataschi* did become proud owner of very expensive long range focus Stewart Warner 16-millimeter *eiga* flic movie camera, latest western technologies, circa '35. Oh, Jack, irony of *do* path of life's flow!

"Lucks next season, Moe!" I did call out as he left to join peers. "I root for Senators!"

"Don't waste your breath, kid!" Moe ripostes. Har. Hee. "I suspicion my playing days could be over sooner rather than later, Yosh! Hey," he did add, "Good luck on your *shiken jigoku* — " how we say, big final exams prior to graduation, than which qualify for collegiate admissions, reet? — "Crack those books, and don't fritter away too much time in Asakusa watching those Hollywood *eiga*, huh?"

"*Daijubo!*" I did yell, and, "Trust me, Moe!"

"Here's hoping *Jizo* keeps his eye on you, kid!" *Jizo*, Jack, Buddhist deity guardian, like unto babysitter for childrens. And thus it were we did part, reet, Jack?

"And was Mr. Morris Berg pleased to have your gift of *hanko* ?" *Papa-san* asks me.

"Reet, Daddy. He said to say anks-thay loads, and as how you is real artistic with *sho* you designed for his moniker, reet?"

"Mr. Morris Berg is most generous with his words," Daddy says, looks down at hands in his lap, traditionalist *Nipponshikki* response to praise.

"Are we not shamed by the magnitude of the *Amerikajin's* gift to our son?" Mama queries.

"The worth of *o-miyage* lies in the sincerity of the giver, not the cost of what is presented," Daddy says, and *Mama-san* looks down at her hands, *Nipponshikki* response to chastisement deserved for foolish utterance.

"*Yosho-san*," says my sis Iko, "can you now create your own *eiga* here in our house? *Yosho-san*," says my baby sis *Iko-san*, "create the *eiga* for me! When it is the day of *hinamatsuri* you can make an *eiga* of all my *ningyo* dolls when I display them to celebrate the Doll Festival of Girls' Day!"

"No can do, Sis," I tell her, "as how you can't find film stock for a gizmo like the Stewart Warner in *Dai Nippon*, besides which it ain't no *eiga* in a lot of *ningyo* dollies all dressed up sitting on a shelf for your pals to come look at on *hinamatsuri*, reet?"

"I am not pleased to have this large *gaijin* thing in our house," *Mama-san* says. "It should be put away out of sight in the cabinets where we store the *futon* when we are not sleeping, so that no visitors may chance to see it!"

"Aw, Mama!" I say.

"What your mother says contains wisdom, my son," says *Papa-san*. "There are those in positions of authority in *Dai Nippon* today who would think ill of one even for the possession of a gift given by the *Amerikajin*. Do not show an expression of mocking disbelief on your visage, my son! You read what I am compelled to write in the editorial columns of *Japan Times*. On every street corner in Tokyo, gramophones play the ugly Song of the Three Human Bombs in celebration of the incident contrived by our Kwantung Army at Mukden, and now there is even public agitation that urges the prohibition of the teaching of *Eigo* in our schools! The Hundred Millions are encouraged to spy on one another and make reports to the *kempei*! My son, do not exult too openly in the distinction you have earned by your association with the *Amerikajin* athletes! This may not in the end prove to have been a good thing in the troubled times we experience in *Dai Nippon* today."

"Hear your father, *Yosho-san*!" Mama says. "He expresses the fears I have known since first we encouraged you to study *Eigo* and permitted you to view the *harukai gaijin eiga* in Asakusa District!"

"*Yosho-san*," Iko is saying, "please create the *eiga* of all my *ningyo* dolls if ever you obtain film for your fine camera!"

Jack, I did tell them: "Folks! Folks, it ain't nothing bad going to *hochee* happen! Ain't I done good what was laid on by Native Land Loving School, not to fail to mention Mr. Sato of Imperial Ministry of Education? Ain't I done had personal audience in company of *honcho* diplomatic factotums at Imperial Palace, and me but sweet sixteen years aged? Ain't *wataschi* now gots clout via Yank embassy, than which Moe Berg did promise, than which will garner me permissions and *yen* grant-aid support funds for higher-educational education endeavor stateside, Ivy League prestigious? *Daijubo*, folks! Not to worry, Daddy! No need to cry, Mama, you just getting Sis here to commence waterworks weeping in concert, reet?"

"You reveal great certainty as to your future, my son," Daddy says, loud enough to be heard over Mama's tears, *Iko-san's* sniffles.

"Reet!" I did say to my *papa-san*.

"Do not forget that the future may hold surprises in store for you, *Yosho-san*," says he, and, "You have yet fully half a year to complete the pre-scribed course of studies of the first form of Native Land Loving School, and you must study with great discipline and diligence to pass successfully the rigors of *shiken jigoku* examinations, and thereafter will come years of university schooling, either abroad or here in *Dai Nippon*, and thereafter a young man begins the work of his life's career, and are you still so young that you have not thought of the time when you shall marry and continue the name and line of your family?"

"*Daijubo*, Daddy!" I did say—real loud, Jack, so as to be heard over Mama's wail, *Iko-san's* sobbing. "*Daijubo*! Future flow of *do* path of life and times lifestyle all rosy red, folks! Certain for sure lead conduit cinch, reet? Honor and glory shtick for *wataschi*, name, family, *kami*, Hundred Millions, not to fail to mention *Mikado*, reet, folks?"

In riposte to which my daddy did say, Jack: "*Rainen no, koto o iuto, oni ga warau!*"

Meaning of which is, Jack: how we say, don't be talking all about future times unless you want devils to be laughing at you, reet?

Oh, Jack, big ironies to come.

2.

Gooch

"I am lost
somewhere in
Oklahoma."

T.R. Hummer

Says I: "You done good, *Seijo-san!*"

Says Terada Seijo (renowned *irezumi* tattoo artist, reet?): "*Sensei*, it is my pleasure to render satisfaction in the execution of my craft. That you are gratified by the results of my work is ample reward for one whose sole desire is to strive toward the attainment of excellence!"

"Reet!" I say to him, and, "Than which is not to fail to mention premium price top-dollar *yen* I pay? Makes it all the sweeter, laborer worthy of his hire shtick, fair-exchange ethos, reet?"

Terada Seijo (transported on regular-schedule basis via personal limo dispatched from Tokyo Town penthouse) don't say nothing, Jack, as how he is aged old-school *Nihonjin*, embarrassed at crass mention of lucre involved. Terada Seijo (signed to exclusive long-term duration contract, reet?) folds hands in lap, eyes downcast, head bowed — very traditionalist *Nipponshikki* shtick, Jack!

Says I: "Than which is to say, *Seijo-san*, not to rest upon laurels to date, dig? As how I now present new and most likely more difficult challenges to come. As instance, tell me, Terada, what's do you know from Oklahoma?"

"Oklahoma, *sensei*? *Sensei*, I do not know what the strange word might signify."

"Oklahoma! Sovereign state thereof! Gateway to sunny Southwest. Land of cattles, wheats — also petroleums and natural gases. Dust Bowl fame. Immortalized in popular *Amerikajin* culture via musical extravaganza spectacular *eiga* flic, also ensconced in global-wide literatures via saga of Joad family created by Nobel winner personage J. Steinbeck, reet? Oklahoma," says I, "didn't they teach you no geographics when you was schoolboy boy, *Seijo-san*?"

"Oh, *sensei*," says he (Terada Seijo, top tattooist in all of islands of *Nihon*, Jack!), "my education has been scant. My life, *sensei* Mr. Yamaguch, has been devoted to my humble *irezumi* craft, which I learned as an apprentice to my father, as he learned from his father before him."

"Ain't it the truths, sad to say?" says I, and, "Live and don't not learn nothing from it, reet? Tell *wataschi* about it, Jack! Than which signifies task upcoming ain't going to be no portion of confection, *Seijo-san*!"

"I welcome the challenge, *sensei*, confident that, with your guidance and instruction, I shall prove equal to the attendant difficulties!"

"Way to go, Terada!" I say. "Listen up! Oklahoma, reet? Sovereign state thereof. I is talking circa nineteen thirty-six to nineteen forty, dig? I is talking state of Oklahoma, county of Payne, town of Stillwater, environ site of Oklahoma Agricultural and Mechanical College, alma mater mine! Life and times of *wataschi* during which in said duration, circa 'thirty-six to 'forty, *Seijo-san*, I was knowed via nickname handle moniker of Gooch. Can you dig it?"

"Gooch?" queries Terada Seijo.

"Gooch! We can devise us a *sho* calligraph to cover that if needs dictate, reet?"

"You baffle me, *sensei*!"

"No more than myself! Hence comes challenge. Let's us brainstorm some, huh, Terada?"

"I follow your lead, *sensei*."

"Reet," and, "Natch!" I say, and, "As for instances, how's came *wataschi* to matriculate at Oklahoma Agricultural and Mechanical College instead of prestige Ivy League institution—Yale, Harvard, Princeton—more appropriate to talents of aforesaid Student Yamaguchi Yoshinori, honors grad of Native Land Loving School, reet? Big irony, Jack! Listen up, *Seijo-san*!"

Renowned *irezumi* tattoo artist Terada Seijo is all ears, into which orifices I pour narrative sketch of unexpected and ironical turns of events in *do* flow of lifetime.

To include (natch!): *kaigi* interview conference on carpet conducted in offices of Imperial Ministry of Education—standard procedure in process of application by said Student Yamaguchi Yoshinori (*wataschi*, Jack, me!) for scholarship grant support for higher-education studies of *Eigo* lingo, literature, and also culture overseas stateside, reet? To include (natch!) formal permissions. At which said *kaigi* interview congress is present Mr. Sato Isao—oh, ironics abound, Jack! As how aforesaid Mr. Sato, presumably high-level factotum of Imperial Ministry, is, in duration of aforesaid *kaigi* conference on carpet, revealed to be no less than *kempei* counterintelligence clandestine type operative charged with mission of oversight scrutiny of Yank American League all-star barnstorm tour of *Dai Nippon*, circa '35, as related heretofore, dig?

"You were accused by an agent of the *kempei* of espionage, *sensei*?" queries Terada.

"More or less. Six of one, half dozen remaining. Than which is to say they did harbor strongish suspicions of *wataschi's* unwitting — har, har, reet? — collusion in concert with aforesaid Moe Berg to photograph *Nihon-jin gumbatsu* military environs. Which is to say: *Kido Butai* fleet in Tokyo Bay, Ichigaya Heights Headquarters, Eta Jima, etcetera blah. To which said allegation I did plead (natch!) total innocence of ignorance, play dumb in naive schoolboy shtick, reet? Than which is no matters, as how even suspicion is due and sufficiency cause to deny application, not to fail to mention possible retributions of punitive nature to be visited upon self and family also."

"How then did it come to pass, *sensei*, that you were able to journey to America, to this place called Oklahoma?"

"Story of my life, *Seijo-san*, compromise!" says I, and do relate to him as how Mr. Sato Isao, revealed as *kempei* operative *honcho* factotum personage, proposes trade-off: *kempei* suspicions to be duly noted in record, no guilts assigned, nor no static nor flak hassles to reflect upon self, name, nor family, reet? Further, overseas travel permission and grant-support *yen* is granted per request submitted. Flip side of which coin is: *wataschi* don't gets to matriculate at Ivy League. Rather I is dispatched on mission to boonies hick sticks of U. S. of A., which is to say, Oklahoma! Whereat *kempei* desire to locate clandestine operative on site to observe and also report *Amerikajin* preparations for *senso* war in offing. "*Hakko ichui*, Terada!" I say to him. "Eight corners of the world is grandiose vista, reet? Somebody gots to cover Oklahoma for *kempei*!"

"And so you engaged in espionage on behalf of the *kempei* during your sojourn in this Oklahoma?" he asks.

"Did I not? Dig it!"

"Oh, *sensei*" says he, "this seems a sordid tale you would tell me! Oh, I have not thought of such things in so long, the terrible years of the great *senso*! No one speaks now of *hakko ichui*, and all of my acquaintance will themselves to forget the horrible stories told of the *kempei*! Oh, *sensei* Mr. Yamaguch," says he, "those were evil years in our history no man wishes now to remember!"

"More's the pity, Terada," says I. And do proceed to relate relevant facts, pith and gist, explain as how it all depends on who doing the telling, and how, reet, Jack?

Than which narrative — replete with context's aura atmosphere, natch! — follows hereafter. Not to fail to mention inclusion of escalating ironies, both historical and personal, reet? "*Seijo-san*, grab your notebook! Brainstorm shtick, enumerate possible graphics to evoke era, circa 'thirty-six to 'forty, life and times of said Yamaguchi Yoshinori, hereafter knowed as Gooch! Ready?"

"I have but one question to pose, *sensei*?"

"Shoot!"

"What of Mr. Morris Berg, known as Moe? Did he, as he promised, employ his influence on your behalf with the *Amerikajin* diplomatic authorities to assist you in your application to the ministry for permission to travel and monies in support of this?"

I tell him: "I is queried aforsaid Sato to same effect at time of *kaigi* interview interrogation, reet? Riposte was: nary a word said one way or 'tother, Terada! In sum and short, *Moe-san* did shoot *wataschi* through proverbial grease, put me on, pulled pedal extremity, snow-job shtick, done bullshitted little Yosh up one side, not to fail to mention down other. To laugh, *Seijo-san*, as in hardy har and hee! Is we ready to get on with it?"

"I can only say, Mr. Yamaguch, that I am shamed on behalf of the great scholar and athlete personage, and now await your convenience, *sensei*."

"Spilled milks," I say, and, "Reet. Okay. Historicals, as for instance, global-wide economics depression, accompanying social unrests, emergence of aggressive nationalism on world scene shtick, reet? In *Dai Nippon* old chauvinist *joi-i* ethos prospers, than which is personified in personage of *honcho* General Tojo Hideki—nickname: The Razor!—risen to stage front and center via activity in command of Kwantung Army stationed on Chink borders. Can you sketch a caricature thereof, *Seijo-san?*"

"I recall the visage of Premier Tojo, *sensei*. He shaved his head, did he not?"

"Where was I? Reet. Tojo in *Dai Nippon*, Schicklgruber in Germany—*Hitler-san* to you, Terada!—Mussolini, also knowed as *Duce*, in Italy, reet?"

"For these others I shall be compelled to search for period photographs, for I have no vision of them to guide my brush in making patterns, no image for my needles to follow—"

"Don't interrupt, Terada! I is rolling! Historicals, global depression, social unrests, aggressive nationalisms engendering armed-conflict flaps. Trend is begun by glorious victories of Kwantung Army of *Dai Nippon* versus Chinks, establishment of Manchukuo, puppet Emperor Henry Pu Yi. Kwantung Army marches against Chinks, provocation of incident at Marco Polo Bridge, reet? Schicklgruber gloms Alsace, Austria, Munich Pact, blitz of Polacks, *Duce* invades Ethiopia in effort to revive classic glory shtick of ancient Roman Empire, joins hands with *Hitler-san* at throat of France, takes on Greeks circa 'forty, Axis Powers (krauts, dagoes, *Dai Nippon*) sign mutual defense treaty, also circa 'forty, etcetera blah."

"My pen falls behind your tongue, *sensei*," says Terada Seijo.

"And that ain't even the half from it, *Seijo-san!* Than which is to say, don't not forget focus in realm of personals: Student Yamaguchi Yoshinori, dispatched stateside as clandestine undercover counterintelligence operative of *kempei* aboard *Empress of Japan* (big irony, reet, Jack?), bound for San Francisco (how you say: Frisco), therefrom via rail (Santa Fe, Jack!) to Oklahoma City, whereat *wataschi* transfers to M.K.&T.—Katy Line—north to Stillwater, county of Payne, A & M College. Go, Pokes! Go,

Punchers! Ride 'Em, Cowboys! — whereat and wherein said context *wataschi's* monicker handle is transmogrified to: Gooch!"

"*Sensei* — "

"Listen up! In context of which historicals, said Gooch (*wataschi*!) passes four years of study, straight-A grades (natch!), active campus life and times lifestyle — frats and sororities, intercollegiate athletics, development of close personal *enryo oyabun-kobun* friendships with fellow matriculants: Stevie Keller (a.k.a. Mighty Mouse, a.k.a. Yukon Strongboy), co-ed Miss Clara Sterk (a.k.a. Petty Girl) — which is to say, *kokoro*, Jack, how you say, romantical love interest. Ah, heartbroke is I, *Seijo-san*!"

"*Sensei*, I am confused!"

"No more than me, Terada! And also not to fail to record espionage activities on behalf of *kempei*, photos and notes taken in observation of campus R.O.T.C. corps, Flying Aggies flyboys, conveying same periodically to aforesaid Mr. Sato Isao, frequent visitor to collegiate environ in guise as field representative of phony facade front org, Japan–America Friendship Society, reet? Rendezvous in remote hick sticks boonies environ of village of Perkins, Oklahoma — ah, *Seijo-san*, heartbroke, heart breaking am I even as I speak!"

"*Sensei* — "

"Dig, Terada! Can you draw picture of pulchritudinous co-ed Miss Clara Sterk, also knowed as Petty Girl? Can you limn N.C.A.A. 116-lb. wrestler grappling champ (four years running, cinch certainty for 'forty Olympiad!) Stevie Keller, also knowed as Mighty Mouse, not to fail to mention Yukon Strongboy? Can you depict Flying Aggies biplane trainer aircrafts aloft in vast expanse of Oklahoma sky? Can you render shapes of blackjack oaks and cottonwoods in dead of winter solstice near rural village of Perkins, Oklahoma? Can your inks capture intellectual squint of close-set small eyes of Gooch's main mentor, venerable Professor Os Southard? Can needles evoke imposing posture demeanor of diminutive Dean Timothy J. Macklin? A & M Prexy Paul Klemp?"

"*Sensei*," says Terada Seijo, "you agitate yourself unduly! And I fear there is insufficient skin on the whole of your body to contain the profusion of images you call up from the memories of your life there in the distant place called Oklahoma!"

"Reet," says I, and, "Than which predicament dictates we wax selective, exercise editorialist skills, as with Moviola *eiga* flic mechanism, reet?"

"It is imperative, *sensei*!"

"Reet! Okey-doke. So. Where to commence?"

Kinestasis: Gooch.

No joke, Jack! Gooch. Me (*wataschi*!). Foto Joe. Gooch. Yoshinori ("Gooch") Yamaguchi, reet? Think I'm kidding? Would I pull your leg? Put you on? How we say: never *hochee*, Jack! Gooch!

Dig:

Cut to: long shot. How, in cinematic *eiga* flic-biz, we say, establish and also cover. Gander.

Stateside. America's Great Southwest. Oklahoma, Jack! Town of Stillwater (county of Payne). Oklahoma Agricultural & Mechanical College. A & M campus, Jack, alma mater mine!

Circa 1936–1940.

Jump cuts (sound collage): Yoshinori ("Gooch") Yamaguchi, class of 1940. Hail to thee, old alma mater! Ride 'Em, Cowboys! Go, Pokes! Go, Punchers! Maroo, Maroo, Marack, Marack, Hurrah for Gold, Hurrah for Black! Go Black and Gold (Beat O.U.!)! Delta Sigma Kappa, ever-loyal sons and brothers we! Big irony therein!

All that good collegiate shtick, Jack!

Gooch Yamaguchi, A & M class of '40. Bachelor of Arts (English and American Literatures and Language), Summa Cum Laude, Delta Sigma Kappa (jockstrapper frat, Jack!). B.M.O.C. (along with gridiron greats, Loving brothers — Carl and Wayne; wrestling phenom Mighty Mouse Stevie Keller, a.k.a. Yukon Strongboy — top protégé of legendary Coach E. C. Gallagher, N.C.A.A. 116-lb. champ four years consecutive; great roundballer Jesse Cobb McCartney (full-blooded Cherokee, Mr. Iba's first hardwood All-American). Gooch Yamaguchi. Name incised on bronze plaque Honor Roll, hallowed walls of Old Central — big irony, about which more to come later!

Redskin, Jack, A & M yearbook, 1940 edition. $5.00 Yank specie (payable with tuition and fees each autumn *tsukimi* semester!). Published each May (end of *hanami*, reet?).

Zoom to close-up, *Redskin* cover (1940 edition). Bas relief, stylized figures of athletes in symbolic action. Football: modeled on composite of gridiron greats, Loving brothers, Carl and Wayne, sensational wingbacks, Jack, ran for four TD's between them in '39, year we almost beat arch-rival hated O.U. Sooners. Basketball: suggests Jesse Cobb McCartney, Mr. Iba's initial All-American, poised for two-handed set shot, full-blood Cherokee. Wrestling: obvious likeness of phenom Stevie Keller, a.k.a. Mighty Mouse, a.k.a. Yukon Strongboy, four years running N.C.A.A. champ at 116 lbs., cinch certain for '40 Olympiad — big irony of which is there ain't none of same due to circumstances of global *senso* conflict of nations lying await in midst of *do* flow of future's path, reet?

Pan to small figure, subordinate to jocks, reet? Slow zoom to very close-up. Freeze! Cheerleader, yell-captain, midair splits, megaphone, A & M banner (black on gold), A & M logo affixed to turtleneck sweater — Gooch!

Great cover, Jack! Looks not unlike like unto carved in stone, cast in bronze (big irony!).

106

Pull camera back, hold. Cover opens. Pages begin to flip — as in Oklahoma wind blowing from off-camera (joke: how's come north wind to blow so hard in Stillwater Town, Jack? 'Cause, Jack, O.U. Sooners — hundred miles south in Norman environ — suck!).

Pages flip.

A & M Prexy Paul Klemp (very presidential: rimless specs, hair parted down middle, Rotary pin on lapel), diminutive Dean Timmy J. Macklin (small chair engenders illusion of larger stature), Professor Os Southard, chair of Department of Languages and Literatures (high forehead signifies keen intellect in addition to male pattern baldness, small eyes behind pince-nez specs indicate penchant for close critical analyses) — administration, faculty, clerical staff factotums, etcetera blah. Facsimiles of signed letters of congrats to all grads of 1940 (best wishes for success in life in face of future's challenge as presented by global turmoils — Schicklgruber in Europe, Mussolini in Abyssinia, depressed state of nation's economics, not to fail to mention *Dai Nippon* depredations in China and Manchuria, reet?): Governor William (a.k.a. Alfalfa Bill) Murray, sovereign state of Oklahoma, not to fail to mention Honorable E. P. Walkiewicz, long-timey incumbent Republican Mayor of Stillwater Town.

Campus Personalities: Pistol Pete (a.k.a. Frank Eaton), sixgun with notches on butt for outlaws and others dispatched whilst serving as federal marshal for Indian Territory, handlebar moustache, ten-gallon hat, friendly folksy twinkle shinning through killer-glint of tiny eyes — great campus character, Jack! Rides up front, on top, homecoming parades (Go, Pokes! Beat O.U.! Go, Aggies!). Sergeant-Major Tommy Turner, vet of Spanish–American *senso*, not to fail to mention Argonne (wheezy voice resultant from inhalation of mustard gases, reet?) flap of Great War, drill master for Pershing Rifles, R.O.T.C. corps advisor, sponsor of Scabbard & Blade honorary *gumbatsu* militarist frat, first to propose formation of Flying Aggies (A & M student aviation club — irony of which to come hereafter!). Miss Samantha Woods, aged and revered maiden lady mistress of campus post office. Et alia. Etcetera blah.

Pages flip in Oklahoma wind from north (O.U. Sooners suck!).

Fall Campus Beauties (as judged from photos submitted to Don Ameche, star of stage, screen, radio): A & M co-eds, ladies fair, Jack! Moselle Harrison, Ligea McCracken, Salome Corcoran, Clara ("Petty Girl") Sterk (Campus Queen for 1940!).

Campus Orgs: Hell Hounds and Ag-He-Ruf-Nex (rival men's cheering sections, Gooch Yamaguchi only A & M student ever granted dual membership!); Peppers (co-ed cheering section, Cheer Captain Miss Clara ("Petty Girl") Sterk); Pershing Rifles (canvas puttees, campaign hats, Sam Browne belts, water-cooled .30 caliber rapid-fires, Springfield '03 shoulder-arms, cavalry sabers, Sergeant-Major Tommy Turner calling hoarse cadence — mustard gases inhaled at Argonne, Jack! — on dusty drill field alongside Lewis Stadium); Scabbard & Blade (attired in full-dress garb, escorting Fall Beauties to annual Military Ball); Flying Aggies (slouched in shade of biplane's wings, leather helmets and jackets, long silk scarves, dangling goggles), about which more later, concerning ironies, reet?

Block & Bridle Club (this were Aggie-land, Jack!), Varsitonians (Big Band Sound!), Newman Club (mackerel snapper minority amongst Baptists and Methodists, both hard and softshell), Dairy Club, Future Farmers of America, Mummers (big production of 1940: *The Barretts of Wimpole Street*, second choice after *Waiting For Lefty* ix-nayed by conservative and diminutive Dean Timmy J. Macklin); *Daily O'Collegian* staff; Aggie Debaters (resolved: "A True American Looks to the Challenge of the Future Rather than Lamenting the Mistakes of the Past"); Aggie Cinemaphiles (founded 1937 by Y. ("Gooch") Yamaguchi, natch!); Chess Club (campus wimps!) . . . etcetera blah blah. You get the idea, reet, Jack?

Pages flip faster.

Greek Life: Lambda Phi Alpha, Kappa Alpha, Sigma Phi Epsilon, Alpha Kappa Psi, Sigma Nu, Alpha Gamma Rho, Farmhouse (quintessential Aggies, Jack—cowshit on boots, goat-roper's feather in band of ten-gallon hat, chew Red Man, expert judges of livestock, research methods of artificial insemination of swines, etcetera), Kappa Delta, Kappa Alpha Theta, Chi Omega (campus lovelies!), Tri Omicron, Sinfonia (music makers, reet?), which is not to fail to mention Delta Sigma Kappa— campus jockstrappers, B.M.O.C., ever-loyal sons and brothers we—irony!

Aggie Sports: Football (Coach Jim Lookabaugh, changed system from Notre Dame Shift to Single Wing, almost beat O.U. Sooners in '39 via superlative performances rendered by Loving brothers Carl and Wayne, cheered on by team mascot yellleader Gooch Yamaguchi); Basketball (25–1 record circa '39–'40 season, Mr. Iba's dynasty in place, all-time legendary coach Iron Duke Hank Iba, Jack! Great hardwood roundballer Jesse Cobb McCartney, full-blood Cherokee, first-ever A & M All-American!); Wrestling (perennial N.C.A.A. champs, natch, mentor is mythic Coach E. C. Gallagher, star is stellar Stevie ("Mighty Mouse") Keller, a.k.a. Yukon Strongboy, 116-lb. class national champ four years consecutive—too young for '36 Olympiad, none held in '40 due to global *senso* war, reet?).

Pages flip.

Portraits. Class of '41, Class of '42, Class of '43 (ironies to come include most therein not to graduate due to universal draft commenced in 1940). Class of 1940, graduating seniors, Jack! Pages slow, cease to flip. Freeze. Gander, Jack!

Cut to very close-up, freeze it! Soundtrack: mix of crowd cheering at football game (Lewis Stadium), male choir sings Alma Mater, female chorus competes with O.A.M.C. Anthem, ragged voices heard chanting Prexy's Yell; Ride 'Em, Cowboys, Go, Punchers, Go, Pokes, Go, Aggies.

Dig:

Gooch. Me. *Wataschi*. Gooch, Jack! Yoshinori ("Gooch") Yamaguchi. I kid you not!

Dig this Gooch (circa 1940):

Portrait of the grad, how we say in *eiga* film biz, bust shot, reet? Gooch.

Dark suit, white shirt, tie in Windsor knot—Man in the Arrow Collar, reet? Sharp. Clean. Standing tall, like six o'clock, Jack! Hair brush-cut, all the rage in Aggie-land circa '40, as how Warner–Pathé News, not to fail to mention March of Time newsreels at local cinemas (two, Jack, Aggie and Mecca!) is always showing clips of Schicklgruber's SS and Gestapo on parade, crew-cut all.

Dig new specs on Gooch! Nearsighted at age two and twenty years aged (congenital: recall *Papa-san's* pince-nez!), said malady accelerated from cracking textbooks in dim light of midnight oils. Not to fail to mention sitting long hours to view double-feature *eiga* flics—Asakusa District, Aggie, Mecca, reet? Round lenses, black bone frames—not unlike like unto Tojo Hideki's—har!

Most solemn expression in large eyes behind specs, resultant doubtless from *Nipponshikki* heritage, but his lips—this Gooch!—is pulled back in big *sumairu* grin (teeth like unto sugarlumps, Jack!)! Happy Gooch! Oh, happy Gooch! Circa 1940, graduation pic, Oklahoma Agricultural & Mechanical College. Happy, happy Gooch (circa '36 to '40)!

Gooch: Valedictorian, class of 1940, Phi Eta Sigma, Sigma Tau Delta, Phi Kappa Phi (honoraries all, Jack—stripe up trouser leg, chevron on sleeve, this Gooch ain't no *baka*!). Outstanding Male Student (1937, 1938, 1939, 1940); Most Spirited Aggie (1937, 1938, 1939, 1940); Most Likely To Succeed (co-winner with Stevie Keller), Class of 1940; elected Class President (co-winner with Clara ("Petty Girl") Sterk)!

You get the idea, reet, Jack? B.M.O.C.

Oh, happy Gooch.

I work from memory—*Redskin* (1940 edition) lost whilst flying upside down over USS *Oklahoma* (circa 1941), irony of which more about later, reet?

From memory, Jack.

> Oklahoma A & M Campus
> Town of Stillwater
> County of Payne
> Sovereign State of Oklahoma
> U. S. of A.
> 5 September 1936

Dear *Papa-san, Mama-san,* Baby Sis *Iko-san*:

I, *wataschi*, your loving son and also bro, Yamaguchi Yoshinori, ensconce myself upon wooden chair at deal table by sole window of room in Maggie Nelson Frosh Residence Hall to address myself to you-all (how we say here in Oklahoma—collectivist pronoun, reet?) there in distant *Dai Nippon*, in this, *wataschi's* inaugural missive to folks at home.

Than which is to say—how we say in *Nihonju*—as bloated new harvests moon (*tsukimi*, reet?) rises high in vastness of Okie sky above A & M campus (Stillwater Town, county of Payne), I, Yamaguchi Yoshinori, commence this first of many letters home to you, folks, my revered parents Mr. & Mrs. Yamaguchi, not to fail to mention beloved kid sis Iko.

Than which is to say, in quiet wee hours past midnight (clock in Old Central tower bongs two even as I inscribe above!)—fellow matriculant roomie (about whom more follows hereinafter later, reet?) fast aslumber in upper bunk bed—I, Yamaguchi Yoshinori, write to you to convey greetings (natch!), much love (also natch), and tug of *hara* belly's emotion gnawing at innards vitals, how we say, homesickness shtick.

Than which is to say: I does miss you, folks!

Please, first, to forgive abovementioned sentiments, absence of *Nipponshikki* decorums taught me by you and venerable and revered mentors of Native Land Loving School. Big irony, Daddy, in that *Yosho-san* is stateside less than fortnight, already, how we say, going native, reet? Reeling under assault of *gaijin* culture-shock shtick, reet?

Also please, *Papa-san*, to forgive your son self-serve indulgence of scribblings in *Eigo*, reet? As how I figure I do needs all possible practice in order to keep up with demanding scholastic studies, and do trust in you, Daddy, to translate with facile ease into *Nihonju* for Mama and Iko. For which assistance, all thanks due (natch!).

Where was I?

Okay. *Amerikajin*-style, I sit on plain wood chair at deal table (view of moon, sky, A & M campus greensward, faint black silhouhette of Old Central clock tower visible against black skyline etcetera blah) to write you this letter home. All quiet in Okie-land, folks, except save for hourly chime of aforesaid Old Central time-piece, howl of wind (you gets used to it, not unlike like unto background music of *shamisen* at *geisha* party, reet?), minimalist snoring of sleeping roomie fellow matriculant personage named Steven Keller, than which who is native of hick sticks village hamlet of Yukon, Oklahoma, fellow frosh and already renown campus personage (a.k.a. Big Man on Campus—B.M.O.C.) due to established reputation for wrestling grappler prowess—116-lb. avoirdupois class—considered strong candidate for N.C.A.A. crown even as he trains hard daily to begin season.

Okie-style salutation: what's up, folks? Everything coolish back there in *Dai Nippon*? Is whole political scene in *Dai Nippon* still in flux ferments due to undue influence of *gumbatsu* militarists, not to fail to mention *zaibatsu* plutocrat fatcats wielding *kinken* clout influences via *genkin* cash doled out in support of intensified rearmament efforts?

In sum and short, Daddy: what's happening in *Dai Nippon* since *wataschi* done departed island shores aboard *Empress of Japan* bound for San Francisco? Please to write and fill me in on all details, including pith and gist foci, reet? As how you knows I ain't interested zilch squat's worth in politico guff stuff, *Papa-san*, but folks here stateside (fellow matriculants and co-eds, mentors, local community yokels) is steady querying me as to what's going on in (how we say stateside) Land of Rising Sun, reet?

Mama-san: I miss you, Mama!

Than which is to say, please to know your son, Yamaguchi Yoshinori, wakes up each morn so far in expectations of sniffing fast breaker repast cooking over *hibachi* fire in our paper house. Only to realize upon full awakening that fast breaker requires trek across campus to dining hall (located in basement of Boggs Agricultural Building, said edifice named for now long-dead and since-forgot prof once famed for developments of technique for artificial insemination of swines — said technique complicated, involving long tube, rubber gloves, good wind and strong stomach, etcetera blah — considered scientific breakthrough to advancement of condition of all humankind, reet?), whereat I am served repast cafeteria style on tin tray, said viands consisting consistently of scrambled eggs, fried strips of swine flesh, big dollop of mush composed of grits cornmeal, occasional variation of pancakes (breadstuff with texture of flannels, Mama) or oatmeal, than which we feed to horsies in *Dai Nippon*, reet?

Mama: I does miss you!

Sis *Iko-san*: your big bro misses you, *Iko-san*! All day, every day, I spiel the *Eigo* with fellow matriculants, co-eds, mentors, casual confabulations with local-yokel citizenry of Stillwater Town (county of Payne, reet?), to juncture now I begin to dream dreams of *Dai Nippon*, our paper house, you, Sis, said dreams coming now in *Eigo* lingo, and thus think oft of you laughing little girl's *sumairu* laugh when I speak same with Daddy, you saying as how we sound like unto donkeys braying, reet?

Your big bro do miss you, *Iko-san*!

Clock in Old Central tower strokes 3 in ante-meridian even as *wataschi* writes to you now, dry wind flows steady out of north (sovereign state of Kansas environ, homeland of *honcho* politico Alf Landon, than which who is predicted to unseat Prexy Roosevelt, reet?), assigned roomie Stevie Keller (a.k.a. Yukon Strongboy, a.k.a. Mighty Mouse) snores softly in upper bunk bed of our room here in Maggie Nelson Hall, huge *tsukimi* Okie harvest moon casts yellow light out of black sky vastness upon campus greensward below my sole window — and I do think — homesickness shtick! — upon you, Daddy, Mama, Iko, so far away from me in *Dai Nippon*, reet?

Hey, which is not to forget to say to you, convey to Daddy for conveyance thence to me, how does you like them *o-miyage* souvenirs I done sent you? Big box of same should arrive prior to this epistle if mail boat don't not founder in briny deep, reet? Beanie I sent is exact likeness like unto that which I (in company of all fellow frosh matriculants of Oklahoma Agricultural & Mechanical College, reet?) is required to affect, doff when addressing upper-class personages — collegiate tradition shtick here in Okie-land, function of which same is to establish, maintain, and also enhance school spirit, about which more later, reet?

I do miss you, folks!

And so, what of *wataschi* (me, your son Yamaguchi Yoshinori, matriculant in good standing, class of '40, Oklahoma A & M, reet?), reet?

Than which is to recognize you shall not have yet received lengthy missive composed whilst aboard *Empress of Japan* (natch) since boat mail requires five and twenty (sometimes thirty!) days. Prolonged sea voyage is now dim memory, frankly boresome, folks! Tedious Pacific crossing is abated momentarily only by stopover in Honolulu (Hawaiian Islands, *Amerikajin* colonialist possession, howsomever many *Nihonjin* folks living there also) for exchanges of mail, passengers, take on fuel oils and foodstuffs for second leg of voyage to San Francisco—than which supply stop is accomplished at Pearl Harbor installation.

Debarkation at San Francisco (*Empress of Japan* passes beneath awesome span of Golden Gate Bridge!), reet? Hereinafter follows (from notes scribbled on scene) first impressions of stateside (San Francisco, Santa Fe rail passage to OKC, transfer thereat to M.K.&T. shuttle line, arrival in Stillwater Town, reception, commencement of campus life and times lifestyle as matriculating student in good standing, A & M College, class of '40), said impressions' effect on sensibility of Yamaguchi Yoshinori (*wataschi*!) like unto, how we say in regards to cinematic *eiga* flic technique (what's playing in Asakusa theaters these days, Daddy?), swish-pan, reet? As follows:

U. S. of A., folks, *Amerikajin* homeland, everything is maximist twice life-sizes, reet?

I do recall enormity of Yank American League all-star *besuboru* athletes well (I scan box-scores, but Moe Berg ain't in Senators' lineup—maybe on injured reserve status?), but did assume grossness of their statures to be function of strenuous activities and special nutritions, reet? Not so, folks! All *Amerikajin* (with but few excepting, to include notably personages of assigned roomie Stevie Keller and revered academic dean, Timothy J. Macklin) is enormous, folks!

Confession: for split-second, minimalist *ma* moment's instant, I did think to myself (Yamaguchi Yoshinori, taking *sanpo* walk through streets of Frisco surrounded by giants sporting large schnozzes, ears a-ring with babble of *Eigo* slang idioms!)—I did think: *Yosho-san*, best you climb back up gangplank of *Empress of Japan* for return trip to *Dai Nippon*, go back home to family and paper house, forget lifetime's *do* path of life to date devoted to blear-eye midnight oils burning study of *Eigo* lingo, *Amerikajin* culture via viewing import *eiga* flics in old *No* and *Kabuki* and *Bunraku* theaters, Asakusa District!

Forget, Yamaguchi Yoshinori, I say to self—neck sore from gandering upwards at big-schnozz giant pedestrians on streets of Frisco, skyscraper edifices to rival Imperial Hotel and also Dai Ichi building! Forget signal honors bestowed for scholastics achievements (stripe up trouser leg, chevron on sleeve!), forget distinction when chosen on pure merit basis to serve as guide-interpreter for visiting barnstorm tour of Yank American League *besuboru* all-star greats team (Cornelius McGillicuddy, Bambino Babe Sultan of Swat Ruth, Iron Man Lou, et alia, not to fail to mention Morris ("Moe") Berg!) circa but a year ago, reet? Forget!

Forget even honor of personal audience with *Mikado* (har and hee!), direct descendant of Sun Goddess *Ameratasu* (which is to note I am fast losing impulse to stand, face east, perform kowtow here in room of Maggie Nelson Hall, A & M campus, Old Central clock tower scarce visible against black vastness outside my sole window, wee hours, reet?). Forget, I say to myself, good fortune of grant-support *yen* bestowed by Imperial Ministry of Education to enable higher-educations venture studies stateside (not to fail to mention disappointment at Oklahoma land-grant institution in place of Ivy League prestige school — reason for which I need not rehash, reet?).

I do 'fess up, folks, to unseemly non-*Nipponshikki* episode. I did stop in my tracks, there on Frisco streets, think serious to retrace steps to dockside, reboard *Empress of Japan*, come homeward to you in *Dai Nippon*. Go home! I think: return to who and what you is, Yamaguchi Yoshinori!

And (natch!) I do not, reet? I think: you is got opportunity for advanced study here stateside (A & M College, Oklahoma, sovereign state thereof — can't be so bad even if but third or fourth or fifth or sixth rate, reet?). Grab it and run, *Yosho-san*! I did think. Which is not to fail to mention (between you and me only, Daddy, secret we keep from Mama and Iko) attendant complexities attending upon special arrangement agreement bargain struck with Mr. Sato Isao of Imperial Ministry (har!), reet, Daddy?

Howsomever, I do not (natch!) turn back to reboard *Empress of Japan*. I say to self: you is not no longer who you once was, Yamaguchi Yoshinori! Thus it were thence I did purchase ducat, board Santa Fe bound for OKC, reet? Hence thus it is I sit here ensconced on wooden chair at deal table in room in Maggie Nelson Hall (wind from northward, light snoring from personage of assigned roomie Mighty Mouse Yukon Strongboy Stevie Keller), composing this, inaugural missive home to you there in *Dai Nippon*.

Train ride eastward (Sante Fe Super Chief) is frankly boresome interlude, folks! I do prove unable to consume comestibles offered for sale (prices higher than feline's back — Okie idiomatic, Daddy!), feel embarrassment at attentions of Negroid personage who schlepps travelers' baggage — how we say, porter, also slumber car attendant (Negroids, Daddy: *Amerikajin* personages not unlike like unto *Dai Nippon Burakumin*, how we say, untouchable hamlet peoples, reet? *Amerikajin* very fond only of, how we say, *shiroi* pale epidermis, reet?), also intimidated by hostile and indifferent miens of fellow passangers (Yank rail travelers, folks, much given to playing of cards with accompanying wagers, drinking of alcohol-base libations than which are served by Negroid porter personages in, how we say, club car, and also dozing in coach seats, to include much loud snores, coughing, sneezing, but nobody spits on floor due to availability of cuspidors provided).

Boringness, folks!

Transfer in Oklahoma City station (how we say Okie-style: OKC, Ok City, The City, etcetera blah), board M.K.&T. (Katy Line) north for Town of Stillwater, county of Payne, reet?

Notable Incident Worth Detailed Reportage: at Stillwater station (early-morn arrival, reet?), conductor personage addresses me as I gather baggage for debarkation, reet?

Says he (black uniform, gold trim on cap, ticket-punch device in hand, big watch suspended on long chain): "You getting off here, is that right?"

Says I (*wataschi*, journey-wearied folks, seat-sitting sore, not to fail to mention sore in need of *sento* hot bath!): "Reet," and, "Town of Stillwater, county of Payne, what's it says on my ducat, reet, Jack?"

Says he: "I knowed your ticket was for Stillwater, what I'se wondering was what you was going to Stillwater for? You fixing to open you one of them laundries does shirts by hand and all maybe like down to Oklahoma City?"

Says I (journey-wearied, seat-sore): "No way, Jack! I is come all the way, via surface sea and also rail transport, from Empire of Japan, reet? Allow me to intro self, Mr. Esteemed Conductor: you looking at Yamaguchi Yoshinori—"

"Yama the which?" he interjects.

"—come to Stillwater Town, county of Payne, sovereign state of Oklahoma, to matriculate as member of class of circa 1940, reet? Agricultural and Mechanical College, dig? Man, I is student personage; how you say, Joe College, reet?"

"You ain't a Chinese?" queries conductor personage.

"Not hardly, Jack! We all look same to you, reet? Common mistake, occurred more than once on streets of Frisco, sovereign state of California, than which wherefrom I is just departed via Sante Fe Super Chief, reet? *Nihonjin*," I say, and, "How you say, personage of Japanese extraction origins, reet?"

"Jap," says he. "You the ones causing all the hell getting after them poor Chinese back there and all, huh?"

Dig, folks: I is journey-wearied, seat-sore from long train ride across U. S. of A. vastness vista, reet? Mind-boggled is I by race of giants in giant land shtick, reet? And even in early morn, sun burns down out from empty sky over Okie-land, reet? Perspirations beading on brow, accumulating in pits of arm, crotch also—I hustle baggages to exit coach, conductor personage in pursuit.

"Not me, Jack! Never *hochee!*" I say over my shoulder as I schlepp baggages, and, "Flap with Chinks is endeavor of militarist *gumbatsu* cats, Kwantung Army *budo*-types, Jack, *katana* longsword rattling of *hakko ichui* eight corners of world under single roof of *Dai Nippon* trendiness now rampant amongst Hundred Millions back home, reet? Me, Yamaguchi Yoshinori, ain't political, dig? Please to be forgiving abruptness, as how I needs must get off here before I miss stop, reet?"

"Goochie?" says he. "Well, I never heard of no Japs going to school up to the A and M college no more than no niggers ever done! I did hear tell they letting in damn Indians if they can play sports good these days." Whilst I debark coach, deposit baggages on station platform, conductor personage adds, "I don't guess I never even seen me a Jap before in all my life I seen some Chinese operates a laundry down to Oklahoma City, but if I ever seen a Jap before now I never knowed it when I did. You-all look alike, it seems like you'd want to get along better over there, don't it?"

"Takes discerning scrutinies to distinguish," I tell him. "Narrow and more slanty baby blues, more pronounced prominence of cheekbones, lighter shade hue of epidermis pigments, reet?"

"Gooch-something, you say," says he as locomotive hisses steam, wheels squeal, coaches lurch.

"Reet," says I, looking round about for welcome-reception person-ages. "Yamaguchi. Goochie. Gooch for short if you likes, reet?"

"I'd say short," says conductor factotum as train begins to slide away from platform. "I'm reading in the papers about you-all Japs causing wars over there all the time now, but damn if I can see how if ain't none of you no bigger'n you! Hell, Gooch-whatever, you ain't no bigger'n a minute. I got me a nephew ain't but twelve year old, he's big as you and weighs in a sight more to boot!"

"*Sayonara!*" I call to him as train picks up speed, and, "How you say: so long, Jack, reet?"

Can you dig it, folks?

M.K.&T. train pulls out of sight (heading ever northward, next stop is village hamlet environ of Perry, reet?), locomotive steam-mist dissipates in hot humid air, I stand admidst baggages, sweating into suit under searing rays of early-morn sun streaming down out of cloudless-sky vastness. As small assemblage of ragamuffin children (bare feet dirty with red clay dust, shaggy hairdos, runny noses – big schnozzes) and platform local-yokel loungers (overall clad, tobacco chewing, snuff dip-ping, work shirted, clodhopper shoes, reet?) assembles to gander and gawk apparition of unfamiliar (hence: exotic) Oriental personage (me, Daddy, *wataschi!*) arrived on OKC train, I is approached by pince-nez spectacle-wearing gentleman personage attired in three-piece suit, high white collar, fedora – thin whispy hairs grown long in compensation for premature male pattern-baldness straggle down – small (intelligent!) baby blues behind specs, said personage awash with perspirations in aforesaid heat of morn, reet? He bears papers in pale hands, unfolds same to address me, reads:

"I'll have to assume you're our young Mr. Yamaguchi? I'm Professor Southard of the A and M Department of Languages and Literature."

I render ten-degree kowtow bow, say: "I is. Call me Gooch for short, reet, prof?"

"Gooch?" says Prof Os Southard, looks at paper again.

"Gooch," I iterate, and we enact *Amerikajin* howdy handshake (than which I is at ease to execute via countless instances so dramatized in Yank *eiga* flics, also from personal experience with American League *besuboru* all-stars circa just last year, reet?), after than which we do schlepp bag-gages to town's sole taxicab (motorized *jinricksha*, folks!) for short trip through town on Main Street to A & M campus, Maggie Nelson Hall.

So: whilst I remain (natch!) your son, Yamaguchi Yoshinori, I is now, for duration (four years, folks!) of higher-educational sojourn here state-side, knowed as Gooch. I will endeavor to try to remember to render *kanji* calligraph I is devised for said moniker handle, just for funs, in this my inaugural missive home to you-all there in *Dai Nippon*.

Gooch: you dig the ring of it as much as me, folks? Gooch!

Even as I write to you, folks, assigned roomie Mighty Mouse Yukon Strongboy Stevie Keller stirs in upper bunk bed (do he dream of grap-pling heavier and faster opponent, of rural environ village of Yukon from whence he emanates?), says (slumber-heavy voice), "What the hell are you doing up, Gooch? It's the middle of the night still!" After which he resumes supine posture, also light snore.

Where was I? Highlight of first weekend is Saturday-afternoon official-welcomes ceremony staged downtown Stillwater (corner of Sixth and Main, reet?), focus of which is no other than *wataschi* (Gooch!) — occasion of which is fact I am first-ever student of foreign origins to matriculate at A & M, reet? Big doings, folks! Not unlike like unto *matsuri* festive welcome of arriving Yank American League *besuboru* barnstormers at Yokohama dockside circa last year, reet?

Featuring: speech of official welcomes enunciated by Honorable E. P. Walkiewicz, long-time incumbent mayor of Stillwater Town, who concludes peroration by proffering me (Gooch!) symbolic (pasteboard cutout painted with silver gilt, reet?) key to municipality. Also official howdy handshake — I note Hizzoner's palm horny-hard as rice-paddy peasant's, Daddy! — and oversize Alf Landon button. Says he: "We want you to feel like that Stillwater and A and M is your home away from home, son, and hope your days here as a Aggie will serve to help international intercourse between your country and these great United States of America! My own folks come across the Atlantic from Poland two generations back, and we done just fine here, and, 'course you can't immigrate like we done 'cause of the quotas and all, but I know you going to do real good here in your studies!"

Than which is followed by applause of assembled, to include student officer *honcho* types representing joint Pan-Hellenic frats and sororities, not to fail to mention scattering of local-yokel citizenry attracted by Yank flags and A & M spirit banners — sad to say, no *Hinomaru* round sun flags on hand, reet? Also members of Aggie Spirit Band, than which renders Stars and Stripes Forever — no *Kimagayo* nor *Kaigun* March sheets musics on hand (natch).

Than which musics is followed by brief seconding remarks tendered by A & M Academic Dean Timothy J. Macklin — first *Amerikajin* adult I confront no taller than me, Daddy! Not to fail to mention A & M Prexy Paul Klemp — substance of which declamations is as how advent of *wataschi* (Gooch) as matriculating student marks onset of new eras in internationalist dimension of education mission at venerable A & M institution of higher learning, than which promises bright future, in that said new dimension will enable A & M (also Oklahoma and whole of U. S. of A.) to share fruits of advanced democratic civilization with backwards nations of world, thus hopefully avoiding tensions such as now plague globe (asides refer to Schicklgruber, Mussolini, and *hakko ichui* phenom in *Dai Nippon*, reet?), possible by-product of which might could be increase in overseas markets for Okie products such as wheats and cattles and swines, than which go begging presently in depressed markets, thus all served to mutual advantages, etcetera blah.

Scattered applauses followed by photo op pic posings: Gooch with staunch Republican Landon supporter Mayor E. P. Walkiewicz, Prexy Paul Klemp flanked by Gooch and diminutive Dean Timmy J. Macklin, said photos published in Sunday edition of Stillwater *News–Mess* (joke, Daddy!) *shimbun*, than which clips from same I clip to enclose herewith — mayhap you will wish to mount same in family photo album for personal archive chronicle record, reet?

What's else?

Collage of campus life: registration for classes (I enroll in frosh composition, college algebra, Oklahoma and *Amerikajin* histories, biological science — to include lab in which we dissect froggies — and special tutorial, topics to be arranged, conducted by main mentor Prof Os Southard. Routine of Maggie Nelson Hall habitation: assigned roomie Mighty Mouse Yukon Strongboy Stevie Keller, meals taken in cellar dining-hall cafeteria located in aforesaid Boggs Agricultural Building. Campus Social Scene: Aggie Spirit Rally conducted in anticipation of upcoming football (Beat O.U.!) and wrestling (A & M cinch certain to repeat N.C.A.A. title, natch!) and roundball seasons (Iron Duke Coach Hank Iba promises winning ways on hardwood!) — to include bonfire sing-songs, cider and doughnuts (*Amerikajin* snack repasts, Mama), and mixer dances — I do but watch, reet?

Not to fail to mention frat and also sorority rushes activities, in which context I hasten to add your son Gooch is considered cinch for tap from Delta Sigma Kappa (jockstrappers, Daddy) due to sponsorship of assigned roomie Stevie Keller! Also to note further evidences of Gooch's success in A & M campus social whirl: I audition for and attain memberships in cheering spirit squads, both Ag-He-Ruf-Nex and also Hell Hounds, said orgs devoted to inspiration of A & M athletic contingents of all sports in annual quests to vanquish hated downstate arch-rival O.U. Sooners — which is also to note *wataschi's* status as adjunct member of A & M Reserve Officer Training Corps (Yank *budo*-style training entity, Daddy), said R.O.T.C. under direction of Sergeant-Major (U.S. Army Retired) Tommy Turner, beloved campus personality (on par with Pistol Peter Frank Eaton and aged campus postmistress spinster Samantha Woods — big social-scene whirl, folks!

Wonder of which is, your son — call me Gooch over here, folks! — is huge boffo success! No day passes but than which good wishes camaraderie feeling of fellow student peers and also co-ed females is conveyed to me, as for instance:

Stevie Keller: "Gooch, you know, I'll tell you honest, I never figured a Jap could be such a nice guy as you are!"

Miss Clara (a.k.a. Petty Girl) Sterk: "Oh, Gooch, you're so smart in English class, and you're just as cute as a button!"

Can you dig it, folks?

Anything else? Oh, folks, the *eiga* flics I seen since arrival in Stillwater Town! *Big Broadcast of 1936, Broadway Melodies of 1936, The Thin Man, Modern Times, Angel, A Night at the Opera, Klondike Annie, The 39 Steps* — oh, folks, this going to be a great four years for the viewing of *eiga*!

Old Central clock rings five times — wind ceasing from north — roomie Stevie Keller turns over in sleep (upper bunk bed, Maggie Nelson Hall) — my baby blues grow heavy, folks, hence needs must conclude this, my inaugural epistle home.

Papa-san, Mama-san, Iko-san: I do miss you, folks!

Howsomever, despite attendant complications attending, joy and success of safe arrival, happy events, etcetera blah all conspire to impart sincere confidence in me, your son (Gooch!) that I shall cinch certain attain to intended goals of honorand-glory shtick for self, name, family, *Dai Nippon*, reet? And sign myself your son (with new-style Yank *hanko* signature),

Gooch!

P.S. Daddy, do incoming mails to *Dai Nippon* pass through censorship scrutinies these days? Reason I query: tomorrow eve I shall sojourn to nearby rural hick stick boonies village hamlet of Perkins, Oklahoma, thereat to rendezvous with Mr. Sato Isao, who presents self via letter (taken by me from trembling liver-spotted hand of aged and venerable campus Postmistress Miss Samantha Woods) as liaison factotum personage representing Japan—America Friendship Society, reet? Than which meeting I shall report in full in next epistle, providing you flash me, how we say stateside, high-sign indicating *daijubo* not to worry concerning censorships complications in postal system of *Dai Nippon*, reet?

Love to all!

G.

Dig:

I, Gooch, stand waiting under leaf-barren limbs of twisted blackjack oak tree, sheltered from unceasing wind out of north by cluster of cottonwoods, west bank of Cimarron River, air gritty with dust of Colorado and Kansas blowing by, environ of rural hamlet hick stick boonie village of Perkins—ten miles west of Stillwater Town (county of Payne, etcetera blah), U. S. of A., reet?

Moon waxing toward obesity of *tsukimi* harvest dimension is sole source of illumination. Rippling waters of Cimarron reflects silver gilt of moonlight back up to black dust-filled vastness of Okie-land sky, unceasing north wind whispers nonsense through cottonwoods, shakes leaf-barren limbs of blackjack oak, slow-moving waters of Cimarron (much reduced due to Dust Bowl drouth conditions, exposing sandbars, rocky riverbottom) engenders faint trickling noise.

And am met by appointed personage, as follows:

"Student Yamaguchi Yoshinori?" says aforesaid Sato Isao, emerging from depths of cottonwood grove, reet?

To which greetings query I did riposte: "You got it, Mr. Sato. Me, myself, and I. Where's you come from, *sensei*?"

Says he (approaching nigh, small *sumairu* smile on thin lips): "Greetings, Student Yamaguchi Yoshinori! Suffice it to say that I am here at our appointed hour and location. Let us, henceforth, Student Yamaguchi Yoshinori, agree that it shall not be for you to put questions, on any subject, to me? Rather, it is I who shall pose questions. You, Student Yamaguchi Yoshinori, shall, I trust, endeavor to provide accurate and comprehensive answers thereto. Do we understand one another, Student

118

Yamaguchi Yoshinori?"

"Reet. Excepting save how's come I gots to schlepp all the way out here in the boonies to meet you? If you're so-called field rep of Japan–America Friendship Society, than which *kempei* front org is sponsoring me at A & M, how's come you don't just drop by campus when we needs to confabulate, Jack?"

"Do not," says he, "Student Yamaguchi Yoshinori, permit your immersion in the daily life of the barbarian *Amerikajin* to lead you into impertinence and lack of decorum — the absence of *enryo* we so rightly prize in our beloved *Dai Nippon* — which *gaijin* qualities so characterize their behavior. Maintain your regard for *Nipponshikki*, Student Yamaguchi Yoshinori!"

"Reet. Duly noted. Orry-say. By the way, they calls me Gooch here now."

"Gooch? What is . . . Gooch?" asks Mr. Sato Isao.

"Short for Yamaguchi, reet? *Amerikajin* Okie-style collegiate nickname moniker, dig?" Mr. Sato makes his *sumairu* smile bigger, there in moonlit rural environ of village of Perkins, dust-laden wind blowing through cottonwoods, blackjack oak's bare boughs, Cimarron (slowed to trickle in drouth phenom, reet?) flowing below bank whereon we stand.

"Gooch," says Mr. Sato Isao, clandestine *kempei* counterintelligence operative. "Gooch. Yes, it has the flavor of their ugly language on one's tongue, does it not?"

We pause, silent, listen to wind, trickle-sound of Cimarron waters over rocks, around exposed sandbars, moonlit. When I do not riposte, says he: "Just so. And it occurs to me, Student Yamaguchi Yoshinori, that there is a delightful humor implicit if I were to choose this Gooch as your code identity to employ in the reports I submit to my *kempei* superiors. Is that not amusing, Student Yamaguchi Yoshinori? The barbarian *Amerikajin* mock you with this ridiculous corruption of your family name, but we shall in turn mock them by this irony I create in naming you Gooch for official intelligence communications! Thus shall we together mock their ignorance of our mutual effort to prepare the way for their defeat should they ever dare to interfere with the sacred destiny of our beloved *Dai Nippon* as our glorious empire strives toward the triumph of *hakko ichui*! Just so," says Mr. Sato Isao, and, "Are you able to enjoy as much as I this irony we create at the expense of these *gaijin*, Student Yamaguchi Yoshinori?"

"Reet," I say, "as in hardy har and also hee, reet? Irony shtick. Tell me about it, Jack! Except as how I do think they intend nickname moniker as affectionate diminutive form of address."

"Just so," Mr. Sato says, and, "And now to the purpose of our appointment here in this isolated and desolate place. Tell me . . . Yamaguchi Yoshinori — tell me, Gooch — have you succeeded in establishing a secure rapport in your relations with the *Amerikajin* in the academic and social life of this absurd excuse for an institution of higher learning, this Oklahoma Agricultural & Mechanical College? And what is the bizarre hat you wear upon your head? Is it some decadent new fashion of the *Amerikajin* youth whose confidence you seek to gain by emulating their foolish sumptuary habits?"

Says I: "That is my frosh beanie, Jack! Prescribed attire accessory for all matriculants, fall semester, class of 1940, reet? Collegiate shtick, so as to provide visible communal *enryo* fellow feeling amongst said matriculants, also enabling upper-class *honchos* to engage in appropriate hazing harassments, as for instance, aforesaid do accost me on campus, demand I sing A & M anthem, recite cheers to be employed in concert when Poke athletic teams engage hated downstate arch-rival Sooners of O.U. on playing fields, spiel names of A & M revered administrators such as Prexy Paul Klemp, diminutive Dean Timmy J. Macklin, identify legendary campus character eccentrics like unto beloved ancient aged and enfeebled Postmistress Miss Samantha Woods, campus mascot Frank Eaton, also knowed as Pistol Peter, Coach Iron Duke Mr. Henry Iba, hardwood roundball mentor, et alia etcetera blah."

Mr. Sato Isao renders biggish *sumairu* smile, expels breath-hiss prior to speaking. "Ah so, Student Yamaguchi Yosh—"

"Call me Gooch, reet, Jack?"

"—Gooch, then. So. It would appear you have done well in your effort to infiltrate the *Amerikajin* infrastructure. I am pleased."

"Reet," I say, and, "*Wataschi* didn't graduate top of his class at *Aikyojuko* Native Land Loving School for nothing, Jack! Gooch ain't no *baka* dummy dope slow-study, reet? Still early days on, but I figure me to be cinch certainty for *ichiban* straight-A grades, blowing roof off all tests and pop-quiz scores to date, have it from, how we say, horsie's mouth Professor Os Southard, main mentor and also frosh comp instructor as how I is best essay author—notwithstanding minor problems in *Eigo* idiomatics—Prof Os says Gooch is best student he is seen in coon's age, meaning of which is indeterminate long duration, reet?"

"Excellent, Gooch! Yes, I shall call you Gooch! It shall be my personal amusement when we converse, our own small humor."

"Reet, ironies," I say, and, "Social whirl hereabouts promises equivalent promise of great successes in offing also. I is already, how we say, buddy-buddy best pal friend of assigned roomie Stevie Keller, also knowed as both Yukon Strongboy and Mighty Mouse, fellow frosh matriculant and renowned grappler at 116-lbs. avoirdupois weight class, than which who you'll doubtless get to gander come 'forty Olympiad scheduled now for Tokyo Town, reet?"

"The confidence of this *Amerikajin* student is deemed important by you for the success of our design, Gooch?"

"Reet! Strongboy Stevie is already A and M *honcho*, how we say, Big

Man on Campus—irony of which, in passing, is as how he is sole fellow frosh male matriculant small as me, reet? You don't get it?" I query when Mr. Sato don't show *sumairu* smile of amusement. "I guess you gots to dig *Eigo* slangs to twig humors therein, reet? Anyhoo, Mighty Mouse Stevie is done pledged to use his personal clout influences to get me rushed and pledged by same frat eager to enroll him, Delta Sigma Kappa, campus jockstrappers—"

"This is a secret society?"

"Sort of," I tell him. "Than which will doubtless open door of social acceptance welcomes opportunity for yours truly, Gooch, enable me to move in best circles, observe and gather such info as you deems of use in intelligence observation shtick scam."

"Admirable!" says Mr. Sato, hisses loud breath intake.

"Not to fail to mention I is in process of developing Platonic-style *enryo* friendship with co-ed fellow frosh Miss Clara Sterk, also knowed as Petty Girl, already, not unlike like unto Stevie, renowned on campus—in her case for pulchritudes. How we say, real looker, reet?"

"Ah!" exclaims Mr. Sato, snickers. "But do you not, Gooch, find the *Amerikajin* females revolting in appearance, their characteristic scent disgusting to one's olfactory sense?"

"You gets used to it," I tell him. "Noses, how we say, beak, honker, schnozzola, don't look so big after a while, and usual stink smell of raw meat is masked among refined types by applications of heady perfumes, musks, lotions, toilet waters."

"But they are so tall! I personally experience no erotic response to females who tower above me in stature, and they are shameless, exposing the napes of their necks to entice male attention, are they not, Gooch?"

"Cultural-relativities shtick," I tell him. "Yanks admire bosoms, some is leg men. Each to his own, reet? No accounting for tastes, as in *Amerikajin* anecdote concerning widow woman who kisses porcine. You don't get it?"

"Enough triviality, Gooch," says Sato Isao. "It is clear that you have done well, and prospects for ultimate success appear excellent! Now pay close attention to the instructions I shall give you."

"All auricular orifices, how we say in *Eigo*, little pitchers endowed with same, reet?" Mr. Sato don't get it, Jack. And proceeds to convey particulars of espionage assignment assigned me, Gooch. As follows:

"In addition to maintaining a general surveillance of local political developments—"

"Honorable E. P. Walkiewicz, staunch Republican incumbent mayor of Stillwater Town, do assure me Alf Landon is cinch certain to topple socialist Roosevelt come November."

"Please do not interrupt! In addition to your general surveillance of political activity locally, make it your custom to read the local *shimbun* editorials daily. For example there are two areas of interest to me and my superiors of the *kempei* we would have you scrutinize closely."

"Reet," and, "Than which is?" I say.

"First, make it your duty to be cognizant of developments in the activity of the Reserve Officer Training Corps, the paramilitary student organization on the campus of this pathetic excuse for an institution of learning —"

"Reet! R.O.T.C., also knowed as rot-cee, A & M student doughboys, perform basic marching drills on campus greensward, practice saluting and other military courtesies, hold class on small-group infantry tactics, wear uniforms emanating from circa Great War era, conduct ceremonial raise and also lowering of flag to bugle-call accompaniment — strictly for laughs outfit org, Jack! They don't even gots real weaponry to train on, employing dummy wooden rifles, reet?"

"You interrupt me once more, Gooch!"

"Orry-say," I say, "but what's interest of *kempei* in R.O.T.C.? I mean, like, rot-cee, no can compare with *budo*-type studies all little nippers back home in *Dai Nippon* is prescribed since *wataschi* was kiddie. Rot-cee, Mr. Sato, only reason matriculants of A & M elect same is to draw down stipend to finance educational endeavors in light of dearth of *genkin* cash in current economics depression crunch, reet?"

Mr. Sato Isao (clandestine *kempei* counterintelligence operative operating in mufti guise as roving U. S. of A. field rep of phony-baloney Japan–America Friendship Society, beneath leaf-barren branch of blackjack oak, shelter of cottonwood grove, bank of Cimarron River, environ of rural hick stick boonies hamlet village of Perkins, Oklahoma, north wind carrying Dust Bowl dust in moonlit late-eventide air) smiles indulgent *sumairu*, says: "Gooch, you are but a tender youth aged a mere eighteen years, is this not so? Just so. It is unlikely you shall appreciate the intricate complications of political and military intrigue, Gooch. You believe the *Amerikajin* Reserve Officers Training Corps to be no more than it appears, a gathering of foolish *baka* students who assemble to play a game of soldiering —"

I interject: "I gots it straight from horsie's mouth in personage of assigned roomie buddy pal Stevie Keller, than which who desires to become member of aforesaid rot-cee, and I seen them drilling out of step, don't know lefts from right. I seen dummy wooden rifles, done smelled them old Great War uniforms from mothball storage — Jack, I could take me a platoon of little nippers out of *budo* studies in *Aikyojuko*, run rot-cee off campus with but one big *banzai* assault —"

"Again you interrupt me, Gooch! You are no doubt correct in your estimation of the current state of their military readiness. But it is the task of the *kempei* — of you and me and our superiors, even unto our great leaders headquartered back in *Dai Nippon* at Ichigaya Heights, Gooch — to be ever alert to any alteration in this condition. Am I lucid, Gooch?" he queries.

"You is," I say, "but I still say A & M rot-cee is to but laugh, hardy har and hee hee, reet?"

"And did you not, Gooch, think Mr. Morris Berg was but a superannuated player of the *besuboru?*"

"Reet. Okay. You gots me there. Orry-say."

"Just so. You will, then, observe the activities of the Reserve Officer Training Corps. Inform yourself, through your friendship with this Stevie Keller personage, for example, of ongoing developments, and you will report these developments to me, with full particulars, in such manner and with such frequency as I shall hereafter prescribe. Do you understand me, Gooch?"

"Reet. We is attained to *keiyaku* agreement."

"Further, you will learn all you are able of a new organization, inaugurated only this year on the campus of this wretched mistake of an institution of higher studies, this Oklahoma Agricultural & Mechanical College, which organization is devoted to the study and practice of aviation."

"You talking Flying Aggies," I say. "I read announcement inviting interest in A & M campus *shimbun, Daily O'Collegian.*"

"Just so."

"They gots but one old rickety Great War vintage biplane, Spad, reet? Purchased as obsolete from U. S. of A. Army Air Corps, strictly recreational club activity, Jack, not unlike like unto Debate Club, Glee songsters, Block and Bridle horsie riders, reet?" Mr. Sato Isao renders big hiss breath intake of breath, smiles big *sumairu.*

"We believe," says he, "the *Amerikajin* now commence, under the leadership of the plutocrat Roosevelt, to prepare for armed conflict in opposition to our beloved *Dai Nippon.* We believe, I and my superiors in the *kempei,* that the barbarian *Amerikajin* will eventually combine with the hated colonialist English and French to thwart the inevitable expansion of our Greater East Asia Co-Prosperity Sphere. We believe it is all but a certainty that the grand design of *hakko ichui* will bring us one day to face the armed forces of the *Amerikajin* somewhere in the Pacific."

"You gots to be kidding!" I say, "I mean, we fighting the Chinks, long-term-struggle shtick, mighty Kwantung Army bogged down in north China vastness, reet? Okay, so maybe might could be we press on southwards, bump up against Hong Kong, French Indo-China, even India, Asia for Asians shtick. But where we going to confront U. S. of A. interests, Jack?"

"Gooch," says he, "you are a young man, and yet you have studied the geography of the world, have you not? What of the Philippine Islands? What of Guam, Gooch? What of the islands of Hawaii? What of the Aleutian Islands? Your thinking is clouded by your long study of the crude *Eigo* language, I fear, your reason muddied as this stagnant river at our feet by your viewing of corrupting *eiga,* your intellect further stunted now by your immersion in their decadent culture here in this desolate place called

Oklahoma. Do not presume, Gooch, to an understanding of things beyond your tender wisdom. Resolve only to do as you are instructed!"

"Reet. I going to give it my best shot, Mr. Sato."

"Just so," says he, and, "And by so doing, you may rest assured that your minuscule effort will contribute to the triumph of our beloved *Dai Nippon*, and in this you shall have earned honor for your name and family, and shall prove a loyal subject to our sacred *Mikado*!"

Dig this, Jack! There, circa mid-September 1936 (onset of *tsukimi*, reet?), under leaf-barren branches of blackjack oak, sheltered from dust-laden north wind by clump of cottonwoods, rural environ of hamlet village of Perkins, Oklahoma. We stand in darkness (moon sole source of illuminations, Dust Bowl dust gumming baby blues, gritting in toothies), execute slow and protracted kowtow of reverent subservience in direction of westward — site of far-off sacred Chrysanthemum Throne of Sun Goddess *Ameratasu's* direct descendant, reet?

Kowtowing, I did think: say it ain't not so! Say it ain't so I done devoted long hours of midnight oils study to grammars, syntax, vocabulary of *Eigo* lingo, drill pronunciations at my *papa-san's* knee! Say it ain't so I is done glommed all spare *yen* to pay for ducats to view stateside *harukai* import *eiga* flics, hustling *chogee* across Tokyo Town to Asakusa District, picking up on idiomatics and also slangs, reet? I is thinking: Moe, say it ain't so! Say it were not as how you was *Amerikajin* espionage operative in guise facade of Yank American League all-star *besuboru* barnstorm squad member, circa '35! Thinking, Jack: Mr. Sato, say it ain't so as how you is *kempei* clandestine counterintelligence operative in mufti guises of Imperial Ministry of Education factotum, now reappeared here (Oklahoma!) in persona personage of phony-baloney Japan–America Friendship Society liaison roving field rep!

I think: Student Yamaguchi Yoshinori, say it ain't so! Gooch (A & M matriculant in good standing, class of 1940!), say it ain't so!

Fact, Jack: it is so, reet?

Big ironies. Than which is to say, way the mop flop, cookies crumbles, course of *do* flow, reet? Than which is to say: unfortunate paradigm of events snares individual (me, Jack!) in nexus of historical events unfolding, reet?

"I suggest to you," says Mr. Sato Isao, "that such intelligence as you obtain be committed to memory. This will, in most instances, suffice, for has not your education in the excellent schools of *Dai Nippon* magnificently prepared you to memorize significant facts?"

"Reet. One thing I do good is memory rote learning and recitation shtick."

"In the event that you suspect your memory will prove unreliable, should the information be of such volume and complexity as to lead you to doubt your ability to retain it, you may write memoranda—always, of course, in *Nihonju*, which will ensure their security against any scrutiny by the *Amerikajin* who presume you their comrade, for what ignorant *Amerikajin* dolt will know how to read our graceful *kanji*?"

"Zip. Zilch. Squat. None," I say.

"And then you have only to await my periodic summons. Gooch—ah, it does amuse me, this name we designate as your *kempei* identity!—Gooch, you need only await my summons, and thereafter convey all particulars to me at our scheduled rendezvous. Would you put any last queries to me before we part now, Gooch?"

I say: "One thing. Does my daddy Mr. Yamaguchi know what all I'm doing for the *kempei* here in Okie-land?"

"Your father," says Mr. Sato Isao, "is ignorant of particulars. I think it likely he entertains at least a general and superficial understanding of our relationship, Gooch. This is unavoidable. Your father," says he, "is not deemed entirely reliable with regard to his *bushi* patriotic sentiments. Perhaps, like you, Gooch, his loyalty and love of country have been tainted by his lifelong association with things western, a result of his intimate knowlege of the *Eigo* language? The *kempei* is aware of the inquiries he has made to learn what he can of who I am. No matter. I only enjoin you not to share your activities on behalf of the *kempei* with him or any other member of your family, Gooch."

"Duly noted."

"Have you additional queries?"

"Nope."

"Then I take my leave of you, Gooch. Return to your life as a student at this absurd imitation of a place of education, this Oklahoma Agricultural and Mechanical College, and take joy in your *hara* belly that you serve *Dai Nippon* as one of the many who are here in the midst of the despicable *gaijin* barbarians as the eyes and ears of our empire!"

"Reet," I say, and, "See you," and, "So long," and "Dig you later, reet, Jack?"

"Ah!" says Mr. Sato, "I have almost forgotten!" He reaches inside his coat, extracts fat unmarked envelope, hands same to me, reet?

"What's this?"

"Money," he says, "*genkin. Amerikajin* currency in an amount ample to generously support your subsistence. Expend it at your discretion." I feel thick pad of bills, greenbacks, lucre, kale, cabbage, moolah, betwixt my fingers, hear crispy crackle of banknotes, bucks, the necessary ready, dough, reet?

"Anks-thay," I say, and, "Where you off to now, Jack?" Mr. Sato smiles large *sumairu* in moonlight, reet?

"I journey eastward. I go to visit with your counterparts matriculating at the venerable institutions known as the Ivy League. We are many, Gooch, but our patriotic resolve and our discipline make us one! *Banzai!*" cries out Mr. Sato Isao to black vastness of Okie-land sky. A dog barks far off, howls, barks, is silent.

"Onward and upward, go with *do* flow, reet?" I say, turn back, stroll *sanpo* shank's mare toward Stillwater Town (county of Payne, sovereign state of Oklahoma, circa 1936 *tsukimi!*).

I kid you not, Jack! How it were, mid-September '36, reet? Gooch. *Wataschi. Kempei* counterintelligence clandestine espionage operative operating in guise as Gooch, frosh matriculant in good standing, Oklahoma A & M, class of 1940, reet? Assigned spy mission shtick, R.O.T.C., fledgling Flying Aggies aviation sport club. Irony of which is I is instructed to rely on memories — me, Gooch, memory-trained — I do work strictly from recall, reet, Jack?

Oh, say it were not so!

Fact, Jack: it were so.

Jump cut:

A & M Campus
Stillwater Town
County of Payne
Sovereign State of Oklahoma
U. S. of A.
24 December 1937

Dear Folks:

I your son (and big bro, Sis!) greet you there in far-off *Dai Nippon* from here in distant Okie-land — *Nihonjin*-style, reet?

As how: as small cold moon of harsh *fuyu* winter season casts frigid beam down upon frozen snow crust currently covering Okie vista vastness, bitter wind out of northerly orientation (Kansas plains, reet?) knifes through A & M campus, Old Central clock tower bongs ten plus one times as signal of approach to midnight, I take up Nr. 2 Ticonderoga yellow pencil, apply same to pulpy page of Big Chief tablet, commence near year's end (eve of *Kurisumasu* Yule, reet?) this my epistle home to you-all, reet?

How we say, Yank-style: Hello *Papa-san*, Hello *Mama-san*, Hello Sis *Iko-san*!

How do things shake in Land of Rising Sun? Been a whiles since you put brush to rice paper to write me, Daddy! Hope and trust nix amiss? Doubtless you is busy preoccupied with pressures of *Japan Times* toils responsibilities (like to peruse your editorials, Daddy, but A & M library don't gots subscription to foreign *shimbun* due to stringent budgets resultant of economics crunch cutbacks of Depression syndrome, reet?) How goes fervent ferment of politics of *Dai Nippon*, Daddy? Doubtless you continue compelled to echo *hakko ichui* guff stuff? We gets only vaguest of vagaries reported in local *News-Mess* (joke: har!), to include

126

so-called Rape of Nanking at hands of 7th Division of Kwantung Army, reet? Big flap *shimbun* coverage here, natch. Sad to say *Amerikajin* sympathies is 100 per cents empathetic with Chinks.

To which I say: whatever, reet?

As how Gooch (yours truly!) is done come to profound conclusion via profundity of introspections, reet? I decide: world is very strange place, Daddy! Constant unceasing flaps of politico-economy-militarist shtick, reet? Kwantung Army, upon pretext afforded by incident at Marco Polo Bridge, doubtless stimulated (if not instigated?) by extreme *joi-i Yamato Damashii* chauvinism rampant amongst Hundred Millions, presses Chinks, outrages global-wide sensibilities via such as Nanking debacle. In Old World Europe, Shicklgruber, Mussolini, Limeys, Frogs, Russkies all steady in flaps turmoils over Rhineland, Saar, Alsace–Lorraine, Ethiopia, Moscow Trials, etcetera blah blah blah. Stateside, Yanks expend energies in frustration of Depression, rage versus socialist FDR government outrages in Washington (D.C.), labor-union strifes in Detroit City factories (Mr. H. Ford engages in lockout tactics, blue collars respond with sit-ins!), etcetera etcetera blah blah!

What's right-thinking reasonable sane personage to do and also think, Daddy?

Riposte: ignore such, reet?

Can you dig it, folks? Justification reason rationale therefore: life too short to bother self to distracted distraction with spheres of public flaps, reet? Say I: a man gots to tend to his knitting, hoe own row, get on with it, perform necessaries, make life for self amidst *do* flow despite flaps rampant as reported in *shimbun* all round about, reet?

What I mean to say, folks: your son Gooch (also still Yamaguchi Yoshinori, natch!) is done now enjoyed full nine plus ten years of life and times, than which period of temporal duration has enabled aforesaid Gooch to see something of eight corners of world, reet? Done seen it is in constant continual unceasing flap of politics etcetera blah! Gooch know life contains great promises of satisfactions, as in dignity of name and ancestral lineage (*kami*, reet?), filial love engendered (also familial!) by security of family circle (you, Daddy, and also Mama and Iko!), higher order of serious endeavor worthy of life's totality of efforts (*Eigo* lingo!), minimalist joys of spare-times hobby (*eiga* flics!) — which is not to fail to mention particulars of personages and experiences confronted through vagaries of events, than which refers (natch!) to oddness opportunity of stateside U. S. of A. sojourn (Okie-land!), than which is enriching source of life's richness, same creating storehouse memories to enjoy in dotage years inevitable when geriatrics facts reduce scope and tone of active activities, reet?

Life and times, seen big-picture style, flap mess hassles, reet? Seen close-up (as in *eiga* flic frame!), life is, how we say in *Dai Nippon, Eija Nai Kai* — ain't it good! In short and sum, aged now fully nineteen years old, I wax philosophical, concluding: I is a happy man, folks, and do intend to continue so as such, reet?

On local-yokel scene, revered mentors of A & M faculty currently reduced to receiving remunerations in form of scrip coupons specie good only with local merchants (in lieu of shortaged greenbacks, reet?), also including commodity handout rations: peanut butter, lard, hard cheeses, soy flour, etcetera blah. Says Gooch's main mentor Prof Os Southard, if situation pejorates, he will be compelled to seek enrollment on rolls of Civilian Conservation Corps now employed on campus — I think to comfort him with advice to emigrate to *Dai Nippon*, excepting, how you tell me, Daddy, teaching of *Eigo* also in serious decline there, reet? Sorry sad on behalf of Prof Os (natch!), but do Gooch really care?

A & M administration, in personages of Prexy Paul Klemp and diminutive Dean Timmy J. Macklin, announces new program permitting stony-flat-brokes students to matriculate on credit, deferring tuitions to be repaid in future, when, as Dean Tim says, things gots to look up as how they can't get no worse, reet?

Gooch? I does not really care, as how I am, through newfound total life philosophy (aforementioned) enabled to view even loss of Okie topsoils to Dust Bowl winds as minor hassle (grits in pearlie whites, particles itch under eyelids, red dust collecting in aural orifices, reet?). I do confess to minimalist guilt twinges, as how — as you well know, Daddy! — I am never short of *genkin cash*, due to support from Japan–America Friendship Society (Mr. S. I., reet?). Bills in plain envelopes continue conferred on regularly scheduled visits to rural Perkins environ, reet? Than which ready necessary lucre moolah enables me to live high atop swine (money for cafeteria meal tickets, *eiga* flic ducats, attire and assorted necessaries and luxuriants, reet?) So it go, flow of *do*, Daddy!

And if not concerned for flaps public and communal, what then, folks?

Personals, *Papa-san*! Than which I summarize in gist and pith below:

First, Gooch (*wataschi*!) now established as personage of scholarly renown on A & M campus, folks! What I mean, grades straight-A in all subjects undertaken to date, reet? Main mentor Prof Os Southard confides I am likely prospect candidate — providing I do maintain excellence performance tradition throughout — for valedictory distinction of class of 1940, reet? Only *minken* competish for same kudo is personage of Miss Clara (a.k.a. Petty Girl) Sterk, than which who happens also to be close friend (fellow *Eigo* major, reet?), and appears also to be *koibito* romantic sweetheart type mutual interest of Gooch's *oyabun* best friend buddy pal Stevie Keller (a.k.a. Yukon Strongboy, a.k.a. Mighty Mouse), about which duesome (threesome, counting Gooch!) I relate more hereinafter.

Note: exceptional scholarly efforts and achievement might could be source of social stigmata here on A & M campus, folks, than which odium I evade via active participations in wide range array of org memberships, reet?

Example: sport life.

Facile mode of measure for passage of time, year by year, I learn, is seasonal recreations, intercollegiate style, reet? As follows:

Fall semester begins football, weekly schedule of contests versus various neighbor institutions. As how, season opener pits A & M Aggie Cowboy Puncher Pokes against Central State Teachers College (easy warm-up win!), followed weekly on successive Saturday venues at home and away in contention with such as Drake, Washington U. (Missouri Show-Me State!), U. Washburn (Kansas), Kansas Aggies, Baylor of Lone Star State Texas, culminating in yearly doomed effort to defeat hated arch-rival downstate Sooners of O.U. How we say, Big Game, reet?

Matsuri festive event staged at revamped Lewis Field, same preceded by big bonfire pep and spirit rallies — featuring Gooch! — hopes at high crest for '36 meeting due to new game strategies of double wingback offense as devised to dethrone hated Sooners, reet? A & M boasts advent of prime-rated gridiron newcomers (fellow class of '40 members!), Loving bros, Carl and Wayne, reet?

Big *matsuri* doings, Daddy! Entire A & M student body (natch!) on hand to follow cheers led by (you guessed it!) Gooch! To include notables: Honorable Governor Alfalfa Bill Murray (wildcatter, tycoon-type, Daddy, *Amerikajin zaibatsu*, than which who misfortunately lost fortune in Black Monday stock crash of circa '29, hence doffed headgear into Okie-land politics ring to recoup assets, hails from Ponca City, forty miles northward — than which is also home of Miss Clara ("Petty Girl") Sterk, about which whom more later, reet?); A & M Prexy Paul Klemp (seated on governor's left hand, fifty-yard line, natch!), looking utmost presidential in snappy fedora concealing hair parted in middle, vest and watch chain, wire rim specs; Honorable Mayor E. P. Walkiewicz (seated on governor's right, as how U. S. of A. politicos precede academics in status strata, reet?); diminutive Dean Timmy J. Macklin (seated behind guv, hence not visible from gridiron sidelines as how Governor Murray is large man — typical *Amerikajin* size, Daddy! — hence concealing diminutive Dean Tim — I wonders, do Dean Timmy have any view of game thus blocked?); around which, not unlike like unto celestial satellites drawn to major-density planetary body, is seated A & M faculty (admitted to Lewis Field on complimentary freebie ducats, as how Depression economics — faculty salaries reduced last three years running, Daddy! — precludes purchase of admission by revered mentors, reet?), to include also town, county, and other state notables (Chamber of Commerce, Rotary, Kiwanis, Woodmen, Odd Fellows, etcetera blah) on hand.

Can you dig it, Daddy? Day is briskish (close to *tsukimi* season!), light breeze out of north too gentle to affect flight of pigskin bladder, Okie sun burns bright — cloudless (no sign of break in Dust Bowl drouth, natch) blue-white sky vastness. A & M Spirit Band whips up crowd spirits via spirited renditions of "Ride 'Em, Cowboys" fight song, whilst among spectators circulate vendors of Coca-Cola, RC and Moxie nonalcoholic bottled libations, also exploded corns and groundnuts available for ingestion.

Ceremonials: opposing squads do face-to-face shtick on fifty-yard line, exchange howdy handshakes to signify sportsmanship intent (like unto kowtow greetings, reet?), stand back with hands over heart organs (all rise!) for rendition of *Amerikajin* national anthem as Stars and Stripes is raised on end-zone flagpole — said flag-elevation performed by Pershing Rifles (R.O.T.C.) honor guard under command of Sergeant-Major Tommy Turner, about whom and which more later.

Gooch: I stand straight in politeness deference posture to *Amerikajin* patriotism shtick (natch), feel strains of solemn musics vibrations like unto electrical tinglings in innermost bones—I confess, Daddy, I imagine musics to be *Kimagayo*, close baby blues tight shut to think upon you-all, of *Dai Nippon*, even envision *Mikado* (hee, reet?) on Chrysanthemum Throne. Tug of homesickness brings all but tears to Gooch's baby blues. Might could be sentimental sloppy *ma* moment of non-*Nipponshikki* sadness, reet? Except anthem concludes, Spirit Band breaks out with "Ride 'Em, Cowboys," opposing teams (clad in helmets and padded like unto ancient *samurai* armors) line up for kick-off commencement of contest—time for Gooch to spring into actions, folks!

Dig it, Daddy! Fifty-yard line marker, A & M sidelines bench (close by scrubs, coaching staff), it is your son, *wataschi*! It is Gooch than which who leaps into active activity to lead cheers! You would be proud, I dare to speculate, *Papa-san*, to see me so, center of event, focus of collectivist crowd attentions!

I grasp black-on-orange A & M gonfalon, reet? Stand before bleachers, wave banner, lead a thousand throats in time-honored cheers (like unto *banzai* chorus, reet?), run to and also fro, leap and otherwise cavort—I lead schtick for campus cheer orgs (Hell Hounds, Ag-He-Ruf-Nex, Peppers—co-ed, captain of which is Clara "Petty Girl" Sterk, reet?), twirl A & M banner!

We do "O.A.M.C." anthem, the Prexy's Yell, a locomotive for the team, a personal for coach, personals for vaunted Loving bros Carl and Wayne, do Ride 'Em, Cowboys, Go, Pokes, Go, Aggies, Go, Punchers! On gridiron turf, I hear smack of pad on helmet, referee's whistle, grunt and groan of contestants not unlike like unto *sumo* wrestlers locked in test of strengths and balances, reet? Before and above me in bleachers seating I lead a thousand throats in *banzai*-type cheers, see A & M flags wave in response to my gonfalon, view fanatic fans clad in orange and black beanies (totems of symbolist support of team, reet?), clang of odd cowbell as A & M struggles downfield in quest of end-zone score!

Can you dig it, folks? Oh, happy happiest of happy am I thus so! Happy, happy Gooch!

Than which is not to fail to mention aftermaths bittersweetness resultant from loss (24–14) to hated Sooners, reet? Sad to say, Loving bros Carl and Wayne, to include new double wingback offense, avail not, even to no avail is thousand throats hoarse with cheering (led by Gooch!). How we say here in Aggie-land, folks, wait till next year, reet?

End of (natch) disappointing football season brings advent of round-ball and grappling, reet? Than which means change in A & M fortunes from gridiron mediocrity (Pokes finish 4 and 4, reet?) to excellences of hardwood and mat!

Former is manifest in Missouri Valley Conference cage crown bestowed upon Aggie squad, led by already-legendary coach Iron Duke Hank Iba, reet? Oh, we is formidable on hardwood, Daddy! Squad is led by vaunted probable All-American choice sharpshooter guard Jesse Cobb McCartney, F.B.I. (full-blood Amerind), recruited to A & M from Otoe-Missouria tribal rolls, only matriculant on campus with dermis of hue duskier than Gooch's, reet? Puncher Pokes finish '36–'37 season at 16 triumphs, but 3 debacle defeats, take Missouri Valley laurel as aforementioned, reach semifinals of N.I.A. tourney only to be thwarted in overtime loss to New York Gotham U. contingent enjoying advantage of playing in amenable confine of Madison Square Garden, reet?

Roundball season: busy time for Gooch, folks! In addition to midnight oils burned incessant to maintain scholastic averages, I is also waterboy factotum for b-ball quintet, reet? Meaning: sit close to Iron Duke Mr. Iba, in company of benchwarmer scrubs, keep towel and water jug at ready for time-outs, at which times I caper onto hardwood, pass towel around, dispense refreshing sips from jug, add exhortations towards victory to Mr. Iba's instructions as to how to work stall-game strategies resulting in easy lay-up hoops, reet?

Which is also to mention as how I is also mascot of stupendous (undefeated!) wrestling squad. At mat-side for all matches, pounding floor with flat of hand as ref counts out pin-fall effected (without fail!) by Mighty Mouse Yukon Strongboy best friend buddy pal Stevie Keller, 116-lbs.-avoirdupois sensation—Miss Clara Sterk (member of Mat Maids cheer section, subgroup of Peppers, reet?) at my side to share delight in Stevie's inevitable win, reet?

Long story truncated to pith and gist, folks, Poke matmen grapplers are (natch) Missouri Valley and also N.C.A.A. champs, perfect record unblemished in dual, triangular, and also quadrangular meets—hated downstate rival O.U. Sooners devastated by 48–3 laugher score, Poke Punchers led by legendary mentor E. C. Gallagher—I assure Strongboy Stevie as how Hundred Millions going to love him come circa '40 Olympiad in Tokyo Town (*koki nisenroppyakunen Orimpikku*), reet?

Do. Can you not dig it?

So thusly do flow *do* of life and times here, folks. First calendar year (plus) of A & M matriculation—to present moment wherein I sit alone in otherwise empty Delta Sigma Kappa frat house, eve of *Kurisumasu* Christmas 1937. Time-space measured best by seasonals sport (mediocre football, ever-improving roundball, eternally outstanding wrestling—*besuboru*, sad to say, is but intramural amusement here—and I think only seldom from Morris "Moe" Berg!). Historical flaps globalwide flap me not, Daddy. Due to *do* concept of life's philosophy for conduct of life and times, reet? Happy Gooch!

What's else? Hour creeps late, Daddy, clock in Old Central tower soon to emit dozen bongs, midnight, advent of *Kurisumasu* Yuletide. Only small hard *fuyu* winter moon casting cold light on frozen thin snowcrusted campus expanse, shriek of Blue Norther wind wails at windows of deserted Kappa House I alone occupy in solitary caretaker-status solitude, reet? What's else to say?

In passing, Daddy, know I prosper material- and financial-wise via greenback dollar funds support provided by Mr. S. I., field rep of Japan–America Friendship Society (har!), said remuneration transmitted at periodic rendezvous in appointed locale (banks of Cimarron River, environ of rural hamlet village of Perkins)—need I say more? Hint:

Of late I note recently expanded (from two battalions to four, reet?) R.O.T.C. org commanded by Sergeant-Major Tommy Turner (Great War vet, U.S. Army Retired, reet?), and also mention *sanpo* strolls I take outside Stillwater Town to new airport constructed by Civie Conservation Corps to view ground-school activities of Flying Aggies Aviation Club (sole Spad aircraft not yet certified airworthy, reet?). All this above mentioned, source of possible shames, reet, Daddy? I need say no more! Yet I do not despair!

Ancient old-timey Yank custom, folks: on turn of old year to new (*o-shogatsu* upcoming soon!), *Amerikajin* all pledge vows of endeavor for year to come, than which is noble signification of intent to attain to personal moral amelioration of aforesaid pledge, reet? Me (*wataschi*, your son, Yamaguchi Yoshinori, knowed now and here as Gooch!), I follow suit as follows:

I vow to continue to burn midnight oils, excel in excellence of all scholastic tasks, vie even to defeat sole *minken* academic competish Miss Clara Sterk, win ultimate valedictory laurel to be dispensed upon graduation come circa 1940!

I vow to cultivate ever-closer and more profound camaraderie with all fellow A & M matriculants (to include co-eds, observing decorums, natch!), especially Delta Sigma Kappa bros, not failing to mention special friends Stevie Keller and Clara Sterk!

I vow to persist in lifelong-to-date efforts toward total mastery of *Eigo* lingo (including idioms, slangs, Okie regionalisms), to include regular attendance at screenings of all *eiga* flics booked at Aggie and Mecca theaters, than which viewing serves in aid of aforesaid!

I vow to not flap in response to flaps global and/or localist!

I vow to fulfill contracted responsibilities encumbered by Japan–America Friendship Society (ironical har!) grant-scholarship support (need I say more?), executing same so as to avoid potential taints of shames or embarrassment — which is to say, Gooch going to do what he gots to, merit honor-and-glory shtick despite all!

I do vow to be happy (Happy Gooch!) in pursuit of life's direction dictated by new-found *do*!

Must be more I could pledge, folks, but I hear Old Central clock ringing in Yule *Kurisumasu*, fingers cramped on shaft of Nr. 2 Ticonderoga nub, buff pulpy page of Big Chief tablet blurs words, back sore, baby blues a-burn from lamplight, reet?

And so I close (*Nihonjin*-style, reet?) this my year's-end (circa 1937!) epistle, Daddy.

As small hard moon of *fuyu* midwinter casts cold light down from Okie sky vastness, revealing thin frozen crust of snow (will melt-off ease Dust-Bowl drouth come spring?), Old Central clock tower clangs turn of *Kurisumasu* Yule, accompanied by shriek of eternal north wind howling southward through A & M campus, here in Stillwater Town (county of Payne, sovereign state of Oklahoma), so far from you, where I, your sole son, affix my *hanko* signature Yank-style to this missive, thusly:

Gooch (a.k.a. Yamaguchi Yoshinori!)

Happy Gooch, reet, Jack? Can you dig it? Circa 1936 to '40. How it were, Jack!

132

How we say, *mise-en-scene*:

World-wide globalist flaps continue (natch!) to flap, reet? In Europe, Schicklgruber foments agitations, *Anschluss* shtick with Austria, Munich Pact, etcetera blah—peace in our time (hardy har and also hee!), reet? Mussolini (a.k.a. *Duce*) tests napalm versus swarthy Ethiops, civil strife rages in Iberia, etcetera blah. Edward abdicates throne to marry paramour (Mrs. Simpson, reet?), succeeded by younger bro Georgie; *Hindenburg* blimp burns at Lakehurst (sovereign state of New Jersey!), Mid-Continent Petroleum Refinery (Tulsa Town) experiences labor strike brouhaha, etcetera blah blah!

Daily Oklahoman and *O'Collegian shimbun* pay scant attentions to events of Far East, than which I follow via my daddy's epistles (handed to me from aged and trembling liver-spotted hand of Miss Samantha Woods, venerable A & M campus postmistress, reet?)—than which Asian environ flaps include unbroken string of glorious victories of Imperial Kwantung Army versus Chinks, Showa Restoration coup failure in Tokyo, Anti-Cominterm Pact signed by Schicklgruber and *Dai Nippon* (circa '37), Prince Konoye becomes premier of *Dai Nippon* in last feeble effort to control *gumbatsu* militarist chauvinist politico factions provoking Hundred Millions, etcetera blah!

In sum and short pith and gist: global world-wide flaps continue (natch!) to flap, Jack!

What's do *wataschi* care! Dig: I, Gooch, matriculant in good standing of Oklahoma Agricultural & Mechanical College, Class of 1940, is Happy Gooch, reet? Promising candidate for valedictory honors laurel, loyal bro of Delta Sigma Kappa jockstrapper frat, budding B.M.O.C. via membership in Hell Hounds and also Ag-He-Ruf-Nex cheering spirit orgs, mascot of N.C.A.A. champs (natch!) Aggie grappler squad, best buddy bosom pal of 116-lbs.-avoirdupois wrestling phenom Stevie Keller (Mighty Mouse, Yukon Strongboy!), Platonic-style confidant of A & M campus beauty (also sole academic *minken* competish!) Miss Clara ("Petty Girl") Sterk—what's do I need for caring for flaps, Jack?

Reet—not to fail to mention as how Gooch is also clandestine subrosa *kempei* secret police counterintelligence operative, than which for I receive generous dollar greenbacks support via phony-baloney sponsorship of Japan–America Friendship Society, said funds transmitted at periodic Cimarron River (rural Perkins village environ!) rendezvous by Mr. Sato Isao, society field rep (har!), reet?

Do I sweat it? *Daijubo*, Jack! Never *hochee*! As how I, Gooch, is found, how you say, equilibrium of balanced existence—*yoin, dantai, ma, do*, reet? Circa '36 to '40, Jack, I am but Happy Gooch, and flap no flaps for flaps global or localist!

Dig:

A & M campus (Town of Stillwater, county of Payne, sovereign state of Oklahoma), end-of-semester wind-down, time of approaching *shiken ji-goku*, final examinations hellishness, reet?

Than which is extended *ma* period of severe stresses for Kappa House jockstrappers, anxious to maintain athletic eligibilities, reet? Hence it is time wherein I, Gooch, come to fore in ranks of ever-loyal frat bros. Due (natch) to rep I establish and maintain (via midnight-oils labors) of Quiz Kid scholastic invincibility. Dig:

Cut to: Kappa House (ever-loyal bro we, reet?), fast breaker table, new day in offing, life and times of *wataschi* Gooch Yamaguchi, Joe College-type, circa April '38 (*hanami*).

Ever-loyal bros assemble in dining room to partake in camaraderie concert of day's initial repast, served up on heaped platters by motherly matron-type cook (Mrs. Erna Haas—widow of recently deceased math mentor Prof Adolph Haas—position sinecure of Kappa Housemother-Cook bestowed by benevolent A & M administration in lieu of husband's death benefit, than which *genkin* funds reside in limbo due to retrenchment Depression's economics), to wit: slippery-fried (in butter) fried eggs (over easy, Jack!), thick bacon slab rashers, scratch biscuits awash in viscous white gravies, choice (milk or acid-black coffee) of beverage—long table exudes heady aromas of eggs and rashers, steam cloud arises from biscuits inundated by gravies, aforesaid stimulating night-engendered appetites of hearty growing jockstrapper lads gathered, reet?

"Chow down!" shouts footballer Carl Loving.

"Lemme at it!" says roundball letterman Ned Whitcomb.

"Son, I could eat me the ass end out of a damn skunk!" says 189-lbs.-avoirdupois grappler Gary Lee Stringer (also, natch, N.C.A.A. champ and '40 Tokyo Olympiad hopeful).

"Watch the boardinghouse reach, jag-off!" says best bosom pal Stevie Keller as Gary Lee jostles Stevie in exuberance of quest for nearest basket of scratch biscuits, adding, "Ain't you forgetting something, Stringer?" and, "Come on, Wayne, do it so's we can scarf and get it to hell done with, okay?"

Clatter of plates and utensils, scrape of chairs (I, Gooch, slip into seat beside Stevie) cease as gridiron great Wayne Loving, Kappa House student-chaplain, stands at head of table to pronounce mandatory benediction over waiting repast.

"In Jesus name," says Wayne, folding huge hands in prayer, head bowed, "we ask Thee, Father, to bless us all and ever' one, and bless these vittles to the nourishment of our bodies, and ask—"

"Amen!" choruses loyal bros. Table erupts in clash-clatter of plates and utensils, boardinghouse reaches grope for food platters, thereafter followed by smack and crunch of mastication, thump of swallows, beverage gulping, same punctuated by table banters, as follows:

134

"Save some gravy for the white folks, okay, asshole?"

"Hey, shit-ass, you got a piece of egg stuck on your lip. You mind, you're making me fucking sick, okay?"

"Look who's talking who always chews with his mouth open!"

"You ever notice how flour gravy looks just like jizzum?"

"Can I have your biscuit if you don't want it, Gooch?"

"Hey, Gooch-face," says Gary Lee Stringer, "'fess up, wouldn't you druther eat this shit than fishheads or whatever they eat where you come from?"

"Did I or did I not tell you to keep your dumb mouth off Gooch?" says bosom pal buddy Stevie.

"No sweats, Stevie," I say, and, to Gary Lee, "Gary Lee, man, I is done told you before, reet? Head of piscatory organism most succulent and nutritional portion. Cultural relativity shtick, Gary Lee! Come visit me if and when's you qualify for circa 'forty Olympiad in Tokyo Town, Jack, I teach you how's to consume heads, also not to fail to mention fishes pickled the way my mama does it, reet? Also *shushimi*, raw-style, reet? Also *hatsugatso*, Gary Lee, how you say, bonito, sliced raw served up on *take* bamboo leafs, fresh caught in merry month of May upcoming, of the excellent gustatory delights, Jack!"

"Sure thing," says Gary Lee, and, "And don't be calling me Jack, I told you before! Anyway I'd have to eat it with sticks I suppose, right, Gooch-face?"

"Never *hochee*, Gary Lee! As how *hashi* chopsticks requires finesse motor coordinations. You like to spill more food in your lap than even now with knife and forks, reet?" Said riposte evokes chorus of appreciative guffaws—hardy har and hee.

"That's telling his redneck goat-roper ass, Gooch!"

"Put that in your pipe and smoke it, Stringer," says Stevie.

"If you was a foot taller and a hundert pounds heavier, I'd whup your yellow ass, Gooch. And you too, Keller."

"Nothing but fear and common sense holding you back, scrotumnose," Stevie says, rising from table—reference to schnozz is especial insult, as how Gary Lee suffers chronic severe acne vulgaris.

"Relax, Stevie, *daijubo*," I say, and, "Gary Lee just joshing, reet?"

"And maybe I just don't like his unfunny jokes," Stevie says.

"The trouble with you, Gooch-face," says Gary Lee Stringer, "is every time I pull your chain a little turd from Yukon who's too big for his britches puts in his two cents' worth."

"Can we just fucking eat fucking breakfast without a fucking squabble, you guys?" says hardwood standout Ned Whitcomb.

"Next jerk cracks wise, me and Carl will kick us some royal ass!" says Wayne Loving—than which gridiron personage weighs approximately 210 lbs. avoirdupois. In combination with bro Carl, totality exceeds 400 lbs. weight, thus silencing banter.

Kappa House fast breaker table camaraderie, reet? Circa April (*hanami*!) 1938.

Okay, Jack, sad to say, I 'fess up, *wataschi* Gooch is not universally popular B.M.O.C., reet? To wit, 189-lbs.-avoirdupois grappler Gary Lee Stringer exhibits marked antagonisms, expresses same via cracks wise — asks at fraternal repasts (as aforesaid) does I miss diet of fishheads, weeds, rice, asks is it true that amongst (how he say, Japs) *Nihonjin* female vaginal organ is oriented horizontal (wider spread, tighter it gets), etcetera blah.

To avoid intensifying confrontations, I respond always with big pearlie whites *sumairu* smile, ripostes of nonconcern to turn aside wraths. I reply, for instance, as how I, Gooch, lack knowlege of female-type anatomy (being yet virgin pure innocent, reet?), but promise to inform him by direct postal communication of hard facts if and when I apprehend same, reet?

Says Gary Lee (jaw firm, fists clenched), "You just better not try losing your cherry with one of our women, you might could get your stones cut off, get me?"

"Never *hochee*, Gary Lee," I say with big accompanying *sumairu* smile, "as how prenuptials intercourses is strictly non-*Nipponshikki*. How you say, most uncool, reet?"

"Is that why you're always sniffing around Clara Sterk like a little boy dog, Gooch-face?"

"You misapprehend, Gary Lee. As how Miss Petty Girl is but good friend classmate Platonic-style, reet? In additions to which aforesaid, co-ed matriculant is pre-engagement frat pin signified partner of best pal bosom buddy Strongboy Stevie, reet?"

Says Gary Lee Stringer: "I don't understand a word you're saying half the time, you little yellow dwarf!"

"Say not so, Gary Lee!" I do riposte with big *sumairu*. "I speak only of the idiomatics *Eigo* English vernacular slangs, Jack!"

"And don't call me Jack, I told you more than once, pencilneck!"

Can't not please all the folks all the time — sad to say, reet? I riposte softly to turn aside potential wraths, smile big *sumairu* exhibiting pearlie whites — flap not. So what's if not universally popular B.M.O.C., reet? So what's if small pale prevarications necessitated upon select occasions, reet? Happy Gooch. Circa April (*hanami*) 1938. Happy Gooch, Jack!

Dig it:

English literary classicals, reet? Beowulf (in translations, natch!), Bede, G. Chaucer, Spenser, W. Shakespeare (natch!), Pope and also Swiftian satiricals, Defoe et alia. Thrice-weekly class meetings, master mentor Prof Os Southard, assigned reading (mostly abridged), short critical papers, major documented essay, midterm and also final examinations (idents and short essay responses), borderline grades to be determined by instructor's subjectivist evaluation of quantity and quality of discussion participations, reet?

Where *wataschi* Gooch shines, Jack! Example:

Prof Os Southard: "And so what is Swift doing when he casts his satire in such bizarre terms? Hands? Let's not always be seeing the same hands up all the time, people! Gooch, let Clara answer this one."

Clara ("Petty Girl") Sterk: "I think Swift does it to dramatize his criticisms of the politics and the social morality of his times."

Prof Os: "Allright. Can anyone take it any further than that? No one? Okay, Gooch."

Gooch (*wataschi*, me, Jack!): "Honorable Mentor Prof Os, and also fellow peer matriculants, I submit J. Swift do resort to bizarreness extremities in characterization of Yahoos as manifestation of effort to view fellow *Igirisujin* Englishmens as if wholly alien folk, like unto anthropologist amongst primitives, as how dramatic distortion technique shtick enables author hisself to see said foibles as cited prior by Miss Clara, reet, Prof?"

"That's very interesting, Gooch," says Prof Os, after than which he proceeds to explicate my insight for benefit of fellow matriculants and co-eds.

"I still don't get it," says class dunce dimwit dummy John ("Jake") Millstone (mammoth 268-lbs.-avoirdupois footballer sadly lacking speed or quickness, hence perennial benchwarmer scrub, reet?).

"Goochie," whispers Clara sotto voce aside, "you're so smart sometimes it's scary!"

Can you not dig it, Jack? Gooch, class standout (in concert with Clara, as aforesaid), sits up front to bask in benevolent gaze of master mentor Prof Os, hand up for every question, writing assignments submitted on time without fails, first one done with pop quizzes, reet? Where I do shine, Jack!

Mise-en-scene: English lit classicals, thrice-weekly. Master mentor Prof Os Southard — thinning blond hair grown long to comb over forehead in futile effort to conceal creep of male pattern malady, rimless pince-nez specs catching light (April, Jack!) of bright Okie sun from high windows, suit with vest (shiny over shoulders, in seat of pants), open text in one hand, chalk in other. Paces before assembled enrolled, writes on blackboard, poses provocative queries, looks in vain among raised hands for arms outstretched not emanating from Gooch (me, Jack!) nor Clara, reet? Oh, Jack, long way removed from rote daily recitations and *tachiyomi* read aloud whilst standing at attention shticks of Native Land Loving School routines!

Classroom ambience auras: odors of chalk dust, sweeping compound, desk and floorboard varnish, bodily effluvias of assembled (mild perspirations engendering strong stench of characteristic *Amerikajin* raw beef in warm weathers!), sun blaze at windows striking highlights on Prof Os' pince-nez, glint of midair suspended dust motes, sound of assorted feets shuffling, page turn and flip, scratch of pen nibs recording lecture notations, occasional hallway passerby, song of mockingbird from campus greensward not unlike like unto playing of distant nose-flute, reet?

Number 2 Ticonderoga, Big Chief tablet at ready in event of sudden unexpected worthy insight from thin bloodless lips of Prof Os, I sit prim, back straight, knees together, baby blues atwinkle, slight *sumairu* smile of intelligent appreciation expressed to encourage lecturing master mentor — on my desk's surface is carved chronicle of previous A & M matriculant generations: OU Sucks, A & M Sucks, English Sucks, I Love Winnie Bersch, Sigma Chis Eat at the Y, Jocks Are Dum, Go Pokes, FDR Sucks, So Does Landon, Winnie Loves Me!, Go Punchers! Not to fail to mention assorted Greek-letter logos and sundry witty asides, reet?

Banjo clock ticks loud high on wall (portraits of G. Washington, A. Lincoln, W. Shakespeare, C. Columbus, Honorable Governor of sovereign state of Oklahoma William (a.k.a. Alfalfa Bill) Murray) — Time, Jack! Circa April '38, each tick of banjo clock like unto small *eiga* flic freeze frame, unending in memory — from which I work, Jack! — always past, present, passing . . . past and gone, reet?

"Miss Clara," I tell her, "Strongboy Stevie says as how he will dig you at luncheon scarf, or, failing same, after grapple practice, reet?"

"Thanks, Goochie. Hey, you're a sweetie pie, do you know that?"

Miss Clara (a.k.a. Petty Girl) Sterk, reet, Jack?

I do 'fess up, Jack, said co-ed personage constitutes ever increasing distraction from academic scholarly concentration (study of English lit classicals), reet? Clara Sterk, Jack — honey-blond hairs cut short to frame visage like unto cloche hat. Sheen on same evidences strict hygienic daily shampoo. Eyes pale bluish, gold lashes and brows (like unto ripened wheats), epidermis tan-gold by virtue of exposure to Okie sun, lips glossed with dark red cosmetics, color of which is matched by fine-groomed nails of both hands and toes, reet?

I assert, Jack — even in confines of classroom stifling warmth! — characteristic *Amerikajin* raw beef stink is fully obscured by Shalimar scents I observe her to periodically daub behind ears, on wrist-pulses, base of long throat, reet? Which is not to fail to mention her schnozz is not overlargish, rather, how you say, button snub, which is also not to fail to mention shaved nape of neck alluringly displayed as she bends over desk beside me, Jack!

138

"Goochie, you're such a doll! I could just eat you up sometimes!" declares Miss Clara ("Petty Girl") Sterk.

"Reciprocal, Miss Clara, most assuredly assured!" I riposte with huge Platonic-style *sumairu* smile.

On lapel of crispy-starched white blouse, she wears best bosom buddy pal Stevie's frat pin (Delta Sigma Kappa, ever-loyal bros we!), reet?

Old Central tower clock marks end of hour-long class period. I stand, gather text (*Anthology of English Literary Masterpieces*, Jack!), Big Chief, Number 2 Ticonderoga, wrap same in *Nihonjin*-style *furoshiki* cloth to make easily portable bundle, reet? I bid Miss Clara adieu, inform her I will not join her and Stevie this eventide due to conflicting necessity, prepare to merge with exiting throng of enrolled when mentor Prof Os summons me to his desk.

"Gooch," says he, "I have a message for you from Dean Macklin."

"Reet," I say. "What is scoop, honorable prof? I mean, like, Gooch is all auricular orifices."

"The dean," says Prof Os, "asked me to ask you to come over to his office in Arrington Hall as soon as my class was dismissed. I don't know what this is all about, but I think you'd better get over there right away, all right?"

"Reet. Sounds solemn seriousness, reet? How we say, *kaigi* conference of official business shtick. Hope I isn't done somehow pissed in grits, Prof."

"He didn't confide the purpose when he gave me the message. Just go. And you shouldn't repeat things you hear on campus without being sure of what they mean, Gooch. Piss isn't a polite word, Gooch."

"Reet!" I say, and, "Anks-thay, prof! I will note same. Is micturate preferred usage of decorum? Evacuate bladder? Wring out kidney? Take whiz? Drain reptile? Howsomever, Gooch will check it out! Also, anks-thay for most excellent lecture and discussion today, Prof!"

"I appreciate the compliment, Gooch. I wish I had twenty of you and Clara instead of all these redneck goat-ropers! And no, it's just generally not a subject one mentions in polite discourse."

"Reet," I say, and, "Never too late to learn niceties of *Eigo* English complexities! I promise to remember, give no utterance to, how we say, *tachishoben* urinations wee-wee, reet? Lingo, prof, words, funny strange, reet? Howsomever, Gooch is off, bee-line to Dean Tim's office!" And flash big *sumairu* smile, render five-degree deference bow to *sensei* master mentor, proceed thereafter to egress, reet?

Gooch, Jack! Semi-B.M.O.C., reet? A & M campus, circa April '38, dig? I cross greensward in direct direction of Arrington Hall (domicile of higher-educational hierarchical *honcho* administration) fast as short legs (shank's mare!) permit — how we say, *chogee* (fast, Jack!), reet? Can you dig it?

Gooch: looking good, Jack! Strictly Joe College collegiate image shtick. Hair styled in new crew-cut brush fashion (as in Ivy League fad popularized by Schicklgruber storm troopers mode), a-twinkle baby blues now aided by advent of bone-frame specs (as in Tojo Hideki mode, reet?), crisp starched white shirt closed at collar with polka-dot bow tie (as in Eddie Cantor mode), lightweight Hell Hounds logo cardigan, white-ducks slacks, thick wool socks, saddle shoes (as in *kempei* operative mode!) — Joe College collegiate Gooch, Jack!

One arm deployed to schlepp *furoshiki* bundle, I keep other free to gesture big howdy-hello greetings wave to fellow matriculants and co-eds who greet Gooch as I traverse greensward past Student Union, Boggs Hall, Theta Pond (largest rubber-bottom lake in U. S. of A. — hardy har Aggie joke, reet?) in bee-line line toward Arrington Hall designated *kaigi* conference rendezvous with diminutive Dean Timmy J. As follows:

"Hello there, Goochie!" calls out Miss Ligea McCracken, semirival campus beauty to Miss Clara — strictly no true *minken* competish, Jack, as how her schnozz is peninsular!

"What say, Gooch?" shouts current (class of '38, reet?) valedictory laureate Harrison C. V. Bell — than which whose scholarly rep fast fades in comparison with frosh-soph years' accomplishments achieved by *wataschi* (Gooch!) and Miss Clara, reet?

"Are you going to help me study for math like you promised, Gooch?" inquires Miss Salome Corcoran — also potential campus beauty rival of Miss Clara (no *minken* competish, Jack, as how she exudes choking stench of uncooked meat, her cologne inadequate to squelch, reet?). "You know I don't have any head on my shoulders for arithmetic! Come on, Goochie, you promised!" she pleads as I stride rapid strides past in haste to attend *kaigi* meet appointed — also not to fail to mention desire to attain upwind orientation relative to Miss Corcoran, reet? All which is to say: B.M.O.C.. Of the social popularity, Jack!

"My man, Goocha!"

"So how's the Goocher today?"

"Goocherino!"

"Goochingham!"

"Slow down, Gooch, you'll work up a sweat! Where's the fire?"

Visage-splitting *sumairu* affixed in place, I riposte en passant:

"No sweats, Miss Salome! Gooch will be there with bells on, *soroban* abacus in hand to provide promised aid, reet?"

"Hello, Ligea!"

"Can't not say it, Harrison C. V.!"

"Dig you later, cats!"

"Don't hold me back, Jack, gots to meet with *honcho* Dean Tim instanter!"

"Excuse, please, folks, must *chogee* to appointed *kaigi* conference as appointed, reet?"

Happy Gooch!

Jack: to my surprise, awaits me not only aforesaid diminutive Dean Timothy J. Macklin, but also present is A & M Prexy Paul Klemp, than which personage is seated ensconced in Dean Tim's chair—diminutive Timmy, as appropriate to relative status stature, is compelled to stand at prexy's side, backdrop to which duo stand flags of A & M and sovereign state of Oklahoma, not to fail to mention Stars and Stripes, also to note framed photos of FDR and Governor William (a.k.a. Alfalfa Bill) Murray adorning wall, reet? "Gentlemen," says secretary-receptionist Mrs. Merle Sare, "our young Mr. Gooch is here for his appointment," and closes sanctum door behind me.

I advance on carpet, restrain culturally induced impulse to execute thirty-degree kowtow bow, striking rather pose of formal informality, stifling hiss-intake of surprise-shock breath, firm abdominal *hara* belly muscles in preparation for atmosphere of seeming impending solemnity seriousness engendered by stony visages of Prexy Paul and Dean Timmy, reet? How we say, Jack, hardened *hara* belly, seat of emotions, is steeled to absorb assaults of tensions, from which control of same is engendered requisite *enryo* dignities appropriate to given occasion, reet?

"Hello and good tidings to you, honorable academic administrative *honcho* personages, on this day of April—sad to say as how showers bringing flowers are to date inadequate to break Dust Bowl drouth!—reet?" I say.

"Gooch," says Prexy Paul, "Dean Tim here suggested I join you-all for your little chat here."

How it were, Jack!

"Gooch," says Prexy Paul, "you-all know we mighty proud of how good you done here since you come to A & M."

"We're all very proud of your record here at A & M," mumbles Dean Timmy.

"And I won't deny we was worried some when them Jap–America Friends folks come asking us to admit you to the college."

"There were no precedents, Gooch," mutters Dean Timmy.

"What with money tight as a bull's ass in fly-time since 'twenty-nine, and that damn Rosenfeldt and his wife in the White House, they's even talk about wanting to let the niggers down to Langston at Guthrie come on up to A & M to save on budgets, to which I for one say over my dead body!"

"And we're committed to a full-blooded Indian for Mr. Iba's team," says

Dean Tim (reference is to roundballer great surefire bona-fide All-American probability Jesse Cobb McCartney, F.B.I., of Otoe-Missouria tribal ancestry, reet?).

"But you come recommended real high by that there Sato fella, and since your tuition and costs is all paid up in advance so's you couldn't be no burden that way, we took us a chance flyer on you, didn't we, Gooch."

"Risks," whispers Dean Tim.

"Than which for same I express deep unceasing gratitudes, honorable academic administrators!" I jump in—*hara* in turmoils not unlike like unto Okie twister roaring across drouth-struck vastness wastes, reet? Like: as how *wataschi* is thinking—is jig up? Cover blowed? Is I, Gooch (Yamaguchi Yoshinori!), abouts to be revealed as clandestine *kempei* counterintelligence espionage operative, shamed, expelled from ranks of A & M class of 1940, handed steerage-class ducat home to *Dai Nippon*, disgrace for self, family, name, *kami*, and Hundred Millions to boot? No joke, Jack!

"But you done real good, Gooch," says A & M Prexy Paul Klemp (widereputed close personal friend and politico-style ally of Honorable Governor William (a.k.a. Alfalfa Bill) Murray, hence—natch!—important academic administrative leadership *honcho* in statewide Okie higher-educational realms.

"Your scholarship is outstanding, and your social adjustment is exemplary," grumbles diminutive dean.

"Aw, shucks, it weren't nothin'!" I say, rub toe of saddle shoe over carpet nap as appropriate *Amerikajin* gesture of embarrassment at said direct praises, reet?

"And I'll 'fess up," says Prexy Paul, "I get me a real proud feel right down deep where the real me lives when I see you out there rooting on our Aggies with the Hell Hounds and Ruf-Nex, Gooch. The last time we played the damn Sooners, even Alfalfa Bill hisself says to me, that little Jap's got him more spunk and pep as any six real Aggies!"

"O.U. sucks!" I interject, and, "Go, Punchers!"

"We were so pleased when the Kappas rushed you, Gooch," says Dean Tim from corner of his mouth.

"Though I'll also 'fess I worried some again then about reactions by some folks when you got to being right in there at fraternity and sorority mixers and tea dances and co-ed pep rallies and all."

"Oklahomans," adds Dean Timmy in sotto voce aside, "tend to be very aware of race and color and religion and national ethnic origin. It's a cultural thing, Gooch."

"Delta Sigma Kappa," I say, "ever-loyal bros we!"

"Which brings us right down to the nut cuttin' nub of why the dean here asked you to drop by today," says Prexy Paul.

"There's been an allegation, a complaint, Gooch," says Dean Timmy Jr., chin down on chest.

"Thousand pardons, honorable administrator *honchos!*" I cry, and, "In advance, begging humbly of the forgiveness for whatsoever!" and, "What is I did done, Jack?"

"Clara Sterk," says Prexy Paul.

"You seem to see a lot of Miss Sterk, don't you, Gooch?" says Dean Tim through closed pearlie whites.

"Reet," I say, and, "Miss Sterk, also knowed as Petty Girl, Pledge Leader of Chi Omega, captain of Peppers spirit and cheer org, fellow language and also literature major, current co-leader for class of 'forty academic average as posted each semester end by A & M Registrar, reet?"

"We wondering some, Gooch," Prexy Paul says, "since a other party is brought it to our attention, just what the, like, say, tone of your relationship with Miss Clara Sterk is?"

"What are your intentions, if any, with regard to Clara, Gooch?" adds Timmy Jr., looking at flags on standards behind desk.

"Strict platonism!" I ejaculate, and, "Miss Clara is frat pin pin-mate almost enfianced of best buddy bosom pal Stevie ("Yukon Strongboy") Keller, also knowed as Mighty Mouse. In said threesome trio context, honorable administrators, we is good friends only. Honest Amerind, honorable personages! I ain't done nothing to merit censures in aforesaid regard, reet?"

Pause in confabulation, Jack: hiatus in *kaigi* conference meet, reet? A & M Prexy Paul Klemp peers through pince-nez pinched perched on tip of pointy schnozz; diminutive Dean Timothy J. Macklin clears bronchial and also sinus passages, gazes at coffee-table tome as if struck by sudden interest in ruination of ancient Greece and Rome; I loosen *hara* tummy muscles — as how, Jack, they don't gots nothing on me, reet?

Says Prexy Paul: "We had us a little talk about this very same thing when you first come to us, you recollect, Gooch?"

"In this very office," slurs dean.

"Word for word!" I tell them, and, "Advent of first foreign origins alien student enrolled at venerable A & M College is occasion of problematics, to wit, ambience of cultural chauvinism rampant in sovereign state of Oklahoma, reet? How you say, honorable personages, 'Okies don't much like foreigners nor niggers nor Jews and Catholics nor Bohunks,' reet? Thusly, you did caution Gooch friendly warnings, keep meathooks off Caucasian co-ed meat. Dast not, I recall you tell me, try to get stinky on dinky, dip not wick in flesh forbidden lest consequences dire, to include expulsion and rapid swinging door hit me in the ass on way out back to *Dai Nippon* results therefrom, reet? Than which is not to mention shames and disgraces and also political embarrassments to good name of venerable A & M institution."

"Something like that," says diminutive Dean Timothy, staring into wastebasket interior.

"Verbatim damn near!" says Prexy Paul, smiles *sumairu* smile at me through foci of double-barrel pince-nez on schnozz. "This boy is a pure-dee wonder for memorizing what he's been told, Timmy!"

"Than which facile facility," I tell them, "I owes to my revered mentors of alma mater Native Land Loving School, honorable personages!"

"And you done kept your pecker in your pants all this time since, have you, Gooch? Even rubbing up close to all them little sorority gals at the mixers and such?"

"Escorting Clara Sterk about the campus between classes, Gooch?" asks dean, eyes affixed to desktop.

"Scout's honor!" I assure them, and, "Dig, honorable academic *honchos*, Yank *Amerikajin* female co-ed personages present no attractiveness of erotics variety to us *Nihonjin*, reet? As how aforesaid female co-eds possess for us repulsive odor akin to uncooked beeves. Also not to fail to mention we consider same, how you say, mud-fence ugly, due to oversize proboscises, reet? Also consider said womens shameless via unabashed exposure of neck napes, result of popular fad pixie haircuts cuts now all the rage at A & M."

"Is that a fact?" says Dean Tim to wall, and, "I sort of assumed you'd give almost anything to get your hands on white women, Gooch."

"Beef?" queries Prexy Paul. "You sure you don't mean fish?" Laughs big Okie hardy har har, reet?

"If I'm lyin' I'm flyin', and you don't not see no wings on Gooch, reet?"

Second pause in *kaigi* conference meet ensues, Jack. Prexy Paul Klemp muses introspective, looks to Dean Timmy, than which personage avoids presidential scrutiny, examines fingernails. I, Gooch, stand easy, *hara* belly in state of total relaxed relaxation. Jack: I did contemplate possible sources of allegation complaint responsible for *kaigi* call up on carpet, reet?

"I'll buy it. How about you, Tim? Speak up like you got a pair, damn it, Timmy!"

"Plausible," stammers diminutive dean.

"Dast I pose query, honored *sensei* sirs?" I ask.

"Shoot," Prexy Paul says as Dean Tim nods.

"Dast I inquire as to which specific personage accuses me, Gooch, of aforesaid carnal transgressions and or intents?"

"Confidential, personnel matter," says Dean Tim to portrait of Honorable Governor William ("Alfalfa Bill") Murray.

"That'd be telling, Gooch. And 'sides, it happens the little bird what told Timmy here about it also happens to outweigh you way too much for you to do anything about it, would be my guess. Let's us just forget this little trip to the woodshed. No harm done. And go on about your bidness, okay? You keep on rooting our Aggies the way you do, and keep doing good in your studies and all, enjoy drilling along with the R.O.T.C. and Flying Aggies boys — I also hear tell you see all the movies comes to

Stillwater, is that right, Gooch?"

"Reet," I say. As how info requested not forthcoming is already clear to *wataschi* as point of Prexy's pointy schnozz, obvious like unto brown wart on dean's visage. As ushered toward door by crab-walking diminutive dean — man with a plan, Jack! — I is casting about for conceptions of appropriate retributions revenges, reet? I is thinking: 189-lbs.-avoirdupois grappler bigot redneck goat-roper Gary Lee Stringer (natch!).

"Say there, Gooch," says Prexy Paul as I depart. "Is it truly true what they say about the monkey on them Oriental gals, they sideways? Haw haw!"

"The Prexy's joshing you, Gooch," whispers diminutive Dean Timothy.

"Reet," I riposte, and, to Prexy Paul, "Reet, *sensei* prexy *honcho*! Wider separates the legs, more constricted becomes said monkey. Har! Hee!"

Dispensing politic *sumairu* smile for Mrs. Merle Sare as I exit Arrington Hall administration edifice, I emerge upon greensward A & M campus, resplendent in light of bright Okie sunshine, reet?

I does assert: Happy Gooch! *Yoin. Ma. Do*, reet? Than which is, in context of said juncture in life and times of Gooch, complicated by necessity of actions required versus Gary Lee Stringer, false accuser, than which whose calumny dictates I assert sacred honor shtick, *Nihonjin*-style, redeem self, name, family, *kami* etcetera blah. How?

Trust Gooch to find means to end, Jack!

Moderate irony, Jack: I, Gooch, matriculant in good standing (valedictory hopeful!), A & M class of '40, Joe College collegiate semi-B.M.O.C., reet? Said Gooch does vow *budo*-style revenges upon gross crude rednecker personage, reet? About which more hereafter!

"Hey, Gooch!"

"Hi there, you cutie-pie Goochie!"

"Hey, Joe, what 'a you know?"

"Hey, Gooch, you eating lunch at the Campus Grill or back at the frat house?"

Gooch. Semi-B.M.O.C. Traversing A & M campus greensward toward Student Union, reet? Big *sumairu* smile, *furoshiki* bundle (text tomes, Big Chief tablet, etcetera blah) under one arm, other free to wave big howdy-style greetings waves. Responding automatic in kind:

"Felicitous salutations, Jack!"

"Just got back from Kokomo!"

"In due time, reet? As how I needs must repair to campus post office to post missive to folks back home, reet?"

Thinking, Jack: retaliation shtick necessary to exert upon personage of 189-lbs.-avoirdupois grappler Gary Lee Stringer, reet? What's to do?

How, Jack?

As how redneck goat-roper big grappler Gary Lee is too large, also too strong, not to fail to mention too fast for *wataschi* to risk frontal direct challenge and assault, reet? Also at risk is degree to which Gooch remembers good *budo* stuff (*jujitsu* moves, etcetera blah) taught by revered mentors of Native Land Loving School—I did not pay close heeds, Jack! In light thereof, how's to proceed?

Alternatives include: notify Gary of vengeance shtick intention via threatening epistle, signed in blood to show absolutist sincerities? Call Western Union, arrange for same to deliver *wakazishi* short sword suggesting to Gary Lee *seppuku* suicide shtick as face-saver redemption for dastardly calumny? Never *hochee*, reet? Blab tattle-tale story to Strongboy Stevie, requesting he employ good offices to induce vaunted Loving bros Carl and Wayne to, how you say, kick living excrements out of Gary Lee as *oyabun-kobun* service to bosom pal buddy Gooch? Latter is, Jack, tempting, but misfortunately would constitute denial of Gooch's *on* responsibility—hence shameful, reet?

Quandary, Jack!

"Who is that? Step close so's I can see who it is. My eyes don't see so good no more! Is that you, little Gooch person?" queries Miss Samantha Woods, aged venerable A & M campus postmistress.

"Reet," I say to Miss Samantha, extract sealed missive from *furoshiki* bundle, rewrap same, extend to her shaking, liver-spotted hand.

"I thought so," says she, and, "At first I thought it must be one of the little girls, you're so small. And I suppose you got another one of them big fat letters with all the henscratch writing on it you want mailed home to your people, do you?"

"Reet, Miss Samantha-*san*, it are me, Gooch."

"You're a one for writing them letters," says she, takes sealed epistle in bony crone fingers, places same on postal scale, commences protracted ordeal of reading scale to calculate postage freight costs, reet? "Seems like folks should go to school close to home so's they don't have to be always writing letters all the time. Back in 'ninety-six when I come here, ever'body was all Stillwater folks and from the county, some of them."

"Who's that you're jawing at, Sam?" says voice from behind back of counter dimness environ, after than which wherefrom emerges personage of Frank Eaton, a.k.a. Pistol Peter, A & M campus celebrity, retired federal marshal, perennial mascot leader of homecoming parade, eccentric and much-beloved figure of legendary wild-west lawlessness era Okie territorial days, reet? He is garbed (natch!) in customary costume: ten-gallon hat, fringed vest, chaps, pistol belt and holster (firing pin long since removed from famous notched Colt .44 as public safety measure). "Oh," says Pistol Peter Frank Eaton, "it's the little Chinee they let come to school to

146

A & M."

"Reet, Honored Frank," I say, watch Miss Samantha lean close, squint over Coke-bottle-bottom specs to read scale.

"In my day you was all cooks or setting up laundries in the Cimarron Strip to do washing for outlaws and Indians," says Frank, and, "I never knowed a Chinee could read nor write nor hardly speak plain American in my day, I'll tell you."

"This one can write, and don't hardly do a thing besides if all these big letters is any sign," says Miss Samantha.

"Reet, Venerable Frank," say I, and, "Than which era epoch in which you was sole legal official westerly from Fort Smith, reet?"

"Don't get him started," says Miss Samantha, and, "Now you've got me confused, and I've got to start all over from scratch weighting this fat letter, Gooch!"

"Orry-say, Miss Samantha."

"Indeed I was the law, and no badman nor drunk Indian nor ever any Chinee for certain dast challenge me!" says Pistol Peter Frank, withdraws notch-handle Colt .44 (firing pin long since removed, natch!) from holster, hefts and twirls same on triggerfinger.

"Now you've gone and done it! I'll have to hear it all again like I have a thousand times before," says Miss Samantha, and, "Now where was I before I lost my concentration?"

"Those were bad days in Oklahoma Territory," Frank is saying. "See these here notches I cut me on the grips?"

"I do see same, Pistol Peter!"

"Ever' one is a man I killed. Most all of them badmen and drunk Indians, but nary a Chinee I recollect."

"Lordy, you've gone and set him off, Gooch!"

"Shot ever' one with this here Colt smoker. Some in the gut, some in the face, one I got in the side of his head, smack dab through his ear! I don't think none of them was never any Chinee as I recollect, but it's been so many years a man disremembers!"

"Lean over the counter and take a look yourself, Gooch, I just can't see that close up no more no matter how I strain with these old eyes."

"Two ounces?" I read on scale, and, to Pistol Peter Frank Eaton, "Reet, quicks-draw shtick, reet? Call villain from out saloon, face same down in midst of dusty street, as how chronicled in western horse-opera genre *eiga* flics, reet?"

"Some," says Frank.

"Tell me another, you old liar!" croaks Miss Samantha.

"Two ounces avoirdupois, Miss Samantha," I remind her, as how aged and trembling A & M postmistress is knowed to suffer wavering sensibility, symptom of creeping inexorable senilities onrush.

"I said some, Sam," Pistol Peter says, and, "Most I bushwhacked. Hid out where they kept their mount tied, picked 'em off when they come to ride off. Or I come in on them when they was eating or squatting in the two-holer to where they couldn't reach for a weapon. Or I could always wait for when they got liquored up. One I got me at night, which is tricky shooting, but there was moonlight to help."

"That's better," says Miss Samantha.

"Really? No guff stuff, Frank?" I ask. "Duplicity tactics? Sneak attacks? Blow bad men away via subterfuges and also guiles?"

"Damn straight!" says he. "You're a Chinee, so you wouldn't understand the ways of it. It was life or death, and Hanging Judge Parker give me a job of work to do, didn't he? There's no dishonor in it when you're treating with scum the way I was away back before statehood! It's the American way: you got a job to do, you do it as best you can, no if's, and's, nor but's! Except a Chinee heathen probably won't understand the ways of it, 'cause you was all washing clothes and cooking grub for these same scum I had to bring to justice for Judge Parker if I wanted to earn my found and get on in the world, see?"

"What," queries Miss Samantha Woods, "was I doing just a minute ago? Did you give me a letter to mail a minute ago? Aren't you that little Gooch fella's always mailing the long ones to your people?"

"Reet, Miss Sam," I say to reorient aged postmistress. To Pistol Peter Frank Eaton, I say: "Anks-thay, Revered Frank! Please to permit me to shake your hand hearty in appreciation, reet? As how you is done been biggish help to Gooch!"

"I don't mind if I do," says Frank Eaton (a.k.a. Pistol Peter) as I pay Miss Samantha postal freight charge. "I never had truck with no Chinee much, seeing as how I never had one cook for me nor wash my duds. But I'll press the flesh with any honest law-abiding man in the territory! When I came off the trail and needed my britches washed there was this widow gal in Fort Smith wasn't particular—"

"None of that!" interjects Miss Samantha. "You'll not talk your filth in my post office, Frank Eaton! And you scoot, young man, before you hear what you shouldn't!"

Can you dig it, Jack? How to proceed, direct from mouth of equine, reet? About which more later.

How it were, Jack: circa April 1938, A & M campus, reet? Late-afternoon calmness descends with tolling of Old Central tower clock, hot Okie sun dips lower in cloudless pale-blue sky vastness to create long shadows on greensward—fellow matriculants and co-eds repair to sylvan brink of Theta Pond (world's largest man-made rubber-bottom lake!) for casual flirtations confabulations, to Student Union for coffee and also Coke dates, some (elitist few, Jack!) to A & M library to crack tomes in preparation for soon upcoming *shiken-jigoku* final-examinations hellishness grind, reet?

Gooch (*wataschi*, Jack!) ambles feckless-style to Lewis Field turf (site of unceasing gridiron disappointments versus hated downstate arch-rival Sooners!), than which locale also serves in off-season as training ground for ever-increasing more active activities of A & M paramilitary orgs – R.O.T.C. and Pershing Rifles drill team, reet?

As I approach, in distance becomes visible sole aircraft of Flying Aggies aviation club, hum of Spad motor as fledgling student pilots practice landings and takes-offs at nearby Stillwater Town airport (constructed by Civie Conservation Corps), engine hum faintly audible, like unto insect buzz in remote Okie prairie wastes.

Gooch (I kid you not, Jack!), matriculant in good standing (sure bet for valedictorian!), Oklahoma Agricultural & Mechanical College, class of '40 – also (necessities necessitate!) secret clandestine *kempei* counterintelligence operative engaged in performance of duly entrusted mission, than which is honorable service in service of *Dai Nippon hakko ichui* grand design, reet? Ironies abound, Jack!

In far end-zone confines, Pershing Rifles, crack troop honorary ceremonial drill team practices cadenced moves, slowmo and extended silent count parade manuevers, said rehearsals accomplished with wooden dummy rifles due to lamented shortage of Real McCoys, reet?

At fifty-yard line (center of field, whereat is conducted ritual gridiron coin flip to determine kicksoffs sequences, reet?) are gathered R.O.T.C. corps, same clustered about personage of Sergeant-Major Tommy Turner, U.S. Army Retired (decorated vet of Great War flap, invalided via mustard's gas, etcetera blah). I approach fringes of aforesaid corps, hear Sergeant-Major Tommy perorate, as follows:

"Gentlemen," says he, "this is a great day for us all here at our A & M! I have been promising you this day would come, and here it is, and now you will see some real-life soldiering instead of all this military courtesy and map reading and squad tactic theory and other such pussy garrison-duty stuff!" Small ripple of hardy har guffaws from cadet corps, reet?

I slip through thronged – "Oh, hey, Gooch!" – "Hello, Gooch, you missed formation." – "You don't have to step on my toes, Gooch, just ask and I'll let you by, okay?" – penetrate inner circle, wherein Sergeant-Major Tommy stands, hands on hips, crowbar tucked under one arm not unlike like unto swagger stick; on turf at Sergeant-Major Tom's feets repose two large (coffin-like size, Jack) wood crates, than which bear varied stencil-ink inscriptions: War Department, Ordnance, This Side Up!

"We are done," Sergeant-Major Tommy is saying, "with simulated firing exercises, gentlemen. Because there is boo-coo ammo on its way to us right now, so we'll not just be disassembling and assembling and deploying our two water-cooled thirties any more either, and we for darn sure will not be pointing sticks at pretend targets and making firing noises with our lips as we practice squeezing off a round properly. No sir! Now," says Sergeant-Major Tom, takes crowbar from armpit, strikes blow on crate lid, "we will learn marksmanship, and we will fire official qualification for record, and we will fire transition range when we get one set up out in the boonies, and we will learn about the basic infantry weapon hands-on instead of out of a field manual."

Sergeant-Major Thomas Turner (U.S. Army Retired): gauntness, reet? Wears campaign hat headgear (strap under sharp chin), high collar buttoned, breeches and puttees, reet? Voice not unlike like unto file's rasp (due to mustard's gas inhaled in Great War flap conflict) on dry Dust Bowl Okie air. "Gentlemen, you are about to feast your eyes on a precision instrument, and I assure you you will be made familiar with its proper prescribed maintenance. Do we all have our rods and patches and oil with us today like we were ordered?" Chorus of assents accompanied by uplifted, waving cleaning rods. He jabs crowbar under crate lid, says to me, "Well, hi there, Gooch! I thought I noticed you missing when I took muster formation today. Hell, you don't want to miss out on this, son. You can tell your grandbabies you were here the day they finally came!"

"Reet," I say, and, "Greetings honorable non-com mentor," and, "Orry-say for tardiness, problems on my mind, reet? So what's doing, *sensei* sarge?"

"Just you be patient and wait and see for yourself, Gooch." He prizes upward with crowbar — snap, crackle, pop splintering of wooden lid, than which yields to reveal rows of rifles, Jack, than which shoulder-fires gleam dully in fading Okie sun, said glisten due to patina of grease encompassing aforesaid guns, reet? Small chorus of cheers and also whistles (oohs and ahs!) accompany revelation of new-arrived long-awaited weaponry. "How's that for a sight for sore eyes, Mr. Gooch?" asks Tommy, big *sumairu* smile creasing craggy visage.

"Reet," I say, and, "Neat!" and, "Top shelf, Sarge Tom!"

"That, gentlemen," says he to assembled cadet corps, like unto big gridiron huddle confabulation, "is the Queen of Battle! You are looking at the Springfield nineteen-oh-three rifle, thirty caliber, bolt-action, as accurate a piece as exists in the world today, and I don't give a hoot for all your Garands and Browning semi-automatic things they like to talk up these days. Boys," says Sergeant-Major Tommy Turner, "I put a few Huns out of their misery with one just like those, and I'd wager you could do the same if that Austrian paperhanger gets fractious." Chorus of whistles, cheers!

"Slick," I say to Tommy, and, "Swell," and, "Hot stuff, reet?"

"You bet you," says he, and proceeds to organize details of fatigue to extract Springfield shoulder-arms from crates, commence cleaning of Cosmoline grease pack therefrom, log in serial numerals, etcetera blah. "Now you'll get a chance to see some real army training, Mr. Gooch."

"Reet. I will inform bosom buddy pal Stevie Keller of auspicious event, as he plans to soon join cadet corps to earn commision, having hurdled National Guard enlistment obstacle."

"You do that. I figure enrollments are going sky high once the word's out we've got us actual hardware to fire and drill with now. Every patriotic redneck at A & M's going to want to be a soldier right sudden's my guess. Too bad you're not a citizen, Gooch, I'd make room for you even if you are undersize and underweight and don't act like you know hayfoot from strawfoot most of the time. Your friend the famous wrestler Keller got in the National Guard, and he's not a hair taller or heavier than you are. 'Course I did hear a shithouse rumor he had to stuff himself with bananas and Kool-Aide and stand on his tippy-toes to make it, but that's between you and me and the stump what we do for our athletes, huh?"

"Reet, sarge! Lamentably sad to say I did neglect to pursue *budo* militarist studies offered by revered mentors back home in *Dai Nippon*. Temperament unsuited to martial lifestyles, as how I did fritter youthful salad days of youth away on study of *Eigo* English and import *eiga* flics, reet?"

"Just as well," Sergeant-Major Tommy Turner says, and, "The ones escape this one'll be the lucky ones. You'll be going back home when you graduate, I suppose, but I got money says most of these cadets will be seeing action sooner rather than not."

"War?" I query. "*Senso*? You think current global flaps eruption in world-wide conflicts involving U. S. of A. likely, *sensei* sergeant-major?"

Pershing Rifles honorary ceremonial drill team continues to march to and also fro in end-zone environ, armed with but dummy rifles and (natch!) dress sabers as how they suffer lowest priority for actual ordnance. A & M R.O.T.C. cadet corps cavorts on gridiron turf, wiping Cosmoline from new Springfield shoulder-arms, play at *chambara* swordfights with cleaning rods, snicker and clack noises of bolts worked back and also forth. Roar of Spad aircraft engine oppresses overhead as Flying Aggies student pilot performs low-flying wing waggle buzz of Lewis Field—disciplined Pershing Rifles ignore same whilst R.O.T.C. cadets take mock aim and snap off pretended shots at swooping aircraft, than which pilot thereof is visible, leather helmet and goggles, white scarf trailing in slipstream.

"Wiseacre!" says Sergeant Tommy, "Thinks he's the Lafayette Escadrille! I'd speak to somebody about that horseplay if I thought it'd do any good."

"*Senso*? War?" I repeat. "Say not so, sarge-*san*! Worldwide global brouhahas unlikely ever to extend to remoteness of continental U. S. of A., much less unto remote interior environ of sovereign state of Oklahoma, reet?"

"The world's shrinking, Gooch," he says, lays gnarled hand on my shoulder in gesture of paternalness camaraderie, reet? "I wish I was kidding sometimes, but I can read the signs of it. Today we have our new Springfields, and ammo for them and the water-cooled thirties in the pipeline. Don't you read the papers and keep up with politics, Gooch? Next thing'll be mortars, artillery before you know it. I'm not spoofing you. And more and up-to-date planes," says he, squinting up into Okie sky vastness at departing Spad aircraft, silhouette against declining sun, reet? "Billy Mitchell was right," he says.

"No stuff guff?" I say, and, "Straight poop from group, not to josh Gooch, Sarge?"

"Bank on it. And they'll be regular army officers, all brass and Sam Browne belts a mile wide, coming in here to run the show before you can say Jack Robinson." Glaze of misty-eyes sadness regret shows briefly in visage of Sergeant-Major Tommy Turner (U.S. Army Retired), wounded vet of Great War mustard's gas, reet? "But," says he — misty glaze evaporates — "there's a silver lining always, Gooch! They'll be needing the likes of old war horses like me to show them how it's done right!"

"Reet."

"Well," says he, "I have to get some good order and discipline started here before it turns into pure grab-ass. You take care, Gooch. Get your education, take your diploma when they give it to you, and go home. I understand you're quite the student. Go on back home to your folks and enjoy the good life with all them geisha gals, huh?"

"Reet, *sensei* sarge."

"And remember the first rule of soldiering I taught you."

"Reet," I say, "never volunteering. Also, if as how it ain't alive, paint it. Than which is not to forget yardbird's credo, if you can't consume same nor fornicate, micturate thereupon, reet?"

"Haw haw! What a memory you got, Gooch!" laughs file-rasp (mustard's gas burns scarring esophagus) laugh of Sergeant-Major Tommy Turner. "You hanging around to give us a hand cleaning these new pieces?"

"Orry-say, no can do, Sergeant Tom. As how I needs must repair to grappler mat practice. I vow to pass good word of new-arrived shoulder-fires to buddy pal Strongboy Stevie. Busy eventide awaits *wataschi*, sarge," I tell him, "much to perform, reet? Howsomever, permission to pose query?" I ask.

"Fire away."

"In martial experience you experience, *sensei* sergeant, what ethic prevails governing strategies for assault upon enemy?" "Just like I teach everybody. Find cover first, and deploy on high ground if you can find it."

"Reet!" I say, and, "Anks-thay, sarge!" Render sharp salute and receive reciprocal same, step out smartly about-face at route-march pace. Depart turf of Lewis Field, direction of Gallagher Hall gymnasium as dusk falls upon A & M campus — circa April 1938, reet?

152

Ironies, Jack!

Grapple practice, reet? A & M, Jack, perennial N.C.A.A. undefeated champs under coaching mentor legendary Coach E. C. Gallagher, reet? Dig:

Largish room in basement of Gallagher Hall (legendary coach's legend already manifest in edifice moniker, reet?) — upstairs is hardwood court upon which vaunted roundballers of Iron Man Duke Mr. Henry ("Hank") Iba cavort in winter seasons. Cellar environ floor is covered with big mats, like unto oversize *futon*. At opposite ends of same are situated (respectively) barbells and hoists for weight training, lockers (note: unlocked, Jack!) for storage of street apparel and gym bags — grapplers doff latter attire to don jerseys, tights, and shoes, thereafter engage in group calisthenics to warm up musculatures, pump blood into same via barbells and hoists, how you say, get loose as gander, reet?

Thereafter by pairs repair to mats area to practice takedowns, escapes, positions most suited to accumulation of riding time (winning points margins earned thereby in close matches, Jack!), shoots and lunge moves, arching of back (reliance on strong neck muscles) to create bridges effects, thus avoiding pins even in postures of submission, reet? Whilst squad works out thusly, Coach E. C. Gallagher moves about offering fine pointers of strategy and tactic, urging ever-greater expenditures of energies effort, inspiring enthusiasms via exhortations, etcetera blah.

Throughout all which above-mentioned, Gooch sits on sidelines, proffers towels and waterbucket when requested (orange halves during actual duels meets, reet?), engage in casual banter confabulations. As follows:

"Come on, Gooch, give it a try," says Yukon Strongboy Stevie, "I'll let you start with me pinned and see if you can keep my shoulders down for a three-count. A two-count?"

"Never *hochee*, Mighty Mouse!" I riposte, and, "As how I done told you most recent, I am lover, not combatant, reet?"

"I'm getting tired of hearing you say that, you know?" says Gary Lee Stringer.

"It is to josh, Gary Lee," I tell him. "I rely on brain quickness in lieu of nonexistent physicality endowment, reet?"

"Which is you're saying you're chickenshit. Right, Gooch?"

"Consider the source and ignore him, Gooch," says Stevie, and, "Pick on somebody your size why don't you, Stringer."

"Not to worry, *daijubo*, Stevie Strongboy," I tell bosom pal buddy as he joins me to wipe perspirations from brow, wet whistle at waterbucket. "As how I do not provoke, Gary Lee no doubt doubtless feeling frustrations despair of possible athletic eligibility threat in event grade-points plummet after upcoming *shiken jigoku* final exams, reet?"

"I don't give a rat's ass what he's feeling," says Stevie. "He's cruising for a bruising. I'm about subject to ask one of the Lovings to hand him his head," and, "You studying late with me and Clara at the library? Oh, that's right, I forgot. You're going on one of your long walks to look at the damn stars and all tonight."

"Reet. Probably take in flic at Mecca after practice, *Snow White and the Seven Dwarfs* playing tonight, big Disney Walter animation extravaganza, take *sanpo* stroll to view *hanami* moon thereafter."

"You kill me, Gooch," says Strongboy Stevie. "That's a movie for kids."

"Young at hearts, reet, Stevie?" I say, and, "Is you heard hot poop scoop from R.O.T.C. cadet corps? Big shipment of Springfield 'oh-three shoulder-fire weaponry is done been delivered this day, same bringing much joy to soul of *sensei* Sergeant-Major Turner Tommy."

"I already heard," says Stevie. "Just my shit luck. I enlist and then they get rifles and start field training like it's the regular damn army or something."

"Fun and games shtick," I say. "*Budo* stuff guff all steer excrement, reet?"

"That's easy for you to say. You're not looking at National Guard duty when you graduate." Than which confabulation is interrupted by legendary Coach E. C. Gallagher, than which personage inquires if bosom pal Stevie is under delusion that this is sorority tea dance or Coke date, or, perchance, does said Stevie recollect assemblage is devoted to refinement of grappling skills in preparation for upcoming renewal of duel Bedlam Series match versus hated downstate arch-rival O.U. Sooners? "Sorry, coach," says Stevie, returns to mat; I grin *sumairu* grin at Coach E. C., sidle casual-style nonchalant to end of room area whereat reside team lockers—first step in execution of planned plan, reet?

Dig it, Jack: circa April '38. Grappler practice, reet? Sounds of labored respirations, exertions grunt and also groans, occasional vernacular vulgarity articulated as expression of frustration, whoop of exuberance, whistle blasts and shouts from Coach Gallagher. Oppressive odor of perspiration-soaked tights, jerseys, jockstraps, clank of barbells and hoists, rattle-clang of dipper in waterbucket, thwack of towel. Than which session concludes with final exhortation from Coach E. C. to walk off sweat, cool down musculatures prior to shower, perfunctory caution that collective skills at all weight classes must improve if certitude of victory over hated Sooners, not to fail to mention N.C.A.A. regional and national finals, is to be realized—also strong caution to watch weight!

First step of planned plan accomplished, Gooch departs, carrying *furoshiki* bundle (loaded, Jack!). "Digging you later, Stevie," I say, and, "Convey greetings from Gooch to Clara, inform same as how I will dig her in class anon on the morrow, reet?"

"Still catching that dumb movie and walking around looking at stuff?"

"Reet," I say, and, "Amongst other things."

"Hey!" I hear Gary Lee Stringer, emerging from shower, "Who the hell swiped my gym bag? Where's my damn bag, man? Hey, come on, guys, help me find my stuff, okay?"

"Find your own shit, Stringer," I hear Strongboy Stevie respond.

"Hey," says Gary Lee, "is somebody trying to be funny? I'm not leaving until I find it, man! I got my study notes and everything in there, man!"

Gooch thinks: seek and find, Jack! Try looking in *benjo* sanitary facility, behind commode stool, reet? Hardy har har! Also: hee hee! Do you dig it, Jack?

Circa April '38, reet? *Hanami*. Except as how moon of spring only minimally available for traditionalist viewing shtick. Than which orb is obscured by scudding cloud cover (sign of frontal weathers bringing rains to ease Dust Bowl drouth gripping Okie-land vastness prairie?). Than which—*hanami* moon, Jack!—Gooch is not on prowl to view nohow, reet? Plan, Jack! Dig it:

Gooch: esconced obscured from casual views of passing passersby, shrubbery to one side at end of quaint wooden footbridge spanning inlet of Theta Pond (world's largest man-made rubber-bottom lake—hee!)—full darkness of eventide prevails over environ of A & M campus. Therein (ensconced obscured, Jack!) I unwrap *furoshiki* bundle, removed preselected attire: black turtle-neck pullover, black dress trousers, black brogans (double-thick soles and heels, reet?), black hose, not to fail to mention scarf of same dusky hue.

Not unlike like unto medieval *samurai* donning armor garb, Gooch doffs Hell Hounds sweatshirt, chino slacks, saddle shoes, white wool sweatsocks (fold same, wrap in *furoshiki*, stash same in shrubbery fastness), clad self in aforesaid sumptuary blackness, reet? Total effect of which same (scarf over face—only baby blues visible, Jack!) is near-invisibility in Okie-land A & M campus black eventide darkness—like unto legendary *ninja* assassin-types, Jack! Thereafter: wait.

Crouch in shrubs (foot of footbridge over Theta Pond inlet), eavesdrop on passing passersby, than which include last campus stragglers returning from Student Union Coke dates, library brainstorm cram-jam study sessions in preparation for upcoming *shiken jigoku* final-exam hellishness, not to fail to mention one pair of *koibito* sweetheart lovers (love ecstacies in remoteness of Theta Pond environ completed—pond's rubber bottom lining reinforced and augmented!), to include one, then another solitary *sanpo* stroller. Gooch, near-invisible in *ninja* blackness garb: waiting, watching.

Plan, Jack! Alibi shtick is solid, as how Strongboy Stevie will (if necessitated!) witness said Gooch did signify intent to attend Mecca to see *Snow White and the Seven Dwarfs*, reet? Than which *eiga* flic I is already done viewed; thusly, I can quote dialogues, summarize plot line if necessary, reet? Mecca box-office personage will testify as to aforesaid Gooch's presence, as how I done gone (*chogee*, Jack!) there, purchased ducat (sneaked out fire-door egress, repaired in haste to Theta Pond locale!).

Whilst Gary Lee Stringer is done been seeking gym bag, reet? How long it did tooks you, Gary Lee, to find aforesaid canvas bag (containing street attire, study notes, etcetera blah) stashed clandestine behind *benjo* toilet facility commode stool? Hee! Hee! Hee! Also har.

Passing of passersby traffic slows, ceases. Followed thereafter by solitary solitudeness. Is Gary Lee Stringer done found bag too soon, gone home to Kappa House whilst Gooch purchased *eiga* flic ducat, viewed opening logo credits of Disney Walter animation extravaganza? Is Gary Lee Stringer done crossed wood footbridge bridging Theta Pond inlet whilst Gooch eased out fire door egress of Mecca Theater?

No time for doubts, Jack! Gots to conclude strategies of plan tactic. Hope for best, trust to lucks, go with *do* flow, reet?

Expert advice is clear: bushwhack from cover (Pistol Peter Frank Eaton!); take high ground (Sergeant-Major Tommy Turner!). How to apply aforesaid wisdoms to personage of detested dishonorable calumniator redneck goat-roper big Gary Lee Stringer? 189-lbs.-avoirdupois grappler is formidable objective opponent enemy, reet? Neck of same is wide as skull. Shoulders bulge like unto twin drumlins. Arms and legs is like trunks of aged pine trees of *Dai Nippon*. Wherein lies high ground bushwhack from cover advantage required by Gooch, Jack?

I, Gooch, conclude: baby blues, schnozz, terminus of spinal bones, testicular gonad family jewels—all which lie vulnerable to *budo* attack tactics, unprotected by musculatures, reet? Whereupon I cogitate (work from memory, Jack!) in effort to recall specifics of *budo* unarmed assault procedures, than which (sad to say!) I failed to pursue with diligence whilst matriculating at alma mater Native I and Loving School.

Dig it: solitary solitude, crouched near-invisible (*ninja* blackness garb!) in shrubs at foot of footbridge spanning Theta Pond inlet, entire duration of which interim is endurance of *hara* belly tensions nervousness anxieties. Oh, I did think: where is you, Gary Lee?

Than which personage approaches along shore of Theta Pond, blacker blackness of hulking silhouette against blackness of Okie sky vastness (*hanami* moon scuds behind clouds), aforesaid whistling poor rendition (off-key) of "Yes, We Have No Bananas"—as clodhopper footsteps thump-clump upon wood of wooden footbridge. I discern gym bag pendent from one hand (checked *benjo* commode stool at long lasts, reet, Gary Lee?), thus limiting aforesaid's responsiveness potentials to but one free meathook hand.

As Gary Lee Stringer reaches foot of footbridge, I emerge from foliage (near-invisible *ninja* garb!)—only in last *ma* moment's instant does I recall to refrain from uttering big *banzai* yell (to induce paralysis fright, reet?), as how silence is vital to calculated anonymity.

I rely on memory, Jack! As follows:

Vengeance revenge assault commences with, how we say, *Ujo Nai Homa*, Big Horsie Kick (how you say: Cincinnati Left Jab, reet?), delivered with hard brogan toe to juncture of said Gary Lee's testicular region. Gary Lee (surprise to me, Jack!) utters no utterance expressive of appropriate pain nor shock — said personage merely doubles up, drops gym bag (instinctive, reet?), clutches at groin region as if to douse by smothering sudden fire outbreak. At which instant I deliver *Iki Ka Da* (Swift Striking Crane, Jack!) — how you say, like unto *eiga* personage Moe the Stooge, move to eyes, first and second digits extended rigid. Than which provokes shrill scream (like unto Okie tornado warning siren alarm) from lips of Gary Lee — he relocates hands from groin to baby blues, midscream, reet? Than which scream I interrupt with delivery of *Funiji Fukiken*, Smithy's Hammer Blow, directing same to his prominent *Amerikajin* schnozz (how you say: snotlocker). At which instant (blood spouts from out Gary Lee's nostrils) I execute basic *judo* trip-fall — 189-lbs.-avoirdupois grappler Gary Lee Stringer tumbles to ground — bigger they is, harder they falls, reet?

At which juncture I pause: gots to catch breaths, Jack, reassert control over *hara* belly excitements verging on hysterics brink! I look about (near-invisible!) to ascertain solitudes continues, check Gary Lee, than which who writhes on ground (one hand now grasps groin region, other pressed to baby blues, screaming muffled now by choking blood from busted schnozz filling open mouth).

I think: I, Gooch, redeem honor of my name, family, *kami* ancestors, avenge in full for slander perpetrated by aforesaid personage now in pain and shocks of assault!

I conclude execution of planned plan with *Gi Rodo Gin* (Dragon's Tooth Sinks Deep, Jack!), kick delivered to base of spinal bone. How you say, assure opponent enemy is down for count, reet? Blow of brogan to spinal base elicits only loud huff of breaths exhalation, said bigot goat-roper slanderer personage now reduced to sobbing moans, involuntary quivers, reet?

Whilst Gary Lee Stringer rocks side to side, not unlike like unto tortoise desiring to flip off backside, I repair to stashed *furoshiki* bundle, extract preprinted placard (shirt cardboard, Jack, untraceable!), than which I affix with safety pin to back of Gary Lee's letter-sweater, than which reads: *Aggie Wrestlers Suck. Go Sooners.*

Than which bravado guff stuff, I calculate, will provide added incentives to A & M grapplers in upcoming Bedlam Series duel match, not to fail to mention N.C.A.A. regionals and finals — also not to fail to mention placing suspicions for assault upon hated downstate arch-rivals, reet?

Hee. Har.

I think (*chogee* across dark deserted A & M campus, shank's mare, near-invisible in *ninja* mufti costume): this I did do to redeem honor of self, name, family, *kami*, etcetera blah. Also honor of Miss Clara ("Petty Girl") Sterk (A & M campus beauty, co-valedictorian — to date! — of class of '40), semienfianced via frat pin pinning to Mighty Mouse Yukon Strongboy Stevie Keller, best bosom pal *oyabun-kobun* buddy of Gooch, reet?

I think (as *hanami* moon, circa April 1938, eludes me behind cloud-scud): if I am fighter, mayhap I shall yet prove to be lover also, reet?

Dig it, Jack: wee small hours of night (*hanami* moon lost behind cloud cover — rains coming to slake parched Okie-land Dust Bowl prairie dusts?), I stand before Kappa House (ever-loyal bros we!).

I think: what is you done done this night, Gooch? Honor-and-glory shtick? I think: Gary Lee Stringer! Miss Clara Sterk (fast aslumber in Chi Omega House, but one block away on Sorority Row, reet?). Mighty Mouse Yukon Strongboy Stevie Keller. Morris Berg (Moe, say it were not so!). *Papa-san. Mama-san. Iko-san.* Agricultural & Mechanical College (Stillwater Town, county of Payne, sovereign state of Oklahoma, U. S. of A.). Empire of *Nihon.* Gooch (*wataschi*)!

Oh, Jack, I did contemplate big ironics of life and times lifestyle!

I enter Kappa House (near-invisible!), ascend silent in sock-feets to second-floor room, wherein I kneel at bedside bunk (Strongboy Stevie aslumber in upper), clap hands gently to summon *kami* — does they hear me when I clap so soft, so far away from me in distant *Dai Nippon*? — begin to whisper sotto voce aside, reet?

I say: "*Kami* of name and lineage, hear Gooch, also knowed as Yamagu-chi Yoshinori, humble personage gots what for to tell you of, reet? I is, this day, done did a thing might could merit merits, benevolence of *kami* concerns for future fortunes upon *do* path of life of yours truly. Avenge vengeance shtick against bigot redneck goat-roper calumniator for slan-derous allegation assertion lodged with *honcho* A & M administrator facto-tums, reet? For than which anks-thay to venerable and revered mentors of Native Land Loving School for instruction in *budo* martial strategies and tactics, smattering of which sufficient I recall, enabling success of aforesaid vengeance venture. Simultaneous, I, Gooch, needs must 'fess up to betray-al of *Amerikajin* hosts, than which results of previous betrayal of *Dai Nippon* via self-conscious and willing cooperations with Moe Berg — "

"Gooch?" says Strongboy Stevie, leans out from upper bunk. "You just coming in, man?"

"It is me, Stevie," I say, doff *ninja* garb, proceed to hit lower bunk hay.

"What the hell were you doing there on your knees, Gooch?"

"Like, bedtime prayers shtick."

"Oh. Sorry. Is all that black get-up part of it? Hey, man, you missed it! You ain't heard about Stringer? He got the crap beat out of him by some O.U. guys, right on campus, over by Theta Pond, man!"

158

"No stuff?" say I, and, "Calamitous debacle misfortune, reet? Said Gary Lee expected to recuperate instanter?"

"He's in the infirmary. They don't know if he'll be able to wrestle regionals or not yet. He for damn sure won't wrestle the Bedlam this week. Those fucking Sooners are going to be hurting for this one, I can tell you that! Everybody on the squad's out for blood for this one!"

"Reet. Damnable shame for Gary Lee. Go, Pokes! O.U. Sucks! Ah so," I say, "must needs get minimalist shuteyes, Stevie. Relate details of catastrophics in light of new morn, reet? Sleeping tight, Stevie."

"Yeah. Goodnight, Gooch," says he, and, "See you in the morning," and, "Did you look at your moon or whatever like you wanted?"

"Somewhat only," I riposte, "as how clouds obscure same, reet?"

"Yeah, maybe it'll rain for a change. Oh, hey, you probably didn't hear this, either. Somebody heard it on the radio, the Olympics are cancelled for nineteen forty, man! Because of you guys having that war with China. Can you believe that crap? I'm a cinch for the Olympics, and they stop them because of a damn war! Who the hell can figure anything in life, huh, Gooch?"

"Oh, Stevie," I say, "orry-say, man! So sorry for this, Stevie, who could prognosticate flap with Chinks!"

"Well, it sucks," says he. "But it's not your fault, Gooch. Get some sleep."

"Reet." I think: Oh, Stevie, sad to say, say it were not so '40 Olympiad will not come to pass in Tokyo Town—*koki nisenroppyakunen Orimpikku!*—ironies, Jack! I think: sleep tightly, Mighty Mouse! Do not permit louses to bite, Miss Clara! Gary Lee: hee and har! Oh, Jack, flaps global, flaps localist, life and times *do* is six of one, half-dozen remaining, reet? Oh, Jack, where is *do* philosophics of life's pathway when most needed!

Oklahoma A & M Campus
Stillwater Town
County of Payne
Sovereign State of Oklahoma
U. S. of A.
31 December 1938

Dear *Papa-san, Mama-san, Sis Iko*:

Nihonjin-style, I take Number 2 Ticonderoga in hand, apply fresh-sharpened point thereof to lined page of Big Chief tablet, send year's-end greetings home to you-all in *Dai Nippon* from far-distant Oklahoma, reet? As Old Central tower clock bongs Westminster-style chime of quarter past eleventh hour of ultimate day circa 1938, your son Gooch (a.k.a. Yamaguchi Yoshinori!), do greet you on eve of *o-shogatsu* New Year, lamentably unable to join you in ceremonial rice cakes etcetera blah rituals.

Once more, folks, I, Gooch, write to sum up pith and gist summation of yet another successful year's experience of Joe College collegiate shtick, reet? As witness:

Scholastic-endeavor shtick proceeds on schedule, according to grand design ambition plan for academics excellence laurels. I, Gooch, now upperclassman (junior!) sit atop class standings (than which is not to fail to note I share same lofty eminence still with co-leader of class of '40 Miss Clara — a.k.a. Petty Girl — Sterk, about which whom more hereinafter, reet?).

And continue to enjoy status as certified genuine B.M.O.C., result of aforesaid outstanding academic achievements in concert with varied array of various social-org participations. I hold to *do* view of life's purposes and meaning. *Yoin* experienced in *ma* moments, reet? With such revisions therein as dictated by circumstances encountered.

Than which leads me to open discussion of potential cultural controversies, reet?

Daddy: mayhap best you not translate following remarks into *Nihonju* for Mama and *Iko-san*, reet? As how I express only tentative thoughts, expressing same in part for need for your wise and also sage councils. And to clarify said thoughts toward greater clarity when contemplation of translation of thought to actions becomes (mayhap!) appropriate, reet? Like unto, how we say, thrust of tongue into eye-tooths precludes ability to see what is said.

To wit:

Papa-san, I, Gooch, your son, bearer of family name and hopes of future honor-and-glory shtick, entrusted with obligations to preserve dignities undamaged of ancestral generations who reside in spiritualist *kami* attendance upon us — I, Gooch, do understand and fully accept *Nipponshikki* traditionalist burden of responsibility shtick, reet?

Than which, at present moment of present-ness of life and times of *wataschi* Gooch, aged now full twenty years of age, approaches prospect of prospective consideration of entry into condition of matrimonials, reet? And as how I envision plans you plan for time of my return to *Dai Nippon*, reet? Than which doubtless includes contemplation of *omiami*, how we say, traditional arrangement of nuptials contract.

Forgive Gooch, *Papa-san*, if I broach subject requiring *enryo* restraints and decorums, delicacy of which, *Nihonjin*-style, dictates silence!

And, like: I know as how it is *Nipponshikki* tradition shtick for you, *Papa-san*, head of paper household, to take total charge of *omiami* business, select matchmaker to engage in systematic researches to locate suitable helpmeet mate prospects for your sole son (me, Gooch!), to include inquiries (discreet!) into said female personages' ancestral lineage as how to determine suitability out of concern for dignity, decorum, and honor of family histories, not to fail to mention baby blues peeled for undesirable hereditary characteristics latent or blatant, than which possess potentials for future eruption among offsprings engendered in children, grandchildren, etcetera blah, such as feeble minds, misshapen limbs, ugly faces, etcetera blah. Than which fraternalistic authority is therefore to appoint representatives to undertake *omiami* negotiations with selected eligibles, present recommendations, haggle for dowry, leading to formal ceremonial meetings of parties concerned

160

(me, Daddy, to include selected female personages!), iron out details as to relative family status, etcetera blah, reet? At which point, everything settled, I take ink brush from your hand, inscribe *hanko* signature on *omiami* contract—thereafter to live happily ever after (move in with you and *Mama-san*, natch!).

And, Daddy, I do accept above-cited, reet?

Except. . . .

As how, *Papa-san*, particulars of particular events and personages, context here (A & M campus, sovereign state of Oklahoma, U. S. of A., reet?) conspire and combine to present problematics situation I relate hereinafter for your deliberations. To wit:

Miss Clara (a.k.a. Petty Girl) Sterk, reet? Miss Clara, Daddy! Clara Sterk: fellow co-ed matriculant, A & M class of 1940. Currently co-leader (in concert with wataschi Gooch!) in academics standing (4.0 grade-point), possible co-valedictorian of aforesaid '40 graduating class—in short (same height as me, Daddy!), female co-ed personage of distinctive intellect prowess: brain, greasy grind, worms who consumes tomes, reet? The gal ain't no *baka*, Daddy!

Than which is not to fail to mention Miss Clara's tangible achievements in realm of campus social-org activities.

To include: executive office-holder (vice-prexy!) of Chi Omega sorority; captain-elect of Peppers co-ed cheer and school spirit squad counterpart to Hell Hounds and Ag-He-Ruf-Nex; thrice choosed official Campus Beauty (in company of other select few co-eds—none of which cannot hold even flickering candle's flame to Clara, Daddy!), full-page sepia-tone photo portraits published annually in *Redskin* annual (leaning delicate and demure against rough bark of blackjack oak, feeding ducks and gooses coy on bank of Theta Pond, prone in simulated distracted posture of study on campus greensward grass), reet?

All of which aforementioned above, Daddy, is to say: Miss Clara Sterk—"Petty Girl," I repeats, is affectionate informalist monicker handle denoting great pulchritudes, reet?—is feminine personage of distinguished accomplishments in realm of A & M collegiate life-realm.

Not unlike like unto *wataschi* Gooch, Daddy.

Than which is not to fail to mention integrity of Miss Clara's pedigree—than which includes respectable and affluent parentage (her daddy is oil wildcatter success associate of Bill Marland, Okie oil tycoon, reet?) renowned in environs of city of Ponca City (40 miles northward from Stillwater Town) as patrons of culture (big contributor to funds to erect larger than life-size effigy statue of sage-philosopher-star of stage, screen, and radio Will Rogers—lately deceased circa '35), example of good civics citizenship (confidant of Honorable Governor William—a.k.a. Alfalfa Bill—Murray!), and economic ostentation (Clara tells me her daddy owns both Ford flivver and La Salle limo). To sum pith and gist: no flawed chromosome nor gene neither in Miss Clara's ancestry, Daddy!

Not unlike like unto Gooch, reet?

Does you dig my drifts, *Papa-san*?

Additional element of relevance, Daddy: whilst I do grant and stipulate to widespread *Nihonjin* evaluation of *Amerikajin* female personages as, how we say, mud-fence ugly (raw-beef smell, oversize schnozzes, not to fail to mention lack of proper inhibitions, including indecent exposure of erotic nape of neck, loudness of laughter, failure to exhibit appropriate subordination in company of male personages, etcetera blah), said Miss Clara exerts peculiar effect upon me (your son Gooch!).

Beyond citation as how Miss Clara defies inclusion within stereotyped *Amerikajin* stereotype — any odor is masked by strong scent of Shalimar scent, Clara's nose is, how we say, snub pug, I do assert I sense — daily more intense in her presence (side by side in classes, together at A & M library study tables, in company of Stevie Keller at Greek-org sociabilities), subtle aura of attraction — near-glandular assault upon my sensibility!

Please to forgive indiscretion and ineptitude of above-mentioned, *Papa-san*! Like, bear with Gooch further, reet?

Miss Clara Sterk: grace and line of movement, like unto expert stroke rendered by *sho* calligrapher's brush. As for example, exquisite curves discernible where gullet joins jawbone, crook of elbows, flow of wrist-bone animated by inscribing classroom lecture notations on pad, flexibility of ankle (adorned with gold-plate slave chain — bearing Stevie Keller's initials!) as saddle-shoe-clad toe points when one limb crosses the other — I hesitate, Daddy, halt, refrain from enumerating further instances for fear of violation of decencies via reference to as yet unspoken and more intimate anatomical regions!

Miss Clara Sterk: exactitude of design in miniature, reet? Like unto *bonsai* pine, intricacy of crane executed in *origami* folded paper construct, *ikebana* arrangement of florals, detail of tiger's eye as limned on best-grade silk, reet?

To wit: minuscule convolutions of pinkish auricular orifice, from which hangs pendant fleshy-pink (pierced for jewels!) globe of lobe, reet? Fine threads of eyebrows (plucked by tweezers to enforce symmetry, coloration reinforced by cosmetic pencil!), thin as hair from weasel's tail. Twin nostrils which pulse with intake and also exhale of life's breaths! Teenie-weenie dimples at knuckle junctures whereat fingers join hands! Unfailing match of fingernail (also toes when wearing open sandals in summer!) lacquer with lip paint!

Oh, Daddy! Nights aslumber, I dream oft more now of such (Clara!) than of my home and family in *Dai Nippon*! Does you catch my drifts, *Papa-san*?

And beyond exquisite design symmetry of Miss Clara's mere corporeal physicality, Daddy, I needs must not fail to mention essence than which animates said personage's personality, reet? To wit:

Highlights sheen upon swaths of her wheat-gold hairs tossed careless, struck by rays of sun burning bright high above in Okie sky vastness. Sparkle-twinkle flash of her baby blues, wink and blink and bat thereof! To hear Miss Clara Sterk laugh, Daddy, is like unto tinkle of *furin* windchimes which do hang on our *engawa* porch of paper house in far-off *Dai Nippon*, reet?

Oh, Daddy!

How we say here, *kokoro* sentiments, *wataschi* Gooch falls — is fallen! — noggin-over-feets in love with Clara ("Petty Girl") Sterk!

Can you forgive, *Papa-san*, un-*Nipponshikki* of above-mentioned articulation than which is so unseemly? Please, Daddy, not to translate aforesaid into *Nihonju* for Mama or Iko, reet?

And I assert as how I, Gooch, can take joy in such indulgence in *kokoro* romantic sentiments. I do incorporate same into contemplation of *do* philosophy of path of life and times now and hereafter, reet? Except for, how we say, mitigations and extenuations complicating same, reet? To wit:

Stevie (a.k.a. Mighty Mouse, a.k.a. Yukon Strongboy) Keller, reet?

Stevie Keller, 116-lbs.-avoirdupois undefeated (to date) grapple champ of Missouri Valley Conference and also N.C.A.A. (three years running!), solid leaden conduit cinch for U. S. of A. Olympic squad (irony of which is now there won't be none due to cancellation of Tokyo Town Olympiad due to senso flap with Chinks!). Mighty Mouse, Daddy, absolute B.M.O.C. of A & M Aggie campus! Also loyal Delta Sigma Kappa bro (sponsor of Gooch — breaking frat tradition color-line — even Jesse Cobb McCartney, bona-fide roundball All-American pick don't gots rushed by no frats due to Otoe-Missouria aboriginal ethnicity heritage!)!

Yukon Strongboy, *Papa-san*: Gooch's best bosom pall buddy ruff, reet? Roomie roommate of Maggie Nelson Hall, Kappa House since thereafter, I provide him with vital assistance with math studies (teach him how to use *soroban* abacus when he runs out from fingers and toes to count, Daddy!), drill him on dates, names, and environs for mandatory prescribed course in Oklahoma history, dictate literary compositions (books reports), etcetera blah, as how to enable best pal to maintain athletic eligibility status, reet?

Stevie and Gooch: we is, how we say, gruesome twosome duo on campus, Daddy! Attend gridiron and hardwood contests, grapple practices, duel and tourney matches, view Aggie and Mecca *eiga* matinee flics oft in concert, sup side by side seated at Kappa House table, go to frat stag poker smokers, sorority open-house socials, tea dances — I sit like unto fifth wheel wallflower (how we say Okie-style: mammary glands on boar swine, reet?) on Student Union Coke dates he enjoys with Miss Clara, Daddy!

In short (like unto Gooch, Stevie, Clara, diminutive Dean Timothy J. Macklin, all of like size, reet?), best bosom *oyabun-kobun* buddy pal of Gooch, reet?

Hence: complication, *Papa-san*! Stevie is semienfianced (frat pin pinned, bestower of gold-plate slave chain anklet last *Kurisumasu* Yule) of Clara Sterk — probabale future upshot of which is: when Stevie graduates (1940 coming, Daddy!), attaining to Okie National Guard officer commission as source of financial enablement to tide over Depression economics, Mighty Mouse Strongboy will execute *Amerikajin*-style *omiami* marriage (justice of peace to avoid expense!) with Petty Girl, duo hie off in southerly direction to rural environ vicinity of village of Yukon, Oklahoma (close by Norman, home of hated rival Sooners), there to live happily ever after.

And I, Gooch (*wataschi*, your sole son!) will return to islands of *Nihon*, reet?

163

What's to do, Papa-san? Will you advise, please (and keep word strictly mum, as how Moe Berg used to say)? Where, I query, is wisdom of *do* philosophy when most in need thereof, reet? Where is *yoin*? Where is *ma*? Advise, Daddy, please!

Okay. Safe to translate to *Nihonju* for *Mama-san* and Iko that which follows hereinafter, reet? To wit:

Nothing much to say, reet, folks? Global world-wide flaps continue (natch!) to flap: Schicklegruber and *Duce* Mussolini snooker Chamberlain (who claims peace in our time at Munich, settling Sudeten brouhaha), glorious and heroic Imperial Kwantung Army continues string of unbroken victories (like unto A & M grapplers, reet?) versus Chinks — how long before Chinks must throw in towel, Daddy? Franco gains edge in Iberian *senso*, whilst, in U. S. of A., Republicans rant at possibility prospect of FDR third-term socialist-style government (Honorable E. P. Walkiewicz, mayor of Stillwater Town, cites threat of dictatorship on horizon if Rosenfeldt wins again in '40).

Local-wise, Civie Conservation Corps completes digging of huge man-made Lake Klemp (named for A & M Prexy!), than which Stillwater Chamber of Commerce lauds as certitude to make of Stillwater environ resort attraction rivaling Miami and Niagara Falls. Not to fail to mention invented by A & M faculty personage Prof Ned Lawry, than which innovation, termed "parking meter," is lauded as sure-fire generator of tax revenues for urban municipalities currently suffering shortsfall due to depressed economics, reet? Also not to fail to mention dramatic re-doubling of size of A & M R.O.T.C. cadet corps (from four to eight battalions!), arrival also of regular *Amerikajin* army officer cadre to take charge thereof — than which is personal loss of status stature for Sergeant-Major Tommy Turner, than which whom is thereby reduced to limited duties.

R.O.T.C., Daddy, now equipped with Springfield shoulder-fire weaponry, new air-cooled .30-caliber rapid-fires, portable mortars, etcetera blah, will spend next summer academic calendar hiatus on extended field manueverings at Ft. Sill — much to chagrin of Cadet Stevie! Flying Aggies aviation clubbers now proud possessors of Link Trainer device, schedule to sign contract soon with federal government War (*senso*) Department for training of pilots, reet?

All than which latter above aforesaid proves of great interest to personage whose name I need not articulate, reet? Suffice to say, *Papa-san*, Japan–America Friendship Society has of late increased amount of *genkin* scholarship support funds to Gooch, reet?

Otherwise: all well here, folks. And how is you, *Mama-san*? *Iko-san*, does you burn midnight oils, do good in scholastics? I confess to yet-lingering *hara* belly sadness of homesickness longing, folks, even after more than two years away from you here in distant Oklahoma, reet? 1940 (Empire Foundation Day, 2,600 years of Imperial Way, coming same time as Gooch's graduation!) coming soon, reet?

Meanwhiles, I keep schnozz to grinding stone, also clean, convey to you herewith and herein all due familial respects and sentiments, to include greetings to *kami* who reside in *tokonoma* alcove *butsudan* altar in our paper house. Next time you clap hands to summon same, say hello for me, Gooch, in Shinto, reet, folks?

Past hour of midnight now, folks—echoes of Old Central tower clock Westminster-style gongs fade over greensward of deserted A & M campus—matriculants all gone home for holidays. Stevie and Clara, even as I write, attend big *o-shogatsu* New Year Eve bash party hosted by her parents in city of Ponca City, but 40 miles northward, reet?

And so close this, my year's-ending epistle to you, folks. And sign my *hanko* signature, your son—

Gooch

Cut to: campus greensward, Agricultural & Mechanical College, Stillwater Town, county of Payne, sovereign state of Oklahoma, circa September 1939, reet? Dig it, Jack!

Can you not dig it? Circa September '39, reet? A & M campus, first day of classes, final year of collegiate life and times of *wataschi* (me!), Gooch, Jack!

Green campus greensward lies lush, watered by seasonal rains easing Okie Dust Bowl drouths (at long last!), grass thick under steady strong sun beaming bright down out of blue-white sky vastness (than which same is dotted here and also there by tufts of clouds' fleeciness), normal seasonal Okie heat swelter mitigated by cooling surge of Rocky Mountain airs descending from northerly (O.U. Sucks!) out of Colorado and Kansas prairie expanses. Blackjack oaks still sport deep summer green leafages, mockingbirds perched therein, scissortails (Okie state bird, Jack!) cut flight patterns in balmy air—overall ambience aura effect of idyllic paradisiacal peace and contentments—how we say, good to be alive, Jack!

September 1939, first day of classes, than which includes initial organizational orientations meeting of Prof Os Southard's advanced seminar (masterworks of *Igirisujin* English and Yank *Amerikajin* lits, reet?)—enrollment by invitation and/or permission of instructor only, Jack! Than which class meet concludes as follows:

"I think that covers it," says main mentor Prof Os, and, "Does everyone know what to expect now? Okay, I won't hold you until the bell today. Go on and enjoy this weather while it lasts, people." Than which pronouncement is followed by slap of notebooks closings, dropped pencils clatter, shuffle of books gathered (I wrap materials in *furoshiki* bundle cloth, reet?), stomp of feets exiting, etcetera blah.

"See you later, Goochie," says Clara Sterk.

To which I riposte: "Miss Clara? You have scheduled appointment than which you needs must hie off in haste to rendezvous?"

"I told Stevie I'd meet him at the Union for a Coke. Do you want to come along, Gooch?" says she—we stand in hallway of William Mills, Jr. Humanities Building, outside door to Prof Os' seminar room, reet?

"So nice the weathers, Miss Clara," I tell her, and, "Shames to sequester selves within whilst unseasonal coolth creates balmish spring-tide temperature! Will you not join me for greensward stroll or loll? How we say in *Dai Nippon*, Miss Clara, come along on little *sanpo* walk with *wataschi* Gooch?"

"I would," says she, "but I told Stevie I'd meet him at the Union after Southard's class got out."

"Please, Miss Clara," I say, and, "As how Prof Os is done emancipated us early, Strongboy Stevie will not sit expectant for yet half the hour's duration, reet? Please, Miss Clara," I say, "I would confabulate with you."

"Is it important?" she asks, then renders me big *sumairu* smile—ah, Jack, my heart breaks, breaking, broke!—says, "Okay. For a little while until I have to meet Stevie. You're such a card sometimes, Gooch!"

Thus it were, Jack!

We traverse (side by side: I clutch *furoshiki* bundle under arm, Miss Clara carries her tomes like unto shelf beneath chests, reet?) William Mills, Jr. Humanities Building hallway, egress to campus greensward vista, walk sidewalk past Old Central (shadow of clock tower is cooler shady slice against balm-warm greensward green, reet?), cut off concrete to walk upon grasses yet spongy from recent rainfalls, meander in direction of distant Theta Pond.

"Ultimate year as A & M matriculants for us, Miss Clara, reet?" I say.

"Isn't it hard to believe, Gooch?" she says. "Time goes so fast it seems like to me. Sometimes I feel like just yesterday we were all walking around scared, wearing those silly frosh beanies we didn't dare take off except when an upperclassman stopped you and made you sing 'O.A.M.C.' and do all the cheers. Oh, Gooch," says she, "sometimes it almost makes me want to cry when I think how soon it'll be when we graduate and all go away and don't come back next fall!"

"Reet," I say, and, "Time flying. Future coming. *Ma* moment rife with *yoin* resonances in which we abandon collegiate life and times lifestyle, proceed in direction of *do* path of career shtick, etcetera blah. Than which perception endows even present instance with nostalgia tinge, reet?"

"I guess," says Clara Sterk. We pause, look back at lofty Old Central clock tower monolith against Okie sky vastness.

"Old Central," I say, and, "Thereon, upon bronze placard, will be inscribed names of outstanding student personages, class of 1940."

"We'll all be there forever, won't we, Gooch, even when we've gone away forever, you and me and Stevie, like the way we're all together all the time now!"

"Reet!"

"Oh, Goochie!" says she, and, "I wish you didn't have to go home all the way over on the other side of the world when we graduate next spring! I sure hope you'll be able to come back for a visit, or when we have class

166

reunions at Homecoming! We're going to write lots of letters back and forth, aren't we, so it won't be like we're saying goodbye forever, is it!"

"Reet."

Dig it: circa September '39, first week of classes, A & M campus, recent summer rains and northerly air mass coolth render atmosphere ambience of balmish paradisiacal idyllicness, reet? I, Gooch, class of '40, take *sanpo* stroll on lush green greensward (vague direction of Theta Pond, reet?) with Miss Clara ("Petty Girl") Sterk (co-valedictory candidate with Gooch, than which whom said co-ed personage I do love with fullest *kokoro* romantical sentiments, Jack!).

Miss Clara Sterk: ah, Jack, my heart is broken, breaks, breaking!

Bright beaming sun ascending high in blue-white Okie sky vastness expanse strikes silver-gold highlights in wheat-gold of her hairs! Tiny tendrils — how you say, saliva curls, reet? — dangles from creamy porcelain of her ears, flounce of newstyle horsie's-tail coiffure reveals fetching glimpse of downy nape of her neck! Darkened arch of her plucked brows, long silky lashes, do frame depthlessness of her blue baby blues — wink, blink, bat, flash! Little flare of her nostrils set in pert snub pugness of her schnozz as she breathes deep of balm-warm air's freshness! Miss Clara's bee-stinged full lips (encarmined glossy blood-red, Jack!) part to reveal rows of even pearlie whites! Sun-dress straps cross perpendicular to curve of her peach-tanned shoulders, and upon the satin dermis of her exposed arms I note faint bleached hairs fine as weasel's tail *sho* calligraphy brush! Above shelf she makes of her text tomes (shames upon Gooch!), I sneak peek into shaded cleft of her bosoms cleavages! Her hips do swell under skirt, recede to twin symmetry of her shining legs, than which limbs terminate in platforms of her small feets, ten toes tipped with blood-red paint (to match — natch! — hue of her finger-ends and also lips)!

I work from memory, Jack!

Miss Clara ("Petty Girl") Sterk: circa first week of classes, Oklahoma A & M campus, September 1939 (senior year, Jack!) — in balm-warm mid-morn air's ambience atmosphere, hard by Theta Pond environ, pervades scent of Shalimar perfume, reet?

"I'll miss you, Gooch. We all will."

"Will you sit upon greensward with me, Miss Clara?" I query, and, "I will spread *furoshiki* cloth thereon to preclude grass stains encroachment upon your frock," I say.

"You're always so sweet, Gooch, I think you're the nicest person I know," says she, and, "I've got to go in a sec if I'm going to meet Stevie on time."

And we did sit side by side upon green spongy grass greensward, A & M campus, September '39 (I spread *furoshiki* beneath her!). "Miss Clara," says I, "you do wear always upon your garment Mighty Mouse Stevie's Kappa pin, reet?"

"He'd be so hurt if I forgot ever," says she. Nearby environ of Theta Pond, fellow matriculants and also co-eds do stroll and loll.

"And encircling lower limb is ever Strongboy's slave-chain anklet, reet?"

"I just love it," says she, and, "He was so sweet to spend so much money for it!" In still green-leafed branches of blackjack oak trees and also cottonwoods on marge of Theta Pond, mockingbirds sing for unseasonable mild weathers.

"You and Stevie is semienfianced, reet?"

"It's all but official," ripostes Miss Clara, and, "He can't afford a ring, so we didn't say anything to my parents last New Year's, but everyone knows, anyhow. If he gets his National Guard commission next year he'll get a bonus, so maybe I'll have something to show off to everyone even before you have to take off to go home, Goochie."

"Miss Clara," I say. Then pause, summon *hara* belly courage—forgive me, *Papa-san*, forgive me, family *kami*, for non-*Nipponshikki* audacities!— to speak further. Balm-warm air of September '39 is cut by flight of insect-devouring scissortails, reet? "Miss Clara," I did say, "in *Dai Nippon* whencefrom I come, custom of marriage is, how we say, *omiami*, reet? Meaning, matter of negotiations conducted formal style in solemn sober *kaigi* conference confabulations, delegations confer in representations of families concerned, research lineages, settle dowry via haggle hassle, consult respective *kami* ancestral spirit ghosts to ensure future domestic conjugal tranquilities, etcetera blah."

"And I think it's just so cute the way you do things the way you're always telling me, Gooch!" says she, and, "It's why I just love you to death, Gooch, because you're so different and still such a neat guy!"

"Reet!" I say, and, "Miss Clara, do you surmise you will be happy in lifelong life and times marriage yoke with Stevie Keller?"

"Oh, I just know we will, Goochie!" says she, and, "Oh, I know Stevie's no great brain like you, and it's tough getting married with steady jobs so hard to come by, but my daddy says things are getting better even if Roosevelt is practically a communist, and he knows some people down in Yukon can get me a teaching position as soon as I graduate, and if Stevie gets his commission the way he's supposed to, we'll be fine!"

"Miss Clara Sterk," I say—ambience atmosphere is one of paradisiacal idyllicness, green greensward grasses, tree leafages, birdsong and also flight, bright ascending Okie-land sun in blue-white balm-warm sky vastness, Theta Pond environ (Old Central tower like unto *kami* spirit guardian looking down from high thereupon!), scent of Shalimar scent, reet? I say: "Miss Clara Sterk of Ponca City, Oklahoma, co-valedictory candidate sole *minken* competish for laurel versus Gooch, I, Gooch Yamaguchi, declare I love you, reet?"

"And I love you too, Goochie!" says she, jumps up from greensward, clutches books to chest, kneels to kiss me (Gooch!) on cheek, says, "You're so sweet and so cute, I wish I could take you home with me sometimes and just keep you on a shelf with my knickknacks! I think you're the very best friend I have in the whole world, even including my sorority sisters, and you're so smart in class, and you know so much about movies! Gooch, I always wanted to have a twin brother, did you know that? And if I did, I'd want him to be just like you! I love you I swear as much as if you were my little twin brother! Bye now," says she, and, "If I don't scurry I'll be late for Stevie! Hope your book wrapper thing's not too dirty from this damp grass! Bye, Goochie!"

And thereafter runs—*chogee*, Jack!—across A & M greensward in direction orientation of Student Union, reet?

Do you not dig it?

Jack: my heart breaks, breaking, broke, broken!

Dig: campus greensward (true green via summer rains easing Dust Bowl drouths), trees on marge of Theta Pond yet leafed green, bright burning sun high in blue-white Okie sky vastness, bird chirp and also flight thereof, air balm-warm via coolthness of northerly air masses, totality of ambience atmosphere infused with lingering scent of Shalimar, reet?

Miss Clara ("Petty Girl") Sterk vanishes in direction of A & M Student Union.

I, Gooch, think (heartbroke, Jack!): mayhap though I am fighter (reference to *ninja*-style assault on redneck goat-roper big 189-lbs.-avoirdupois grappler Gary Lee Stringer, reet?), I sure ain't not no lover, Jack!

Than which is not to fail to mention as how circa September '39 is also, reference Schicklgruber blitzkrieg-style invasion of Poland, how you say, WW II—how we say in *Dai Nippon*, *senso*, reet, Jack?

Oklahoma A & M Campus
Stillwater Town
County of Payne
Sovereign State of Oklahoma
U. S. of A.
31 December 1939

Dear *Papa-san*:

I, Gooch, your son (a.k.a. Yamaguchi Yoshinori!), take Nr. 2 Ticonderoga in hand, apply point thereof to lined pages of Big Chief tablet, commence this, my year's-end epistle to you, *Nihonjin*-style, reet? Thus:

As bitter cold Blue Norther wind shrieks at my Kappa House window (edifice empty except save for me, Gooch), carrying from out of Kansas and also Colorado expanses load of thick driven snows to blanket A & M campus, I, your son, heir to name of family *kami*, take pencil in digits to write, begging your forgiveness, and to convey to you via this missive the peace and serenity restored to you, than which I is done so dishonorably disturbed of late recent passing months.

Daddy: my *hara* belly hurts me for shames I is caused you (how we say here: heart-bust, reet?)! I do concede herewith, hereby, and also herein, as how I is guilty of most non-*Nipponshikki* sentiments and also behaviors, reference autumnal incident concerning Miss Clara (a.k.a. Petty Girl) Sterk I did relate in confidences to you. And I do thank you, in all familial deferences due, for your mercies to *wataschi* in not passing on aforesaid shameful info to *Mama-san* nor Sis Iko neither—anks-thay, Daddy!

What's to say, Daddy?

Perhaps it is as how I am too long in tenure durance here so far away from *Dai Nippon*, not unlike like unto little kiddie lost, how we say, baby in forests of Okie cultural wasteland desert? Unduly influenced by insidious dramatic influences of *Amerikajin eiga* flics I view on regular schedule at Aggie and also Mecca theaters (not to fail to mention courting duos on marge of Theta Pond), aforesaid depicting freewheel style of sophisticate *kokoro* romances, hence inducing me, Gooch, to attempt same in conjunction with Miss Clara Sterk?

Perhaps it is I was but seduced by extraordinary feminine pulchritudes of said Miss Clara (campus beauty!)—no, Daddy, not to bestow blames upon her, as how she didn't have nary a inkling, reet?

Perhaps it were but grand design of *do* path and philosophy of life did dictate me to do this shameful thing? Aforesaid predestination shtick calculated to chastise Gooch for arrogance ignorance innocence presumptions? Hence, howsomever, thus corrected I is now prepared the better to proceed toward future life and times lifestyle?

Than which is not to fail to mention that all cause for concern concerning said dishonor is now mooted, reet? As how Miss Clara Sterk (a.k.a. Petty Girl) and Mr. Stevie Keller (a.k.a. Mighty Mouse, a.k.a. Yukon Strongboy) is done formal-style proclaimed official enfiancement (ring purchase dependent upon attainment of Okie National Guard officer commission by latter aforementioned 116-lbs.-avoirdupois grapple champ), due to, how we say in *Eigo*, tie hitch knot, upon graduation in springtime merry month of May (late *hanami*), circa '40, reet? Happy duo plans, says *shimbun* announcement in local *News-Mess* (har!) to establish domicile in southward region of Yukon village, Oklahoma (natch!), whereat Miss Clara has impending secondary institution pedagogical appointment. Said sinecure is resultant via her daddy's clout influences, reet? Strongboy Stevie to seek commercial opportunities as available.

So it ends, *Papa-san*. How we say: so be it amen, reet?

Old Central clock clangs dozen times—new year (*o-shogatsu*!) and also decade of 1940, *Papa-san*! And I dare say, aged one and twenty years, time seem to pass ever the more swift, Daddy!

Howsomever, much of mundane newsworthiness to report, but what's do I care, reet, Daddy?

World-wide global flaps continue (natch!) to flap apace, reet? Iberian Republican Popular Front succumbs to Franco, Schicklgruber allies hisself with Uncle Joe Stalin to whack Polish Poles, sits now in sitzkrieg-style Phony War versus France and *Igirisujin* English, Imperial Kwantung Army continues (natch!) victorious advances versus Chinks—ain't they never going to surrender to us, Daddy? — *senso* in China now full blast under new *gumbatsu* Premier Tojo Hideki (he the one also knowed as The Razor, Daddy?), whilst stateside, Republicans all but *kichigai* insane angered over FDR running for third term etcetera blah blah.

What's do I care?

Local-wise, R.O.T.C. continues expansion activities, Flying Aggies fly over A & M campus to train U. S. of A. Army Air Corps flyboys — all than which I report to personage of Japan–America Friendship Society, than which whose moniker I need not articulate. But what's to care — *daijubo*, reet?

How does you envision future era, Daddy? Your son as *shimbun* scribe like unto you? Diplomatic-corps *honcho* factotum employed by *Gaimusho* Imperial Foreign Ministry? Big-business *zaibatsu* exec? I have of late oft even thought of career endeavor in thriving *eiga* flic industry of *Dai Nippon* (still gots Moe Berg's Stewart Warner camera there in our paper house, Daddy?). Perhaps as man-in-middle type factotum, Toho Company rep for *harukai* stateside imports? Har har — and also hee, reet, Daddy?

What's ever, with grace and guidance of my *Papa-san*, oversight assistance of benevolent family *kami* spirits, precision tool of *Eigo* lingo — than which now I am all but master of! — how we say stateside, can't go wrong for being right, reet?

Well. Late, Daddy. I do confess to weariness of spirit and also corpus. All apologies for curtness, I sign off with *hanko* signature — until mid-May circa '40! — your son,

Gooch

Cut to: circa May 10, 1940.

Tenth day of May (merry month thereof, late *hanami*, reet?), 1940, U. S. of A., sovereign state of Oklahoma, county of Payne, Stillwater Town, campus greensward (good spring rains engender green grasses and blackjack oak leafages) of Oklahoma Agricultural & Mechanical College — commencement, Jack! How we say: no more recess, no more tomes, no more mentor's disapproving mien — graduation day, Jack!

End of matriculation, end of collegiate Joe College life and times shtick — end of Gooch, reet? Dig it:

Mise-en-scene is early afternoon, A & M campus, temperatures arisen already to high nineties (Fahrenheit) under blazing bright sun high in clear blue-white cloudless Okie sky vastness. Assembled students and faculty (not to fail to mention assorted *honcho* dignitaries!) perspire not unlike like unto swine in Ottoman spa, clad all in black gowns and mortarboard headgears (orange tassels pendant therefrom, reet?).

Than which ceremonial participants proceed in ritualist academic processional, route march pace timed to strains of "Pomp and Circumstance" as rendered by Aggie Spirit Band (augmented by selected instrumentalists drawn from ranks of A & M Varsitonians, Big Band Sound dance band), entourage led (natch!) by A & M Prexy Paul Klemp (diminutive Dean Tim Macklin carries mace of authority, reet?) from out of Lewis Field staging environ, traversing greensward to close by Old Central, whereat lofty clock tower provides minimal but growing slice of dark green shade relief from swelterheat.

Procession halts, grads filing into rows of folding chairs, A & M faculty and administrative *honchos* ascending wooden steps to join dignitaries awaiting on platform dais. Families and friends and assorted wellwishers and also mere curious local yokels arrayed out upon greensward expanse behind class of '40, than which remains standing for playing of *Amerikajin* national anthem (Aggie Spirit Band augmented by Varsitonians) whilst Pershing Rifles honor-guard contingent (real Springfield '03 shoulder-arms, Jack!) raise Stars and Stripes and also Okie state gonfalon—said contingent under command of Sergeant-Major Tommy Turner, said personage resplendent in full-dress uniform adorned with Great War campaign ribbons.

Anthem strains diminish, give way to occasional mockingbird chirp, faint stir of raised flags in stifling air as A & M semiofficial self-appointed chaplain (Baptist, natch!) Reverend Lyle Bates articulates overlongish benediction calling upon Christian deity for blessings upon all gathered for solemn and also joyous occasion, peace on earth in these our troubled times, daily breads, etcetera blah blah amen.

"The class of nineteen and forty will please to get seated, please," says A & M Prexy Paul Klemp.

Can you dig it, Jack? It is circa May 10, 1940, reet? I, Gooch, sit ensconced on folding chair, first row (flanked left by Miss Clara Sterk, right by best pal bosom buddy fellow Kappa bro Stevie Keller, reet?)—how we say, best seats in house, Jack.

High above Gooch burns hot ball of sun (perspirations descend from tight mortarboard headgear—orange tassle pendent!—collects in collar, flows from armpits beneath black gown, collects in waistband, trouser crotch, beads on legs, backs of hands (wherein I clutch program!), feets smolder in brogan oxford shoes, reet? I look up at Old Central clock tower (shade cast shields only *honcho*-types on platform dais), red brick ivy-covered edifice masked by huge gray tarpaulin at ready for impending unveiling revelation of new bronze placard bearing names to join roster of previous generations of outstanding A & M grads. I squint, grimace against piercing sunlight to gander assembled *honchos* on raised platform dais. Not unlike unto still-pic photo printed in Stillwater *News-Mess shim-bun* special A & M graduation exercise feature article:

At lectern stands A & M Prexy Paul Klemp, notes in hand, alongside small table bearing heaped diplomas (how we say, dermis of sheeps) and hot-off-press copies of 1940 *Redskin* annuals, same to be handed to grads individually upon moment of crossing platform to commence, reet?

Stage right of standing Prexy Paul is seated A & M administration and also faculty, to include: diminutive Dean Timothy Macklin (minimalist stature nondramatic whilst in seated status), legendary figures Coach Iron Duke Mr. Henry ("Hank") Iba, E. C. Gallagher—gridiron mentor absent due to recent nonrenewal of contract as result of failure to defeat hated pigskin downstate arch-rival O.U. Sooners (successor yet to be named, reet?).

Stage left are *honcho* honored dignitaries in attendance by invitation, to include: Honorable Governor William "Alfalfa Bill" Murray (scheduled to unveil Old Central bronze placard yet concealed by tarpaulin), Honorable E. P. Walkiewicz, Mayor of Stillwater Town (keynote speaker), campus personalities—Pistol Peter Frank Eaton attired as Old West federal mar-shal—including notched sixgun minus (natch!) firing pin—Miss Sa-mantha Woods, aged venerable campus postmistress, Sergeant-Major Tommy Turner—than which is not to fail to mention Mr. Sato Isao, field rep factotum of Japan–America Friendship Society (har and hee!), nor also bevy of U. S. of A. military officers attached to R.O.T.C. and Flying Aggies student-aviator club, et alia etcetera blah.

Can you not dig it, Jack? I, Gooch, think: Gooch, ends now Joe College collegiate life and times! Ends now, this day (10 of May, circa '40!) long-desired higher educational venture in stateside U. S. of A.! Now, this day (whilst Prexy Paul Klemp introduces guests, summarizes pith and gist of program to come), ends that which than was once (long-ago, far-away *Dai Nippon!*) glorious and promising enticing future time! Which is to say: than which was future, then present, this day becomes past's pastness, Jack.

Gooch thinks: ironies, Jack! Lifelong childhood innocence study of *Eigo* lingo at my *Papa-san's* side on *tatami* mat in our paper house, uncountable viewings of Yank *harukai* import flics (Asakusa District, Jack!)—ends now! Opportunities shot at bluebird, brass ring selection as interpreter-guide (audience with *Mikado*—har!) for American League all-star *besuboru* barnstorm squad (Moe Berg!), collusion in espionage mission entered upon out of overzealous desire for stateside Ivy League (Boola, boola, Go, Tigers!) study, relegation to Dust Bowl drouth-struck plains of Okie-land, A & M (cow college, Jack!) matriculation, clandestine *kempei* operative role—oh, ironies, Jack!—now ends.

I glance leftward, perspiration-glossed cheek of Clara Sterk (rosy-flushed in sun swelter, miasma of Shalimar scent, damp drooping saliva curl!)—ah, Jack, heartbroke is Gooch! Rightward, I note visage of Mighty Mouse Yukon Strongboy Stevie Keller (beneath black gown, clad in Okie National Guard uniform for impending presentation of commissions)—

173

oh buddy best pal, ever-loyal Kappa bros we! I swivel on folding chair, gander rows of fellow grads, class of '40: Loving bros (Carl and Wayne), Jesse Cobb McCartney (F.B.I.), Hell Hounds and Ag-He-Ruf-Nex comrade peers, assorted grapplers, roundballers, gridders — on horizon beyond Theta Pond, heat's shimmers dance.

I think: Gooch! Ends now, this day, reet? I think, do philosophic path of life is twisted course through tangled forest, ironies awaiting around each turn. I think, in this moment, *ma* is not stasis of serene awareness of ambience; rather, sense of separation of selfhood, isolation and anomie, reet? *Enryo* is not balanced harmony of relations; rather, distances imposed by deceits. *Yoin* is not balanced harmony's resonance; rather, silence of shames, pain of confusions. Gooch. Ends (circa 10 May '40!) now.

Says Hizzoner Mayor E. P. Walkiewicz (Republican): "This here generation of college students graduating faces the biggest challenges in the whole entire history of mankind! Not only is they not any jobs much out there hardly unless you're lucky, and our state's agriculture is half blowed away in dust storms, but we got us a dictator of our own near as bad as old Hitler sitting in the White House thinks he can get hisself elected for life, so even though I don't guess it's hardly fair to politic in this here occasion, I'm here to tell you if you don't want your kids growing up socialists and communists, you'd better get behind someone like Taft or Wendell Willkie if you don't want us getting involved up to our necks ever' day in foreign alien wars and corruptions!"

I think: Gooch, where is gone little nipper Yamaguchi Yoshinori? Where is Mr. and Mrs. Yamaguchi's little boy, Yosh? *Yosho-san!*

"Scripture teaches us there will be wars and rumors of wars," says *honcho* bird colonel of regular army R.O.T.C. cadre, "so I understand the honor that is mine, assisted by Sergeant-Major Tommy Turner, who I think you all know and admire here on the campus of Oklahoma Agricultural and Mechanical College, to present commissions as reserve officers of the army of the United States, in the rank of second lieutenant, these commissions to be active in the Oklahoma National Guard under its commander-in-chief the Honorable Governor William Murray, to the following distinguished members of the class of nineteen forty. . . ."

I watch bosom pal Stevie stand, doff black robe and mortarboard (replaced by visored hat — how you say, pooper scooper, reet?), join select fellows to ascend wooden steps, stand at attention posture on platform dais whilst Sergeant-Major Tommy Turner affixes gold bars to epaulets — I note light in Miss Clara's blue baby blues, mist of misty tears (oh, Jack, heartbroke!) as Mighty Mouse Yukon Strongboy joins fellow peer shavetails in rendition of first salute to bird colonel R.O.T.C. *honcho.* I think:

where is gone Student Yamaguchi Yoshinori, top scholar—stripe on leg, chevron on sleeve—of Native Land Loving School? I think, where is callow innocent than which whose sole joy was highest marks attained in form, rote memorization of *Eigo* idiomatic slangs gleaned viewing import *eiga* flics? Gone, I think, is ambitious youth so honored by distinction of selection as guide-interpreter to barnstormer Yanks (say it were not so, Moe!), not to fail to mention honor (har!) of audience with *Mikado* (hee!)!

"It's my honor," says Honorable Governor Alfalfa Bill, "'cause I always been believing in educations for our young folks here in the great state of Oklahoma, to pull this here cord and show you-all the names of the grads is judged most outstanding for good grades and honors and school spirit by A & M's faculty and administration. Now these here names is going to grace the walls of Old Central here for all time to come, carved out in metal on a plate and all for anyone as wants to can look up and see who the best ones is!"

Honorable Alfalfa Bill yanks lanyard, tarpaulin falls in heap to green-sward green—cheers, applause (tired, muted by extreme high-nineties temperature, reet?)—revealing names of outstanding honored grads. Amongst which (natch!), just below that of Clara Sterk, I read: *Yoshinori "Gooch" Yamaguchi*. Weary cheers and hands-claps.

I think: where is gone eager enthusiastic frosh Gooch alighting upon Stillwater Town railroad platform, wearing obligatory frosh beanie? Where is gone Joe College collegiate sentiments—Go, Pokes, Go, Punch-ers, Ride 'Em, Cowboys, Beat O.U.? Oh, where is Gooch (circa '36, '37, '38, '39)? Gone, Jack!

"The salutatorian of the class of 1940, Miss Clara Sterk, will now read the Class Will and Prophecy," says diminutive Dean Timothy J. Macklin (minuscule stature evident by evidence of mortarboard-clad noggin par-tially concealed by lectern, reet?).

Do you dig it, Jack? Miss Clara drops from contention in *minken* com-petish for co-valedictory laurel via sole grade of B bestowed by Prof Os Southard in final lit seminar, spring '40 semester, aforesaid resultant from Miss Clara's preoccupation with enfiancement and nuptials planning tensions.

I think: Clara! Even perspiration drenched, delicate as *sho* calligraph, small not unlike like unto *bonsai*, exact as *origami* crane! Clara! I sniff waft of Shalimar miasma dissipate via osmosis in stalled superhot air of high-nineties temperature of midafternoon (May 10, '40!). Clara! I think: vow, Gooch, to love her not unlike unto twin sister, not unlike like unto *Iko-san*! I think: know, Gooch, you is not a lover!

Says Miss Clara (reads from prepared script, reet?): "And to the A & M classes of nineteen forty-one, nineteen forty-two, and nineteen forty-three, and to all the classes who follow in our footsteps in the future to come, we leave our love and devotion to Oklahoma A & M, and we predict for you the challenges of learning and of the future we all enter this day in the Year of Our Lord Jesus Christ nineteen hundred and forty!" Heat-enervated cheers and scattered smatter of claps enfeebled by heat-stifle. "And now," says Clara, "it's my pleasure to introduce the valedictorian of the A and M graduating class of nineteen forty—"

"Go get 'em, Gooch!" whispers Strongboy Stevie (gold shavetail bars glint in white-hot afternoon sun) in my ear.

"—having compiled a perfect straight-A grade record through four years of study. Summa cum laude, Phi Kappa Phi honorary scholastic service fraternity, Sigma Tau Delta, Phi Eta Sigma, voted Most Popular Male Student and Most Spirited Male Student, well," Clara says, "if we had a Phi Beta Kappa chapter at A & M, he'd be that too! And I just want to say personally that he's my favorite person except for one"—heartbroke, Jack!—"and I know everyone just loves him as much as I do, and I'd like to say how much he's contributed to make our four wonderful years at A & M so wonderful—"

"You'd think damn near," whispers Stevie, "you was the one instead of me she was marrying up with, Goocher!"

"Reet," I did say, Jack.

"—I give you my very best friend who I know will be my friend for life, and a dear friend and now loyal alum of A & M and America too, and I know will make us all proud of him in our future lives, it's my pleasure to introduce to you our very own. . . ." Miss Clara pauses to lick lips, get pronunciation right, reet? "Yoshinori Yamaguchi, who came to us all here at A and M from the Land of the Rising Sun, Japan, four years ago, and made us all love him! And we call him just plain Gooch! Come on up here, Goochie!"

Do you dig? *Ma*, reet? Moment of stasis (rise from folding chair in first row, ascend—perspiration awash!—wooden steps, render minimalist kowtow deference bow to dais delegation, receive big perspiration-clammy hug from Miss Clara—Shalimar!): who I was, what I is, what's to come, reet, Jack? *Ma*: zip, zilch, squat, zed, zero. Oh, in moment of collegiate life and times triumph, so unhappy Gooch, sad struck with *yoin* awareness of host of ironies implicit therein, reet?

Says I (extemporary, Jack!): "Reet. First off, all due deferences respects to revered faculties and administration *honchos* present, than which is not to fail to mention dignitaries of political and also social renown. Welcome all, reet? How we say back home in *Dai Nippon, yokoso*, folks! Next up, *wataschi's* personal anks-thay and kudos to all mentors and fellow matriculants and also co-ed females, class of circa '40. Like, anks-thay for providing stimulating educational ambience atmosphere aura enabling humble Goochness to attain honors you so graciously bestow thereon, reet? How we say in *Nihonju*, deep in my *hara* belly is enkindled burning embers of gratitudes to all contributing thereto! How we say, *arigato*, folks! What's else?"

Shaded by lengthening shade of Old Central clock tower, I look out upon rows of '40 grads, black-clad, sagging in folding chairs under heat-weight. Theta Pond horizon shimmers. Mockingbirds silent in silence, scissortails grounded, blackjack oak leafage droops limp. Up front, Clara and Stevie squint up at me. What's else to say? Anybody, I do wonder, truly attending to spontaneous-style obiter dicta of Gooch?

"Aforesaid speakers," I say, "declaim of world-wide global flaps, economics stagnations, formidable obstacle challenges also. Reet. I add only: not to underestimate power of individual initiatives, old-fashioned frontier Okie-style *Amerikajin* virtue values, reet? I say to you fellow grads, class of circa 'forty, it remains to self to create selfhood, reet? We is what's we does, fellow peer Aggies! I say to you: how we say in *Dai Nippon*, pause and sniff blossoms, reet? *Ma* moment steady slipping away. Look around you, Jack! How we say, *yoin*, catch subtleties of emanations emanating from all about. *Enryo*! We say, establish proper decorum relations in all relationships, reet? Not to fail to mention big picture of *do*, than which is *Nihonju* lingo signifying course of actions taken in life and times lifestyle sojourn. In sum, fellow peer Aggie grads of both genders, class of nineteen forty, open baby blues wide apart, look around, do right by others not unlike like unto Gold Rule rule, reet? Therefore, in sum and short, pith and gist, get on with it, Jack!" Faintest ripple of applause rises from heat-sodden black-clad grads assembled.

"In concluding," I say, "I conclude as how we must face future time with traditionalist A & M Aggie spirit, reet? As how: Go, Pokes! Go, Punchers! Ride 'Em, Cowboys! Beat O.U.! How we say, *banzai*!" I shout to furnace-like Okie sky vastness—Aggie Spirit Band (augmented by Varsitonians) strikes up "Fields of Waving Wheat" fight-song, segues into O.A.M.C. anthem, all standing to sing (Pershing Rifles Honor Guard salutes with '03 Springfields) as I descend wooden steps, resume spot on front row seating for presentation of sheep's dermis diplomas.

Jack, I did think: bye-bye; so long, been good to know you; see you around, reet? Dig you later, cats! Oh, going, Jack, going, gone! Past gone, present becoming pastness, future becomes present. How we say, *sayonara*, reet? Can you truly dig it, Jack?

What's else? Remains only to relate final informal-style congress of grads, faculty, administrative *honchos*, politicosocial luminaries, families, friends, wellwishers, assorted mere curious localist yokels, aforesaid personages milling in confines of shade slice cast by Old Central clock tower (than which bongs thrice), partaking of reception repast snack of cookies and Methodist-style (no booze!) pink punch.

"Oh, Goochie, your speech was so neat! It just breaks my heart you can't stay long enough to come to the wedding! Are you positive you have to take right off in the morning?" says Clara.

"Sad to say," I say, and, "Also fragmenting mine, Miss Clara."

"It'd be swell to have you there, Gooch," says Stevie. "If it wasn't for my folks and Clara's probably too throwing a hissy, you know I'd ask you to stand up with me as best man."

"Reet," I say, and, "Looking good in National Guard uniform, Shave-tail Stevie," and, "There in *kami* spirit, reet? Thinking upon nuptials ritual whilst I traverse continent westward to 'Frisco aboard Santa Fe, reet? Orry-say about cancellation of Olympiad, Stevie, we might could have rendezvous reunion in Tokyo Town otherhow, reet?"

"Yeah," says he, "well, sometimes life kicks you in the butt, huh, Gooch?"

"I don't want him going over there if there's going to still be your war on, Gooch," adds Miss Clara.

"Reet."

Ma. Stand still in place, Jack. Shaded slice of A & M campus greensward, May 10, 1940, reet?

"Gooch," says Prexy Paul Klemp (diminutive Dean Timmy in wake, natch!), "I want you to meet the governor of the state of Oklahoma, son! You can tell your grandkids about it! Bill," says he to Honorable Alfalfa William, "shake the hand of the best all-around student I seen in all my days heading up A and M! I'll admit he don't look like much, but this little Jap is a pure-dee whiz-bang for getting A's and joining in activities with true Aggie spirit!"

"Congratulations!" says Honorable Governor Bill, takes my hand in both his, executes big howdy handshake squeeze, reet? "I didn't make head nor tails either one from what you said up there, but I'll take the prexy's word it was on the money. Yama-something was it?"

"Gooch," I say, and, "Honored and humbled is I to make your acquaintance, revered politico *sensei*." Roving *News-Mess* photog snaps pic, reet? Gooch in double handclasp of Governor Alfalfa Bill, Prexy Paul beaming benevolent thereon, Hizzoner Mayor E. P. Walkiewicz close by, not to fail to mention Prof Os Southard, and also diminutive Dean Tim hidden from view by rangy mayor.

"It's not going to be the same trying to slam some literature into the heads of these rednecks without you there to keep it going, Gooch," says

Prof Os.

"Send me glossy print, please," I say to photog, hand him *meishi* calling card bearing home address, reet? "As how I assemble pics and *shimbun* clips to chronicle Okie sojourn in family album."

Yoin: look about, receive nuance emanations resonating out of totality context, reet?

"Gooch," says 189-lbs.-avoirdupois grappler Gary Lee Stringer, "I know we never got off on the right foot all the time we're supposed to be Kappa brothers and all, and I had me a lot of time to think on it getting healed up after them O.U. sonsabitches wrecked me that night at Theta Pond, and I 'fess I never give you a square deal, so I hope you'll take my hand as a friend or at least not enemies and we can sign each other's *Redskin* and all, okay?"

"Reet, Gary Lee. Life and times too short to nurse grudgery, reet? Orry-say for truncation of your grapple season!" We shake howdy handshake, exchange secret Kappa brotherhood grip, inscribe respective *Redskin* annuals with *hanko* autographs, etcetera blah.

Enryo: achieve balanced reciprocities in all relationships, reet, Jack?

"Sincere congratulations, Gooch," says Mr. Sato Isao (frockcoat, striped trousers, spats, opera hat), emerges from throng. I render kowtow bow, reet?

"Anks-thay, *Sato-san*. Like, surprised to see you here this day. Don't hardly recognize you except in dark on bank of Cimarron River, rural Perkins village environ."

"It is my pleasure and duty as the designated representative of the Japan–America Friendship Society," says he (big *sumairu* sneer), "to present myself at the various commencement exercises at which our young men of *Dai Nippon* undergo the quaint and awkward *Amerikajin* rituals. Even now I must haste away, west to California, then east, to Harvard, Yale, Princeton, Amherst, and elsewhere."

"Reet," I say, and, "Guess I won't be seeing you no more after today, reet?"

"It is not for me to say," says Mr. Sato. "But I am empowered to state that my superiors of the *kempei* are well pleased with you, Gooch — forgive my laughter, your *Amerikajin* name always inspires mirth! It is to those functionaries that you may look for guidance in your future activities, Gooch!"

"I been, like, thinking of maybe going in for journalism, like my *Papa-san*, get on with one of the provincial *shimbun* maybe."

"Gooch," says he, "I should not be surprised to learn that wise personages at Ichigaya Heights may find endeavors better suited to serve the ends of *hakko ichui* than scribbling editorials in *Eigo* for some obscure *shimbun* in our provinces! No, Gooch, I think you must accept that destiny holds a finer purpose for one of your considerable talents and experience!"

"Reet," I say, and, "We better stop gab-fest in *Nihonju*, huh? Like, everybody staring, reet?"

"I haste away from this wretched, sweltering place," says he. "I long for the cool ocean air of California to eradicate the memory of the oven's heat of this blistered prairie!"

"You gets used to it."

"Again," says Mr. Sato Isao, "my congratulations to you, not only upon the excellence of your performance of your mission — what great advantage it is to *Dai Nippon* to know all we know of these barbarians! — but also upon your scholastic triumph! With such young men as you in the service of *Dai Nippon*, who shall hope to prevail against us?" And departs with aside comment on sickening stench of warm uncooked meat, bowing mini kowtow left and also right to extricate self from throng, reet?

Do: philosophical path of life and times. Where is *wataschi* going in future, which is not to fail to mention question as to mode of transport, reet, Jack?

Dig it: circa May 10, 1940. Circulate to exchange *hanko* signatures in *Redskin* annuals (not to forget X of Pistol Peter Frank Eaton, spidery sprawl scrawl of shaky-handed Miss Samantha Woods, block printing of Sergeant-Major Tommy Turner, flourish of Mr. Iron Duke ("Hank") Henry Iba, Loving bros Carl and also Wayne, All-American roundballer full-blood Otoe-Missouria Jesse Cobb McCartney, new-commissioned Shavetail Stevie — natch! — Miss Clara — oh, heartbroke, Jack!), etcetera blah.

Above mentioned experienced whilst all the while pondering implications implicit in *ma* moment in historical flow of *do* path, reet? As for instance:

10 of May, 1940, Jack — fifty-years anniversary of founding of Oklahoma Agricultural & Mechanical College (cornerstone of Old Central dedicated circa '90), and also, back home in *Dai Nippon*, Empire Foundation Day, Jack, 2,600 years celebration of *Kodo* Imperial Way dating all the way back to, how we say, *Yamato*, ancient name of *Nihon*, reet? Which is also not to mention global-wide flaps yet flapping: glorious Imperial Kwantung Army still (natch!) advancing victorious versus stubborn Chinks, whilst in Europe, sitzkrieg Phony War terminates with Schicklgruber invasion of Belgium (also clobbering Dutchmen), to include impending fall of France — not to also fail to mention signing of Berlin-Rome-Tokyo Axis Pact, reet?

Oh Jack, big ironies to come! About which more later.

From memory, Jack! Make up what's I done forgot, reet?
Gone, man.

Letters gone, burned up in our paper house in a big fire circa '42 (Jimmy Doolittle's daring-do flyboys off the *Hornet*). *Redskin* issue of 1940 gone, fell out of my haversack whilst flying upside down over the U.S.S. *Oklahoma* (circa '41). Big fires! Big ironies, about which more to come later.

Mr. Sato Isao, Moe Berg (not to fail to mention Sultan of Swat, Gehrig, Jim Foxx et alia etcetera blah) — gone, Jack!

Stevie ("Mighty Mouse") Keller (a.k.a. Yukon Strongboy), Clara ("Petty Girl") Sterk (heartbroke is I, Jack!), gridiron greats Loving bros, Carl and Wayne, also gone (Iwo Jima, Jack, how we say, *Ogasawara*, Sulfur Island), Jesse Cobb McCartney (full-blooded Otoe-Missouria certified roundball hardwood All-American!) gone — Anzio beachhead! Gooch (Y.Y.). All gone.

Happy Gooch, circa 1936–1940, Oklahoma Agricultural & Mechanical College, gone. Gooch, name cast in bronze on A & M Honor Roll, hallowed Old Central walls, removed with metal grinder and sandblaster, circa '44 (due to escape of daring and resourceful Mighty Mouse Strongboy from Philippines Islands durance vile, return via Australia to stateside carrying news of chance Corregidor reunion with *wataschi*, reet?) — hence, gone! Gooch: face and name removed from library copies of 1940 *Redskin*! All gone.

Go, Pokes. Go, Punchers. Go, Aggies. Ride 'Em, Cowboys.

Oh, happy, happy Gooch!

Not unlike unto as if how he never was, reet?

Motto: *mono no awari*. How we say, sad resignation to injustice of life, Jack!

Meaning: like, way the cookies crumbles, mop flop, true course of *do* flow's path of life and times lifestyle evolving eventually in *ma* moment's ultimate awareness, reet?

Tell me about it, Jack!

3.

Lieutenant
Benshi

*katte kabuto
no o woshinieyo:*
in the moment
of victory,
tighten
your helmet
strap

"*Sensei*," says renowned *irezumi* tattoo artist Terada Seijo, come via *wataschi's* personal limo from Yokohama to check condition of current state of handiwork, "I am pleased to announce all swelling of the flesh has subsided without complication. Further, the stage of peeling and flaking of the epidermis is all but concluded. I can, *sensei*, whenever you deem it appropriate, proceed to formulate a design to be applied to the lower portion of your back when you have indicated your approval."

"Reet," I say, and, "Than which will leave only vastness of my ever-wider-spreading ass, canvas more than adequate to contain conclusion of chronicle of life and times of *wataschi* Foto Joe Yamaguch, up to and including present *ma* moment, reet? Remind me to save you a good spot for your *hanko* signature seal calligraph, *Seijo-san*, as how it ain't but fair excepting save you gets to flash your moniker as artist when hide goes up for display on wall of Wantanabe Museum, reet?"

"*Sensei* Mr. Yamaguch," says Terada Seijo, "the honor of the task itself is sufficient reward for my humble effort!"

"Than which is not to fail to mention profuse *yen* I is forking over, reet? *Daijubo, Seijo-san*! Not to fret, as how I make joke, joshing-levity shtick. Hand me my *kimono*, there, will you, it's getting chilly as Okie eventide in *tsukimi* autumnal season in here, Jack!"

Can you dig it? Tokyo Town penthouse, thirty stories high above smog haze pollution, personal accommodations adjoining corporate headquarters, Foto Joe Yamaguch Productions, Inc., cinematic conglomerate (*monsho* sign of carp, swimming upstream, highly stylized rendition, reet?) — me, *wataschi*, fabled legendary *eiga* flic film mogul Foto Joe Yamaguch, stretched out prone and buck bare-ass skinny-dip naked nude on tea table for expert examination by renowned *irezumi* tattooist Terada Seijo.

I pose query to you, Jack: is it not passing strange — humongous irony! — to what a man can come in course of *do* flow of life and times?

185

"If you will permit it, *sensei*," says he—I grant said allowance with wave of hand, reet?—"I dare to venture the opinion that this, your design which I execute with my modest skills—"

"Come off it, Seijo, you the best! Like, I gots the good word on you direct from seafarers in every port city, Jack! Never understate virtues, nor fail to blow horn, all that old-timey *Nipponshikki* guff stuff, dig? When you gots it, flaunt it, *Seijo-san!*"

"You embarrass me, *sensei*," mumbles Terada Seijo, averting aged baby blues, rubbing noggin with both hands whilst I stand in day of birth's suit to don household-style lounging *kimono*, reet?

"You was saying?"

"Indeed, *sensei*. That I opine that the appearance of your flayed skin following your demise—may we avert the day by folding a thousand paper cranes!—upon the walls of the Wantanabe Nautical Museum will surely strike visitors as the most remarkable available for viewing. The others," says he, "are all of course traditional schemata, dragons and tigers, courageous carp swimming against the stream's current, blazes of chrysanthemums, likenesses of the Sun Goddess *Ameratasu*, *samurai* warriors, the forty-seven *ronin*—"

"Reet," I say, "but will they dig what they gander? Face it, Seijo, it comes down to this: is it, like, too personal to get message across?"

"Ah," says he—Mr. Terada Seijo, great *irezumi* tattoo artist famed in every dockside and wharf environ in islands of *Nihon*. "Ah," says he, "I do confess, *sensei*, I can only pray to my *kami* that your meaning will prove lucid! Forgive me, Mr. Yamaguch, but I possess no expertise in this regard. I am but a craftsman, only a man of modest skills with tinted inks and electrically powered needles—"

"Reet! Like, not your job to figure significance of bits and pieces, piths and also gists, reet?"

"Perhaps if you were to write something, *sensei*, a monograph to be displayed in company with your flayed skin, so that visitors to the Wantanabe Nautical Museum might read it as they viewed my handiwork, and thus comprehend—"

"Ix-nay!" I say, and, "Nothing on paper, nor no pics neither, as how it don't do not endure, Jack! Not unlike like unto *eiga* flic film stock, acetone celluloid base, too subject to burning, big fires all the time possible, dig?"

"Then I must confess I am at a loss, *sensei*."

"No more than me, *Seijo-san!* Dig: half the time I feel not unlike like unto *hanashika* professional storyteller than which who don't can be certain sure how's it going to come out until I reach conclusion's end, reet? Like, every time I tell it, seems like different distinct yarn, reet?"

"*Sensei*," says he, "it is the story of your life! How could you not know whereof you speak?"

"Hee hee!" I laugh. Also har.

186

"Okay," and, "reet," says I. "Listen up! Take notes, sketch on your pad there as and if spirit moves thereto, reet? As how we going to talk about *senso*, going to make us some pictures of, how we say in *Eigo*, WW II — we going to render the Big One, Jack."

"It is not a subject I enjoy to think upon, *sensei*."

"You and the rest of what Tojo and other *honcho* types did used to call Hundred Millions — than which in fact there wasn't more than seventy million *Nihonjin* to start with, reet? Anyhoo. Ready, *Seijo-san?*"

"Proceed at your pleasure, *sensei*."

"Reet. I always does. Than which is doubtless probable possible source of half my troubles. Where was I? Reet. Okey-dokey, dig as follows!"

Than which follows is brainstorm shtick, reet? Run it up flagpole, observe who kowtows. Toss it around, note whereon it do stick. Like, shotgun, see what's we hit, then call it target. I tell Terada Seijo:

Task is hopeless, Jack! Too much to tell, not enough space available on *wataschi's* lower back (saving buttocks expanse vastness for post-*senso* era, reet?), images overlap and flow not unlike like unto camera collage-dissolve sequence. Oh, *Seijo-san*, where to begin, reet?

Issen gorin draftees? *Nihonjin* yardbird grunt Sad Sacks, reet? Cannon fodder, Jack! Reception of *aka gami* red letter informing aforesaid of greetings from *Mikado*, to include *genkin* cash *yen* money for transport to Eta Jima basic-training site enclosed. Ritual last meal of red rice served prior to departure (aforesaid dons thousand-stitch belt for trip, signifying willingness to die for cause, reet?)

Jack: where is space for tableau of *atsumari*, how we say, fall-in formation muster? Stand tall like unto six o'clock in ranks for *tenko* roll call, *banko* count-off, chant of *Chokuyu* Imperial Rescript, face eastwardly direction of Imperial Palace for choral recitation of *reihan* oath of imperial homage, reet? Sing for fast breaker (*nigirimeshi* rice balls and sardines, *hango* mess kit in hand) verse or two of *Umi Yakuba*. Flesh out scene, how we say in *eigo* flic show-biz, dress set, reet?

Add *katana* longswords for *budo* officer-types, Arisaka rifles, Nambu rapid-fires. All very *Yamato Damashii*, Jack! Most stirring *gumbatsu* martial spirit of *hakko ichui*, natch! Than which is not to fail to mention two-plus million dead (subtract from seventy million true count of fabled phony-baloney Hundred Millions!), reet?

Where is scope of *wataschi's* skin to accommodate vaunted *Kido Butai* fleet en route from Kuriles for brilliant attack (*Tora*, Jack!) on, how we say, *Pearu Halbol*, Z-flag flapping in Pacific breeze (not to fail to mention *Hinomaru* and also Sunrise Flag). Dub music track: *Kimagayo* anthem (natch!), *Kaigun* March. Depict early Sunday antemeridian sky over Honolulu thick with planes of *Dai Nippon* (Zekes, Betties, Aichi dive bombers, also Val, not to fail to mention Nakajima, Jack!).

Oh, certain sure, Jack, insert good times-successes roll! After glorious imperial victories over Yanks in Philippines, flight of $50,000 General — how we call him, *Makassar* — insert light moments: arrival of transports from *Dai Nippon* bearing cargoes of *moga* prostitutes (how we say: Comfort Women), U.S.O.-style Encouragement Shows also, natch! Not to fail to mention *Eigo* lingo broadcasts of "Zero Hour" radio, Mrs. Iva d'Aquino (Tokyo Rose, Jack!). Not to fail to mention successful lightning thrusts versus Wake Island, Singapore, Aleutians, Hong Kong — and (natch!) continued perpetually on brink of total victory advance of Kwantung Army toward Chunking, reet?

Dast not fail to mention reversal of *senso* fortunes! Guadalcanal, New Guinea Kokoda Track debacle, Midway, Coral Sea, Great Marianas Turkey Shoot, Bismarck Sea, Leyte Gulf — simultaneous with Yank Marines-led island-hop campaign — *Sekigahara* war's decisive battles continue, *Ketsu Go* final defense of home islands following upon Okinawa and *Ogasarawa* (Sulfur Island — Iwo Jima, Jack!) — quick cuts to *yake tsuchi jidai* Burned Earth Period of clockwork bombings by *bee nijo koo* B-29s: can *Mikado* have been mistaken to undertake *senso* (ask remainder of phony-baloney Hundred Millions back home)?

Oh, Jack, not to fail to effect vivid representation of *kamikaze* Divine Wind flyboys volunteering for assignments via entering circle next to name on flight-school rosters, aforesaid adorned with *hachimaki* headbands reading: All Lives to Fatherland, and also: One Plane, One Warship!

Certain sure not to neglect to render *Enola Gay* releasing *genshi no bakudan* A-bomb on Aioi Bridge target (Hiroshima, Jack!), *pikadon* flashboom illuminating whole scene totality, reet?

Get cracking, Seijo! Hump stumps, Jack! I tell him: time on wing, space available limited!

And where (not to fail to mention!) is space for me, *wataschi*, Jack? How depict former Student Yamaguchi Yoshinori, former Gooch (A & M class of '40), now immersed in aforesaid context as Lieutenant *Benshi* — *benshi*, how we say, he who explains, reet? Historical cinematographer documentary docudrama style, dispatched on personal mission for Premier Tojo Hideki (a.k.a. The Razor, Jack!) to create *eiga* flic chronicle of glorious triumphant realization of *hakko ichui*? Than which is not to fail to mention role after circa late '44, personal rep of *Mikado* (Hirohito, Jack, knew him from way back — har and hee!), dispatched to record new chronicle, *Nippon Maketa* flic — how we say, Japan is Defeated, reet?

Get cracking! Spot on wall of Wantanabe Nautical Museum awaits *wataschi's* hide — time fleets, Jack! How we say, gots to *chogee*, reet, Seijo-san?

Kinestasis: Lieutenant *Benshi*.
Because, like, I always gots to explain, reet?

Circa '41 to '45, Jack.

How we say, WW II (*senso*!). Lieutenant *Benshi* on account of I gots to explain to everybody: *honcho*-types in Ministry of War (Ichigaya Heights, Jack); brother officers intent upon achieving glory for *Mikado* and *Dai Nippon*, also honor for selfs and ancestral *kami*, family names, etcetera blah (various locale environs in Southern Seas Theater); semianonymous under-derlings assigned to assist in conduct of specified tasks (creation of *eiga* cinematic docudrama documentation of grandiose *hakko ichui* design — bringing eight corners of world under roof of *Dai Nippon*, and also *Nippon Maketa* — Japan is Defeated — oh ironies!) associated with wartime missions, reet?

Lieutenant *Benshi*. Me, Jack.

Dig: *benshi*, old-timey silent *eiga* flics in *Dai Nippon*, said personages stand up next to silver screen, explain to audience what's happening, reet? Like, narrative coherence, point out subtle patterns of imagery, light-dark motifs, observations on moral significance, etcetera blah. *Benshi*: all gone with advent of soundtracks to film studios in *Dai Nippon*, circa '32 abouts. But, like I gots always to explain things, like, how we say, Big Picture, for *honcho*-types, brother officers of Imperial Army, assigned underlings. What's in a name, reet? Dig:

Cut to: *kaigi* conference room, Imperial Ministry of War, Ichigaya Heights (Tokyo Town), circa summer of '41. *Take* bamboo shades raised to admit sunlight, striking reflections on lacquered surface of conference table, air heavy with authority of *honchos* present — brass hats, Jack!

Present: Premier-General Tojo Hideki (very coolish cat, slit-eyes behind round specs, shaved noggin, makes tent of fingertips, listens, says nothing); Major General Kammu Fujiwara — military commander for *Domei* (how we say, Board of Wartime Info, reet?), fat man, Jack, butterball, lard-ass, frogface, liver-lips — I is talking ugly, Jack!

And (natch!) me. *Wataschi*, Jack, Sub-Lieutenant Yamaguchi Yoshinori (just out from boot camp at Eta Jima, looking good in new uniform of Imperial Army, to include officer's collar tabs!), trying not to clank sword whilst standing at attention to riposte to queries posed by abovementioned — very awkward still in management of *katana* longsword, Jack, than which is obligatory sidearm apparel for officer types, Imperial Army.

Props (two): elaborate proposal submitted to *Domei* through channels by Sub-Lieutenant Yamaguchi Yoshinori, said document conveying as how his talents can best be of valued service to *Dai Nippon* in conflict (almost certain!) to come, signed in my blood as traditionalist *Nipponshikki* indication of total sincerities, reet? And also intelligence dossier devoted to life and times to date of Yamaguchi Yoshinori, forwarded to *Domei* upon request from offices of *kempei* secret service intelligence-gathering agency of *Dai Nippon*, reet? Than which dossier is strictly (natch!) confidential.

Dialogue:

Fujiwara: "It has been the assumption of the military manpower authorities that you might most productively serve *Dai Nippon* in the capacity of a combat interpreter in the event—" (smiles *sumairu* at me, at Premier-General Tojo; no response from T. — coolish customer, Jack!) — "the Hundred Millions should come to find themselves engaged in armed conflict with the British *Igirisujin* or the *Amerikajin*. In addition to your fluency in *Eigo* resulting from your education in—" (Fujiwara pauses to recollect, flips dossier open to refreshen memory) — "the place called Oklahoma, there is regretfully some question as to your acuity in matters requiring sensitive perception and subtle insights. I have reference here—" (pauses again, finds page in dossier) — "to your unfortunate association with Mr. Morris Berg, also known as Moe, the *Amerikajin* athlete. This was in nineteen thirty-five."

Me: "*Honcho sensei* general, that is a bad rap, reet? Like, I was but a kiddie, little nipper, reet? What's did I know? Besides in addition to which, I was told by a party on the inside as how my work for *kempei* counterintelligence as clandestine operative stateside did put me in good graces in all the right places, not so?"

Fujiwara: "You have reference to Mr. Sato Isao?"

Me: "I does indeed! *Isao-san*, he said as how he'd get it squared on record and all, set me straight with *kempei* factotum folks, *sensei* general!"

Fujiwara (checks dossier, closes it, raps it with hairy knuckles — sound of knuckle bone rapping on lacquered sun-reflecting surface of long table in *kaigi* conference room, summer sunbeams of circa 1941 coming in windows resultant from raised *take* bamboo curtains, Ichigaya Heights, Imperial Ministry of War, Tokyo Town, etcetera blah): "There is a summary report authored by Mr. Sato, the thrust of which is that your service to him in the place called. . . ."

Me: "That's Oklahoma, *sensei* General. Agricultural & Mechanical College, class of 'forty, summa cum laude, valedictory kudo, straight As all the way—"

Fujiwara (*budo* authoritative style, reet?): "It is unnecessary to recite your scholarly accomplishments, Lieutenant Yamaguchi! The question before us is the validity of the rationale of your proposal." Taps proposal with hairy knuckle bone.

Tojo: (don't say nothing, Jack, very coolish customer — than which is why they call him The Razor, reet?).

Me: "Can I, like, try to explain, *sensei* general?"

Fujiwara: "With brevity, please, lieutenant. The premier is a man with enormous responsibilities in this momentous epoch in our history! This audience is a sign of his depthless desire to do all necessary to the attainment of *hakko ichui*."

Me (kowtow bow to Fujiwara, same to Tojo — my *katana* clanks against my leg; very inept with mandatory longsword, Jack!): "Reet! First off, interpreters is, how we say in *Eigo*, ten cents per twelve, reet? Than which is not to fail to mention as how *Domei* gots photographers and also combat artists up proverbial *Amerikajin* wazoo—begging illustrious pardons for resort of vulgar idiomatic slangs. What's I'm offering you here—" (nod noggin in direction of proposal on *kaigi* conference table)—"is a cinematic *eiga* flic archive, coherent narrative docudrama documentary of whole shooting match, how we say, Big Picture, reet? I mean, it's going to be some time passing prior to attainment of *hakko ichui*, even with glorious victories unceasing, as in, say, like, China since all the way back to '31 Mukden Incident, Marco Polo Bridge triumph thereafter, than which is not to fail to mention big win at Nanking, reet? I mean, Co-Prosperity Sphere is reaching out in all directionals, ain't so? Going to take us some time and doing, *sensei honcho* general!

"Howsomever, give me the stuff, budget itemized in my proposal, cameras, film stocks, a few bodies to crew, office here in *Dai Nippon*—Tokyo Town preferred!—to process and also edit screen rushes as they come in from wherever, transport available to hit locations environs as called for, maybe also for second-unit jobs of work, *wataschi* Sub-Lieutenant Yamaguchi Yoshinori can give you a *eiga* filmic record of ultimate triumph of *Dai Nippon* as will last forever as tribute to honor and glory of Hundred Millions, *Dai Nippon*, and also not failing to mention, *Mikado*—" (Fujiwara and Tojo stand (natch!), join me in kowtow in direction of Imperial Palace)—"and the name of *Ameratasu* the Sun Goddess than which who is source of all we is, reet?"

Fujiwara: "Admirable, lieutenant. Even noble, though such exuberance is typical of the young and seldom justified in the cold light of deliberation through which the wisdom of responsible leadership manifests itself."

Me: "Reet, *sensei* general, but I kid you not, this would be a first! I mean, this is a shtick like nobody nowhere ever envisioned as precedent! I is talking thousands of miles of *eiga* flic footage, mountains of film cans, national *matsuri* holidays in the future when the whole Hundred Millions knocks off work to view series of *eiga* flics chronicle glory of *Dai Nippon*, big doings make *Tanabata* festival celebrating seventh day of seventh month of lunar calendar look not unlike like unto weenie roast, reet? I is talking the big-timey show-biz, general!"

Tojo: (don't say nothing, Jack, but I seen his little eyeslits blink behind them specs!).

Me: "Like, I'm talking about a special unit of Imperial Army, dig? Organization and logistics, that's your thing, but I can see it, say, housed under benevolent bureaucratic wing of, say, *Akio Jessoji* Artists National Service Association, reet? Dig: cinematic *eiga* strike force, always at readiness state, on the go! Like, some big thing comes off in China, we get the word, *wataschi* Sub-Lieutenant Yamaguchi goes to action status—cameras and also crews on location for actuality shoots in a matter of hours, getting

191

that good footage, mobile labs to develop rushes, slap together rough cuts, whiz it all back to *Dai Nippon* for final edits, synch in soundtracks—"

Fujiwara: "Restrain yourself, lieutenant! An excess of enthusiasm is always unseemly, not *Nipponshikki*! As to details, rest assured that the *sensei* premier and I will consider all aspects. You may be excused, Sub-Lieutenant Yamaguchi. Unless—" (turns to Tojo, dips fat noggin in deference due)—"there are further questions?"

Tojo: "I would ask this young man from whence comes his conviction that he is adequately qualified to carry out this grandiose scheme? Ambition is necessary, even laudable, but without the requisite abilities, is simple foolishness."

Me: (don't say nothing, Jack, 'cause I is shaking in my puttees, squeezing *take* bamboo sheath of my *katana*, trying to come up with appropriate riposte, reet?).

Fujiwara: "The *sensei* premier-general has addressed a question to you, lieutenant!"

Me (swallow hard, lick lips prior to articulating): "Reet. Because. As how, *sensei honcho* premier, ain't nobody in *Dai Nippon* knows the *eiga* flics like I do! I mean, *wataschi* been *baka* crazy cracked hooked on *eiga* since I was but a teeny-tiny little nipper tot toddler, prior even to matriculation at Native Land Loving School, reet? I mean, ain't nobody amongst all Hundred Millions digs the *eiga* like I does!"

Tojo: (mum, Jack—blinks eye-slits, makes Amerind teepee from fingertips, nods shaved noggin at Fujiwara).

Fujiwara: "That will suffice, lieutenant. Excuse yourself, please."

Me: "I mean, if I might could just explain, how honor-and-glory shtick and all ain't nothing unless Hundred Millions folks knows about it, reet? And *eiga* flics, Jack, flics shows folks the way it were, how it is, see—"

Fujiwara: "You are dismissed, lieutenant!"

Me: (salute, sword bangs against my leg, about-face, depart smartly, *katana* swinging askew, Jack!).

Tojo: (mum—why he is also knowed as The Razor!).

Dig, Jack: how I did try to explain, *benshi*-style, to said *honchos*. Circa summer of '41, just out of Eta Jima boot camp, armed only with B.A. degree from Oklahoma A & M, not to fail to mention *katana* longsword and also rapid-developing *ma* moment's awareness of ironics implicit in all things—proposing big cinematic *eiga* gig as pure-dee scam scheme to keep out from China boonies, wherever, avoid front-line combat interpreter assignment, reet?

Explain. Not unlike like unto old-timey *benshi*, reet, Jack?

Cut to: Back seat of Nakajima (two-seater dive bomber, Jack!) twin-engines, cockpit open to facilitate lensing (hand-holding Moe Berg's

Stewart Warner 16-millimeter, as how jerry-rig camera mount on fuselage is proved inadequate via testing for stability versus flight vibrations, reet?) – 1,000 feet up over blue Pacific, Jack! Over my shoulder, 250 miles northward, out of sight now, *Kido Butai Tora* task-force flotilla (thirty-three vessels) waits on us, deck of the *Akagi* off which we did fly, sailed out of Hitokysyu Bay (Kuriles), *honcho* Grand Admiral Yamamoto in command (Chuichui Nogumo holding stick of lead bomber!), hundred and five aircrafts – Zekes, Betties, Val, and also Nakajimas, than which latter carry Long Lance torpedos, reet? Thirty ain't coming back home to deck of the *Akagi* nor none other ship of line, Jack!

Heading southeast into sunrise, reet? Circa 7:49 antemeridian, Sunday, 7 of December 1941 (December 6, Tokyo Town time, reet?). Pearl Harbor (*Pearu Halbol*), Jack. Global-wide conflict flap – how you say, WW II (not to fail to mention simultaneous invasion by Imperial Army of Malay Peninsula – do it up right!)!

Wataschi. Me. Lieutenant *Benshi*, reet?

Engines noises so loud in open cockpit, gots to shout to pilot – Imperial Navy hotshot flyboy air ace with record kills in China aerial campaigns in support of Kwantung Army, Lieutenant Commander Heihachiro Sugihara, gung-ho for attack, sad to say than which whom is most upset distressed at noncombat photographic mission assigned. Which is to say, Jack, he don't get the Big Picture, reet?

Gots to shout into slipstream to be heard.

Like, Oahu coming up dead ahead, Honolulu visible in dissipating mist of morn, Yank vessels lined up like unto ducks in Payne Country Free Agricultural Fair shooting galleries in harbor, morn's sunlight silver on water, sky filled with planes of *Dai Nippon* like unto locusts coming after wheat's crop in Okie Panhandle, reet?

"Sugihara!" I yell into slipstream, "like, hang back, man, I needs must get me some cover shots of first strike, dig?"

"This is without honor!" says Lieutenant Commander Heihachiro Sugihara, hotshot flyboy ace hero of Chink campaigns, throttles back engines.

"Hold steady!" I cry, get excellent establishing shot as first wave of bombers, torpedo planes following, let loose on dockside wharf facilities, Wheeler Field, and also Schofield Barracks, sending up smoke's plumes as backdrop. "Great!" I shout, watch second formation of strike wing peel off to begin attack run, good composition balance in Stewart Warner's viewfinder frame. "Now," I scream into rushing wind, "pull out and circle attack perimeter so's I can get me a comprehensive pan, Sugihara!"

Lieutenant Commander Sugihara yanks back on stick, climbs above gray smoke's pall beginning to form over Honolulu, drift inland over sugarcane and pineapple fields on sea breezes, dips wing to start slow circle of scene of destruction, attack clearly already great success, how you say, milk run all the way, reet? "Steady!" I shout, and, "Them *honchos* going to flat fall off their *tatami* when we screen these rushes back on the *Akagi*, Jack!"

Sugihara, big China campaigns air ace—holder of Supreme Order of Chrysanthemum, Military Order of the Golden Kite, etcetera blah—holds Nakajima craft in gradual perimeter sweep, sound of bombing faint as distant thunder on Oklahoma prairie threatening gully-washer and also toad-strangler deluge, reet? He turns in his seat to speak to me, fur trim on canvas flying helmet shivering in wind. "Where is honor to be found in this? What can you know of *bushido* martial honor, you cannot even manage your longsword gracefully on parade!" says Lieutenant Commander Heihachiro Sugihara, Imperial Navy air ace flyboy. "I am a senior pilot of demonstrated skill and courage," says he to me—high over Oahu, Jack!—"It is my place by right to lead an attack wing! *Dai Nippon* achieves historic glory this day. We bring the eight corners of the world under our roof, but I am shamed, my aircraft unarmed, my sole duty to ferry a taker of pictures, a maker of *eiga* amusements, while my valiant and daring comrades destroy the *Amerikajin* on the ground far below us! I am shamed. I earn no honor for *Dai Nippon*, no respect for my name. I dishonor the *kami* of my family!"

Like, I gots to explain, *benshi*-style, to him, reet?

I lean close to his ear to be heard against wind's rush of slipstream, fumble in the haversack betwixt my knees for another film magazine (canisters packed in tight, wedged with personal copy of *Redskin* (1940 edition, light reading in spare odd moments aboard *Akagi*, voyage from Kuriles, reflect on good old days gone bygone—nostalgia shtick, Jack). I say, "*Sugihara-san*, you don't understand, man! Like, first off, if we had ammo you'd be wanting to fire your wing cannons, strafe, reet? Vibrations therefrom resultant render lensing impossible! Hey, let's us fly down for some close-ups footage now! Than which is not to fail to mention more profound considerations, *Sugihara-san*! Listen up, Jack, I'll explain to you how it work, this good honor-and-glory shtick, reet?"

Lieutenant Commander Heihachiro Sugihara dips Nakajima's schnozz, dives toward Schofield Barracks, whereat-and-upon fleet and highly maneuverable Zero aircrafts strafe panicked troops on grassy quads—I get sharp footages: khaki-clad Yank G.I. *issen gorin* running for covers, pathetic resistance in manifest form of few die-hards on barracks roof with rifles, track of bullets chewing up quad turf as we follow in wake of Zero making low-flying pass at targets of opportunity—wind-rush slipstream, gun-chatter, cannon-burst, ubiquitous bomb explosions all about shake fuselage, blur vision in Stewart Warner's viewfinder, smokes thickening.

"Dig, Sugihara," I yell at him—explain!—"What's we doing here is vital, reet? I mean, like, would I have *honcho* Premier-General Tojo's warrant if it were not so? Okay, honor and glory for *Dai Nippon*, Jack, but who's to know if we don't get it on film, in the can, cut and edit, add musics, screen it for Hundred Millions back home?"

"Honor," says the lieutenant commander, "lies in what a man performs as his duty. What can you know of this? You are educated among the *Amerikajin* barbarians! You speak their *Eigo*! You are not *Nipponshikki!*" He jerks back on stick, climbs, camera almost goes over side into drink, reet? We head for Wheeler Field, big fires of burning Yank aircrafts, fuel and also ammo dumps.

"Okey-doke," says I, "zilch, zip, squat, I grant you, but I is talking differences between what's is and how you view it on silver screen, reet? Big day for *Dai Nippon*, mayhap *Sekigahara*, war's decisive battle, reet! But is it, like, what's we done did, or what Hundred Millions see got did? I mean, if you don't see cottonwood felled on river's bank, do it really fall?"

"I shall attain to no honor this day!" Sugihara says. I shoot almost straight down on Wheeler Field, rows of Yank aircrafts going off in flames like unto firecrackers on 4 July Okie-land parade celebration, hangers collapsing, oil stench from smoke of burning fuel, bombs, and also ammo caches exploding not unlike like unto counterpoints.

"They going to love this back at Ichigaya Heights!" I cry. And, "Think about it, *Sugihara-san*. Did I not lens you stepping into cockpit on deck there on the *Akagi*? Will I not lens you climbing back down, arms raised in big *banzai* cheer when we get back? In betwixt," I shout in his ear, "won't I cut together all this glorious victory over *gaijin* barbarian *Amerikajin*? What's Hundred Millions folks going to think about who gots good honor-and-glory shtick when this *eiga* flic screens? Heavy musics track, reet? *Kimagayo* national anthem? *Kaigun* naval march? What's folks going to think about who gots the glory when I do a slick super of you, looking all heroic, behind Sunrise Flag waving in ocean's breeze, Jack? Who gots the glory when my flic plays Asakusa District back home in *Dai Nippon*, Sugihara?"

It takes a sec for it all to sink in — Lieutenant Commander Heihachiro Sugihara is, see, like the real thing, reet? Flyboy hotshot air ace pilot of Chink campaigns. He is thinking it gots to be real to be true.

We climb for orientation view of *Pearu Halbol* (Pearl Harbor), ships burning, listing, sinking, torpedo planes swooping low to slip Long Lances into blue Hawaii waters.

"I have not thought of this which you explain," says *Sugihara-san*. "What you have said is most interesting, lieutenant."

"Why," queries I, "does you think all them guys in the junior officers' mess on the *Akagi* is calling me *benshi* when they crack wise, Jack?"

"I confess I have not considered that," he says. We come in low behind attacking Val torpedo bomber.

"Would I pull your leg? Tug your chain? Heap upon you excrement of bullock?"

"I will ponder these things you have said, *Benshi*," says Lieutenant Commander Heihachiro Sugihara, "but I cannot believe you can make honor and glory from nothing with your *eiga*. I have won distinction in China, and if this day should not prove to be *Sekigahara*, if there shall be battles to fight in the days to come, I shall strive to win renown for my efforts!"

"Reet," I say, and, "now, when I give you the word, flip this baby over, and we'll track the next Long Lance all the way across the harbor to its target, dig? Great stuff already in the can, man!"

"Be certain your seatbelt is secure, and hold tightly to your precious *gaijin* camera, *Benshi*," he says, snaps the Nakajima's stick—we roll over, I find Long Lance torpedo's wake in viewfinder frame as blood rushes to my noggin, reet? And certain sure not to fail to mention, Jack: feel my personal copy of *Redskin* (1940 edition!) begin to slip out from haversack betwixt my knees!

Wherefrom—sad to say!—it did fall, plummet downwards, into burning hulk of listing and also sinking U.S.S. *Oklahoma*—like, Jack, got burned up in a big fire, reet?

Cut to: Philippine Islands, Jack. Bataan Peninsula, late April (*hanami*—big irony, reet?), circa '42.

Milieu: *hakko ichui* coming to be, Jack! 14th Imperial Army (*honcho* General Masaharu Homma in command), 43,000 strong, is done whipped up on the Yanks, reet? *Amerikajin* finished on Bataan, Dutchmen done give up in East Indies, *Igirisujin* limeys yield in Burma, Malaya, Singapore, Hong Kong—*hakko ichui* on schedule!

Than which is not to fail to mention die-hard Yanks, stragglers from Bataan, still holed up in rock tunnels of Corregidor fastness fortress, aforesaid under continuous heavy assault of glorious 14th Imperial Army—Dugout Doug MacArthur, how we call him, $50,000 general (reported prewar salary, reet?), a.k.a. *Makassar-san*, is already cut and run in P-T boats for Australia, leaving Skinny Wainwright in command of 11,000 survivors of futile but brave Yank Bataan Peninsula defense campaign.

Bataan Peninsula, rugged boonies, Jack! Thirty miles long, fifteen wide, two roads only, mountains down the middle, reet? Tough country, not unlike like unto Cookson Hills of Oklahoma, excepting save for jungle foliage, hot in April as Panhandle in July, humidity added—*wataschi* feels perspirations gather in collar, armpits, crotch, soaking chest—like, hot, dig?

Lieutenant *Benshi*. I gots always to explain.

Bataan Peninsula, circa late April '42 (*hanami*). *Wataschi* is out in the boonies, Jack, scouting locations for second-unit productions, big *eiga* flic on preproduction schedule (as result of rave reviews of *Pearu Halbol* assault docudrama, reet?), tentatively entitled *Down with the Stars & Stripes*, treatment and rough-draft script approved personal by *honcho* Premier-General Tojo Hideki (Ichigaya Heights), big documentary propaganda shtick designed for Hundred Millions back home in *Dai Nippon* to chronicle and celebrate glorious triumph of Homma-led victorious 14th Imperial in Philippine campaign, reet?

So: I is hoofing it shank's mare in boonies, scouting out remote locations for second-unit work, accompanied by sole companion Private (how we say, *issen gorin*, cheapest small-coin cannon-fodder yardbird) Matsunaga Yutaka, than which who is veteran vet of P.I. fighting, recently detached from victorious 14th Imperial, assigned as personal aide-de-camp dog robber batman to *wataschi*.

Matsunaga Yutaka, Jack: farm boy, like unto redneck goat-roper Aggietype, drafted by *aka gami* red-letter greetings from *Mikado* right out from rice paddy — village yokel from Shikoku Island, rural hick sticks boonies environ of *Dai Nippon*, not unlike like unto, say, Perkins, Oklahoma, reet? Illiterate (natch!). Nickname which I did bestow upon him is Gopher, from *Eigo* "gofer," cinematic nomenclature — nickname derives from effort to create rapport, howsomever untranslatable to *Nihonju*, and also as reflection of awareness of Gopher Matsunaga's extreme buck teeth pearlie whites, reet? Hence: Gopher.

Private Gopher Matsunaga, Jack: Simple Simon-type, reet? When not schlepping my *katana* long sword for me, sings *Umi Yakuba* marching songs learned from boot camp (Eta Jima), as in:

> Across the sea,
> Corpses in the water;
> Across the mountain,
> Corpses heaped upon the field;
> I shall die only for the *Mikado*,
> I shall never look back!

Benshi. Gots to explain to him.

Dig:

I is tramping shank's mare the boonies of Bataan Peninsula to scout up locations for second-unit production, reet? Sweating like unto hog in Okie Panhandle in August, environ's climate like unto Cookson Hills with jungle growth added.

Gopher Matsunaga says to me, "*Sensei* Lieutenant *Benshi*, I do not understand what we seek."

"Gopher," says I, "we looking for sites suitable for lensing, reet?"

Issen gorin Private Gopher (a.k.a. Yutaka) Matsunaga says, "But why do we not simply go to where we fought if you wish to make the *eiga* of the *senso*, Lieutenant *Benshi*?"

"Gopher," says I, "quit your bitching, reet? And keep that *katana* from dragging in the dirt when you schlepp it! Remember, Jack, this is prime duties you gots here with me, reet? Would you druther be schlepping your Arisaka rifle in the final assault on Corregidor? Would you druther be humping a Nambu up them rocks whilst the *Amerikajin* socked in them tunnels tries to shoot Mrs. Matsunaga's little boy Gopher's head off his shoulders?"

"I obey your orders without question, *sensei* Lieutenant *Benshi*, but only protest I do not understand why we must find a place to make the *eiga* where no battle was fought."

"Gopher," says I (Lieutenant *Benshi*, reet?), "I will explain it to you one more time. This environ is mostly all mountains and jungles, not to fail to mention swamps, reet?"

"It was terrible to fight the *Amerikajin* in the jungle," says Gopher Matsunaga. "We could not see to aim our rifles in the dense growth. Hundreds of my comrades died all about me in the mud and slime of the swamps. The terrible heat swelled their bodies until they burst, and there was a horrible stink of men dead in the heat. We were not able to help the wounded, and they cried until they too died. We were not able to bury, the dead *Amerikajin* we found in the jungle as we advanced. We, bayoneted their wounded where they lay to stop the noise of their crying—"

"Reet!" says I to stop him, as how *issen gorin* Private Yutaka (a.k.a. Gopher) Matsunaga is only a illiterate redneck goat-roper rice-paddy farm boy from Shikoku Island and will rap on about battles he has fought—touch Section 8, reet? "Reet, Gopher," I say, "but that is how it really were, dig? This *eiga* flic we going to lens is a big production, high priority at Ichigaya Heights Imperial Ministry of War Headquarters, so we can't be shooting no big scenes in the jungle nor swamps, nor not neither on no mountain slopes."

"I do not understand, Lieutenant *Benshi*."

"Listen up, Jack! What we needs is big open clearing. Place we can stage, like, final glorious and victorious *banzai* charge, dig? We get us a mess of extras, borrow a bunch of General Homma's boys from the Fourteenth, dress them up right, costumes, clean uniforms, new sandals, leggings, tunics, forage, caps, long swords for budo officers, fixed bayonets on each and every Arisaka for the *issen gorin*, new-issue Mauser pistols for non-coms. Line them up, send them running *chogee* right into the camera, waving the Sunrise Flag and also *Hinomaru*, mix us up a soundtrack, Nambu rapid-fires, crack of Arisaka, random mortar rounds dropping in, satchel charges, big music theme behind it, *Kimagayo* anthem, *Kaigun* March also, maybe special score we can commission back in *Dai Nippon* if budget allows. Dig?"

I think he don't not dig, Jack!

Private Gopher Matsunaga stands there in blistering heat of the sun, thick humidity air aura, late April '42, lets my *katana* drag in the dirt. Says to me: "It was not like that, Lieutenant *Benshi*. We heard no music when we fought the *Amerikajin*. We sang the songs they taught us at Eta Jima because we were frightened, yet afraid to show our fear. I do not think you can make the *eiga* of this, *sensei* lieutenant."

"Reet," says I, "you can't make no *eiga* flic shows the way it really were, even cutting actualities documentary footages together. The thing is, Gopher," I tell him, "what the *eiga* is is something Hundred Millions folks back home can believe were real, dig? Folks back home in *Dai Nippon*, *honchos* up at Ichigaya Heights, you think they want to see the Fourteenth Imperial Army singing *Umi Yakuba* so as not to be messing their pants when Yanks shoots at them? You think your *mama-san* and your *papa-san* back on Shikoku Island wants to see Homma's boys rotting in the alien Bataan mud? Never *hochee*, Gopher! What Hundred Millions folks in *Dai Nippon* like to view is glorious Fourteenth doing all that good *bushido* guff stuff shtick, flags waving, officers leading with longswords out, hear the boom-boom like counterpoints against *Kimagayo*! That's how they wants to remember it, can you not dig?"

"I shall not forget the truth of it," says Private Gopher Matsunaga — like he's talking to hisself instead of to *wataschi* Lieutenant *Benshi*, Bataan Peninsula boonies, late April of 1942, reet? I think: touch Section 8 as result of traumatic battle experiences experienced in Philippine campaign.

"Don't be so certain sure, Jack," I says, "'cause time do funny things, Gopher-*san*! Might could be, distant future, you is a old man has to chew your noodles twice 'cause your gums can't grind even them *udon* no more, you won't remember nothing except what's I lens in this *eiga* flic, reet? Your grandchildren say to you, 'Tell us, *Papa-san*, from the glorious victory you won on Bataan against the barbarian *Amerikajin*,' could be all's you can think to say is, 'Hey, like I forget, kiddies! Go gander that boffo *eiga* flic, *Down with the Stars & Stripes* if you want to dig how it were!' Reet?"

Benshi, Jack. I explain, but he don't not dig! *Issen gorin* Private Gopher (a.k.a. Yutaka) Matsunaga, Jack, all's he says is, "I do not think I shall live to become an old man, *sensei* lieutenant. I do not believe in my *hara* belly that I shall ever return to my village on Shikoku Island. I truly believe I shall have to die for the *Mikado* in this great *senso* in quest of *hakko ichui*, as they told us all at Eta Jima when we learned to be soldiers."

"Reet," says I, as how it is too hot to stand talking, trying to explain to this redneck goat-roper hick-sticks rice-paddy farmer boy. "Pick up my damn sword out from the dirt, Jack!" I say, very *budo* officer-style, reet? "Let's us keep moving, Gopher, we gots to find us that site to stage the big *banzai* charge."

Gone, Jack. *Benshi, honcho*-types, *budo* officer bros, underlings assigned to assist. All gone.

Motto: *mendokusai* — how we say, they done had it, bit the big one, reet?
Meaning: nothing ain't nohow permanent in life and times, no matter howsomever you explain same, Jack!

Cut to (flashback style, reet?): circa April 1, 1942 (Fool of April, reet?), Ichigaya Heights (Tokyo Town), headquarters of Imperial Ministry of War, reet? Than which is also locale of personal headquarters of premier of *Dai Nippon* (whilst also holding simultaneous rank of general derived from last command of Kwantung Army yet engaged in seeming-eternal flap versus Chinks, reet?), Tojo Hideki — nickname: The Razor.

Than to which site is summoned *wataschi* (me, Jack!), Sub-Lieutenant Yamaguchi Yoshinori, on scene for personal *kaigi* privy conference confabulation session with aforesaid *honcho* Premier-General Tojo, *wataschi* standing tall (looking good like unto six o'clock) in unform: olive-drab forage cap (red star thereon), tunic of identical hue (than which is not to fail to mention epaulets and collar tabs signifying shavetail officer rank, reet?), Sam Browne-style belt and shoulder strap (regulation Mauser pistol removed from holster, checked at door with *kempei-tai* military-security minions), breeches-style *monpei* riding trousers and tight-wrapped puttee leggings, issue brogan kicks — than which is not to fail to mention mandatory *budo* officer's *katana* longsword in *take* bamboo sheath I schlepp in sweat-slippery palm.

Can you not dig it, Jack?

It is *wataschi* (me!), Sub-Lieutenant Yamaguchi Yoshinori, *aka gami* red-letter draftee shavetail officer of Imperial Army of *Dai Nippon*, but three months returned from victorious *Kido Butai* attack upon Yank naval and also air installations of, how we say in *Dai Nippon*, circa big *senso* WW II era, *Pearu Halbol*, reet?

Dig it, Jack!

I (me!) — circa April 1, 1942 (*hanami* time), how we say in *Eigo*, April's Fool, reet? I stand tall at attention posture in sole presence of *Dai Nippon* supreme *honcho* Premier-General Tojo Hideki (a.k.a. The Razor!), Ichigaya Heights (Tokyo Town!), *kaigi* conference confabulation chamber, *take* bamboo blinds down tight to darken aforesaid interior environ, thus facilitating 16-millimeter screening of final edit print version of docudrama *eiga* flic (than which I is done entitled: *The Bright Beams of Ameratasu Shine with Benevolent Approval upon the Advent of Hakko Ichui!*) I did lens (from back seat of unarmed two-seater Nakajima dive bomber, Jack!) over *Pearu Halbol*, than which extensive live actuality footages (supplemented by staged shtick, reet?) I is done been editing in jerry-built Tokyo Town studio, than for which purpose I stand whereat and when I stand, to screen finished *eiga* flic, like, premier for Premier, Jack.

200

How it were:

Me (I, *wataschi*!), Sub-Lieutenant Yamaguchi Yoshinori, on carpet (than which there ain't none—floor of *kaigi* conference confabulation chamber screening room is floored with tiles, upon which clanks my *katana* longsword) in present presence of *Dai Nippon* Premier-General Tojo Hideki—armed only with *budo* longsword and ever-increasing sense of big ironies of life (as result of same revealed by life-and-times ironic experiences to date, reet?), not to fail to mention Oklahoma A & M Bachelor of Arts degree.

Present: Sub-Lieutenant Yamaguchi Yoshinori, Imperial Army (current status: extraordinary assignment, reet?).

Present: *honcho* of all *Dai Nippon* Premier (and General!) Tojo Hideki (a.k.a. The Razor!), than which personage sits shaved-noggin, round horn-rim specs, in best (sole!) seat in house, anticipatory to screening viewing.

Props: in addition to aforesaid projector, reel, portable screen, sound system speaker stowed beneath table, also note thick *kempei* dossier folder ensconced on lap of Premier Tojo (than which personage is ensconced in sole chair in chamber, reet?).

Dig you must, Jack! As how this day, April's Fool, circa '42, I did receive, official-style, my WW II *senso* wartime moniker, which is to say, Lieutenant *Benshi*—he who explains, reet? As follows:

"I greet you, Sub-Lieutenant Yamaguchi Yoshinori," says Premier-(*honcho* of all *Dai Nippon*!) General Tojo Hideki, and, "Perhaps it would be well for you to lay aside your longsword? I find the noise you make with it distracting."

"Reet," say I, and, "Like, orry-say and also thousand pardons, *sensei* premier, but, like, I still don't seem to gots the hang of schlepping it everywhere I go, trying to salute and also keep in step marching and all." I unhitch cord affixing *katana* to my belt, lay same softly on conference confabulation table so as not to mar lacquered surface thereof.

"Regrettable," says *honcho* Premier-General Tojo. "One would have assumed you might attain to at least a minimal competence in trivial matters such as correct military deportment. But, then, you were not educated for a martial life, is this not so, lieutenant?"

"Reet," I riposte, and, "Orry-say. But, hey, I'm, like, still working on it, giving collegiate-style effort, reet?" and, "Nope, no *budo* in me, *sensei*, as how I majored in *Eigo* lingo and literatures ever since my little-nipper days at Native Land Loving School. Me," I tell him, "*wataschi* is strictly *aka gami* red-letter conscript-type officer." He smiles little *sumairu* at corners of thin lips, nods shaved noggin at me. I render (natch!) thirty-degree kowtow bow to signify totality of deference and also subservience shtick demanded of situational *enryo* relationship in context.

I mean, Jack, dig it! Here is I. Fool of April Day, circa '42, shavetail non-*budo* sub-lieutenant of Imperial Army of *Dai Nippon*, unarmed (*katana* longsword is on conference confabulation table, reet?) except save for embryonic developing sense of sensitivity to life's big ironies. Standing tall on tiles like unto six o'clock before *honcho* of all *Dai Nippon* Premier-General Tojo Hideki (a.k.a. The Razor), amidst *senso* now under way full three months — string of total victories of which create aforesaid person-age's great popularity with Hundred Millions.

"It has been some time since last we met, has it not, sub-lieutenant?" says he.

"Reet. Since way back mid-circa '41, as how I was just done finished Eta Jima boot camp and also officer leadership training course, than which I regrets to say did not, like, take so good, reet?"

"And at our initial meeting you presented a rather radical proposal," says he, tapping thick *kempei* dossier ensconced on his lap with manicured nail of forefinger.

"Reet," say I, "to you, *sensei* premier-general, and also General Whozis-I-forget-his-moniker, sad to say."

"General Fujiwara," says Premier-General Tojo, and, "I thought it well to dispense with his presence today. I do not enjoy," says he, "and I presume you do not, to conduct our affairs under the scrutiny of a man whose eyes remind one in startling fashion of a frog's." At which juncture aforesaid *honcho* Premier-General Tojo Hideki stops a beat for effect, grins (small!) *sumairu*, exposing pearlie whites (sharp, Jack, like unto rodent's — why they call him The Razor) — it is joke, same at expense of fat froggy-face General Fujiwara, device employed to put *hara* belly tense shavetail sub-lieutenant at ease in present presence of *honcho* eminence, how you say, establish rapports. As in har and also hee, reet?

"Enough of levity, Yamaguchi Yoshinori," says he — grin ceases in-stanter! — "You have, I believe, a work of *eiga* cinema to present for my viewing?"

"Reet. sixteen-millimeter, thirty minutes, black and also white, than which I apologize for, as how *senso* now in progress is done cut off *Amerikajin* color film stock *harukai* imports, natch, and *Nihonjin* imitation stuff thereof comes out grainy and also, sad to say, lacking in true color-ations, reet? Howsomever, what's you is about to gander, *sensei* premier-general, is composite docudrama. Actualities lensed on location, by hum-ble *wataschi*, same augmented by cover shots, dramatized transitions, sound and musics tracks I done scrounged from commercial studios here in Tokyo Town, reet? Total effect of which — " I begin to explain when he interrupts.

"May we not simply view your effort, sub-lieutenant, and permit me to pose queries as and if I feel the need or desirability of exposition?"

202

"Reet," I say, stand at projector. "Like," I add, "I can freeze frame or adjust focus for you anywhere you want to look close, explain, how we say, rhetoric of *eiga* flic lingo, reet?"

"Let us," says Premier-General Tojo Hideki, "proceed."

"Reet!" I flip toggle switch, stand to at projector as opening credits logos and musics score (*Kimagayo* anthem, natch!) begins:

Opening shot, reet? Sunrise over Fujiyama (mounting volume of *Kimagayo* as taken from version recorded by Toyama National Military Band, aforesaid platter picked up cheap at flea market fire sale), followed by rapid dissolve to Sunrise Flag super over Mt. Fuji's snowy peak, followed by super of title calligraphs logo: *The Bright Beams of Ameratasu Shine with Benevolent Approval upon the Advent of Hakko Ichui!*

"Dig, *sensei honcho* premier-general," say I over soundtrack, clatter of projector's sprockets, "as how title graphic indicates sun coming up over Fuji is possible actual presence of Sun Goddess giving nod to glorious venture, not to fail to mention Imperial Navy's Sunrise Flag super points to *gumbatsu* military nature of said enterprise, reet?"

"I am quite capable of reading our language, sub-lieutenant," says he as flic cuts quick to long shot, slow pan of naval armada under way, rugged coastal hills visible in far distance, voice-over (*wataschi*, Jack, me, natch!) announces: *Dai Nippon's invincible Kido Butai steams eastward to enact the celestial destiny of our divinely inspired mission to unite the eight corners of the world under one roof!*

"That," says Premier-General Tojo Hideki, "is not the *Kido Butai* fleet."

"Reet," I explain, "and that ain't Hitokysyu Bay in the background neither, as how *kempei-tai* security was tight as, how we say in *Eigo* Okie-style, bull's anus in season of fly hatch, reet? They wouldn't let me lens nothing until we hit international waters point of no return. So I done cribbed this from old newsreel footages from way back circa 'twenty-two during famed infamous Washington Naval Conference, reet?"

"Will audiences not recognize the antiquated vessels we see before us?" he queries as voice-over (me, Jack!) says: *Not since the historic defeat of the barbarian Russians a generation ago has the world seen so formidable an assemblage of sea power!*

"You know," I riposte, "and I know, and, like, Imperial Navy *honchos* will know, but your average man on the street, Hundred Millions John Q. Public-*san*, he won't know, reet, *sensei* premier-general?"

Eiga flic cuts quick to series of jump cuts of *Nihonjin* sailor swabbies engaged in action drills—strapping on helmets, climbing ship's ladders, sealing hatches, coiling hawser ropes, loading and also elevating deck guns (close-up of shell rammed home, locked in breech!), *budo* officers on bridge scanning horizon, etcetera blah blah as voice-over (who else, Jack?) says: *The officers and seamen of the mighty Imperial Navy are ever alert to the threat of attack by our barbarian enemies!*

"That," I tell him, "is training-exercises shtick I done lensed down in Sasebo right after I got back from *Pearu Halbol*. Had to beat off volunteers with a stick when I put out casting call for midshipmen to pose on the bridge with them binoculars."

"The Imperial Navy," says he, "already received universal plaudits for their role, yet it was the army, under my command here at Ichigaya Heights, which conceived and ordered the strike against the *Amerikajin*. Admiral Yamamoto is fast gaining in popularity, while the Hundred Millions agitate over the delay in our conquests of China and the Philippine Islands."

"*Daijubo, sensei* premier-general!" I assure him, and, "Gander this!" I say as voice-over (me, natch!) says: *Meanwhile, the ever-vigilant and enlightened leadership of Dai Nippon monitors the master strategy of hakko ichui from within the fastness of the impregnable headquarters located at Ichigaya Heights!* Shot is big sand table, relief map, surrounded by *honcho* staff officer-types, at center of which congregation stands aforesaid Tojo Hideki, pointer in hand, mouth moving, reet? "Recognize anybody you know there, *sensei* premier-general?" says I. Hee, reet? Not to fail to mention also har! Screening room is too dark to be sure if he grins *sumairu* grin not unlike like unto feline consuming excrement.

"Where was this photographed?" queries he. "That is not Ichigaya Heights!"

"Reet!" I say. Voice-over (*wataschi*, for certain sure!) says: *Premier-General Tojo Hideki, ever mindful of the sacred trust he holds by gift of a grateful and loving nation, given to his hand from the hand of our beloved Mikado, assumes total command of the coordination of joint military efforts!* "That's *Nihon Eiga* newsreel archive stock footages, shot over in Mukden back when you was first running the show for the Kwantung Army's first campaign versus Chinks, reet?"

"Ah!" says he, and, "I did not recall it at once when it first came into view."

"And let me say, looking good!" I tell him, and, "You ain't aged a day since then, *sensei* premier-general! Also, most folks don't look as good on film as in the flesh, but you're, like, naturally photogenic, reet?"

Quick cut to wardroom of attack carrier, reet? Collage of flyboy types assembled for enemy ship-recognition drill, silhouettes of Yank cruisers, destroyers, flat-tops, aerial photos of Pearl Harbor docks, Wheeler Field, Schofield Barracks, etcetera blah. "That," I tell premier-general *honcho*, "is actuality stuff! On board *Akagi*, reet? Somewhere in Pacific, steaming easterly to jump-off point. Note countenances of flyboys, *sensei* premier-general? I must of edited ten-to-one shot ratio to get them expressions of confident intensity."

"It is unnecessary to explain technicalities unless I request it, sub-lieutenant," says he. Says voice-over: *The enthusiastic warriors of Dai Nippon eagerly anticipate the moment of Sekigahara that is imminent!*

"Just thought you'd like some inside info as to how it's did, reet?" Voice-over: *Their comrades prepare the attack aircraft for launching!*

Cut to swabbies rolling out bombs and also torpedoes, arming wing guns and nose cannon, raising planes on elevators from hangar decks, etcetera blah. "I had to do six takes to get one good one here," I say, "as how light was so lacking in them elevator shafts, sky overhead overcast and all, reet?" Music track cuts to *Kaigun* March simultaneous with cut to Sunrise Flag stretched in Pacific breeze on main mast of attack carrier *Akagi* — hold and slow zoom to Sunrise Flag close-up as voice-over says: *The preordained moment of decisive action arrives in the hours before dawn a scant 280 miles from the Amerikajin target!* Same followed by venerable and historic Z-flag running up to join Sunrise and also *Hinomaru*.

"Dig, *honcho* premier-general," I say. "Too dark to lens anything against sky vastness in wee morn hours before attack launch, so I splice in footages shot day before on practice runs, reet? Shot is too brief to allow audiences to question same."

"I cannot listen to the film if you do not refrain from speaking, sub-lieutenant!"

"Reet," and "Orry-say," I say as *eiga* flic cuts to attack launch ceremonials — flyboys gather with ship's officers on *Akagi* flight deck to quaff ritual *sake* cups, exchange kowtow bow wishes for good luck, flyboys donning *hachimaki* headbands over flight helmets, aforesaid adorned (extreme close-ups to facilitate reading, reet?) with *Hinomaru* red ball of sun and varied conventional calligraphies in *kanji:* One Life Pledged to Victory! All Effort Devoted to the Triumph of Dai Nippon! May Ameratasu Bless My Mission! I Destroy the Gaijin Enemy on Behalf of My Mikado! May My Aircraft's Engine Function Properly Today! etcetera blah blah.

"That's not available light you see there, premier-general," I tell him, and, "but note how I had pick-up swabbie film crew holding arc-lamps statue-still as how not to give away artificialities of illumination, thus rendering illusion effect of flyboys and ship's officers also squinting into sunshine."

"Praiseworthy," says he.

"Now note marked shift in narrative pace," I say, "as how leisurelike decorum of *sake* quaffing ceremonials segues via upbeat tempo of *Kimagayo* anthem theme motif reintroduced to signal same, fast pace action of attack launch, reet?"

"To be sure," says he, and, "Must you explain everything, Sub-Lieutenant Yamaguchi?"

Kimagayo comes on loud, accompanying jump cuts: flyboys running across deck to climb in aircrafts, swabbie signalmen waving planes into launch order, props firing, turning, spinning, long shot of deck swarming with taxiing planes, cut to ship's officers on bridge — dramatic full shot of Lieutenant Commander Sugihara Heihachiro (my pilot, Jack!) standing on wing of Nakajima, looking into dawn's light, stepping into cockpit (close-up of hand hitting ignition switch), deckhand swabbie removing wheel-chocks, *Sugihara-san* waving jaunty wave of goodbye from cockpit, reet?

"That," I tell him, "is Lieutenant Commander Sugihara Heihachiro, big flyboy decorated air ace hotshot sky-jockey famed already in Chink campaigns."

"Must I learn the name of each individual depicted?" asks Premier-General Tojo.

"Orry-say," I tell him, "but I promised Sugihara I'd put in good word for him, as how he was all dismayed he had to fly unarmed so's I could lens attack actualities, concerned as he was for honor-and-glory shtick for name and family etcetera blah."

Series of quick cuts: signalman drops semaphore flag, aircraft revs engine, heads down deck, prop wash flutters signalman's clothes. Assembled swabbies on sidelines raise big *banzai* cheer, signalman wags semaphore flag, aircraft picks up speed, *banzai* cheer chorus, wipe screen to silhouettes of aircrafts leaving carrier *Akagi's* deck, ascending to assume formations heading eastwardly, glinting in glow of morn's first direct sun.

Aloft, says voice-over (me!), *the attack planes of Dai Nippon proceed to their unsuspecting target!*

"That stuff on the deck of the *Akagi* was all shot out of sequence, most of it," I say, "but this next segment is all the actual actuality, *honcho* premier-general."

"Will you not be silent?" he queries.

"Just thought you'd like a little background," I say, and, "Thousand pardons and all, reet, *sensei?*"

Cover shots follow. *Kido Butai* as seen from aloft — keep it brief as how vibrations of Nakajima makes for blur. Aircrafts in formations as seen from above, below, and also alongside (quick cut over Sugihara's shoulder to show fuel and altitude gauges, gloved hand on stick!), expanse vastness of Pacific to eastwards, waves reflecting highlights of full sun of morning, reet?

"I got my doubts about this transition," I tell him, "as how duration of flying time requires commensurate conventionalized illusion of time duration on screen, reet? I might could fill in with some more voice-over dub to tease audience with suspense, but, how we say, on the other hand, slow pace here is good contrast with launch and upcoming rock 'em and also sock 'em attack actualities. What's you think, premier-general?"

"Have I indicated impatience, save for your interruptions? And how shall I think at all if you do not cease speaking, sub-lieutenant?"

"Reet," I say as *eiga* flic cuts to coastline of Hawaiian archipelago, voice-

206

over says: *The designated target emerges on the horizon in the light of Amera-tasu. The decisive battle commences!* "Sorry to butt in again, but wanted you to know I dubbed all the sound effect in studio." Than which sound-track—engine whine of diving torpedo planes, whistle of falling bombs, explosions, chatter of rapid-fires, boom of nose cannons, comes on before *honcho* premier-general can riposte.

Attack sequence is full eight minutes, reet? Pearl Harbor dockside, Yank ships listing and burning—Wheeler Field, Yank aircrafts parked in conve-nient rows on runways to explode not unlike like unto firecracker strings—Schofield Barracks, khaki-clad Yank *issen gorin* run across grassy quad turf for cover from strafing fire—quick cuts over Sugihara's shoulder to pro-vide illusion of buttons pressed to release bombs, fire rapid-fires.

I try to watch *honcho* Premier-General Tojo Hideki watching actuality footage of Pearl Harbor attack—no response betrayed in dimmed screen-ing room—they don't call him The Razor for nothing, Jack!

"See that torpedo running just under water's surface!" I say, and, "We got that flying upside down bung over appetite, *sensei*! Oops! Orry-say to pop off again!"

"And what vessel is that which was struck by the torpedo?" he asks.

"That," I tell *honcho* leader of all *Dai Nippon* Premier-General Tojo Hideki (a.k.a. The Razor), "is the U.S.S. *Oklahoma, sensei.*"

After than which instant (circa Fool of April Day—*hanami!*—1942, Jack!), I say no more during duration of screening of *wataschi's* first *eiga* flic (docudrama) screening (*The Bright Beams of Ameratasu Shine with Benevolent Approval upon the Advent of Hakko Ichui!*—thirty minutes, black and also white).

Dig: I stand to at pre-*senso* Bell & Howell projector, watch (in dimness of *kaigi* conference confabulation chamber, Ichigaya Heights, Imperial Ministry of War, Tokyo Town!) Premier-General Tojo Hideki watch remainder of flic. I does not comment on long shots of smokes arising from Honolulu (dockside, Wheeler Field, Schofield Barracks) environ, explain no more explanations concerning transition footages portraying *Tora* strike force returning for rendezvous with *Kido Butai* fleet (intercuts of visage of Lieutenant Commander Sugihara Heihachiro turning in cock-pit to smile big *sumairu* smile at me, very close-up, reet?). I wax not expository as how planes landing on deck of *Akagi* was shot two days prior to attack in context of takeoff and return drills shtick to keep flyboys on toes alert. I elaborate no elaborations as to difficulties encountered in getting ship's personnel cooperations—all hands caught up in joyous cele-brations of *Tora* success—in staging return triumph ceremonials (*sake* cups, *banzai* chorus, Z-flag in wind on *Akagi* main mast, etcetera blah), call no attention to long shot of *Kido Butai* steaming westerly into sunset towards Home Islands home port.

As how, Jack, I (me, *wataschi*!), Sub-Lieutenant Yamaguchi Yoshinori (a.k.a. Gooch, A & M class of 1940!) am dumb-struck with awe-inspired sense of big ironies of life, reet?

As how *honcho* of all *Dai Nippon* Premier and also General Tojo Hideki sees my docudrama *eiga* flic, but I feel only *yoin* resonances (1940 *Redskin*, replete with *hanko* classmates' autographs, falling from between knees whilst upside down over U.S.S. *Oklahoma*—got burned up in big fire, Jack!), feeling vacuum sensation of *ma* interval in life and times when design of pressure of inexorable historical forces impinge upon individual's fate—I am silent in sudden awareness of *do* path's life and times lifestyle shtick: Moe Berg, Mr. Sato Isao, Oklahoma Agricultural & Mechanical College—Miss Clara!

Oh, Jack, say it ain't so! Like, all's I wanted to do was see all the *harukai* Yank import *eiga* flics, speak, read, and also write the *Eigo* English lingo! Can you dig it? Big ironies, Jack. About and of which more to come as follows:

Thus: I stand to, silent, whilst flic runs off reel—final scene of *honchos* (Premier-General Tojo center stage, natch!) raising *sake* cup toast—"*Hai!*" says The Razor, recognizes old Kwantung Army footages from *Nihon Eiga* archive—dissolve to freeze frame of repeat opening shot, sun bright over Fuji's peak, roll credits, than which is followed by blank screen, clatter of projector sprockets.

"Tell me, sub-lieutenant," says he, "how many times did I see your name appear among those listed as responsible for the creation of this *eiga*?"

"Only seven," I say, and, "Producer, director, writer, cameraman-cinematographer, research, voice-over narration, and also film editor, reet? You think it's maybe, like, too many, *sensei* premier-general? I can cut it back some in the editing studio on the Moviola if you want, but I was just, like, doing it up Hollywood *Amerikajin* style, credit where credits due, reet?"

"Just so," says he, and, "It strikes me as not *Nipponshikki* to display one's name so blatantly upon the face of an artifact which presumes to chronicle so glorious a moment in the collective national history of the Hundred Millions."

"Then you like my *eiga* flic?"

"Indeed, but I do request that you remove your name where it appears so often. I should much prefer the film's audience to be able to read something on the order of: *Prepared for the Edification of the Hundred Millions by the Authority of Premier Tojo Hideki*. Yes, I think that would be considerably more appropriate!"

They don't call him The Razor for nothing, Jack!

"Reet," I say, and, "and, like, with the assistance of Sub-Lieutenant

Yamaguchi Yoshinori, Imperial Army of *Dai Nippon?*"

"Learn to content yourself, sub-lieutenant, with the inner satisfaction that comes of the knowlege that you have performed your duty completely and with loyalty to those to whom our beloved *Mikado* has placed you in a posture of subservience."

After we rise, perform kowtow in directional of Imperial Palace, I ask: "No credit at all? Zip? Zilch? Squat?"

"You are an excellent young man by all reports, Sub-Lieutenant Yama-guchi," says he, "and I foresee a happy and successful future for you, one which will bring honor and glory to your name and family. You have yet, I regret to say, to learn the virtues of humility and deference that are so vital to a martial way of life such as the Hundred Millions have embarked upon. Need I say more?"

"Nope," I say, and, "Ix-nay, *sensei!*" and, "Coming over loud and clear, *honcho* premier-general!" I say, and, "Like, I been away stateside for a long time, so it'll maybe take me a while to get with *Nipponshikki* and also *bushido budo* ethos, reet? Like with my longsword, I'm steady working on it, *sensei.*"

Irony, Jack! Like, I don't even gots a screen credit for first-ever *eiga* flic I ever made, reet? Than which further irony is: aforesaid *eiga* flic is (natch!) not no longer extant, reet? Got burned up in a big fire (circa 1944 — Burned Earth Period, how we say, *yake tsuchi jidai!*). Oh, say it were not so!

"Indeed," says *honcho* Premier-General Tojo Hideki, "I find your *eiga* a most excellent effort, and foresee that it will contribute greatly to our propaganda effort to maintain and enhance the confidence of the Hundred Millions in the ultimate success of the great *senso* we pursue. You are aware, are you not, sub-lieutenant, that, despite the unbroken chain of victories enjoyed by our combined armed forces, some faint-hearted among us worry that our hostilities with the *Amerikajin* will prove our undoing?"

"Reet," I say. "*Nihonjin* folks can dig whipping up on, like, *Igirisujin* British, but Yanks is different story. U. S. of A., *honcho* premier-general, big country, let me tell you from horsie's mouth, as how I been over a good half of it riding on Santa Fe and also M.K.&T. railroads, reet? Also as how Hundred Millions feel friendships feeling for Yanks, like, how we adopt their *besuboru* as national sport of *Dai Nippon* and all."

"I have already decided to ban that decadent *gaijin* sport from the life of the Hundred Millions, at least for the duration of the *senso*. It will soon be forgotten in the throes of the conflict. But it interests me that you also doubt the wisdom of our attack upon the *Amerikajin*, sub-lieutenant," says he, and, "Yet, is not the certainty of ultimate victory already evident in events to date? Can we question the lucid paradigm of history? Consider, sub-lieutenant, have not the armies of *Dai Nippon* swiftly vanquished the Dutch in the East Indies, the French in Indo-China, the hated colonialist *Igirisujin* in Burma, Malaya, Singapore, and Hong Kong? Their vaunted navy sailed against us, and we sank both H.M.S. *Repulse* and also *Prince of Wales* on one and the same day! And we have decimated the *Amerikajin* fleet, disabling eight battleships and three cruisers at Hawaii, with the loss of but thirty aircraft, as your *eiga* so effectively dramatizes. And let me say how prudent of you it is not to mention our losses at *Pearu Halbol!*"

"Anks-thay, *sensei*."

"*Dai Nippon* holds sway from the Solomon Islands, to our south, to the *Amerikajin* Aleutians; we are the masters of Asia for five thousand miles from Burma to the *Amerikajin* island called Wake! Even now our army and navy are poised to strike in New Guinea, and from there we shall invade Australia and New Zealand. From Burma, the *Igirisujin* colonial empire of India will fall to us! How is it possible for you and others of infirm faith to doubt the invincibility of *hakko ichui*, sub-lieutenant? Please, speak freely, for I am curious as to the thinking of such as you among the Hundred Millions I have been chosen to lead."

"Reet," I did say, Jack, and, "well, like, for openers, we been whipping up on the Chinks since circa 'thirty-one, still ain't made them yell uncle, reet?"

"China is vast! The Kwantung Army, which I had the honor to command, occupies more territory there with each day that passes!"

"Reet," I did tell him, Jack, and, "And so's U. S. of A." I mean, Jack, like, he done asked me, reet? "We is done caught Yanks trousers-lowered style at *Pearu Halbol*, not unlike like unto *ninja*-style assault, but they ain't give up, last I hear from Philippines campaign."

"General Homma," says he, "leads more than forty thousand gallant soldiers on the Bataan Peninsula. His victory is assured. Bataan will yield to us, sub-lieutenant, and thereafter the last of the *Amerikajin* will be destroyed on their rocky bastion called Corregidor — the vain fifty-thousand-dollar General *Makassar* has already fled to Australia in cowardly fashion, boasting like a magpie that he will return to defeat us, even as we press the harder against his doomed, abandoned troops!"

"Reet. You knows best, *honcho* premier-general," I did say, and, "I is only a *aka gami* red-letter conscript gots a talent for *Eigo* lingo and making the *eiga* flics. I can't even schlepp my *katana* longsword in good *budo* style, reet?"

Premier-General Tojo Hideki — a.k.a. The Razor — smiles little *sumairu* (sharp little pearlie-white choppers, Jack!) at me in dimness of *kaigi* conference confabulation chamber screening room, taps my *kempei* dossier with his folded ivory fan — stylized symbol, like unto *katana*, of ancient *samurai* status, reet? Says he: "And how shall such as you serve the cause of the Hundred Millions in this *senso*, sub-lieutenant?"

"Search me!" I did say, Jack.

"Shall we send you to join General Homma's Fourteenth Imperial Army in Bataan's jungles, in the capacity of a combat interpreter, employing your considerable facility with the *Eigo* and your rich experience in the barbarian *Amerikajin* culture to interrogate the hordes of prisoners we shall surely capture?"

"I keep," I did tell him, "flubbing dub with longsword."

"Shall we," says he, "assign you to some quiet and dusty clerk's desk, there in obscurity to read and translate such intelligence documents written in *Eigo* as the *kempei-tai* secure as we advance upon Australia and New Zealand?"

"It's a thought."

"Or," says he, "we might employ you as an assistant to the valuable Mrs. Aquino, to aid her in preparing the "Zero Hour" programs we broadcast to demoralize the *Amerikajin issen gorin* who still resist us in the jungles of Bataan even as we speak here?"

"I could dig that," I say, and, "As how it don't bother me none as how it's not *Nipponshikki* to work under female personage, reet?"

"No," says *honcho* Premier-General Tojo Hideki, smacks my *kempei* dossier with folded ivory *samurai* fan. "No," says he, and, "I contemplate a more substantial role for you in the achievement of the destiny of the Hundred Millions! Are you prepared, Sub-Lieutenant Yamaguchi Yoshinori, to enter upon a task of astounding historical significance?"

Jack: was I not? "Reet!" I say, and, "All the same to me," and, "What's I gots to lose, *honcho sensei*?"

"You may stand at ease, sub-lieutenant," he says, "and do allow your longsword to remain on the table until you depart — I have no desire to witness further awkwardness —" little sharp-toofer *sumairu* — "I would have us consider some particulars of your career before we discuss the possibilities of your future. Please be so kind as to raise the blinds so that we may look upon one another as we speak with candor."

"Reet." I go to windows, pull cord to lift *take* bamboo blinds — bright midday sunlight of *hanami* time (Fool of April Day, circa '42) rushes into *kaigi* conference confabulation chamber. *Honcho* Premier-General Tojo lays aside *samurai* fan to open my *kempei* dossier, sifts documents therein, reet?

"There is," says he, "nothing to alarm us in your family history, though I note your father's penchant for things western."

"My daddy," I say, "is a very progressive guy, hip to all modernist-era trends, expert in the *Eigo*, whence from I come by my talent honest. *Papasan* is done boiled the rice pot, *saikatsu*, writing the editorial page for *Japan Times*, but he's strictly *Nipponshikki* off the job, *honcho sensei* premier-general! You should see, wears regulation prescribed *monpei* outfit with pride now, natch, but even pre-*senso* when he clad hisself in them three-piece suits and snappy fedora lids, not to fail to mention low-cut brogans, when he got home to paper house from the *shimbun* office each eventide, doffed the western threads, put on his *kimono*, sat down on the *tatami* to practice his *sho* calligraphy, whip out a few *haiku* poems. My daddy and my *Mama-san*, and my kid sister *Iko-san* too—" I commence to utter when he raises his small hand to stop me.

"I have said there is nothing substantial in your family history to alarm me, sub-lieutenant! Do not offer explanations where none are requested."

"Orry-say."

"And I note with satisfaction," says he, picking up copy of my school-matriculation report from dossier sheaf, "that your record of scholarship at our renowned Native Land Loving School is exemplary, save for the notable exception of the prescribed military studies, of course."

"Stripe up my leg, chevron on my sleeve, *honcho sensei*! I just never got with the *budo* program, reet? Like, I was *kichigai* crazy cracked hooked on *Eigo*, not to fail to mention all them *harukai* import *eiga* flics—"

"Again," says he, "there is no need to explain! Be assured that *Dai Nippon* takes pride in the outstanding accomplishments of its youth. Our greatest care is that such potential be nurtured in the proper development, that it bear the fruit of an honorable maturity."

"Anks-thay," I did say, Jack.

"But," says he, "we must give special attention to the events of the year nineteen thirty-five, as reported herein—" he points to dossier contents— "by one Mr. Sato Isao."

"Reet," I say, and, before he can say more, "We been over that already once right after I got out from Eta Jima, last year. I was just a little nipper kiddie, *honcho sensei*. I mean, what's did I know, reet? Sato and my school prefects never told me nothing, and I was, like, all agog as how here I were but sweet sixteen years old aged, picked out special to serve as interpreter-guide for visiting Yank American League *besuboru* all-star barnstormers. Dig it: Student Yamaguchi Yoshinori, got choosed to hobnob with *Amerikajin* sport greats as reported at length in *Yomiuri Shimbun*. Legendary semi-immortals, George Herman Ruth, also knowed as Babe, Bambino, Sultan of Swat, Man of Iron Louis Gehrig, I called him Lou, *sensei*! Vernon, also knowed as Lefty, Gomez—"

"We must not neglect to mention a Mr. Morris Berg," interjects he, "which personage was, and perhaps still is—we have no information as to his subsequent whereabouts or activities—known by the diminutive appellation of Moe?"

"Reet. But how could I know he was fluent in *Nihonju*? I was just a kid, sweet ten and six aged! He told me he just wanted to see the sights, tourist shtick."

"Did not this Morris Berg photograph military installations and activi-

212

ties?"

"Sort of," I say, "in the background, like."

"And did he not display a remarkable knowlege of our national life, a brilliant fluency in our language?"

"He promised to put in a good word for me with the Yank embassy folks," I say, "grease the skid so's I'd get me Imperial Ministry of Education *yen* grant support to go stateside for higher-educational education – I was but sweet sixteen, all innocence, premier-general!"

"And did he not, upon his departure from *Dai Nippon*, make a gift to you of his expensive and technologically advanced motion-picture camera?"

"Reet," I say, "but that was just *o-miyage* souvenir, same one I used to lens flap at *Pearu Halbol*, Stewart Warner with long range focus lens, reet?"

Dig it, Jack! I is thinking: *wataschi's* posterior is long bamboo grass than which The Razor going to trim short. I is thinking: excrement is in propeller of electric cooling device! I is thinking: *wataschi*, Razor going to send you packing to Bataan boonies to combat interpret for Homma's 14th Imperial whilst Yank defenders take aims with Springfield shoulder-fires on Mr. and Mrs. Yamaguchi's little boy, Yosh!

"The *kempei*," says *honcho* Premier-General Tojo, "concluded that you had perhaps . . . perhaps unwittingly collaborated in an *Amerikajin* intelligence mission against *Dai Nippon*."

"So what if even mayhap so?" I query. "I mean, *Kido Butai* pulled off *Tora* assault sneak attack, no harms did, reet? Ain't no Yanks about subject to bomb *Dai Nippon*. You said your own self, *sensei, Amerikajin* on last legs on Bataan, reet?

"Despite this questionable activity, the Imperial Ministry of Education did sponsor your studies among the *Amerikajin*."

"Reet," I did say to him, Jack, "but just between you and me and also tree's stump, *honcho* premier-general, I think it were *kempei genkin* cash *Sato-san* was slipping me under blackjack oaks, banks of Cimarron River, rural Perkins, Oklahoma, environ, reet?"

"Sub-lieutenant," says he, but I do not cease spiel, as how *yoin ma do* congruence sense of life and times accumulating ironies converge in *hara* belly tense anxieties to inspire flush inspiration of expression I cannot eschew, reet?

"No Princeton Tiger, Harvard Yard, nor Yalie shtick matriculation permitted, reet? Where was clout influence pull grease of vaunted influential Morris Berg – also knowed as Moe – when I need him? Sato, *honcho sensei*, he did dispatch *wataschi* as matriculant at remote obscure Oklahoma A & M, strictly cow college located in one-horsie wide-spot-in-thoroughfare provincial Stillwater Town, county of Payne, reet? Than which aforesaid—"

"Silence!" shouts *honcho* Premier-General Tojo Hideki, and, "You will refrain from speaking!" and, "Are you so deficient in *budo* discipline as to ignore an express command from a general officer of the Imperial Army?" Said personage (The Razor, Jack!) displays sharp-pointy chopper pearlie whites, grips ivory *samurai* fan in one hand like unto hilt of *katana* longsword whilst fanning air with *kempei* dossier documentation sheaf with the other. I hit (natch!) posture of attention—straight like six o'clock!—render thirty-five degree kowtow bow of submission subservience.

I think: *wataschi*, you is done immersed pedal extremity in proverbialist canine's dung, than which substance The Razor will now rub your schnozz in, reet, Jack?

"It is just this, your evident inability to exercise a prudent control of your tongue, which gives me pause when I come to decide if you can be entrusted with a task of historic significance, Sub-Lieutenant Yamaguchi Yoshinori," says he, and, "It is just this seeming flaw in an otherwise admirable character which doubtless motivated Mr. Sato Isao of the *kempei* to send you to a less than excellent school to study among the *Amerikajin*, and to test your loyalty with a counterintelligence assignment!"

"I done real good at it though, *sensei*!"

"Again you speak when you should listen!"

"Orry-say, *sensei*," I whisper.

Premier-General Tojo Hideki hisses big breath intake hiss, closes baby blues behind black bone-frame round specs, bows shaved chrome-dome noggin before speaking.

"Indeed," he says, and, "Once again your scholarship was exemplary, both a credit to the honor of *Dai Nippon* and a humiliation to your barbarian *Amerikajin* fellow matriculants, who, if they were not the shameless *gaijin* they are, would be dishonored by their inferior academic performance."

"Reet," I say, "Phi Kappa Phi, Phi Eta Sigma, Sigma Tau Delta, Dean's List and also Prexy's four years consecutive, not to fail to mention valedictory laurel, but they ain't all redneck goat-ropers, *honcho sensei*, as how fellow co-ed matriculant Miss Clara Sterk, also knowed as Petty Girl, only lost out to me by a fraction of a grade-point, as how main mentor Prof Os Southard—" I self-stop, reet? As how premier-general personage is looking look at me as might could indicate intention is to discard ivory *samurai* fan, reach for longsword. How you say in *Eigo*, Jack, eye of fish, dig? "Orry-say again," I add, hit attention posture, render kowtow bow.

Says he—following upon lengthy impregnated pause, reet?—"What need have we of the *kempei* to compile and maintain a security dossier on one such as you? What need is there for our Mr. Sato to inscribe so many pages with the record of your scholastic achievements and your dependable and valuable service in the counterintelligence mission of *Dai Nippon* during your time among the *Amerikajin*? What need have I to review your career with you when I have only to utter a word and you will inundate my ears with explanations and apologies and trivial elaboration! No," says he. "When I open my mouth, do not speak again unless and until I command you." Like, the man is steamed.

"I order you, Sub-Lieutenant Yamaguchi Yoshinori, upon your sacred oath of loyalty, to stand at attention in absolute silence and to listen to me as I explain to you the historic mission in the service of *Dai Nippon* that I have determined, despite all my misgivings, to entrust to you! Are you able to heed my command? No, do not signify by speaking! Bow, once, so that I may be reassured."

What's to do, reet, Jack? I is but two and twenty years of age aged — Fool of April Day (*hanami*!), circa 1942. Unarmed save for *yoin ma do* awareness of life's big ironics, only this day come to articulation manifestness. I (*wataschi*, me!), Sub-Lieutenant Yamaguchi Yoshinori, Imperial Army of *Dai Nippon* (a.k.a. Student Yamaguchi Yoshinori, a.k.a. Gooch!), render crisp forty-degree kowtow, Jack!

"It is my wish," says *honcho* Premier-General Tojo Hideki, "to create an historic chronicle in the form of an *eiga* — "

"Reet!" I interrupt.

" — that shall serve as a record for the posterity of the Hundred Millions of the celestially ordained triumph of *hakko ichui*."

"I is your man, *honcho sensei*!" I say, but he don't cease spiel, reet?

"I conceive that it shall, in the manner of your *eiga* devoted to our brilliant victory over the *Amerikajin* at *Pearu Halbol* — "

"I can see it! I can see it, epic global-wide scope, cast of millions, coloration by technicolor!" I say.

" — depict *Dai Nippon's* subjugation of the barbarian eight corners of the world."

"I is already visualizing visuals, *honcho* premier-general!" I say, and, "Alternate soundtracks in myriad lingos, thousands of prints for world-wide distribution, coordination of premier screenings, massive promo effort thrusts, box-office *oatari* boffo smash assured!"

"Do you consider yourself equal to so great a task, sub-lieutenant?"

"But try me!" I say, and, "Does ursine defecate in forest? Is Papacy prelate not member in good standing of mackerel-snapper faith?"

"It will doubtless require a complex logistical structure," says he.

"Reet. Levy on personnel available from *Nihonjin* commercial studios, comb out file dossiers on skilled technicians currently performing *issen gorin* conscript service, budgetary itemizations to finance venture, not to fail to mention research staff toward reconstruction of events to date — start back circa 'thirty-one Mukden Incident, *honcho sensei*?"

"You pledged on your oath to listen in silence, sub-lieutenant!"

"Orry-say, but this is opportunity I been waiting on, fondest hopes, wild-most dreams, shot at bluebird and also brass ring, not to fail to mention honor-and-glory shtick, reet? Thousand pardons!" I say, resume attention posture, render kowtow, reet?

"Though you will proceed under my direct command authority and will report directly to me alone, this operation will develop only gradually, for it is said that small feet shall attempt only short steps."

"I can but dig it!" I is unable to refrain from saying.

"If you would but recognize the sagacity of stopping your mouth when others speak!" says he, and, "I have determined the most propitious beginning is to create first an *eiga* to dramatize the surrender of the stubborn *Amerikajin* who still attempt to resist us in the Philippine Islands."

"Than which, sad to say, however, ain't yet happened yet though, reet, *honcho* premier-general?"

"Yet this will come to pass! The campaign in Bataan Peninsula has been long and costly in both lives and treasure. I would not have the Hundred Millions despair at this. Thus, such an *eiga*, in the manner of the one devoted to *Pearu Halbol*, shall be created to persuade all of *Dai Nippon* that *hakko ichui* proceeds at an appropriate pace."

"I do dig," I tell him, "minimize casualties, accentuate-the-positive shtick."

"Just so. And you will commence your work immediately. My staff will arrange transport by air to the Philippines for you at once."

"I was, like, hoping, *sensei*," I say, "for some furlough time as how to visit family in our paper house for a while before I pitch in shoulder-to-wheel syndrome, reet?"

"You will depart at once," says he, and, "You will apply by the warrant of my personal seal for the necessary support and cooperation from General Homma's field headquarters on the Bataan Peninsula—"

"Wouldn't it be better to, like, work out of Manila, *honcho sensei*, as how bullets flying likely to disrupt concentrations on task at hand?"

"You will follow my orders, and you will do so without expressions of dissent!" says he.

"Reet."

"So," says he, "you understand your mission, Sub-Lieutenant Yamaguchi Yoshinori?"

"Reet! Lens *eiga* flic of Homma's boys whipping up on Yank defenders of P.I. Aforementioned to serve as prototype for series thereof to capture on celluloid glorious destiny of *Dai Nippon* fulfilled via *hakko ichui* schema."

"It is well. And," says he, "are you conscious, as I am, sub-lieutenant, of the great moment we share, of the import of this day, not only for the Hundred Millions, but for all of humanity in the future to come? We make permanent what is only a fleeting instant in the eternal passage of time!"

"*Hai!*" I say, and, "At least I think so, reet?"

Says he: "I suspect that mankind will look back upon this day and wonder that so grandiose an accomplishment began so humbly."

"Reet. Honor-and-glory shtick for name and family, etcetera blah."

Honcho Premier-General Tojo Hideki stands up, lays down *kempei* dossier and ivory *samurai* fan, faces east (directional orientation of Chrysanthemum Throne, Imperial Palace, natch!), shouts: "*Tenno Heika Banzai!*" Bows, reet?

Than which ejaculation I (natch!) join in chorus: how we say, Jack, "Long Live Emperor," reet?

I mean, like, what's else to do, reet, Jack?

"You will require," says Premier-General Tojo Hideki, "a code designation to facilitate our communications via radiogram if your reports of progress are to penetrate the bureaucracy that necessarily insulates one in a position of responsibile leadership such as I occupy, sub-lieutenant."

"Reet," I say, and, "Call me whatsoever."

"A most appropriate nomenclature occurs to me," says he, and, "When it was my honor to command the heroic Kwantung Army in Manchukuo, I was concerned that my troops should be provided with suitable entertainments to occupy the hours not devoted to training exercises. It was I, for instance, who initiated the transport of *moga* prostitutes from *Dai Nippon* to our encampments on the Chinese border."

"Reet. Comfort women, populace of which populated Happy Fields Yoshiwara District of Tokyo Town, reet?"

"Just so. I find that a contented soldier performs his duty with true zeal. I also caused to be brought from *Dai Nippon* a selection of *eiga*, mostly of the *chambara* martial variety, to inspire *budo* spirit in my troops. I also brought performing companies of acrobats and musicians for the amusement of my officers and the *issen gorin*. I recall now the *benshi* who in those early days accompanied the *eiga* sent to us. Do you know of the *benshi*, sublieutenant?"

"Reet," I say, and, "*Benshi*, old-timey silent flic days, *benshi* stand up beside the screen and explain *eiga* to audience, reet? As how illiterate *Nihonjin* Hundred Millions can't read *kanji* captions. Obsolete with advent of soundtracks. *Benshi* all gone, *sensei*."

"Just so," he says, and, "I designate your code name to be *benshi*! Do you perceive the humor of this, sub-lieutenant? You may smile if you feel so inspired — I am not a humorless man, Sub-Lieutenant!"

"Reet," I say. "Hee hee. To laugh, *honcho* premier-general, reet? I does dig it: *benshi* steady explains, reet? Reference *wataschi's* loquacity. Junior officers' mess aboard carrier *Akagi* did crack wise with same, reet?"

"Just so!" says he. *Honcho* Premier-General Tojo smiles *sumairu* revealing sharp chopper pearlie whites. To laugh, Jack. "I dismiss you now. We have no more time to spare for levity. You will wish to bid your family

217

farewell and prepare for your journey to Bataan. *Sayonara*, Sub-Lieutenant *Benshi!*"

"Last query," I say. "Where's aforesaid Mr. Sato Isao now? Like, I ain't heard from him since departure from stateside, reet?"

"Ah," says Tojo Hideki, "I regret to inform you he perished in the attack upon Hawaii, where he had been dispatched on a mission of great importance prior to our heroic strike. He gave his life for the Hundred Millions, earning much honor and glory for his family and name!"

"Reet," I say, and, "Too bad, like, reet?"

"All losses grieve me," says he, and, "I recall that I composed a poem in his memory when I learned of his demise, so ironic was it, to have been killed by the bombs launched by the planes of *Dai Nippon* whose mission he facilitated by the intelligence he gathered beforehand. Such is the irony of one's *do* path in life, *benshi*, is it not so?"

"Reet. You wrote a poem?" I query.

"Of course," says he, and, "Did you not know, *benshi*, I am, like your esteemed father, a poet?"

"Could have fooled me, *sensei*," I say, and, "So long and also see you later, reet?" And did render kowtow, retrieve longsword from conference confabulation table, salute, about-face (*katana* clanks on floor tiles!), departing smartly. They don't call him The Razor for nothing, Jack!

Do you dig it? *Ma. Yoin. Do.* Life-and-times ironics, reet? Lieutenant *Benshi*—me, Jack! Circa Fool of April Day (*hanami!*), 1942, reet? Oh, say it were not so, Jack!

What's did I know? What's else to do except save do as inscrutable forces of historical flaps global-wide do dictate, to which end I did bid sad goodbye to family—*Papa-san*, *Mama-san*, Sis *Iko-san* (paper house, Tokyo Town!), catch slow boat troop transport (no aircrafts available), destination of which is metropolis of Manila.

Thus it were, Jack, I, Lieutenant *Benshi*, sat packed to bulkheads with *issen gorin* replacements for Masaharu Homma's glorious 14th, composing rough-draft script of first full feature-length *eiga* flic I will lens on Bataan Peninsula—title: *Down with the Stars & Stripes*.

Thus it were I did sit aboard aforementioned slow boat troop transport out of Yokohama (bound for Manila!), considering life's ironies to date and also future's unknowns in state of relative calmish *enryo*. Rough out rough draft *eiga* flic script, listen to *issen gorin* cope with sea voyage boredom via singing choral verses of *Umi Yakuba* (Eta Jima boot camp song):

> Across the sea,
> Corpses in the water;

Across the mountain,
Corpses heaped upon the field;
I shall die only for the *Mikado*,
I shall never look back!

I did think: Lieutenant *Benshi*, you must gots to be living right! As how now no danger of front-line combat-zone endangerment, no need to lens actualities footage (unlike unto *Pearu Halbol* flap attack!), entire P.I. propaganda flic *eiga* can be staged dramatic scam, reet? Than which to effect I communicate via military-radio frequency as follows:

Date:
8 April 1942

To:
Premier-General Tojo Hideki
Ichigaya Heights Headquarters
Imperial Ministry of War
Tokyo
Dai Nippon

From:
Lt. *Benshi*
Producer, Director, Writer, Cinematographer
Imperial *Hakko Ichui* Cinematic Documentary Chronicle
Manila
Philippine Islands

Arrival on scene aforesaid above coincidentally coincides with end of armed *Amerikajin* opposition to glorious and also victorious 14th Imperial Army on Bataan Peninsula (surrender of Corregidor expected to follow soonest hereafter, reet?).

I, Lieutenant *Benshi*, propose to proceed instanter with liaison assistance of Homma Manila Hq. staff to scout locations for lensing *eiga* flic *Down with the Stars & Stripes* in area of aforesaid Bataan remoteness, complete with script rewrite, assemble available actuality footages, recruit crew, proceed to casting etcetera blah.

How we say, *sensei, Eija Nai Kai* — like, it couldn't get no gooder, reet, *honcho* premier-general?

Congrats (natch! to you, also General M. Homma, exultant *issen gorin aka gami* red-letter conscript troops of glorious and also victorious 14th Imperial, and also to Hundred Millions folks back home in *Dai Nippon* — government handing out caramels to little nippers to celebrate? Also please to say hello in High Court *Nihonju* (natch!) for me personal to *Mikado* when next you meet for high-level official confabulations, and please also say hello to my folks Mr. and Mrs. Yamaguchi (also Sis *Iko-san*!) should you run into them on streets of Tokyo Town whilst enjoying *sanpo* stroll. Tell them, please, I, their sole son and big bro, Lieutenant *Benshi*, is fine, suffering some in intense heat and also humidities of P.I., than which puts even Okie-land sun-baked vasteness in shade.

Hey, *sensei! Hakko ichui* on schedule per your prognostications, reet?

Where next? India? Australia? New Zealand?
Tenno Heika Banzai!

After than which dispatching above-cited, I proceed to *honcho* General Masaharu Homma's Manila Hq., reet? Lamentably, said *honcho* general is away on present duties (seige of Corregidor, reet?), expected back immediate upon Yank surrender. Staff *honcho* factotum types is still busy trying to clean up after much-lamented destruction of Manila (on scale of circa '37 so-called Rape of Nanking by 9th Army), thus unable to provide beyond bare-minimum transport and personnel assistance — latter is manifest in form of one *issen gorin* Private Matsunaga Yutaka (a.k.a. Gopher) as factotum aide-de-camp dog robber assistant to accompany me (Lt. *Benshi!*) southwards to Bataan to commence remote locations scout trek, reet?

Than which proceeds apace, all whilst I exist in info vacuum, than which persists unbroken until end of April — progress of work much impeded by refusal of Yank Corregidor die-hard holdouts (under command of Lt. General Skinny Wainwright) to succumb to assaults of now-exhausted battle-wearied 14th Imperial. Than which info barrier breaks first week of May (merry month of!), circa '42, via radiogram from Tokyo Town, delivered personal to *wataschi*, as follows:

Date:
6 May 1942

To:
Lt. *Benshi*
Hakko Ichui Eiga Mission
Bataan Peninsula
Philippine Islands

From:
Premier-General Tojo Hideki
Ichigaya Heights Headquarters
Imperial Ministry of War
Tokyo Prefecture
Dai Nippon

I am reliably informed by *kempei-tai* military intelligence operating in the front lines held by the victorious 14th Imperial Army of *Dai Nippon* that the fall of Corregidor fortress to our heroic warriors is expected at any moment. I order you to cease your present activity with regard to the *eiga* tentatively entitled *Down with the Stars & Stripes* and to proceed at once to General Homma's field headquarters in the immediate vicinity of Corregidor. There, you will, with the cooperation and support of General Homma's staff, devise to create an *eiga* documentary of the impending Corregidor surrender.

It is imperative that you create this *eiga* as soon as the *Amerikajin* surrender is received, and that it be transported as soon as possible for presentation to the civilian populace of the Hundred Millions of *Dai*

Nippon, whose infinite patience and matchless martial spirit have been sorely tried by both the unexpected duration of the conflict in the Philippines and the heavy losses in killed and wounded suffered by the 14th Imperial Army at the hands of the barbarian defenders. So dire is the situation that I add, in most strict military confidence, that, although General Homma is still officially accounted a national hero on the scale of (here I must transgress the virtue of modesty for the sake of candor!) myself, Admiral Yamamoto, and General Yamashita (the latter for his brilliant defeat of superior *Igirisujin* forces at Singapore), I shall recall him and remove him from command in official disgrace once our final victory is realized. Thus it is that the *eiga* you create of the *Amerikajin* surrender of Corregidor shall be such as to both obscure the public memory of General Homma and reinstill the necessary *kirijini budo* fighting spirit among the masses of the Hundred Millions of *Dai Nippon*.

Let me now append a personal message to you, Lieutenant *Benshi*:

Has the news of the dastardly 18 April bombing raid launched against our capital city of Tokyo reached the rural areas of Bataan, where I presume you conduct your current (and now postponed!) duties? The cowardly *Amerikajin*, led by one Col. James Doolittle, were able to reach the shores of *Nihon* from the carrier *Hornet*, which steamed from *Pearu Halbol* to within only a few hundred miles of our coastline.

This vicious assault was clearly intended, not as a blow struck at legitimate military targets, but as a terrorist attack upon unarmed and unsuspecting civilians.

The raid was inept in its execution; a survey of the bombing pattern establishes the probability that the *Amerikajin* bombardiers mistook the chimneys of Tokyo's countless *sento* public baths for those of small factories. Thus, there was no significant damage wrought upon even our vital industries. The only casualties were civilians, and these resulted primarily from the fires following upon the bombing.

Lt. *Benshi*: I regret to inform you that among the list of those killed in this futile and pointless carnage appear the names of your father, your mother, and your sister. I have made a personal effort to confirm the report, and thus can assure you there is no mistake or ambiguity possible.

I convey to you my sincere personal sympathy, in addition to that of the *Mikado* and the entire Hundred Millions of *Dai Nippon*. The names of your parents and sister are now inscribed on rice paper and affixed to the shrine at Yasukuni, emblematic of their eternal inscription in the memory of *Ameratasu*, where throngs of your fellow *Nihonjin* repair daily to honor their ascent to the state of *kami*. Your family, along with the other civilians killed by the evil *Amerikajin*, have made an honorable sacrifice equal to that of our heroic warriors of the Imperial Army and Navy who have given, and will yet give, their lives on behalf of our sacred *hakko ichui* destiny. May this example of your loved ones serve to inspire you to ever-greater effort in the performance of your duty!

Postscript: Most recent *kempei-tai* intelligence communications from our glorious Kwantung Army in China inform me that several of the crews piloting the planes of the Doolittle force have fallen into our hands there. Further, interrogations conducted reveal the probability that the *Amerikajin* were guided to their targets over Tokyo in large part by reconnaissance photographs quite possibly obtained by one Morris (a.k.a. Moe) Berg, who we now confirm is an operative of the *Amerikajin* Office of Strategic Services. You will, of course, remember Moe Berg from your association during the year 1935! This information cannot be absolutely confirmed, but it is my assumption that it would prove of interest to you. Know, finally, Lt. *Benshi*, that I intend, when the press of my duties permits, to compose a *haiku* to express my compassion for your loss.

Tenno Heika Banzai!

Papa-san! Mama-san! Iko-san! Tojo, say it ain't so! Oh, Moe, say it is not so! Oh, Jack: big ironies of life! What's to say thereof? Except save, due (possible!) to *eiga* footages I did assist Moe Berg to lens (circa '35!), due to Doolittle raid on Tokyo Town (*hanami!*), *wataschi* Lieutenant *Benshi* (a.k.a. Yamaguchi Yoshinori, a.k.a. Gooch!) is rendered, how we say in *Nihonju, munako*—orphan child of no name, reet? *Ma. Yoin. Do.*

"Saddle up, Gopher," I say to *issen gorin* Private Matsunaga Yutaka, "as how we gots to *chogee* on down to Corregidor, reet?"

"Lieutenant *Benshi*," says he, "I thought we had yet to discover more sites suitable to make the great *eiga* which will show our victory over the *Amerikajin* here in Bataan. Why now do we go where the fighting still rages? I do not know if I am capable of taking up my rifle to fight against the *Amerikajin* again, Lieutenant *Benshi*. I am told by my comrades that this place called Corregidor is all but impregnable, and that thousands of *Nihonjin issen gorin* and also officers will die for the *Mikado* if we are to capture this fortress. I do not know if I have the *hara* belly courage to die for my *Mikado* here so far from my home and family, Lieutenant *Benshi*!"

Jack, I did tell him: "Will you put a cork in it, Gopher! Stuff a sock in it, Gopher! Grab my longsword and pack our gear! Hump your stumps, Jack! Gopher, move it before I gots to get real *budo* on you and, like, kick your keester, reet?"

"Lieutenant *Benshi*, are you well? You appear shaken, Lieutenant *Benshi*. Have you read something in the radio message I brought you that has alarmed you?"

I said: . . . Jack, I do not remember what I did say!

Suffice to say Private Matsunage (a.k.a. Gopher) Yutaka, rice-paddy-raised *Nihonjin* redneck goat-roper farmer boy from hick sticks boonies rural village environ of Shikoku Island, *issen gorin aka gami* red-letter conscript draftee cannon fodder dogface grunt destined to perish on *Ogasarawa* Sulfur Island (Iwo Jima, Jack!) for his *Mikado*, done took up my *katana* longsword, packed our traps, and we done went *chogee* in direct direction of Corregidor, reet? Than at which place I did lens Yank surrender to Homma's 14th.

Big life ironics, reet, Jack?

Got burned up in a big fire. Jimmy Doolittle's flyboys, B-25's launched off deck of U.S.S. *Hornet* (than which vessel happened by happenstance to be out to sea on training run during *Pearu Halbol* devastation of Yank Pacific fleet). Pinpoint targets (*sento* public baths chimneys looking not unlike like unto small factory smokestacks) with aid of photos lensed (16-millimeter Stewart Warner with long range focus lens) by Morris (a.k.a. Moe) Berg, third-string bullpen warm-up catcher for Senators of Washington (D.C.), than which personage is clandestine O.S.S. operative in guise of touring Yank American League *besuboru* all-star squad (circa '35) – aforesaid Moe guided by official (personal audience with *Mikado*, Jack!) interpeter Student Yamaguchi Yoshinori.

Moe! Tojo! Say it were not so!

Along with family photo album, all pics of Daddy, Mama, Iko (Ueno Park, *hanami*, circa '28!), along with revered mentors' reports of excellence in academic pursuits at Native Land Loving School (stripe up leg, chevron on sleeve!) of said Student Yamaguchi Yoshinori. *Iko-san's* big bro *Yosho-san*. Mr. and Mrs. Yamaguchi's little boy Yosh! Gone. Got burned up in big fire, Jack!

Not unlike like unto 1940 edition of *Redskin* (Go, Pokes! Go, Punchers! Beat O.U.!), A & M College, burned up in fire (result of Long Lance torpedo than which failed to catch *Hornet* at dockside!) aboard U.S.S. *Oklahoma*, circa December '41 – than which great victory for *Dai Nippon* begins commencement of, how you say, WW II (*senso!*), reet? Celestially destined commencement of *hakko ichui* grandiose design – than which global flap brings *wataschi* (Lieutenant *Benshi* – *munako* orphan child of no name!) to Corregidor fortress environ (May 8, 1942), Philippine Islands (hot like unto Okie Dust Bowl with humidities added), final defeat of barbarian *Amerikajin* die-hard defenders, ultimate triumph of *Dai Nippon* – oh, it is to laugh, reet?

As in: har har. And also hee.

"Why did you burn the radio message I delivered to you, Lieutenant *Benshi*? Was the message one to alarm you or cause you grief?"

"Got burned up in a fire," I did say to him.

"I do not understand," says he, and, "Do you hear the noise like thunder, Lieutenant *Benshi*? Those are the enormous *Amerikijin* cannons my comrades tell me they shoot at us from the Corregidor fortress, even larger than those that rained death upon my comrades of the Fourteenth Army when we fought on Bataan in the jungle and in the swamps."

"I ain't deaf!" I tell him, and, "Keep your coolth, Gopher, we ain't subject to enter no combat! I gots the straight scoop poop info from *honcho* Premier-General Tojo as how the Yanks is surrendering instanter, reet? *Daijubo*, Gopher!" I tell him — not to fret. Eight corners of the world soon united under roof of *Dai Nippon*, everything pretty soon now hunky-dory, peace on earth era of plenty via Greater East Asia Co-Prosperity Sphere etcetera blah blah. How we say — *Eija Nai Kai* — ain't it so good how's it can be, Jack?

Cut to: field headquarters, 14th Imperial Army of *Dai Nippon* (tip of Bataan Peninsula, hop, skip, and also jump across water from Corregidor fortress), circa 8 of May, 1942, reet?

"You are the one," says *honcho* General Homma Masaharu, "identified in the radiogram I received from Ichigaya Heights as Lieutenant *Benshi*?"

"Reet, *sensei* general," say I, and, "Lieutenant *Benshi*, come, *honcho* Premier-General Tojo's *hanko* signed warrant in hand, to lens *Amerikajin* surrender ceremonials out on yonder rock —" I nod noggin in directional of Corregidor fortress — "than which they tells me is about subject to proceed instanter, reet?"

"The surrender," says General Homma Masaharu, "is already accomplished. The *Amerikajin* General Wainwright telephoned me before this morning's dawn. Did you not note the quiet that fell upon us when the firing ceased? Are you truly an officer of the Imperial Army?" he queries, and, "How is it you do not wear your longsword? And who is this *issen gorin* who attends you with it and cannot stand at attention in my presence without twitching as though he were feebleminded?"

To which I riposte: "Reet. Commissioned by Imperial Rescript upon satisfactory completion of Eta Jima locale training. Sad to say, how-somever, *sensei* general, *wataschi* never did get hang of hanging *katana* on belt in proper *budo* style, reet? *Honcho* leader of all *Dai Nippon* Premier-General Tojo — I calls him *Hideki-san* — was gracious enough to overlook aforesaid failing when he appointed me per official *hanko* warrant on special-duty-mission status, reet? My man there is one of your boys, Private Matsunaga Yutaka, than which whom is shade Section Eight whacko *baka* as result of Bataan campaign combat experience experienced — the boy sees *Amerikajin* even in his dreams, hears guns shooting at him even in silences, hence necessary to cut him some slacks, *sensei*. I mean, please-to-forgive shtick and all, reet? Aforesaid *issen gorin* personage was assigned to me by your rear echelon staff back at Manila as assistant, how we say, grip, to schlepp my longsword, *eiga* motion-picture camera, and assorted gears."

"Ah!" says General Homma Masaharu — *honcho budo* commander of 14th Imperial Army, now at long last after four plus months victorious in Philippine Islands conquest campaign. "Ah," says he, and, "We have fought bitterly for many months, and now you come from Tokyo to make the *eiga* that will show how easily we vanquished the *Amerikajin?*"

"Reet. Something like," I tell him, Jack.

Says he: "For months we have endured the privations of war, fighting and dying for the *Mikado*, and at the moment of triumph comes a non-combatant without martial skills to make a spectacle of the delivery of our enemies into our hands! How appropriate," says he, "that the political generals at Ichigaya Heights, who know no more than you of what we have undergone, turn our suffering and sacrifice into a cheap propaganda amusement for the Hundred Millions of *Dai Nippon!*"

"Ain't it always the way?" I say, and, "Just following orders, *honcho* general!"

Dig: as how General Homma Masaharu, *honcho* commander of 14th Imperial, is wise to situation's situation, reet? As how, vaunted victory over Yanks is done took too long, cost too much lives and also materiel, thus done slapped damper down on Hundred Millions *senso kirijini* martial ardor engendered by previously rapid sequence of unbroken victories — Tojo in Korea (how we say: *Chosen*, reet?) and also China, Yamamoto at *Pearu Halbol*, Yamashita versus *Igirisujin* at Singapore, etcetera blah. Aforesaid *honcho* General Homma Masaharu is wise as to hot-water status with Ichigaya Heights Ministry of War *honcho* superiors. Show me a worried man: Homma Masaharu, brow furrowed, baby blues sunken, hairs thinned, not to fail to mention heat's humidities engendering perspirations gathering in lines in visage, dotting aforesaid wrinkled brow, creating sweat rings in armpits of tunic.

Says he: "My triumph turns to ashes in my mouth! I had sworn to take the fifty-thousand dollar *Amerikajin* General *Makassar* back to *Dai Nippon* in chains, and to present him as a gift of *senso* to the *Mikado* —" note, Jack: no kowtows required at mention of direct descendant of Sun Goddess under combat field conditions, reet? — "and thusly to humble the reputations of the politicians who rule at Ichigaya Heights! But *Makassar* eluded the net of ships I cast about Corregidor, and now I shall have only the inferior-ranking Wainwright as a prize to symbolize my victory! Even as we seize the point of his last resistance, the coward *Makassar* is safe in Australia, where he makes broadcasts over the radio and continues to assure his troops, who lie at my feet there, just across the water, that he will send them reinforcements sufficient to repulse us and drive us back to Manila and into the sea! Oh, I shall avenge myself upon his command when I have them disarmed and helpless before me!"

"Reet," I say, and, "*Daijubo, sensei!*" and, "Australia might could be next — *Hideki-san* didn't say in last missive I gots personal from him — *hakko ichui* on schedule, reet?"

"If this is so, I will not be permitted the honor of the command," says he, and, "No, history has decreed that *Makassar* and I have passed one another by on the *do* of our lives!"

225

Dig Big Irony of which is to come, reet, Jack?: as how Dugout Doug MacArthur had aforesaid Homma Masaharu executed, circa '46, reet? As retaliation for atrocities attendant upon so-called Bataan Death March and subsequent sufferings imposed upon Yank prisoners taken in P.I. What's to know? What's to do, Jack?

"I have no time nor any inclination to discuss such things with you, Lieutenant Who-Calls-Himself-*Benshi*. I am ordered by Ichigaya Heights to cooperate with you. There are eleven thousand *Amerikajin* and their Filipino cohorts gathering to stack their arms at the entrance to the Malinta Tunnel over there, even as we speak, the remnants of *Makassar's* command and some few reinforcements which arrived only last November, the only support he received before we launched our attack. So, tell me what you require to make your *eiga*, Lieutenant *Benshi*, and tell this idiot *issen gorin* who serves you to cease his twitching or I shall strike him with my scabbard! Oh, you are no soldier, that is evident! Tell me, Lieutenant *Benshi*, is your sole skill the making of *eiga*? I wonder that you can be of any service to *Dai Nippon* if all you are capable of is creating popular amusements!"

Jack, I did tell him: "I is also fluent in *Eigo* lingo, *honcho sensei* general, to include idiomatics and slangs, once served as interpreter-guide upon personal appointment by *Mikado* hisself, and, thereafter, operating in alien *gaijin* terrain of Stillwater Town, county of Payne, sovereign state of Oklahoma, did meritorious service stateside amongst barbarian *Amerikajin*, whose surrender you takes today, as clandestine *kempei* counterintelligence operative, reet?" And I did tell him, Jack, outline of scenario I is done devised to lens Corregidor surrender ceremonials — than which contains (all unbeknownst to me, natch!) big irony, than which follows:

> MUSIC: *Kaigun* Naval March
> ROLE LOGOS: WHITE DEVILS' COLONIALIST IMPERIALISM CRUMBLES BEFORE THE ONSLAUGHT OF *HAKKO ICHUI! AMERIKAJIN* MERCENARIES HUMBLY SURRENDER TO VALIANT FORCES OF *DAI NIPPON!* WESTERN BARBARIANS' CULTURAL AND ECONOMIC POLLUTION OF GREATER EAST ASIA CO-PROSPERITY SPHERE ENDS IN FINAL DEFEAT AT CORREGIDOR FORTRESS! *YAMATO DAMASHII! TENNO HEIKA BANZAI!*
> MUSIC DOWN TO BACKGROUND.
> JUMP CUTS TO ACCOMPANY VOICE-OVER: Stock footage of *Igirisujin* colonial empire life (*Igirisujin* attired in white tropicals play at cricket; *Igirisujin* ladies in garden hats, full skirts, sip tea on veranda, attended by Asian servants); Dugout Doug MacArthur reviews formation of puppet Filipino Constabulary; *Amerikajin* army officers play golf at Manila Country Club, Filipino caddies schlepp bags; *Amerikajin* officers lounge in wicker chairs with drinks served by Filipino messboy, balcony overlooking Manila

Bay—typical preprandial (a.k.a. Blue Hour) cocktails imbibition; swish pan of Filipino school kiddies pledging allegiance to Stars & Stripes; Caucasian overseer directs coolie labor (Malay rubber plantation? tea field of India? logging in Burmese forest?); *Amerikajin* enlisted men cavort drunkenly in company of Asian *moga* comfort women—if available in captured Signal Corps or "March of Time" archive footage, if not, stage same in Manila with Yank P.O.W.'s and localist talent?); etcetera blah blah.

VOICE-OVER: Asia for Asians! *Yamato Damashii!* Triumph of *Nipponshikki* ethos! *Hakko ichui* liberates the brown and yellow-hued peoples of the Greater East Asia Co-Prosperity Sphere from the hated domination of decadent, alien cultures of the barbarian West! *Hakko ichui* destines the Hundred Millions of *Dai Nippon* for the mission of leadership of all Asia toward a glorious and honorable future of economic plenty and social order and tranquility! The realization of our sacred heritage is at hand! Following rapidly upon the liberation of *Chosen, Manchukuo,* and China, our Imperial Army and Navy have wrought successive defeats upon the *Igirisujin* at Singapore, the Hollanders in the East Indies, the French in Cochin China, and now, the arrogant *Amerikajin* who presumed to impede the celestially decreed progress of the Empire of *Nihon!*

CUT TO: still pic, *Nihonjin* naval aircraft poised in midflight above burning, sinking Yank vessels at *Pearu Halbol* dockside (scavenge from initial docudrama segment!).

VOICE-OVER: The sons of *Ameratasu* destroy first the ineffectual *Amerikajin* fleet!

CUT TO: stock footage, long shots of Imperial Army on march (Chink campaign if no available Bataan Peninsula actualities on hand).

VOICE-OVER: Now we conclude the struggle of the courageous Imperial Army in the Philippine Islands with a stunning, effortless capture of the last *Amerikajin* forces yet resisting from within the seemingly impregnable fortress of Corregidor! The cowardly defenders give up their arms to the command of the heroic 14th Imperial Army!

CUT TO: Pan of informal ranks of 14th Imperial *issen gorin* wielding Arisaka rifles, bayonets affixed, gathered atop typical Corregidor fortress blockhouse, arms raised in series of choral cheers:

   Tenno Heika Banzai!
   Tenno Heika Banzai!
   Etcetera blah.

"*Sensei honcho* general," I tell him, "I needs, like, forty or fifty of your *issen gorin* boys. If somebody can mayhap stop them looting long enough? Clean uniforms, if possible. Than which is not to fail to mention I needs you to, like, form Yank prisoners up in ranks, at attention posture, reet? Find me some for sure gots bandages, walking wounded, reet? Dirtier the better. And don't let your ordnance boys glom all them captured weaponries until I get me a shot of big heap of Springfields — maybe get a line of Yanks to walk by, toss their shoulder-fires and also sidearms on the pile? Also please one squad of your bestest, boys who can take direction for flag lowering and also raising. Gopher!" I shout over my shoulder, "stand by with them film magazines, Jack!"

"The *Amerikajin* General Wainwright and his staff," says General Homma Masaharu, "I insist you photograph them in your *eiga* for all to see how I have in the end subjugated them!"

"*Daijubo!*" I assure him, and, "I gots a scenario roughed out for that will flat knock them off their *tatami* up there at Ichigaya Heights, *honcho* general! Gopher," I say, "stick close to me, and do not — I repeats — do not lose my sword!"

"It is strange to me to see the *Amerikajin*, so many of them, so close to me," says he, and, "We seldom saw them close to our ranks when we killed one another on Bataan."

"Reet. *Sensei* general, can you get me them boys I needs? Hang in there, Gopher," I say, "we gots us a job of work to do today, reet?"

> CUT TO: Long shot, Corregidor fortress (Stars & Stripes flapping in sea breeze — if available; inventory Yank Signal Corps archives in Manila prior to Tokyo Town final-edit sessions?).
> MUSIC: *Kimagayo* anthem (do 14th Imperial have marching band for visuals?).
> CUT TO: Flag ceremonials — track Stars & Stripes descending pole, flag ripped off lanyard, torn by exuberant *issen gorin* in show of spontaneous emotions — aforesaid under casual supervision of company-grade *budo* officer; *issen gorin* unable to restrain *hara* belly joy, trample Stars & Stripes under feets; close-up of shredded flag ignited by anonymous hand bearing taper, flames erupting.
> MUSIC: Increase decibels of *Kimagayo*.
> CUT TO: Long shot, squad of very *budo issen gorin*, responding to orders of field-grade office (sword drawn, on parade posture of attentions like unto six o'clock!), raises *Hinomaru* Sun Flag and also Sunrise Flag; cut to close-up of flags flapping; series of jump cuts: visages of *budo* officer-types, *issen gorin*, all chin up, eyes raised (baby blues misty, asparkle with ecstacies of ecstasy!) to flags, big *sumairu* smiles; cut to throngs of *issen gorin* led by *budo* officers of 14th Imperial, Arisakas and *katana* raised in *banzai* choruses audible mix with *Kimagayo* etcetera blah.

"Whilst you form formations of *Amerikajin* prisoners before entrance to Malinta Tunnel, *honcho* general," I say, "me and Gopher will take *sanpo* stroll casual-like and shoot cover shots to establish milieu, reet? Can you not restrain your boys from looting jag until we get footages in can, *honcho* general?" I ask, and, "Follow me, Gopher!"

Dig it, Jack: Corregidor fortress rock is like unto landscape of moon, craters and rubble of aerial and artillery bombardments unremitting during durance of siege, reet? Blockhouses cracked and torn like unto Okie-land dwellings in aftermaths of tornado twister, cave entrances collapsed, Yank guns spiked in emplacements, burned vehicles, every which way is atmosphere aura of dusty dust hovering in superheated air under harsh sunlight — cinders and ashes, Jack.

"This is a terrible place to fight and die, I think, Lieutenant *Benshi*," Gopher says, and, "The air is thick, as it was in the jungle swamps of Bataan, but I think there was here no place to flee and hide from our cannons and bombs except in the caves and tunnels where a man might be buried alive."

"Reet. Now let's get up on high ground and lens one slow pan of whole shebang, Gopher."

> VOICE-OVER: The *Amerikajin* commander Major General Jonathan Wainwright, often addressed as Skinny, left to perish with his famished and exhausted troops by the cowardly $50,000 General *Makassar*, variously addressed as Dugout Doug, presents his sword in abject humility to General Homma Masaharu, commander of the 14th Imperial Army!
> (Note: Ask Tojo if I gots to cut Homma from frame in editing process)

"Gopher," says I, "hand my *katana* to *honcho* General Wainwright there. Skinny — okay if I call you by affectionate nickname moniker handle, Skinny? Nothing personal intended, reet? Skinny, please to accept my longsword, reet? When I calls for action, please to hand aforesaid in turn to *honcho* General Homma here, reet? General Homma," I say, "you take my longsword proffered by *skinny-san*, step one giant step rearwards. Skinny, you might could, if you don't mind, render General Homma a smart salute, very *budo* style, reet? *Sensei* general, you return Skinny's salute."

Skinny Wainwright don't say zilch, takes my *katana* from Gopher Matsunaga, holds it in both hands — like unto awkward as *wataschi* when I essay to schlepp same on parade, reet?

"I have never been so close to an *Amerikajin*," Gopher says, and, "He is the height of two *Nihonjin*, but he smells like rotted meat, and his nose is very big!"

"Shut up, Gopher!" I say, and, "Bigger they is, harder they hit canvas, reet?" and, "Don't be ethnocentric, Gopher! Any questions, General Homma?" I query.

"What shall I say to the *Amerikajin* Wainwright?" asks Homma Masaharu. "Shall I laugh with contempt at him? I will not salute an officer who has failed to inspire his command to victory! He is disgraced, and should have burned his colors and committed *seppuku* rather than yield like a woman of no virtue!"

"Reet," I say, and, "Will you at least try it my way, *sensei* general? Like, might could be our *eiga* flic's gonna be screened global-wide. Just give him hard *budo* stare, breath hiss intake of contempt, as if how playing *hara* belly game, stony-stoics shtick, reet? No dialogue in script. Very *Nipponshikki, honcho* general!"

"Let us do this foolish thing, Lieutenant *Benshi*," says he, "and be done with it. The *Amerikajin* Wainwright must be taken to my field headquarters on Bataan to make a radio broadcast calling for the end of all armed opposition to *Dai Nippon* in these islands."

"Reet," I say, and, to Wainwright, "Skinny, any questions before I roll camera?"

Major General Jonathan (a.k.a. Skinny) Wainwright don't say nothing, reet? Stands stoop-shouldered, old-style campaign hat (like unto Sergeant-Major Tommy Turner's!) on his noggin, empty .45 holster (sidearm already looted by one of Homma's staff factotum personages) hanging open on his web belt—needs a shave, shirt perspiration soaked (natch!), both hands gripping my *katana* to control tremors' tremble.

"Reet!" I say, put baby blue to viewfinder, frame Skinny and Homma. "Action!" I say, hit lever of Stewart Warner 16-millimeter—Moe, say it were not so!—hear grind of gears close to my ear. "That's a wrap, gents!" I cry, even though *honcho* Homma don't take direction, don't return salute from Skinny Wainwright, reet?

Dig: irony of above-cited scene I create via *eiga* flic filmic medium. As how Skinny Wainwright is good foot taller than *honcho* Homma, ordinary procedure would be to stand said *sensei* Homma on box (alternative: stick Skinny in trench, not unlike like unto female leads opposite Alan Ladd) to equivicate relative respective statures, reet? Except as how I is mindful—sacred-mission-duty shtick!—of Premier-General Tojo Hideki's plans for Homma recall and also decommission in lost face disgrace (desire to preclude hero-status equivalencies with Tojo-Yamamoto-Yamashita troika)—hence I allow tall skinny Skinny Wainwright to tower towerlike over diminutive Homma: effect on screen is not unlike like unto adult reluctantly weary gifting small truculent boy with toy sword.

What's do Homma know? Abovementioned is easier than total elimination via cutting-room floor. All in the technique, Jack. I mean, go with *do* flow, reet?

> VOICE-OVER: Reeling from the unremitting assault of the heroic 14th Imperial Army, 11,000 demoralized *Amerikajin* troops, their ranks ineffectually augmented by reluctant conscripts pressed into service by the puppet Filipino government, present themselves, utterly devoid of fighting spirit, to surrender at the entrance to Corregidor's cavernous Malinta Tunnel, the deserted headquarters of the cowardly $50,000 General *Makassar*. Grateful to be free of the terror of battle, the *Amerikajin* and their Filipino cohorts are

relieved to become the captives of *Dai Nippon*!

CUT TO: (After cover shot of Malinta entrance) long slow pan of rank upon rank of *Amerikajin* officers and *issen gorin*, Filipino Constabulary types — expressions of fatigue, apprehension, facial tics, numbed resignation — get a few *sumairu* if possible! — etcetera blah blah.

Than which is easier said than executed, Jack! — requiring assistance of *honcho* General Homma's staff factotums to keep victory-flushed *issen gorin* and combat officers of 14th Imperial out of frame, reet? Than which personages can only with difficulty be restrained from looting assembled P.O.W.s — how you say, liberating personal property of Yanks and also Filipinos, to wit: currencies (Filipino and also greenback *genkin* bucks!), Lucky Strike, Old Gold, and Phillip Morris ciggie smokes, Zippo lighters, wristwatches, rings, shoes, web belts, puttees — in short pith and gist, anything useful or valuable — how we say, *o-miyage* souvenirs, reet?

Than which impolite and criminal acts of liberation is oft accompanied by pushing, shoving, cuffing, slaps, threatening gestures performed with *katana* longswords and Arisaka bayonets (cutting off buttons and brass, also ranks insignia), muzzles of Arisakas and also Mauser pistols carried by *Nihonjin* noncoms in wooden holsters waved beneath P.O.W. schnozzes, reet?

Than which is not to fail to mention accompanying verbalist taunts verbalized in *Nihonju*, and also smattering of crude vulgar *Eigo* lingo snatches. To wit:

"Look upon the *Amerikajin*! They are large, and they stink, but they fear us!"

"Roosever eat shit!"

"Babe Ruth eat shit!"

"I cannot remove the gold ring from the finger of this *Amerikajin baka*! May I borrow your sword, *sensei* lieutenant, so that I might cut off his finger?"

"Stand away from the prisoners!" shout factotum staff officers of *honcho* General Homma's staff. "Stand away so that the lieutenant is able to make his *eiga* pictures! Return to your squads and platoons!" they cry, slap visages, whack shoulders and also backsides with *take* bamboo sword scabbards.

"Why does the lieutenant make the *eiga* of the *Amerikajin*? Let him photograph us so that our families in *Dai Nippon* may see that we have captured all these barbarians without harm to ourselves!" cry the combat officers and *issen gorin* of 14th Imperial Army.

What's to do, reet? I lens slow pan, reload magazines, select selected prisoners for brief close-ups. To facilitate same, I employ *Eigo* banter badinage to effect rapports, as follows:

231

"Hey, Joe, what's you knows? Just returned from Kokomo?"

"How abouts that DiMaggio, reet?"

"Mac, seen any good flics of late?"

"Buddy-ruff, look at birdie camera's lens, give me big grin like unto feline consuming excrements, reet?"

"Where you hail from, sarge?"

"Smile for folks back home, reet, Jack?"

"Did you ever think you'd grow up to be movie star?"

"Is Wee Bonnie Baker done cut any new platters?"

"Anybody here from Oklahoma?"

Yanks is sorry-looking sight, Jack. Most skinny as Wainwright due to short rations of siege durance, uniforms dirty, motley of Army, Navy, Marines, Army Air Corps — stragglers escaped to Corregidor during final Bataan push. They look askance when I speak, or stare back, like as if how they do not see *wataschi*. Some wounded, heads, arms, and also feets bandaged. All in need of shave and a haircut (two bits!). Few riposte to verbal sallies.

"Fuck off you little yellow fuck!" says burly Marine sergeant.

"Hey, sarge, don't get mad on me, Jack! I'm just doing my job, reet?"

"You speak American almost," says swabbie sailor who stands with hands in dungaree pockets, like unto as if how it were cold in dust-laden heat swelter of Corregidor rock,

"Reet! Come by it honest from my dear departed daddy, than which who is undeserving victim of *senso* war not unlike like unto you, sailor boy! Which is to add I is done honed lingo to fine fluency via four years duration stateside, Jack! Ever been to Oklahoma, sovereign state of, sailor?"

"Oklahoma?" says he, and, "We had us some Okies came in with the last reinforcements on the *Coolidge* just before the shit hit the fan. I seen 'em back before we bugged out of Manila, but they're probably all dead or run off into the hills with the Huks if they're lucky."

"Reet. Can you give me just wee tiny *sumairu* smile for birdie in camera? Say cheese," I say.

"I never thought it would happen. They said we'd be relieved. Even MacArthur said we'd be relieved when he shoved off in those P-T's. He said he'd bring relief back with him!" says Yank captain wearing Corps of Engineers brasses.

"Reet," I say. "You ever heard this one?" and sing to tune of "Battle Hymn of Republic":

> Dugout Doug MacArthur
> Lies a shakin' on the rock,
> Safe from any injury
> Or any sudden shock!

Yank captain commences to weep, reet? Embarrassed, I cease banter badinage, move on. "Mom's pie made of apples!" I say in effort to lift spirits of dejected Yanks, get attentions on camera lens. "World Series! Lucky Strike Green is done departed for *senso*! Wee Bonnie Baker! Chattanooga Choo-Choo! Blues in the Night! Betty Grable! Fighting Irish! Eleanor Roosevelt! Deep in the Heart of Texas! Empire State Building! Give My Regards to Broadway! Bobby Soxers, reet?"

"Lieutenant *Benshi*," asks Private Gopher Matsunaga (schlepping film magazines and my longsword, reet?), "is it truly the *Eigo* you speak to these defeated *Amerikajin*? It sounds to my ear like the donkeys in my village!"

"Reet." I think: *Iko-san*! Oh, say it were not so, Jack! *Papa-san! Mama-san*! Say it were not so!

"Finish making your *eiga*, Lieutenant Who-Calls-Himself-*Benshi*," says factotum member of *honcho* Homma's staff. "The *sensei* general is anxious to transport his prisoners across the water to join those already held on Bataan, for there is a long march to be made to bring them to the camp that awaits them near Manila. Can you not make your intricate camera make pictures more quickly, Lieutenant?"

"Reet," I say. Think: Moe, say it were not so! And, "Anybody here from Oklahoma, sovereign state of?" I shout at Yank formations, baby blue to viewfinder.

"Oklahoma?" says nearby Yank *issen gorin*, and, "Who wants to know? This shavetail's from Oklahoma, but I think his brain's scrambled from the shelling too bad to remember. I'm from Wisconsin," says he, and, "You looking for guys from Wisconsin too, or just Okies?"

Oh, dig it, Jack! Big irony of life, reet? Corregidor fortress rock (P.I.), circa 8 of May, 1942 — me, Jack (*wataschi*!), formerly Student Yamaguchi Yoshinori (got burned up in a big fire, Doolittle raiders off *Hornet*, along with paper house, family album, reports of revered mentors of Native Land Loving School, *Papa-san, Mama-san, Iko-san*!),formerly Gooch (A & M class of 1940 — *Redskin* got burned up in a big fire aboard U.S.S. *Oklahoma, Pearu Halbol* flap commencement of WW II global-wide senso conflagration), now Lieutenant *Benshi*, engaged (personal *hanko* signature seal warrant of *honcho* Premier-General Tojo Hideki, Ichigaya Heights) in creating *eiga* propaganda docudrama (*hakko ichui*!) flic of final Yank surrender with 16-millimeter Stewart Warner (*o-miyage* souvenir gift of Morris ("Moe") Berg — say it ain't so, Moe! — clandestine Office of Strategic Services counterintelligence operative — say it ain't so, Sato!), reet?

Big irony, Jack!

As how: I look into viewfinder, frame visage of diminutive Yank second louie — baby blues vacant, in bad need of shave and a haircut (two bits!), dirty uniform, expression not unlike like unto sleepwalker awakening in

233

nightmare-style context of surrender brouhaha flap.

I look through viewfinder, frame and focus close-up of aforesaid visage of Yank: Second Lieutenant Stevie (a.k.a. Yukon Strongboy, a.k.a. Mighty Mouse!—cinch sure bet for '40 Olympiad—*koki nisenroppyakunen Orimpikku*—originally scheduled for Tokyo Town!) Keller. Can you dig it?

"Stevie?" I say, lower camera. "Hold this, Gopher!" I say, and, "Stevie, is it you? Oh, say it is not so, Stevie! Gopher," I cry, "take this and hold it, Jack!"

"Lieutenant *Benshi*," says he, "how am I to carry all the film supply and also your longsword in addition to the big camera?"

"Guard it with your life!" I say, set Stewart Warner on rocky-dusty ground rubble at my feets, step between ranks of Yank officers and *issen gorin*. "Strongboy? Mighty Mouse?" I say, and, "Stevie, is it truly you in this place? Oh, long time no see, Yukon Strongboy Stevie!"

"I told you he's shellshock," says anonymous Wisconsinite Yank P.O.W.

"Stevie-*san*!" I say—think: say it ain't so! I think: big ironics of life and times! I think: Stevie Keller! Clara—yet heartbroke, Jack! I think: Oklahoma Agricultural & Mechanical College! Go, Pokes! Go, Punchers! Go, Aggies! Beat hated downstate arch-rival O.U. Sooners who suck wind from out of north! Oh, say it were not so, Jack!

"Didn't I just now tell you he's shellshock brain-scrambled?" iterates anonymous Yank Wisconsinite *issen gorin*. But Stevie blinks, looks at me, blinks at me, leans forward for close-up scrutinization of my visage. "Stevie," I say, "it is me, best bosom pal *oyabun-kobun* ever-loyal frat bro roomie, Gooch."

"Gooch?" says Stevie.

"Reet!" I shout, clasp his bony shoulders—siege-shortened rations is done diminished already diminutive 116 lbs. avoirdupois four years consecutive N.C.A.A. grapple champ's physique. "Reet, Stevie, it is me, *wataschi*, Gooch!" I did cry.

"Gooch," says he, and, "How's come you're here, man? You're one of them?" he says, checks out my uniform. "You're one of them been killing us ever since we got off the boat in Manila Bay? You're one of them knifed us in the back at Pearl Harbor, Gooch!"

"Reet!" I cry, give him big frat-bro ursine-style hug.

"What the hell's this, old home week?" queries anonymous Yank Wisconsinite.

"Gooch!" says Stevie, blinks, spits into dusty rock-rubble of Corregidor fortress at my feets. "Damn Gooch!" he says, and, "You fucking dirty little slant-eye fuck-stick traitor son of a bitch bastard, it's you been killing us ever since we come to this shit-hole!"

"You know this Nip, lieutenant?" asks anonymous Wisconsinite Yank prisoner.

"I know him for a back-stabbing traitor—" says Stevie.

"Oh no, Stevie!" I interject, and, "You gots it all wrong, Strongboy! Is big coincidence-style ironicalist twist of forces historical and globalist engenders chance rendezvous here! I is strictly noncombatant—"

"—and if it's the last thing I do I'll get his dirty yellow traitor ass for it!" says Stevie.

"Does this small *Amerikajin* threaten you, Lieutenant *Benshi*?" says Gopher Matsunaga. "Shall I summon one of the staff officers to restrain him? His demeanor is threatening to you, I think."

Than which factotum member of *honcho* Homma's staff steps up, says, "You must complete your *eiga* at once! *Sensei* General Homma's patience is exhausted! The *Amerikajin* captives must be assembled at the fortress wharves for transport to Bataan!"

"Reet," I tell him. "Stevie, not to worry! *Daijubo*, reet? You going back over to Bataan Peninsula to begin incarceration durance shtick up at Manila, reet? No sweats, dig?" Officers and *issen gorin* of 14th Imperial commence to herd Yank P.O.W.s over rocky rubble of Corregidor in direction of wharf environ—said activity accompanied by overly enthusiastic and impatient shove, push, slap, and also threats with bayonet and longswords.

"*Chogee!*" shout the officers and *issen gorin* of 14th Imperial. "*Chogee*, Yankee shit!" they shout, push, slap, prod with bayonet and longsword.

"Saddle up, lieutenant," says anonymous Wisconsinite, and, "Stick with me, lieutenant. I'll show you how to come out on the other end of this alive and kicking," and, "We ain't dead yet, are we, lieutenant?"

"What is it?" queries Strongboy Stevie, "Is it more killing us again now?"

"Not to fear, Stevie!" I say. "Gooch coming with you, reet? Count on me, Mighty Mouse!"

"Gooch," says he, "it was you killing us all the time," and, "I never would of thought it was you with them killing us all this time."

"Lieutenant *Benshi*," says Gopher Matsunaga, "we have no more film remaining with which to make more of the *eiga*. What shall we do now, Lieutenant *Benshi*?"

"The *sensei* general orders you to disengage yourself from the captives and depart his command area!" says factotum member of Homma's staff.

"I guess they'll be killing us now, or maybe not until later," Stevie says. "Are you the specific one going to kill me, Gooch? How many of us you killed so far, Gooch?"

"Lieutenant *Benshi*," says Gopher Matsunaga, "am I to continue to accompany you or must I rejoin my comrades? I would rather stay with you, Lieutenant *Benshi*! I know the fighting is over now that the *Amerikajin* are our prisoners, but I fear they will send me elsewhere to fight and

235

die, perhaps to China or up in the mountains to fight the savage Hukbala-hup, who are said to cut off the heads of all *Nihonjin issen gorin* who fall into their hands! May I remain with you, Lieutenant *Benshi*?"

"You ain't dead yet, you just look like it, lieutenant," says anonymous Wisconsinite. "Just stick close, I'll keep an eye on you. Talk to your old buddy Nip here and see if he can't put in a good word for us to get some water and something to eat, huh?"

"Gooch," says Mighty Mouse Strongboy, "Gooch's been killing us just like the rest of them all this time. I wish I could talk to Clara and tell her how it was you killing me, Gooch, but I ain't had mail since I come off the *Coolidge*."

"You gots it all wrong, Stevie," I tell him, and, to anonymous Wisconsinite, "Disregard what-all he says. Brain scramble shellshock Section Eight, reet? We is best bosom buddy pals, A & M class of 'forty, reet? Delta Sigma Kappa, ever-loyal bros we!"

"I don't even know this shavetail hardly to talk to," says Wisconsinite *issen gorin*. "I guess I took pity on him 'cause he's so teeny—if he was yellow and buck tooth he could half pass for Nip himself."

"Obey the *sensei* general's order at once!" screams factotum *budo* member of *honcho* Homma's staff.

"What shall I do, Lieutenant *Benshi*?" asks Gopher Matsunaga. "If you allow them to take me back to my comrades, who will carry your sword for you?"

"Gooch, you damn back-stabbing traitor!" says Stevie.

"Keep baby blue peeled for Strongboy Mighty Mouse Stevie, please," I say to Wisconsinite, and, "I will rendezvous with you on Bataan, reet?" To screaming factotum—waves unsheathed longsword—I say: "Inform *honcho* General Homma I do mean to schlepp along with P.O.W. convoy to complete *eiga* lensing. Inform said personage that I, *wataschi*, Lieutenant *Benshi*, operate as personal operative of *honcho* leader of all *Dai Nippon* Premier-General Tojo Hideki, Ichigaya Heights, reet?"

"We can make no more *eiga*, Lieutenant *Benshi*," says Gopher Matsun-aga, "for I have told you we have no more film supply for your camera."

"And take," I tell factotum staff officer, "this *issen gorin* back to his outfit, reet? Be gentle, as how the boy is touch brain scrambled shellshock from rigors of jungle combats. I work strictly solo from here on!"

"The *sensei* general will not be pleased," says *budo* factotum.

"Do you send me to China to fight, or against the Hukbalahup in the mountains above Bataan, Lieutenant *Benshi*?" Gopher asks as I take film magazines and my *katana* from him. "Ah, did I not say to you long ago that I knew I should have to die for my *Mikado* far away from my home village?"

"Reet," I say, and, "Stay coolish, Gopher. *Daijubo*." To Stevie, who joins throngs of Yank P.O.W.s shuffling toward Corregidor dock wharves, progress accelerated by push, shove, slaps, and also bayonet and longsword prods, "Hold on, Stevie! Ride 'Em, Cowboy! Gooch-ness coming with you!"

"Rot in hell, traitor Gooch!" he ripostes.

"You all discombobulated, Stevie! Shellshocks-syndrome shtick, reet? Not to sweats! *Daijubo*, ride barges to Bataan, casual *sanpo* stroll thereafter to Manila environ, *senso* war over now, made in shade quaffing tepid lemon-flavored drink, reet?"

"I got a hunch," says anonymous Wisconsinite, "this is gonna be a long day."

I saddle up, clutch Stewart Warner (say it ain't so, Moe!), film magazines (*hakko ichui* footages!), follow after, *chogee* pace over bomb-crater, dust-thick rocky rubbles of Corregidor fortress, longsword askew.

Irony, reet, Jack?

What's did I know?

Circa 8 of May, 1942—final Yank surrender of Philippines Islands conquest campaign, reet? Than which is not to fail to mention: also date of Battle of Coral Sea (carrier *Shoho* and several Imperial Navy destroyers lost!), reet? What's did I know, Jack? Which is not to fail to mention yet further irony—dig:

Eiga docudrama (*hakko ichui!*) I did not lens, reet? As how, as reported to *wataschi* by Private Matsunaga Yutaka (a. k.a. Gopher), all available film stock on hand in Bataan environ boonies is got used up in Corregidor lensing (same dispatched from *honcho* Homma's field headquarters up to Manila for processing)—hence and thus it were I did fake it. How you say, vamp shtick, reet? Than which is to say I did accompany humongous throng (20,000 minimums!) of Yank and also Filipino Constabulary P.O.W.s on *sanpo* perambulation up sole road out of Bataan Peninsula toward Camp O'Donnell destination. All the while pretending to lens (empty film magazine in Stewart Warner, Jack!) as guise-ploy to justify *wataschi's* presence on scene.

How you say: so-called Bataan Death March, reet, Jack?

Dig:

"Who are you, and what do you do here, lieutenant?" queries *budo* infantry captain commanding company of rear-echelon 14th Imperial *issen gorin*. "You do not wear the collar tabs of any regiment of the Fourteenth Army—you are not authorized to speak to prisoners without my permission! As I am your superior in rank, lieutenant, it is my responsibility to tell you that you wear your sword as if it were an embarrassment to you!"

"All due deferences and respects, *sensei* captain," I tell him, "but, like, buzz off, reet? I is Lieutenant *Benshi*, personal staff of *honcho* supreme commander of all *Dai Nippon* Premier-General Tojo Hideki—do the name

237

strike a bell or other familiar note? Check it out with *honcho* General Homma if you won't take my word for it—which is to say, if you don't mind if he hands you your head back on tea tray for impertinence, reet? Also I carries said *Tojo-san's* personal *hanko* warrant on off chance you is literate, dig?"

"What is that which you hold up to your face and aim in the direction of my *issen gorin* and the *Amerikajin* prisoners? Is it a weapon?" asks *budo* infantry captain commanding rear-echelon prisoner troop escort company contingent.

"Quaint device, pre-*senso* manufacture, for making the *eiga*, reet, Jack? Never seen one before? *Sumairu*, I'll maybe make you famous up at Ichigaya Heights. I didn't catch your name, captain?"

"Do not aim your device at me! See that you do not impede my command! My name is of no concern to you, Lieutenant Who-Calls-Himself-*Benshi*!" After than which exchange aforesaid *budo* captain sheaths longsword, beats strategic withdrawal retreat from my vicinity, vents frustration by grabbing *take* bamboo stave wielded by one of his *issen gorin*, whacking at slow-moving P.O.W.s.

What's do I, Lieutenant *Benshi*, know, reet? Among which boundless context of ignorances is mood of rear-echelon *budo* officers and *issen gorin* of 14th Imperial detailed to escort Yank prisoners north all the way to Camp O'Donnell on shank's mare foot. Among which aspects of mood is distinct attitude of unrestrained vengeance impulse resulting from heavy losses inflicted by Yanks and Filipino cohorts during unduly and unexpected prolonged lengthy campaign for Bataan Peninsula. Which impulse is expressed as brutal-style retributions visited upon said P.O.W.s (push, slap, shove, blows delivered with sword scabbards, rifle butts, *take* staves)—which is not to fail to mention (say it were not so!) lethal thrusts of bayonets and also *katana*, occasional shot fired point-blank from muzzles of Arisaka rifles and also noncoms' Mauser pistols drawn from wooden holsters! All than which barbarity is, sad to say, sanctioned by *Nippon-shikki budo samurai* code ethos, than which decrees disgrace-dishonor shtick for soldiers who surrender and also fail to show *kirijini* fighting spirit in struggle unto death, reet?

Hence: how you say, Jack, so-called Bataan Death March.

"Well," says anonymous Wisconsinite *issen gorin*, and, "Well, well, well, well. If it ain't the friendly little Nip can almost talk American! Hey, Lieutenant Keller," says he to Strongboy Mighty Mouse Stevie, "look who's come to join the clambake!"

"Reet," I say, and, "No small task locating you in midst of hordes afoot shank's mare heading northerlyward, Stevie," and, "How you making it, Mighty Mouse?"

238

"Gooch," says he, "is it now you're going to kill me? They started in killing us all again Gooch, so I was wondering when you'd get here to stab me in the back with your big sword. Take a picture of me when I'm dead and send it to Clara so she can see it was you did it, traitor Gooch!"

"Oh, Stevie, were it not so!"

"Don't mind him, Mr. Nip," says Wisconsinite *issen gorin*, "I took care of him good so far, huh? He wanted to jump off the scow on the way over from the Rock, but I never let him. He's small, but he's a wiry mean fucker even if he is half starved! He's whacked out from all the barrages on the Rock, plus which also the heat's getting him, I think."

"I is here!" I say, and, "Gooch here, Stevie! Troubles behind us, guys!"

"Somebody better watch him, he wanders off one of your Nip pals is as likely to shoot him as not, or stick one of them long shivs up his ass. A ways back down the road, Mr. Nip," says anonymous Wisconsinite, "I seen them shoot a Gyrene in the head for drinking the ditch water all the water buffaloes pee in. Can you slip us a sip of water, Mr. Nip?" he asks. "I think this sun's getting to me a little, too. Can you say how long's it going to be before they feed us some chow?"

"Not to worry. I mean to rescue best bosom pal buddy Stevie Keller single-handed style, and you to boot in bargain, reet, Wisconsinite personage?"

"Are they ever," asks anonymous Wisconsinite *issen gorin*, "gonna let us take a break in the shade and give us some chow and a drink of water? I ain't so sure I can hack it much farther, Mr. Nip."

"Gooch," says Strongboy Stevie, "why don't you just kill us now with your big sword? What's the good walking us until we drop, or is that your plan to kill us slow this way, Gooch?"

"Hang in, boys!" I tell them, and, "I promise to give you my field ration when same are issued to Fourteenth Imperial escorts, reet? Very nutritious combat standard fare," I tell them, "Box lunch, four *nigirimeshi* rice balls, three pickled sardines, dried kelps. *Umai*, how you say, yum yum, reet? Now," I say, "take each one sip from my canteen to wet whistle, than which I will refill at first potable source we pass, reet? Ditch waters unsafe to imbibe, same polluted by Filipino barrio sewages, not to fail to mention micturation of beast of burden buffaloes, as aforementioned."

"I ain't so sure I can wait, Mr. Nip," says Wisconsinite, and, "The louie here ain't going to make it if we don't get him out of this sun, Mr. Nip!"

"Call me *Benshi*," I say.

"His name's Gooch," Stevie says, and, "I'll make it just to keep you from the satisfaction of killing me, Gooch!"

I tell him: "Stevie, think on pleasanter things to divorce sensibilities from rigor of heats and dusty dust rising out of road. Think upon Miss Clara! Think like unto me of good old days bygone! A & M campus, reet? Go, Pokes! Go, Punchers! Ride 'Em, Cowboys! I would share nostalgia shtick had my nineteen forty *Redskin* not been consumed by big fire at *Pearu Halbol*, reet? Think upon vaunted N.C.A.A. championship laurels you did garner four years running, Stevie! Think how, now that *senso* war is over for you, you will anon again regain grappling forms and condition, return to Miss Clara, return to Okie-land vastness vista!"

"This little fart was a wrestler?" queries anonymous Wisconsinite. "He don't look there's enough of him left now to pass the draft-board physical."

Bataan Death March, Jack!
Conditions of extremist duress intensified by unremitting heat-swelter of overhead sun — not unlike like unto outdoor graduation ceremony (May 10, 1940!), A & M College, scorcher sun effect exaggerated by humidities and permanent dusty dust cloud raised aloft from road by feets of 20,000 Yank and Filipino P.O.W.s — not to fail to mention rear-echelon 14th Imperial escort contingent — numbers reducing by the minute due to atrocity attritions (push, shove, slap, bayonet and sword, Arisaka and Mauser!), utter absence of food stores, dearth of potable waters, debacle resultant from confluence of miscalculation blunders, etcetera blah blah blah!

"Stevie?" I query, creep close to examine recumbent form in thick moist dark of Bataan eventide. "Stevie, are you wakeful? As I foretold, Stevie, I come to share box-lunch ration supper with you! Rice, pickled sardine fishes, kelps, Stevie, make you grow big and strong yet once more again! Wake and consume same, Stevie!"

"He's either asleep or else he's croaked," says anonymous Wisconsinite *issen gorin*, and, "I'm not sure myself if I'm awake or dead already and just dreaming I'm awake, Mr. Nip. I been walking so long it feels like my dogs are still going one in front of the other. I'm fearful if I go to sleep I'll never wake up. Everyone's dying after they lay down and go to sleep here, Mr. Nip. Can you spare a sardine for an old friend, Mr. Nip?"

"I'm awake, Gooch," says Stevie, "I just can't sit up. How long did you make us march, Gooch? Are you killing us now tonight or in the morning when we wake up, Gooch?"

"Eat," I say to them, and, "Scarf! I have also fresh water, purified via boiling over sentry fires. Did I not vow I should return to you with sustenance? Eat and imbibe now," I say, divide rice, sardines, kelps betwixt them. "Hard day, tough row to hoe on road today, reet? Eat, imbibe, slumber, sweet dreams of pleasanter things, ready to press on upon the morrow, boys."

They do not riposte. I hunker beside them on edge of drainage ditch (whereat 14th Imperial rear-echelon escorts did decree march halt due to eventide advent, reet?), listen to them chew and also swallow my box lunch, gulp from my canteen.

All about us in the Bataan dark sound the moans and also groans of those who die now as they lie prone on the road beside ditches, succumb even as they experience first respite from rigors — say it was not so, Jack!

I think: *Papa-san! Mama-san! Iko-san!* Moe! Mr. Sato! Tojo! I mean: how came I (*wataschi*: Yamaguchi Yoshinori, Gooch, Lieutenant *Benshi*!) to this time and place here (circa May '42!)?

"What's all that jabbering they're saying over by them fires, Mr. Nip?" asks Wisconsinite *issen gorin*.

"They do speak even as we," I tell him. "They do speak of home and families they long for back in *Dai Nippon*, and of the rigors of this day's protracted stroll, and express joy and satisfaction to think we draw closer to Manila environs where all shall doubtless receive surcease."

"Is that a fact? That's good to hear. That fish sure hit the spot, Mr. Nip. I think I'll maybe get me some shut-eye now."

"Don't believe anything he says," says Strongboy Stevie, and, "That's Gooch! I know him for what he is."

"Oh, Stevie!" I say.

"All the same, I'm for sacking out," says Wisconsinite *issen gorin*, and, "Goodnight, Irene," says he.

"Permit not bugs to bite," I say, and, "Stevie, may we not confabulate before we rest against the morrow's rigor? Tell me, Stevie, how it came to pass that you is here? Was it not doubtless inexplicable and inexorable forces at large in global world-wide historical flaps results we should be so mis-met in this environ even more wretched than rural Okie-land Panhandle wastes? Stevie?"

After long silence — insect chant, mosquito whine, faintest breeze astir, *Nihonju* boastful braggart natter at sentry fires, expiring ejaculations of Yank and Filipino P.O.W.s all about us in Bataan darkness — he says: "I never figured on it, Gooch. You must of known all along, but I never. I had it going good for me! Clara got on teaching at Yukon, the very same high school I went to myself when I was a kid. I did some work for her daddy, and I had my Guard commission money coming in, it was going good for me, Gooch! Then you started in over here and in Europe and all, and they had the draft all of a sudden, and Roosevelt federalized the Guard, and wham bam thank you ma'am they took me and shipped me on the *Coolidge* over to Manila. I still never figured on it, really."

"Oh, Stevie!" I say, and, "It was not *wataschi* Gooch did do this! I am *aka gami* red-letter conscript like unto you, reet? Blame not Gooch!" But he do not attend my words, Jack. Mighty Mouse Yukon Strongboy Stevie Keller, second lieutenant, Okie National Guard (federalized by FDR!), weak from hungers privations of Corregidor fortress siege, weary from protracted combat campaign retreat down Bataan Peninsula, perhaps likely shellshocked brain scrambled from unceasing artillery bombardments undergone whilst sheltered in rock tunnels—not to fail to mention exhausted by day-long perambulation (Death March, Jack!), continues to speak as if I (*wataschi*, Lieutenant *Benshi*) is not there with him in Bataan eventide's darkness.

"At first we didn't do nothing, just bivouacked in tents out to Clark Field. One time MacArthur inspected us in person. We didn't think nothing of it until you back-stabbed us at Pearl, and the same day it hit the fan at Clark. Bombs," says he, and, "When they told us it was Japs then I knew it was you, Gooch. You know," he says, "I even wrote Clara a letter from Clark once before you done it, how I'd maybe try to write you a letter in Japan and might could be we'd have a reunion over here before my tour was up and we went back home stateside, like we used to talk about we'd do when I came to Japan for the Olympics before they shit-canned them because you-all were making wars over here, Gooch."

"Oh, Stevie!" I say, and, "It was not I! I only serve to create the *eiga* flic docudramas, Stevie! I even schlepp longsword utterly lacking in *budo* aptitude, Strongboy! It is ironicalist twist of *do* flow's path of lives, Stevie," I did tell him.

"I need to sleep," says he. "Will you kill me with your sword while I'm asleep if I let myself fall asleep, Gooch? Stragglers on Bataan, Gooch, we heard you cut their heads off when you caught up with them. The worst of it on the Rock wasn't half starving or even getting killed by the barrages, it was not sleeping because you never let up shelling us, did you know that, Gooch? I'm going to sleep, I don't care if you kill me or not while I'm asleep," says he.

"Stevie," I say, "remain wakeful but a moment more! Attend me, Stevie! Do you not recall good old days bygone gone by? A and M? Go, Pokes and Punchers? Beat hated downstate arch-rival Sooners to south? Do you not recall how I did speak to you of *do* life philosophy I did evolve? Than which was to live in *enryo* harmonies, *ma* moments of personal sensitivities awareness of *yoin* resonances emanating in concert with immediacy's exquisite exactitude all round about? No good, Mighty Mouse! It don't feed bulldog, Stevie! Look to what a pass such *do* path has led us! I confess failure of life's philosophy, Stevie, situated here just as you, sadness and bitterness reflections introspection all that remains! Stevie, I have suffered also severity of *senso* war's absurdness! My daddy, Stevie! *Mama-san*! Kid Sister Iko! Gone from me, Strongboy! Got burned up in a fire by Yank flyboy Jimmy Doolittle, reet? I is now *munako* orphan child of no name! Yet I do recollect our camaraderie circa 'thirty-six to 'forty, reet? I do recall you did interpose yourself in protectivity against such as crude rude redneck goat-roper Gary Lee Stringer and others who would have denied me frat bid of Delta Sigma Kappa membership tap. And thus it is I shall perform in like manner for you! Stevie?"

I essay to look close, discern in Bataan eventide's darkness if, like unto recumbent prone slumbering Wisconsinite *issen gorin* at his side, he sleeps.

"Know, Stevie," I say, lean close to his ear, "that I is not without abilities to manifest my vow. I is now Lieutenant *Benshi*, Imperial Army of *Dai Nippon*, and carry warrant inscribed with personal *hanko* signature seal of *honcho* Premier-General Tojo Hideki, supreme commander of all *Dai Nippon*, reet? Thus it are I do speculate I may mayhap prove yet to perform wondrous feats! Know, Yukon Strongboy Mighty Mouse Stevie Keller, out of regard for you—ever-loyal bros we, reet?—and also innocent platonic-style eternalist love of beloved Miss Clara, I even now devise plot ploy to effect your liberation from current durance of incarceration at hands of these *Nihonjin* rear-echelon redneck types picketed all about us. Know I will remain in proximity to assure you and Wisconsinite buddy pal adequacy of food and drink nourishments until we do reach Camp O'Donnell destination. Thereat and thereafter, I shall effect your liberation! Do you dig it, Stevie?"

I lean close, listen, hear rise from parted lips of fastasleep Stevie a distinct snore.

"Ah, Stevie, you do not attend! Howsomever, nevertheless I shall as vowed!" I look up into black sky of Bataan night's blackness—sole illuminations flickering of picket sentry fires, diminished *Nihonju* chatter natter—breath deep of moist thick air, address only my own self, reet?

"I, formerly Student Yamaguchi Yoshinori, formerly Gooch, now Lieutenant *Benshi*, will betray grandiose celestially ordained design of *hakko ichui* to effect your salvation, Stevie, even as I did betray old alma mater mine A & M College via clandestine *kempei* counterintelligence activity, even as I did betray—all unbeknownst unwitting at onset!—*Dai Nippon* and also *Mikado* via collaboration with Moe Berg."

He slumbers, and save except for 14th Imperial rear-echelon *issen gorin* walking perimeter sentry picket duty, I (*wataschi*!) alone is yet wakeful. I huddle alongside slumbering Stevie and also anonymous Wisconsinite (ditchside, Bataan Peninsula, circa May '42!), clutch my longsword and Stewart Warner 16-millimeter camera (no film, Jack!), vow to keep watch over them, shoo away mosquitos which whine, mayhap inflicting malarial infections, reet? I did say: "Stevie, if necessitated on the morrow, I will, if necessary, schlepp you *onbu* style, how you say, piggy-back, reet? Trust me, Stevie!"

I did think: *Papa-san! Mama-san! Iko-san*! Moe! *Sato-san*! Tojo! Stevie! Clara!

And I did weep sad bitter tears—how you say, waterworks, reet, Jack? Thus it were I did weep for loss of all that might could be and also was, all in sweep of life and times to date, all brought to naught zilch zip diddly squat via sheer force of ironicals oppressing inscrutable *do* path. Old *Nihonjin* proverbial proverb: whilst crying, stung by bee in the face. Dig it! Irony, Jack. About which more to come. As follows:

Date:
15 June 1942

To:
Premier-General Tojo Hideki
Headquarters, Imperial Ministry of War
Ichigaya Heights
Tokyo
Dai Nippon

From: Lt. *Benshi*
Hakko Ichui Docudrama Mission
Manila City
P.I.

Sensei honcho Premier-General:

I write to notify you as how final edit of Corregidor surrender *eiga* flic segment of *hakko ichui* chronicle is all but complete (how we say, in can, reet?) — how you like this title: *The Sun of Ameratasu Sets upon the Last Bastion of Decadent Amerikajin Colonialist Presence in the Greater East Asia Co-Prosperity Sphere: Hakko Ichui Proceeds According to Prognostication!*? Final masterprint thereof (title logos effected with startling effect glass-shot over pan of rock fortress, assembled captives, reet?) will be dispatched to you for screening via first available military aviation transport from Clark Field anon — hope you can dig it, *honcho* premier-general!

Howsomever non-*Nipponshikki* immodest of me so to blow own horn, I do consider said *eiga* flic true cinematic gem, as how structure thereof enables same to be viewed as newsreel short subject (not unlike like unto *Amerikajin* "March of Time") and also open ended so as to permit for incorporation into larger epic *hakko ichui* saga, not to fail to mention possible inclusion of select segments into feature-length *Down with the Stars & Stripes*, than which *eiga* flic production was interrupted by need to lens Corregidor surrender actualities per your instruction, reet?

Assuming your continued benevolent sponsorship of abovecited feature-length *eiga* flic aforesaid, I means to proceed instanter to nearby (Manila City environ, reet?) Camp O'Donnell P.O.W. incarceration facility, there to conduct big-scale casting call — as how, *honcho* premier-general, inclusion of selected selection of Yank officers and also *issen gorin* taken captives on Bataan and Corregidor will bestow persuasive aura to depiction of triumph of *Dai Nippon*. We talking boffo spectacular *oatari* smash hit flic!

Thus *wataschi* humbly requests you flag Manila HQ of Imperial 14th to authorize releases of spoils of *senso* war loot materials: uniforms, weaponries (firing pins removed, natch!), etcetera blah, for employment as wardrobe-costuming for props authenticity.

With blessings of *Ameratasu* and good available natural light, I speculates to bring *Down with the Stars & Stripes* in, within budget (natch!) in time for timely next photo-op assignment: Australia/New Zealand conquest? Please to advise as and also if appropriate, reet?

Otherwise, all well here save for reluctance of Homma replacement

14th commander *honcho* General Teranchi Hisaichi to deploy officers and also *issen gorin* at my behest for remote locations shoots, same due (so he say!) to dangers attendant upon presence in P.I. boonies hick sticks of armed Hukbalahup resistance to occupation forces of *Dai Nippon*, reet? Could you not jack up aforesaid *honcho* Teranchi, Premier-General, induce said *budo* personage to cooperate more fully with *wataschi*?

I await upon your return radiogram (with *hanko* signature seal to effect instanter desired results!) and close with wish for your prolonged good healths and brilliantness of celestially inspired supreme-style leadership of all *Dai Nippon*!

Tenno Heika Banzai!

Lt. *Benshi.*

Mise-en-scene: 4 July 1942, reet? *Senso*, Jack! WW II. *Dai Nippon* poised for massive mobilization strike southwards (via New Guinea!) against Aussies and also New Zealanders (how you say: Anzacs), reet? Grandiose decreed design of *hakko ichui* remains on schedule—despite unforeseen setbacks (omelet's creation necessitates destruction of eggs) at Coral Sea flap, than which did include losses of carriers *Akagi* (aboard which *wataschi* did sail to *Pearu Halbol*, Jack!) and also *Kaga*, not to fail to mention sister ships *Horyu* and *Soryu*, and cruiser *Mikuga*, reet? How we did say: *daijubo*, reet?

Cut to: circa 4 of July, 1942, Camp O'Donnell (Manila City environ, P.I.) incarceration internment facility for 5,000 Yank P.O.W.s—former Yank installation converted intact to aforesaid purpose and also function via erection of high barb-wire fence enclosure, construction of sally-port-style main gate, guard towers each 500 feets on perimeter (wherein are ensconced 14th Imperial *issen gorin* with binoculars, not to fail to mention mounted Nambu rapid-fires on half-cock).

Dig it, Jack!

Main compound (like unto campus greensward, save for absence of green grasses, same diminished to dusty dust via passing feets of P.O.W.s), wherein P.O.W. denizens is summoned at behest of *wataschi* (Lieutenant *Benshi*!), called out from deep shade of barracks domiciles to bright white-heat of P.I. midsummer midday sun: not unlike like unto Graduation Day, A & M campus, May '40—ah, big ironics, Jack!

Dig:

I (*wataschi*!), Lieutenant *Benshi*, stand above assembled in main compound, decorum and also demeanor of Yanks assured by 14th Imperial personnel at ready in guard towers. I hoist megaphone to my mouth, deliver following peroration, as follows:

"Greetings, gents! How we say, *aisatsu* salutations from outside world!

I call you out in midday midsummer sunshine—hot as Okie Panhandle with tropical humidities augmenting—to shoot you bona-fide four-square strictly good deal, reet? Okey-doke! How many here like to enjoy easy-money detail assignment to be conducted outside enclosure fence than which defines durance vile herein, huh? Let's see show of hands, Joe!"

(Yank P.O.W.s: sullen group, Jack! Sad to say, condition thereof is evident decline even from state exhibited on Bataan shank's mare trek. Most hatless, also shoeless, clad in skivvy shorts, ribs displayed under dark-tanned skin due to loss of avoirdupois resultant from incarceration mini-malist-rations diet, reet?).

"No takers? Hey, listen up, Yank dogface *issen gorin! Wataschi* Lieutenant *Benshi* talking to you! I is talking significant tangible respite relief from slammer tenure context, boys! Talking good chow! How many here weary from once-a-day *nigirimeshi* rice ball and occasional fish-head soup menu fare? Anybody interested in change from bean-curd swill and pumpkin's mash served daily by camp chefs? Anybody like to scarf three squares per from pre-*senso* pack rations of C and also K, said vitals straight from confiscated war's spoils stores stashed in Manila City warehousing? Who here do dig to pig out? Let's see hands raised, boys!"

(Here is noted flickers of alertness in large deep-sunken eyes, upturn of visages, bones prominent against hollow cheeks, pinched mouths twitch agape, shuffle of bare foots in compound's dusty dust)

"Boys, I are Lieutenant *Benshi*, official docudrama *eiga* flic cinematographer in personal service to *honcho* Premier-General Tojo Hideki—Hideki Tojo to you!—gots his *hanko* seal signature warrant right here in hip pocket! Hey, guys!" I tell them—shout through megaphone (not unlike like unto leading A & M cheer in big game versus hated arch-rival down-state Sooners). "Guys, *senso* war over for you, past bygones past and gone by, reet, Joe? What say we kiss and make up? I mean, like, give *wataschi* benefit break of doubts, reet?"

(Foots shuffle in dusty dust, sunken-eye squints against blistering over-head sun of midsummer midday—oh, Jack, things at sorry pass bad way at Camp O'Donnell!)

"Lacking volunteers volunteering, I gots to choose chosen, reet? Like, I is talking shower baths, delousing, quinine pills, light duties, mint-fresh khaki and also fatigue uniform garbs for all concerned, opportunity to participate in creation of boffo box office *oatari* smash *eiga* flic, no lines to memorize as how all audios to be studio dubbed—hey, chance to be movie stars!"

(No takers, Jack! I turn to 14th Imperial *budo* officer liaison type, say, "Break out prisoner manifest roster, I'll pick me half a hundred random-style.")

Says he: "This is irregular, Lieutenant Who-Calls-Himself-*Benshi*!"

"Jack," I did say to him, "you looking to argue with *honcho* Premier-

General Tojo's *hanko* signature seal warrant? I knowed a man once who did — name of Homma Masaharu!"

Casting call, reet? Than which is only (natch!) guise ploy to include Second Lieutenant Stevie (a.k.a. Yukon Strongboy, a.k.a. Mighty Mouse!) Keller in *eiga* production cast of characters.

Dig it, Jack: circa 4 of July (Glorious Fourth!), '42, Camp O'Donnell (Manila City environ, P.I.), small field table set up in deep shade under eave of P.O.W. barrack domicile, at which sits ensconced *wataschi* (me, Jack!), Lieutenant *Benshi* (producer-director etcetera blah) to conduct pro-forma perfunctory interviews with Yank prisoners assembled from camp manifest roster (furnished grudgingly) — P.O.W. queue order and also decorum maintained by squad of 14th Imperial *issen gorin* wielding *take* bamboo staves, which is not to fail to mention camp *budo* junior officer in command of detail, than which who waves sheathed *katana* longsword, reet? As follows:

"You is Corporal Bobby Grummond, Corps of Engineers, reet?"

"Yes sir. I hope I didn't do nothing to get called out for this detail, sir. I been keeping my nose clean, and I been sick too ever since we got here, so's I ain't fit for duty, sir," says Corporal Bobby Grummond.

"At ease, *sensei* corporal," I say, flash big pearlie whites *sumairu* — establish rapports, reet? "Tell me about yourself, Bobby-*san*. Like, thumb-nail sketch shtick, résumé of interests and also hobbies stuff."

"Bow to Japanese officer when speaking!" screams *budo* 14th junior officer-in-command — strictly stage accent *Eigo*.

"Ix-nay on the kowtow shtick!" I tell him in *Nihonju*, and, "Casual tone vital here if I gots to guestimate potential of *Amerikajin* for cinematic *eiga* role performances, reet?"

"I command these prisoners assembled at your request, and I insist they behave with established rules of military courtesy!" ripostes he, and, "All captives must bow when speaking to *Nihonjin* officers and guards. Failure to so deport themselves is punishable!" says he. Corporal Bobby Grummond hits forty-five degree kowtow, shoulders hunched to receive corrective blow of sword scabbard.

"Wrong, *budo* lieutenant personage!" I say, stand up from field table, withdraw oil-paper *furoshiki*-wrapped warrant from hip pocket, thrust out same, aggressive-style, reet? "I holds total creative control option on this project, lieutenant, as explicitly explicit over *hanko* signature seal of *honcho* supreme leader of all *Dai Nippon*! Must I needs say more?"

"You will destroy the camp's discipline, and thus threaten its security," says he, but do lower sword scabbard.

"And you is subject," I tell *budo* 14th Imperial lieutenant, "to throw kibosh wet blanket on delicate and sophisticated significant project of utmost military and cultural urgency than which might could rouse ire of aforementioned *honcho* Premier-General Tojo Hideki! What is it with you, Jack? Does I gots to send radiogram to Ichigaya Heights or place call to *honcho* General Teranchi in Manila City Malacanang Palace headquarters to secure ongoings cooperation assistances?"

"I take no responsibility for the security of our prisoners if you defy my authority, Lieutenant Who-Calls-Himself-*Benshi*!"

"Reet," I tell him, and, "So noted," and, to Corporal Bobby Grummond, "Straighten up and fly level, Bobby-*san*! No need to cringe here. Where was we? Reet. Tell me all about yourself."

"Like what, for instance, sir?"

"Like, where you from come, Joe? What's you did do in civie life and times prior to *senso* flap? Ever worked as thespian before?"

"I'm from Cleveland, sir," says he. "I enlisted when I couldn't find no job. Jobs was scarce in Cleveland if you didn't have no qualifications in 'thirty-eight, sir, in case you didn't know."

"Tell me about it, Bobby!" I flash pearlie whites *sumairu*. "Couldn't have been no worser as how Oklahoma, sovereign state of. Believe it, Jack!"

"I got took," says he, "right down on the dock across the bay from the Rock. We was trying to get to the Rock, but we couldn't get this little motorboat started up. We was still farting around with this here diesel engine when you come on us, so all's we could do was put our hands up and hope you didn't chop our heads off like we heard shithouse rumors you was doing to everyone you caught on Bataan. Then I got sick marching up here, drinking bad water and malaria. I been sick ever since we got here, so I can't do heavy-duty details, but I ain't going on sick call. They put you in the infirmary here, almost everyone goes in comes out with your little toes turned up, and I'm just trying to keep my nose clean until it's over and go back to Cleveland unless I reenlist if there's still no jobs. How long you think this war's gonna last, sir?"

"Tell it to the Marines," I say, and, "Search me, reet, Jack?" and, "Forces historical and global-wide beyond ken of individual. Impossible to speculate as to potential ironics yet to come. Done any acting, Corporal Bobby Grummond?"

"Like in plays and that?"

"Reet!"

"No. I don't remember. I was in this, like, pageant, once in grammar school. I was the lion. I had to say some stuff in, like, a lion's voice, roaring—but it wasn't a regular play or anything, and the teacher said I didn't roar good enough, so another kid got to do it. It was just a pageant, they called it."

"Experienced, but miscast," I say, make marginalia note on camp's prisoner-manifest roster. "I think I can use you, Bobby-*san*," I tell him, and, "I see you as, like, adjutant aide-de-camp dog robber striker type,

Bobby Grummond. How you like promotion to shavetail rank? Make you second louie, dog robber to cinematic *eiga* Yank commanding officer who leads command to ignoble debacle defeat in Bataan campaign, reet? Can you display servile obsequious expression on your visage?"

"Huh?"

"Never mind, you is perfect for part!" To *budo* 14th lieutenant, I say, "Escort this *Amerikajin* corporal to thespian segregation area, reet? And don't let me hear from no slap-kick-shove shtick!"

"I forswear responsibility for security!" says he, and, "I accede to your request only under duress!"

"Reet," I say, and, "Go with *budo* personage, Bobby Grummond, man, I'll dig you later when entire cast assembles for script read-through. *Daijubo*, Bobby," I say, and, "Strictly light duties coming up! Next!" I shout to prisoner queue, look down line of Yank P.O.W.s in search of countenance of Second Lieutenant Stevie Keller, Jack.

Dig: casting call (circa 4 of July, 1942!), commencement of production of *Down with the Stars & Stripes*, feature-length propaganda *eiga* flic docudrama to memorialize brilliant (howsomever delayed by stubborn defense!) victory of *Dai Nippon* (14th Imperial Army, reet?) over *Amerikajin* colonialist forces in Bataan Peninsula campaign.

Mise-en-scene: Camp O'Donnell incarceration internment facility (Manila City environ, reet?), late afternoon midsummer sun of P.I. overhead (humidities thick air aura), compound area baked to dusty dust, buzz of blackflies (also mosquito whine!) attracted to open *benjo* latrine trenches (gross stench thereof also — natch!) — across compound in isolation situation locale is situated makeshift infirmary (thatched roof, open sides) wherein lie *Amerikajin* P.O.W.s expiring from combination of malnutrition, malaria, beriberi, dengue fever, and also untended combat wounds, not to fail to mention mistreatment!

Ah, say it were not so, Jack!

In deep dark shade slice beneath eave of barrack P.O.W. domicile sits (ensconced at rickety field table) *wataschi* (Lieutenant *Benshi*!), longsword trailing in dust, camp prisoner-manifest roster damp-softened with humidity moisture — engaged in guise ploy plot routine shtick toward purpose of locating best buddy bosom pal Strongboy Stevie Keller (than which whose moniker on manifest roster I circle, reet?) — aforesaid toward purpose plan of aiding and also abetting said Mighty Mouse's liberation from durance vile (betrayal of *Dai Nippon hakko ichui*!), long queue of Yank P.O.W.s, all said procedure designed to gull attendant *budo* 14th junior officer in command (*issen gorin* alert with Nambu rapid-fires mounted aloft on guard towers, not to fail to mention barb-wire enclosure fence) — how you say, cover baby blues with woolen veil, reet, Jack? As follows:

"What's your handle moniker, Joe?"

"Technical Sergeant Peter Tracy, sir, Army Air Corps."

"No need to bow to me, Pete, as how I ain't not no *budo* type, reet? Can I call you Pete?"

"Really? You speak pretty good English for a Jap, sir. My friends call me Jiggs, like in the funnies, Maggie and Jiggs?"

"Reet," I say, and, "Maggie and Jiggs. Katzenjammer Kids. Little *mun-ako* Orphan Anne. Any relation kin to Dick Tracy? Har! Also L'il Abner. Major Hoople too! Ah, Jiggs, I do think upon good old days bygone stateside!" Jack: by virtue of which said chatter and also natter I do establish rapports, reet?

"You one of them Nisei, sir?"

"Nope," I say, "*Nihonjin* Hundred Millions bred and also birthed. But did a stint stateside, higher-educational education endeavors, Oklahoma Agricultural and Mechanical College, class of nineteen and forty, reet? Ever heard tell from my alma mater A and M, Jiggs-*san*?"

"That's the one," says Technical Sergeant Peter (a.k.a. Jiggs) Tracy, "always had the good basketball teams. I never went to college, but I followed sports close. A and M was as good as anybody except for maybe the Whiz Kids from Illinois."

"Reet! A & M Aggies, legendary great roundball mentor Coach Henry ("Hank") Iba, also knowed as Iron Duke Mr. Iba! Knowed him personal! How you like to be in movies, Jiggs?"

"Search me," says he, and, "They're saying we'll get chow and no kicking around from the guards, but the rumor is it's all horseshit to get a detail for some dirty work."

"Would I put you on, Jiggs? Look upon me, Jiggs! Is this visage before you one who would proffer you bullock's excrement on silver tray?"

"If it's really what they're saying and not shit detail, I give a rat's ass," says he.

"Reet," I say, and, "Go with *do's* flow, Jiggs-*san*!" and mark aforesaid's name on manifest roster.

Impossible (sad to say—wish it might could have been otherhow!) to accept all comers at Camp O'Donnell casting call, reet? As how: parameters imposed by budget bottom line (Ichigaya Heights), tight production schedule (Australia and also New Zealand next and also soon), not to fail to mention limitations on Yank uniforms and gear (wardrobe and props) supply available as *senso* spoils of war stashed in Manila City warehouses dictate no more than fifty roles (to include extras, cameo walk-ons, featured speaking parts), reet? Than which is not to fail to mention inappropriate appearance of majority of Yanks auditioning, reet? As follows:

"Seaman First Class John V. Vos, sir. I'd really like to be in your picture if I could, sir."

"Reet. Tell me, John Vos, what happens to your noggin? *Budo* guards rough you up a little too rambunctious? Hey, and also cease to bow to me, reet?"

"No sir, I got burned real bad when you hit us on Manila Bay. I was on the gunboat *Maxson*, just anchored out in the bay. We mostly ran patrols to keep the Flip smugglers from having a field day whenever they felt like it. Eighth of December, I just got off night watch, crapped out in my bunk, and this Judy bomber come in low over the water and dropped one down our stack. I got burning oil on the whole side of my head when I was going up the ladder to the hatchway to jump ship. I was one of the lucky ones even got overboard before she foundered," says Seaman First Class John Vos, and, "I was in sickbay when you all took Manila. I was one of the lucky ones; you shot all the bedfast. I been here since even before they put up the fence around O'Donnell. I even helped build it. This one corpsman medic here, he says I'm probably gonna get gangrene, my ear and cheek and neck and all, but there's nothing to do except keep it wrapped to keep the flies off me, except now my bandage's like stuck to me so I can't take it off to air it unless I soak it, and you won't let us have hardly enough water to drink, which we have to boil it first to keep from getting parasites."

I do look upon Seaman First Class John V. Vos (stands before me at attentive posture, shirtless, shoeless, skivvy shorts, pus-caked bandage-wrapped noggin, swelling thereof—not to fail to mention rot-stench! —closing one eye, discoloration of dermis on one side). Ah, Jack! I say: "Regrets all up the wazoo, Seaman John V. Vos, but can't use you in this *eiga* flic, reet? Just not right for imagined ambience I seek."

"Why not? I can do whatever you need me to, sir!"

"Orry-say," I say, "but it don't look good to exhibit injured decrepit Yanks when filmic logic dramatizes *Nihonjin* triumph over vigorous how-somever cowardly *Amerikajin* manhood specimens."

"I was hoping maybe I could get some medicine out of it," says Seaman First Class John V. Vos as he is returned to general camp populace, and, "They been predicting I'd kick the bucket from the first day I got took in sickbay, but I ain't dead yet, wise guys!"

"Captain Clifford Eimon? Orry-say, Cliffie, can't use you. Put on some avoirdupois poundage, maybe next time, reet?"

"Blow that out your bunghole," says Captain Clifford Eimon (Regular Army West Pointer die-hard defender type, only captured upon occasion of mass surrender of Corregidor rock fortress, reet?). "How the hell gain weight on a rice ball a day and that fish-gut soup if you're lucky you give us, you fuck!"

"Truly sorry, Captain Cliffie," I say, "not my department, reet? Facts remains fact, you too svelte slender to look right schlepping Springfield oh-three shoulder-fire with full field pack and also tin-pot helmet."

"Says you," says he, and, "I toted a Browning Automatic Rifle all the way down Bataan to the Rock, and I'd still be kicking ass with it if Wainwright hadn't of give up on us!"

"I'll note you in script marginalias as possible alternate understudy. Bestest I can do, Cliffie. Next!"

"Private Walter Hintz, United States Army."

"Greetings, Uncle Wally! How you like—"

"I give you my name and rank, and you can have my serial number if you want it, otherwise I got shit to say to you!" interjects Buck Private Wally Hintz.

"Don't blame *wataschi*, okay, Wally? I am same as how you, Joe, inextricably entangled in global-wide matrix of *senso* flap historical forces confluences, reet? Let's be friends, Walter!"

"Stick it where the sun don't shine!" says Private Walter Hintz, U.S. Army.

"Three squares per diem, de-louse and hot *sento* baths, clean and also new uniforms, light duty—"

"Fuck off, slant-eyes!" says he, and, "And that goes double for Tojo and Hirohito the both of them!"

"What does this huge ugly *Amerikajin* say?" asks *budo* 14th lieutenant. "Did I hear him speak the ineffable name of the *Mikado*?"

"Button your lip, lieutenant, I'll parley the *Eigo* here," I tell him in *Nihonju*, and, "Some folks is just plain camera-shy. Return this Yank to general populace, and don't even think about from swinging that *take* bamboo sword scabbard at him, reet? Next!" I holler at P.O.W. queue, squint against blinding late-afternoon midsummer sun dazzle (horizon foliages dances in heat waves' shimmer!), looking for diminutive stature and distinctive visage of Mighty Mouse Yukon Strongboy Stevie Keller to appear.

Than which confrontation confabulation follows as hereinafter, thusly:

"Stevie!" I say, and, "Greetings and felicitous salutations, Strongboy Stevie! Oh, these many hours here perspiring in minimalist shade relief cast by barrack domicile eaves has I awaited to see you in assembled queue throng, Stevie! It are *wataschi*, me, Stevie, Lieutenant *Benshi*—formerly Gooch!—come to Camp O'Donnell to find you as I did foretell upon occasion of rigor of prolonged *sanpo* perambulation here hence from Bataan, reet? Stevie, do you not recognize me? Stevie, you are even further, sad to say, diminished in avoirdupois by incarceration internment privations! Oh, Stevie-san, would this were not so, best bosom buddy pal of days bygone gone by!"

252

"Gooch," says Mighty Mouse Yukon Strongboy at last, "I suppose I'm supposed to bow to you, huh, Gooch?"

"Never *hochee*, Stevie!" I assure him. "No kowtow for Lieutenant *Benshi* — strictly egalitarian modes for *eiga* flic casting call. Stevie, is you struck serious ill?"

"How's come you come here, Gooch?" he queries, and, "You're killing us all just fine, the ones you didn't kill on the march. You didn't need to come personal, Gooch."

"Stevie, you persist in bassackwards perceptions, man! Step closer, Stevie, for I would impart confidentials, reet?"

"You can have no use for this sickly small *Amerikajin*," says *budo* 14th lieutenant-in-command. "This one is no larger than a boy, and see how he cannot stand without wavering, and how empty are his eyes — this minuscule *Amerikajin* belongs in the infirmary where he can expire quickly and so not waste the rations we bestow upon the prisoner corps!"

"Will you but cease to kibbitz!" I shout at him, and to Stevie in *Eigo*, "Stevie, I did hope you shall have recovered from shellshock brain scramble effects of Corregidor fortress assaults! Does you hear and also dig what I say, Stevie?"

"Of what use in your *eiga* can such a one as he prove?" asks *budo* lieutenant, and, "I have seen you reject prisoners of exemplary health and vigor, Lieutenant Who-Calls-Himself-*Benshi*, in addition to those exhibiting wounds and the open sores which afflict us all in this climate! If you choose this one to join those you will take out of the camp to make your *eiga*, he will surely expire, and this will cause great confusion if you return fewer *Amerikajin* than the number with which you depart."

"Stand at ease, Stevie," I say, and to *budo* 14th lieutenant in (natch!) *Nihonju*, "Neglect further to zip your lip, lieutenant, and your name goes direct via radiogram to Ichigaya Heights! For your info, I gots to have one looks like he's on his final legs and also of diminutive stature to play role of Yank commander so as to depict same in subservient posture to Fourteenth Imperial officer than which to whom he surrenders in scenario, reet? I don't want no long tall Skinny Wainwright type towering over *Nihonjin budo* commander. Same depicts *Amerikajin* as undistinguished and also non-*budo* — not unlike like unto comic-relief shtick in midst of high tension *senso* docudrama flic, reet?"

"You're a day late and a dollar short, Gooch," Stevie is saying. "I feel like I'm dead already and I'm just dreaming I'm still alive. How'd it all happen like this, Gooch?" he asks. "I tried a long time to figure it, you betraying us and all, but it don't make no sense to me. Does it make sense to you, Gooch?"

"Your *eiga* will prove absurd!" says *budo* lieutenant, and, "Even the most ignorant of the Hundred Millions in some isolated fishing village will not believe such a one as this would exercise command even among the *Ameri-*

kajin cowards who fled in the face of our heroic attacks!"

"What is you, a critic?" I ask. To Stevie in (natch!) *Eigo*, "Mighty Mouse best bosom buddy pal ex-roomie ever-loyal frat bro of mine! Lean close! I shall confide confidences in utmost confidentiality, reet? Can you keep secret, Stevie?"

"Gooch," says he — Second Lieutenant Stevie Keller, Okie National Guard (federalized!), a.k.a. Mighty Mouse, a.k.a. Yukon Strongboy: shirtless, shoeless, skivvy shorts, makeshift hat of woven *take* bamboo grasses atop noggin to preclude sunstrokes. Also much and severe diminished in avoirdupois weights via rice-ball fish-gut soup P.O.W. menu fare, doubtless yet touch shellshock brain scrambled (Corregidor rock fortress bombardments!), vacant eye demeanor indicating anomie and also perhaps malarial or dengue fever ravages.

"Stevie," I say, stand, step closer (dragging longsword!) to whisper confidential confidentialities, "I come to effect your liberation from endurance of durance vile, reet? *Wataschi*, former Gooch of good old A and M class of 'forty days bygone gone by, now Lieutenant *Benshi*, come to rescue you single-handed style shtick, Stevie! Do you not dig it?"

I did tell him, Jack! As how once outside looking in at Camp O'Donnell perimeter enclosure fence, on location to lens *Down with the Stars & Stripes* feature-length *eiga* flic docudrama segment of grandiose cinematic *hakko ichui* chronicle, as how three squares per diem a day Yank rations of C and also K pre-*senso* packaging, not to fail to mention de-louse and daily *sento* hot baths, quinine and also sulfa pills medicinals, health and heartiness of pre-*senso* grappler conditions will be restored, reet? After than which I do intend to release him homeward in direction of U. S. of A. stateside sanctuary.

"You and me you're saying, Gooch?" says he. "I suppose we'll just walk away from the guards on top the water all the way across the Pacific Ocean, is that what you're saying, Gooch?"

"Ix-nay, Stevie! Listen up good!" I tell him: as how security bound to be lax lackadaisical at remote location shoot, hence facilitating A.W.O.L. over-the-hill desertion departure in direction of distant mountains whereat and wherein reside budo Hukbalahup aboriginals who yet contest conquest of *Dai Nippon*, than which aforesaid aboriginals is notorious and also infamous for effecting escapes and also evasions of Yanks on the run.

"Sad to say, I can't split with you, Stevie," I say, "as how said Huks like to divide noggin from shoulders of such *Nihonjin* as fall into misfortunate proximity therewith, reet?"

"I don't trust you, Gooch," says he, and, "You back-stabbed us, you're probably going to do it again, aren't you, Gooch? I'd as leave rather stay here and be killed in O'Donnell with my own people than off in the boonies with you and be killed by you."

254

"No, Stevie! Buddy pal of mine, here for certain sure you subject to expire! Already you relinquish too much avoirdupois poundage, appear not unlike like unto proverbial starving Chink, reet? Not to fail to mention malarial and dengue fever ravages, jungle-rot crud as causes nonhealing eruptions of skin ulcerations also. Also not to fail to mention neglect and also mistreatment afforded by *budo* rear-echelon officers and also *issen gorin* who serve as warders, reet?"

"I'd sooner wait it out than go with you, Gooch," says he. "When I wake up at night when the lice and mosquitoes and blackflies is eating me alive, I wish I was dead a lot, but remember Clara's in Yukon waiting on me, and they say maybe you'll let us have our Red Cross packages one of these days, or get our mail to us. No, Gooch," he says, "I can tough it out here if the war don't last too long."

"Stevie-*san*, P.O.W. shtick might could go on indefinite, reet? Who can say which shall have been course of history when future becomes past pastness, Stevie? *Dai Nippon* triumphant, Stevie! *Hakko ichui* scheme scam succeeds, man! Already we vanquish Yanks and *Igirisujin*, not to fail to mention Dutchmen, Frogs, Chinks, reet? Next and soonest comes fall of Anzacs, after than which India is scheduled next — Stevie, what and if U. S. of A. loses *senso* war to *Dai Nippon*, when shall you have been released from durance vile for repatriation return stateside to Clara and Okie-land Yukon domicile?"

"You shit and fall back in it, Gooch!" he ripostes. "There's no way you can beat us once we make our mind up to whip your ass!"

"Reet," I say, and, "Come out of incarceration internment with *wataschi* Lieutenant *Benshi*, Stevie, effect escape by my connivance, rendezvous with vaunted *budo* Hukbalahup resistance in mountains of P.I., restore healths to hale and also hearty pre-*senso* grappler conditioning, Stevie! This I promise to come to pass, best buddy bosom pal of mine!"

I tell him, Jack! Persuade him *senso* war flap might could go on decades to come, *Dai Nippon* might could possibly emerge victorious — what's did I know, Jack? — odds against ultimate survival in Camp O'Donnell argue in favor of accepting liberation and evasion to Hukbalahup far mountains sanctuary.

Circa 4 of July, 1942, Camp O'Donnell (Manila City environ), casting call, reet? Yet additional ironies to come, Jack!

"Okay, Gooch," says Mighty Mouse Yukon Strongboy Stevie, "I'll go with you, but I ain't being in your damn dirty movie you say you're making, and I ain't trusting you no farther than I can throw you in the shape I'm in now, just so you know."

"Reet!" I say. "Hey, Stevie, if as how all goes as prognosticated, sooner rather than tardy you confabulate in person with Miss Clara, give her warmest greetings from days bygone classmate Goocher, reet? Also explain to A and M alma mater faculty and administrative *honchos* and also alums as how Gooch came via ironical and inexorable forces historical global-wide to be here-and-now Lieutenant *Benshi*, reet? Not to fail to mention sad personal losses of family—Daddy, Mama, Iko!—in Doolittle raid conflagration! I is *munako* orphan child without name, Stevie! Also convey to aforesaid how I do miss bygone days gone by, nostalgia shtick, wish it had not been thusly, reet?"

"Too bad about your folks, Gooch," and, "Sure I will, Gooch," says he. "I'll tell everybody about you here and at Corregidor making your pictures of them burning the flag and how you was at Pearl you were telling me. I'll tell everybody all about you, trust me to do it, Gooch!"

"Reet! Great, Stevie! Hey, not to fail to mention, where is anonymous *issen gorin* native of Wisconsin Badger State than which who did accompany us on prolonged *sanpo* perambulation northward from Bataan, Stevie? I would add him as extra bit player to *eiga* cast, effect liberation in duet tandem with you, as how I did vow."

"The guy from Wisconsin? He's dead, Gooch. He couldn't take the kicking around when we got here to O'Donnell, so he slugged a guard and ran off and you caught him and chopped his head off for a punishment. Right out there in the middle of the compound in front of everybody," Stevie says. "They made us watch, for a lesson, they said it was. He wasn't the only one, either."

"Ah, Stevie!" I did say, and, "Oh, that it had not been so is my wish in fervency, Stevie!"

"Don't you worry, Gooch. I'll tell everyone all about it if I ever make it back home. Trust me to do it, Gooch!"

Dig it, Jack! Above-cited prophecy is replete with ironics, reet? Gross and minuscule. All of which same is (natch!) all unbeknownst to me (*wataschi!*), Lieutenant *Benshi* (a.k.a. Student Yamaguchi Yoshinori, a.k.a. Gooch!), circa 4 of July, '42, reet? Dig:

> Date:
> 30 August 1942

> To:
> Lt. *Benshi*
> *Hakko Ichui Eiga* Mission
> c/o Hq., 14th Imperial Army
> Malacanang Palace
> Manila
> Philippine Islands

> From:
> Premier-General Tojo Hideki
> Headquarters

Imperial Ministry of War
Ichigaya Heights
Tokyo Prefecture
Dai Nippon

Lt. *Benshi*:

Know that I am less than well pleased upon receiving repeated reports from the Manila headquarters of General Teranchi Hisaichi indicating your most irregular deportment in the conduct of your assigned mission. In addition, I am informed that you are, it appears, responsible for a grave breach of military security; know that this most recent event has led me to the brink of ordering the cancellation of your ultimate mission and your transfer to a combat unit of the 14th Imperial Army, where, it might be hoped, you could better serve the sacred cause of our *Mikado* and the Hundred Millions of *Dai Nippon*.

To be precise, it is reliably reported to me that you have grossly abused my personal warrant, conveyed to you only to facilitate the execution of your duties. I am informed that you have repeatedly and with impunity flaunted my *hanko* seal to the detriment of correct military order and discipline, thus shaming superior officers who seek only to follow the code of *bushido* in their behavior. My personal warrant, Lt. *Benshi*, was not conveyed to you to permit you to violate the norms of military courtesy, nor to allow you to circumvent the normal administrative procedures established by the 14th Imperial Army! If it is true, as it is reported to me by more than one source, that you have spoken with flippancy to senior officers and that you have confiscated vast amounts of materials and manpower without respect to the wishes and needs of others (however genuine and fervent is your desire to create the *eiga* that is your mission!), then you have brought shame upon both yourself and my own reputation!

Know that I am most disturbed, most severely agitated, by the report that your careless and casual deportment in the production of *Down with the Stars & Stripes*, so unwisely undertaken in a rural location distant from adequate security (and dangerously in proximity to regions controlled by the savage Filipino aboriginals known as Hukbalahup!) has resulted in the loss of a prisoner of war, the *Amerikajin* 2d Lt. Keller, S., Know, in mitigation, that I have received your personal account rendered to General Teranchi's headquarters to the effect that you pursued the escaping *Amerikajin* officer and personally dispatched him with a stroke of your *katana*; know also that my informants express serious doubt as to the veracity of your account, and that I, personally, find I must exercise my poet's imagination to its fullest extent to conceive your performing such a deed, given your well-known ineptitude with the longsword and other weapons of war. I do not accuse you of fabricating your report, but cannot bring myself to feel wholly confident in its total dedication to the truth of the events you assert transpired in the mountainous jungle you so unwisely chose as the site at which to create your *eiga*. I will assume, to your advantage, that the escaped *Amerikajin* officer Keller, S. perished in the jungle terrain into which he disappeared.

257

Were I convinced that you were in any degree responsible for the loss of this prisoner, know that I would not hesitate to order your court-martial and summary execution – I am not informally known as The Razor without justification!

Lieutenant *Benshi*: the implications of these several reports, in addition to the press of recent events in the course of our celestially decreed *senso* in pursuit of the realization of the national goal of *hakko ichui*, dictates that I postpone indefinitely the production of *Down with the Stars & Stripes*. You will, immediately upon receipt of this radiogram, cease all attendant production activity!

You are ordered to present yourself in all haste to General Teranchi's headquaters in Manila City, where you will board the first available air transport for New Guinea, where you will present yourself at the field headquarters of General Horii Tomitaro, commander of all combined imperial forces there.

In strictest military confidence, I inform you that your assignment is to accompany General Horii on his imminent campaign to cross the mountain wastes of New Guinea in order to prepare the way for our invasion of Australia from Port Moresby. *Hakko ichui* proceeds as ordained by *Ameratasu*!

Is it possible for you, Lieutenant *Benshi*, or for any who do not share my responsibilities, to appreciate the awful burden I bear as supreme commander of *Dai Nippon*, answerable only to the *Mikado* for my decisions? I think not! Oh, if there were but some means available by which I might express the attendant intricacies and obstacles! Poetry, I assure you, does not suffice!

The losses suffered by our Imperial Navy at Midway and Coral Sea are most recently compounded by additional losses at Cape Esperance and in the eastern Solomons – we do not even inform the Hundred Millions civilian populace of the sinking of the carrier *Ryojo* for fear this intelligence might dampen their admirable and vital *kirijini* fighting spirit. Given this, what can be said of the unexpected and shameful defeat suffered by the Imperial Army on the island called Guadalcanal, also inflicted by the barbarian *Amerikajin*? Of 30,000 *issen gorin* engaged there, we succeeded in evacuating, in great shame, but 13,000!

Know, Lieutenant *Benshi*, that the path of exalted leadership is a rocky one, not unlike the very *do* of life itself, its course twisted and often veiled in mists! Thus it is that I demand of my subordinates that they behave with a demeanor which will preclude adding to the weight of the terrible yoke I carry. Thus it is I caution you to conduct yourself in more appropriate *budo* manner in your relationship with General Horii and his staff on New Guinea! His victory – and your depiction thereof in the *eiga* you create as it unfolds before your eyes – is essential to the maintenance and enhancement of morale among the Hundred Millions of *Dai Nippon!*

Tenno Heika Banzai!

Do you dig it, Jack? Midway, Coral Sea, Cape Esperance, Guadalcanal, New Guinea – how you say: handwriting-on-the-wall shtick, reet? Twist

258

and turn of *do* path of life, misty vista of course of history, inscrutable to he who scrutinizes future-ward vainly. Big ironies, Jack!

Than which is to say: commencement of chronicle of defeat of *Dai Nippon*, reet? Than which is not to fail to mention betraying of *hakko ichui* by Sub-Lieutenant *Benshi* (me, Jack!) via scripted escape of Mighty Mouse Yukon Strongboy Stevie Keller (shavetail second lieutenant, federalized Okie National Guard!) in vicinity of close proximity of mountain terrain environ than which is infested with Hukbalahup aboriginals engaged in ongoing opposition to imperial forces of *Nihon*.

Said I: "Farewell, Stevie! Give regards to Miss Clara, not to fail to mention also all administrators, faculty, and fellow alums of A and M, reet? Convey my regrets for *senso* flap than which so discombobulates all concerned. Stay hid in daylights, travel only in eventide's dark, present self to first Huks you confronts, than which aboriginals you will recognize via humanoid bones worn in schnozzes as decorative embellishments, not to fail to mention long bolo knifes carried for purpose of killing *Nihonjin*. Be well, Stevie, *wataschi* Lieutenant *Benshi* will mayhap dig you later again at later juncture down *do* road of life. So long, Strongboy!"

Said he (much restored to vigor via *eiga* flic production regimen of three squares captured *senso* spoils of rations C and also K, quinine and also sulfa pill tablets, clean uniforms, etcetera blah): "Sure, Gooch. I suppose I'm supposed to be grateful to you, huh? Don't worry," says he, "I'll tell them all about it, Gooch."

"Reet," said I as he did slip into jungle foliage, and, "Not to fail to mention sad saddening loss of my daddy, mama, and baby sis, reet? Also danger I did court on your behalf in phony-baloney scenario for escape I did concoct to relate to Fourteenth Imperial headquarters in Manila City in the morn, reet? So long, Stevie!"

Irony of which contained therein I relate hereafter (to wit: as how Mighty Mouse Strongboy Stevie did rendezvous with said marauding Huks, than which who did convey said Stevie to distant small island of P.I. archipelago, wherefrom he was took by U.S. Navy P-T patrol recon boat, than which did convey best bosom buddy pal to Australia (Down Under, reet?), wherefrom thence he was transported stateside across Pacific, debriefed in detail—first word of, how you say, Bataan Death March!—given rehab and medical discharge with lifetime service-connected disabilities pension. Grappler days (natch!) over, Jack. All than which (reference wartime propaganda flics produced in '44 and '45 by Hollywood, reet?) leads to depiction of *wataschi* (me, Jack!) in series of commercial feature-length *eiga* — *Destination Tokyo*, *The Purple Heart*, *Thirty Seconds over Tokyo*, *Back to Bataan*, *Yank on the Burma Road*, *Betrayed from the East*, *Behind the Rising Sun*, *First Yank in Tokyo*, etcetera blah. Where was I, Jack?

Chronicle of *senso* WW II defeat of *Dai Nippon*, end of *hakko ichui* shtick! As (long story rendered semishortish) follows, Jack:

Jump cuts: chronological chronology of *senso* — WW II! — circa August '42 to and through mid-July '44, reet?

Umi Yakuba (than which little ditty is taught to all *issen gorin* as part parcel of Eta Jima boot-camp training and also *budo* indoctrinations):

> Across the sea,
> Corpses in the water;
> Across the mountain,
> Corpses heaped upon the field;
> I shall die only for the *Mikado*,
> I shall never look back!

Than which is not to insist on disasters unabated (mitigation of same essential to contextual ironics). As how at Rabaul (New Britain Islands): good duty prevails up to late in '43, reet? Principal *Nihonjin* operational air and also naval base of operations, all *issen gorin* off duty as of 1700 hours, leisure time provided for by regular transport service from *Dai Nippon*, than which brings singers and also dancers (how we say: Encouragement Shows), not to fail to mention volunteer *moga* prostitutes (how we say, Jack: comfort women), *eiga* flics produced in aid of wartime propaganda *kirijini* fighting spirit morales (to wit: *One Plane Has Not Yet Returned, Five Scouts, The Story of Tank Commander Nishizumi, Mud and Soldiers, The War at Sea from Hawaii to Malaya, The Story of the Camp*, etcetera blah — said slickie flics produced by big-time expanded budgets domestic studios — totaly unlike like unto in-the-field actualities efforts of *wataschi* Lieutenant *Benshi*, Jack!); minuscule amenities afforded, as in daily *sento* hot baths, Cherry and also Golden Bat ciggie smokes, Asahi beer, Suntory whiskies ration, standard imperial military menu fare (sardines, rice balls, and seaweed kelps, natch) augmented by trade with native aboriginals for bananas (yes we don't got some!), papayas, mangoes, breadfruits — than which is not to fail to mention ever-present drawbacks in form of bad waters supply sources engendering diseases (to wit: dengue and scarlet fevers, malaria — natch! — dysentery; how you say, Jack, drizzling shits G.I. Trots). Also assorted tropical-environ jungle-climate cruds causing boils, fungi on dermis, nonhealable ulcer sores.

Still and all, Jack, fighting spirit morales (*kirijini!*) of 100,000 plus officers and *issen gorin* garrison on scene remains elevated, as witnessed in popular assemblages to accompany aviation sortie takeoffs, said ceremonials exuberant with *Hinomaru* flag waving and *banzai* choral cheers — all which same is, natch, prior to Yank aviational devastations wrought thereafter, as by legendary air ace Major Richard (a.k.a. Bing) Bong et alia.

Radiogram message from Tulagi (Guadalcanal outpost), circa 7 of August, 1942: *Large force of ships, unknown number of types, entering the sound. What can they be?*

Answer: the Yanks is coming, Jack!

Battle of Ilu River, reet? Colonel Ichichi Kujono in command—instanter upon losing 800 plus *issen gorin* in vain river-crossing night-fighting tactic, aforesaid *honcho budo* personage did burn regimental colors and commit *hara kiri* belly-slit shtick as expiations of shames brought to reflect upon Imperial Army, *Dai Nippon, Mikado* etcetera blah. Holograph on the wall, Jack!

Not to fail to mention General Hyatake Haruyoshi, than which less-than-*budo* commander-in-chief did desert his troops, cut-and-run bug-out to Bougainville fastness sanctuary, reet?

Anonymous *issen gorin* diary entry (Battle of Bloody Ridge, reet?): *We are nothing but skin and bones, pale wild men. I have become like a primitive man.*

Guadalcanal (courtesy of Yank 2d Marine Division), Jack (circa August '42 to and also through February '43, reet?), how we say: Island of Death. Than which moniker handle emanates from phenom of 23,000 *issen gorin* dead from ranks of original 36,000 Imperial Army contingent on scene.

Last radiogram message from Tulagi extant: *Enemy forces overwhelming. We will defend our posts to the death, praying for eternal victory.*

Can you dig it, Jack: *Yamato Damashii* fighting spirit (*kirijini!*) of Hundred Millions of *Dai Nippon*, reet?

Umi Yakuba (second verse):

> If I go on the sea,
> My corpse will dissolve in the water;
> If I go in the mountains,
> My body will be covered with mosses;
> I will have died for my *Mikado*,
> I will have gone with no regret!

Mikado (har and also hee, reet?), upon receipt of *kempei-tai* military intelligence info informing aforesaid Celestial Presence of evacuation of Guadalcanal: "What is now your intention with regard to the conduct of this *senso*, Premier-General?"

Tojo (don't call him The Razor for nothing, Jack!): "I shall endeavor to halt the westward course of movement of our *Amerikajin* enemies, and will proceed, as *hakko ichui* dictates, on schedule to the invasion and conquest of Australia."

Big irony thereof and therein: New Guinea, Jack! General Horii Tomitaro in command, en route on march to cross humongous mountain jungle wastes in drive on Port Moresby (jump-off to Australia), infamous famed Kokoda Track campaign, reet? Circa '42 to and also through April '44, route of march beset by unmitigated and unprecedented debacle disasters due to climate and terrains, also harassment by aboriginal head-hunter cannibal types! Resultant (natch!) in turn-around and disorderly withdraw retreat back north on Kokoda Track from juncture but twenty miles short of Port Moresby objective — sad to say, aforesaid *honcho* General Horii hisself is done got drownded in attempt to ford rushing raging torrent mountain stream, now pursued by Yanks and also Aussies dispatched from Down Under by *Makassar-san*, Dugout Doug MacArthur.

Highlights of New Guinea debacle defeat: Butcher's Corner, whereat 638 *issen gorin* succumb to Yank air-cooled rapid-fires, said casualties resorting to employment of deceased comrades as rampart bulwarks parapets to return fire, snatching brief slumbers in close proximity of dead, than which who bloat and subsequently burst under hot sun in kunai grass — can you not dig it, Jack?

Than which is not to fail to mention Buna-Gona, whereat Imperial Army of *Dai Nippon* sustains loss of 100 *issen gorin* per diem daily to starvation privations.

Dairy entry of one *issen gorin* Wada Kuyoshi (K.I.A. thereafter at Sananda): *It is about time we received some Divine aid. It seems all the grass and roots have already been eaten. Will the Mikado not beseech Ameratasu and also his family kami to assist us in our predicament?*

Aside: circa 16 of October, 1942, three captured crewpersonages from Doolittle raider roster executed for atrocity crimes in Shanghai — *Papa-san! Mama-san! Iko-san!* Oh, Jack, I tell you: ain't no surcease of sorrows in vengeance revenge shtick!

Circa March '43, Jack: Battle of Bismarck Sea — loss of forty Imperial Navy vessels (not to fail to mention 45,000 *Nihonjin issen gorin* swabbie sailor boys introduced to locker of legendary David Jones thereby!). Imperial Navy of *Dai Nippon* withdraws heavy ships remaining from once-formidable *Kido Butai* task force to safer waters sanctuaries of Islands of *Nihon*. Than which is to say: termination of plans for invasion and also conquest of Australia, Jack!

Circa November '43, reet? Bougainville, Jack: 7,000 *issen gorin* — members of 6th Division famed infamous for so-called Rape of Nanking, circa '37! — meet fabricator (not to fail to mention innovative defensive strategy tactic, *takotsubo* octopus traps — how you say, foxholes wherein in wait lies solitary *issen gorin* wielding Arisaka shoulder-fire, concealed under woven palm-leaf *tatami* lid to spring forth and bushwhack passing G.I. grunt dogfaces, reet?).

Than which is also not to fail to mention (also circa November '43 – bad month for *Dai Nippon*, Jack!) Betio Atoll, also knowed as Tarawa, reet?

Honcho Admiral Shibasahi Keiji in command (2,600 *issen gorin* at the ready, and also willing and able): *A million men cannot take Tarawa in a hundred years!*

Wrong, Jack!

Seventeen (count them, Jack!) *issen gorin* survive assault of U.S. Marine island-hopper amphibians under command of Chesty Puller (Medal of Honor designate, reet?).

Honcho Admiral Shibasahi Keiji (final radiogram message dispatched to Ichigaya Heights): *Our weapons have been destroyed. From now on everyone is attempting a final charge. May Dai Nippon exist for ten thousand years to come!*

Official communiqué (Imperial Ministry of War, Ichigaya Heights): *We are saddened by the loss of the valiant defenders of Betio Atoll, and officially acclaim them as the Flowers of the Pacific. Tenno Heika Banzai!*

Lieutenant Furano's Poem:

> The young cherry blossoms
> Fall from the branches
> At the highest moment of their glory
> With no regret.
> Myself, like a broken petal,
> I will scatter my bones
> In the mountains
> Or on the ocean's surface.
> The dawn is bright
> With the joy of reunion
> With my dead comrades
> At the Yasukuni Shrine!

Circa 1944, Jack: Kwajalein, Guam (glommed from Yanks with relativist ease in wake of *Pearu Halbol* victory, 9 of December 1941, reet?), not to fail to mention Saipan.

Saipan: not to fail to mention Battle of Philippine Sea, how you say: Great Marianas Turkey Shoot (four hundred plus *Nihonjin* aircrafts zapped from sky's vastness, as against dozen and a half odd Yank flyboys).

Aside: here perished Lieutenant Commander Sugihara Heihachiro, one-time disgruntled *budo* Chink campaigns hot shot air ace sky-jockey hero chauffeur on photo mission at *Pearu Halbol* – remember him, Jack?

Which is also not to fail to mention (ah, would it had not been thus so!) *Nihonjin* civilians (how you say: feather merchants) suicide leap to deaths into sea off high cliffs of Marpi Point to avoid incarceration internments durance vile in clutches of barbarian *Amerikajin*, reet?

Honcho General Saito (in command, final radiogram to Ichigaya Heights instanter prior to face-saver *seppuku hara kiri* belly-slit): *I advance to seek out the enemy. Follow me!*

Twenty-nine thousand *issen gorin* expire, Jack! Not to fail to mention Saipan provides air-strike distances to *Dai Nippon* Home Islands, dig?

Mikado (har!) to Premier-General Tojo Hideki (upon reception of *kem-pei-tai* intelligence info of aforesaid Saipan debacle): *Hell is upon us!*

Aside: can you not dig it, Jack? Utter and also complete reversal of fortunes of *senso* war, reet? Chronology of ongoing inexorable inescapable defeat of *Dai Nippon* (to include—natch!—frustration of celestially decreed grandiose *hakko ichui* design)—oh, yet further big ironics to come, about which further follows hereafter immediately concerning personalist deviation in *do* course of life and times of *wataschi* Lieutenant *Benshi*.

Motto of which is, Jack: *issun saki wa yami*, than which means—one inch in front of your visage, all is dark's darkness, which is to say, future impossible to prognosticate, Jack!

Date:
18 July 1944

To:
Lt. *Benshi*
Hakko Ichui Eiga Mission
Southern Seas Theater of Operations

From:
Premier-General Tojo Hideki
Imperial Ministry of War
Ichigaya Heights
Tokyo Prefecture
Dai Nippon

Lieutenant *Benshi*:

I can only hope that this, my ultimate official communication with you, reaches you at whatever distant outpost you reside at presently. Know that I am cognizant of the difficulties you have experienced as a result of the long series of schedule changes ordained by me in an effort to utilize your capacities as a maker of *eiga* in a location where the armed forces of *Dai Nippon* might inflict a crushing and final defeat of our *Amerikajin* enemies—ah, Lieutenant *Benshi*, please know I understand the frustrations you have encountered in your desire to create the *eiga* chronicle of the triumph of *hakko ichui* . . . the island called Guadalcanal, New Guinea, Bougainville, Betio Atoll, Kwajalein, Guam, and now the disaster of Saipan! Know, Lieutenant *Benshi*, that it is my most sincere wish that it all might have been otherwise!

Know also that, even as I struggled each day to the utmost extent of my abilities to meet the crises arising from this horrendous and unforeseen series of military misfortunes, I did find time to review the reels of *eiga* film you have so faithfully dispatched to my attention here at Ichigaya Heights, and that I did present numerous examples of your excellent achievement to the *Mikado* personally and did explain to him the noble purpose we intended for this, our joint venture. It is the *Mikado's* response to your *eiga*, the reels depicting the heroic defenses offered by the armed forces of *Dai Nippon* at Guadalcanal, New Guinea, and elsewhere as I have enumerated herein above, that occasions this last radiogram from me to you, Lieutenant *Benshi*.

Know the *Mikado's* wishes, and the impending circumstance of my resignation from the office of premier of *Dai Nippon*. . . .

Know, Lieutenant *Benshi*, that when I have composed this communication you read somewhere in the vastness of the Pacific Southern Seas Theater — and have affixed my *hanko* signature seal beneath what I have written, I shall be conveyed in my staff car to the Imperial Palace, where I shall enter the Sakurada Gate, there to be received in formal audience by the *Mikado*, to present to him my written resignation from the office of premier. The entire matter, in the aftermath of the disgrace and shame of the defeat at Saipan, which will enable the barbarian *Amerikajin* to conduct aviation sorties now directly against the Home Islands, is of course prearranged. I shall be succeeded by Koiso Kunaiki, to whom you will direct any future communications of an official nature, Lieutenant *Benshi*.

Know, then, Lieutenant *Benshi*, that the *Mikado* directs me to order you, as the last act of leadership attendant upon the office I resign so soon, to avail yourself of any available transport, and to return to *Dai Nippon* and present yourself to the new premier installed here at Ichigaya Heights. Premier-designate Koiso, I understand, will arrange an audience for you with the *Mikado*, who has asked expressly to personally issue your new orders. I will add, as inspiration to you as you attempt the hazardous journey home along routes constantly under fire of the *Amerikajin* naval and air forces, that the *Mikado* recalls your first audience with him in 1935 in the company of the party of *Amerikajin* athletes, and finds in the work you accomplished under my direction since *Pearu Halbol* a potential for further valuable service on your part to our nation and the Hundred Millions.

Tenno Heika Banzai!

Postscript: Lieutenant *Benshi*, forgive me for appending a personal note to this radiogram. I am now an old man, past the possibility of attaining new honor and glory like unto that which came to me in Manchukuo and in the brilliant victories that only evaded us since 1942! I go now, disgraced and shamed, to enter private life in my house, to write *haiku* to express the wisdom I have learned on the long, ironic *do* course of my life to this terrible moment. Can you appreciate the bitterness, anger, and depression I feel, Lieutenant *Benshi*? No, I think you cannot; you are a young man, and the *do* of your life will surely be long and strewn with good fortune like the petals of the cherry blossoms that litter the gravel paths of Ueno Park during *hanami* — has not the *Mikado* chosen you for what will doubtless prove a task of great significance? Ah, Lieutenant *Benshi*, I will hope and trust you are not so young as to neglect to pause in the onrush of your life's quest, that you will sense the *ma* that surrounds you and will feel its *yoin* resonating. Do not forget that our lives are charmed, predestined by the influences of *Ameratasu* and the *kami* who attend us. Know, Lieutenant *Benshi*, that we are not responsible for our fates and should not be so arrogant as to assume the guilt and blame for the missions we fail to bring to satisfactory ends! Thus it is that I, an old man now, fallen from the heights of honor and glory, accept the disgrace and shame all will surely shower upon me like the rains of the typhoon! I will enter private life, contemplating, writing poetry—but you are a young man and will not understand what I have written as postscript to this last radiogram, Lieutenant *Benshi*.

    Tenno Heika Banzai!

    T.H.

Do I not dig, Jack? Hee! Also har! Big ironies, Jack, following hereafter, reet?

Date:
3 August 1944

To:
Premier Koiso Kunaiki
Headquarters, Imperial Ministry of War
Ichigaya Heights
Tokyo Prefecture
Dai Nippon

From:
Lieutenant *Benshi*
Truk
Caroline Archipelago
Field Hq, Southeast Pacific Fleet
Imperial Navy of *Dai Nippon*

Sensei Honcho Premier Koiso:

Greetings and salutations, not to fail to mention most sincere hearty congrats to you upon occasion of your exalted elevation—doubtless much deserved!—to office of *honcho* premiership of all *Dai Nippon*! Than which is not to fail to mention adding fervent hopes this radiograms arrives at Ichigaya Heights, given difficulties of commo (not to fail to mention transports!) with Home Island under current *senso* conditions of Yank intercepts of four-fifths of all vessels and/or aircrafts attempting journey, reet? To which is also necessary to add *wataschi's* firmest firm conviction misfortunate fortunes of *senso* war which did sad to say plague sadly departed predecessor ex-Premier (still General, reet?) Tojo (a.k.a. The Razor) Hideki will doubtless under your inspired supreme leadership turn about and resume course of glorious progress and progression toward triumph of *hakko ichui* grand design as predetermined and destined by no less than Sun Goddess *Ameratasu*, reet?

Allow me to intro self: I is Sub-Lieutenant Yamaguchi Yoshinori

266

(code name: Lieutenant *Benshi*!), Imperial Army of *Dai Nippon*, currently attached (strictly casual transient status) to Southeast Pacific Fleet Hq. here on Truk (Southern Seas Theater), said locale resultant upon strategic relocations (not to say retreat!) from Rabaul, than which remove was occasioned by Yank island-hop by-pass maneuver leaving 100,000 *issen gorin* and also *budo* officer swabbie sailor boys with, how we say in *Eigo*, omelet on visage, reet? Not to fail to mention cataclysmic catastrophe (straw snapping camel's hump, reet?) loss of Admiral Yamamoto (national hero of Hundred Millions in aftermath of brilliant *Pearu Halbol* victory!) to enemy's aircrafts whilst on recon mission flight. Anyhoo, here is I, *honcho sensei* premier!

Than which is not to fail to mention my surprise and also delights to know *Mikado* hisself request to see my visage back in *Dai Nippon*! To be candid frankly, I is done been thinking as how cinematic *eiga* chronicle of *hakko ichui* was dead equine beaten further by series of false-start productions truncated by unremitting Yank assaults, failure of imperial forces to achieve celestially preordained victories appropriate for narrative *eiga* depiction, reet?

Dig: looking forward to meeting you soonest anon!

And *daijubo, sensei honcho* Premier Koiso! Not to perspire over seeming snake-bit inability of armed forces of *Dai Nippon* to halt Yank advances since circa mid-'42, reet? Despite reversals seemingly ceaseless in *senso* fortunes of war, inimical (to say least!) to *Dai Nippon*, *Yamato Damashii kirijini* fighting spirit remains elevated aloft here on Truk! To wit: current popular ditty sung by all *issen gorin* as they scan sky's vastness vista and also ocean horizons on ever-alert lookout for approach of *Amerikajin* assault forces—

Come out,
Nimitz and *Makassar*!
Then we will send you
Tumbling down to hell!

Catchy, reet? Than which is not to fail to mention all on scene wear thousand-stitch belts (as on Guadalcanal, New Guinea, Betio Atoll, etcetera blah!).

Than which is also not to fail to mention minimalist diminishment of morales factor due to *benjo* shithouse rumors rife to effect that *Amerikajin* air sorties wreak devastations on Home Islands from recently obtained Saipan airstrips, also that ashes of deceased *issen gorin* is no longer delivered to grieving kins via taxicab (with attendant appropriate pedestrian hats doffed, kowtow, etcetera blah), now comes parcel post to avoid depressing Hundred Millions civie populace due to exponential increase of K.I.A. numbers—any truths to all this guff stuff, *sensei honcho* premier? I look forward to hearing all straight poop scoop when I gets to Ichigaya Heights.

In closing prior to conclusion, please to convey my greetings to *Mikado* when next you confabulate, reet? Tell said celestial personage I, Lieutenant *Benshi*, formerly Student Yamaguchi Yoshinori, also recall our meet in '35, and anticipate renewing service to *Dai Nippon* with true deep *hara* belly's joy! Dig you later, *honcho* premier!

Tenno Heika Banzai!

Lieutenant *Benshi.*

Cut to: Tokyo Town, *Dai Nippon*, circa late August 1944, reet? *Wataschi* (Lieutenant *Benshi*, Jack!), returned to Home Islands (no personalist home, Jack, as how paper house got burned up in previous big fire, circa '42) after two years plus absence on military *giri* duty. Journey from Truk accomplished via combo of sea and air hitchhike-style travels from Carolines via Bonins and Okinawa, same endowed with big dosage of Lady Luck luck enabling *wataschi* to evade Yank air and also sea interdiction.

Circa late August '44, Jack: beginning of *yake tsuchi jidai*, how we say, Burned Earth Period—Yank bombing sorties based now on Guam in Marianas archipelago, followed thereafter by day and also night round-the-clocks emanating from airstrips on Tinian and also Saipan, reet?

One long blast (sirens and factory whistles) for warning—Yanks is coming!—shorts to signal commencement of attack (everyone runs *chogee* for shelters)—one long to mark termination of raid. Usual schedule is daily betwixt noon and one o'clock postmeridian, eventide raids less predictable, reet? Jack: we talking ceaseless big fires (not unlike like unto traditionalist Flowers of Eido conflagrations tradition in spades!)!

Tokyo Town (circa late August '44): Hundred Millions populace howsomever appears yet to maintain strong *Yamato Damashii kirijini* fighting spirit—to wit, fave-rave ditty sung (not to fail to mention also hummed and whistled!) by *monpei*-clad civilians as they do *chogee* to shelters, emerge after all-clear whistles to douse fires and scrutinize rubbles for deceased and also injured survivors (to tune of "Buffalo Gals, Won't You Come out Tonight?"):

> Why should we fear air raids?
> The sky over *Dai Nippon* is protected with iron defenses!
> For young and old it is time to stand up!
> We welcome the honor of defending *Dai Nippon*!
> Come on, *Amerikajin* aircraft! Come many times!

Catchy, huh?

Dig it, Jack: *wataschi* Lieutenant *Benshi*, returned home from two years plus *giri* duty on Pacific front, debark vessel at bomb-damaged Yokohama wharfside dock (irony, as how no band musics accompanying, reet?), perambulate *sanpo* shank's mare to Tokyo Town (schlepping camera and also *katana*), traverse urban environ—*monpei*-clad feathermerchant Hundred Millions civilians too busy cleaning up after daily big fires to convey greetings, to Ichigaya Heights, wherefrom *wataschi* (after scolding for non-*budo* appearance!) is dispatched (charcoal-fueled pre-*senso* Plymouth staff car sedan) to Nijubashi Plaza, Sakurada Gate (oh, ironies, Jack!),

Imperial Palance, domicile of *Mikado* (har!), Hirohito (hee!), direct descendant of Sun Goddess *Ameratasu* (hardy har!), than which celestial presence (hee hee!) awaits Lieutenant *Benshi* in personal audience—which is not to fail to mention as how said confabulation confrontation takes place in confine of imperial bomb shelter—as how stray Yank missiles is done landed of late in imperial gardens, reet? As follows:

"Greetings, Sub-Lieutenant Yamaguchi Yoshinori," says *Mikado*, "or is it perhaps proper that I should address you as Lieutenant *Benshi*?"

"*Aisatsu* salutations, *Mikado*," I riposte, and, "Reet," as I hit full kowtow, concerned lest I bump schnozz on floor in dark dimmed lack-of-light ambience of imperial bomb shelter—"*Benshi* is my name, cinematic *eiga* chronicle of glorious triumph of *hakko ichui* design decreed by *Ameratasu* for all *Dai Nippon* is my game."

"Do not attempt to prostrate yourself at full length upon the floor here, Lieutenant *Benshi*," says he, and, "I regret to say the chamber is filthy. The management of the Imperial Household has become exceedingly lax in these dire times, and I confess that I have ceased to bestow my attention on such mundane matters when events so threaten the ruin of *Nihon*."

"Reet, *Mikado*," I say. "Cold and clammy down here, stale airs, utter absence of ceremonials amenities as how I does recall from first time we met, circa 'thirty-five."

"Be at your ease, Lieutenant *Benshi*. Let me look upon you in this poor light. Ah, you are greatly altered by the long time that has passed since I first set my eyes upon you—has it indeed been nearly nine years since the day I spoke to the precocious boy chosen to serve as guide and interpreter for the visiting delegation of renowned *Amerikajin besuboru* athletes? I confess I was not wholly pleased when Premier Tojo banned the sport throughout *Dai Nippon* last year, but it was my principle then to leave the conduct of this *senso* to the constituted authorities. So it is that time changes all things, not excluding ourselves, Lieutenant *Benshi*. And do please lay aside your longsword, for I observe you are not comfortable holding it at your side."

"Anks-thay, celestial divinity," I say, set *katana* on sole *kaigi* conference confabulation table whereat is seated *Mikado* to receive me, reet? Big clank sound echoes loud in minimalist dim and also damp confine of imperial bomb shelter.

"And there is no need to hold your large *furoshiki* wrapped bundle, Lieutenant *Benshi*."

"Double anks-thay, son of heaven," I say, set Stewart Warner, wrapped in oil-cloth *furoshiki* to guard against salt-air corrosions of long risky Pacific voyage home, next to longsword. "Tool of trade," I say, "duly inspected by factotum guard on guard outside, than which who said as how it was okey-doke to bring along herein, reet? 16-milimeter camera, sentimental value gift, gifted to me as *o-miyage* souvenir by Morris Berg—also knowed as Moe—remember Moe Berg, *Mikado?*"

"*Hai!*" says *Mikado*, and, "He is the *gaijin* I was later informed understood even the High Court *Nihonju* with which we conversed in those days so long ago."

"Reet," I say, and, "Wish as how it had turned out otherhow, as how aforesaid personage Moe-*san* did engender all my woes subsequent with *kempei.*" *Mikado* waves subject away with royal hand and also arm gesture, says:

"Let us not speak of that long past misfortune. We have something more urgent to discuss. I am pleased that you appear well, even though time has transformed you from a precocious boy to a man of broad and rich experience of this great *senso* that brings such hardship upon the Hundred Millions, Lieutenant *Benshi.*"

"Reet. Likewise, *Mikado*. I mean, like, you looking good. Ain't aged a day from how you looked riding white horse Snow White in ceremonial pic my dear departed *Papa-san* kept on the wall of his office at *Japan Times.*"

"It is kind of you to say this, Lieutenant *Benshi*," says he, "but I suspect you mean to flatter me."

"Reet, *Mikado*," I did say.

"I have perused the comprehensive dossier concerning your activities which is maintained by the *kempei*, Lieutenant *Benshi*," says *Mikado* (har and hee, reet?).

"Reet," I say, and, "Natch. But I can explain all the gigs and black marks, *Mikado*! Like, I didn't wise up to Moe Berg's counterintelligence espionage scam at first, and when I did—I was but sweet sixteen years old aged, reet, *Mikado*? Dig, *wataschi* was pure *kichigai* crazy cracked eager to get stateside for higher-educational education endeavors, study *Eigo* and view all the new *eiga* Hollywood flics on first run, reet? I wanted Ivy League, but fobbed off to obscure cow college Oklahoma A and M as punishments for Berg flap, reet? Howsomever, whereat, A and M campus, Stillwater Town, county of Payne, sovereign state of Oklahoma, I did with enthusiasms aid *kempei* regional clandestine counterintelligence operative Mr. Sato Isao versus *Amerikajin gumbatsu* militarist establishment, to wit Pershing Rifles, R.O.T.C., and also Flying Aggies, which is not to fail to mention as how subsequent thereto, I is done carried out *eiga* docudrama mission assigned personal by ex-*honcho sensei* Premier and also General Tojo Hideki, than which is not to fail to explain loss of one prisoner of war Lieutenant Stevie Keller whilst engaged in remote location shoots site in production of feature-length *eiga*—"

"There is no necessity," interrupts *Mikado*, "to manifest the implications of your code name, Lieutenant *Benshi*! I only wish you to understand that I am cognizant of all that has transpired in your life, a notably remarkable series of events for one so young, is it not?"

"Reet!" I say, and, "Orry-say for the spiel, *Mikado*!"

"And please to understand that I am not unmindful of the personal loss you have sustained in this *senso* — "

"Reet. *Papa-san, Mama-san*, Sis *Iko-san*, got burned up in a big fire inside our paper house, circa *hanami* nineteen and forty-two," I did whisper to damp echoing walls of imperial bomb shelter interior environ.

" — and it is just this, the death and suffering visited upon my loyal subjects, which occasions my summoning you here today, Lieutenant *Benshi*." *Mikado* pauses, reet? Takes big breath hiss intake, covers celestial visage with royal hands — shoulders slumped — says (imperial voice muffled by hands over mouth): "Ah, Lieutenant *Benshi*! How fervent and vain are my daily prayers to *Ameratasu* and the *kami* of my ancestors that none of this had come to be!"

"Reet, tell me about it, *Mikado*," I did say, and, "Like, I can but dig it!"

What's to do save except stand at relative ease, *katana* and also Stewart Warner camera on table, await upon imperial wisdom to manifest tangibility in words, reet? Dig it, Jack!

"What is your estimation of the likely course this *senso* will take in the months or even years to come, Lieutenant *Benshi*?" he queries. "Speak candidly to me. You have observed events at close hand all across the Pacific since our initial victory at *Pearu Halbol* — tell me what you foresee, Lieutenant *Benshi*."

"With bark off?" says I. And, "No jives? Minus conventional prescribed *Yamato Damashii* sentiments and also slogans, *Mikado*?" When *Mikado* nods royal noggin in affirmative, I say:

"*Nippon maketa, Mikado*!" How you say, Jack: *Dai Nippon* is done been whipped to frazzle, reet? "*Pearu Halbol* was strictly fluke flashing in pan lucky sucker punch. Might could have worked if Yank carriers had been moored dockside with battlewagons, destroyers, cruisers, but they was out to sea patrol maneuvers, hence escaped and evaded conflagrations."

"And yet we vanquished the *Amerikajin* in their bastion at Corregidor," says he, "and drove the Fifty-thousand-dollar General *Makassar* in disgrace to Australia!"

"Reet," I say, "was I not there on scene? But it took *honcho* Homma twice so long as how it should, losses to Fourteenth Imperial too great to justify cost accounting investment to win on bottom line, reet? Thereafter, Imperial Army and also Navy ain't won zip zilch diddly squat! Coral Sea, Midway, Bismarck Sea farce debacles, *Nihonjin* swabbie sailors don't dast now take big ships out of Home Islands waters for fear from introduction absent ceremonials to David Jones, reet? Guadalcanal Island of Death,

New Guinea, Bougainville, Betio Atoll, Kwajalein, Guam, Saipan, Tinian, Philippine Sea, Marianas Turkey Shoot, you name it, *Mikado: Nippon maketa*, reet? Where is *senso* heroes of Hundred Millions now? Homma sitting to home in paper house twiddling opposable thumbs in disgrace. *Tojo-san*, also knowed as The Razor, writing *haiku* poems to express wisdoms he done gleaned whilst leading all *Dai Nippon* up primrose *do* path to defeats unceasing, not to fail to mention *honcho* Admiral Yamamoto lost at sea over Rabaul."

"What you say is true," says *Mikado*, "but my generals and admirals remind me that we have more than a million *issen gorin* in good fighting spirit in China—"

"What's good," I query, "of vaunted Kwantung Army when it don't dast try to cross ocean waters to defend *Nihon* for lacks of air cover to get them home, *Mikado*? Which is not to fail to mention as how Kwantung Army been slugging Chinks since circa 'thirty-one, still ain't won *Sekigahara* decisive victory! Island-hopping Yanks coming, *Mikado*! Philippines likely next—Dugout Doug *Makassar* going to make good and redeem promise to return, reet? Thence Bonins? *Dai Nippon* thereafter! Dig it, *Mikado: Nippon maketa*!"

Can you not dig this, Jack? It is me, *wataschi*, Lieutenant *Benshi* (a.k.a. Student Yamaguchi Yoshinori, a.k.a. Gooch!), telling straight to direct descendant of Sun Goddess *Ameratasu* the *Mikado* as how *Dai Nippon* going down tube, into porcelain *benjo* sanitary convenience in global-wide *senso* flap debacle, reet? Imperial bomb shelter, late afternoon, August 1944, opening weeks of *yake tsuchi jidai* Burned Earth Period B-29 (*bee nijo koo!*) raids daily on Tokyo Town. I kid you not, Jack!

"Lieutenant *Benshi*," says he, "I tell you in strict confidence, upon your oath of loyalty to me and to the Hundred Millions, that your opinion is shared by me and several of the more moderate of my many advisors. Yet, there will be no surrender! Do you perceive the implications of this fundamental contradiction, Lieutenant *Benshi*?"

"We getting whipped, not unlike like unto doom faced eternal by A and M Aggies when versus hated O.U. Sooner downstate rivals on gridiron—than which is to say, fatty chances, reet? What's else to do save except throw in towel, raise aloft white gonfalon?"

"Perhaps you are not sufficiently *Nipponshikki* to comprehend, Lieutenant *Benshi*? *Dai Nippon* will never capitulate to the hated *Amerikajin* and their allies! The Hundred Millions, led by our generals and admirals, inspired by the *samurai* code of *bushido*, will resist our enemies to the last man, woman, and child! All will wear the thousand-stitch belt! Even now, as the *Amerikajin* rain death and destruction upon us from their aircraft each day, as they sink our vessels and exterminate the legions of the

Imperial Army all across the Pacific, the *gumbatsu* militarists devise strategies to prolong the conflict!"

"Won't wash, *Mikado*!" I did say, and, "Whacko *kichigai baka* crazy cracked, reet? Going to arm Hundred Millions with *take* bamboo spears to resist Yank Marine amphibians coming ashore on Home Islands? Loony tunes, *Mikado*!" I tell him. "Bughouse, reet? Women and also kiddie little nippers going to don thousand-stitch belts versus artillery and also napalms? Screws loose amongst *budo gumbatsu* types, *Mikado*!"

"Yet this will come to pass, Lieutenant *Benshi*," ripostes he. "At Ichigaya Heights they plan Operation *Sho Go* to defend our Philippine conquest when the Fifty-thousand-dollar General *Makassar* returns with his armada from Australia to avenge his humiliation! Already the *kaigi* conference chambers at Ichigaya Heights are noisy with the talk of *Ketsu Go*, the final defense to the death of the islands of *Nihon*, Lieutenant *Benshi*!"

"*Mikado*," I did tell him, "time to give it up, fold hand, punt! You the onliest one can do it, *Mikado*!" I did say, Jack!

"No," said he, and, "*Nippon maketa*! I am but a mere mortal, Lieutenant *Benshi*, not the divinity the Hundred Millions think me! What can but one small voice do? *Nippon maketa*. We shall all fight to the death. *Dai Nippon* will disappear when our enemies have killed the last of the Hundred Millions, and with them will disappear the Chrysanthemum Throne that has endured for over two and a half thousand years! Is it not sad, Lieutenant *Benshi*?"

Long impregnated pause in confabulation, reet? Do you not dig, Jack?

I is thinking: The End, reet? Finish. All she inscribed, Jack! End of Lieutenant *Benshi* (also of Student Yamaguchi Yoshinori, not to fail to mention also Gooch!), end of Hundred Millions, end of *Dai Nippon*, which is not to fail to mention end of so-called *Mikado* — wimpy mere mortal concerned foremost for end of Chrysanthemum Throne etcetera blah. Dig: this is fashion in which world ends — going to get burned up in big fires, accompanied by *Mikado's* whimper and also simpers, reet?

"Lieutenant *Benshi*," says *Mikado*, "do you hear me, Lieutenant *Benshi*?"
"Reet."

"Your mission has been to record the triumph of the grand design of *hakko ichui* with your *eiga* camera, is this not so?"

"Reet," I say, "than which is pure farce absurdist in lights of disaster debacles unceasing since mid-circa 'forty-two. End of *hakko ichui*," I say, "end of cinematic *eiga* flic docu-drama mission shtick."

"Indeed," *Mikado* says, "*hakko ichui* is only a memory that mocks those who dreamed it. And yet, Lieutenant *Benshi*, there is a service you can perform for *Dai Nippon*."

"Such as?" I ask. "Combat interpreter, not to fail to mention *budo* thousand-stitch belt officer leading *issen gorin* versus Yank invaders with longsword in hand."

"No. Listen to me, Lieutenant *Benshi*! Forget, if only for a moment, what I have told you, what you must not share outside the walls of this filthy chamber where we hide from the *Amerikajin* raiders!"

"Reet," I say, "all auricular orifices, *Mikado*."

"If *Dai Nippon* is fated to disappear from the global family of nations, still there is honor in the tenacity of our refusal to capitulate to the *gaijin* barbarians, and the peoples of the world who survive us may be brought to know and honor our resolve. For this to be, there must be a record of the inexorable course of our extermination. What better means to this end than for you to continue your mission, now to create a chronicle of the demise of an ancient and once-glorious empire!"

"You talking *eiga* flics, *Mikado*?"

"I am charging you with an awesome responsibility, Lieutenant *Benshi*! I lay in your capable hands—for I have viewed the wondrous *eiga* you created at *Pearu Halbol* and elsewhere—the honor of recording for the world's posterity the death throes of a nation whose existence was decreed to extend for ten thousand years by the Sun Goddess *Ameratasu*! To you, Lieutenant *Benshi*, shall go the honor and glory attendant upon ensuring that mankind shall never forget us, though the generations of men to come will no longer look upon the race of *Nihonjin*. Are you equal to the historic task I set you, Lieutenant *Benshi*?" asks *Mikado*.

Can you dig this, Jack?

"Carte blanche?" I query. "Total creative control? Screen credits as deemed appropriate? Budgetary adequacy?"

Circa late August 1944, Jack!

"I'll need your personal *hanko* signature seal warrant, *Mikado*, sixty-six petal chrysanthemum *monsho* crest, reet?"

Imperial bomb shelter, palace grounds, Tokyo Town, *Dai Nippon*.

"No *budo* interferences with production, reet? Studio facilities for editing and also dubbing. Direct line of communication to Imperial Palace for consults, bypassing bureaucracy factotums, reet? Transports and logisticals priorities?"

End of *hakko ichui* project, commencement of *Nippon maketa* endeavor.

Says *Mikado*: "Are we agreed then, Lieutenant *Benshi*? Have we

274

achieved *enryo?*"

Says I: "Reet, *Mikado!*" and, "Hey, I'll need that imperial *hanko* signature seal warrant instanter, reet?"

At which juncture clammy minimalist confines of imperial bomb shelter is invaded by remote whistle and siren blasts, voices of factotum imperial guards at bunker door. "It is the *Amerikajin* aircraft," says *Mikado*, "coming again to rain death and destruction upon the Hundred Millions. We are safe here, Lieutenant *Benshi*, for the only bombs that fall near the palace are not aimed at us but fall by mistake away from their targets in the city. Did you know the *Amerikajin* formerly took aim at our *sento* public bath houses, Lieutenant *Benshi*? I am told they mistook the chimneys of the furnaces that heat the bath waters for those of small factories they assumed produced munitions."

"Reet," I said;. "*Bee nijo koo* from off Saipan and also Tinian airstrips. They gots lots better photo recon now than in circa 'forty-two when Jimmy Doolittle's boys hit us off the *Hornet*. You think this is bad, *Mikado*, wait and see if they gets airstrips in the Bonins, you will see big fires!"

Said he—*Mikado*, Jack (har and also hee, reet?): "I do not expect to remain in Tokyo Prefecture, Lieutenant *Benshi*. I am advised to remove the Imperial Household to my resort dwelling at Hayama, which lies two dozen miles to the southwest, on Sogami Bay. I seek the serenity that abounds there and the leisure that will enable me to pursue my passionate interest in ichthyology." Study of fishes, reet, Jack?

"Lucky you, *Mikado*," I did riposte.

Cut to: circa August '44 up to and also to include early September (onset of *tsukimi*) 1945, Jack—cinematic *eiga* docudrama created as chronicle of defeat (*Nippon Maketa!*) of Empire of *Nihon*, aforesaid assuming (natch!) total extermination of *Nihonjin* race (to include 2,600-years-old Chrysanthemum Throne, reet?), than which said endeavor is sacred-trust-mission shtick entrusted by (no less than, Jack!) *Mikado* (hee and har!) hisself to *wataschi*. Me, Jack! Lieutenant *Benshi* (a.k.a. Student Yamaguchi Yoshinori, a.k.a. Gooch!).

Can you not dig big ironies inherent, Jack? I mean, *Mikado's hanko* signature seal warrant in hand (instanter response thereto from *honcho budo*-type factotums upon flashing same), I hop-skip about Southern Seas Theater of Operations as military transports allow (sea surface and also air!), lens actualities as occasioned by advance of Yank-led allied forces driving to unconditional victory, than which progress and process is lengthy and problematic via resistances of thousand-stitch belt (to the death, Jack, *kirijini*, sword in hand!) *issen gorin* led by *budo samurai*-spirit (in mode of legendary forty-seven *ronin*, reet?) *honcho* officers.

Than which is not to dwell upon morbidities, Jack—as follows jump-cut style:

Peleliu, Jack—Battle of Bloody Nose Ridge debacle defeat, than which disaster is simultaneous with news of demise of *honcho* Admiral Yamamoto Takagi (architect of glorious long-past triumph at *Pearu Halbol*, reet?). Aforesaid national hero of *Dai Nippon* dies in air whilst on recon flight over Rabaul Imperial Navy headquarters—hand that pushed button what activated wing-mounted rapid-fires unknown, though suspicions point to Yank air aces Major Richard (a.k.a. Bing) Bong (forty kills!) or possible also Major Thomas (a.k.a. Tommy) McGuire, Jr. (thirty-eight kills!), latter of which awesome aviational duo perishes over Philippines hereafter, reet?

Than which segues (natch!) to circa October '44, Battle of Leyte Gulf, than which debacle defeat initiates anticipated return of boastful braggart (man of his word, Jack!) $50,000 General (a.k.a. Dugout Doug!) *Makassar*—said *Makassar-san* did publish promise via inscribed matchbook covers and also ciggie smoke packs dropped by air, latter which is muchprized by Imperial Army *issen gorin* as superior (Lucky Strike, Old Gold, call for Phillip Morris!) to *senso*-rationed *Nihonjin* smokes. Howsomever, Operation *Sho Go*, how we say, Operation Victory Defense of Philippine Conquest (long-past, circa '42) is (natch!) doomed to fail (witness fall of Manila, evacuation in hastes of 14th Imperial Hq. from fabled Malacanang Palace, circa February 1945), reet?

So goes *Sho Go*, Jack! Much actualities footage in film cans, dispatched with retreating 14th staff to Home Islands for subsequent editing and also dubbing.

Than which is not to fail to mention notorious infamous famed Divine Wind fiasco farce—how we say, *kamikaze*: all lives to the fatherland shtick, reet? As follows:

Cut to: October 1944—how we say, *tsukimi* time of viewing swollen fat harvest moons, reet? Sample segment (script fabricated from unedited *eiga* flic actualities footages), as follows:

Open: cover shot, slow pan, Kyushu or northern Ryukus airstrip; zoom to long shot, row of Imperial Navy aircrafts (Val dive bombers, Zekes, Zeros, Bettys, assorted single-engine pre-*senso* scout and recon planes), than which is to say—hasty assemblage motley air flotilla gathered in Home Islands from amongst remainder of once-vaunted Yank-decimated aviational forces of *Dai Nippon*, reet?

Music: *Kaigun* March (natch!); super Sunrise Flag flapping in fanengendered air to simulate sea breezes.

Voice-over: *honcho* Admiral Takijuio Onishi (inspired author of Imperial Navy Divine Wind Special Attack Unit—*kamikaze*, Jack!):

Just as, in ancient times, *Ameratasu* sent a terrible storm to sink and drown the armada dispatched against the Chrysanthemum Throne by the Mongol barbarians, so, in the name of the *Mikado*, do we unleash the flower of our gallant youth to destroy the vessels of the barbarian *Amerikajin* who sail toward our sacred shores! We salute the glorious young men of *Dai Nippon* who step forward eagerly to offer their lives in willing sacrifice for the *Mikado! Tenno Heika Banzai!*

Music: fade out *Kaigun* Navy March.

Cut to: slow pan, full shot, ranks of Imperial Navy Aviation School, class of October 1944—flight suits and cloth helmets (straps adangle to suggest casual indifferences to solemn *hara* belly tensions).

Voice-over: class of October '44 choral rendition, a cappella, of class song (author unknown!), *Doki No Sakura*—how we say, Jack: We Are the Class of Cherry Blossoms!:

We fall from the branch
As though in autumn's chill wind,
But our end brings honor and glory
To our families' names and *kami*!
Happily our bones and flesh mingle
With the enemy dead in their ships beneath the sea;
We are the cherry blossoms
Who destroy the *Amerikajin*
On whom we descend,
Smiling and laughing as our spirits
Join our fallen comrades in triumph
At the Yasukuni Shrine,
Where we live forever!

Cut to: extreme close-up, class roster, very slow pan down list (audience enabled to read names: Hideyoshi Takako, Aizawa Hirota, Fukuda Nonaka, et alia); freeze frame midst of roster, follow with ink brush passed hand to hand as grads signify volunteer status via inscribing circle above name—triangle signifies otherhow (about which more below, Jack!).

Cut to: bust shot, four, five, maybe half-dozen volunteers donning *hachimaki* headbands (hold long enough to enable audience to read *kanji* calligraphy: One Plane, One Enemy Warship!; My Life for the Mikado!; I Bring Death to the Amerikajin Sailors!; Mother, Father, I Will Rejoin You in the Eyes of Ameratasu! etcetera blah blah).

Cut to: half-dozen (dozen?) volunteer grads at work on small field tables and *tatami* mats in field tent, ink pots, brushes, rice-paper scrolls, composing farewell *haiku* to post to next of kin.

Cut to: long rank of grad volunteers, attired in full flight garb, lifting small ceremonial cups of *sake* in departing toasts to *Mikado*.

Voice-over: choral class of October, circa '44, cheer: *Tenno Heika Banzai!*

Jump cuts: row of parked aircrafts (as established in prior cover shot)—

ground crew *issen gorin* scramble to remove chocks, spin props, checking undercarriages for secure attachment of 500-pounders—volunteer grad pilots stepping up on wings, seated in cockpits, sliding canopies shut—interior close-up of cockpit—stripped instrument panel.

Cut to: full shot, one plane after another accelerates down airstrip, takes off; track with camera until attack formation disappears into sky's vastness vista over coast (Kyushu or northern Ryukus, reet?).

Cut to: assembled ground crew *issen gorin* led by *budo* officer in command, hands raised, lowered, raised in ceaseless unmitigated enthusiasms of choral cheers.

Voice-over: *Banzai! Banzai! Banzai!* etcetera blah.

Cut to: aforesaid abovementioned Sunrise Flag aflap in fan-engendered sea breezes.

Music: *Kaigun* March (muted!).

Voice-over: *honcho* Admiral Takijuio Onishi—inspired author of Imperial Navy Divine Wind Special Attack Unit (*kamikaze*, Jack!):

> So invincible is the fervor of the Class of Cherry Blossoms that fully one half of the despicable *Amerikajin* Task Force Number 58 has been destroyed or disabled by their heroic, sacrificial attacks in but one month's time! Let none, thus, among the Hundred Millions dare to despair, or to doubt the inevitable victory of *Dai Nippon* which *Amera-tasu* has decreed will fall to us as surely as the blossom falls from the bough upon the advent of *tsukimi*!

Fade out, reet?

"Lieutenant Who-Calls-Himself-*Benshi*," says *budo* Imperial Navy officer in command (circa October '44, Kyushu or northern Ryukus airstrip, reet?), "I think it would be well if you were to accompany a formation of our Cherry Blossoms; an aircraft can be found with fuel sufficient for you to fly at their side and make your *eiga* of their attack upon the *Amerikajin* vessels and return you here."

"Ix-nay," I say, and, "Put me down for triangle signification, reet?" And, "What if them Yank swabbie gunners mistooked *wataschi* for one of your Cherry Blossom grads? What happens to big *eiga* flic docudrama if you loses producer-director-scriptwriter-cinematographer, huh, Jack?"

"And is your *eiga* more important than our valiant Cherry Blossoms, Lieutenant-Who-Calls-Himself-*Benshi*?" queries *budo* Imperial Navy officer in command.

"Reet!" I say, and, "Damn bet you!" and, "Want to gander again at *Mikado's hanko* signature seal warrant, Jack?"

Than which is, how we say, a wrap, reet?

Nippon Maketa: Japan defeated, reet?

Witness: *Ogasawara*—how we say, Sulfur Island (circa February and also March 1945, reet?). Iwo Jima (as in sands thereof), Jack!

Honcho budo officer in command Kuribayashi Tadanichi (last message received via radiogram therefrom): "I will die here." Than which he did. Aforesaid *honcho budo* Kuribayashi Tadanichi, along with (natch!) *issen gorin* and fellow *budo* officer-types terminated by Yank Marine assault force employing to said effect two (count them, two!) tons of explosive explosives per *Nihonjin* defender.

Nippon Maketa.

Witness: Okinawa (circa April to and through June 1945, reet?)—100,000 *issen gorin* and *budo* officer-types expire, not to fail to mention loss of 7,000 plus *Nihonjin* aircrafts (final last operational air forces available at disposal of Ichigaya Heights *honcho* bureacratic tacticians).

Honcho General Adashi (*budo* officer in command, reet?): "My officers and men all followed my orders in silence without grumbling, and when exhausted they succumbed to death with the grace of flowers falling in the wind. I then made up my mind not to set foot on my country's soil again, but to remain as a clod of earth in the Southern Seas Theater with my 100,000 officers and men, even if a time were to come when I would be able to return to *Dai Nippon* in triumph."

Than which he did not (return!), Jack!

Nippon Maketa.

Not to fail to mention once more oft-mentioned *yake tsuchi jidai* Burned Earth Period, reet, Jack? Circa February '45, Yank B-29's *bee nijo koo* now based on Tinian and Saipan airstrips begin intensified round-clock bombing of Home Islands.

Dai Nippon hit parade hit (circa Burned Earth Period):

Why should we fear air raids?
Our big sky is protected with iron defenses!
For young and old, it is time to stand up!
We are blessed with the honor of defending the homeland!
Come against us, enemy planes!
Come many times!

Nine of March, 19 and 45: Big Fire, Jack! Hundred thousanddead in Tokyo Town, rivaling losses of Great Kanto Plain Earthquake of circa '23. Paper houses burn, earth burns, air burns, Jack! All got burned up in Big Fire!

Nippon Maketa: Japan defeated, Jack!

Date:
27 July 1945
Year 2605 of The Chrysanthemum Throne

To:
Lieutenant *Benshi*
Southern Seas Theater of Operations

From:
The *Mikado*
Imperial Household
Hayama
Sogami Bay
Dai Nippon

The *Mikado* causes the following communication to be inscribed and dispatched to you by the most rapid available means:

Lieutenant *Benshi*:

Doubtless word has reached even the most remote corners of the Southern Seas Theater of hostilities (now, alas, not so remote as once they were!) of the horrifying suffering which has been visited upon my loyal Hundred Millions since the intensification of the enemy's daily efforts to destroy *Dai Nippon* from the air above us. I will not clutter this epistle with needless detail, for even to contemplate the scope of the pain and death we experience makes my *hara* belly heavy with grief—let it suffice for me to say that you would not recognize your native city were you to return here, Lieutenant *Benshi*!

Only the confines of my Imperial Palace and grounds appear immune, at least for the present, from the depredations of the merciless *Amerika-jin* raiders (save for an occasional misdirected fire-bomb missile which falls into the imperial gardens or orchards, burning even the innocent blossoms and tender fruit buds to cinders and ashes!). For this reason, I remain at Hayama, where I continue to enjoy my passion for ichthyology.

I cause this epistle to be inscribed and sent to you to request that, in the name of *Ameratasu* and the Hundred Millions, you return at once to *Dai Nippon*, but not to the environs of Tokyo or Yokohama, which are now unsafe to serve as sites for the monumentally significant task you perform at my request.

Rather, having consulted with various of my personal military advisors, and with the appropriate authorities at Ichigaya Heights, I have identified a locale where you may repair in relative security to continue your great work—I am assured you will not be molested where I intend you should relocate, for, like our ancient city of Kyoto, the *Amerikajin* appear to have determined to spare this place I name, doubtless because they mean to preserve it as a treasure to pillage when they launch their invasion of *Dai Nippon*.

Thus it is, Lieutenant *Benshi*, that I request you employ the imperial warrant I have bestowed upon you to obtain immediate transport to the city of Hiroshima, where facilities for the continued progress of your work will be waiting in readiness for your arrival. Once established there, please communicate with me so that I may know the status of your project and so that I may continue my efforts to assure you receive all possible and necessary assitance, as my own activities as an ichthyologist permit.

280

By the *hanko* seal of the *Mikado*.

Tenno Heika Banzai!

Cut to: circa 6 of August, 1945, reet? Hiroshima City, Jack! Got burned up in a big fire. How we say: *Pikadon* — boom flash of atomics bomb (how you say: Little Boy, missile dropped from *bee nijo koo Enola Gay*, flying from off Tinian airstrip). *Pikadon*: big fire boom flash burns up 200,000 of Hundred Millions, one fell swoop, reet? Circa 6 of August, 19 and 45 — 8:15 antemeridian o'clock, reet? *Nippon Maketa*. Dig:

Date:
7 August 1945

To:
Mikado (personal!)
Imperial Household
Hayama
Sogami Bay
Dai Nippon

From:
Lieutenant *Benshi*
Hiroshima City (what's left from it, reet?) Environ
Dai Nippon

Celestial Divinity Personage:

I, Lieutenant *Benshi*, reporting direct to you as per previously received instruction, do harbor but faint hopes and wishes fond locally disrupted communication facilities suffice to transmit this my epistle, and do beg your royal indulgences of sad news it is *wataschi's giri* duty to impart. . . .

Circa 6 of August, '45, reet? Environ of Kabe (satellite suburb from Hiroshima City): I say (to sleepy taxi jock Hattori Ichizo): "Dig, Jack, I is on *Mikado's* business, reet? Do I gots to flash flourish you imperial *hanko* signature seal warrant to get indivisible attentions and also cooperations? Come on, man, run me into Hiroshima. I'll see to it you gets voucher for twice going rate of fare, reet?"

Says he (sleepy-eye taxi jock Hattori Ichizo, roused in wee predawn slumber hours by *wataschi* — confabulation occuring in dark's darkness of aforesaid personage's humble paper abode domicile): "*Sensei* lieutenant of the Imperial Army — "

"Call me *Benshi*, reet?"

" — it is not in my power to convey you into the city until dawn's light emerges from the east! The *kempei-tai* forbid civilian vehicles on public streets until the day's light is fully upon us. Be reasonable, *sensei* lieutenant of the Imperial Army!" says sleepy-eye taxi jock Hattori Ichizo, and, "I am not able to read, and so your paper you wave in front of my eyes means nothing to me, *sensei* lieutenant! Please allow me to go back to sleep. Come back in the morning after I have consumed my meager breakfast, and I shall with delight and enthusiasm convey you to your destination in Hiro-shima."

"Jack," I tell him, "does I not make it clear how urgent it be I gets to town and start in on screening rushes I gots waiting on me all locked down dry and also tight in cans in studio *Mikado* hisself done provided to purpose? Did I not tell you I is just back from extended tour at great personal risk of entire Southern Seas Theater of *senso*? If you can't read *kanji*, does you mean to stand there in skivvies and say you don't not recognize chrysanthemum *monsho* crest nor crane logo neither one?"

"*Sensei* lieutenant of the Imperial Army Who-Calls-Himself-*Benshi*," says he, "I am a poor man who neither reads nor writes. I chauffeur a taxicab for which I am not even granted sufficient fuel coupons by the military authorities in these troubled times. I honor you for your gallant service to *Dai Nippon* in the Southern Seas, Lieutenant Who-Calls-Him-self-*Benshi*, but also beg to inform you that I also have sacrificed both my sons and also a daughter to the cause of the triumph of *hakko ichui*. My eldest son succumbed to an exotic fever contracted while serving with the Kwantung Army in distant China, and the younger, who rejoiced when his *aka gami* red letter came from the *Mikado*, because he would emulate the *budo* life of a soldier his older brother had chosen, was killed in 1941 by the barbarian *Igirisujin* far to the south of us in the place called Singapore, and I delivered their boxed ashes to their mother myself, in my taxicab, from Kobe. My only daughter was so enthralled by the music of The Three Human Bombs that she sailed away on a ship as a *moga* comfort woman. This vessel was never seen again. Doubtless her bones rest on the ocean's floor!"

"Orry-say, Hattori *Ichizo-san*," I mumble.

"So is it not only just that an old, poor, illiterate and also childless taxicab chauffeur should be permitted to slumber through the black night when only our *kami* keep watch? Is it just that I should be roused from my *futon* pallet by a lieutenant of the Imperial Army who calls himself *Benshi* and waves a mysterious scroll and demands immediate and also illegal transport into the city?"

"Reet," I say, and, "*Mikado's* throne been doing okay for two thousand six hundred and also five years. Big *eiga* flic docudrama chronicle of end thereof can wait yet one more day without it melts. Go back to bed, *Ichizo-san*, I'll, like, come back when it's morn, reet?"

"Not prior to eight o'clock, please, Lieutenant Who-Calls-Himself-*Benshi*," says sleepy-eye taxi jock Hattori Ichizo (Kabe, suburb environ of Hiroshima City).

"Reet. Can I leave my *katana* longsword here with you till then? It's enough I gots to schlepp my haversack and this big Stewart Warner 16-millimeter camera, reet?"

Big (not to fail to mention also blatant) irony thereof, Jack! As how, due to fate's fickle digit confabulation confrontation with aforesaid Hattori Ichizo, *wataschi* spends early predawn wee hours of 6 of August, circa '45, twiddling opposable thumbs in surburban Kabe environ, hence on scene at safe (har!) distance (about to enter taxi chauffeured by aforesaid *Hattori-san*) at precise *ma's* historical cataclysmic moment (8:15 antemeridian) of *pikadon* — how we say, big fire flash boom, reet?

Might could like have been, like, purchased farm, sold ranch, kicked pail for *wataschi*, reet? Ironics of *do* path of life and times. Lose some, win some, Jack. Also, live and do not learn! Dig:

> *Mikado*, sad to say, entire *eiga* flic studio generously afforded on-site in Hiroshima City center is gone, reet? Talk about your cinders and ashes, *Mikado*! Poof, reet? *Pikadon*, big fire boom flash done burned it all up! Docudrama *eiga* film canisters gone; studio facilities gone; varied anonymous factotum staff (amongst 200,000, in turn amongst Hundred Millions) gone; Hiroshima City gone. Got burned up in Big Fire *pikadon* yesterday, *Mikado*! Approximate *ma* momoment of cataclysmic *yoin* resonances were quarter past eight (antemeridian). All gone, *hakko ichui* footages along with more recent *Nippon Maketa* actualities lensed at great personal risks on location in Southern Seas Theater of Operations, reet?

I think (circa 6 of August, '45, whilst perambulating *sanpo* shank's mare style amongst cinders and ashes — formerly Hiroshima City):

All gone, Jack! Got burned up in Big Fires. Ironics twists of *do* path of life, contemplated in *ma* day-long occasion for introspective-style reflections upon surroundings (cinders and ashes, Jack!). I did think:

Family photo albums (Student Yamaguchi Yoshinori, *Papa-san, Mama-san*, Sis *Iko-san*, Ueno Park, Native Land Loving School, stripe up trouser leg, chevron on sleeve, Moe Berg and also peer Yank American League *besuboru* visiting barnstormer athletes of renown — circa '35, reet? — audience with *Mikado* (har!) in company thereof, shot at bluebird brass ring success career shtick via grant-supports *yen* granted by Imperial Ministry of Education (*kempei* phony-baloney secret police front facade, Jack!) towards higher-education endeavors stateside — all gone, Jack! Got burned up in fire, Tokyo Town, circa *hanami*, 1942, reet?

I did think: Gooch! Matriculant in good standing (Phi Kappa Phi, Phi Eta Sigma, Sigma Tau Delta), Oklahoma Agricultural & Mechanical College, Stillwater Town, county of Payne, U. S. of A., circa '36 to '40 — Go, Pokes! Go, Punchers! Ride 'Em, Cowboys! Mighty Mouse Yukon Strongboy Stevie Keller — Delta Sigma Kappa ever-loyal bros we! Mr. Sato Isao (Japan–America Friendship Society — har!), *kempei* counterintelligence clandestine operative, greenbacks moola mazuma bestowed in plain brown envelope beneath blackjack oak, banks of Cimarron, reet? Oh, happy Gooch! Miss Clara ("Petty Girl") Sterk—ah, Jack, heartbroke was I for *kokoru* love unrequited! *Redskin* edition of 1940, got burned up in fire aboard U.S.S. *Oklahoma*, circa December 7, 1941. Collegiate life and times lifestyle interval in *do* path, Jack—all burned up in a fire, reet? Gone, Jack. I am, how we say, *munako* sudden orphan child of no name.

I think (amidst cinders and ashes of former Hiroshima City, reet?): *hakko ichui* (cinematic *eiga* docudrama, bring eight corners of world under benevolent roof of *Dai Nippon*—har!), gone. Got burned up in Big Fire *pikadon* boom flash! *Eiga* actuality docudrama treatment of glorious *Pearu Halbol* triumph (commissioned by ex-*honcho* former Premier-General Tojo "The Razor" Hideki), gone, Jack! Surrender of vanquished Yank defenders in vain of Corregidor rock fortress (Skinny Wainwright, Strongboy Stevie!), glorious victory of Homma-led 14th Imperial—gone, Jack. Burned up in Big Fire.

On-site actualities footages (awaiting editing and also dubbing, reet?): Guadalcanal (a.k.a. Island of Death!), Bismarck Sea, Bougainville (insufficiency of *takotsubo* octopus trap tactic, than which failure leads to thousand-stitch belt fight to death *kirijini budo* ethos), Betio Atoll (seventeen *issen gorin* survivors, Jack!), Kwajalein, Guam, Saipan (Marpi Point *Nihonjin* Hundred Millions civilian suicides leap!), etcetera blah. *Eiga* footages in can all burned up in Big Fire!

Peleliu, Philippine Sea (Great Marianas Turkey Shoot!), Leyte Gulf (so goes *Sho Go*, Jack!), Luzon, fall of Manila (hasty evac of Malacanang Palace 14th Imperial Hq., reet?), *Ogasawara* Sulfur Island (Iwo Jima, Jack!)—*Nippon Maketa*! All burned up in big *pikadon* flash boom fires, reet?

Live and do not learn, reet? What's do I, Lieutenant *Benshi*, know, Jack?

> *Mikado*: doubtless you gots all the inside info poop scoop on *pikadon* flash boom, so so sad to say I add to your celestial concerns with bad news of total destruction of both *hakko ichui* (to include all but final edit of feature-length *Down with the Stars & Stripes*, than which *eiga* flic were produced on spec for ex-*honcho* former Premier-General Tojo), and also *Nippon Maketa* actualities footages dispatched from varied on-location locations in Southern Seas Theater.

> *Mikado*: alls I, Lieutenant *Benshi*, gots to show for *eiga* efforts unceasing since circa '41 (good old days, reet, *Mikado*?) is film currently in camera magazine (pre-*senso Amerikajin* Stewart Warner, excellent long range focus lensing capacities), said footage garnered whilst *wataschi* did perambulate *sanpo*-style amidst cinders and ashes (formerly Hiroshima City) during early-morn daylight hours of 6 August (but yesterday, *Mikado*!) in company of sterling character taxi jock personage Hattori Ichizo in vain search for studio facilities, than which, I regrets to report, I learn were located close by Aioi Bridge, than which formerly (prior to *pikadon*, natch!) did span Ohta River—than which I is informed by *kempei-tai* authorities on scene was doubtless target of missile dropped direct thereon by sole Yank *bee nijo koo* observed overhead immediately preceding *pikadon* conflagration, reet?

Anyhoo, *Mikado*, does you gots any instructions for *wataschi* Lieutenant *Benshi*? Any interest in Imperial Household (not to fail to mention amongst Ichigaya Heights *budo* strategy tacticians!) in cinders-and-ashes footages residing undeveloped in trusty Stewart Warner?

Please to advise, *Mikado!*

Cut to: long shot, Hiroshima City environ, milieu established via slow pan from Kabe suburban hillside vantage (in company of taxi jock Mr. Hattori Ichizo, reet?).

Says he: "What was that light which still pains my eyes, Lieutenant Who-Calls-Himself-*Benshi*? Where is Hiroshima City? Is it the end of the world, Lieutenant-Who-Calls-Himself *Benshi*? Oh, look, within the smoke that covers Hiroshima I see fires burning everywhere! Is it an earthquake, Lieutenant-Who-Calls-Himself-*Benshi*? Oh, see the fires everywhere within the smoke!"

I say: "Cool it, *Hattori-san*!" and, "Reet, big fire!" and, "Might could be earthquake, *Hattori-san*, not unlike like unto Great Kanto Plain shocker than which I remembers from childhood days long bygone, circa 'twenty-three. Or might could be fire storm like unto Yank incendiary raid on Tokyo Town last March."

"Lieutenant Who-Calls-Himself-*Benshi*," says he, "if it is the end of the world, why are you and I not harmed? Oh, do you not see the fire everywhere!"

"Reet," I say, lens slow-pan long shot of Hiroshima City environ vista (fires, smoke pall rendering morn's light not unlike like unto eventide!), and, "Did you note sole solitary *Amerikajin* aircraft pass overhead in direction of city center just prior to confrontation of excrement with fan, *Hattori-san*?"

"It is like the fires of hell which the Christian missionaries told me of when I was a boy!" says he, and, "Oh, it may be that they told the truth, though I did not believe them then! Perhaps we are dead and have been relegated to perdition for our sins! Yet, Lieutenant-Who-Calls-Himself-*Benshi*, if this were so, would we not feel great bodily pain, or is the pain inflicted on those in the Christian hell only this terrible vision before us of what was once the city of Hiroshima?"

"Search me, *Hattori-san*," I tell him, and, "Let's us stroll *sanpo* shank's mare down there and see what we can see, lens some actualities footages, reet?"

Mikado: please to advise *wataschi* Lieutenant *Benshi* as to further tasks if any you desire I undertake, reet? I mean, like, all *eiga* flic footages (except save for undeveloped reel in camera magazine, ashes-and-cinders actualities lensed on scene yesterday) gone, *Mikado*! Burned up in Big Fire *pikadon* boom flash—along with Hiroshima City and (natch!) 200,000 some odd from amongst Hundred Millions—how many left of original number these days? Please advise, *Mikado*!

Cut to: full shot, old woman—how we say, *Oba-san*. Said personage approaches camera, attired in charred old-style *kimono*, schlepping pre-*senso* portable sewing machine like unto baby infant cradled in arms, bare feets blistered from treading upon still-hot cinders and ashes of former byways of Hiroshima City, reet? Old woman *Oba-san* speaks to camera frame, as follows:

"Do not go farther into the city, *sensei* gentlemen," says she, "for the city is no more. I alone have been spared. Do not go farther, gentlemen, or you will surely perish in the flames that rage everywhere, as did all who lived in my house and in all the houses on the street that is no more. Go back to safety, *sensei* gentlemen!"

"*Oba-san*," says taxi jock Hattori Ichizo, "we come from the hills of Kabe. Tell us what happened, *Oba-san*!"

Says she (*Oba-san* old woman, bare feets blistered, charred *kimono*, pre-*senso* portable sewing machine cradled baby-infant style in arms): "I sat upon my *tatami* in my house to sew, for I must earn money to feed myself and my daughters-in-law and my grandchildren because the *senso* we fight against the barbarian *gaijin* to achieve the glorious triumph of *hakko ichui* has taken my sons and my oldest grandson to be *issen gorin* warriors far away over the seas to the south. I had just begun to sew a cloth to sell in the open market held each day at the Yokogawa Railroad Station, and then there was a sudden light and a loud noise, and my house and my daughters-in-law and my small grandchildren were burning. It was as if I had slept and awakened to find all save myself dead in the fire, and even my *kimono* was burning, so I took my sewing machine up—for even if all my family is now joined with our ancestral *kami*, still I must feed myself, and without this machine I have no way to buy food save to beg, which is dishonorable. I walked here, and there is no more Hiroshima, for all I have seen since I began to walk are the fires that burn all the houses and burn the bodies of the dead and dying—go away from this place, *sensei* gentlemen, or you will also perish in the fires!"

"*Oba-san*," queries Hattori Ichizo, "was it an earthquake?"

"*Oba-san*," I say, "tell me if you heard, like, an airplane go over about the time light got turned on, reet?"

> *Mikado*: is we now amidst context of final last days of *Nippon Maketa* cataclysm? Any word from Ichigaya Heights? Is Yanks coming ashore on Home Islands even as I scribble this? Is end of *Nihon* (not to fail to mention 2,605 years venerable Chrysanthemum Throne) in offing instanter? Please advise, *Mikado*! I, Lieutenant *Benshi*, await your instructions, reet?

Cut to: medium shot, quick cuts, platoon of *issen gorin* yardbird dogface cannon-fodder soldiers of Imperial Army, seated on muddy bank of Ohta River—intercut close-ups of respective visages revealing countenances swollen with red-gold burns, eyes melted away, empty red-black sockets, etcetera blah.

First *issen gorin*: "Who are you that approaches us? What noise is that like the flutter of a bird's wings you make? Speak! Tell us what has happened, for we are blinded and cannot see!"

Hattori Ichizo: "Oh! My *hara* belly churns with torment! Look at their faces, Lieutenant-Who-Calls-Himself-*Benshi*! They have no eyes! Oh, see how the flesh is burned upon their hands and faces! Ah, let us go away! It is more than I am able to look upon, Lieutenant-Who-Calls-Himself-*Benshi*!"

Second *issen gorin*: "Can you give us water to drink, whoever you are? Please answer my comrade's question, what is the noise I hear? Give us water, please! I had water in my canteen, but I drank it all and still I thirst! Take my canteen, please, whoever you are, and fill it in the river. Is there still water in the Ohta? So intense was the heat I felt that I fear the river is dried up and I shall never find water to drink!"

"I will fetch water for you," says taxi jock Hattori Ichizo, and, "Lieutenant-Who-Calls-Himself-*Benshi*, take a canteen from the belt of another of these poor wretches and come with me to the river's edge so that we may at least give them a refreshing drink in their misery!"

Second *issen gorin*: "My comrades and I thank you, stranger, and I will say a prayer to my *kami* for your kindness in the morning if I am still alive when morning comes again."

Third *issen gorin*: "Is it not still morning? I remember it was morning, and after the *atsumari* muster and *tenko* call of the roll and *banko* count-off, our platoon marched from the barracks to join the schoolgirls impressed to clear firebreaks among the paper houses so that Hiroshima City might not burn as Tokyo did when the *Amerikajin* rained fire down upon that city from the sky last spring. Is it still morning, stranger, or is this perhaps a bad dream I dream while still asleep on the *futon* in my barracks? Tell me, stranger, what hour of the day or night is this?"

"Please come, Lieutenant-Who-Calls-Himself-*Benshi*, help me to bring water from the river! I cannot stay and look upon these men! Why do you not come away and help me, Lieutenant-Who-Calls-Himself-*Benshi*?"

Fourth *issen gorin*: "Stranger, when you have given us water to drink, will you then lead us back to our barracks? We must report to an officer. Our officer was with us when we marched out to work with the schoolgirls to make firebreaks, but he does not answer when we call out his name, so he must have gone away to seek help for us, or perhaps he was killed when the great heat and fire came to blind and burn us."

Second *issen gorin*: "Will you not tell us what noise that is in our ears? We have no eyes to see, but we hear with our burned ears yet!"

Mr. Hattori Ichizo: "Poor young man," says he, "you hear only what we hear, the crackling of the fires that rage all about us, even to the river's edge, and the cries of those in pain, like yourself, poor young soldiers of the Imperial Army!"

I say: "Go schlepp the man some river waters, *Hattori-san*, I'm busy lensing, reet?" and, "Ain't no barracks left to lead you to, Jack! Ain't squat left. Zip. Zilch. Goose eggs, reet? Barracks, *honcho budo* officer types, Hiroshima City—gone, Jack! Burning up even as I palaver, Big Fire ubiquitous," and, "What's you hearing is drive gear from Stewart Warner camera, pre-*senso harukai* Yank import manufacture, Jack, film running on sprocket gears in magazine, making *eiga* flic actualities if minimalist available light due to smoke and also dust if air's aura don't put kibosh thereon, reet?"

> *Mikado*: please to forgive ramble semicoherence of this my missive. Like, all facilities in Hiroshima City (cinders and ashes!) in confused chaos condition. Without first highest priority status afforded Lieutenant *Benshi* via your *hanko* warrant, no chance to dispatch radiograms—even now, *Mikado, budo kempei-tai honcho* factotums on scene in command berate *wataschi* for clogging emergencies radio channels, reet? Hard to say if incoming epistles might could make it through. Howsomever, I is content to stand by, await word from Imperial Household—is you still studying fishes at Hayama resort domicile?—please advise instanter, *Mikado*!

Says he (Hattori Ichizo, taxi jock personage, reet?): "I will go no farther with you, Lieutenant-Who-Calls-Himself *Benshi*. I am too old, my *hara* belly is too sick to wander in this smoldering rubble and see more of what we have seen! Goodbye, Lieutenant-Who-Calls-Himself-*Benshi*. I wish you good fortune in whatever purpose you intend with the *eiga* pictures you make of this horror! Oh, I think it may be the end of the world, as the Christian missionaries foretold!"

"Suit yourself, *Hattori-san*," and, "Keep coolth, reet?" and, "Hey, wait a sec! Hold on, *Hattori-san*! Go over there by that wall. There. See that, like, black shadow on the bricks? Like, point at it whilst I frame you center-frame."

"What is it?" queries Mr. Hattori Ichizo. "Why do you wish to make an *eiga* picture of this? Have you not already enough pictures of the fires and broken walls and corpses strewn in the streets and alleys of Hiroshima?"

"Gander close, *Hattori-san*. Don't you recognize the shape? That's a silhouette, Jack! Somebody, one amongst Hundred Millions, was standing there, Jack, silhouette gots burned into brick wall when light came on, fired in bricks by fire flash boom, reet?"

"Ah!" screams taxi jock Mr. Hattori Ichizo, waves arms at camera—I cease lensing instanter—runs away, hop-skip stride to avoid stepping in hot rubbles cinders and ashes with *geta* clogs. Howsomever strictly *daijubo* no sweat as how I done already gots shot I sought, reet, Jack?

> *Mikado*: what's more to say? Burned up in Big Fire, reet? All gone. Than which is not to say countless survivors, folks lucky (not unlike like

unto *wataschi*!) to live in suburban Kabe, Koi, Noboricho, Nagatsuka, and also Ushida environs. Than which is also not to fail to mention numerous survivors even in center-city locales, some close by Aioi Bridge, than which is reputed by reliable *kempei-tai* sources I consult to have been target of sole solitary Yank *bee nijo koo*. *Mikado*: I ask, to what ends, reet? I mean, like, not the end of the world, reet? Query, *Mikado*, is: why?

Cut to: city center, cinders and ashes (Hiroshima, Jack!), circa 6 of August, 1945. Red Cross Hospital (still standing, not unlike like unto dome of Industrial Exhibition Hall, ground zero, reet?) — hospital grounds littered wall-to-wall with litters bearing dead, dying, burned and broken, etcetera blah.

Long shot: white-coat-clad medicos and nurses move amongst aforesaid casualties to dispense water, coat burns with salves, wrap open wounds. *Mise-en-scene* is dim lit resultant from rubble dust residue suspended in atmosphere, same thickened by smoke haze derived from continuance of fires blazing ubiquitous (*kempei-tai honchos* already on job, organizing bucket brigades to douse embers), remote late morn's sun illumination augmented adequate to allow lensing by aforesaid conflagrations, reet? Than which is not to fail to mention (impossible to catch on film, Jack!) pervasive stink-stench of burned fleshes, singed hair assaulting olfactories (medicos, nurses, impressed civilians, Imperial Army garrison *issen gorin* fatigue squads all armor selves against same via hankies and *furoshiki* clothes tied across mouth and also schnozzes) — circa 6 of August, '45. Big *pikadon* fire boom-flash aftermaths, Jack.

"Hey, Doc," I say to white-coat-clad personage who kneels to hold shallow pan of water to scorched lips of litter-recumbent civilian (baby blues swole shut by facial searing), "is this the Red Cross Hospital? I'm looking for Imperial Army *eiga* flic studio, new facility established most recent by Imperial Rescript. Can you, like, give me directions thereto?"

Says he: "I am not a doctor. I am as yet only a student of the medical arts, but you see I do what I can to ease this suffering. What are you, lieutenant of the Imperial Army, that you make your way aimlessly among the litters bearing your dead and dying countrymen? Why do you take pictures? Throw away your camera, lieutenant, and do what you can to help us!"

Can you dig it, Jack? White-coat-clad student medico is, how you say, touch Section 8, semispaced by reason of shock state induced by vision of hordes of terminal injured, complicated, doubtless, by frustration of inability to afford succor, reet? Dig:

"Like to lend hand, Jack. But, like, I is on the *Mikado's* business here, reet? Lensing *eiga* flic record than which mayhap is *Nippon Maketa* docu-drama actuality, purpose of which is to communicate global-wide suffer-ing and also sacrifice, honor-and-glory shtick, of Hundred Millions, high-est-priority significance, dig? Don't tell anyone I told you, as how mum is word. Now, can you clue me which way to Imperial Army cinematic studio facilities? And, hey, call me *Benshi*, reet?" He (white-coat-clad stu-dent medico, hankie knotted over visage to filter stink-stench) holds pan of water to scorched lips of litter patient, than which who's tongue is too swelled to speak. And do not seem to hear my words, reet?

Says he: "I can do nothing beyond dispense water to the thirsty and apply salve to their burns! Within there are two surgeons who sew torn flesh and amputate crushed limbs, but we have no medicines, for the pharmacy was razed by the explosion! Oh, lieutenant, how is it you are able to witness all this, and not apologize, as I do, for not sharing this suffering? How is it that you do not throw away your camera and do what you can to assist?"

"Orry-say," I tell him, and, "Hey, this is Stewart Warner pre-*senso* Yank manufacture, gifted to me by renown personage whose moniker you might could recognize if I told!" and, "*I wa jinjutsu*, Jack!" — how you say, medicine is the art of compassion, reet? — and, "I done told you, Doc, highest-priority mission on behalf of *Mikado* hisself! Want to gander his personal *hanko* warrant? Hey," I add, "if you can't point me to studio, where's nearest extant military *honcho* authority headquarters? Like, where does I go to send a radiogram to Tokyo Town, Jack?"

"I cannot stand idly and talk to you, lieutenant," says he, and, "Oh, how is it that you and I were spared this fate? I was asleep on my *futon* and woke only when the walls of the student dormitory collapsed about me, crush-ing and killing all my comrades — how is it you do not apologize to these unfortunates who lie at our feet, lieutenant?"

Semispaced Section 8 brain scramble shock state, reet? Finds expression knee-jerk response style in traditionalist *Nipponshikki* embarrassment at inexplicable phenom of good luck doubtless unearned and also unde-served. Dig it, Jack!

"*Do* path ironical twists," I tell him, and, "Don't knock it, reet? Go with flow, Doc! Way cookies crumbles and also mop flop! Hey, look at camera when I call for action, reet?"

"Ah!" says white-coat-clad student medico — addressing scorched-lips-eyes-swelled-shut anonymous personage to which he proffers drinking water in shallow pan — "Forgive me, brother," says he, "for my dishonor-able failure to share your pain! Can you forgive me my lack of injury, brother?" he queries, and, "Drink, brother! Can you not open your lips wide enough to drink? Will your tongue not let you swallow even a drop?"

290

Extreme close-up: shallow pan with water tipped to scorched lips which fail to part, water spills, slides down blistered chin. Fade to black, reet?

Mikado: I wait, trusty Stewart Warner 16-millimeter with exposed film magazine (cinders and ashes!) at hand, ready and willing to depart to wheresomever you decrees. Where to next, *Mikado*? Combat assignment? Wield *katana* longsword in leadership of Hundred Millions remainder, thousand-stitch belt *budo* style versus Yank assault invasion of Home Islands? *Kempei-tai* intelligence interpreter slot (any openings up at Ichigaya Heights, *Mikado*?)? But to say the word, *Mikado*, I'd as leave depart Hiroshima Prefecture environ soonest, reet? As how peculiar effects noted amongst us who got off whole and also sound—to wit: hairs falling out, uncontrollable regurgitations spasms (how we say in *Eigo*, chuck up), high fevers, G.I. Trots, loss of appetites, general *darui* weariness, finger digits bloating with pus, etcetera blah. Anyhoo, *Mikado*, please to advise Lieutenant *Benshi!*

Than which is not to fail to mention ditto Big *pikadon* Flash Boom (a.k.a. Big Boy!), Nagasaki Town, circa 9 of August, 1945, reet, Jack? Than which is to say, not unlike like unto Hiroshima (cinders and ashes!), got burned up in a big fire.

Date:
16 August 1945

To:
Lieutenant *Benshi*
Hiroshima City
Hiroshima Prefecture
Dai Nippon

From:
The *Mikado*
Imperial Household
Imperial Palace
Tokyo
Tokyo Prefecture
Dai Nippon

The *Mikado* orders that these, his exact words, be transcribed and dispatched for your immediate attention:

Lieutenant *Benshi*:

Forgive me, Lieutenant *Benshi*, for my delay in responding to your recent epistle. I confess that your touching personal account of the destruction visited upon the once-beautiful (and innocent!) city of Hiroshima only added to the intense anguish felt by all in my household occasioned by the flow of *kempei-tai* intelligence reports seconded to my attention from Ichigaya Heights. And the horror of Hiroshima, so catastrophic as to seem surely unique, was so soon doubled by the devastation of Nagasaki—oh, Lieutenant *Benshi*, so painful was the prospect that all the cities of *Dai Nippon* would in turn be subjected to this barbarous new weaponry unleashed by the *Amerikajin* that I determined, in concert with many of my closest advisors, to spare the Hundred Millions such further suffering by accepting the Allied peace terms of unconditional surrender!

I hope and trust you will see, as I and my loyal counselors do, Lieutenant *Benshi*, that though *Dai Nippon* has lost much honor by my decision, I have ensured the survival of our race and nation — and hope and trust also that you join me in my vision of a glorious and honorable future in store for the Hundred Millions under the merciful administration of our *Amerikajin* conquerors. Thus it is, I observe, that even the greatest misfortune may bring unanticipated opportunities: from our shameful defeat may yet come untold benefits! Is not the *do* path of all men's lives wondrous in the rich complexity of ironies with which we are so unexpectedly confronted?

I presume, Lieutenant *Benshi*, that you were among those who gathered beside their radios and at the amplifiers mounted in public places throughout the villages and cities of *Dai Nippon* to hear my recorded announcement of surrender but two short days ago? I need not iterate my message to the Hundred Millions urging them to look with hope to the future, and to strive for the honor and glory that so characterize our long history.

Let me only assure you that there were many, fanatic in their *bushido* dedication to fight to the death of all, who sought even to prevent the broadcast of the *Mikado's* Imperial Rescript! I thank *Ameratasu* and my household *kami* they did not succeed, and my *hara* belly is heavy with regret and sadness for the several thousand who have resorted since then to *seppuku* out of a mistaken sense of shame and dishonor for our defeat!

To respond to your repeated concern for your next assignment, Lieutenant *Benshi*, I tell you that I envision no purpose, in light of recent events, to your further service to the Chrysanthemum Throne. Even as I dictate this epistle to you, Lieutenant *Benshi*, arrangements for the peaceful and orderly arrival of the *Amerikajin* conquerors are being negotiated. While I am assured they will be merciful in their deportment toward the Hundred Millions, I am also confident they mean to exercise justice according to their wisdom, and thus there exists the possibility that retribution will be visited upon individuals the *Amerikajin* deem most directly responsible for Allied losses incurred during the just-concluded hostilities.

Given this possibility, and the relative prominence of your activities at *Pearu Halbol* (I am told the *Amerikajin* call this *Nihonjin* victory a "sneak attack" in *Eigo*!) and at Corregidor (I refer to the so-called March of Death which followed upon our triumph), it might be well for you to seek now a surely welcome obscurity. It is possible, for instance, that the *Amerikajin* will feel most wrathful toward those who enjoyed their hospitality prior to hostilities. I can inform you that various individuals active as agents of the *kempei* in the United States prior to the outbreak of *senso* have shed their identities to escape attention in the days to come!

To this prudent end, please consider this epistle your official notification of demobilization. I only wish that I were able to afford you more tangible assistance, but you must know that my own capacities are seriously curtailed now. I take small comfort in the certainty that a young man of your proven ability and initiative will be the equal of any adversity you encounter in the post-*senso* era we all enter.

Thus it is I wish you all good fortune and success in the years ahead, even as I address you for the last time as Lieutenant *Benshi*, and thank you personally, and on behalf of the Hundred Millions you have served in the name of *Ameratasu*, and bid you goodbye fondly.

By the hand and *hanko* seal of the *Mikado*.

Tenno Heika Banzai!

Postscript: My advice to you concerning the undeveloped *eiga* film of the Hiroshima experience — would it not be in the best interest of all if this chapter in our history were forgotten? Destroy your *eiga* film, Lieutenant *Benshi* (if I may address you by this name one additional time?), as the *pikadon* destroyed all the *eiga* archives assembled in that unfortunate city, as you told me your personal photographs and other mementos were destroyed in (so long ago it seems now!) 1942. I hasten to add the above should not be construed as an imperial directive! It may be you could facilitate your situation with the Allied authorities if you were to present them with this *eiga*; it may even be that one day in the inscrutable future we ourselves might desire to include your *eiga* in some archive memorializing the harsh fate of the Hundred Millions; it may even be that, some day far distant in time, you may yourself value it personally as a macabre souvenir of your youth. To conclude, I am not able to advise you!

By the hand and *hanko* seal of the *Mikado*.

Tenno Heika Banzai!

Can you not dig it, Jack? End of global-wide *senso* (WW II, reet?), end of *wataschi* Lieutenant *Benshi*! With both bang and also whimper, reet?

Than which is not to fail to mention final ironics. Than which is, what's do future hold in store for *munako* orphan child of no name (a.k.a. Student Yamaguchi Yoshinori, a.k.a. Gooch, a.k.a. Lieutenant *Benshi*!) — where to go, what's to do, reet?

Cut to: circa 28 of August, 1945, Atsugi Airfield (fifteen miles distant from Yokohama), initial Yank Occupation Force personnel — one Colonel Tench, U.S. Army, in command, arrives in *Dai Nippon*. With him is 150 *Amerikajin* in 16 planes, aforesaid greeted by *Nihonjin* welcome party led by *honcho* Lieutenant-General Arisuye Seizo (all *sumairu* smiles and appropriate deferential kowtow bows, natch!), said delegation followed by (circa 30 of August) $50,000 General Dugout Doug *Makassar*.

Passing note aside: formal surrender staged aboard U.S.S. *Missouri*,

Sagami Bay, circa 2 of September—first days of *tsukimi* moon viewing season, reet, Jack?

Unremarked on scene during ceremonials is *wataschi* as casual unofficial observer, reet? Having doffed (natch!) Imperial Army uniform—how you say, in mufti—and (natch!) *katana* longsword, retaining only Stewart Warner 16-millimeter camera as possible aid in endeavors to come, dig?

To conclude: Hundred Millions (minus *senso* losses of two million *budo* officers and *issen gorin*, not to fail to mention one million feather-merchant civilians!) spared by *Mikado's* decision to fold cards and punt. Which is not to fail to mention accompanying salvage job effected with respect to 2605 years aged Chrysanthemum Throne, reet? Than which is to say: every oscillating richard for his own self ethos clue conveyed to *wataschi* with dramatic emphasis—probable likely key to future endeavors as yet unforeseen. I mean, like, looking out for numeral *ichiban* number one, reet, Jack? As related hereafter following.

Final note (bang and whimper, cinders and ashes!): popular phrase slogan catchword oftenmost heard uttered (tone of profoundest bafflement) by Hundred Millions (minus three!) in era immediately following upon surrender—"Can the *Mikado* have been mistaken all these years?"
To which I do riposte: "Jack, ain't you heard? *Mikado* ain't Celestial Divinity *Mikado* no more! By order of *Makassar-san*! I kid you not!"

Do you not dig crazy ironics thereof, Jack?

4.

Foto Joe Yamaguch

"There's no business like show business!"

Ethel Merman

Says I: "How much space we gots left on my dermis there, *Seijo-san?* Hold mirror aloft so's I can gander, reet?"

Says he (Terada Seijo, tattooist par excellence of Yokohama dockside wharf environ, on exclusive contract retainer—big *yen*, Jack!—to complete *wataschi's* neck-to-thighs backside panorama mural of life and times—full colorations!—same to be gifted by deceased—when appropriate!—to Wantanabe Nautical Museum, reet?): "*Sensei*, I fear the space remaining will scarce suffice to depict, however stylized the rendition, all the years of your rich experience following upon the end of the great *senso* to the present instance!"

Says I (Foto Joe Yamaguch!): "Look again, *Seijo-san!*" and "Value of overindulging self-indulgent gratification of appetites lifestyle, reet? Buns broad as tabletop adequate for *o-cha* tea ceremonial, room to spare, *Seijo-san!* Here, take your mirror back, Jack! Like, hurts me to look upon excessive adipose excess, reet?"

"I fear you are mistaken, *sensei*," says he, "for the years to be encompassed are too many, the memorable events of your public success are of such magnitude as to deserve a far more extensive depiction than can possibly be contained even upon your ample fundament, if you will forgive my so saying, *sensei!*"

"*Daijubo* no sweats, *Seijo-san!*" I tell him, and, "Trick is to render period in question summation-style, reet? How we say in cinematic *eiga* flic world, quick-cut, collage, super shots, swish pans, reet? Trust me, *Seijo-san!*"

"As always, *sensei*," says he, "I defer to the wisdom of your mature judgment."

"Reet!" I say, and, "He who has gold rules, reet?"

I do tell him, Jack: overall scheme theme is, how we say, Jimmu Boom, reet? Miraculous economics recovery of *Nihon* in post-*senso* era, than which is not to fail to mention cultural rejuvenation and nurturing to fruitions of democratic political ethos under benevolent despotic administrative leadership of *Makassar-san* (a.k.a. $50,000 General, a.k.a. Dugout Doug), aforesaid *honcho* personage working out from former insurance conglomerate headquarters Dai Ichi Building, downtown Tokyo Town, reet? Than which enables Hundred Millions — no-longer-sacred presence of *Mikado* still (natch!) ensconced on Chrysanthemum Throne (free of former burdensome Imperial responsibilities to pursue fishes research and writings proclivities, reet?) — to reenter global-wide family of nations as peaceful peace-loving sibling. I is talking Jimmu Boom, Jack!

"Ah, Mr. Yamaguch, how wondrous rich is the life you have enjoyed!" says Terada Seijo.
Obvious deduction to be made therefrom: he do not dig, reet? No sensibilities rendered sensitive to chronicles of ironics (large and small!) I is done enumerated so far, reet?
"Is you done forgot fires large and small I relate to you, Jack? Listen up, *Seijo-san*! We gots the lots to do, time short and shortening, carcinomas ravaging *wataschi's* innermost organs — heart, liver, kidneys, *hara* belly-lining etcetera blah in decline apace, dig? Ready?" I query.
"I shall," says he, "attend your words and make the relevant notations. As before, I shall then return in the limousine you so generously provide at my disposal to my establishment in Yokohama to devise the schema of the comprehensive design so as to impose a coherence of symmetry which will be both faithful to the particulars you impart and reflective of the animating principle they manifest."
"Easy for you to say, Terada!" Dig: he do not dig. Terada Seijo waits, ink, brush, rice-paper scroll at ready, for *wataschi* to speak spiel, reet?

I tell him: render me, how we say, *nawanoren* — how you say, juke joint, gin mill, watering hole, urban roadhouse, hangout dive — render me, Terada Seijo, neon lights lit, down-home shitkicker musics, wall-to-wall *hosutesu moga mama-san* B-gals astride barstools. Render generations faceless and also nameless anonymous post-*senso* Yank *Amerikajin issen gorin* dogface draftee G.I.s on prowl for the night — render me famed (now lost to all but memory's recall due to big fire!) Eta Jima Strip — render me Texas Bar, *Seijo-san*!

"*Sensei*, might you not, with the excellent education you attained as a youth, and later, in the land of the *Amerikajin*, have matriculated at one of the many new universities founded after the great *senso*? With your fluency as a speaker of *Eigo*, you might well have become a great scholar and

298

teacher."

"Words," I tell him, "words in books, on paper, reet? Ever watch how words burn in fires large and small, Jack?"

Render me, I tell him, Eta Jima (formerly Imperial Army of *Dai Nippon*, reet?) Yank training facility. Render new-style Quonset hut barracks, firing ranges, parade grounds, N.C.O. Leadership Academy classrooms, Brigadier General Jeffie Walker, Army of U. S. of A. in command. Render yearbook annual scam (inspiration derived from A & M alma mater *Redskin*, reet?), *genkin* cash grafts off topside rendered beneath table.

"Is you hearing me good, *Seijo-san*?"

"I wonder, *sensei*, that you did not write your memories of the great *senso* to share with our new nation? Was there not, is there not still, a curiosity among the citizenry of *Nihon* concerning the observations and reflections of those, the great politicians and military leaders, who have shared their experience with us? Yet, who among them can be imagined to have seen and done so much, to have journeyed throughout the Southern Seas, to have conversed with so many notable personalities, including even the *Mikado* —"

"He writes about fishes now!" I say, and, "Stuff cork in it and get on with job, Seijo!" I tell him, and, "Past is past, bygones gone, dead and also buried along with three from amongst Hundred Millions."

Render me free-lance life and times lifestyle on the hustle, budding Horatio Alger career-quest shtick financed by sale of Moe Berg's Stewart Warner camera, reet? Render *wataschi* on the bricks wearing out *geta* clogs in search for paying gigs. Render me lensing births and also baptism Shinto ceremonials shtick, graduation rituals, weddings, not failing to mention also funerals, also holidays such as *hatsu mode* first shrine visits of new year, *hari-kuyo* needle masses held by housewifes, *hinamatsuri* doll's festival, *koinobori* Boy's Day (boys flying carp streamers), *tanabata* seventh day of seventh month, etcetera blah blah blah! Render *wataschi's* endeavors unceasing in search of big break, cash-flow trickles, hedged bets and risk-plunges, late-night tourist-class transports schlepping to on-location remote shoot sites, minimalist accounts kept in pocket-size ledger, hand-to-mouth.

"Can you dig it, *Seijo-san*?"

"I wonder, *sensei*, that you have made no effort, now, in the leisure and affluence of your maturity, to renew the acquaintances of your youth?"

"Past is pastness. You didn't hear me first time I masticated cabbage, Terada?"

"What of your comrades and mentors of Native Land Loving School? What of the *besuboru* celebrity Mr. Morris Berg, known also as Moe?

Though he would be of a very advanced age, still he might be alive somewhere in the land of the *Amerikajin* across the ocean. Even though you were orphaned by the demise of all your family, Mr. Yamaguch, still you might enjoy the camaraderie of old friends."

"What I said, Jack, bygones!"

"And what of the once-renowned wrestler Mr. Keller Stevie, and Miss Sterk Clara, who perhaps only failed to requite your love for her because she did not understand the nature of your sentiment? Did the legendary Yukon Strongboy indeed escape to Australia and from thence to his native country across the Pacific?"

"Will you get on with it, Jack!" I say, "Reet, Mighty Mouse Stevie got back to Okie-land, recommenced conjugal domesticity life and times, Miss Clara at his side—sad story that, not unlike like unto all the rest, reet? Come on, *Seijo-san*, we gots to be getting after Jimmu Boom era, reet?"

"And what of the *issen gorin* named Matsunaga who you called by the name of a rodent? What of the gallant aviator who accompanied you on your mission to *Pearu Halbol*?"

"Got burned up in fires large and small. Ironicals, dig, *Seijo-san*?"

Render me small-time strictly-from-famishment *yakuza* punk Ando Hirobumi! Render me first feature-length commercial *eiga* flic venture *Hands and Feet of Death*, circa '71! Render *wataschi* scraping barrel's bottom for last *yen* to produce prints, distribute same, render Foto Joe Yamaguch clapping hands to summon *kami* to pray for assistance toward recoup of investment, than which is not to fail to mention profits margin, reet?

"You listening good, Seijo?"

"And I do wonder, *sensei*," says he (Terada Seijo, *irezumi* tattooist par excellence famed far beyond Yokohama environ), "that you mention no association with the annual events held in Hiroshima to commemorate the horror of the *pikadon* and the subsequent suffering, even to this present day, of the *hibakusha* survivors who gather each sixth of August to celebrate City of Peace Day—are you not, as a result of your coincidental trek through the burning old city that day, one of them, Mr. Yamaguch? Is it not certain that all the bodily ills you suffer now were caused by the *pikadon's* mysterious after-effects?"

"Been back, more than once," I tell him. "Done lensed gatherings of Mushroom Club Society of Microcephalic Children, not to fail to mention *Orizurukai* Folded Crane Club, not to fail to mention Children's Memorial, likeness effigy of Sasaki Sadako, than which who died ten years after *pikadon* whilst endeavoring in vain to no end to fold a thousand paper cranes to prolong life and times against leukemia ravages, reet? Been back, Terada! Free-lance gig hustles on the bricks, Ground Zero Cenotaph, Peace Museum, assembled throng heads bowed in silence for full minute's duration at eight-fifteen A.M. precise—cinders and ashes, Jack!"

Render! Render me. . . .
"You listening, *Seijo-san*?"

Motto: *shikata ga nai*. How we say, like, it can't not be helped, reet?
Meaning: like, Jack, *do* flow of life's path goes whereto it will, despite
efforts otherhow, dig?

Circa, say, 1948, reet? Tokyo Town, Jack, than which at said venue is
held grandiose (big spread in all *shimbun*, natch!) war-crimes trials, twen-
ty-eight *Nihonjin* standing tall in dock to accept sentencing upon convic-
tions (natch!) of *senso* atrocities, to include torture of helpless prisoners
(Bataan Death March, Camp O'Donnell, etcetera blah!) and conspirator-
ial complicity in planning and also conduct of formerly glorious *hakko
ichui* effort to conquer globe. Said legal proceedings proceed in all legality
(natch!) under close scrutiny personal supervision of *honcho Makassar-
san*—how we say now, S.C.A.P. (Supreme Commander, Allied Powers)
—operating out from Dai Ichi Building headquarters, reet?
    Bottom line: half-dozen plus former *honcho* Premier-General Tojo Hi-
deki condemned to execution, remainder to incarceration in durance vile
for varying durations, dig?
    In short and sum, pith and gist, Jack: assorted former *gumbatsu* and also
zaibatsu personages selected to pay piper, thus slaking Yank lust for justice,
reet? In short, good time (*ma* moment!), circa '48, for personages associated in close association with *hakko ichui* endeavor (except saving *Mikado*,
natch!) to run close to ground, seek cover, low-profile shtick, reet? *Wataschi* way ahead of this game, Jack!
    Than which is to say, circa 1948, I is distanced safe from Tokyo Town,
ensconced at Eta Jima environ locale, site of central U.S. Army training
facility, reet? Which is not to fail to mention new incarnation of *wataschi*
under aegis of new post-*senso* moniker (designed to confuse potential
interested Yank military-justice investigator-types), to wit: Foto Joe!

Dig: longish story truncated—from proceeds proceeding from *oyama*
black-market sale of Moe Berg's pre-*senso* Stewart Warner 16-millimeter
eiga camera, *wataschi* garners *yen* sufficient to afford purchase of pre-*senso*
Yashica 35-millimeter still camera, complete with real leather gadget bag,
to include also film supply. Not to fail to mention civvie feather-merchant
garb to replace now nonfashionable *monpei* uniform of Imperial Army of
Dai Nippon. Also: trademark beret, aviator shade specs, black leather jacket, black turtle's neck, slacks of like hue, black spade-toe kicks (double soles
and heels), reet? Also, adequate initial supply of various business cards—
how we say, *meishi*—such as:

Foto Joe Says:
Risk a Buck, G.I.!
Send a Pic Back Home!
Catch Passing Moment on Film!

Not to fail to mention coda:

Terms Strictly Cash and Carry!

What I mean: gots to make do with what's you gots, Jack? Here is *wataschi*, *munako* orphan child of no name (formerly Student Yamaguchi Yoshinori, formerly Gooch, formerly Lieutenant *Benshi*!), possible candidate to provide partial satisfaction of Yank post-*senso* justice lust. Gots to make my nut, reet? What's else save but for manifest of ingenuity in utilization of photog and also *Eigo* lingo skills? Jack: everybody gots to be somebody!

Thus it were: circa 1948, Eta Jima environ locale, attired in aforesaid attire designed to attract customer attentions whilst concealing substantive self from scrutinies (beret, turtle's neck, leather jacket, spade-toes!), gadget bag and pre-*senso* Yashica slung, I sally forth upon business venture, environ of soon-to-be-famous famed Eta Jima Strip — how we say: *karyukai* red-light gin mill juke joint roadhouse district sprung to life (from cinders and ashes of total defeat and also destruction of *Dai Nippon*!). As follows:

Say, circa 1948, 1949. Typical day's routine shtick, reet, Jack?
As how, awakened from slumber late in the day by summons of Mrs. Hino Takako, landlady personage, from which said personage *wataschi* rents *futon* pallet space in lean-to attached to her small paper house (than which edifice suffered but minimalist damage in big *senso* fires, same repaired and restored with scrap materials salvaged from Yank garbage dump close by Eta Jima barracks locale).
Says she (Mrs. Hino Takako, old auntie *Oba-san* widow lady, reet?): "Mr. Foto Joe! Mr. Foto Joe, wake and arise from your *futon*, for it is now past three o'clock, and you must be up if you are to arrive at the *nawanoren* where you make your photographs of the *gaijin issen gorin* and their disgraceful *moga* women who shame the honor of *Nihon*!"
Can you dig it, Jack? Mrs. Hino Takako, old *Oba-san* auntie widow woman, keeps lupine spectre from her paper domicile via rents *yen* I render for space in lean-to attached. Mrs. Hino Takako, poor as ecclesiastical rodent, yet dismayed only as how she ain't gots *yen* as yet adequate to purchase traditionalist *kimono* garb at *oyama* black-market price, thence compelled to continue to sport *senso*-style *monpei*, laments loss of national honor and glory aura of *Nihon* due to total unconditional defeat at hands of barbarian *Amerikajin* (not to fail to mention assorted allied powers also)

302

now occupying occupation status, dig?

"Good morn, Old Auntie," says I, and, "Anks-thay for the basin of water and towel," and, "Three in postmeridian already? Time do fleet, reet, *Oba-san*?"

"Foto Joe," says she, and, "Why do you call yourself by this *gaijin* name? Had you no parents? Were you given no family name to honor with the deeds of your life? What must your *kami* think of you? An able man of your years might surely find some other work that would not contribute to the decay of our once-glorious culture!"

"Reet!" I tell her, and, "Gots all burned up in fires. Come on, Old Auntie *Oba-san*, give Foto Joe a break. Just trying to make my nut, gots to go along to get along, reet, Mrs. Hino?"

"Had I a son like you, Foto Joe," says she, "I should forbid him to walk in the street where the *Amerikajin* soldiers and their *moga* women gather in the filthy and noisy *nawanoren*! Ah!" she laments (Mrs. Hino Takako, Old Auntie *Oba-san* widow lady landlady, reet?), "*Nihon* is doubly disgraced! *Ameratasu* surely frowns upon us, and the *Mikado* cannot be pleased!"

"Reet," I tell her, and, "*Mikado* like everybody else now, looking out for *ichiban* number one numero uno. He studying fishes up to Hayama resort domicile except save when he ain't calling social-style hat-in-hand on *Makassar-san* at Dai Ichi Building office suite. Ain't you heard, Old Auntie? *Mikado* is done forswore direct descent lineage from Sun Goddess, no longer a deity, puts his pants on one leg at a time just like *wataschi* and also you in them *monpei* breeches, reet?"

"You blaspheme," says Mrs. Hino Takako (Foto Joe's landlady), and, "The Imperial Rescript broadcast was a lie!"

"Would *Mikado* lie?" I query. "Was *Mikado* mayhap mistook to undertake *hakko ichui* endeavor? Do *Makassar-san* fib? Say not so, *Oba-san*!"

"*Makassar-san* is a great warrior," allows Mrs. Hino Takako, "but he is also a barbarian. Who shall I believe if I cannot believe the *Mikado* or *Makassar-san*? Ah!" she do lament, "*Nihon* is cursed by her *kami*, and there is no right or reason to be found in all the world!"

I tell her: "Now you talking, Old Auntie! Reet!" I tell her. "Everything global-wide gone sheer pure *kichigai* crazy cracked insane bughouse bonkers! Like, what's wisdom of big fires, reet?"

"I cannot converse with you, Foto Joe!" she says. "You are like all the young men and women of *Nihon* today—your tongue is corrupted by the donkey's noise of the *Eigo* you speak with the *Amerikajin*! You are no longer *Nipponshikki*, and behave no differently than the foul-smelling *gaijin*!"

"I been told the like of it before, *Oba-san*. Your problem, Old Auntie," I tell her, "is you don't acclimate, reet? Go with *do* flow, Mrs. Hino!"

She don't riposte, reet? Only laments: thumps breastbone with clenched fists, covers visage with palms, turns away, hobbles arthritic back inside her repaired restored paper house, attired in old *senso monpei* breeches and tunic due to inability as yet to afford black-market *oyama kimono*.

I acclimate, Jack!

To wit: perform morn's ablutions (towel and basin of water provided by landlady), taking extreme care combing hairs into new long-hairs style, slicked down to form badass D.A. with Brylcreme—purchased on *wataschi's* behalf at Eta Jima Post Exchange reet?—don black turtle's neck shift, pegged-cuff black slacks, like-hued spade-toe kicks, leather jacket, hoist gadget bag (pre-*senso* Yashica 35-millimeter, film rolls, receipt slips, *meishi* business cards therein!), hit *benjo* for tinkle, set off on *sanpo* walk to garner wherewithal than which feeds bulldog and also retards lupine.

"Foto Joe!" calls Mrs. Hino Takako after me from door of her paper house, "Will you not take your breakfast meal with me in my house? I have *nigirimeshi* rice balls and a piece of fish purchased in the *oyama* market!"

"Anks-thay but no thanks, *Oba-san*," I tell her. "Gots to get with it, commence to harvest straws whilst sun is up, reet? I'll glom me some of them *instanto ramen* precooked dehydrated *udon* noodles is all the rage in the *nawanoren* on the Strip."

"Ah!" she laments, "The Hundred Millions eat the food of the *gaijin*! Indeed, all the world is *kichigai*!"

Tell me about it, reet, Jack?

Daily-routine shtick (circa '48, '49, reet?), Eta Jima *karyukai* red-light gin mill roadhouse watering hole—Strip, reet? Hour is four in postmeridian, juke joint *nawanoren* open for business, Jack! How you say, early fowl garners nightcrawler—Foto Joe amongst first on scene. As follows:

Pop in (bop-style stride sanpo stroll strut, reet?) Texas Bar for quick-fix breaking of fast via order of new Jimmu Boom Yank-style precooked dehydrated *instanto ramen udon* noodles, served up steaming in plastic bowl by Texas Bar bartender-owner personage Arai Kikuo (*issen gorin* vet of Kwantung Army, survived *senso* with nary a scratch, never heard shot fired in anger, reet?), than which who says:

"Good evening, Mr. Foto Joe. It must be four o'clock, for you are here. I can only admire the discipline and diligence you exhibit in your enterprise, Foto Joe!"

"Reet," I say, and, "Big blackjack oaks from little acorns do sprout, even in parched Okie red clay soils. Gots to be man with plan, as how my dear departed *Papa-san* did always advise me," and, "Must be a slow night coming, nobody here but us chickens and also the *hosutesu*, reet?"

Says he: "*Ona hideri wa nai*"—there ain't never no dearths of womens— "Will you drink a beverage with your noodles, Mr. Joe?"

"Asahi," say I, "if you gots a bottle cold, *Kikuo-san*."

"I regret to announce I no longer offer Asahi for purchase, Foto Joe.

The *Amerikajin* prefer their Schlitz and Pabst and Miller brands which are contained in metal canisters, even though I must ask a far higher price to purchase these in the *oyama* market. I hope soon to effect a relationship with an *Amerikajin* who will be willing to smuggle beer to me from the Post Exchange, which will reduce my costs. Now, even the *moga hosutesu* ask for imported beer, for they think it renders them more attractive to the *Amerikajin issen gorin*."

"Go with *do* flow, *Kikuo-san*," I say, and, "I'll pass on the libation tonight. Gots to watch the *yen*, reet?"

"Ah, Foto Joe," says he, "your thrift is admirable! I am confident you shall yet become rich as the *zaibatsu nariken* new-rich who increased their fortunes many times while you and I fought and bled for them in the *senso*."

"I can but try," I say to Arai Kikuo, Kwantung Army vet who suffered nary a scratch, reet?

"I too shall one day be wealthy if I am able ever to become as fluent as you in speaking the *Eigo*, Mr. Joe. Truly, you have a great gift of speech in their difficult language, and it is evident to all who know you that the *Amerikajin* are fond of you for this and this causes the volume of your commerce with them to be ever larger."

"Reet," I say, scarfing plastic bowl of steamy hot (*umai* delish!) pre-cooked dehydrated *instanto ramen udon* noodles with bamboo *hashi* chopsticks (included in cost!).

"Tell me, Mr. Foto Joe," says Texas Bar bartender-owner personage Arai Kikuo — red vest, white shirt, black bow tie and arm garters to achieve Yank-style aura appearance image, reet? — "how and where did you attain to your fluency in *Eigo*? I know you are secretive with respect to the history of your life, but if you confide in me I vow never to reveal what you tell me. Were you perhaps a prisoner of the *Amerikajin*? Were you one of those who studied the *Eigo* as a schoolboy prior to the ban upon such study shortly before the *senso* began? Or are you a genius who is able to learn a barbarian speech simply by listening to the talk of the *issen gorin* and reading their *Stars & Stripes shimbun*?"

"Might could have been, six of one, half dozen the other, *Kikuo-san*," I tell him, and, "Them as say don't not know, whilst them as knows ain't saying, reet, Jack?"

"Ah, Mr. Foto Joe, you are an enigma!"

"Reet!" I riposte. "As in wisdom uttered by Leroy Paige, also knowed as Satchel, Negroid *Amerikajin* legendary great *besuboru* fireball moundsman but recently acquired by Amerinds of Cleveland squad: keep low profile, don't look back, as how might could be somebody diminishing interval betwixt you, reet?"

Dig it: circa '48, '49, Texas Bar *nawanoren*, Eta Jima *karyukai* juke joint gin mill watering hole roadhouse red-light—Eta Jima (soon to be famed, Jack!) Strip.

Interior is dim-lit via candle flicker as how in late '40's early-days era of Jimmu Boom economic miraculous recovery miracle, electric powers ain't turned on till fall of eventide's full darkness. *Wataschi* is amongst earliest opening-time arrivals on scene, than which include only bartender-owner personage Arai Kikuo and also bevy of *hosutesu moga* B-gal prostitutes—never a paucity of womens, reet?—seated at tables to await Yank G.I. *issen gorin* scheduled to depart Eta Jima barracks confines at hour of five. Than which *mama-sans* render final adjustments to cosmetic enhancements of pulchritudes: tighten falsie bra straps to assert cone shapes—how we say, PX Chest, reet?—smoke *oyama harukai* import ciggie smokes (Old Gold, call for Phillip Morris, Chesterfield, Lucky Strike)—engage in minimalist banter exchange with Foto Joe (me, Jack!) to pass time passing. As how:

"Mr. Foto Joe, why do you not make our photographs unless we are in the company of the *Amerikajin issen gorin?*"

"You gots the *genkin* cash, honey," I tell her, "Foto Joe gots the time and also film-loaded fast-speed pre-*senso* Yashica, satisfactions guaranteed or *genkin yen* refunded cheery-style, reet?"

"Will you accept Occupation Currency, or must you have only *yen*, Joe? Poor Joe," says she, "has not yet learned how to convert Occupation Currency in the *oyama* to *yen*! How shall your commerce thrive if you deal only in worthless *yen*, Joe?"

"I is working on the problem, sweetie pie," I tell her, and, "Give Foto Joe time, all things possible to he who strives and also has patience, reet?"

"Oh, Joe," says another, "do not always talk of money! Make a photograph of me and my friends for love, Joe!"

"Orry-say," I say, and, "No *genkin*, no pic, reet? *Kokoru* lovey-dovey sentiments don't sustain bulldog nor retard entrance of lupine quadruped, reet?"

"Foto Joe!" says yet another *moga hosutesu* B-gal prostitute *mama-san*, "You consider us beneath your dignity! I think you are like the Yanks who disdain us save when they wish to drink and dance and sleep together!"

"Mr. Foto Joe behaves as if he were one of the *Amerikajin*," says yet another. "He thinks because he can converse so easily in their *Eigo* that he is no longer *Nipponshikki*! You are one of the *Eigo-ya* who wish to be thought *Amerikajin*, and so flaunt their *Eigo* speech!"

"Say not so!" I do riposte. "No offenses intended nor aspersions cast. Like, everybody gots to make him or her's nut, reet, baby-*san?*"

"You are both arrogant and indifferent, Foto Joe," says another, "but know that I strive to learn the *Eigo* as well as you, and when I speak it fluently I shall beguile one of the Yank *issen gorin* to make an *omiai* marriage with me and take me with him to his country across the ocean when he departs *Nihon*, and I shall live as an *Amerikajin* and be affluent and lazy, and the arrogant indifference of all the *Nihonjin* who now scorn us for fraternizing will no longer vex me!"

"Good lucks, sweetheart," I tell her, and, "More's powers to you if and when. And welcome to it, doll-baby, as how mayhap I been there before. Might could be it ain't all what's it cracked up as, reet?"

"Did you indeed reside amongst the *Amerikajin*, Joe?"

"Teach us to say more words in the *Eigo*, Joe!"

"Hear my pronunciation, Mr. Joe. Tell me if I enunciate correctly."

"Reet," I say, pause in Texas Bar *nawanoren* doorway egress. "Let's hear you, lover."

"Suck and fuck ten dollars Occupation Currency, my place, G.I.," says she in *Eigo*, and, "Do I not sound as though I were already *Amerikajin*?"

"Reet," I riposte. "I mean, like, accent needs hone, but syntax is crystal lucid. Congrats, *Mama-san*! Continue to crack tomes, burn midnight oils. Study is prayer, and also pain equals learning, reet?"

"Joe, you know that at midnight I shall lie on a *futon* with the Yank who gives me ten dollars Occupation Currency!"

"The mysterious Mr. Foto Joe mocks us!" they say, and, "He teases us in the manner of the Yank *issen gorin* who teach us to speak obscenities for their amusement!" they say, and, "I will not permit you to make a photograph of me this night when you return to the Texas Bar with your camera, Foto Joe!"

I say: "Way cookies do crumbles. Not to fail to mention how mop flop," and, "Dig you later, ladies. Time now to place shoulder bone to grinding surface, schnozz to wheel, dark of eventide falling upon Eta Jima environ, reet?"

Jump cuts: circa '48, '49, Eta Jima (soon famed!) Strip environ, hours of Yank military off-duty eventide dusk and full darkness, reet? Foto Joe (a.k.a. Student Yamaguchi Yoshinori, a.k.a. Gooch, a.k.a. Lieutenant *Benshi*!) in performance of hustling-nut shtick — beret (eventual trademark lid, reet?), black turtle's neck tunic and leather jacket and pegged trou, spade-toes of like hue, aviator shade specs, badass D.A. coiffure, gadget bag slung, pre-*senso* Yashica at ready, Jack! Success of same highly dependent upon glibness spiel of *Eigo* confabulation style, alertness to *ma* moment's ambience to create favorable commercial *enryo* relationships. As follows:

"Hey Yank!" I shout above victrola music-noise emanating from gin mill *nawanoren* entrenceway (not to fail to mention clank, clang, and also the pinging of new Jimmu Boom *Nihonjin* post-*senso* popularity rage for pinball machines generated in *pachinko* parlors), wherein favorite musics accompaniment is (big irony, Jack!) old *senso* favorite *Kaigun* Imperial Navy March theme song, reet?

"Yank!" I shout, and, "Jack, I mean you, reet? You there, Honorable

Private First Class Jones Martin, don't you not recognize visage of old Foto Joe than which who did take your pic whilst you did enjoy throes of three-day pass but a fortnight ago, man?"

"You talking to me, Nip?" queries Private First-Class Jones Martin (native of Cincinnati Town, draftee *issen gorin* high school dropout, reet? Gots to put the moniker handle to the visage to make it in this biz, Jack!). "I'm Marty Jones," says he, "but who the hell are you and how's come you know to call me by my name, Jap?"

"Oh, Jones Martin," I say, dig in gadget bag, withdraw stack of still pics, shuffle to locate likeness of aforementioned Jones Martin. "Sad it do render old Foto Joe's heart and also *hara* belly to think so soon you is done plumb forgots him, man! Here, Jones Marty-*san*, gander this! Recognize anybody therein depicted, Honorable Private First Class Jones?" I flash pic (snapped in confines of Dolly Bar fortnight prior, reet?).

"Hey, that's me!" says he, and, "Damned if I remember posing for that. Cripes, was I wasted!" says he, and, "How much you asking for it, Nip?"

"Already yours, Jones Marty," I say. "Bought and paid for but an instant before I clicked shutter, reet? Been looking for you all these many nights since to deliver same. Foto Joe," I tell him, "word is bond, satisfactions guarantee, reet? Enjoy in good healths, Jones Marty," I say, and, "Where you been so long gone, buddy pal? On sick call penicillin dosage as result of conjugal infection contracted from unclean *moga mama-san?*"

"I been confined to quarters for drunk and disorderly on account of I was A.W.O.L. sleeping it off must of been the night you took my picture. Hey, this is pretty neat, Nip! Who's the *mama-san* I'm leaning on so I don't fall on my face? I could use me some of that gash after all the time I been sitting in the dayroom while everybody's out getting their ashes hauled regular!"

"Six of one, half-dozen the other," I say, and, "All look alike to me too, but might could be this one's moniker is Fumiko-*san*, reet? Check out Dolly Bar, reet, Jack?"

"I'll do that," says Private First Class Jones Martin (Cincinnati native *issen gorin* high-school dropout, reet?), "and thanks for giving me this. Usually you give a Jap money you don't see his ass ever again in life."

"Satisfactions guarantee!" I tell him, and, "Strictly *genkin* cash and carry! Here, take my *meishi* card. Tell all your buddy pals back in barracks, Foto Joe, perambulating photog, candid and also posed, *sanpo* pic snapper extraordinaire of Eta Jima Strip environ, on scene nightly with fall of eventide dusk and dark, reet?"

Can you dig it, Jack? Customer service, reet? Foto Joe's motto: product delivery (in person!) certifiable! Create good wills, generate repeat and return trade, word-of-mouth advertising—forget yesterday, stay on ball today, tomorrow follows not unlike like unto dawn's light in wake of eventide darkest dark. Thus it were I did build hustle nut, reet?

"Hello, boys!" I greet trio of staff sergeants enjoying *sanpo* stroll down Eta Jima Strip sidewalk. Like, money and passes in pockets, window-shopping *nawanoren* entranceways in search of congenial atmospheric auras (than which is to say: adequacy of unoccupied *moga hosutesu* B-gal *mama-sans*, reet?). "Allow me to intro self, Yanks! Foto Joe's my handle, reet? Whom does I have pleasure of addressing?"
"Get the fuck out of my way, you little gook fucker!" says one.
"Maybe he's a pimp," says another, and, "Ask him does he know the best place here to find us some snatch."
"Take that camera out of my face unless you want me to stick it up your ass, Jap!" says the third.
"Orry-say, Yanks," I say, and, "Did I hear you looking for female-persuasion distaff-side femininity companionships? New in town, boys? Hey, like, welcome to *Nihon*, formerly knowed as *Dai Nippon*, G.I.s!"
"You're right, he's a pimp," says first Yank staff sergeant.
"How much you want to arrange us some cunt?" asks second.
"If he's pimping why's he pointing a camera at us?" queries third.
I gots to explain (a.k.a. *Benshi*!), reet? I tell them: "Foto Joe's the name, snapping pics my game. First night in Eta Jima? Just off boat at Sasebo or mayhap Yokohama? Fly in from Okinawa to Tachigawa? Welcome to islands of *Nihon*, boys! How's about a *o-miyage* souvenir pic to memorial-ize significance of *ma* moment, reet? Shoot you good deal, fellas! Three prints for price of two, reet? Hey, strike posture pose, stand close so's I can fit you all in frame. Smile *sumairu*, guys, you gots big night ahead of you when I aim you in direction of wall-to-wall *hosutesu moga* comfort ladies instanter, reet?"
"You want to?" asks first of second.
"I will if he promises to point us toward some pussy," ripostes third.

Thus it were, Jack! Eta Jima Strip (soon famed!) environ, circa 1948 etcetera blah. Hustle nut, beat cobblestones, diminish shoe leathers (black spade-toes!), assemble *yen*, reet? Long nights, darkness of Eta Jima skies, musics noise of *nawanoren* and also *pachinko* parlors, Occupation Force Yank *Amerikajin issen gorin* and also noncoms, wall-to-wall *mama-san hosutesu moga* comfort women B-gals. . . . Jack, thus it were!

"Good eventide to you, Yank! Nice lady you gots there! Like a pic to remember event thereby?"
"What say, fellas? Having good times on Strip? How's about candid *o-miyage* photo souvenir to send folks back home stateside?"
"Where you hail from out, buddy? Texas! Close by Oklahoma, as in sovereign state thereof, reet? Ever visit county of Payne environ? How

Aggie Pokes doing on gridiron these days, still losing to hated downstate Sooner arch-rivals?"

"Please to print John Hancock moniker handle on dotted line to facilitate delivery, reet?"

"*Yen* only, please, as how *wataschi* Foto Joe ain't yet in business of Occupation Currency exchange. Maybe mayhap you might could be interested in doing little deal with Foto Joe to barter specie at PX? Orry-say, just asking, reet, Yank?"

"Is we having fun, boys? How we say, *eija nai kai*, ain't it good! Like a pic as proofs thereof? Consider, dawn's light brings hangover's headaches, not to fail to mention regrets remorse, reet? Yet, as documented in black and white glossy-finish photo I render you, joy throes of this eventide eternalized, reet?"

Thus it were—long nights etcetera blah, Jack.

After midnight, Victrola musics and also *Kaigun* Imperial Navy theme song noise fading, foots-sore and spirit-weary, *wataschi* Foto Joe perambulates shank's mare *sanpo* empty streets and alleys back to domicile (lean-to *futon* rental space attached to restored repaired paper house of Mrs. Hino Takako), reet?

Says she (from within confines of paper-house environ): "Who comes now walking at this late hour of the night before my house like a burglar?"

I riposte: "*Wataschi*, Mrs. Hino. Who else? Relax and resume slumbers, *Oba-san* old auntie. It's but Foto Joe come home from night-long labors hustling nut, reet?"

"Ah," says she, "Mr. Foto Joe, who will not reveal his true name even to the poor widow who rents him space for his *futon!*"

"Reet. Go back to sleep, *Oba-san*, as how Foto Joe's canine pedal extremities is tired, buttocks dragging, and tasks yet to execute ere I recline."

"Will you," says Mrs. Hino Takako, "at this late hour, when soon the blackness of night will be broken by dawn's first light, now prepare your pans of evil-smelling chemicals to make the photographs of the *Amerikajin* conquerors and their disgraceful *moga?*"

"Reet."

"Ah!" cries old *Oba-san* widow woman landlady Mrs. Hino Takako from her *futon* within paper house, "had I a son, I should not allow him to wander the night like a thief or an outcast! I should not permit him to mix noxious chemicals in the dark to make photographs of *gaijin* soldiers and prostitutes!"

"Reet," I say, and, "If wishes was fishes, *Mikado* would doubtless study same, not to fail to mention as how porcines might could fly not unlike like unto Nakajima aircrafts, reet, Old Auntie?"

310

"Mr. Foto Joe," says she, "did you fill your leather bag with the *yen* of the *gaijin*? Are you now a man of affluence because you walk the street that shames the name of Eta Jima and all our *kami*?"

"Not yet, Mrs. Hino. Bricks from straws and also mud, great blackjack oaks from itty bitty acorns, reet? Give wataschi but time and a few breaks, *Oba-san*," I tell her, "I might could surprise even you, reet?"

"Goodnight," says she. "It is time for decent citizens to be asleep."

"Sweet dreams," I tell her, and, "Don't not let cockroaches nibble."

So it did go, Jack. Night in and also out, Foto Joe (a.k.a. Student Yamaguchi Yoshinori, a.k.a. Gooch, a.k.a. Lieutenant *Benshi*), ensconced in context of Eta Jima environ — secure locale remote from Tokyo Prefecture (whereat eight and twenty ex-*honcho* personages endure durance vile for commission of *senso* crimes atrocities, courtesy of S.C.A.P. *Makassarsan*, reet?). Than which is not to fail to mention Mrs. Iva d'Aquino (a.k.a. Tokyo Rose) residing also in slammer for *senso* anti-*Amerikajin* propaganda broadcasts ("Zero Hour," reet?). What I mean: keeping low profile, Jack!

And who is to say *wataschi's* go with *do* flow nut hustle might could not mayhap have continued ad infinitum, Jack? Save except for (as always!) ironics of ironical twist than which alters course of life-and-times chronicle. To wit: advent of personage otherhow obscure, which is to say, *moga hosutesu mama-san* comfort woman B-gal named Matsumoto Yoko, reet?

How it were:

Cut to: *karyukai* red-light gin mill juke joint watering hole roadhouse Eta Jima Strip (now very soon famed!), circa 1 of January, 1950. Dig:

Texas Bar *nawanoren*, wee hours of blackest night darkness, revels of Yank-style New Year's Eve celebration ceremonials now ended, reet? G.I.s heretofore assembled in record numbers departed (gone back to Eta Jima base barracks to sleep it off, gone off in company of selected wall-to-wall *mama-san hosutesu moga* B-gals to engage same upon *futon* etcetera blah). Musicians of new feature attraction Hatta Yoshizawa Country Western Dance Band also departed, pockets filled with *chippu* tips money for rendering repeated renditions of "Auld Lang Syne," "Goodnight Ladies," and "Deep in the Heart of Texas." Newly acquired Seeburg juke plays Kitty Wells recording of "You're Uptown Tonight Where All the Bright Lights Shine," reet?

Texas Bar *nawanoren* is, how you say, shambles, as in, shot at and missed, shit at and hit, Jack. Tables and chairs askew, stools overturned, former littered with myriad empty beer cannisters (*oyama* market Schlitz, Pabst, and also Miller's High Life), overflowed ashtrays, not to fail to mention floor is not unlike like unto same, bestrewn with ciggie smoke butts, confetti and streamers and paper hats (launched in abandon of throes of twelve midnight sharp exultations, reet?), beer puddle spillages, etcetera blah.

Circa 1 of January, 1950, Jack: Yanks and *hosutesu*, also Hatta Yoshizawa Band musicians, noise of shitkicker music, paper horns blowed at midnight, all faded to silence surrounding Kitty Wells singing "You're Uptown Tonight Where All the Bright Lights Shine," not to fail to mention faded to silence are also 108 bells rung in Eta Jima Town to mark *Nihonjin* New Year Day celebrations ceremonials, how we say, *o-shogatsu*, reet? To include ingestion of ritualistic *mochi* rice cakes etcetera blah.

Enter Foto Joe—black-clad not unlike like unto *ninja*-style *gorutsuke* assassin or also thief-outcast, leather gadget bag chock-full jam-packed from sales receipts, film supplies exhausted—New Year's Eve eventide revels create big demand for pics both candid and posed, reet? Thus: enter Foto Joe, pedal extremities canines burning, buttocks dragging, etcetera blah.

To what end? Who's to say, Jack! Moment of *ma* respite in nut-hustle labors endeavor? Desire to, how you say, masticate fatty tissues in casual confabulations with fellow humankind. Stop and smell rosebuds *yoin* resonances? Whatever, reet?

Enter Foto Joe, Texas Bar *nawanoren* post-revels shamble, there to discover interior environ deserted save for work-wearied presence of bartender-owner Arai Kikuo, aforesaid personage commencing clean-up chores, reet?

"Happy New Year's to you, *Kikuo-san*," I say, and, "T'was rough night, reet?"

"Foto Joe," says he, "I wondered if you might not return to my Texas Bar yet once more this night before I had restored my property to a decent condition and closed and locked the shutters. Where have you been since you left just after the hour of midnight, Joe?"

"If it's anywhere, I was at it," I tell him. "Dolly Bar, Rhumba Bar, Sin Itoro's, Rising Sun Lounge, Jack, I been every place! Done shot up all my films, popped my last flash, wrote last receipt, give away ultimate *meishi* card. Gots to get it whilst getting's good, reet, *Kikuo-san*? Looks to me like you done turned you some big *yen* yourself, Jack!"

"Ah!" says he, "It was a glorious night for my commerce, Joe! The Yanks spend their Occupation Currency freely, and I shall realize a fine profit for this night's work even at the wretched rate of exchange I receive for scrip in the *oyama*. But I confess it saddens me that I cannot myself celebrate *o-shogatsu*. At midnight the *Amerikajin* were so boisterous, singing their songs of nostalgia for old friends, blowing on the paper horns I procured through the Eta Jima Post Exchange, kissing all the *hosutesu*, I was unable even to hear the one hundred and eight bells ring throughout Eta Jima, and I consumed no *mochi* this New Year Day, Foto Joe."

"Forget it, *Kikuo-san*," I tell him. "All that traditionalist *Nipponshikki* guff stuff is but old headgear in Jimmu Boom times now, reet? Still enjoyed by old auntie *oba-san* ladies like unto my landlady Mrs. Hino, man, but us ambitious young folks is gots to concentrate on feeding bulldog, assembling capital risk venture piles."

"Joe," says he, "I suspect you are a man of little sentiment! Truly, I reaffirm my prediction that you shall one day be wealthy! If only you were willing to accept the Yanks' Occupation Currency to exchange at the *oyama*, this might occur soon!"

"I'm working on it, Jack!" I say. "Come on, *Kikuo-san*, it's already first day of new year nineteen and fifty. We both in prime time of lifetimes, reet? Set 'em up. I'll buy you a real libation! Gots any Yank *harukai* import Scotch left behind the bar, that good stuff you treat military police provost with so's he don't rule you off-limits? None of that cold *o-cha* tea slops *moga* gull G.I. *issen gorin* into treating."

"Will you not offer to buy me a drink also, Mr. Foto Joe?" says small voice from dim-dark corner-table recess of Texas Bar *nawanoren*.

"Who dat say dat?" I ask, slip off trademark opaque aviator shades, squint to envision personage of *hosutesu* seated therein and also thereat, reet?

"It is I, Matsumoto Yoko," says she, and, "And will you buy me a drink to celebrate this first day of the new year I am certain holds great fortune in store for me, Mr. Foto Joe?" she queries.

Do flow, Jack! *Ma* moment in which *wataschi* Foto Joe pauses in midst of frantic frenetic nut hustle (circa 1 of January, '50, *o-shogatsu!*), atmospherics (interior of shambled Texas Bar *nawanoren!*) conducive to *enryo* sense of richly subtle relationships reciprocities (bartender-owner Arai Kikuo, *hosutesu moga* B-gal *mama-san* prostitute comfort woman Matsumoto Yoko, reet?)—what I mean to say, Jack, subsequent ironics, as follows hereafter. As in adage aphorism of Yank impressario Barnum P. T.: one borned every minute—not to fail to include *wataschi* Foto Joe, Jack! Dig:

"I must restore the cleanliness of my establishment if I am to be ready to welcome my customers tomorrow, Joe," says Arai Kikuo, and, "Drink with the little *moga* if you wish, Joe," says he, "I will make a gift for the new year to you both from the last bottle remaining of the *harukai* imported White Horse Scotch I reserve for the Yank officers of the military police corps."

"Anks-thay, *Kikuo-san*," I say, and, "I'll owe you one, reet?"

"Come and sit with me, Mr. Foto Joe," says small voice from out dim-dark corner-table recess, and, "Perhaps the surprising generosity of *Kikuo-san* indicates great fortune awaits us both in this new year. Come, sit with me here, Mr. Foto Joe."

"Reet." I cross littered and beer-spillage puddle bestrewn floor, take chair opposite (tiny table for two—knees gots to touch, Jack!), say, "I don't recognize you, sweet thingness. You come here oftentimes prior to this eventide?" and, "Thought I knew all the *hosutesu* on the Strip, but new talent constant inflow makes for confusions, reet?"

"I have only just journeyed to Eta Jima from my village in Eisaku Prefecture, and this is indeed my first night to come to the street of the *nawanoren*, but already I know the renowned and mysterious Mr. Foto Joe, for you were identified for me earlier tonight by my new friends, who have all gone away to sleep with their *Amerikajin*."

"Do tell," I say, hoisting glass of *harukai* import White Horse Scotch served up by bartender-owner Arai Kikuo. "Here's dirt and water meld in your baby blues, *Mama-san*! Down hatch, reet? Over portal of lip and pearly whites, be alert, *hara* belly—it comes!" She laughs—as in, hee hee.

"Mr. Foto Joe!" says she, and, "I observed you all through this night as you came and went and came back again to this *nawanoren*, and I saw how you teased and taunted my *hosutesu* friends to pose for the many photographs you made with your camera. You will need time simply to count all the money you received this night, Mr. Foto Joe!"

"Reet," I say, and, "Just doing my job, *Yoko-san*. Okay to call you *Yoko-san*, lovey-dovey? All the B-gals knows me, hon!" and, "Don't let it fool you, I gots plenty overheads expense comes off topside, reet?" She laughs, Jack.

"Mr. Joe," says she, "your manner of speech is as amusing as my friends told me! Some even call you *baka*, but most like you and say you tell no one the truth of your origins. Some say you taught the *Eigo* to yourself by conversing with the *Amerikajin* when they first came to *Nihon* as conquerors and by viewing their *eiga* at the Eta Jima Post Exchange Theater, and that you can read their *shimbun* as well as they. Others say you were most probably a prisoner of the *Amerikajin* for a long time during the great *senso*. *Kikuo-san* once told one of my new friends he believes you once lived among the *Amerikajin* or the *Igirisujin* across the oceans."

"Reet. So what's does you think, newly-arrived-on-Strip *Yoko-san*?"

She laughs, Jack! Says: "I do not think you are *baka*, Joe. Have I your permission to address you as Joe? I also doubt you were ever a soldier in the *senso*, for I knew many former *issen gorin* of the Imperial Army in my village, and I cannot imagine you ever exhibited the *budo* virtues of a soldier! And it is too fantastic to imagine you ever resided in the land of the *Amerikajin* or the *Igirisujin*, Joe!"

"So?" I query.

"I am content to laugh at the ease with which you joke with the *Amerikajin*, as I might if I could speak their *Eigo*, and I can only admire your enterprise in earning so much money for making their photographs, though I am told you will only accept *yen* in payment. And I am happy to

314

enjoy the laughter you cause in me by your manner of speaking, Joe!"
Laughs. Hee hee, reet?

"Smart cookie," I tell her, and, "Them as don't know do the saying,
whilst them in know don't not say, reet?" And, "Bring us another round,
Kikuo-san!" and, "This one's on me, Jack!"

"Ah!" says Kikuo Arai, "How am I ever to complete my work if you
both sit here and drink as if it were yet early in the evening of the last day of
the old year! Joe," says he, "why do you not celebrate *o-shogatsu* with this
moga who is too young and inexperienced to find herself a Yank? Take her
to your *futon*, Joe, and leave me to the completion of my tasks!"

Hosutesu B-gal *moga* comfort woman *mama-san* Matsumoto Yoko
laughs—hee, also har!—says: "Oh, my friends all tell me Mr. Foto Joe will
not share the pillow on his *futon* with any woman! Is this true, *Joe-san?*"

Say I: "To date, reet. But, what's the hecks. I mean, like, it's first day of
new year *o-shogatsu*. I is done heard hundred and eight bells ring, but
scarfed nary a *mochi* rice cake, reet? Come on, *Yoko-san*, I is done spent too
many eves of new years solitary far away from home! Let's us *sanpo*
perambulate shank's mare! I'm game if you is, reet?"

"Can I believe what my ears hear?" queries Arai Kikuo.

"Hee hee!" laughs Matsumoto Yoko, says, "Have you any Occupation
Currency with which to pay me, Foto Joe? I have vowed not to accept *yen*.
We must agree on a price for your pleasure!"

"Let's us," I did tell her, "do it just this one time for *kokoro*. How we say
in *Eigo*, do it for love, reet, *Yoko-san?*"

Kokoro, Jack! How you say, love sentiment, reet? Circa wee dawn darkest
hours of night, 1 of January, 1950 (*o-shogatsu!*), Eta Jima environ. What's
do *wataschi* Foto Joe (a.k.a. Student Yamaguchi, a.k.a. Gooch, a.k.a. Lieutenant *Benshi!*), aged one and thirty years—prime of lifetime life and
times—know from *kokoro* heart-felt love sentimentalities, Jack!

What I mean: *wataschi* knows his *mama-san* Mrs. Yamaguchi cooking
up *umai* yummy yum *nigirimeshi* rice balls over *hibachi* charcoal coals in
kitchen of his paper house; *wataschi* knows kneeling on *tatami* mat beside
his *papa-san* Mr. Yamaguchi, read-aloud shtick drill from editorial columns of English-language *Japan Times shimbun* to polish perfect *Eigo*
pronunciations—oh, reet, *wataschi* knows his baby sis *Iko-san* playing with
her *ningyo* dolly, mocking donkey's bray of *Eigo* phonemes; *wataschi*
knows worship-from-afar-off strictly platonic mode (in reference to Miss
Clara ("Petty Girl") Sterk—ah, heartbroke was I, Jack!). Thus *wataschi*
knows embarrassment mortifications of mistaken intentions resulting in
said Miss Clara's sisterly reciprocal sentiments impass, reet? What I mean:
what's do I know from *kokoro*, Jack?

What I mean is: like, circa 1 of January, '50, *wataschi* Foto Joe is
homeward bound via *sanpo* shank's mare perambulation in close company

of *moga hosutesu* B-gal *mama-san* Matsumoto Yoko (newly arrived to hustle nut on Eta Jima Strip from remote rural hicks sticks village environ locale of Eisaku Prefecture), than which is inexplicable phenomenon of *wataschi's* life and times, Jack, explained mayhap only as *ma* moment of respite from nut-hustle labors, minimalist deviation in *do* flow of ironics than which I relate — what I mean is, *futon* ecstacies shared (first and last, Jack!) in *ma* moment (aged one and thirty years old!) of supreme *enryo* intimacies — but one more *yoin* resonance in, how we say, *temei wo shirii*, totality of total life's experiences, reet? As follows:

"Oh!" cries out *wataschi's* landlady, old ecclesiastical-rodent-poor widow woman *oba-san* old auntie Mrs. Hino Takako, "who approaches my household in the dark early hours of *o-shogatsu*, laughing and talking loudly? Are you inebriated revelers who have strayed from the sinful street of Eta Jima into my yard? Speak, or I shall call out for the neighborhood watchman to come to my assistance!"

"Relax, Mrs. Hino. Maintain coolth," I say, and, "It ain't but *wataschi* Foto Joe coming home from nut-hustle labors, gots a friend with me going to spend night with me in my lean-to, reet?"

"May I know the name and gender of your guest, Foto Joe?" says she from within confines of her restored repaired paper domicile.

"Ix-nay," I tell her, and, "None of your beeswax, Mrs. Hino!" and, "Resume slumbers, *Oba-san*," and, "What's you ain't cognizant of can't not inflict injuries, reet?"

Matsumoto Yoko, Jack? She laughs: as in hee hee, not to fail to mention hardy har!

"Ah!" laments *wataschi's* landlady, Mrs. Hino Takako. "Now is my shame complete! My tenant, the enigmatic Mr. Foto Joe, brings a *moga* into my household! Had I a son such as you," says she, "I should tear out my hair and smear my face with ashes for shame!"

"Reet," I say — Matsumoto Yoko laughs, Jack! — "Orry-say, Old Auntie, but these is new-style post-*senso* Occupied Japan Jimmu Boom times. Go with *do* flow, Mrs. Hino! Dig you later on the morrow's morn anon, reet?"

"Foto Joe," says Matsumoto Yoko, laughs, "the old woman speaks to you as if you were a small child, not a man fully grown!"

"Reet. Enter my humble abode, *Yoko-san*. I'd sing you chorus of traditional *Nipponshikki* song of welcome-to-domicile shtick, except as how it's late and might could wake neighbors, reet?"

"Oh," says she — laughs, Jack! — "your abode is even smaller than my parents' house in our village in Eisaku Prefecture! Is not one's life wondrous?" she queries. "I am to share the *futon* of Mr. Foto Joe, the famed and mysterious photographer of *Amerikajin* and *hosutesu* in Eta Jima, and I find he lives in a tiny room with scarcely space for his *futon*, and his landlady is an old shrew who chastises him as though he were a small boy!

My first night in the town of Eta Jima proves truly remarkable!" says she.

"Reet," I say, and, "Life and times full of surprises unexpected, ironic and also otherhow, reet?"

"*Joe-san,*" says she as we recline (unclothed!) upon my *futon* — noggins sharing pillow, reet? — "I would have you know that it is only because you are the first man I lie beside in Eta Jima that I do this for *kokoro* and thus do not demand you pay me a high fee for my company. Know that I have come, like my *hosutesu* friends, to earn money in large amounts and to enjoy the exciting life among the *Amerikajin* on the street of the *nawan-oren*. Know that never again will I do this for *kokoro*, Joe! I am a poor girl with no education who comes here from a remote village, but I am inspired with great ambition, and perhaps one day I will surprise everyone with my success. Know, mysterious Mr. Joe, that you pay me no fee for this only because it is the first time for me in Eta Jima, and because it is *o-shogatsu*, and so to be generous may bring me good fortune in this new year!"

"Reet!" I did tell her, Jack, and, "Know what you mean, *Yoko-san*! Ambition shtick. Honor and glory to family name and also *kami*. Been down the *do* road, honey-bunch! Go with *do's* flow, *mama-san*! In passing, be aware of competitive rates prevalent on Strip these days, reet?"

"Ah, Joe," says she, "come upon me now, for the hour is late, and your landlady will surely embarrass us if we lie together into the full light of morning. Come upon me, *Joe-san*!"

"Reet," I did say, and, "Like, you gots to show me fine points of procedural process. As how, this is pristine occasion for *wataschi*. I mean, like, I is done traversed globe near global-wide, Southern Seas Theater throughout *senso* duration, but never got around to it prior to present *ma* moment, reet? Like," I did say to her, Jack, "show me, *Yoko-san*, as how I don't know from legumes about *kokoro*. How we say in *Eigo*, *o-shogatsu* first day of new year, I make you present of *wataschi's* maraschino, reet?" How it were:

"There! There, Joe! Slowly! What is your haste?"

"*Yoko-san*!"

"Thus, *Joe-san*! You are in such haste! Lie fully upon me, Joe, for I am strong and will not break!"

"*Yoko-san*!"

"Put your face close to mine, Foto Joe! Feel my breath in your ear! Shall I place my tongue in your ear, Joe?"

"*Yoko-san*!"

"Oh, now, Joe! I feel you so far within me! Now, Joe, now, now! Ah, Mr. Foto Joe!"

"*Yoko-san*!"

"Ah, lie a bit longer upon me, Joe! Hear how your breath is hard and swift! Do you feel how our flesh clings? Joe?"

"*Yoko-san?* Is it over? Did I did it? *Yoko-san!*"

Etcetera blah, reet, Jack?

Kokoro, Jack! How it were, reet? What's did I know? How you say, live but don't learn nothing thereby, reet? *Kokoro?* I think not, Jack! *Wataschi* Foto Joe did this night (wee darkest predawn hours of *o-shogatsu*, circa '50!) yield up maraschino of virgin innocence (aged one and thirty years of age old, Jack!) to newly arrived in Eta Jima town *hosutesu moga* B-gal *mama-san* Matsumoto Yoko—but I do allege it were not *kokoro*, Jack!

Rather: consider it *ma* moment of deviational respite in *wataschi's do* flow of life and times lifestyle, ephemeralist aberration *kichigai* temporary-insanity shtick. Live, but do not learn thereby, reet?

"*Joe-san*, are you asleep?"

"But resting baby blues, sweet's pie. Like, wondering if I did do it right, proper form and all, reet?" She laughs, Jack!

"Oh, *Joe-san*, why do the men I lie with always wonder if they have behaved correctly? Be assured you do it as well and also as ineptly as any I have known, Joe!"

"Reet. Take your word for it. Sleep now, *Yoko-san*, as how dawnlight arises in east instanter, landlady personage Mrs. Hino certain sure to raise, how we say, stink ruckus, if you yet abide with me come postmeridian hours."

"The mysterious Mr. Foto Joe, famous on the street of the *nawanoren* in Eta Jima! Is it true I am the first woman with whom you have ever lain upon your *futon?*"

"Reet. What's the diff?"

"Ah! But I am a special person, not like my *hosutesu* friends of the Texas Bar who laughed at me tonight because I am newly arrived from the country and because I did not know how to speak to the *Amerikajin* to entice one to share a pillow with me for a price."

"You'll learn. Week, two. Trust Foto Joe: you'll be posing for pics candid and posed with Yanks, dragging down all that Occupation Currency scrip specie to exchange in the *oyama* black market, reet?"

"Do you think, *Joe-san*," she says, rising up from *futon* on one elbow, "that I am like all the rest of the *hosutesu*, that I will be content to work each night on the street of the *nawanoren* until I have saved enough money to move to a village and buy a shop or a small restaurant? Do you think I am an ordinary foolish *moga*, Foto Joe?"

"Sad to say," says I, and, "I think you ain't but a kiddie, aged eighteen or nineteen years old?"

"Seventeen," says she, "but I confess I say I am twenty when anyone asks

318

my age."

"Reet. Aged seventeen years old. Hence you ain't but scarce done playing with *ningyo* dollies."

"I am inspired by lofty ambition!" says she, and, "Though I cannot read or write, and I cannot speak the *Eigo*, I will study and learn these things, and when I am proficient and I have saved enough of the money I earn in the *nawanoren*, I shall be ready to execute my ultimate scheme for success in my life!"

"Than which is?" I query.

"You will mock me with laughter if I reveal this to you."

"Ix-nay," I say, and, "Scout's honorific, cross *hara* belly and heart both in sincere hope of expiration, reet?" She laughs, Jack.

"I shall," says she, "find an appropriate *Amerikajin*, one who is young and handsome and does not smell too strongly of raw beef, and who has a nose smaller than most, and who comes of a good family, and I shall beguile him until he proposes a marriage to me, and then I shall journey with him across the ocean, and there I shall live with him in the land of the *Amerikajin*, and I shall have the comfort and joy of living the life I have seen depicted in the imported *harukai eiga* and in the colored pictures published in the *shimbun*, and I shall grow old in a condition of happiness and affluence!"

"No stuff?" I query, and, "Reminds me of my dear departed baby sis — *Iko-san* was her handle, reet? Used to steady be singing a song our *mama-san* teached her, as how she wanted to grow up to marry a man like my daddy, live in a paper house with him and their kiddies, reet?"

"And did your sister do this, *Joe-san*?"

"Nope. Big fire, circa 'forty-two, cinders and ashes, when you was just a little nipper, sweetness," I say, and, "Here's wishing you lucks, babes." And, "Go to sleep now if you don't want to appear wan when you hit Texas Bar on the morrow's eventide to find you your Yank, reet?" I say.

"You mock me, Mr. Foto Joe, but I might as easily scorn you!"

"Mrs. Hino doubtless eavesdrops," I try to interject, but she don't listen, reet?

"Everyone in the *nawanoren* knows I am but an ignorant girl from a poor village, but what of you, Foto Joe? Has your life been so sordid that you are ashamed to reveal its history?"

"Matter of security," I say, but, Jack, she ain't hearing me, reet?

"And though you enjoy a fine commerce with the *Amerikajin*, there are those who consider you *baka* because you accept only worthless *yen* for your photographs!"

"I'm working on that one, hon," I try to say.

"And what of your future life, mysterious and *baka* Mr. Foto Joe?" says she. "Have you no ultimate scheme for your old age? Will you forever be only Foto Joe who wanders Eta Jima's street of *nawanoren* to make stupid photographs of *moga* and *Amerikajin issen gorin*? If you will not speak of your past, have you the candor to tell me of what is to come, Mr. Foto Joe who mocks my ambition?"

"Truth told," I say when I dig she's done yakking, "I ain't give it much thought, reet? I mean, like, I had me big plans when I was but your age, sixteen, seventeen years, but give up same due to circumstances unforeseen and mitigating—big fires ubiquitous," I say.

"You speak riddles!" says she. "Perhaps you would do well to devise a plan for the remainder of your life, *Joe-san*."

I say: "Like, I'll think on it, reet? You ready to slumber, cuteness?"

"Come closer to me, Joe," says she, "for the night is very cold, and perhaps my warmth will provoke you to attempt once more what you have just done for the first time. Is it not probable a second occasion will give you greater confidence in your new ability?"

"Might could," I say, and, "Anyone ever tell you you gots a scrumptious nape to your neck, Miss *Yoko-san*?"

"And take notice also," says she, "how much larger than usual are my breasts, much larger than most of my *hosutesu* friends. I am told the *Amerikajin* value large breasts. Is this so, Joe?"

"Reet," I tell her, and move snuggle-close on *futon*, Jack!

Jack: all things (good and also bad!) come to end—usually ironical in portent—reet?

"Foto Joe!" calls out landlady *oba-san* Mrs. Hino Takako, knocks on my lean-to door. "Foto Joe, are you awake, or do you still entertain yourself in the lodging you rent from me with the shameless *moga* who laughed loud enough to wake my neighbors in the night? Wake, Foto Joe, for it is late in the afternoon and you must depart for the street which disgraces all of Eta Jima!"

"I is up!" I tell her, and, "Doing busy beaver and also honeybee-style labors lo these many hours, Old Auntie! Don't open door. I is developing pics in here, reet?"

"And does your *moga* assist you in your work, Foto Joe?"

"Relax, Mrs. Hino, she's long gone. Done perambulated off *sanpo* shank's mare to find her friends for breakfast *chogee* style quick as her high heels go upon advent of first dawn light, reet?"

"Truly?" she queries.

"Would I yank your aged venerable limbs, *Oba-san*?"

"That is well," she says, and, "The gossips of this neighborhood will be denied the satisfaction of seeing a fallen woman in my home! Tell your *moga*, Foto Joe," she says through closed door (I develop pic negatives in chemical-stink minimalist interior environ atmospherics, reet?), "that she is not welcome in this heretofore virtuous household. Do you attend my words, Foto Joe?"

"Loud and clear, Roger wilco and out, reet?"

"I expressly forbid you ever again to bring your *moga* or any other from this city's sinful street as a guest to my house, Foto Joe!"

"You got it, *Oba-san!*" I say, and, "Never *hochee* nevermore, reet?"

"Do you promise me, Foto Joe?" she asks—voice decibels volume reduced, mouth close to door.

"Reet."

"Is it that you now experience regret and remorse for your debauchery, Foto Joe? Have you resolved to behave with acceptable decorum as a result of your night of abandon?"

"Ix-nay," I tell her, and, "Like, odds indicate contra against possible long-shot freebie *kokoro* ecstacies sentiments ever again, reet? Hard fact of life and times even in current Jimmu Boom good times economics, Old Auntie," I say.

"Ah!" says she, "What should I do were I cursed with a son such as you, one who reduces all decency to a consideration of *yen!*"

"Logics fallacious," I say. "Hypotheticals contrariwise to known available data, Mrs. Hino. Forget it, reet? Past is pastness. Go with *do* flow, reet? Now, please to depart my doorway, as how I gots me a small fortune in pics to develop and also print—very busy on Strip in context of Yank *o-shogatsu* celebratory revels. If you lets in day's light, Mrs. Hino, Foto Joe subject to drops a bundle, reet?"

O-shogatsu New Year's Eve, circa January 1, 1950—hats and also horns Yank revels—not to fail to mention *kokoro* (freebie!) ecstacies of *futon's* shared pillow. Night to remember, Jack!

What's did I know, reet? Aged but one and thirty years old (circa '50), I think: Foto Joe, will your garb eternal be beret, opaque aviator shade specs, black jacket, turtle's neck, pegged trou, spade-toe kicks of like hue? I think: *wataschi* Foto Joe, has *do* flow path of life and times come to ultimateness here within *nawanoren*, gadget bag shoulder-slung, Yashica at ready, upon (soon famed!) Eta Jima Strip?

"Joe, you little zipperhead slant-eye midget fucker!" cry Yank clientele in effusive eventide greetings. "You got them pitchers you took of me and my main man with them broads in the Rhumba Bar last weekend?"

"Foto Joe," asks Texas Bar bartender-owner Arai Kikuo, "how is it that you never appear to weary, as I do on occasion, of this unremitting quest after affluent security we pursue each night?"

"*Joe-san*," says *hosutesu* B-gals, "my friend *Yoko-san* hints that you shared a *futon* with her. Is this so? We will not believe this unless you can show us a photograph as proof, for we know you have no interest in women, Joe!"

I say: "Show me your *yen*, Jack, I show you your pic, reet?" and, "Defecate or vacate *benjo* stool, G.I., as how I gots your likeness here in my bag—is you gots the *yen*?" and, "*Sumairu* big smile for camera, Yanks! How you say, like unto feline masticating turds, reet?"

I say: "Go with *do* flow, *Kikuo-san*," and, "Evacuate kitchen if temperatures oppress, reet, *Kikuo-san*," and, "Trouble slumbering, *Kikuo-san*? Try counting *yen* and also scrip specie instead of sheeps, reet?"

I say: "Them as say don't know from legumes, them as knows strictly observe mumness, reet, ladies?"

I say: "Hello, *Yoko-san*! Ain't seen you much past couple weeks on Strip, reet? Where and also how you been keeping, babes?"

Says she, "Ah, Joe! Did I not foretell, that night and early morning we lay together on your *futon*, that I would find an appropriate *Amerikajin* who might prove my destiny for a wonderful life to come across the ocean?"

"Reet."

"It is possible I have already found this man. Do you know the *Amerikajin issen gorin* who is named Buck Private Walter Everett Kennedy?"

"Never heard of him," I say, "but, like, I works from memory of visages, pay little heed attentions to moniker handles."

"Perhaps you have not yet made his photograph," says she, "for he came to *Nihon* only shortly before I journeyed to Eta Jima from my village. I will bring him to the Texas Bar soon, and you can make a photograph for us, Joe. Will you do that?"

"Warn him I accept *yen* only, no scrip," I say.

"Ah, Joe," she says, "I think he is a proper man for me to make an *o-miai* marriage with. He is of course very tall, like all his *issen gorin* comrades, but his nose is no larger than usual among the *Amerikajin*, and he smells only very faintly of uncooked meat!"

"Sounds," I say, "like as if he is positive pure dreamy boat heartthrob cutie pie matinees idol."

"More significant, Joe, is that he appears already beguiled by me. He says often and with much zeal in his voice that he loves me as he has never loved another—this a friend of mine did translate for me, Joe! And he is very jealous that I come to the *nawanoren* on the evenings when he cannot come to Eta Jima from his barracks. My friend has told him that I do this only to earn Occupation Currency, and already I have a box that begins to fill with scrip, Joe! I shall save a great amount and then exchange it all at one time in the *oyama*. Also, Buck Private Walter Everett Kennedy speculates that if he and I were to have a child, would it resemble him or me the more. Or so my friend translates his words to me."

"The man," I tell her, "is doubtless head over heels, anus over appetite, Swoon City, reet?"

322

"He is at present confined to his barracks for the infraction of returning tardy to his duty after a night with me on my *futon*, but he sends me assurance he will be free to join me in but two weeks. Meet us here at the Texas Bar, Joe, and I will present to you Buck Private Walter Everett Kennedy, who says his family is an honorable one which earns its livelihood in the place called Hattiesburg, Mississippi, by means of cutting down forests of small trees from which paper is made."

"Boy hidey!" I say, and, "For certain sure said personage is how we say in *Eigo*, rosy-neck yeomanry salt of earths blue-collar, scarce one to grace *shimbun* social-register society page stateside!" and, "Mississippi, as in sovereign state thereof, never been there myself, but hear as how it is deity's own half-acre, reet? So," I say, "how's your *Eigo* progress?"

"I learn rapidly," says Matsumoto Yoko, "under the tutoring of Buck Private Walter Everett Kennedy. Listen to these words, Joe: If the good lord made anything better than quim, he must of kept it for hisself," she says, and, "Do I enunciate well, Foto Joe?"

"Reet," I tell her. "Not unlike like unto native spieler."

Thus it were, spring of 1950—*hanami* time (big ironies of life!), reet? *Wataschi* Foto Joe is thinking: *wataschi*, is it not mayhap opportune juncture in temporal span of life and times lifetime to initiate actions, given possibilities fate's fickle digit destines you is arrived at ultimate destination (aged one and thirty years old, Jack!) on do path?

"Foto Joe!" cry out *hosutesu moga* B-gal comfort women within Eta Jima Strip *nawanoren*, "Why are you so somber, Foto Joe? Why do you seem of late so incapable of jocularity? If it is true that you did indeed share your *futon* with Matsumoto Yoko, was the experience so unpleasant as to prevent your smiling as you go about the Strip to conduct your commerce with the Yanks, *Joe-san*? Choose one of us, *Joe-san*," they tease (circa *hanami*, 1950, reet?), "and you will experience the transport that comes of sharing your pillow with a *moga* of mature years and seasoned skills! Come on, Joe!" they greet me. "Smile!" they say, and, "Choose your favorite from among us, and you will learn how to be happy with the delights of *kokoro*!"

"Reet," I tell them, and, "Don't not jerk my chain, nor pull limb, reet? Too busy, gals, gots to perambulate *sanpo* shank's mare down Strip, hustle after nut, reet?"

"Mr. Foto Joe," says Texas Bar bartender-owner Arai Kikuo, "are you ill? The *moga* speak of how sad you appear as you go about the *nawanoren* with your camera. Have you received unpleasant news, *Joe-san*?"

"Feeling glum, chum," I tell him. "Got a feeling denominated as blues, reet?" and, "Feeling suddenly lower than whale's excretion, than with resides on bottom of Pacific with David Jones and also *Kudo Butai* Imperial fleet, *Kikuo-san*."

"Is it the *moga* Matsumoto Yoko, Joe?"

"Doubtful," I say, and, "Rather, might could be I envision life and times shtick here and now, *ma* moment of decision as to settle down in *enryo* relationship with good woman, raise kiddie offsprings and get respectable shtick, than which do require female personage thereto, reet, *Kikuo-san*?"

"Ah, Joe, there is never a dearth of women!"

"Reet. Than which adage I keeps telling self."

"Mr. Foto Joe," says *wataschi's oba-san* landlady widow woman Mrs. Hino Takako, "a change has come to your demeanor. Had I a son who behaved with such lack of animation, I should advise him to consult a physician or a fortune teller and also to pray to his *kami* to ease his spirits!"

"Reet."

"Are you an unhappy man, you, Mr. Foto Joe, with all the *yen* your commerce brings you, and with a landlady such as I, who worries on behalf of her tenant?"

"Anks-thay," I say, and, "Who would ever of thunk it of *wataschi* Foto Joe, reet, Old Auntie?"

Cut to: interior environ, Texas Bar *nawanoren*, circa springtime (*hanami!*), '50, reet? Joint is, how you say, but jumping, reet? On bandstand, Hatta Yoshizawa Country Western Band renders unceasing medleys of shitkicker favorites. Crowded minimalist atmospherics thick with ciggie smoke, bar, booths, not to fail to mention also tables-for-two filled with off-duty Yanks, wall-to-wall *mama-san hosutesu*, bartender-owner Arai Kikuo busy as legendary handicapped interior decorator serving up stateside *harukai* import *oyama* canisters of malt beverages, reet?

Enter *wataschi* Foto Joe: beret, opaque aviator shade specs, black turtle's neck and leather jacket, pegged trou and spade-toe kicks of like hue — gadget bag (natch!) shoulder-slung, pre-*senso* Yashica at ready, reet, Jack?

"Foto Joe! *Joe-san!*" cries out voice of Matsumoto Yoko — *Yoko-san*, reet? — "Joe, I am so pleased to see you! Come to our table, Joe, for I would present to you the man of whom I spoke, Buck Private Walter Everett Kennedy!"

Can you not dig it? Oh, Jack, I do hereby allege it was not *kokoro* love sentiments!

"Greetings and also salutations, reet?" I say, and, "Pleasure's all mine, G.I.!" and, "*Yoko-san* been talking you up something fierce, Honorable Buck Private Kennedy," and, "How you keeping, *Yoko-san*? Still hoarding all that good scrip specie in a box toward big day of *oyama* highest rate of exchange?"

324

"Joe," says she, "do not jest," and, "Is he not a most wonderfully appropriate *Amerikajin* for the purpose I confided to you? Talk to him for me, *Joe-san*, for my *Eigo* is still so poor, and my *hosutesu* friends you can see are all too engaged to translate for us."

"What's I'm supposed to say to him, babes? I mean, like, you say words, I'll move lips not unlike like unto Charlie McCarthy dummy, reet?"

"Oh, Joe," says she, "ask him if he truly loves me, and ask him also if he has yet to speak to his *oyabun* superiors to ask permission to make a marriage with me, and ask him to describe the large house in which we shall reside together in the place called Hattiesburg in Mississippi."

"Reet," I say, and, to Buck Private Walter Everett Kennedy, "Joe's the name, photo's my game, nice getting to know you, reet?" hold out my hand for big Okie-style howdy handshake.

"I know about you," says he, "you're the Jap ever'one calls Foto Joe takes pitchers of ever'body in bars here. I seen you a couple times when I used to was always be hanging out on the Strip before I met up with Yoko. Was it you used to was her boyfriend once or something?" he queries.

"Ix-nay," I riposte. "Just old acquaintance, reet?"

"Is he not just such a man as I foretold I should find to take me across the ocean to a wonderful life, Joe?" says Matsumoto Yoko.

Says he: "She still can't talk for shit. I always got to be steady asking some whore to tell me what she's talking. I just was wondering if you used to was her boyfriend or what," says Buck Private Walter Everett Kennedy, "on account of she's always saying your name a lot is what made me wonder, see?"

Dig it, Jack: Buck Private Walter Everett Kennedy. Yank Mississippi rosy-neck good old boy *issen gorin*, not unlike like unto Aggie matriculants of alma mater Oklahoma A & M (Go, Pokes! Go, Punchers! Beat O.U.!), Texas Bar, Eta Jima Strip, circa '50 *hanami*, than which personage *Yoko-san* — it were not *kokoro*, Jack! — projects as agent of *do* flow life plan leading toward future affluence stateside comfort securities etcetera blah.

It is, how you say, to laugh, Jack.

"So, Honorable Buck Private Kennedy Walter Everett," I say, "Miss Yoko bids me query you, like, do you still love her — how we say, harbor sincere *kokoro* sentiments therefor, reet?"

Says he: "I never knowed a woman like Yoko before, man," and, "Women to home won't let you get to first base even unless it's you tell 'em you want to get married up with them in the damn Baptist Church. Fuck that shit!" Says he: "Me and some good old boys buddies of mine drove out to Soso in this one old boy's daddy's pickup once and screwed a nigger gal we had to give two damn dollars each before she'd do it, but what I mean, white women won't let you touch and don't even hardly like you looking at it neither. Man," says Buck Private Walter Everett Kennedy, "I love it here! Onliest thing I don't like is I'd just as leave Yoko didn't come around these places on the Strip whoring when I ain't got a pass to get off base when I'm restricted to barracks. Tell her she knows damn well I'd given her more money if it wasn't they busted me from Pfc. and cut my payday down."

"Reet," I say, and, to Matsumoto Yoko (*daijubo* no sweats for *wataschi* to effect rapid gear-shift lingo to lingo, reet?), "Loves you all to death, hon, but don't cotton to Strip *moga* hustle you pursue, reet?"

"Joe, tell him I love him also, though I should marry him even if I did not, and that I work only to accumulate large sums to contribute to our comfort and security when we go to live as husband and wife in the place called Hattiesburg in Mississippi."

"Jack," I tell him, "it's like, her dowry she's hustling, reet?"

"The which?" he queries. I explain (Lieutenant *Benshi*, reet?). "Dowry? Who in hell's she marrying she needs to get a dowry?"

"Best I can figure, Buck Private Kennedy Walter Everett," I tell him, "you yourself sole so designated, reet?"

"Me?" says he, and, "Shit and fall back in it, Jap! You don't know nothing about Mississippi," says he. "My old daddy'd flat kill my ass if I brought me home a slope gal for a wife!"

"What does he say in response, *Joe-san*?"

"Reet," and to Matsumoto Yoko, "He says as how he's subject real soon to initiate red-tapes bureaucracy paperworks process toward nuptial permissions instanter, lovey doves."

"But I tell you, Mr. Jap Foto Joe," says he, "I don't mind trying to get me enough to last me all my life whiles I'm here!" Can you dig it? Grabs her (thigh's inner surface!), ursine hug embraces, kisses (tongue extended!) her direct on aural orifice, reet?

"Did I not tell you I should beguile an appropriate *Amerikajin*, Foto Joe?" says she—laughs—hee, har, reet?

"Come on, Yoko," says he, "let's us go off and get with it on that mattress before I do it in my drawers right here."

I say: "As how trio creates horde, dig you later, reet, folks?"

Hanami, Jack! Circa springtime, 1950, reet? I did think: Foto Joe, is it not opportune *ma* moment juncture in life and times lifetime span of *do* flow path to alter status? I think: Foto Joe, you gots you *yen* adequate to contract construction of smallish paper house, ensconce helpmate therein, engender kiddies (thus providing son and heir to light funeral fire, reet?) — who more likely to purpose, I did think, than aforementioned Matsumoto Yoko, than which *moga hosutesu* herself does seek but *ushi* domestic conjugal *yoin* stabilities within *enryo* relationship, reet?

Jack, what's did I know? *Wataschi*, aged but one and thirty years of age old. Live, how you say, but don't not learn nothing thereby, reet?

"Mr. Foto Joe," says *wataschi's* old auntie *oba-san* widow woman landlady Mrs. Hino Takako, "it is a great pity you have no parents, for if this were not so, your father might contract with a reputable *nakodo* matchmaker to arrange a suitable *o-miai* marriage arrangement with a woman of respectable name for you, and the influence of a seemly wife might lead you to abandon your shameful activity in quest of *yen!*"

"*Joe-san*," says Texas Bar bartender-owner Arai Kikuo, "if your discontent results from a simple yearning for the pleasure of a woman on your *futon*, can you not afford with all your *yen* to purchase the occasional favors of as many *moga* as you desire? And if what troubles you is the solitude of your life, and you seek a more continuous relationship, can you not as well afford to establish a mistress in some house in Eta Jima where you might go for companionship whenever the need came upon you?"

I did think: Foto Joe — a.k.a. Student Yamaguchi Yoshinori, a.k.a. Gooch, a.k.a. Lieutenant *Benshi*! — if neither chances nor not also circumstances proffer solutions, is it not dirty though necessary job you gots to do your own self?

Jack: please to dig it was not *kokoro* sentiments heartfelt — wholly unlike like unto instance of Miss Clara ("Petty Girl") Sterk! — which, as follows, did motivate *wataschi*. Say: *wataschi* Foto Joe did only seek to seize misunderstood *ma* moment awareness of mistaken *yoin* in midst of *do* flow path, did endeavor due to inadequacy (aged one and thirty years!) of ironical perspective mind-set to bring heretofore chaos course of life and times to end in acceptable — howsomever so humble, Jack! — stasis, reet? As follows:

Late spring (*hanami*, Jack!), circa '50, reet? Late hours of eventide, Jack, interior environ of Texas Bar *nawanoren*, Yank *issen gorin* clientele returned to Eta Jima barracks confines (or elsewhere in company of *mama-san hosutesu* to enjoy *futon* transport ecstacies, reet?). Present on scene: bartender-owner Arai Kikuo, *moga* B-gal Matsumoto Yoko, and (natch!) *wataschi* Foto Joe, reet?

"Joe," says Arai Kikuo, "shall I serve you and the *moga* something to drink? I have ample stores of the *harukai* imported *oyama* White Horse Scotch whiskey reserved for officers of the Yank military police."

"Thanks but no thanks, *Kikuo-san*," I say, and, "Mayhap later if celebration ceremonials eventuate as hoped, reet? Meanwhiles, give us a tad privacy."

"I shall be busily engaged in cleaning this establishment to be ready for tomorrow's commerce," says he, "and I promise my ears shall be stopped against such words as you may exchange with the *moga, Joe-san*."

"Reet," I tell him, and, "Anks-thay," and, "I owe you one, *Kikuo-san*."

What's did I know (aged one and thirty years!), reet, Jack?

"Like," I did say to her (Matsumoto Yoko, *moga hosutesu* B-gal *mama-san*!), "anks-thay for coming out so late in eventide to requested rendez-vous, *Yoko-san*."

Says she: "Good evening, Joe. *Kikuo-san* conveyed your message to me yesterday, and so I have come where and when you asked, but know that I would otherwise even now be with my betrothed, Buck Private Walter Everett Kennedy, and I have no doubt he will be angry with me for refusing to accompany him this night. He will think that I am lying on my *futon* with another *Amerikajin issen gorin*, and this always enrages him."

"Reet," I say, and, "Orry-say," and, "Listen up, *Yoko-san*," I tell her, "as how I gots serious business shtick to confabulate, reet?"

"Oh, Joe," she says, "you are ever so mysterious in your conversation! Do you know that you are a legend in all the *nawanoren* of Eta Jima? In each place I go when I am at work with my *hosutesu* friends, they talk of Foto Joe, and they speculate as to the size of the fortune in *yen* you have surely accumulated, and each *nawanoren* reserves a space on the wall to post the photographs you are unable to deliver to your customers — what can the mysterious and legendary Mr. Foto Joe desire from me?"

"Reet," I say, and, "Try to deliver every pic I'm paid for, but some Yanks just flat disappear, reet? So I sticks them up, like adverts, reet? Minimalist chronicles of Strip life and times passing-scene revelries." She laughs, Jack — hee hee, reet? And when she does not riposte, I say, "So, *Yoko-san*, how it's going by you? Still saving all your Occupation Currency scrip specie in big box toward projected *o-miai* marriage dowry sum?"

She laughs, says: "Indeed! My friends who translate the words of Buck Private Walter Everett Kennedy tell me he promises very soon to ask for permission to make our marriage, and when this permission is granted, I shall take all my *Amerikajin* scrip to the *oyama* and exchange it for *yen* at the most favorable rates, and then I shall journey to his home across the ocean to live the life I have dreamed of — oh, Joe," says she, "it appears certain all shall come to pass as I predicted to you that night of *o-shogatsu*!"

"Ix-nay!" I say, and, "How we say in *Eigo*, blowing smokes out your spout, reet? Than which is to say, never *hochee*!"

She don't not laugh nor *sumairu* smile neither at that, reet, Jack?

Says she: "What do you say to me, Joe? Why do you say such things to me! Oh, you are a cruel person, *Joe-san*!"

I tell her: "Listen up!"

I did tell her: as how Buck Private Kennedy Walter Everett is strictly rosy-neck good old boy shit-for-brains no goodnik, reet? As how in Mississippi (sovereign state thereof!), he don't not dast schlepp home *Nihonjin* whore personage as helpmeet mate, reet? As how life she dreams of stateside is not unlike like unto village hicks sticks boondocks rural environ of Eisaku Prefecture she did flee for Eta Jima Jimmu Boom times for economic opportunities nut hustle, reet?

I did say: "*Yoko-san*, Buck Private Walter Everett Kennedy is low-class no-class-at-all pulpwood cutter, thus destined to rude crude scratch-for-living hands-to-mouth existence mode not unlike like unto durance vile, reet?"

"I have beguiled him! He loves me!"

"It ain't but that you is premier womans he ever shared *futon* pillow with — except save for Negroid *moga* — ain't no *kokoro* about it, reet?"

"I shall cross the ocean with him! I need not even purchase the PX Chest because my breasts are so uncommonly large — this you know! I shall have enough money when I exchange my scrip in the *oyama* that I will be able to afford the surgery which removes the skin about my eyes, and thus none will then recognize that I was born *Nihonjin!*"

"He is, like, putting you on, *Yoko-san*. He is, like, shooting you through proverbialist grease, handing out line, dig? Shooting bullock, *Yoko-san!*"

Said she: "Oh, Foto Joe, why do you say cruel things to me! You make me weep, and it is not good of you to do this cruelty! You lie, Joe, you say cruel lies to make me weep!"

"Joe," says bartender-owner Arai Kikuo, "why does the *moga* weep and tear at her hair?"

"Relax, *Kikuo-san*," I tell him, and, "*Daijubo* no sweats, reet? Like, *wataschi* Foto Joe can handle situationals, reet?" To her, *moga hosutesu* B-gal *mama-san* Matsumoto Yoko, I say, "Terminate waterworks, reet? Listen up, *Yoko-san*, as how I gots what for serious to convey, reet? Is you digging my words, Yoko?" I query.

"I listen," she says, "and I hear, but my eyes flow at the cruel lies you speak to me, Mr. Foto Joe!"

"Listen up," I say, and, "Hear words of wisdoms I glean via one and thirty years life and times I relate to you, *Yoko-san*," and, "Dry baby blues, *mama-san*," and, "Pay attentions to Foto Joe, reet? Listen to me, Yoko, as how preamble as follows is designed to state case favorably on behalf of *wataschi* toward proposition I propose thence, reet?"

"I listen, but I no longer know if you are my friend, *Joe-san*, for your cruel lies concerning Buck Private Walter Everett Kennedy so burden me with despair."

I tell her, Jack! I tell her: "*Wataschi* is not Foto Joe, Yoko! *Wataschi* is *munako* orphan child of no name, sad to say, result thereof of twists personal and historical global-wide, same resultant derived doubtless from chaos of *do* flow path of life and times, reet? Can you dig it, *Yoko-san*?

329

Listen up!"

Jack, I tell her—from Student Yamaguchi Yoshinori, reet? I tell her from Mr. and Mrs. Yamaguchi's sole son and heir, pride and also joy little Yosh (*Yosho-san!*), outstanding matriculant of Native Land Loving School. I tell her from paper house wherein resided little Yosh, *Papa-san*, *Mama-san*, Baby Sis *Iko-san*! I did tell her from *Amerikajin* national pastime sport of *besuboru*—ever heard, I did query, from names of legendary American League all-star greats George Herman (a. k.a. Babe, a.k.a. Bambino, a.k.a. Sultan of Swat!) Ruth? Louis (a.k.a. Iron Man!) Gehrig? Vernon (a.k.a. Lefty!) Gomez? Ever heard from Senators of Washington (D.C.) third-string bullpen warmup catcher goes by handle of Morris (a.k.a. Moe!) Berg?

"*Joe-san*, you baffle me with these strange names!"

"Reet!" And I tell her, Jack! I tell her from Moe Berg's 16-millimeter Stewart Warner *eiga* flic camera with long range focus lens, lensing *Kido Butai* fleet at anchor in Tokyo Bay, Ichigaya Heights headquarters, Eta Jima training facility—"Environ whereat we sit ensconced nearby even as we confabulate, reet, Yoko?" I tell her from Ambassador Joe Clark Grew, from Mr. Sato Isao (Imperial Ministry of Education—har!), from personal audience with *Mikado*.

"Do you say to me that when you were but sixteen years of age you were presented to the *Mikado*, *Joe-san*?"

"Reet! Listen up!"

Jack: I tell her from lifelong *kichigai* craze for *eiga* flics and also *Eigo* lingo. I reveal *hara* belly-deep desire for higher-educational education endeavors stateside, promise of Moe Berg's clout influences to attain necessary funding to fund same etcetera blah.

"And did you cross the ocean to the land of the *Amerikajin* to pursue your study, Joe?"

"Did I not?" I explain (*benshi* style!) as how *kempei* complications preclude Ivy League matriculations, dictate enrollment at obscure cow college institution as first foreign student ever admitted, Oklahoma A & M (Go, Pokes!), class of '40, reet?

"So what is sometimes rumored of you is true, *Joe-san*? You did live among the *Amerikajin* in this distant place called Oklahoma?"

"Reet. Sovereign state thereof—not all that far from Mississippi!" I tell her. "Dig, Yoko: having betrayed *Dai Nippon* traitor-spy style, I did thence betray Yanks also, reet? Sheer-necessity shtick, *Yoko-san*, *genkin* cash in plain brown envelopes conveyed by aforesaid Mr. Sato in guise of Japan–America Friendship Society field rep, banks of Cimarron River beneath blackjack oaks, rural Perkins village environ, reet? Can you dig it, *Yoko-san*?"

"And the *Amerikajin* called you by the name of Gooch?"

"Reet!"

Jack: I tell her from return to *Dai Nippon*, circa June of '40, reet? From *aka gami* red-letter draft greetings from *Mikado, budo* officer training (courtesy Imperial Army!) at Eta Jima — "Same environ nearby where even as I speak we sit ensconced, reet, Yoko?"

"I should not," says she, "have imagined you a soldier, Joe, and never an officer."

"Me neither. Ironicals, reet?" I tell her, Jack, from grandiose *hakko ichui* eight corners under single roof flic docudrama *eiga* scheme scam I concoct to evade combatant status. I tell her from *honcho* Premier-General Tojo Hideki. I did tell her from Lieutenant *Benshi*, reet? I say, "How we say, he who explains, reet? Named for old-timey silent flic days before your time, reet?" I tell her from A & M yearbook annual *Redskin*, 1940 edition, lost in big fire aboard sinking U.S.S. *Oklahoma* whilst on mission to lens glorious *Tora* initial triumph of grandiose *hakko ichui* design.

"You are a veteran of the historic victory at *Pearu Halbol, Joe-san*? I find this assertion so difficult to credit!"

"Was I not? Noncombat status, natch, ensconced in back seat of Naka-jima bomber craft — unarmed, reet? — said aircraft chauffeured by Chink campaign air ace flyboy jockey Imperial Navy Lieutenant Commander Sugihara Heihachiro, personage, sad to say, later lost in Great Marianas Turkey Shoot debacle defeat, reet? Before your time, *Yoko-san!*"

I tell her: from 14th Imperial Army, *honcho* General Homma Masaharu commanding — also later hanged by *Makassar-san!* — P.I. campaign, from feature *eiga* flic *Down with the Stars & Stripes*, from circa May '42 Corregidor rock fortress surrender ceremonials staged for lensing on scene, from *do* flow fate's rendezvous with Stevie (a.k.a. Yukon Strongboy, a.k.a. Mighty Mouse!) Keller thereat, from so-called Bataan Death March, from Camp O'Donnell durance vile casting call, subsequent escape connived for Strongboy Stevie — "Hence, I did betray *Dai Nippon* once more again, reet?"

"But where are all the *eiga* you made of the great *senso* throughout the Southern Seas if what you tell me is true, *Joe-san?*"

"Gone," I say, "Big fires, reet?" I explain: from massive cinematic archives (*Hakko Ichui, Nippon Maketa!*) incinerated in studio facility located close by Ground Zero *pikadon* Flash Boom, Hiroshima City, from holocaust aboard U.S.S. *Oklahoma*, from Jimmy Doolittle's daring dash flyboy raid off deck of *Hornet*. "Gone," I did tell her, "along with *Papa-san, Mama-san*, Sis *Iko-san*, nineteen forty edition *Redskin*, family photo album, not to fail to mention three from amongst Hundred Millions, not to fail to mention also Student Yamaguchi Yoshinori, Gooch, and also Lieutenant *Benshi*, reet?"

Jack: what's did I not tell her, *hosutesu moga* B-gal comfort woman *mama-san* Matsumoto Yoko, circa late spring (*hanami!*), 1950, reet?

"And in the year nineteen forty-four you were granted a private audience with the *Mikado*, Joe?"

"Reet. *Yake tsuchi jidai* Burned Earth Period. Old pal of mine now engaged in concerted fishes study research and also writing, reet?"

"I do not know if I am able to believe all this you have said of yourself, *Joe-san*. If it is true, still it is as great a riddle as the enigma you present to all who know of you here in Eta Jima today."

I tell her: "*Yoko-san*, it is *wataschi's* sad-and-happy life and times lifetimes chronicle, reet? It is black-and-white still pics, stacks from *eiga* film cannisters, than which none of survives extant, reet? All reduced to cinders and also ashes, available only from memories, manifest in motley *Eigo-Nihonju* lingo I spiel, reet? It is past's pastness rendered chaotic absurdist via reminiscent perspectives, reet? I call it big irony of life, *Yoko-san!*"

"But why do you relate all this to me, *Joe-san*? And why did you tell me the cruel lies concerning Buck Private Walter Everett Kennedy? Ah, Joe! As always, you seem to jest even when you say you are in earnest!"

I did say: "I is done give my spiel, spoke speech, as how we is come here and now to *ma* moment in Texas Bar *nawanoren*, reet? As how because there is betwixt us possible potential *enryo* reciprocities relationship, reet? As how because, aged one and thirty years of age old, armed only with ironic sensibilities and also *yen* capital, *munako* child of no name orphan *wataschi* does, in prime time of prime of life and times, propose to alter course of future's *do* flow, reet?"

"I do not understand," says *moga* B-gal *hosutesu* comfort woman *mama-san* Matsumoto Yoko.

"Reet. Listen up further!"

Jack, I said to her: "*Yoko-san*, *wataschi* Foto Joe, *munako* child of no name orphan, heretofore than which whose life and times lifetime are chaotic absurdities resultant of ironies big and small, herewith and by *do* proffer to you proposal of *o-miai* marriage, reet?"

Said she: "What have you said to me, *Joe-san*?"

"Listen up! *O-miai* marriage proposal, reet? How we say, come live with *wataschi*, be my *kokoro* love, reet? Establish connubial and also conjugalist blisses within context of *ushi* domestics, reet? In short, pith and gist: tie knot, hitch, splice, man-and-wife shtick. Become honest woman, adapt moniker handle to that of Mrs. Foto Joe, reet? Is you hearing me, *Yoko-san*?"

Says she . . . Jack, she did not say nothing! Zip, zilch, zed, diddly-squat, reet? Jack, can you dig it—she did laugh! Hee! Har!

"*Yoko-san!*" I say . . . I did say as how, after one and thirty years knockabout, *Nihon*, stateside, Southern Seas Theater of Operations, all as unwitting victim of twists ironical, both personalist and global-wide scopes, after series of fires big and small (cinders and ashes, Jack!) rendering all endeavors chaotic absurdist, *wataschi* did desire, how you say, implant roots, settle down to modicum norm stable lifestyle of domesticity shtick, reet?

"*Yoko-san*," I did say, "do me favor not to laugh, reet? Please to consider seriously offer proffered in all seriousness. I am talking paper house we will build, same complete with *engawa* veranda porch, to include *furin* wind-chime bells to signal breezes blowing sylvan. I is talking *tokonoma* niche in wall for ensconcement of family *kami butsudan* and also rice-paper scrolls, *shoji* sliding panel doors, *tatami* whereon to slumber, *futon* to share, *hibachi* in which to ignite charcoal coals to cook *umai* yummies for to scarf. I is talking *geta* clogs stashed outside door, *kimono* for casual attire, to include *obi* sash and *monsho* crests—talking as how to engender little kiddies to light funeral pyres as and when appropriate, reet? Please not to laugh, *Yoko-san!*"

Hee. Hee. Hardy har har, reet, Jack?

"Ah, *Joe-san!*" says she when able to stifle guffaws. "Mr. Foto Joe proposes marriage to me! Joe, either you continue to jest or you are the *baka* fool some in the *nawanoren* of Eta Jima consider you!"

"I is talking," I do iterate, "*Yoko-san, kokoro* heart and *hara* belly sentiments! I is talking *mimikaki* tenderness reciprocities! I is talking formulation, not to fail to mention manipulation, of future time's *do* flow in direction of satisfactions mutual, reet, *Yoko-san?*"

"Foto Joe," calls out Texas Bar bartender-owner Arai Kikuo, "what have you said to cause the small *moga* to laugh like one lost in the depths of insanity? It is well past the hour for me to lock the door and shutters and go to rest against tomorrow's endeavors, *Joe-san*. Can you not take your *moga* and depart soon?"

"Reet!" I tell him.

I did say: "Riposte, *Yoko-san. Kikuo-san* seeks to slumber. How we say in *Eigo*, yes or no, defecate or vacate commode, reet?"

"Then you are truly desirous of making a marriage with me, Joe?"

"In fact and also act. I gots the *yen* if you say when. Speak or eternally maintain silence, reet?"

"Ah, Joe." She shakes noggin, big *sumairu* feline devouring excrement grin, reet? "*Joe-san*, it is you who do not listen to me! Have I not told you since the night of *o-shogatsu* when we first met that I should beguile an *Amerikajin* to take me for his wife? Did I not present to you Buck Private Walter Everett Kennedy of Hattiesburg in the place across the ocean called Mississippi? You did not hear my words, Foto Joe, or else it is that you are a *baka*! How should I agree to marry you when it is destined that I shall marry Buck Private Walter Everett Kennedy, who is, I suspect, sent to me by the *kami* I have prayed to since I was a child in my village? How shall I marry you when it is fated that I shall take my ever-larger box of Occupation Currency to the *oyama* for exchange, and with this ample dowry journey across the ocean with Buck Private Walter Everett Kennedy, there to live in comfort and happiness forever? Ah, *Joe-san*," says she, "it must be true that, despite the profitability of your commerce as a photographer of *hosutesu* and *Amerikajin issen gorin*, the answer to the riddle you present in the *nawanoren* of Eta Jima is simply that you are a great fool for all of your one and thirty years of life! Further, Mr. Foto Joe," says she, "know that I do not believe any of what you have told me of yourself. I think what you have said of yourself, *Joe-san*, is as great a lie as what you have said of Buck Private Walter Everett Kennedy!"

"Do that mean answer is no? Negative? Ix-nay?"

Hee. Har. Laugh of equine, Jack.

"Reet," I did say. "I can dig it. Forget I ever mentioned same, reet, Yoko?"

"Mr. Joe," says Arai Kikuo, "I must insist that you depart, and take the *moga* with you! It will be dawn before my eyes are closed in the sleep that restores me for tomorrow's commerce!"

"Mr. Foto Joe," says she—*moga hosutesu* B-gal comfort woman *mama-san* Matsumoto Yoko—"when I am the wife of Buck Private Walter Everett Kennedy, and we have gone to reside in Hattiesburg in Mississippi in the security of my dowry and his enterprise as a forester, and I have learned to speak the *Eigo* fluently, I shall remember this remarkable experience, and I shall relate it to my children, and we shall laugh together in amusement at the *baka* Mr. Foto Joe who will doubtless then still walk about the *nawanoren* of Eta Jima with his small camera!"

I did say: "Never *hochee, Yoko-san!*"

What's did *wataschi* Foto Joe know, reet, Jack?

Here is I (Foto Joe!), circa late spring (*hanami*!), 1950, reet? Aged one and thirty years, sole owner and also operator of thriving still pic photo scam (Eta Jima Strip, *hosutesu*, Yank *issen gorin*) accumulating sizable venture capital *yen* bundle (waiting on best shot to trade same for Occupation Currency on *oyama* black market), now twice-spurned in context of *kokoro* sentiments—Miss Clara ("Petty Girl") Sterk, not to fail to mention *moga* Matsumoto Yoko—(done laughed at me, Jack!). Past times all past (Student Yamaguchi Yoshinori, Gooch, Lieutenant *Benshi*), dead and buried via series of fires big and small (cinders and ashes, reet?)—so what's to do, Jack?

I do 'fess up, *wataschi* Foto Joe suffered momentary totality sensation of *mu* emptiness vacuum of both intellect and *hara* belly emotions simultaneous, reet? I do confess to utter absence of *ki* energies in bereft contemplation of unknowable *do* path of future life and times to come. I do 'fess up, Jack: *wataschi* Foto Joe did even contemplate oldtimey traditionalist *Nipponshikki shinju* despondent lover's self-destruct suicide, reet? I kid you not, Jack!

Query: what's to do?

Riposte: sit taut, how you say, bide times, as how all things come to he who but attends to opportunities' knock on door of paper house. Than which is to say: not to underestimate ironicals forthcoming via fate's fickle digit, Jack! To wit:

Historical note, reet? Circa June of 1950, Republic of Korea (how we did say, *Chosen*, reet?) environ, locale of 38th Parallel — Kim Il Sung, *honcho* Russki stooge maximum leader of self-styled People's Democratic Socialist Republic of Korea (aforesaid geographical and also political entities divvied up by victors as spoils attendant upon global-wide *senso*, reet?), doubtless acting on instructions of Russki maximum *honcho* Uncle Joe Stalin (a.k.a. Dzhugashvili), did send vast army of liberation across said boundary, than which results in Yank (not to fail to mention United Nations resolution internationalist token contingents) response in kind, than which results in rapid mobilization of minimalist Yank forces at hand on Eta Jima scene (bugles blow "Boots and Saddles" alarum!), $50,000 General *Makassar-san* in command, than which (natch!) requires immediate and massive influx of Yank *issen gorin* and materials, result of which is stupendous expansion of Eta Jima training and logistical facilities to support Korean Peninsula retardation of Commie aggressors, etcetera blah blah blah — can you dig it, Jack?

Than which is to say: we is gots us *senso*, Jack! Than which effect of same is to present to *wataschi* (Foto Joe!) unique once-in-lifetimes entrepreneurial opportunity to invest *yen* nut hustled on Strip, vista rosy red optimistic for fast and also fat get-rich-rapid venture.

Than which is to say: goodbye *mu* emptiness, hello regeneration of *ki* energies, Jack! As follows:

Circa summer of '50, reet?

I say: "*Kikuo-san*, can you put me in contact with *honcho* Yank military-police authorities than which you greases via freebie *harukai* import White Horse Scotch libations on occasions of periodic phony-baloney inspections visits to Texas Bar environ?"

"Ah, Foto Joe," says Texas Bar *nawanoren* bartender-owner Arai Kikuo, "I should have known you would not allow your sad experience with the little *moga* to thwart your enterprise!"

"Reet."

"I will introduce you to the *Amerikajin* provost-marshal himself, *Joe-san*," says he, "for a man of your unflagging energy and enthusiasm for commerce merits any assistance I might provide."

"Reet," I say, and, "Anks-thay," and, "Trust me to make it worth your whiles when vessel I envision ties up at berth."

"May I inquire the nature of the venture you intend to undertake with the Yank military authorities, Foto Joe?" he queries.

"In due times," I say. "If designs of rodents and peoples go not awry," and, "Suffice to say, *wataschi* Foto Joe gots in mind little scam scheme in field of publishing industry, reet?"

"Books?" says he. "*Joe-san*, I do not think the *Amerikajin issen gorin* read books! Do you mean to attempt to garner wealth by selling books to the Yanks, Joe?"

"The kind I'm talking, *Kikuo-san*," I tell him, "ain't for reading, just looking at. How we say in *Eigo*, yearbooks, annuals, photo albums, reet? All pics with minimalist captions thereunder, dig? Everybody in U. S. of A. buys same. Like unto good book Holy Bible. Nobody don't not read them, *Kikuo-san*: just purchase same and stick on tea table as dust-catcher conversation piece, reet?"

"To what end do the *Amerikajin* produce such books, *Joe-san*?"

"Means," I explain, "by which old-timey pastness of past days bygone is preserved as dramatic tangible hedge against *do* flow's future uncertainties, reet? Not to fail to mention function as catalyst for occasional nostalgics shtick self-indulgences."

"Ah," says he, "you baffle me, Joe! You are as great an enigma to me as the Yanks who patronize my establishment. I have engaged in commerce daily with them here in my Texas Bar for four years, and still I do not comprehend their *gaijin* ways!"

Says I: "Me neither, but *yen* is *yen*, reet? Take my word for it, *Kikuo-san*, you think this is Jimmu Boom good times? You ain't seen but from nothing yet, Jack! Ain't nothing like *senso* flaps, howsomever minimalist, to engender climate conducive to business acumen, reet?"

Pith and gist: than which is to say, *wataschi* Foto Joe is saved from prolonged *mu* emptiness doldrum, *ki* energies enthusiasms rekindled, via, how you say, Korean Conflict (a.k.a. Police Action) — circa June of '50 — three years' durance of fires big and small on site across Sea of Japan, Jack! Big irony, reet?

Thus it were: *wataschi* Foto Joe stands tall on carpet for *kaigi* conference confabulation within official office confines of *honcho* Brigadier General Jeffie Walker, U.S. Army, Eta Jima training and logistical facility commander. Aforesaid *honcho* personage is seated ensconced behind enormous desk, surface of which is cleared to receive proposal I propose, reet?

Brigadier General Jeffie: noncombatant (I note lack of *senso* fruit-salad campaign ribbons on Ike jacket, reet?) G-4 (supply) Pentagon staffer, bureaucrat type recently shipped to *Nihon* in quest of career ticket-punch to attain two-star rank—said General Jeffie scrutinizes *wataschi* via mien of skeptic indifference, set adorned with black-and-white photo portrait of President Harry S (don't stand for zilch, reet?) Truman on wall, flags of U. S. of A. and also Eighth Army Command on floor standards, reet?

I do allege, Jack: Foto Joe is not intimidated. What's to perspire when *wataschi* been down this *do* road with likes of *Mikado*, Tojo Hideki, diminutive Dean Timmy Macklin, et alia, reet? Like: Jack, I know from *kaigi* conference confabulation shtick scene!

Howsomever, time for, how you say, nut-cutting nitty-gritties exchange, reet?

Says he: "State your business and depart smartly. I'm a busy man," and, "The shit's in the fan over there in Korea, the damn gooks went and just captured General Dean. If we don't stop them on the Pusan perimeter the Twenty-fourth Division'll have to swim home. But I don't suppose that's any skin off your behind. You've got something you want from me? All you people do," says Brigadier General Jeffie Walker, U.S. Army.

Says I: "To contrariwise, *honcho* general *sensei!*" and, "Name's Foto Joe, photos—candid and also posed—my game, reet?"

"The gentleman from the provost-marshal's office who shall remain unnamed here told me who and what you were. Just get on with it, okay?" says he.

"Reet," I say, and, "*Honcho* General Jeff, I is here to propose little deal scheme scam we might could undertake, how you say, silenced-partner-style. Risks, I does haste to add, all *wataschi's*, reet? All's what I needs from you is under-table sanction guaranteeing monopoly exclusiveness patent for ploy I propose herewith. Benefits go without articulation, shared on per-cent percentage commish basis to be negotiated to mutualist satisfactions, dig? How you say, one hand cleansing other whilst backs is also scratched, reet?"

"I think I get your drift," says he, and, "My intelligence tells me you're quite the businessman out there on the Strip," and, "Be specific," says Brigadier General Jeffie.

"Reet!" I say.

I tell him, Jack: I tell him as how, given sudden unexpected sneak attack (not unlike like unto dastardly *Pearu Halbol*) incursion of Russki-inspired North Korea aggressors across 38th Parallel, followed by series of misfortunate Republic of Korea (supported by minimalist Yank forces on scene) debacle defeats, than which results in current straits-dire stituation—Yanks and battered R.O.K. forces dug in on Pusan perimeter—indicates humongous logistics flow of Yank *issen gorin* and materials from stateside to stem and also reverse surging Red Tide, than which signifies probable exponential expansion of Eta Jima facility whereat and in which wherein we conduct *kaigi* confabulation conference this instant, reet? "Than which," I tell him, "presents side-effect residual opportunities for all concerned. To wit, *honcho sensei* general, you and also me, reet?"

Says he (frown manifests within skeptic indifferent mien): "The situation is piss poor — Foto Joe you said your name you go by is?"

"Foto Joe!"

"I've got my career shot dropped in my lap. I was gathering dust in my crack riding a chair at G-Four in the Pentagon. Do you know what I'm saying? So I pulled a string or two and got orders cut to get me over here, but I've got no pull with Mac's boys in the Dai Ichi Building. Oh no, that's a closed club! He's booked up solid with all the dog robbers got on the bandwagon back in Australia, some of them even as far back as P.I. days, which you probably don't know the first thing about. You don't know what the hell I'm gabbing about, do you, Mr. Foto Joe!"

"Do I not, General Jeff?" I say, and assure him, "I dig to profundity extreme sad-so-sad story of career ironics imposing kibosh on strivings of energetic enthusiast not unlike like unto your own self to get, how you say, leg up on hierarchy ladder of *do* flow's life endeavor, reet?"

"Something like that. I'd like to see MacArthur have returned to the Philippines without G-Four shunting logistics away from the European Theater for his benefit," says Brigadier General Jeffie Walker, and, "Then the gooks hit us from out of the blue on the Thirty-eighth Parallel — you people seem to have a tendency that way, don't you! — I've suddenly got my shot! If we can keep from getting pushed into the ocean, Eta Jima's going to be the G-Four center of the whole damn Eighth Army Command, and I'll get my second star the way an apple falls off a tree for you!"

"Reet!" I say. "Fast and fat, *honcho* general! Keep faiths, Yank men and also materials on the way, future's all but solid certainty bright with glorious triumphs, honor and glory to family and name shtick, reet?"

"Let's hope so," says he, "for your sake as well as ours, Foto Joe. We pull out of Japan, you'll find out what losing feels like! What the hell kind of a name is Foto Joe?"

"We is but what we does, reet, *sensei* general?" say I.

"Whatever," says he, and, "So what's your dirty little angle, Foto Joe?"

And I tell him: standing tall on carpet not unlike like unto six o'clock. *Wataschi* Foto Joe presents yearbook-annual-photo album publishing and sales scam scheme, to include necessary premise sanction than which only he can provide, to include structured sales-pitching opportunities, not to fail to mention enforcement of time-payment payments contracted by repo-depot Yank *issen gorin* cannon-fodder yardbirds en route to peninsular conflict flap, also discouragement of possible *minken* competitions, and (natch!) not to fail to mention slice of pie he stands to attain to thereby, reet? To wit:

"Ten per cent *genkin* cash off topside for you personal, *honcho* general *sensei*, than which, if I calculates probable turnovers accurate, might could be sizable nut to schlepp back home stateside along with major general's star I predicts soon falls on your epaulet not unlike like unto *sakura* cherry blossom dropping from branch in *aki* autumn's initial chill breeze, reet?"

"You're good, you know that, Foto Joe? Make it twenty and you're on!"

"Fifteen, than which also requires codicil enabling me to exchange *yen* for Occupation Currency scrip specie for greenback dollars, thus providing margins of profit via said exchanges to cover incidentals and also overheads, reet?" I did riposte.

Dig, Jack:

Samurai: Eta Jima N.C.O. Leadership Academy & Tactical Training Center (editions issued every six weeks, circa 1950, 1951, 1952, 1953, reet?) — hardbound, stitched and glued binding, high-gloss paper, cover logos in raised script suggestive of traditionalist *kanji* characters bisecting diagonally, not to fail to mention stylized figure of medieval-era *budo ronin* warrior lower-right, aforesaid balanced by Eta Jima Command unit crest (takeoff of Quartermaster Corps shield, reet?) — Jack, *wataschi* talking quality product!

Immediately following upon generous frontpapers (also end, natch!) to allow for classmates and cadre *hanko* autographs, minimalist type as follows:

Published by Foto Joe Enterprises, Eta Jima, Occupied Japan.

Not to fail to mention:

Editor and Publisher: Foto Joe Yamaguch.

Than which is also not to fail to mention publisher's logo, than which is stylized modernist rendition of Yamaguchi family (honor and glory to name and lineage shtick, reet?) *monsho* coat-of-arms: carp swimming upstream (courage in face of adversities, reet?), Jack!

Page 1 is (natch!) three-quarter page format formal photo portrait of Brigadier General Jeffie Walker, U.S. Army, seated ensconced behind massive executive-dimension desk. Caption thereunder (bold types!) is Eta Jima commander's personal-style message to troops, as in:

> On behalf of Supreme Allied Commander General of the Armies Douglas MacArthur, and in the name of the Eighth United States Army, I join with the officers and men of the Eta Jima Non-Commissioned Officer Leadership Academy. . . .

Etcetera blah, reet?

Pages 2 through and including also 7 is rows and ranks of two by three-inch portraits of entire Eta Jima facility command staff and cadre, said section headed by title page: *The Men Who Make the Men!* Jack: totality effect is not unlike like unto individual class grad pics, than which concept *wataschi* Foto Joe adapts to purpose from venerable memory of Oklahoma A & M College *Redskin* (got burned up in a big fire!), prototype for entire scam scheme, reet?

Thereafter follows series of stock stills depicting regimen routines of NCA Academy and Training Center life and times lifestyles. To wit: formations (parade and also fatigue), field and classroom problems underway (logistics, trajectory, mapreading), mess-hall chow-lines (not to fail to mention kitchenfly tent on maneuvers, reet?), weapons familiarization firing, to include levity touches, as in Maggie's Drawers aloft indicating entirety of target missed, anonymous *issen gorin* Yank G.I. dogface yardbird staring with expression of profoundest disbelief into mess-kit contents, drill sergeant snapped with yap agape in process of rendering, how you say, ass-chewing chewing-out to straight like six o'clock trainee at attention posture in uniform-inspection ranks, reet?

Howsomever, ultimate sombre seriousness of Academy and Training Center experiences — we got us *senso* Korean Conflict (a.k.a. Police Action) raging, Jack! — is dramatized by collage of appropriate candids (also stock, repeated in all editions, reet?): sweated visage and fists-gripping climbing rope on confidence and endurance course; trainee asquint at M-1 rifle sight; long vista (shot from fire watch tower for bird's-eye scope) of trainee duos stripped to skivvie shirts for unarmed defense grappling; enraged with blood-lust trainee (cadre instructor scrutinizes same) in midassault of straw dummy with fixed bayonet, etcetera blah blah.

Thereafter follows two-page full spread of graduation class (every six weeks, Jack!) arrayed standing on athletic field bleachers (lush grass and snowcover in foreground signify season at hand, reet?), attired in class-A uniforms, guidon gonfalons aloft, to include (front and center, natch!) Brigadier General Jeffie, flanked by command staff and cadre — caption: *The Professional Know-How and Can-Do Leadership that Wins!*

Tome concludes (circa '50, '51, '52, '53) with facing full-page candid: on left, Brigadier General Jeffie hands diploma sheep's dermis, whilst rendering hearty howdy-style handshake, to graduate noncom (now certified effective combat-effective leader, reet?) — on right, *wataschi*, Jack! Foto Joe on one knee to snap pic, gadget bag and back-up cameras slung, big *sumairu* smile, reet? Caption: *Best Wishes to the Grad from Foto Joe! Good Luck Always!*

340

One hundred pages, Jack (not to include front- and also endpapers for *hanko* autographs!), sales clincher of which is insertion throughout photo text of personal pics of individual Yank *issen gorin* customer in question — standing in chow line, on rifle range, at parade-rest posture in formation ranks, cracking books in midnight oils lamplight, etcetera blah — howsomever immodest, Jack, I do assert product were finest qualities!

Which is not to fail to mention interspersed stock pics of leisure lifestyle life and times enjoyed by Yank *issen gorin* Eta Jima student body circa '50 through to and including '53, reet?

To wit: postcard tourist-style views of Eta Jima environ, to include traditionalist *Nipponshikki* shtick, as in pair of *kimono*-clad girls walking park pathway on *geta* clogs, complete with *obi* sashes and *karakasa* paper parasols, lacquered *geisha*-style hairdo, reet? Also old-timey *oba-san* granny snapped whilst schlepping load of firewood *onbu* piggy-back.

More to point are eventide (available-light photos, Jack!) scenes garnered on (now famed!) Eta Jima Strip, to include exterior crowd scenes — G.I.s on prowl! — and *nawanoren* juke joint gin mill watering hole roadhouse interiors, aforesaid featuring (natch!) Texas Bar, reet?

Half-page spread shows bartender-owner Arai Kikuo, holding bottle of Kurin beer aloft, big toothy *sumairu* grin, caption under which reads: *Welcome to Japan, Soldier!* Not to fail to mention suggestive bevy of *hosutesu moga* comfort women B-gals prostitutes crowding bar and tables, same attired in latest stateside streetwalker call-gal apparel, reet? Caption: *Good Times for All on the Strip!*

Can you not dig it, Jack? I mean, *wataschi* Foto Joe assembles big *yen* (all editions of *Samurai* best-seller sell-outs, exchanges same via General Jeffie's good office for Occupation Currency scrip, said specie reconverted to greenback dollars, than which bucks I further convert back to *yen* at highest *oyama* black-market rates — Jack, I is talking Jimmu Boom good times fast and also fat hands over fists get it whilst getting is good: *Eija Nai Kai*, reet?

Sad to say ironical fact of which is: Jack, all things (good and bad!) do arrive at terminal juncture's *ma* moment. To wit: Korean Conflict (a.k.a. Police Action) flap, reet?

As in: following upon successful defense of Pusan perimeter, *Makassar-san* (a.k.a. Dugout Doug) inflicts Inchon Landing debacle defeat upon unsuspecting Russki-inspired Kim Il Sung North Korea contingents. Commie aggressors retreat not unlike like unto scalded dog to Yalu River, than which inspires influx invasion of vaunted Chink Volunteer Army, than which inflicts debacle defeat of Yanks and United Nations allies at Chosin Reservoir, resultant effect of which is ultimate 38th Parallel stalemate, of which same is complicated by fall of *Makassar-san* (old soldiers never die, Jack!) at hands of Harry S (don't stand for nothing) Truman, than which *honcho* personage is succeeded by Ike Eisenhower, than which who promises, sad to say, peace in Korea. Thus it were, Jack—forces inexorable and also inscrutable, global and historical. We arrive thusly at circa 1953, Panmunjom Treaty truce, than which means end of Korea flap boom times for *wataschi* Foto Joe's publishing scheme scam, reet? As follows:

I say: "*Sensei* General Jeffie, rumors of peace rife in atmosphere's aura, reet?"

Says he: "Wouldn't you just know it? Damn it to hell, damn Harry Truman to hell. If Mac had lasted another six months I'd be a major-general! Goddamn Ridgeway put his own personal crew of ass-kissers in, damn Ike's got to call it off to get re-elected, I'll be getting orders back stateside any day, and then it's ride a desk in Washington until they can pass me over for promotion one last time and farm me out to civilian life!"

"Ever thus was *do* flow's ironical twist, reet, *honcho* General Jeff?" I say. "Which is to say: cut and run time for *wataschi* Foto Joe, reet?"

"The rats," says General Jeffie Walker, "always bail out when the water's rising, don't they? So where'll you go now, Joe? You shifty little dork, I'll give you credit, you could sell books to a blind man! Sometime I'd like to know how the hell you got where you are. What'll you do, Joe, retire and live off your interest? Or maybe you'll invest your wad in something conservative like a couple of whorehouses?"

"Plans," I tell him, "for future time as yet indistinct, reet?" And, "I gots me one last bundle of Occupation Currency to launder, announce suspension of publishing enterprise, then pause to ponder, how we say, *yoin* ambience of *ma* moment, after than which *wataschi* makes, how you say, career move, reet, *honcho sensei*?"

"I predict," he says, "you'll come out of this shit smelling like a rose. Well, no hard feelings, Joe. I got my cut."

"*Genkin* cash," I say, "off top-most accounting, no records to embarrass, reet?"

"So for old time's sake I'll warn you to unload any scrip you've got stashed, Joe. Word's out Ridgeway's going to moot everything in circulation and issue a new specie. There's too damn much of it floating around the economy, so don't sit too long on your assets, okay?"

"Reet," I say, and, "Anks-thay, General Jeffie!" and, "Been swell doing business in concert, and orry-say second star did fail to fall on your epaulet, like unto cherry blossom from off bough, reet?"

"Screw it," says Brigadier General Jeffie Walker, U.S. Army, and, "With my pension and perks and what I raked off with you and a few other enterprising locals I don't need to name, I'll be sitting pretty for life, and the Pentagon and Ridgeway and Ike can all of them piss up a rope if they want peace in Korea so much they don't care who all loses by it!"

"Reet!" And we did part, Jack, with big hearty sincerest howdy-style handshake.

Thus it were: end of Korea flap *senso*, end of publishing scam scheme — not to fail to mention accumulation of significant sum of venture capital *yen* reserve enabling up and also outward move of *wataschi* to free-lance *eiga* flic enterprise, than which leads to present mogul-style role in global-wide world of mass popular entertainments, reet? Than which is not to forget incidentals incidental to departure from Eta Jima environ. Big ironies, Jack! As follows:

Cut to: big fire, Jack — circa '53 *tsukimi* moon-viewing time. Environ of famed Eta Jima Strip (business at all-timey high due to Jimmu Boom and Korean flap Yank troop influx). Specific locale of said conflagration is Texas Bar *nawanoren*, reet?

Dig: wee hours of late eventide (immediately following upon closing time), Strip inhabited only by minimalist stragglers of night's routine revels — inebriate Yank G.I. *issen gorin* barracks bound in hopes of evading M.P. scrutinies, scattering of *hosutesu moga* B-gal *mama-sans* waiting in vain on last chance to glom paying customers for *futon* ecstacies. Than which is not to fail to mention *wataschi* Foto Joe, than which who takes *sanpo* shank's mare stroll perambulation homeward after hard night's labor effecting final shut-down liquidation of publishing scam scheme enterprise (to include last exchange of greenback dollars for *yen* at *oyama* highest rates, reet?).

Wee hour late eventide *ma* moment of *yoin* stasis is broken by fire brigade's claxon shriek, sudden glow of flames' eruption from roof of Texas Bar *nawanoren* — *wataschi* Foto Joe runs *chogee* to scene site, reet?

Absurdist milieu confusions, Jack: firefighters direct blatant insufficient water jets from pumper vehicle tank out and upward to expanding conflagration, inebriate G.I. Yank stragglers (not to fail to mention scattering of still-unengaged *hosutesu moga*!) gather to view blaze — *tsukimi* time to view moon, reet? — congress of aforesaid including (natch!) bartender-owner Arai Kikuo.

"Joe! *Joe-san!*" shouts he at me, "My establishment is consumed in flames before my eyes, Joe!" *Kikuo-san* is (natch!), how you say, all shaked up. Flames now fully engulf Texas Bar edifice structure, reet?

"So," I say to him, "I see, *Kikuo-san*," and, "How's come this to pass?"

"Ah, Joe!" says he — tears-laden baby blues of Arai Kikuo reflect fire's light, reet? "Who can say? I had only locked my door when I saw the first flame and smelled the stench! Perhaps one of the inebriated *Amerikajin* discarded a match or a cigarette in the *benjo*? Who can say what causes this disaster!"

"Are you certain," queries *honcho* fire-brigade commander, "there are no persons remaining on the premises?"

"No one!" cries Arai Kikuo, and, "Nothing remains within except my cash box and all else in the world that belongs to me! Joe," cries he, "I am reduced to the clothes I wear and the few *yen* in my wallet! Joe," says he as roof of Texas Bar collapses inwardly, "I am as poor this moment as the day I returned to *Nihon* from my service with the Kwantung Army! Joe," says he — beats forehead with fists, yanks at hairs, reet? — "what is the meaning of this? Do my *kami* destroy me in the moment of my prosperity to punish me for some grave error or indecorum I committed long ago?"

"Search me, *Kikuo-san*," I say, take his arm, pull him back from conflagration's mounting heat intensity, out of range of airborne sparks, distanced sufficient in event *nawanoren's* facade tumbles into street, reet?

"The sole question now," says fire brigade's *honcho* commander, "is whether or not we shall succeed in containing the fire to this building. I fear it will spread to include the entire block!"

"You ain't insured?" I query Arai Kikuo.

"I foresaw no necessity to justify the expense, Joe!"

"Reet. We never does."

"Ah," blubbers Arai Kikuo, "where is the justice for one such as myself? Why was I spared even the slightest injury during the great *senso*? Why was I permitted to prosper in my commerce only to witness its transformation before my eyes to fire and smoke — oh, Joe, it sounds like the roaring of a great dragon!"

"Reet," I say, and, "No justices in *do* flow's fickle digit tickle, *Kikuo-san*!" Whereupon walls of Texas Bar *nawanoren* descend down upon blazing foundation stones. "Cinders and ashes," I tell him, "one of series of fires big and small, *Kikuo-san*, dig?"

"What?" he queries. "What do you speak of, Foto Joe? Do you mock me with your cryptic tongue? I stand with you, a ruin equal only to the ruin of my establishment, and you console me with enigmas? Ah, Joe, you have no feeling in your *hara* belly! You are a cruel man, Mr. Foto Joe, and a friend to none, just as all the *moga* say!"

Dig, Jack: Texas Bar *nawanoren* is heap of raging timbers (not to mention paper, reet?), heat produced thereby hot like Okie-land midsummer sun against visage, pop and crackle of sparks therefrom threaten entire Strip environ (*tsukimi*, circa '53), wee hour late eventide illuminated by blaze to reveal fire brigade's absurdist efforts, pumper vehicle hosing down adjacent edifices, assembled G.I. inebriates and *hosutesu* B-gals, assorted neighborhood *Nihonjin* local yokels roused from *futon* slumbers, reet?

Says he (now destitute Arai Kikuo): "It is not just, *Joe-san*, that I should be ruined by unmerited misfortune while you and so many others thrive though you are scarcely more diligent and industrious than I!"

344

"Reet," I riposte as he sinks to knees on Strip street cobbles, and, "What's to say nor do save forget and forgive, pack traps, how we say in *Eigo*, haul ass, move out smartly, consider *ma* moment's *yoin* significance, follow *do* flow of future pathway wherever, reet?" And, "Come on, *Kikuo-san*, rise from despairing posture, stand tall like unto six o'clock, dry baby blues, exhibit *budo* traditionalist *Nipponshikki* fortitude in face of adversities, reet?"

"You have no feelings! In your *hara* belly is a great *yohaku* void, a *mu* emptiness! You are as malign as the unjust *kami* who visit this destruction upon me!" he cries.

I say: "Reet. Might could be, *Kikuo-san*. Only ways I know to go, reet? Six of one, half dozen the other. We is who and what than which we is, reet, Jack!" and add, "Hey, like, all them pics I stuck up on your wall is also now cinders and ashes, reet?"

Than which is not to fail to mention — circa *tsukimi* viewing of harvest moons time, autumn '53 — chance circumstance last meeting confabulation with *hosutesu* B-gal *moga* prostitute Matsumoto Yoko, Jack — site scene of which confabulation is self-same famed Eta Jima Strip street environ. As hereafter:

Dig: last day of *wataschi* Foto Joe's residency presence in Eta Jima Town. Hour is high noon, sun in sky dissipates October air chill — I is taking ultimate *sanpo* stroll perambulation down Strip (attempt to fix vision thereof in mind's eye memory for future refs, considering, how you say, vibes of *ma* moment's *yoin* implications, reet?), expecting (natch!) milieu of early-hour emptiness (charred ruin of Texas Bar debacle blaze permeates air with cold-ash and cinder stink!), whereas, much to my suprisement, sidewalks is dense populated with mob of *hosutesu* B-gal *moga* Strip denizens, all than which exhibits state of exaggerated consternations — how you say, ladies of eventide *mama-sans* weep and also gnash pearlie whites, reet, Jack?

I say: "What it is, ladies?" and, "What give, gals?" and, "Hey, like, cease waterworks deluge, be at ease, tell Foto Joe what's it alls about, reet?" and, "Is it *futon* ecstacies commerce been outlawed? Entirety of Strip been nominated off-limits by Yank provost-marshal?"

Says one: "Foto Joe, have you not heard of the currency edict enacted?"

Says another: "*Joe-san*, we are devastated by the unexpected action of the *Amerikajin* military authorities!"

Says yet another: "Joe, we awoke this morning to learn that as of midnight last night the Occupation Currency has been changed — the *Amerikajin* *issen gorin* may exchange theirs for the new bills, but our scrip we hold is suddenly worthless in the *oyama*! We have been cheated of our earnings just as if it were taken from us by thieves who roam in the dark of night, Joe!"

"Reet," I say. "Lucky for me as how I is done washed all mine for greenbacks and thence to *yen* couple days preceding, reet? Like, how we say, little bird clued me, reet?"

Says still another *hosutesu* B-gal *moga*: "Do not waste your words on Mr. Foto Joe, friends! See how he smiles, as if we had told him of good fortune rather than ill! See him smile! Mr. Foto Joe has not lost any money to the deceitful action of the *gaijin!*"

"Reet," I say, and do move on out at *chogee* double-time pace, Jack.

"What," calls *hosutesu* voice after me, "does Mr. Foto Joe care for our sorrow at this loss? It is known in every *nawanoren* in Eta Jima that he will soon go on a journey, never to return, rich with his profits from illicit commerce with the devious *Amerikajin!*"

"Reet!" I shout back over my shoulder. At which juncture—ironics, Jack!—I bump into Matsumoto Yoko. *Yoko-san*, Jack: standing on corner, holding large carton, than which said container contains stacks—I is talking big bucks, reet?—of harlequin-hue Occupation Currency scrip (rubber-banded in block bundles from tens and also twenties denominations!), aforesaid *Yoko-san's* baby blues blurry with waterworks tears free falling.

Ah, Jack! Big ironies of life and times. To wit:

"*Joe-san!*" says she. And, "Oh, *Joe-san*, have you heard of this terrible thing done by the *Amerikajin* authorities? Look, Joe, at what I bear in my arms! It is my fortune, *Joe-san*, all the money I have saved in three years here in Eta Jima! I was a wealthy woman yesterday, Joe, because I was frugal, saving against the day when I should make my *o-miai* marriage with Buck Private Walter Everett Kennedy and go to live in the land called Mississippi, and this morning I learn that I am as poor as the day I left my village! Oh, *Joe-san*, what is to become of me and my dream of my future life now!"

I did say: "Search me, *Yoko-san*," and, "Might should of exchanged scrip hoard for *yen* at *oyama* tad sooner, reet?" and, "Hey, dry baby blues, mayhap Buck Private Kennedy personage is willing to make you honest woman wife even minus lacking dowry inducement, reet?" Jack: she did but weep wail the more effusive.

Said she: "Ah, you have not heard the whole of my pain, Joe! Did you not know that Buck Private Walter Everett Kennedy was given a further year's term of service as a soldier by the infamous edict of the Truman Year decreed when the *senso* began in *Chosen?* Ah, but you no longer frequent the Strip since you took up your commerce on the military base! You have not heard that Buck Private Walter Everett Kennedy was dispatched to *Chosen* to engage in the *senso*, and that I have had no message from him since that day? *Joe-san*, you do not know the whole of my anguish!"

"Reet. Might could be fortunes-of-*senso* shtick. Buck Private personage

346

might could mayhap be, how we say, K.I.A., wounded, even P.O.W. from Chinks, reet?"

"No," says Matsumoto Yoko, "I have made inquiries and learned he was returned unharmed to *Nihon*, and thence returned to his home in the land called Mississippi—I have had a letter written in *Eigo* for me by a professional scribe, and directed it to him there, but no response is forthcoming!"

"Reet," I say, and, "Sad so sad to hear, *Yoko-san*, except save for irony of which is, I did give fair warnings thereof, reet?"

"*Joe-san!*" says she, drops carton containing medium-scale nut fortune— now worthless play-money paper, reet?—into gutter (rubber-banded bound bundles of harlequin-hue scrip free fall). "It is not too late for my life if you still wish me to be your wife! It is said you are now as wealthy as the new-rich *nariken* who attained fortunes in the great *senso*! We might now marry, for you desired no dowry when you asked me so many months ago—"

Jack, I did tell her! I did tell her . . . Jack, memory proves inadequate to accurate recall quotationals!

Suffice to say, I did tell her: ix-nay, *mama-san*! No way, reet? As how, I did riposte, brass ring comes round but once, shot at bluebird is but fleeting. I mean, Jack, is *wataschi* not done learned hard way as how no waterworks lamentations dispel hard facts of life and times lifetime when you comes up day tardy and also *yen* short?

I did say (from memory, Jack!): "Orry-say, *Yoko-san*, reet? As how, heartbroke was I once, circa 1940, than which occurred at gentle hands of Miss Clara Sterk, also knowed as Petty Girl, reet? Heartbroke was I once more, circa '50, reet? Dig, Yoko, life and times ironic need not to strike *wataschi* Foto Joe on noggin to get attention, as in manner of Okie-land mule. Like, orry-say," I did say, Jack!

"*Joe-san*," cried she, "what is to become of me? Is my future to be but a purposeless continuation of my past? Will you not assist me, Joe?"

Than to which I did riposte (words to effect if not verbatims, reet?): "Go with *do* flow, *mama-san*," and, "Search me, *Yoko-san*," and, "Way confection crumble, reet?"

Said she: "Why do you taunt me, *Joe-san*? Why do you turn your face from me in my moment of distress? Is it that you are as cruel as all the *moga* of Eta Jima say?"

"Them as knows don't say, reet?" I say, and, "Them as say don't not know," and, "Like, it was never instance of *kokoro* romanticals betwixt us, reet?" and, "*Ona hideri wa nai, Yoko-san!*" Never a dearth from womens, Jack!

What's to conclude? Jack, it ain't nothing don't endure. No, not peoples nor pics (nor *eiga* flics!) do last, reet? Where, I did ask myself (en route on famed legendary Eido Road toward Tokyo Town, aged four and thirty years old aged, reet?), is peoples, not to fail to mention *hara* belly sentiments (not to fail to mention documentations!) of past times past and bygone gone, *wataschi*? Riposte: gone, Jack! Got burned up in series of fires big and small, cinders and also ashes scattered to eight corners of world. Answer, Jack, is Big Irony of Life, reet?

Query yet persists: what's to do with all that *yen* burning hole in pockets? Riposte is (en route halfway down Eido Road *do* path to Tokyo Town): use it or lose it, Jack!

Meaning: I did decide to enter upon concerted free-lance *eiga* flic entrepreneurial venture. Thus came to be, Jack: Foto Joe Yamaguch Enterprises!

Than which is to say: Foto Joe Yamaguch is my name, *eiga* flics (no job too minuscule, no task too grandiose — references available upon request!) my game!

Thus follows hereafter, how you say, Alger Horatio success narrative — than which is to say I did hustle nut toward exponential increase (Jimmu Boom times in *Nihon*, fast and also fat!), reet? To wit:

Cut to: extreme close-up (how we say, XCU, reet?) for purpose of perusal, throwaway broadside handbill flyer, than which *wataschi* Foto Joe Yamaguch did litter streets and also alleys of Tokyo Town, circa autumn *tsukimi* moon-viewing, 19 and 53, as follows:

Announcing!

Hey, folks! Hereby, not to fail to mention herewith, is hereafter established establishment of—

Foto Joe Yamaguch Enterprises!

(Hey, like, wait, don't discard! Read on, folks!)

Mr. Foto Joe Yamaguch, producer-director, cinemaphotographer, editor and *honcho* chief chef and factotum, announces availability of his considerable service for hire to the general public of Tokyo Prefecture (not to fail to mention greater *Nihon*, to include foreign on-site location shoots — inquire at address below for full particularity, all transactions (natch!) in strictest *Nipponshikki* confidentialness and also decorum, reet?).

Folks, consider:

Life and times is, how we say, but fancy passage — ofttimes also mudfence plain, reet? — nought but the blink of Buddha's eye, split millisecond in the mind of *Ameratasu*, and bird is already aloft. Like, what's gone is gone, reet? Not to fail to mention present *ma* moment already going out *shoji* sliding panel door of paper house. And who's to say *do* flow's future path ain't, like, fraught with stones, curves of hair's pin linear configuration, replete with, how we say in *Eigo* (Okie-land style!), chug-holes, reet?

Folks, 'fess up! Does you feel lost in time's onrushing rush? Does you not feel (oh, I think you does!) as how contemporary post-*senso* fast-pace progress of lifestyle life and times in context of Jimmu Boom boom times (*Amerikajin* influences both comprehensive and pervasive, not to fail to mention profound and subtle, reet?) is, how we say *Eigo* Yank-style, big drag drudge? Does you not feel (certain sure is *wataschi* Foto Joe Yamaguch you does!) life slipping away not unlike like unto greased porcine, than which yields *hara* belly-deep suspicion all is for zip, zilch, zero goose's eggs significance? You smoking *harukai* import *gaijin* highest quality ciggie smokes the more, enjoying disproportionly?

Folks, if your riposte to above-mentioned queries is REET, then Foto Joe Yamaguch Enterprises offer you possible potential palliative partial solution satisfactions!

Hey, out there, all you Hundred Millions, answer me this: what's are signal significant instances of import in otherhow hum's drum all-in-vain-for-nothing daily lives? I mean, what's the use when even *Mikado* is (*Makassar-san's* edict, reet?) no longer deistic deity?

How about new baby in the family (honor and glory to family name, thanks to household *kami*, blessings of Sun Goddess, reet?)?

How's about sole son and heir done passed his *shiken jigoku* exam hellishness (entrance admission, periodic testing, not to fail to mention graduation?)?

Papa-san approached by *nakodo* marriage broker on behalf of family touting highly eligible (university grad, excellent career prospect and benefits of *zaibatsu* corporate headquarters) bachelor boy of impeccable ancestry with *kokoro* interest in eldest female offspring?

Death (sad to say!) of clan patriarch or *oba-san* granny, funeral ceremonials pending?

Get my drifts, folks? Can you not dig?

Than which is to say, in sum and short pith and also gist (how we say, rind removed, reet?), be it ambiguities of firstborn's birth pangs, mixed joy of matriculation and/or graduation, weddings ecstacy vs. kiddies' departure (lose a daughter, gain a son, reet?), solemn hysterics attendant upon inexorable termination of lifetime's vitality (still, suffering is over, reet?) — be's it what's it be (six of one, half-dozen the other), scope and shape and particulars of particular given context needs NOT be relinquished to cinder-ash obscurity of time's past pastness! Repeat: you CAN save same for posterity!

You query: how?

Contact: Foto Joe Yamaguch, Foto Joe Yamaguch Enterprises (see address below; sorry, no phone yet!)

Foto Joe Yamaguch, global-wide experience (B.A. with honors!) *eiga* flic cinematographer (in the game since circa '35!) do hereby and also with offer to contract to lens (16-millimeter latest state-of-craft camera technologies, rapid-zoom precision focus!) said occasions of your election — on-site actualities natural light, studio dramatizations in event of unforeseen ironical circumstances preventing location shoots! — be first in your family, on your block, in your neighborhood, your prefecture, in all islands of *Nihon* to catch and hold tight them most tenderest and also memorable experiences of life and times life on magic scroll of celluloid (up-to-date stock, guarantee not to fade, blister, nor crack when directions for archival storing and periodic presentation is followed – limited warranties available for modest surcharges!)!

To Conclude:

Act Now (discount *bonasu* bonus and doorway prizes to first customers stamping *hanko* signature seal on contract's bottom line, reet?)!

Don't Be Crestfallen Sad Sack in Old Age, Life and Times of Life Gone and Bygone for Good, Reet?

Motto: is it not ironic, folks, as how nothing don't endure? Hey, Hundred Millions, even life ain't permanent, but Foto Joe Yamaguch, via magical illusion of modernist miracle *eiga* flics can give YOU satisfactory illusions to contrariwise, reet?

Do you dig it, Jack? And did it not sell? Dig:

Says Mr. Sugitomo Norio (up-and-coming-on-the-make youngish *Nihonjin* businessman nut-hustler in quest of respect to sanction new-found Jimmu Boom boom times affluence): "Let me emphasize, Mr. Yamaguch, that I am at present only curious as to the probable form your *eiga* recording of my forthcoming nuptials might assume. I wish it clearly understood that some members of both my family and the family of my betrothed are rather conservative people and thus might be expected to respond less than positively to any feature of the ceremony which might be said to conflict with traditional Shinto ritual and decorum."

Says I (*wataschi* Foto Joe Yamaguch): "Reet!" and, "I do dig the most!" and, "Impass potential cultural conflict confrontation betwixt old-timey *Nipponshikki* ethos versus contemporary hip Jimmu Boom boom times fast pace and flash values appropriate to status stature you is done garnered via valiant and also triumphant hustle in quest of *yen* nut, reet?"

"I should not have expressed it so, Mr. Yamaguch," says he (Mr. Sugitomo Norio).

"Reet," say I, and, "Than which is why you gots me, Foto Joe Yamaguch, here to do job of work, reet?"

"I am at least," says he, "willing to entertain your conception of what you might deem fitting."

To which I riposte to wit: "*Sensei* Sugitomo Norio – can I call you *Norio-san*? – cards on table's playing surface, how we say in *Eigo*, down and soiled, let's us commence to begin with answers to series of queries I needs must proffer, reet? Not to perspire, *Norio-san*, as how all ripostes remain in strictest confidence security."

Thus it were, Jack: I did pose queries pointed and casual, establish *enryo* rapports, verify validity of background info than which I does already suspicion, reet? Hence I do ascertain as how his daddy, *papa-san* of aforesaid *Norio-san*, did earn his rice humble-style via ownership of small tug and barge service in Tokyo Bay environ up to and to include post-*senso* era times bygone. After than which, coexistent with advent of *Chosen* flap conflict, aforesaid *Papa-san* Sugitomo did deign to participate in running sea's coast smuggling scheme scam (focus, natch, on Yank ciggies — Phillip Morris, Old Gold, Lucky Strike), than which nut-hustle did lead to *yen* capital accumulation venture fund — *wataschi* can dig this, reet? — at which end did *Papa-san* Sugitomo purchase small fleet of tugs, barges, not to fail to mention seagoing fishing smacks, reet?

"Check me on this, *Norio-san*," says *wataschi* Foto Joe Yamaguch. "Your daddy ain't no *baka* dope just fell off rutabaga wagon, reet? Thus it were he did incorporate increasing maritime venture in order to escape preclusive taxations, did further and thereafter send sole son and heir — you, *Norio-san!* — to higher educational education institution?"

"Meiji University," says he.

"Reet! Wherefrom you did graduate in good standing?"

"I was but a poor scholar."

"Natch! Howsomever, sheeps dermis diploma scroll now occupies *tokonoma* place of honor alongside *kami* scrolls and incense in *Papa-san's* paper domicile?"

"My father constructed a western-style home of fired bricks, and he vows to construct an adjoining structure of the same progressive architecture for me and my wife the moment the wedding is accomplished!" says *Norio-san*, reet?

"Natch! And now, *Papa-san* Sugitomo do intend to, how we say, frost confection, position maraschino atop frozen-dairy delight, via marriage of sole son and heir — you, *Norio-san!* — to eligible daughter of family with, how we say, cut-above ancestral lineage social status stature, reet? Is I right or is I right, *Norio-san!*"

"In all essentials," says he, and, "My bride's family boasts an ancient *monsho* crest, though their wealth diminished greatly during the *senso*. I would only add that it is the mutual wish of my father and myself to endow my wedding with a progressive spirit not inimical to the dictates of Shinto practice, while at the same time we assert our sympathy with the dashing spirit of the new *Nihon*."

"Reet!" I tell him. And I do tell this Sugitomo Norio as how Foto Joe Yamaguch's *eiga* flic docudrama will look on screen, reet? I tell him as how, via craftsmanship techniques I garner over long experiences (references furnished if necessary, Jack), to wit, script continuity, on-site actuality augmented by studio dramatizations (held to minimalist minimum!), direction, lighting, camera angles and tracks — not to fail to mention film stock! — and also editing, *wataschi* Foto Joe Yamaguch will produce cinematic *eiga* phenom worthy of rescreening for progenies unto fourth generation's entertainment and information! "Dig it, *Norio-san! The Glorious Wedding of Sugitomo Norio, as Filmed by Foto Joe Yamaguch Enterprises, Foto Joe Yamaguch, Sole Owner and Proprietor!*"

"It is enticing," he do allow.

Says I . . . Jack, what does I not say to him!

I say: we will have us innovative titles, not to fail to mention credits, melded with traditionalist *kanji* script logos. We will slap on soundtrack mix of dramatic immediacy actualities, traditionalist *shamisen* guitar strains and latest stateside Yank Hit Parade hits. We will inject expositions via intercut still pics from family albums (*Papa-san, Mama-san, Norio-san!*). We will build suspense narration scenarios: bride arising to don wedding *kimono* garb, groom knotting *Igirisujin* Old School tie in crisp Windsor, followed by temple processions, *honcho* Shinto priest personage at prayer to *kami* over incense (gong sounds!), conclude with western-style bash blowout reception—nothing but *harukai* import whiskies on tap!— to conclude with teaser, faint-but-palpable climax (no pun intended, *Norio-san!*) of wedding eventide activities, cutting away but an instant short of *futon* consummation ecstacies (nervous groom *Norio-san* looking sideways to catch peep of disrobing spouse, demure bride hinting at coming attractions via eye-lash batting whilst soundtrack suggest falling silks—fade to black and hold for *kokoru* sighs laid over upbeat musics ("Hot Time in Old Town Tonight"?)—oh, Jack, I did tell him!

"I am enticed," says he.

"Natch! Reet! Affix *hanko* seal signature on dotted line, *Norio-san*, after than which production starts on the morrow!"

Clara! I did think, and also: *Yoko-san!*

Did I not sell, Jack?

"Talk!" I say to them. "Palaver!" I say. "Spiel me a spiel, reet? *Wataschi* Foto Joe Yamaguch is all auricular orifices, than which is not to fail to mention as how time is but *yen.*"

"My son, Isoh," says Mr. Kagoshima Ishido, "has brought great honor to our family's name by virtue of his record as a matriculant at our illustrious Tokyo University."

"Reet," I say, and, "Congrats, *Isoh-san*—mind if I call you *Isoh-san?*" and, "I can dig it, Kagoshima Ishido, not unlike like unto how we say in *Eigo*, Phi Beta Kappa, Dean's List, valedictorian shtick, reet?" Kagoshima Isoh, soon-to-be-graduated as grad of venerable Tokyo University (a.k.a. pre-*senso* days bygone, Tokyo Imperial U., reet?), exhibits appropriate *Nipponshikki* decorums upon hearing direct praise—drops baby blues to hands folded in lap, reet?

"My worthy son's academic attainments," says Kagoshima Ishido, "are not of so elevated a caliber, but I hasten to add, Mr. Yamaguch, that the mere fact of his successful matriculation is a moment in my family's history I deem deserves a recognition beyond the ordinary."

"Reet," I do tell them, and, "Common these days in *Nihon*, reet? Like, gentleman's C average mediocrity median is, howsomever, mark of gentleman, reet? I do dig it, fellas! Like, first generation's college education is,

352

how we say, not for the sniffling at."

"My father," pipes up *Isoh-san* Kagoshima, "is, despite the limitations of his formal schooling, a man of great culture. He composes *haiku* —"

"Reet," I interject;, and, "Certain-sure sign signaling sensibilities subtle and also elevated, reet?"

Says Kagoshima Ishido, "I was prevented from availing myself of a university education by virtue of my service to the *Mikado* and *Dai Nippon* in the great *senso*. I had the honor to serve in the ranks of the glorious Kwantung Army in the rank of captain of quartermaster troops."

"Reet," I say, and, "Crack troopers elite corps, reet? Tell me about it, *Ishido-san!*" and, "School of knocks hard, frequent, and also ironical, not unlike like unto *wataschi*. Hey, I does dig it!"

"Then you suggest," says *Papa-san* Kagoshima, "that you are capable of creating an *eiga* expressive of my son's achievement?"

"And is it true, Mr. Yamaguch," queries young *Isoh-san*, "that you will record the events of my graduation even as they occur?"

Jack, I do tell them!

"Boys," I do say — "you don't mind me calling you boys? Reet!" and, "*Wataschi* Foto Joe Yamaguch will make you firstrate modernist-style post-*senso* Jimmu Boom boom times westernized *eiga* flic docudrama chronicle of soon-to-be-graduated Tokyo U. grad *Isoh-san*. I mean: like, we is talking right up *wataschi's* side street, reet? Boys," I say, "if it's one thing Foto Joe Yamaguch know, it is from collegiate life and times life-style."

"Are you personally familiar with our universities, Mr. Yamaguch?" asks *Isoh-san*.

"I shall desire particulars before I am prepared to engage your services, Mr. Yamaguch," says *Papa-san* Kagoshima.

Jack, I tell them:

"Listen up, boys! *Wataschi* talking wide-angle pan shots of Tokyo U. campus environ, Fuji's peak in background, reet? Foto Joe Yamaguch talking rapid zoom to extreme close-up of *Isoh-san's* visage, expression — coached by directing techniques I learn via long experiences! — of innocence animated by curiosities both intellectual and *hara* belly emotive, reet? Not to fail to mention costuming, pre-*senso* out-of-fashion suit to indicate sincerity. Does you dig? I am talking first day at school, reet?"

"But I am almost graduated, Mr. Yamaguch! How shall you make an *eiga* of my first day as a university student?"

"I am confused," asserts *Papa-san* Kagoshima.

"I is talking illusions, reet?" I riposte. And: "*Wataschi* will be on scene for location actualities shoots, commencement procession, *honcho* Rector's address, ritualist kowtow upon bestowal of sheep's dermis diploma scroll, than which is to say, what ain't real, Foto Joe Yamaguch will fabricate. I mean, what's else is script for, reet?"

"You can do this convincingly?" queries *Papa-san. Isoh-san* is mute— starting already to see *eiga* flic, reet?

"Can I not, *Papa-san* Kagoshima?"

I tell them: scenarios in class and out, midnight oil studies grind stints, cheering section at Tokyo U. *besuboru* contests, campus glimpses alternated with home-life *ushi* domesticities, *Papa-san* and *Mama-san*, siblings' awe of big bro *Isoh-san's* lofty collegiate status stature shtick. . . . Oh, Jack, I do tell them, than which is to say—how I do sell, reet?

I think: Gooch! Go, Pokes! Go, Punchers! Ride 'Em, Cowboys, reet?

Oh, Jack, I is talking Alger Horatio Ragged Richard successes—as in *Nihon* all-time hit parade hit song "Big Bucks," reet?—*wataschi* Foto Joe Yamaguch talking rapid upward curve graphs of sales (not to fail to mention profits margins), talking move into higher socio-politico *zaibatsu* corporate elitist upper-echelons clientele, Jack! Witness:

"I hasten to inform you, Mr. Yamaguch," says Mr. Toga Tomonaga, "that I am but a mere functionary, a representative dispatched by his superiors to evaluate both your organization's logistical capacity to supply the product in question, and, equally as significant to my superiors, the discretion which we can assume you will exercise before, during, and after the fact of your involvement in this project."

Dig: *wataschi* Foto Joe Yamaguch is interviewed, *kaigi*-style, by Mr. Toga Tomonaga, reet? Said personage is button-down-collar *Igirisujin* necktie with crisp Windsor knot *zaibatsu* corporate middle-management *kobun* factotum flunky type, epitome soul of new-style *zaibatsu* corporate functionary spirit characteristic of burgeoning economic miracle of late post-senso *Nihon*, reet?

"Hey!" I say, "Gimme three guesses as to *honcho* superior's identity moniker. Mitsui? Mitsubishi? Sumitomo? Like, blink baby blues thrice if I hit it, reet?"

"For the moment, Mr. Yamaguch," says he, "my superiors should prefer to remain anonymous. I assure you I shall be more candid if a formal contractual relationship appears imminent."

"Reet," I say, "Foto Joe gots where he are today via zipping lips. I mean, like, mum is word, reet?"

"Cost," says *zaibatsu* factotum *kobun* corporate midmanager factotum Mr. Toga Tomonaga, "is not, to my superiors, a concern of crucial proportion, since our government's new and enlightened laws provide substantial taxation advantages in matters of this nature."

"Reet!" I say, and, "*Wataschi* hears you, advertising write-off, *Tomonaga-san*! Okay to call you *Tomonaga-san?*"

"My superiors," says he, "plan to host a visiting delegation of *gaijin* business executives, a consortium of international composition who will, in the not distant future, grace *Nihon* with their presence."

"I do dig it! Been down that *do* road before, *Tomonaga-san!*"

"In addition to providing a memorable occasion of *Nihonjin* hospitality for our distinguished guests, my superiors entertain great hope for the consummation of a far-reaching commercial agreement which bears the promise of opening the markets of the western democracies to *Nihon's* foremost manufacturing corporations."

"Big bucks!" I say, and, "Reet!"

"I will only add, Mr. Yamaguch, that our progressive government is also eager to stimulate the economic vitality so lamentably interrupted and at least temporarily diminished by the unfortunate *senso —* "

"*Hakko ichui* debacle," I interpose.

" — and so my superiors contemplate an evening of traditional *Nipponshikki* diversion to bring together, in a spirit of *enryo* mutuality of purpose, these worthy *gaijin* entrepreneurs, selected members of our progressive government's leadership, and, of course, my superiors themselves."

"Oh, talk to *wataschi, Tomonaga-san!*" I say, and, "I does dig it!" and, "We talking shindig, hoe-down, blow-out, hats and also horns! We talking first-class sky-is-limitation *Nipponshikki geisha* party shtick, reet?"

"You are perceptive, Mr. Yamaguch," says he (Toga Tomonaga, *zaibatsu* midmanager functionary *kobun* factotum flunky, reet?).

"Is I not, *Tomonaga-san?*" I query. And I tell him — than which is to say, Jack, I do sell him!

I sell him: traditionalist *Nipponshikki geisha* party shtick, affair laid on for remote hick sticks countryside (camera tracks limos schlepping honored guests to destination!) *ryokan* inn, camera tracking through decorative garden (sounds of hard heels on wooden bridge over carp pond, grinding path's gravel, silhouette of *torri* Spirit Gate) dim lit (shadows sway in breeze!) by paper lanterns. I sell *shoji* sliding panels opening, honored guests doffing shoes, donning felt slippers, greeted by full-regalia-clad *honcho geisha* lady, apprentice assistants on hand to sing ritualist song of greetings:

> May your family flourish
> For a thousand generations,
> For eight thousand generations!

After than which is offered lacquered trays bearing minuscule minimalist *sake* cups, reet? I sell smooth transition shots of honored guests seated on *tatami* mats at low table, *geisha* song and dance formal-entertainment shtick, serving (close-ups of exquisite chow, to include *fugu* blowfish!) bowls, soundtrack *shamisen* musics, *geisha* moving into stage of restrained flirtations and joke-telling routines, etcetera blah.

Jack, I sell modernist Jimmu Boom boom times touches, to wit: *harukai* import champagne bubbly bubbling and assorted strong spirits splashing in glasses, hand-rolled cigars passed, pierced, and also ignited by *geisha* gals (one per guest!), extreme close-ups of tasty morsels hand-fed to open mouths, raucous laugh hee hee and hardy hars, libidinous exchange of bedroom-eye glances, touchie-feelie slap-and-tickle betwixt guest and *geisha* (suggestion of *futon* ecstasy aftermaths!), inebriated bilingo *Nihonju-Eigo* choral sing-song, attire and also coiffures in disarray (*kimono* falling slo-mo to floor to reveal bared ankles?) — I sell symbolic super cornucopia spewing *yen*, greenbacks, Deutschmarks, pounds sterling, not to fail to mention francs, reet?

Do I not sell?

"Mr. Yamaguch," says *Tomonaga-san*, "I expect I shall be pleased to report to my superiors that your services would be most suitable!"

"Reet!" I say, and, "Not to fail to mention cost-plus contract clause. As how, *Tomonaga-san*, you gets what's you pay for, all taxation deductible write-off scam scheme, reet?"

Can you dig it, Jack? Free-lance *eiga* flic cinematic gigs shtick, aforesaid life and times lifestyle exhibiting fast and fat Alger Horatio and Ragged Richard ascendance upward in parallel *do* flow path coexistent with Jimmu Boom times boom miraculous post-*senso* economics recovery of *Nihon*, reet? Than which is to say Foto Joe Yamaguch Enterprises engages more and more lucrative clientele — *zaibatsu* trade — than which is, howsomever, despite enterprise expansion (staff, facilities, scope of operations), not to fail to mention nut-hustle ethos dictating no job too minuscule, reet? As in:

"*Sensei* Mr. Yamaguch," says rice-paddy farmer Yoshihisa Fujiyoshi — *Nihonjin* redneck rural type (outlying hick sticks environ of Tokyo Prefecture) come to town to inquire personal within as to prices, "I doubt seriously that my widowed mother and my many siblings, for whom I speak, are able to afford your services, and thus it is our interview today may prove a waste of your precious time and energies."

"Reet," I tell him, and, "Call me *Joe-san*, *Fuji-san*," and, "Spiel, *wataschi* is all auricular orifices," and, "Fees flexible and open to haggle dicker horse-trade negotiation, reet?" and, "We loves but to serve Hundred Millions folks, *Fuji-san*!"

"My late father," says he, "was but a humble farmer —"

"Earth's saline," I say, "yeomanry backbone spine of *Nihon*, reet?"

"— but he did attain to a modest prosperity by dint of his labor and

356

frugality. It was his dying wish that I, his eldest son, should arrange a traditional Buddhist funeral for his remains — "

"Shinto," I tell him (rice-paddy farmer redneck hick sticks bumpkin Mr. Yoshihisa Fujiyoshi, come to big city to check out prices), "Buddhist, Animist, Christian, even new-style whacko *Soka Gakkai* Value Creation Academy org converts, Foto Joe Yamaguch Enterprises strictly catholic ecumenicalist equal rights tolerances for all in *eiga* flic endeavor realm, as how camera gots no ideologies, reet?"

" — and so it is my desire, shared by my siblings and our widowed mother, to respect my late father's deathbed request, but, also, to signify the occasion with an observance that will mark his reputation in our village to a degree equivalent to his status among his countless friends and neighbors — "

"Say no more, *Fuji-san!*" I tell him, and, "You talking big fire pyre scene, reet?"

Can you not dig big ironies thereof, Jack?

Thus it were, Jack, circa 1953 to through and to include 1971, reet? In sum and short pith and also gist: Foto Joe Yamaguch Enterprises expands staff, facilities, not to fail to mention activities scope widening, reet? As in significant slice-of-pie piece subcontracted from NHK (*Nippon Hoso Kyokai*, how we say, Japan Broadcasting Corporation, reet?) to lens circa '64 Olympics (*koki nisenroppyakunen Orimpikku* — ironies, reet?).

Upshot of which is: what's *wataschi* Foto Joe Yamaguch to do now, Jack, aged three and fifty years aged old (circa '71)?

Oh, Jack, easy it would might could have been to sit back, hunker on *tatami* and observe adequate (more than!) *yen* cash flow flowing toward comfort and secureness of old age coming sooner before later, reet?

How we say: never *hochee* happen, Jack!

As how, *wataschi* Foto Joe Yamaguch (a.k.a. Yamaguchi Yoshinori, a.k.a. Gooch, a.k.a. Lieutenant *Benshi!*) is, how you say, no *baka* fool. Jack: wisdom teached as how past is pastness bygones (burned up in fires big and small, cinders and ashes!) — thus it were I did look future-ward, squint to envision trendiness of trend fashions, espy bluebird on wing aloft, ear to dirt for vibrations of opportunities knocks, reet? Dig:

Wataschi Foto Joe Yamaguch notes — no *baka* dummy dope, reet? — big post-*senso* (circa '45 etcetera blah) internationalist scope of *kippu uriba* box-office hits of *Nihonjin eiga* flic industry, reet? To wit, big *yen* (not to fail to mention bucks!). Which is to specify instance of purely popular mass successes of formula-style cheapie production low-budgets *Godzilla* and also *Rodan* flics, aforesaid concurrent with Chink success Asia-wide of

Run Run Shaw Enterprise (Hong Kong, reet?) *karate* flics, same spreading across blue Pacific in personage of expatriate matinee idol (sad to say early dead and departed!) Bruce Lee, reet?

Wataschi no *baka* illiterate unable to descry holograph on wall, Jack!

Thus it were, Foto Joe Yamaguch did enter upon humongous capital risk venture as independent *eiga* flic feature-film producer, reet? Than which, as in all endeavors heretofore, (natch!) results from ironic combo of intentions shaped by accidentals of chance's fickle digit—flop of mop, cookie's disintegration!

Thus it were, Jack (circa '71), I did scout about, sniff atmosphere's aura, scrutinize options in quest search for *ma* moment in *do* flow than which might could be instant in which *yoin* resonances dictate juncture in which to strike with incandescent iron, reet?

Than which is not to fail to mention passage of time's interim passage effects upon *wataschi*, reet? To wit: Foto Joe Yamaguch (a.k.a. Yamaguchi Yoshinori, a.k.a. Gooch, a.k. a. Lieutenant *Benshi*), aged now fully three and fifty years of age—what I mean, Jack, bound to be some changes, reet? As in: customary attire donned for daily *sanpo* perambulatory strolls about Tokyo environ is altered to include red beret (in keeping with *eiga* flic producer-director vocational images, reet?), than which also serves also to conceal receding hairline sparseness of hairs—Jack, *wataschi* going bald. Not to fail to mention new-style garb, loud-check blazer jacket (strictly *harukai gaijin* import, natch!), now sporting family *monsho* crest (carp aswim upstream) over left breast pocket, loud-check pattern offset via customary solid-hue ascot cloth in lieu of necktie—Jack, I is talking latest stateside *Amerikijin* Hollywood-style fashion cuts: how you say, dress for the success, reet? To include pastel-shade slacks, portrait complete with two-tone golf-style shoes, reet?

Not to fail to mention (sad to say!) inescapable fact of graduated incremental increase in avoirdupois corpulence—what I mean, Jack, *wataschi* getting hog fat (beer gut flabs love handles, also titties!)! Note also: whilst retaining opaque reflector aviator shade specs, I did also affect solitary oversize diamond pinky ring and gem-encrusted Rolex watch with gold band, plus trademark Cuban cigar.

In short sum gist and pith, Jack, *wataschi* Foto Joe Yamaguch did like, play sumputary role appropriate to status stature, aged three and fifty years aged old, reet?

Cut to: Ginza—how we say in *Eigo*, strip, gut, main drag!—Tokyo Town environ (circa 1971), reet? Eventide atmospherics exultant, than which is to say, scene is jumping, Jack! As in: eventide dark bright-lit via neons flashes, mercantile window displays glow, street crowded with bumper-to-bumper vehicles (*harukai gaijin* Yank and *Igirisujin* British imports: Oldsmobile, Studebaker, MG, Chevy and Ford, Morris, not to fail to mention Caddy and occasional Lincoln, Chrysler, and also Rolls Royce!), chauffeurs of which wax ostentatious via horn blare, brakes' squeal, rubber tires peeling, windows agape to allow radio musics (Yank-style, natch!) to emanate into eventide air, whereat it does meld with polyglot confabulations babble of sidewalk's *sanpo* perambulating stroller throngs — how you say, cruising, reet?

Assembled citizenry from amongst Hundred Millions (no *kimonos*, Jack! — sumptuary norms dictates only latest stateside cuts and weaves to express hippest with-it new-style Jimmu Boom lifestyles affluences) rub-berneck passing autos, pause for peekaboo ganders into interior environs of side-by-side western-style nightclubs (Broadway Lounge, Times Square Club, California Surfer, Chicago Bar, etcetera blah) to include minimalist *nawanoren* gin mill watering hole juke joints (oh, Jack, far surpassing greatest long-gone bygone days of Eta Jima Strip!) and — most important not to fail to mention (soon elaborated!) *pachinko* parlors — how you say, pinball emporia, latest *kichigai* fad craze fashion all the rage sweeping *Nihon* (a.k.a. *Dai Nippon*)!

Dig: *wataschi* Foto Joe Yamaguch perambulates *sanpo* casual-style amidst throng, out for eventide of look-see, baby blues agape, reet? What's for? Jack, who can say?

Cut to: neon-lit interior environ of St. Louis Blues *pachinko* parlor (Ginza, Tokyo Town, circa '71, reet?), atmospherics ambience of which is meld of harlequin-hue neons flashing, ceaseless Seeburg (Yank *harukai* import, natch!) juke musics playing unbroken strings from stateside hit-parade hits, than which is not to fail to mention clack-clatter-clacking of *pachinko* pinball mechanisms in play, reet?

Dig, Jack: interior environ is crowded with, how you say, sociological overflow of rising on-the-rise young new generation of new-style *Nihon's* up-and-coming Hundred Millions youths, reet? Young folks, male and also females alike, *yen* in hand to purchase *gaijin harukai* beers and also wines, gather at small *nawanoren*-style quickie bar. More of same aforesaid cluster in clusters about *pachinko* pinball mechanisms lining three walls to cheer on players thereof, than which who do play with verves, resorting to, how you say, body English, to attain to high scores without onus of, how you say, tilts, reet?

Consider attires, Jack: females affect high spiky heels (open toe, painted nails), net hose, hottest of hot pants and minimalist miniskirts, close-fit sweaters and halter tops displaying cleavages, bared epidermis adorned with junk jewelries, to include sliding bangle bracelets and slave-chains, earring dangles, choker necklaces, finger digits all beringed. Than which is not to fail to mention mascaras employed to minimize epicanthic fold (bosoms also augmented with PX Chest devices for western look!), reet?

Jack, I is talking unforeseen side-effect manifest upon portion of flowers of *Nihonjin* young female-hood rendered via post-*senso* influences of Yank Occupation in context of Jimmu Boom boom times, aforesaid generating gals appearing not unlike like unto bad circa 1930s Hollywood *eiga* flic gun-moll gin mill *moga* Barbara Stanwyck sluttish types, reet? Ah, were it not ironical!

Than which is not to fail to mention masculine counterparts, reet? Jack, *wataschi* is talking younger *Nihonjin* manhoods generation cast in absurdist exaggeration of *Amerikajin* James Dean-style punk juvenile delinquent motorcycle-gang social dropouts mode, reet? I is talking hairs long grown and also slicked back with goo in high-crest pompadours, to include, how you say, saliva curls in midst of forehead expanse. I is talking shitkicker bandana hankies tied about necks, black leather jackets (studded with studs!) worn open to display muscle shirts and, where possible, chest hairs, reet? I is talking slung-low dungarees, shoes affixed with toe-taps and heel cleats, key-chain loops swinging free, reet? I is talking armbands and *hachimaki* headbands sporting *Eigo* logos, as in: To Dig Rock and Roll!, Tickle Me Please Baby, I Am Most!, etcetera blah.

I think: *wataschi*, where now is gone generation of young youths in Imperial Army green-hue (Lieutenant *Benshi*!), Imperial Navy blues? Is it not ironical, Jack, I did think, as how *Nihon* (circa '71) is done come to reside under roof of Yank *gaijin harukai* lifestyles trendy fashion?

Only wisdoms occurring, Jack: go with *do* flow, reet?

Cut to: *ma* moment, Jack!

Dig it: *wataschi* Foto Joe Yamaguch's baby blues zoom to instant close-up focus on individual personage who stands in far corner, from whereat he is able (I but speculate!) to dig scene totality's ambience atmospherics, not to fail to mention also thereby enabling hisself to be seen from all angles of St. Louis Blues *pachinko* parlor—I mean: said personage exudes, how you say, charismatics, reet?

I think: *wataschi* Foto Joe, here is *pachinko* parlor punk personage with instinctive impulse to present self so as to be seen whilst seeing self be seen! Here (there, in corner!) stands *pachinko* parlor punk personage with compulsive needs and also desire for, how you say, self-dramatics, reet?

Dig: above-cited punk young personage poses choreographical casual-style, one shoulder against wall, hands dependent upon narrow hips, one foot crossed over opposing ankle, unlit ciggie adangle from semisneering lips—baby blues half-shut hooded to project indifference disdain toward all St. Louis Blues *pachinko* parlor environ, to include all denizens therein, reet?

I note attire: *hachimaki* headband says Born To Flunk; short sleeves of firehouse red muscle shirt are rolled up to display considerable musculature to best advantages, neckline plunged to exhibit minimalist fuzzy-wuzzy chest hairs; patched and also faded dungarees ride beneath navel's button; sockless pedal-extremity feets shod with Yank *harukai* import brogans with double-thick soles and also high heels, reet?

I think: *wataschi* Foto Joe, this punk-style youth is, how you say, photogenic! Like, good facial bones catch neon illuminations in geometric patterns, oversize baby blues absorb same in illusions of deep depths!

Ma moment, Jack!

I sidle up to above-cited's proximity, whereupon I do flash big *sumairu* smile, proffer gold-brushed-finish Ronson, say, "Need some fire, Jack?"

Dig: said punk personage holds half-beat for drama's effects prior to casting half-hooded baby blues in my direction, reet? Unlit ciggie (Chesterfield, natch!) bobs on lip whilst he speaks.

Says he: "Do you address me, old man?"

"Reet," I say, snap Ronson, proffer flame thereof, and, "They smokes bestest when ignited, reet?"

"I know how to smoke cigarettes," says he, and, "I thank you for your courtesy, old man, but I dare not accept it, for this is my last cigarette. It is of *Amerikajin* manufacture, thus very costly, and I have no money presently with which to purchase more."

"Stony broke flat?" I say, and, "*Daijubo* not to perspire, kid, as how pleased I will be to stand you to a pack, not to fail to mention a drinkie if you likes. What's your pleasure, *boy-san*, White Horse? Johnny Walker Black Label? My treat, reet?" I did say.

Dig, Jack: said *pachinko* parlor punk personage did turn in full turn to me, harden gaze, take hands from hips as if to convey aggressive intention posture, hold full beat prior to articulating insult riposte as follows:

"You are doubtless one of the old degenerates who walk the Ginza in search of boys and young men? Go away from me, old man, for I am no *pam-pam* male prostitute! Leave," says he, "for I am revolted by such as you, and I caution you I am skilled in the martial arts!"

"Reet," I say, and, "Glad to hear from it!" and flash big *sumairu* grin, say, "You gots me all wrong, fella!" and, "You talking to Foto Joe Yamaguch, independent producer-director of *eiga* flics, out for Ginza *sanpo* casting-call stroll in search of talents." I proffer *meishi* business card—not to fail to mention revealing *yen* bankroll wad of *genkin* cash of dimension adequate to strangulate equine, reet? "My card," I did say.

"I regret I am unable to read except in the most rudimentary fashion," says he, and, "Like many of my generation, I am crippled by a lack of education and opportunity, a young man doomed to obscurity and poverty in an absurd society. Forgive me for insulting you, old man."

"Reet! Call me Joe," I say, and, "What's your handle moniker, son?"

"I am called Ando Hirobumi," says he, "but were I the child of wealthy parents instead of the *munako* orphan I am, I could afford to petition for a change in my name, for I detest all things *Nihonjin*, and my *hara* belly's most sincere wish is that I might die and be born again in another nation such as the United States of America, but this is a vain wish, for, as I have said, I am doomed to a luckless fate."

"*Hirobumi-san!*" I did say, Jack. "Cheer up, as how you can't never tell how things might could work out, reet? Ever heard from Lana Turner, discovered by *eiga* flic mogul in, how we say in *Eigo*, drugstore soda fountain? This might could be your *ma* moment lucky big break, *Hirobumi-san!* Tell *wataschi*, would you like to be in pictures? *Eiga*, reet? Flics, *Hirobumi-san!*"

"I do not understand you, old man," says he.

"Call me *Joe-san*," I say, and, "Come on, *Hirobumi-san*, let's us *sanpo* stroll to someplace quiet whereat we can confabulate, reet? I'll pop for ciggies, Yank *harukai* imports, natch! — and drinkies! Also, as how *wataschi* Foto Joe Yamaguch ain't so aged as he looks, let's drop 'old man' appellation, reet?"

Ma moment. Jack, we did confabulate *kaigi* style in little *kissaten* coffee-tea-snacks shop nearby, piths and gists of which exchange follows:

"So," I did say to him (*pachinko* parlor punk-youth Ando Hirobumi), "*do* flow don't flow smooth for you, *Hirobumi-san*, reet?"

"How should my life," says he, "have been other than sad and miserable, old man?"

"Call me Joe!"

"I lack even a family that might have bestowed a name of honor upon me. My father is utterly unknown to me, and my mother was a *moga* who allowed me to wander the alleys of Tokyo when I might have been educated, while she plied her trade. She said she thought my father was one of the *Amerikajin issen gorin* who came to *Nihon* after the great *senso* from a remote place called Colorado. The only grace of my heritage is that the blood of this *gaijin* westerner runs in my veins, and so I do not wholly resemble the race of *Nihonjin*, who despise me for my mixed lineage, for I am taller than most, and my eyes are not folded in the common, ugly manner, and my nose is a bit large, and for this I am grateful, though I have no *kami* to thank for this happy accident."

"Reet," I did say to him, and, "Eurasian look might could appeal to western audiences, than which I spotted right off in St. Louis Blues *pachinko* parlor."

I think: Ando Hirobumi — seated across small table from me in *kissaten* Ginza coffee and tea and also snacks shop, smoking Yank ciggies (Raleigh) I did purchase for him — is rife with charismatics, photogenic, how you say, sex appeals would look mayhap good in heartthrob *eiga* flic aimed at new-style generation of *Nihon* youths, than which emulate *Amerikajin* U. S. of A. lifestyles, reet?

"Ever," I query, "been photographed, *Hirobumi-san?*"

"I have no money for such luxuries," says he, and, "I have often thought I might enjoy to work as a male model in advertising, but how should one such as I, cast aside, despised, denied opportunity, come to the notice of the *zaibatsu* who create the magazines and the *shimbun* and the billboards that now abound in the green landscape of *Nihon*?"

"Reet," I say, and, "So, you're skilled in *budo* martial-arts shtick?" Jack, I did think: *wataschi* Foto Joe Yamaguch can see aforesaid Ando Hirobumi in period historicals *chambara* costumes: *samurai* image, armor and *katana* longsword, reet?

"For a time," says he, "I studied the art of *jujitsu* with a minor master who taught me for a fee paid him by my *moga* mother, so that I might defend myself against those who taunted me for my height and blue eyes and large nose, but this ended when my mother sickened and died of a venereal disease."

"Reet. Sad so sad. Tell me, *Hirobumi-san*, how you feeding bulldogs? I mean, Jack, wherefrom you gets your *genkin* cash?"

"It is ever uncertain," says he. "I am given loans when one of my friends wins money playing *pachinko*, and I have even begged for money of the *gaijin* at Haneda Airport as they depart the terminal in taxicabs, but this is risky, for the municipal police arrest beggars because they say we are a disgrace to the honor of *Nihon*. Before you so generously paid for this meal I have just consumed, I had not eaten for two days, and you saw that I had but one cigarette remaining to smoke."

"Think, *Hirobumi-san*," I query, "you could act?"

"Indeed," he says, "I am confident I could, for often, when my stomach cries for rice and there is no prospect of food, and I fear to beg because there are so many police about at Haneda Airport to protect the honor of *Nihon* from beggars, I content myself with imagining I am other than I am."

"Reet. Like what? Gimme, like, for instance."

"I have imagined that I am an affluent *Amerikajin* who resides in a great metropolis such as New York or Beverly Hills in California. I sometimes imagine I am the lost son of a prince of our royal family. Once I imagined I was a soldier famed for heroism in the great *senso*, one of those who never surrendered, who still fights from the jungles of an island in the Southern Seas, like the legendary *ronin*. And I have also imagined I am lesser things, a student at one of the universities of Tokyo, or even a clerk in one of the large *depato* department stores of the city, or a singer in one of the night-clubs on the Ginza."

"Reet," I say, "vivid rich and varied fantasy lifes!" and, "Ever make pretend you was a movie star?"

"Indeed," he ripostes. "I have stood by the posters which depict scenes from the *Amerikajin eiga* and imagined it was I who held the woman with the golden hair in my arms, I who grasped the pistol or the knife, I who drove the large automobiles at great speed while the songs of the radio station broadcasting all the way from San Francisco played about me."

"Reet!"

And I did think, Jack: *wataschi* Foto Joe Yamaguch gots him, how you say, a live one! I mean: said St. Louis Blues *pachinko* parlor punk Ando Hirobumi is ideal's type, reet? To include: charismatics, photogenics, void of hampering *Nipponshikki* traditionalist sensibilities inhibitions, Yank cast to features resultant from paternalist parentage, desirousness of becoming that than which he ain't, given to fancy's self-indulgent fancies — not to fail to mention semiliterate ignoramusness, reet? Can you not dig it?

"*Hirobumi-san*," I did say, "you gots my *meishi* business card, reet? Be at my office, standing tall not unlike like unto six o'clock, address thereon, bright and early come the morrow's morn, reet?"

"To what end do you wish to see me again, old man?"

"*Boy-san*," I say, "*wataschi* Foto Joe Yamaguch going to put you in feature *eiga* flic movie. *Eiga*! Flics, reet? Son," I did say, "this might could be mutual *ma* moment in *do* flow of our lifes and also times, inauguration of mutual advantage *enryo* relationship, reet? Can you not dig *yoin* resonances in atmosphere's aura, *Hirobumi-san*? Than which is not to fail to mention, please to cease 'old man' appellation. Call me, Joe, reet?"

"Why should I trust what you say?"

I did say, "Here's *genkin* cash advance to signify sincerities, reet? Don't" I say, laying *yen* on him, "to be tardy! Not to fail to mention we will negotiate, how we say, exclusive contractuals, reet, *Hirobumi-san*?"

Circa 1971 (St. Louis Blues *pachinko* parlor, Ginza, Tokyo Town!), thus it were, Jack! *Wataschi* Foto Joe Yamaguch (a.k.a. Yamaguchi Yoshinori, a.k.a. Gooch, a.k.a. Lieutenant *Benshi!*), *munako* orphan child of no name discovers *eiga* flic heartthrob leading man of unprecedented successes boffo *oatari* smash *kippu uriba* box-office *jujitsu* feature film series yet still riding high-tide crests of internationalist global-wide audience popularity (all dubbed in sixteen lingos prior to simultaneous distribution releases) Ando Hirobumi, reet? Than which is to say: Jack, *wataschi* Foto Joe Yamaguch's *do* flow life and times lifestyle path, circa 1971 to present *ma* moment's instance takes off not unlike like unto rocket into stratospherics, reet? Thus it were!

Ah, Jack, what's else to say? Save as how I did risk entirety of capital venture *yen* bundle to shoot cheapie low-budget *jujitsu* (historical periods *chambara* concept scrapped due to preclusive costs for costuming etcetera blah, reet?), *Hands and Feet of Death*, scripted, cast, directed, produced, edited, not to fail to mention distributed (*Nihon*-wide, followed by Chink dubbing for Taiwan, Hong Kong, Singapore, studio-generated soundtrack, followed by biggie-risk *Eigo* lingo dub version released in third-run—to include drive-ins, reet?—outlet houses stateside, success of which engenders sale to *teriberi* television syndication in U. S. of A.) by *wataschi*—who else?—Foto Joe Yamaguch, reet?

Profitabilities of which venture I do reinvest in sequel—not to fail to mention foresight of iron-clad exclusive services (cut-rate!) of leading man heartthrob *Hirobumi-san* (natch!)—than which evolves as paradigm pattern than which persists to date, reet, Jack?

So, what's else to say, except save as how I enter upon *do* flow's path as world-wide cinema *eiga* flic mogul-tycoon, reet? Corporate profits margins exponential increase enables *wataschi* to live, how you say, elevated upon porcine quadruped, reet? Jack: I is talking penthouse vacation-retreat villa mansion domiciles, talking chauffeured limos and private jetsetter transport, talking pick of most toothsome potables and also comestibles—result of which (natch!) is corpulence, not to fail to mention also ill healths resultant of *hibakusha pikadon* survivor's exposure effects (cancer, Jack!)—natch!

I is talking world-wide global-scope renown, name of Foto Joe Yamaguch Productions rivaling Run Run Shaw and also Sir Lew Grade, celebrity fame to far reaches of eight corners of world, Jack!

What's else to say more except save daily routines of life and times lifestyle's *do* flow, reet? To wit:

"Is it your pleasure to rouse yourself now, Mr. Yamaguch?" says head *honcho* household chamberlain butler-valet factotum Herbert Pixton (*Igirisujin* British, reet?). "I really do think it high time you wake, sir. You'll recall you do have a terribly crowded schedule today, sir? Do please rise, sir," says he. "I've drawn a hot bath and scented it just as you like, and of course I've prepared a selection of attires for your consideration," says British *Igirisujin* Herbert Pixton, whilst from penthouse bedroom window I espy sun striking full on peak of Fuji, reet?

"Reet," I tell him, Jack, and, "Tell chef personage I'm in nostalgia-like *Amerikajin* mood for down-home old timey Okie-land style fast breaker, to include hog-jowl, biscuits and white gravies, not to fail to mention three or mayhap four eggs—how we say in *Eigo*, cackle fruits, reet?—toasts thick from sweet butter and jams, coffee hot and also black, heavy on sugars."

"Sir," says he, "I would remind you your physician has cautioned you to observe his prescribed diet designed to reduce and retard the fatty substances threatening your coronary passages." Butler-valet Herbert Pixton, reet, Jack?

"Buzz," I do tell him, "off, reet? Also, schlepp me a cigar stogie to my bath."

"I do feel it my duty in your service, sir, to remind you also that you have been cautioned repeatedly to cease your indulgence in tobacco and alcoholic spirits," says Herbert Pixton, household chamberlain factotum.

"Have you, sir," he queries, "no regard for the alarming condition of your lungs and throat and liver?"

"Get," I do tell him, "on with it, reet?" And, "You only live but once." And, "Not to take life and times lifestyle too serious, as how it ain't nothing endures permanent, reet, Herbie-*san*?"

"Okay," I say to executive amanuensis factotum personage, "lay brief briefing on me. Piths and gists only, reet?"

"It is my greatest satisfaction," says he — executive amanuensis (Tokyo U. honors grad!), reet? — "to follow your direction, *sensei*," says he, commences to read off prepared script whilst I loll, cigar alight, first drinkie of day in hand.

"Preliminary figures received at our New York office, transmitted by satellite telephone only this morning, indicate this month's gross receipts are most promising, *sensei*. The New York office recommends we continue to escalate our promotional effort to maximize ultimate returns for this quarter."

"Ix-nay," I say, and, "We gots stateside handle stabilized. Hold on promotionals expenditures, get on horn to Big Apple, tell them I want proposals for extravaganza promotionals on next release, to include *teriberi* network and radio talk-spots, premier-type stateside tour of *Hirobumi-san* and also leading lady, name of which to be announced when appropriate — we talking six months henceforth, reet?"

"In that regard, *sensei*," says executive amanuensis personage, "I am discreetly informed by your solicitors that Mr. Ando, having somehow learned of the possibility of the *Amerikijin* promotional venture, has indicated he considers resorting to legal means to achieve a new and more favorable contractual relationship for himself."

"Natch!" I say, and, "Ix-nay, defecate and fall rearwards thereinto, reet? Tell legal-eagle shyster-types to slip *Hirobumi-san* rumor word as how *wataschi* Foto Joe Yamaguch is done transmogrified him, not unlike like unto worm into moths, from *pachinko* parlor punk. Thusly reverse process is yet possible, big irony of which," I add, "*Hirobumi-san* might could should ponder, reet?"

"*Sensei* Mr. Yamaguch," says *honcho* maitre d'hotel personage of famed fashionable Golden Samurai restaurant (Tokyo Town eatery, reet?), "you grace our establishment with your august patronage! Be assured I and my staff shall exert ourselves to the furthest extent of our energies and our resources to make this luncheon repast a memorable occasion for you and your honorable guests!"

"Reet," I say, and, to trio of guest freeloaders I invite for business-style (tax deduct!) chow-down at ritzy fashionable (favoraite of Tokyo Town *zaibatsu*, reet?) western-style hash house, "Pull up stump and sit, gents, we'll confabulate whilst we scarf. Order up heedless of prices, tab paid by corporate entity, reet?" as *honcho* maitre d'hotel factotum personage proffers gilt-bound menus. "Start," I tell him, "with round of double-sizer drinkies, *harukai* import Scotch for *wataschi*, natch! Now," I say to seated guests, "what's problems pressing on shooting sites, reet?"

"*Sensei* Mr. Yamaguch," says second-unit director of as-yet-untitled new flic in progress shooting just outside city limits on studio lot, "Mr. Ando Hirobumi presents continual difficulties for my direction. He often presumes to state that his numerous screen credits qualify him to interpret his role without regard for my suggestions, and he also adds eccentric nuances to his portrayal of the hero's character."

"*Sensei*," says *honcho* head scriptwriter, "I asked to be allowed to meet with you today so that I might express my desire to be permitted to depart from the script guidelines you prescribed for me. I feel thwarted in my creative impulses to embellish the shooting script with additional dialogue, and this pains me, for I believe I have conceived of several complications of both character and story line which will vastly improve the aesthetic quality of this *eiga*. Your esteemed assistant producer, who is present to respond to what I say, will not allow me this artistic freedom."

"*Sensei* Mr. Yamaguch," says flic's on-site assistant producer, "I appeal to you as the executive producer, and to your unparalleled business instincts! I have told your director he must rein in Mr. Ando's behavior, for otherwise the production of this *eiga* will be delayed, and I have also insisted to this writer that our endeavor will not allow for innovations, for both the former and the latter threaten to alter the budgetary limitations you have so wisely decreed from the beginning of this project."

"Reet!" I say to them, and, "Listen up, gents! Tell *Hirobumi-san* to shape up and fly correct. Trust me. I will get him on horn soonest instanter, straighten him out like unto six o'clock, reet? Than which is not to fail to mention, fiddle not with approved scripts, dig? How we say in *Eigo*, if it ain't broke, not to undertake to repair, reet?"

"I will greatly appreciate your speaking personally to Mr. Ando," says director.

"I am of course content with your decision, *sensei*," says scriptwriter.

"I felt certain, Mr. Yamaguch," says assistant producer personage, "you would support my position with regard to the governing fiscal imperative!"

"Reet! Take *genkin* cash, run therewith, reet? Ultimate consideration is: do it sell? Riposte, as manifest in quarterly accountings is: we is boffo *oatari* smash *kippu uriba* box-office in all eight corners of the globe, reet? Now," I say as waiter schlepps tray of preprandial libations, "suck up, gents! Drinks on corporate entity, all tax deduct — natch! After than which we will, how you say in *Eigo*, pig out. After than which, *wataschi* Foto Joe is gots pressing appointments back at office, and you-all gots shooting schedule to keep, reet?"

"*Sensei* Mr. Yamaguch," says Chink interpreter personage, "Mr. Hsiao asks me to inform you that he has perused the several extensive memoranda composed after your last conference, and finds them accurate in all details, and for this he expresses his sincere appreciation."

"Reet," I say, and, "So, piths and gists, reet? Is we ready to do deal?"

Across from *wataschi* at corporate headquarters *kaigi* conference table is seated Mr. Hsiao personage, than which who is representative delegate factotum of People's Republic of China Ministry of Culture and Public Enlightenment — aforesaid's visage betrays no response whilst interpreter translates utterance into Chink lingo (oh, Jack, Chinks is toughie customers, how you say, nuts not facile for cracking) — attire is plain homespun tunic with high collar, one-size-fitting-legions pantaloons, rough-cut brogans, reet?

"*Sensei*," says Chink lingo interpreter, "Mr. Hsiao is pleased to say that, though all particular clauses are quite in order, yet, he and the ministry officials he represents continue to ponder the advisability of sanctioning the distribution of your *eiga* within the sovereign territory of the glorious People's Republic."

"Reet," I say, and, "State terms, Hsiao! Larger per cent of grosses to sweeten pot necessary? Technical assistances to upgrade embryonic Chink cinema industry? Something, how we say in *Eigo*, payolas under table to grease sticky spots in politico bureaucracies officialdoms? Name it, Jack, as how *wataschi* Foto Joe Yamaguch is here to wheel deal, reet?"

"Mr. Hsiao," spiels interpreter, "suffers doubts as to the salubrity of the effect of your *eiga* upon the political sensibilities of the peasant and worker masses who would view them. He and those he represents wonder if the themes your *eiga* embody are perhaps contrary to the principles of the orthodox Marxist ideology it is their responsibility to nurture among those masses."

"Reet!" I say. "Tell him ain't a political idea nowhere nohow in no *eiga* produced by Foto Joe Yamaguch! Strictly *jujitsu* melodrama shtick, reet? Tell him as how they can exercise censorship cuts from any footages suspect, reet? Ask him," I say, "how's about trial dry run screenings in select isolated hick sticks rural environ communes? Tell him, Jack," I say, "Foto Joe Yamaguch looking to open mass Chink market to his *eiga* flics, reet? Hence and thus able and also willing to make any and all concessions."

"Mr. Hsiao also mentions," says interpreter factotum, "some concern as to the remnants of ill will among the masses of the People's Republic toward all things *Nihonjin*, this ill will the residue of the many years of conflict beginning prior to the great *senso*. There survives, Mr. Hsiao says, a generation of citizens in the glorious People's Republic which remembers the depredations of the Kwantung Army—"

"*Hsiao-san*," I interject, "bygones is by and gone, reet? Hey, ask him if he'd like appointment with *wataschi's* tailor, reet? My treats, fix him up with latest-style set of duds to take home as *o-miyage* souvenir, reet?"

Can you not dig it, Jack? *Wataschi* Foto Joe Yamaguch, sole owner of flourishing Foto Joe Yamaguch Productions, Inc. (also G.M.B.H.!), life and times lifestyle regimen routine (circa 1971 to date, reet?) in big-timey *zaibatsu* fast-track lane of low-risk high-yield cinematic *eiga* flic corporate enterprise, renown spreading to eight corners of world, reet?

"*Sensei* Mr. Yamaguch," says *honcho* executive amanuensis, "is it your wish that I instruct the chef to prepare dinner at home for you this evening, or shall you dine in the city?"

"No time, Jack! Tell cookie to slap together box lunch-style repast, reet? Cold chickens, white wine, loaf of bread, as how *wataschi* gots to eat en route in limo to Haneda Airport destination for departure, rush visit to Peiping Town, vital *kaigi* confabulation conference discussions with Chink Ministry of Culture, reet?"

"Ah," says he, "is it appropriate that I should congratulate you for having attained a concession for the distribution of your *eiga* in the People's Republic, *sensei*?"

"Ix-nay. Not yet, but trust me to deliver impassioned persuasive sales-pitch spiel, Jack!"

"*Sensei* Mr. Yamaguch," says *honcho* staff accountant factotum personage, "if it is your pleasure, I am prepared to present a detailed summary of the past quarter's figures, in addition to—"

"Bottom lines only, Jack! Piths and also gists. Than which is to say, tell *wataschi* how far in black is we, not to fail to mention, what's per-cent increase in net earnings after costs and minimalist corporate taxations, reet?"

"*Sensei* Mr. Yamaguch," says legal-eagle *honcho* shyster solicitor-type factotum (on annual corporate retainer, natch!), "it is my duty, as a loyal employee sworn to serve you, to emphasize the substantial legal advantages of corporate alliance with the *Amerikajin* consortium, which, I add, it is my considered opinion extends a most generous financial inducement to solicit your acceptance of their merger proposal."

"Never *hochee*! As how, Jack, *wataschi* Foto Joe Yamaguch is strictly solitary solo lone-lupine entrepreneur, reet? As in, how we say in *Eigo*, he who schlepps no partners arrives prior to bird of morn in search of wiggly worm, also less footsore nor arm-weary, reet? Ix-nay to Yank *eiga* merger tender, Jack!"

369

"There is a satellite telephone call for you, *sensei*, a personage connected with the *Igirisujin* British film industry."

"Take message, say as how I'll riposte at convenience, requesting both pith and gist, reet?"

"The executive editor of *Yomiuri Shimbun* has called again, *sensei*, begging you to reconsider your response to his previous entreaty."

"Ix-nay! No interviews, no photo ops. As in manner of legendary screen star Garbo Greta, *wataschi* desires recluse status, reet?"

"Your chef begs me to announce to you, *sensei*, that your luncheon awaits you."

"Reet! Old-timey *Nihonjin* nostalgia shtick fare, *nigirimeshi* rice balls, *sushi* fishes, kelps, scalding *o-cha* green tea—*umai* delish yummy!"

"Mr. Ando Hirobumi is, as you requested, *sensei*, on the telephone, eager to converse with you."

"Let *Hirobumi-san* sit on hold whilst I smoke yet another stogie—how we say in *Eigo*, chill pedal extremities, reet?"

"Is it you I speak with, *sensei* Mr. Yamaguch? I fear our connection is faulty, and thus your voice sounds faint in my ears. Do you speak to me from distant Spain?"

"Reet! Pass word to cast and crew to pack traps, haul posteriors for U. S. of A., sovereign state of Utah, hick sticks rural mountain resort village of Park City, lease on remote location for actualities shoots all set, not to fail to mention no union wages scale guarantee in writing, reet?"

"*Joe-san*, I do not fail to appreciate what you have done to raise me from a condition of bleak oblivion to one of international celebrity, but do you not see that I shall feel desolate if you compel me to journey to this far place called Utah? I have not learned to speak the *Eigo* with any fluency, Joe! How shall I be able, in such an emotional state of anxious depression, to perform with conviction before the cameras? *Joe-san*, do you hear my words?"

"*Hirobumi-san*, *wataschi* in midst of big-timey wheelie-dealer confab *kaigi* with *honcho* Muslim personages, authorities both civil and also religious, in reference to objectional footages outraging localist yokel sensibilities here in Cairo City, reet? I ain't gots time to haggle, *Hirobumi-san*! Get on corporate jumbo jet laid on, schlepp to Utah, sovereign state thereof, you going to love Yank lifestyle—burn midnight oils to hone *Eigo* lingo proficiences en route, reet? Trust me, Jack!"

So what's else to say? Excepting save for final ultimate—not to fail to mention most recent! — big irony of *wataschi* Foto Joe Yamaguch's (*zai-batsu* cinematic *eiga* flic independent producer mogul tycoon renowned in eight corners of world global-wide, reet?) life and times to date. As in: how to explain or otherhow account for twists and also turns ironic in *do* flow's path toward unforeseen (predetermined?) destiny's destination? Where-upon occurs last *ma* moment's *yoin* mayhap containing piths and gists of wisdoms earned via decades-long experentials, reet?

Oh, Jack, it is but to laugh! Har. Hee. As follows:

Dig: circa October 1986, how we say, *tsukimi* time of harvest moons viewing, reet? I — me, Jack! — *wataschi* Foto Joe Yamaguch (a.k.a. Yama-guchi Yoshinori, a.k.a. Gooch, a.k.a. Lieutenant *Benshi*!) — repose en-sconced in back seat *honcho* position of Rolls Royce (vintage Silver Dawn!) limo, therein transported via busy streets of Tokyo Town, aforesaid con-veyance chauffeured (natch!) by personal long-time chauffeur personage, than which who sits behind wheel separated by polished glass (bullet-proofed, Jack!) panel, confabulation betwixt whom and *wataschi* is effect-ed by electronic intercom device, reet?

Says I: "Step on it, reet? As how it ain't not *Nipponshikki* to keep *Mikado* waiting."

To which he ripostes: "Forgive me, *sensei* Mr. Yamaguch, but there is such traffic in the avenues of Tokyo, even of a Sunday, and I confess also that I am very nervous, for I have never before in my life entered the grounds of the Imperial Palace, and so I drive slowly and with care to avoid any mishap."

"What's," I query, "*daijubo* needs to perspire? Imperial Palace environ been open to touring curious public since early post-*senso* era bygone, than which is not to fail to mention *Mikado* ain't even *Mikado* no more, not since late-lamented *honcho* Supreme Commander *Makassar-san* done stripped him from deistic stature status, reet?"

"I know, *sensei*," says chauffeur factotum personage, "that the *Mikado* is no more than a man such as you or I, but my parents and my uncles and my aunts revered him as the descendant of *Ameratasu*, and thus, as a small child in the days immediately following the great *senso*, I learned to feel a great regard for him, and even now, a man of fully fifty years of age, I cannot escape the emotion of awe that fills me as I near the dry moat before the palace gate in Nijubashi Plaza!"

"Reet!" I say, and, "Puts on his bloomers but one leg at a time, reet?" and, "*Mikado* what's ain't no more is old man, how we say, *oto-chan* old grandaddy aged twenty-plus years even beyond *wataschi* Foto Joe Yama-guch, reet?" and, "Relax, Jack, *Mikado* what's ain't no more is only old *oto-chan* than which who studies from fishes, reet?"

"I understand, *sensei*, yet I wonder that even you, for all your sophistication through world travel and great success in commerce, are not at all anxious at the prospect of conversing with the *Mikado* within the very walls of his great palace! Are you not wonder-struck, *sensei*, at the designated honor of Suntory Man of the Year which is officially bestowed upon you by our *Mikado?*"

"Reet," I tell him. "Like, *wataschi* done been there before. As for Suntory kudo, go with *do* flow, reet?" And I turn off electronic confabulation device to finish limo (Silver Dawn!) ride in silence—wherein I did search in quest of *ma* moment's *yoin*—all to no avail, Jack.

I did think (reposed ensconced in Silver Dawn Rolls limo!) as we traverse busy (even of Sunday!) byways of Tokyo Town, circa October 1986, *tsukimi* autumn time of harvests moon viewing . . . Jack, what's to think except save upon ironics large and also minimalist of *do* flow's flow in minuscule *ma* moment whilst limo traverses Nijubashi Plaza, enters Sakurada Gate, conveys *wataschi* to palace entrance whereat awaits (as per express instruction!) sole royal household chamberlain factotum personage as escort to royal audience chamber, reet?

Says he (sole Imperial Palace household chamberlain escort factotum personage—nondescript, Jack, old-timey traditionalist *Nipponshikki kimono* doffed in favor of three-piece buttons-down western-style *zaibatsu* factotum garb—natch!): "Allow me to introduce myself, Mr. Yamaguch. I am Utamaro Inukai, and have the honor and pleasure of serving as a member of the *Mikado's* personal staff. He awaits you even as I speak in the imperial audience chamber. I trust you will note that we have complied wholly with your request that no elaborate ceremony accompany your visit and that, contrary to custom, no members of the public or representatives of the *shimbun* be in attendance."

"Reet. Anks-thay," I say, and, "What's happen with ranks of Imperial Palace *ronin*-style guard corps used to was lined roadway in from Sakurada Gate?"

"The *Mikado* relies with confidence on the municipal police for security," says sole imperial household factotum Utamaro Inukai. "We have long since dispensed with the excess trappings of the imperial household, both in the name of a more economical conduct of the household government as well as in deference to the *Mikado's* progressive recognition of the democratic ethos that animates *Nihon* in today's world family of nations. Further, the *Mikado* is seldom in residence, preferring to stay most often at Hayama on Sogami Bay, where he can more conveniently pursue his studies of ichthyology."

"Reet," I say, "cut costs as how to ensure black inks on bottom line of quarterly accountings, lean and mean," and, "Not nary a trace visible from damages effected by Yank *senso* air raids, not unlike like unto as if how it never did *hochee* at all, reet?"

"Indeed," says he. "The *Mikado* believes it is well not to remind the citizenry which visits the grounds when the Sakurada Gate is opened to the public of that so-misfortunate episode in our otherwise illustrious national history. Further," he says, "it is the mutual desire of the *Mikado* and his loyal staff to establish and maintain an aura about the palace conducive to the impression of beauty upon the beholder's eye, and the creation of serenity upon our guest's spirit."

"Reet," I say, and, "Lawn looking good, not unlike like unto billiards table's brushed felts, not to fail to mention fruit trees twice-sized my memory's, must be sight for sore baby blues when *sakura* cherry blossoms blossom at *hanami*, breezes blowing off from Tokyo Bay through green bamboo grasses, carps aswim in ponds by *torri* Spirit Gate, reet?"

"The visiting citizenry and our countless *gaijin* visitors from the distant reaches of the earth find it so," says he — sole imperial household escort factotum Utamaro Inukai. And, "And permit me now to express my personal congratulations to you, Mr. Yamaguch, upon the imminent bestowal of the designation of Suntory Man of the Year, and to welcome you to the Imperial Palace on behalf of our *Mikado*! Will it be your pleasure to follow me within?"

"Reet! Lead way, Jack!" Over shoulder to personalist chauffeur personage, I say, "Keep motor running. *Wataschi* won't be long absent."

Oh, Jack, I did think — circa October *tsukimi* harvest moons viewing autumn of 1986, perambulating *sanpo* style down dim-lit corridors of Imperial Palace in wake of sole household escort factotum Utamaro Inukai, patent-leathers brogans (Italian *harukai* imports, natch!) echoing on tiles — *wataschi* Foto Joe Yamaguch did think:

Papa-san! Mama-san! Sis Iko-san! Moe (say it ain't so!)! Miss Clara! Strongboy Stevie! *Honcho* Premier-General Tojo! Brigadier General Jeffie! *Yoko-san!*

Et alia etcetera blah, reet, Jack?

I did think: *Yosho-san!* Gooch! Lieutenant *Benshi!* Oh, *wataschi* Foto Joe! Etcetera blah.

Jack, what did I not think in duration of minimalist minuscule *ma* moment en route via dim-lit corridor echoes of Imperial Palace interior environ (circa *tsukimi* autumn moon viewing time, October '86!)!

I did think: gone is little *Yosho-san* Yosh. Gone, Jack, is Mr. and Mrs. Yamaguchi's boy (gone is Daddy and Mama, Baby Sis!), gone Student Yamaguchi Yoshinori (gone stripe and also chevron!), official interpreter-guide by appointment of *Mikado* (than which he ain't no more!) to circa '35 Yank all-star American League *besuboru* barnstormer squad (say it ain't so, Moe!)! I did think: gone, Jack, is Gooch, valedictorian of class of circa '40 (Oklahoma Agricultural & Mechanical College! Go, Pokes! Go, Punchers!), gone, reet? *Wataschi* did think: Jack, gone is Lieutenant *Benshi*

(Imperial Army of *Dai Nippon* — gone!)! But gone is grandiose *eiga* docu-drama *hakko ichui* chronicle, not to fail mention also gone is *Nippon Maketa* archive — got burned up in big fires (*pikadon!*), reet?

"Your Imperial Majesty," says Utamaro Inukai — executes demure kow-tow bow, reet? — "I have the honor to present to you Mr. Yamaguch Foto Joe, who enjoys the prestige of being the nominee of your loyal Economic Council of *Nihon* for the illustrious designation of *Nihon's* Suntory Man of the Year!"

Says he (Hirohito, Jack! — *Mikado* what ain't no more — old aged *otochan* man aged now more than eighty-five years old — studies from fishes full-time!): "Welcome, Mr. Yamaguch, to my household. It is my sincere pleasure to bestow upon you the title of *Nihon's* Suntory Man of the Year for nineteen eighty-six and to congratulate you in the name of all our loyal citizenry for the great achievement of your career! I am confident your family *kami* bask now in the honor and glory you have brought to your name!"

"Reet!" I did say, Jack. And, "Anks-thay, *Mikado!*" and, "Hello, *Mikado*! Long time not to see, reet?"

"Please," says he (Hirohito, Jack, near sixty years ensconced upon Chrysanthemum Throne, formerly a.k.a. direct descendant of Sun Goddess *Ameratasu!*) to staff factotum Utamaro Inukai, "excuse yourself with our gratitude for your service this day. Mr. Yamaguch and I," says he, "should like, I think, to converse in private for at least a few minutes. Do I express your sentiment, Mr. Yamaguch?"

"Reet!"

"Shall we," says he — Hirohito, Jack, *Mikado* what's ain't no more! — "be seated, Mr. Yamaguch?"

"Anks-thay, *Mikado*, but I'll stand. As how *wataschi* ain't gots but few minimalist *ma* moments for confab, limo waiting with engine running preparatory to drive to Haneda Airport whereat awaits personalist jumbo jet for flight to Hong Kong City, big flap negotiations with Run Run Shaw necessitated for settlement of *minken* competitive *eiga* flic distributions throughout Southern Seas region environs, reet?"

"But of course," says he, and, "Allow me then to indulge myself, for I grow more infirm each day as my sunset years advance upon me."

"Reet," I say, "grab stool and hunker, *Mikado*, no ceremonials required for *wataschi*."

Jack: *Mikado* (than which who he no longer is!) is old — I is talking eighty-five years aged! — circa *tsukimi* autumn moon view time. Than which is to say: diminutive wimp-style stature is done further diminished, reet? *Mikado's* hairs laced with white streaks, epidermis faded to sallow rice-paper wrinkles, same spotted with warts and also moles, not to fail to mention tremor in claw-style hands, reet? Traditionalist formal swallow-tail coat doffed in favor of cheapie-cut *depato* department store quality business suit (three-piecer, natch!), patent leathers pumps replaced by floppy slippers, reet?

I did think: where now is *Mikado* Son of Heaven garbed in *budo*-style uniform astride favorite horse (Snow White)?

Says he (seated): "We have both become old men, have we not, Mr. Yamaguch? I scarce recognize in your presence before me now the boy in his school uniform who entered this room so long ago in the company of the *Amerikajin* ambassador Mr. Grew and the host of visiting athletes —"

"Circa 'thirty-five," I interpose, and, "Half a century past and bygone, reet?"

"Indeed," says he, and, "Nor can I descry with these failing eyes the young army officer who managed his longsword with such lack of success."

"Circa 'forty-four," I did interject, "minimalist confines environ of imperial bomb shelter, whilst Yank aircrafts did drop five-hundred pounders, not to fail to mention delayed-fuse and also incendiary missiles, down upon Hundred Millions, reet?"

"Indeed," says he, and, "I fear all traces of the boy and the young man I knew have been lost in the corpulence you have accrued in the interim years."

"Reet," I did say. "Excess avoirdupois is direct resultant effect of prosperities enjoyed in cinematic *eiga* ventures life and times lifestyles, self-indulgence self-evident therein doubtless resultant from desire to get whilst getting is good, as how nothing don't seem nohow to endure otherhow, reet, *Mikado*?"

"Ah, Mr. Yamaguch!" says he. "I see that you, just as I, have learned from a long life that the *do* path we follow is characterized by ceaseless change, the years describing patterns of flux and flow as they proceed —"

"Reet!" I did say. And, "Fires big and small, effacing what's was, engendering what's is and will be in paradigms ironical, reet?"

"We seem," says he — Hirohito (*Mikado* what's ain't no more!) — "to have arrived in our old age at a common wisdom, however different the paths we have traveled. I so often pause in my activities to contemplate the events of my long life! Do you do this also, Mr. Yamaguch?"

"Reet," I say, "strictly from memory recall, as how documentations and other assorted artifacts, not to fail to mention personages, all gone, reet, *Mikado*?"

"Oh yes!" says he, "I do think upon the many exceptional men it has been my fortune to know in this long life, great generals and politicians whose activities astounded the world, whose influence held sway over the nations of the world —"

"Like, as for instance?" I did query.

"I think often," he ripostes, "of old Prince Konoye, who strove always for peace, and of General Tojo, who sought always the pursuit and conduct of war. I think frequently of *Makassar-san*, whose firm hand and clear vision lead *Nihon* from the ashes of defeat to our current international eminence and our domestic harmony and prosperity. I think upon the other national leaders of my generation, of Roosevelt and Churchill, of Hitler, Stalin, Mussolini —"

"Dead and gone!" I did say, and, "Ashes and also cinders, burned up in fires of time, blowed by winds to eight corners of the world, *Mikado!*"

"Indeed," says he, and, "Of what do you think when you retire from your commercial enterprise to ponder what was once and is no more, Mr. Yamaguch?"

"I think," I say to him, "of my daddy and mama, Mr. and Mrs. Yamaguchi, and of my baby sis *Iko-san*, than which who got burned up in medium-size fire in Tokyo Town circa 'forty-two by Jimmy Doolittle's flyboys off carrier *Hornet* whilst *wataschi* was lensing propaganda feature flic *eiga* on remote location. I do think, *Mikado*: from Morris — also knowed as Moe — Berg, than which who lensed flics of targets in *Dai Nippon* later employed by *Hornet* flyboys! I do think of Mr. Sato Isao, *kempei* counterintelligence clandestine operative, of Oklahoma Agricultural and Mechanical College alma mater, class of 'forty, of Mighty Mouse Yukon Strongboy Stevie Keller and Miss Clara Sterk — also knowed as Petty Girl — also knowed as Mrs. Keller! I do think of —"

"Have I said something to agitate you, Mr. Yamaguch?" interrupts *Mikado*. But I is not listening, reet, Jack?

"—*honcho* Premier-General Tojo Hideki, than which who composed *haiku* poems night before he was hanged by *Makassar-san*! I think of: Yank P.O.W.s than which who expired resultant from rigors of so-called Bataan Death March, not to fail to mention Camp O'Donnell rigors of durance vile, reet? *Mikado*: I do think of three millions *Nihonjin* amongst vaunted Hundred than which got burned up in fires big —*pikadon*! — and small whilst engaged in pursuit of grandiose honor and glory shtick via *hakko ichui* scheme scam of conquest global-wide, not to fail to mention than of who no trace remains except save aged relatives conducting visitations at Yasukuni Shrine, not to fail to mention *matsuri* holiday hordes folding paper cranes at annual Hiroshima City doings, not to fail to mention *churen kenabo-to* memorials erected throughout Southern Seas Theater of Operations remote local environs, I do think, *Mikado*. . . ."

Jack, I do not recall all that than which I did say to *Mikado* (who ain't no more) during minimalist final ultimate audience granted for ceremonialist purpose of bestowing Suntory Man of Year honorific, reet?

376

Thereafter followed semilong silence, occasion of tangible aura atmosphere of *enryo* betwixt two aged *oto-chan* old men—*wataschi* Foto Joe Yamaguch and ex-*Mikado*, reet? I do not remember what I did think therein, Jack!

Said he (terminating silence, reet?): "It is true, Mr. Yamaguch, we are old men now, and we have seen and known much suffering and loss in our protracted lives. Thinking of such things," said he, "will surely cast a mood of gloomy pessimism upon one's spirit, and I do confess to knowing moments, now, in the last chapters of the chronicle of my life, given over to just such a mood."

"Reet."

"And yet, Mr. Yamaguch," said he, "but a moment's reflection can persuade one that all things combine over the course of one's *do* path in life toward an end that is, if not serene, at least content."

"As how, exactly, *Mikado-san*?" I did query.

"I at least," said he, "have come to see that, with the tribulations of the past fast fading from my memory, destiny appears to have ordained that *Nihon* should be a nation of great enterprise rivaling the golden age of Jimmu, a nation respected and admired in the world community."

"You putting me on, *Mikado-san*? Mind if I call you *Mikado-san*?"

"Consider, Mr. Yamaguch," said he. "Are we not a people now more populous than ever? To call us the Hundred Millions today is to scant our true numbers! Are we not a people internationally famous for our industriousness and our acumen? Is there a people, even the *Amerikajin* who came to our islands as conquerors only a generation ago, that does not envy our prosperity?"

"Depends," I said, "on who you talking to, *Mikado-san*. You should," I said, "read some of my hate mails, reet?"

Jack, he don't not hear me! Said he: "I myself, though an aged man with ever-increasing infirmities, enjoy a dotage surrounded by loving and loyal subjects, an extensive family to carry on my name and lineage when I have passed, my energies devoted to the fascinating and useful science of ichthyology—"

"Fishes," I did say—he don't listen, Jack!

"—secure in the knowlege that I have maintained the Chrysanthemum Throne with honor for my heirs! And consider, Mr. Yamaguch, the instance of your own remarkable life! We spoke, half a century ago, when you were but a boy, precocious in your learning of *Eigo*, eager for further study! And we spoke in a dark moment in *Nihon's* history, when it appeared to us both that the only course left was to effect a record of the destruction of our civilization so that the world might still know the name of our race and the heroism and sacrifice of our end—"

"Reet."

"— and we meet a third time, surely a last time, for the end of all men draws near to us, Mr. Yamaguch, and you are risen from such origins, from such despair, to a position of such wealth, such fame, such influence — Suntory Man of the Year for nineteen eighty-six, Mr. Yamaguch! You have brought great honor and glory to *Nihon*, and to your name and the *kami* of your family! You are renowned for your endeavors in all the distant corners of the world! Mr. Yamaguch," said he, "might you have dared to dream so illustrious and satisfying an end to your life, which began so humbly, a life in which you stand as a bright example of the human spirit's ability to endure and prevail?"

Jack, I did say to him: "Cinders and ashes, *Mikado-san*! Zip. Zed. Zilch. Zero, reet? Nothing plus also nothing," I did say, "totals sum of nought except save series of ironics big and small, not to fail to mention than which said ironics is fast fading from memory's recall, reet? Sole solitary satisfaction to be gleaned, pith and gist therein, is, given who and also when we is, *Mikado-san*, ain't hardly no more to come, reet?"

"I think, Mr. Yamaguch," said he — claps hands to summon imperial household chamberlain factotum Utamaro Inukai — "it would be well to end our conversation now. You are a busy man, and, doubtless, your affairs in Hong Kong and elsewhere press upon you."

"Reet!" I did tell him, and, "*Tenno Heika Banzai*! Does we still say that, *Mikado-san*? See you around and about mayhap, reet?" I did say — not to fail to mention minimalist kowtow bow I did render to ex-*Mikado* whilst escorted from audience chamber by factotum personage (aghast, natch!), reet?

"Was it truly thus, *sensei* Mr. Yamaguch?" queries Terada Seijo — famed Yokohama *irezumi* tattooist, reet? — "The *Mikado* dismissed you from his presence, and you spoke in such familiar fashion to him?"

"Did I not, *Seijo-san*? Like I said, puts bloomers on but one leg at a time, no longer divine since edict of *Makassar-san*, reet? Knowed him when. Now old *ota-chan* studies from fishes." And, "Past times past and bygone gone, reet?"

"Ah," says he, "it is indeed a story rich in unexpected events and unforeseen turns of fate you relate, Mr. Yamaguch! Inscribed on paper, it would surely be a book to amuse and instruct!"

"Ix-nay!" I say, and, "Nothing burns so good as how rice papers, reet? Than which is not to fail to mention, how we say in *Eigo*, following upon *eiga* logo screen credits, *The End*, Jack!"

"Indeed," says he — Terada Seijo, *irezumi* tattooist of Yokohama wharf dockside district environ, famed amongst *Nihonjin* seafarer maritime swabbies for both conceptions and also executions of panorama-style depictions rendered in bright coloration pigment inks upon epidermis via electric needles — and, "It is well, *sensei*, that you have no more to relate, for we have exhausted the full extent of your available skin, unless, of course, we were to decend below your posterior to include the backs of your thighs — "

"Ix-nay," I say, and, "No need, Jack!" and, "End of story. How we say in *Eigo*: all she inscribed, reet? Period, last sentence in final chapter circa life and times lifestyle *do* path of yours truly *wataschi* Foto Joe Yamaguch."

"It remains only," says he, "for you to look upon the entirety of my work, and to pronounce your satisfaction if, as I pray to my *kami*, you find my design and execution acceptable."

"Not to fail to mention," I say to him, "payment of final installments *yen*, than which is not to fail to mention affixing *hanko* signature seal on contract drawed up in advance by *wataschi's* shyster-solicitor personage on retainer for bequest of flayed hide to Wantanabe Nautical Museum, reet?"

"I await your pleasure, *sensei*," says *Seijo-san* Terada.

Dig, Jack: *wataschi* Foto Joe Yamaguch stretched out prone-style, *hara* belly-down, upon divan (high above Tokyo Town, penthouse privacy environ), how you say, buck-starkly nudist, reet? Alongside divan stands Terada Seijo, wields largish hand-mirrors in both hands, reet? One of same aloft above *wataschi's* backside exposed portion of corpus, other held before *wataschi's* baby blues to catch reflections of reflections as I peruse aforesaid *Seijo-san's* handiworks: emblematic depiction of life and times lifestyle *do* path. To wit:

"Here," says he, "on the back of your neck, we commenced with a rendering of figures and locations representative of your earliest memories. Can you see adequately, *sensei*?"

"Reet! *Papa-san, Mama-san*, Sis *Iko-san*. Little Yosh resplendent in regulation uniform of Native Land Loving School. Paper house. Ueno Park. I can dig it, *Seijo-san*!"

"Here, we render Tokyo's Asakusa District as it might have appeared sixty years ago."

"Reet. *Eigo harukai* import flics screened in old *No* and also *Kabuki* theaters, *benshi* on stage to explain, north of Kanda District!"

"Here you will I hope recognize a stylized headline from the *Japan Times shimbun*."

"*Eigo! Eiga*! Words funny-strange sometimes, reet, *Seijo-san*?"

"Notice how the ranks of the *Amerikajin besuboru* athletes appear to rise out of the sea to the east of *Nihon*?"

"Knowed also, circa 'thirty-five, as *Dai Nippon*, reet? I recognize Moe Berg via profile rendition calculated to enhance huge honker schnozz!"

"Note the minor figure, almost a mere shadow in the background, who follows in the wake of the uniformed schoolboy and the tall *gaijin* with the great nose as they walk about Ichigaya Heights with the large camera?"

"*Kempei* counterintelligence clandestine operative surveillance. Sato Isao!"

"I continue to regret that I was unable to persuade you to allow me to depict the *Mikado* in larger proportion to the surrounding figures."

"Wimp! Diminution of minimalist stature expresses pointed irony thereof intended, *Seijo-san*."

"And I regret" — mirror aloft moves, tips same before *wataschi's* baby blues, reet? — "the scope of my design permitted no space to contain a transition to account for your long voyage across the Pacific."

"How we say in film biz, quick-cut, Jack! Pith and gist, reet?"

"And I confess no confidence in my ability to capture your experience in the place called Oklahoma, since the images are utterly alien to me, *sensei*."

"*Daijubo* not to perspire, you done good, *Seijo-san*! Go, Pokes. Go, Punchers. Beat hated O.U. Sooner downstate rivals."

"The river presented no challenge to my craft, but I should have preferred to place a pine tree on its banks."

"It ain't no true blackjack oak, howsomever close enough to fool all but experts, reet?"

"Have I done justice to the figures of the wrestler and the female called Miss Clara?"

"Stevie! Clara! Oh, you done good, Jack!"

"The longsword is placed parallel to the river's course, and is thus both a comparison and contrast, for I intended the sword's blade should gleam like the water's surface in the sun that shines equally upon *Nihon* and the remote place called Oklahoma. Yet the river speaks of peace and tranquillity, while the sword designates the virtues of *bushido* and the great *senso* —"

"River might could should have been more red to stand for muddy Cimarron, than which speaks from stab-in-the-back deceits, as in clandestine *kempei* counterintelligence spy activity versus R.O.T.C. Corps and also Flying Aggies A and M student aviators, reet?"

"As you say, *sensei*. The fires are, as you insisted, many and of varied scale."

"Big and small! *Pearu Halbol*. U.S.S. *Oklahoma*. Tokyo, circa *hanami* 'forty-two. *Pikadon*! Hey, you done good on Tojo, Jack! Spit's image thereof, shaved noggin, horn-rim specs, also knowed as The Razor, reet? Noose about neck is good touch!"

"I do confess to a feeling of pride in that portrait! Have you heard, Mr. Yamaguch, it is said that in isolated villages on our more remote islands, peasant rice farmers and fishermen pray to Tojo Hideki as if to a family *kami*?"

"Reet. Big irony therein, Jack."

380

"Here," Terada Seijo poised aloft mirror over *wataschi's* extensive (accrued avoirdupois, reet?) buttocks' expanse, "I have isolated the wondrous tale of your fabulous career as a maker of *eiga*."

"Reet. There's General Jeffie, one star only, not to fail to mention microcosmic-scope Eta Jima Strip, to include gaggle of anonymous Yank *issen gorin* and flames engulfing Texas Bar *nawanoren*."

"Have I limned the likeness of the *moga hosutesu* and the famous Ando Hirobumi to your satisfaction, *sensei*?"

"To last tittle and also jot! Even gots *Yoko-san's* PX Chest-scale bosoms, gleam of oil annointing *Hirobumi-san's* musculature evident in *jujitsu* fighting posture pose, rain of Occupation Currency scrip specie is also nice—you done real good, *Seijo-san*!"

"And here—" *wataschi* got to bend neck to catch image reflection of furthest buttock extremity in mirror wielded before baby blues—"I depict two aged men, one small and withered—"

"Ex-*Mikado*!"

"—the other obese, his visage exhibiting the siege of terrible illness assaulting his body."

"*Wataschi*!"

"Then you are pleased with what I have done, *sensei*?" queries famed Yokohama *irezumi* tattooist Terada Seijo.

"Reet!" I say, and, "Good jobs of work, *Seijo-san*!" and, "Life and times *do* path lifestyle, circa beginning to present contemporary *ma* moment penultimate to conclusion," and, "Wisdom expressed thereby is nought but ironics big and small, reet?" Terada lowers mien in *Nipponshikki* gesture of embarrassment upon receiving praises, reet? Renders minimalist kowtow bow, etcetera blah.

"Reet," I say, "Help me up, toss me bathrobe to conceal nakedness, *Seijo-san*. Remains only to fork over final *yen* installments payment, affix *hanko* signature seal on document bequesting flayed hide to Wantanabe Nautical Museum, after than which *wataschi's* personalist limo awaits you below for return journey to Yokohama wharf dockside environ, reet?"

"I consider this, *sensei*," says he, "my finest work of a lifetime devoted to my craft!"

"Likewise by me!" I did say to him, reet, Jack?

So: what's else to say (much less do!)? Remains but to wait upon ravages of terminal afflictions (cancers, renal failures, etcetera blah) to run course—go with disease's *do* flow, reet?

Har. Hee.

Than which is not to fail to mention, occupy interim interval via self-perusal in wall and also ceiling mirrors I install in penthouse bedchamber, reet? Dig: *wataschi* Foto Joe Yamaguch, stripped as how for skinny-dips, standing tall like unto six o'clock to stare over shoulder at shoulders-to-behind-butt panorama of *do* life and times (in colorations!), reet? Har. Hee.

Ah, what's to think, Jack? Except to ponder upon self: Yamaguchi Yoshinori, Gooch, Lieutenant *Benshi*, Foto Joe — what's in a name, reet?

Motto: *shikata ga nai*, how we say, it ain't nothing can be done about it, reet, Jack?

Conclusion: *Oiwa Oude*, how we say, "Song of Happiness," reet? To wit:

> Green pine trees, cranes and turtles,
> You must tell a story of your hard times
> And laugh twice.

Har! Hee!